The
Last
Dark

Stephen R. Donaldson

ॐ

G. P. Putnam's Sons
New York

The Last Dark

The Last Chronicles of Thomas Covenant

BOOK FOUR

G. P. PUTNAM'S SONS
Publishers Since 1838
Published by the Penguin Group
Penguin Group (USA) LLC
375 Hudson Street
New York, New York 10014

USA · Canada · UK · Ireland · Australia
New Zealand · India · South Africa · China

penguin.com
A Penguin Random House Company

Library of Congress Cataloging-in-Publication Data

Donaldson, Stephen R.
  The last dark / Stephen R. Donaldson.
      p.   cm.—(The last chronicles of Thomas Covenant ; Book four)
  ISBN 978-0-399-15920-6
  1. Covenant, Thomas (Fictitious character)—Fiction.   I. Title.
  PS3554.O469L37   2013   2013016784
  813'.54—dc23

Printed in the United States of America
10   9   8   7   6   5   4   3   2   1

Book design by Meighan Cavanaugh

to Jennifer Dunstan,

who stood with me the whole time

and to John Eccker,

who has put in more effort, and has been of more help, than I could ever have expected

and to Robyn H. Butler:

"And they lived happily ever after."

Contents

What Has Gone Before

"The Chronicles of Thomas Covenant the Unbeliever"

As a young man—a novelist, happily married, with an infant son, Roger—Thomas Covenant is stricken with leprosy. In a leprosarium, where the last two fingers of his right hand are amputated, he learns that leprosy is incurable. As it progresses, it produces numbness, often killing its victims by leaving them unaware of infections. Medications arrest its progress; but Covenant is taught that his only hope of survival lies in protecting himself obsessively from any form of damage.

Horrified by his illness, he returns to his home on Haven Farm. But other blows to his emotional stability follow. His wife, Joan, abandons and divorces him to protect their son. Fearing the mysterious nature of his illness, the people around him cast him in the traditional role of the leper: a pariah, outcast and unclean. In addition, he becomes impotent—and unable to write. Grimly he struggles to go on living; but as his despair mounts, he has episodes of prolonged unconsciousness, during which he seems to visit a magical realm known only as "the Land."

In the Land, physical and emotional health are tangible forces, made palpable by an energy called Earthpower. Because vitality and beauty are concrete qualities, as plain to the senses as size and color, the well-being of the physical world has become the guiding precept of the Land's people. When Covenant first encounters them, in *Lord Foul's Bane*, they greet him as the reincarnation of an ancient hero, Berek Half-hand, because he, too, has lost half of his hand. Also Covenant possesses a white gold ring—his wedding band—which they know to be a mighty talisman, able to wield "the wild magic that destroys peace."

Shortly after he first appears in the Land, Covenant's leprosy and impotence disappear, cured by Earthpower; and this, he knows, is impossible. Indeed, the mere idea that he possesses some form of magical power threatens the stubborn disciplines on which his survival depends. Therefore he chooses to interpret the Land as a dream or hallucination. He responds to his new health with Unbelief: the dogged assertion that the Land is not real.

Because of his Unbelief, his initial reactions to the people and wonders of the Land are at best dismissive, at worst cruel. At one point, urged by sensations which he can neither accept nor control, and certain that his experiences are illusory, he rapes Lena, a young girl who has befriended him. However, her people decline to punish or reject him for his actions. As Berek Halfhand reborn, he is beyond judgment. And there is an ancient prophecy concerning the white gold wielder: "With the one word of truth or treachery, / he will save or damn the Earth." Covenant's new companions know that they cannot make his choices for him. They can only hope that he will eventually follow Berek's example by saving the Land.

At first, such forbearance achieves little, although Covenant is moved by both the ineffable beauties of this world and the kindness of its people. During his travels, however—first with Lena's mother, Atiaran, then with the Searoach Giant Saltheart Foamfollower, and finally with the Lords of Revelstone—he learns enough of the Land's history to understand what is at stake.

The Land has an ancient enemy, Lord Foul the Despiser, who dreams of destroying the Arch of Time—and with it not only the Land but the entire Earth—in order to escape what he perceives to be a prison. Against this evil stands the Council of Lords, men and women who have dedicated their lives to nurturing the health of the Land, and to opposing Despite.

Unfortunately these Lords possess only a small fraction of their predecessors' power. The Staff of Law, Berek's primary instrument of Earthpower, has been hidden from them. And the lore of Law and Earthpower seems inherently inadequate to defeat Lord Foul. Wild magic rather than Law is the crux of Time. Without it, the Arch cannot be destroyed; but neither can it be defended.

Hence both the Lords and the Despiser seek Thomas Covenant's allegiance. The Lords attempt to win his aid with courage and compassion: the Despiser, through manipulation. And in this contest Covenant's Unbelief appears to ally him with the Despiser.

Nevertheless Covenant cannot deny his reaction to the Land's apparent transcendence. And as he is granted more and more friendship by its people, he remembers his violence toward Lena with dismay. Thus he faces an insoluble conundrum: the Land cannot be real, yet it feels entirely real. His heart responds to its loveliness—and that response has the potential to kill him by undermining his necessary caution and hopelessness.

Trapped within this contradiction, he attempts to escape through a series of unspoken bargains. In *Lord Foul's Bane*, he lends the Lords his passive support, hoping that this will enable him to avoid the possibilities—the responsibilities—of his white gold ring. And at first his hopes are realized. The Lords find the lost Staff of Law; their immediate enemy, one of Lord Foul's servants, is defeated; and Covenant is released from the Land.

Back in his real world, however, he discovers that he has in fact gained nothing. Indeed, his plight has worsened. His experience of friendship and magic has weakened his ability to endure his outcast loneliness. When he is translated to the Land a second time, in *The Illearth War*, he knows that he must devise a new bargain.

During his absence, the Land's plight has worsened as well. Decades have passed there; and in that time Lord Foul has acquired the Illearth Stone, a bane of staggering power. With it, the Despiser has created an army that now marches against the Lords: a force which the Staff of Law cannot adequately oppose. The Lords need the strength of wild magic.

Other developments also exacerbate Covenant's dilemma. The Council is now led by High Lord Elena, his daughter by his rape of Lena. With her, he begins to experience the real consequences of his crime: unlike the rest of the Council, he can see that she is not completely sane. In addition, the army of the Lords is led by a man named Hile Troy, who appears to come from Covenant's own world. Troy's presence radically erodes Covenant's self-protective Unbelief.

Now more than ever Covenant needs to resolve his conundrum. Again he posits a private bargain. He will give the Lords his active support. Specifically, he will join Elena on a quest to discover the source of EarthBlood, the most concentrated form of Earthpower. But he will continue to deny that his ring has any magic. He will accept no responsibility for the Land's fate.

This time, however, the results of his bargain are disastrous. Using the Illearth Stone, Lord Foul slaughters the Giants of Seareach. Hile Troy is only able to defeat the Despiser's army by giving his soul to Caerroil Wildwood, the Forestal of Garroting Deep. And Covenant's help enables Elena to find the EarthBlood, which she uses to violate the Law of Death. She resurrects Kevin Landwaster, a long-dead High Lord, believing that he will have more power against Lord Foul than anyone living. But she is terribly wrong; and in the resulting catastrophe, both she and the Staff of Law are lost.

Covenant returns to his real world knowing that his attempts to resolve his dilemma have served the Despiser.

Nearly broken by his failures, he visits the Land again in *The Power That Preserves*, where he discovers the full cost of his actions. Dead, his daughter now serves Lord Foul, using the Staff of Law to wreak havoc. Her mother, Lena, has lost her mind. And the Lords are besieged by an army too powerful to be defeated.

Covenant still has no solution to his conundrum: only wild magic can save the Land, yet he cannot afford to accept it. However, sickened at heart by Lena's madness, and by the imminent ruin of the Land, he resolves to confront the Despiser himself. He has no hope of victory, but he would rather sacrifice himself for the sake of an unreal yet magical place than preserve his outcast life in his real world.

Before he can reach the Despiser, however, he must first face dead Elena and the Staff of Law. Although he cannot oppose her, she defeats herself: her attack on him draws a fierce response from his ring—a response which also destroys the Staff.

Accompanied only by his old friend, the Giant Saltheart Foamfollower, Covenant finally confronts Lord Foul and the Illearth Stone. Facing the Despiser's savagery and malice, he at last finds the solution to his conundrum, "the eye of the paradox": the point of balance between accepting that the Land is real and insisting that it is not. On that basis, he uses the dire might of the Illearth Stone to trigger wild magic from his ring. With that power, he shatters both the Stone and Lord Foul's home, thereby ending the threat of the Despiser's evil.

When he returns to his own world, he learns that his new-found balance benefits him there as well. He knows now that the reality or unreality of the Land is less important than his love for it; and this insight gives him the strength to face his life as a pariah without fear or bitterness.

"The Second Chronicles of Thomas Covenant"

For ten years after the events of *The Power That Preserves*, Covenant lives alone on Haven Farm, writing novels. He is still an outcast, but he has one friend, Dr. Julius Berenford. Then, however, two damaged women enter his life.

His ex-wife, Joan, returns to him, violently insane. Leaving Roger with her parents, she has spent years in a commune which has dedicated itself to Despite, and which has chosen Covenant to be its victim. Hoping to spare anyone else the hazards of involvement, Covenant attempts to care for Joan alone.

When Covenant refuses aid, Dr. Berenford enlists Linden Avery, a young physician whom he has recently hired. Like Joan, she has been badly hurt, although in entirely different ways. As a young girl, she was locked in a room with her father while he committed suicide. And as a teenager, she killed her mother, an act of euthanasia to which she felt compelled by her mother's self-pity. Loathing death, Linden has become a doctor in a haunted attempt to erase her past.

At Dr. Berenford's urging, Linden intrudes on Covenant and Joan. When members of Joan's commune seek to sacrifice Covenant, Linden tries to intervene, but she is struck down. As a result, she accompanies him when he is returned to the Land.

During Covenant's absence, several thousand years have passed, and the Despiser has regained his power. As before, he plots to use Covenant's wild magic in order to break the Arch of Time. In *The Wounded Land*, however, Covenant and Linden learn that Lord Foul has altered his methods. Instead of relying on armies and warfare to goad Covenant, he has devised an attack on the natural Law which gives the Land its beauty and health.

The overt form of this attack is the Sunbane, a malefic corona around the sun which produces fertility, rain, drought, and pestilence in mad succession. So great is the Sunbane's destructiveness that it now dominates all life in the Land. And its virulence also serves to mask Lord Foul's deeper stratagems.

He has spent centuries corrupting the Council of Lords. That group now rules over the Land as the Clave; and it is led by a Raver, one of the Despiser's most vicious servants. The Clave extracts blood from the people of the Land to feed the Banefire, an enormous blaze which increases the Sunbane.

However, the hidden purpose of the Clave and the Banefire is to inspire from Covenant an excessive exertion of wild magic. And toward that end, another Raver afflicts Covenant with a venom intended to cripple his self-control. When the venom has done its work, he will be unable to defend the Land without destroying the Arch.

As for Linden Avery, Lord Foul intends to use her loathing of death against her. She alone is gifted or cursed with the health-sense which once enabled the people of the Land to perceive physical and emotional health directly. For that reason, she is uniquely vulnerable to the malevolence of the Sunbane, as well as to the malice of the Ravers. Such evils threaten her to the core.

Although her health-sense accentuates her potential as a healer, it also gives her the capacity to possess other people; to reach so deeply into them that she can control their actions. By this means, Lord Foul intends to cripple her morally: he seeks to make of her a woman who will possess Covenant, misuse his power. Thus she will give the Despiser what he wants even if Covenant does not.

And should those ploys fail, Lord Foul has prepared other gambits.

Horrified in their separate ways by what has been done to the Land, Covenant and Linden wish to confront the Clave; but on their own, they cannot survive the complex perils of the Sunbane. Fortunately they gain the companionship of two villagers, Sunder and Hollian, who help Covenant and Linden avoid ruin.

But Linden, Sunder, and Hollian are separated from Covenant near a region known as Andelain, captured by the Clave while he enters Andelain alone. It was once the most beautiful and Earthpowerful place in the Land; and he now discovers that it alone remains intact, defended from the Sunbane by the last Forestal, Caer-Caveral, who was once Hile Troy. There Covenant encounters his Dead, the spectres of his long-gone friends. They offer him advice and guidance for the struggle ahead. And they give him a gift: a strange ebony creature named Vain, an artificial being created for a hidden purpose by ur-viles, former servants of the Despiser.

Thereafter Covenant hastens toward Revelstone to rescue his friends. When he encounters the Clave, he learns the cruelest secret of the Sunbane: it was made possible by his destruction of the Staff of Law thousands of years ago. Desperate to undo the harm which he has unwittingly caused, he risks wild magic in order to free Linden, Sunder, and Hollian, as well as a number of *Haruchai*, powerful warriors who at one time served the Lords.

With his friends, Vain, and a small group of *Haruchai*, Covenant then sets out to locate the One Tree, the wood from which Berek originally fashioned the Staff of Law. Covenant hopes to devise a new Staff to oppose the Clave and the Sunbane.

Traveling eastward, the companions encounter a party of Giants, seafaring beings from the homeland of the lost Giants of Seareach. One of them, Cable Seadreamer, has had a vision of a terrible threat to the Earth, and the Giants have sent out a Search to discover the danger.

Convinced that this threat is the Sunbane, Covenant persuades the Search to help him find the One Tree; and in *The One Tree*, Covenant, Linden, Vain, and several *Haruchai* set sail aboard the Giantship Starfare's Gem, leaving Sunder and Hollian to rally the people of the Land against the Clave.

The quest for the One Tree takes Covenant and Linden first to the land of the *Elohim*, cryptic beings of pure Earthpower who appear to understand and perhaps control the destiny of the Earth. The *Elohim* agree to reveal the location of the One Tree; but first they paralyze Covenant's mind, purportedly to protect the Earth from his growing power. Led now by Linden, the Search sails for the Isle of the One Tree.

Unexpectedly, however, they are joined by Findail, an *Elohim* who has been Appointed to guard against the consequences of the quest's actions.

Linden is unable to free Covenant's mind without possessing him, which she fears to do, knowing that she may unleash his power. When she and her companions are imprisoned in *Bhrathairealm*, however, she takes the risk of entering Covenant, much to Findail's dismay. Covenant then fights and masters a Sandgorgon, a fierce monster of the Great Desert. The creature's rampage through *Bhrathairealm* allows Covenant, Linden, and their companions to escape.

At last, Starfare's Gem reaches the Isle of the One Tree, where one of the *Haruchai*,

Brinn, becomes the Tree's Guardian. But when the companions approach their goal, they learn that they have been misled by the Despiser. Covenant's attempt to obtain wood for a new Staff of Law begins to rouse the Worm of the World's End. Once awakened, the Worm will accomplish Lord Foul's release from Time.

At the cost of his life, Seadreamer makes Linden aware of the true danger. She then forestalls Covenant. Nevertheless the Worm's restlessness forces the Search to flee as the Isle sinks into the sea, taking the One Tree beyond reach.

Defeated, the Search returns to the Land in *White Gold Wielder*. Covenant now believes that he must confront the Clave directly, quench the Banefire, and then battle the Despiser; and Linden is determined to aid him, in part because she loves him, and in part because she fears his unchecked wild magic.

Rejoined by Sunder, Hollian, and several *Haruchai*, Covenant, Linden, and a few Giants eventually reach Revelstone, where they challenge the Clave. After a fierce struggle, the companions corner the Raver commanding the Clave. There Seadreamer's brother, Grimmand Honninscrave—with the help of a Sandgorgon—sacrifices his life in order to "rend" the Raver. As a result, the Sandgorgon gains scraps of the Raver's sentience. Then Covenant flings himself into the Banefire, using its dark theurgy to transform the venom in his veins. When he is done, the Sunbane remains, but its evil no longer grows.

Afterward, Covenant and Linden, Sunder and Hollian, Vain and Findail, and two Giants turn toward Mount Thunder, where the Despiser now resides. Along the way, Hollian dies. But in Andelain, Caer-Caveral expends his own life to resurrect her by violating the Law of Life.

Gradually Linden realizes that Covenant does not mean to fight Lord Foul. That contest, Covenant believes, will unleash enough force to destroy Time. Afraid that he will surrender his ring, Linden prepares herself to possess him, although she now understands that possession is a great evil.

Yet when she and Covenant finally face Lord Foul, she is possessed herself by a Raver; and her efforts to win free leave her unwilling to interfere with Covenant. As she has feared, he does surrender his ring. But when the Despiser turns wild magic against Covenant, slaying his body, the altered venom is burned out of Covenant's spirit, and he becomes a being of pure wild magic, able to sustain the Arch despite Lord Foul's fury. As a result, the Despiser effectively defeats himself; and Covenant's ring falls to Linden.

Meanwhile, she has come to understand Vain's purpose—and Findail's Appointed role. Vain is pure structure: Findail, pure fluidity. Using Covenant's ring, Linden melds the two beings into a new Staff of Law. Then she reaches out with the restored power of Law to erase the Sunbane and begin the healing of the Land.

When she is done, Linden returns to her own world, where she finds that Covenant is indeed dead. Yet she now holds his wedding ring. And when Dr. Berenford comes looking for her, she discovers that her time with Covenant and her own victories have transformed her. She is now able to face her old life in an entirely new way.

"The Last Chronicles of Thomas Covenant"

In Book One, *The Runes of the Earth*, ten years have passed for Linden Avery; and in that time, her life has changed. She has adopted a son, Jeremiah, now fifteen, who was horribly damaged by the Despiser, losing half of his right hand. He displays a peculiar genius: he is able to build astonishing structures out of such toys as Tinkertoys and Legos. But in every other way, he is entirely unreactive, trapped in dissociation. Nonetheless Linden is devoted to him, giving him all of her frustrated love for Thomas Covenant and the Land.

In addition, she has become the Chief Medical Officer of a psychiatric hospital, where Covenant's ex-wife, Joan, is now a patient. For a time, Joan's condition resembles a vegetative catatonia. But then she starts to punish herself, punching her temple incessantly in an apparent effort to bring about her own death. Only the restoration of her white gold wedding band calms her, although it does not altogether prevent her violence.

As the story begins, Roger Covenant has reached twenty-one, and has come to claim custody of his mother: a claim which Linden denies. To this setback, Roger responds by taking his mother at gunpoint. And while Linden deals with the aftermath of that attack, Roger captures Jeremiah as well.

Separately, Linden and the police locate Roger, Joan, and Jeremiah. But when Linden confronts Roger, Joan is killed by lightning, and Roger opens fire on the police. In the ensuing fusillade, Linden, Roger, and Jeremiah are cut down; and Linden finds herself in the Land again, where she is informed that Lord Foul now has her son.

As before, several thousand years have passed in the Land, and everything that Linden knew has changed. The Land has been healed, restored to its former loveliness and potency. Now, however, it is ruled by Masters, *Haruchai* dedicated to the suppression of all magical knowledge and power. And their task is simplified by an eerie smog called Kevin's Dirt, which blocks health-sense.

Yet the Land faces threats which the Masters cannot defeat. *Caesures*—disruptions of time—wreak havoc, appearing randomly as Joan releases blasts of wild magic. In addition, an *Elohim* has visited the Land, warning of dangers which include various monsters—and an unnamed *halfhand*. And the new Staff of Law has been lost.

Desperate to locate and rescue Jeremiah, Linden soon acquires companions, both willing and reluctant: Anele, an ancient, Earthpowerful, and blind madman who claims that he is "the hope of the Land," and whose insanity varies with the surfaces—stone, dirt, grass—on which he stands; Liand, a naïve young villager; Stave, a Master who distrusts Linden and wishes to imprison Anele; a group of ur-viles, artificial creatures that formerly served Lord Foul; and a band of Ramen, the human servants of the Ranyhyn, the Land's time-wise horses. Linden also meets Esmer, the tormented descendant of Kastenessen, a deranged *Elohim*.

From Esmer, Linden learns the nature of the *caesures*. She is told that the ur-viles intend to protect her from betrayal by Esmer himself. And she finds that Anele knows where the Staff of Law was lost thousands of years ago.

Because she has no power except Covenant's ring, which she is only able to use with great difficulty—because she has no idea where Lord Foul has taken Jeremiah—and because she fears that she will not be able to search for him against the opposition of the Masters—Linden risks entering a *caesure*. Accompanied by Anele, Liand, Stave, the ur-viles, and three Ramen—the Manethrall Mahrtiir and his two Cords, Bhapa and Pahni—Linden rides into the temporal chaos of Joan's power.

Thanks to the theurgy of the ur-viles, and to the guidance of the Ranyhyn, she and her companions emerge more than three thousand years in their past, where they find that the Staff has been hidden and protected by a group of Waynhim, relatives of the ur-viles. When she reclaims the Staff, however, Esmer brings a horde of Demondim out of the Land's deep past to assail her. The Demondim are monstrous beings, the makers of the ur-viles and Waynhim, and their power now threatens the existence of the Arch of Time.

To protect the Arch while she and her companions escape, Linden uses Covenant's ring to create a *caesure* of her own. That disruption of time carries her company and the Demondim to her natural present. To her surprise, however, her *caesure* deposits them before the gates of Revelstone, the seat of the Masters. While the Masters fight a doomed battle against the Demondim, she and her companions enter the ambiguous sanctuary of Lord's Keep.

In Revelstone, Linden meets Handir, the Voice of the Masters: their leader. And she encounters the Humbled, Galt, Branl, and Clyme: three *Haruchai* who have been maimed to resemble Thomas Covenant in his honor. Cared for by a mysterious woman named the Mahdoubt, Linden tries to imagine how she can persuade the Masters to aid her search for Jeremiah. When she confronts them, however, all of her arguments are turned aside. Only Stave elects to stand with her: an act of defiance for which he is punished and spurned by his kinsmen.

The confrontation ends abruptly when news comes that riders are approaching

Revelstone. From the battlements, Linden sees four Masters racing to reach Lord's Keep ahead of the Demondim. With them are Thomas Covenant and Jeremiah. And Jeremiah has emerged enthusiastically from his dissociation.

In *Fatal Revenant*, the arrival of Covenant and Jeremiah brings turmoil. They are obviously real and powerful, yet they give no satisfactory account of their presence. And they refuse to let Linden touch them—or to use the Staff of Law. Instead they insist on being sequestered until they are ready to talk to her.

Meanwhile the Demondim mass at the gates, apparently preparing to destroy Revelstone; but they do not attack.

Shaken, Linden retreats to the plateau above Lord's Keep to await Covenant's summons. There she calls for Esmer, hoping that he will answer her questions. When he manifests himself, however, he surprises her by bringing more creatures out of the Land's distant past: a band of ur-viles and a smaller number of Waynhim, joined together to serve her. Cryptically he informs her that the creatures have prepared "manacles." And he reveals that the Demondim are now working in concert with Kastenessen. But he avoids Linden's other questions. Instead he tells her that she "must be the first to drink of the EarthBlood."

When Covenant's summons comes, Linden meets with him and Jeremiah in their chambers. Covenant speaks primarily in non sequiturs, although he insists that he knows how to save the Land. At the same time, Jeremiah pleads with Linden to trust his companion. Feeling both rejected and suspicious, Linden refuses when Covenant asks for his white gold ring. In response, Covenant demands that she join him on the plateau, where he will show her how he intends to save the Land.

Linden complies. She knows no other way to discover why and how her loved ones have changed. Instead of revealing their secrets, however, Covenant and Jeremiah create a portal which snatches her away from her present. Without transition, she finds herself with them ten millennia in the Land's past, during the time of Berek Halfhand's last wars.

They are near the dire forest of Garroting Deep—and far from the place and time that Covenant and Jeremiah sought. Instead their purpose has been deflected by a man called the Theomach, who appears to have a mystical relationship with time. He is one of the Insequent, a race of humans who pursue arcane knowledge and power in complete isolation from each other: a race whose only shared trait, apparently, is a loathing for the *Elohim*. The Theomach interfered with Covenant and Jeremiah because he believed that their intentions were dangerous enough to attract the *Elohim*.

The result is that Linden, Covenant, and Jeremiah stand in the dead of winter many brutal leagues from *Melenkurion* Skyweir, where Covenant and Jeremiah hope to use the EarthBlood and the Power of Command to defeat Lord Foul permanently.

In desperation, Linden decides to approach Berek for help. She wins the future High Lord's trust by healing many of his injured—and by introducing him to his own new-born health-sense.

Afterward the Theomach accomplishes his own purpose by persuading Berek to accept him as a guide and teacher. To show his good faith, he speaks the Seven Words: a mighty invocation of Earthpower which Linden has never heard before.

With supplies and horses provided by Berek Halfhand, Linden, Covenant, and Jeremiah trek toward *Melenkurion* Skyweir. But when the exhausted mounts start to die, Covenant and Jeremiah transport Linden to the Skyweir through a series of spatial portals. There Jeremiah reveals the magic of his talent for constructs. With the right materials, he is able to devise "doors": doors from one place to another; doors that bypass time; doors between realities. Building a door shaped like a large wooden box, he conveys himself, Covenant, and Linden deep into *Melenkurion* Skyweir, to the hidden caves of the EarthBlood.

Covenant is now ready to exert the Power of Command. But Linden drinks first, remembering Esmer's counsel. She then uses her Command to expose the secrets of her companions.

At once, a glamour is dispelled. Covenant shows his true form: he is Roger Covenant, not Thomas, and he despises all that his father loves. His right hand wields immense power: it is Kastenessen's, grafted onto him to wield Kastenessen's savage might. And on Jeremiah's back rides one of the *croyel*, a succubus that both feeds from and strengthens its host. The sentience that Jeremiah has demonstrated is the *croyel*'s, not his own. Gloating, Roger explains that he and the *croyel* aspire to become gods. Bringing Linden into the past—and bringing her here—was an attempt to trick her into breaking the Arch of Time. So far, she has avoided that danger. But now she is trapped ten thousand years in the Land's past and cannot escape.

A terrible battle follows, during which the Staff of Law turns black. Using her Staff, the Seven Words, and the EarthBlood, Linden opposes Roger and her possessed son. While an earthquake splits *Melenkurion* Skyweir, however, Roger and Jeremiah escape, leaving Linden stranded.

The experience transforms her. She now believes that only Thomas Covenant can save the Land. At the same time, her determination to rescue Jeremiah becomes even stronger—and more unscrupulous.

After an encounter with Caerroil Wildwood, the Forestal of Garroting Deep, who engraves her Staff with runes of power, she is retrieved by the Mahdoubt. Here the Mahdoubt is revealed as one of the Insequent. When Linden is returned to Revelstone in her proper time, she learns that Liand has acquired a piece of *orcrest*, a stone capable of channeling Earthpower in various ways. She also hears that a stranger has single-handedly eliminated the entire horde of the Demondim.

He is the Harrow, yet another Insequent. He covets both Linden's Staff and Covenant's ring, and he has the power to take them by emptying her mind. Fortunately the Mahdoubt intervenes. Violating the ethics which govern the Insequent, she defeats the Harrow, winning from him the promise that he will not wrest the Staff of Law and Covenant's ring from Linden by force: a victory which costs the Mahdoubt her own life. After assuring Linden that he will gain his desires by other means, the Harrow disappears.

Then Linden, her friends, and the three Humbled summon Ranyhyn and ride away from Revelstone. Because she still has no idea where Jeremiah is hidden, her stated intention is to reach Andelain and consult with the Dead, as Covenant once did. For private reasons, she also hopes to recover High Lord Loric's *krill*, an eldritch dagger forged to channel extremes of power too great for any unaided mortal.

Along the way, she and her companions come upon a village which has been destroyed by a *caesure*: a *caesure* which Esmer controls as a weapon against the Harrow. There she learns that the Harrow knows where Jeremiah has been hidden—and that Esmer intends to prevent the Insequent from revealing his secret. At the same time, Roger Covenant attacks with a force of Cavewights. In the ensuing battle, Linden's company is soon overwhelmed. Frantic, she takes a wild gamble: she tries to summon a Sandgorgon. Six of them charge into the fight, routing Roger and the Cavewights, and allowing the Harrow to escape.

Later Linden hears that a large number of Sandgorgons have come to the Land, driven by the rent remnants of a Raver's malign spirit. In Covenant's name, they answered Linden's call. But now they have repaid their debt to him. They seek a new outlet for their own savage hungers, and for the Raver's malice.

When Linden and her companions have done what they can for the homeless villagers, they ride on to Salva Gildenbourne, a great forest which encircles Andelain. There they encounter a party of Giants, Swordmainnir, all women except for one deranged man, Longwrath: their prisoner. When the Giants and Linden's company reach comparative safety, they stop to exchange tales.

The leader of the Giants, Rime Coldspray, the Ironhand, explains that Longwrath is a Swordmain who has been possessed by a *geas*. With nine other Swordmainnir, the Ironhand has been seeking the cause or purpose of his compulsion. After acquiring an apparently powerful sword, he has led the Giants to the Land. Here it becomes clear that his *geas* requires him to kill Linden.

To protect her, the Swordmainnir agree to accompany her to Andelain. But during the next day, they are assailed by the *skurj*, fiery worm-like monsters that serve Kastenessen. Two of the Giants are killed. Yet Liand saves the company by using his *orcrest* to summon a thunderstorm. The downpour forces the *skurj* underground, and the surviving companions are able to flee.

At last, they reach Andelain. The sacred Hills are warded by the Wraiths, small candle-flame sprites that repulse evil by drawing power from the awakened *krill*. Thus protected, the companions hasten to find the *krill*.

During the dark of the moon, however, the company meets the Harrow again. Indirectly he has offered Linden a bargain: if she surrenders the Staff of Law and Covenant's ring, he will take her to Jeremiah. But while he taunts Linden, Infelice, the monarch of the *Elohim*, appears. She argues passionately against the Harrow— and against everything that Linden intends to do. Yet Linden ignores them both as she approaches the *krill*.

There the Dead begin to arrive. While the four original High Lords observe, Caer-Caveral and High Lord Elena escort Thomas Covenant's spectre. Yet the Lords and the last Forestal and Covenant himself refuse to speak. None of them answer Linden.

Driven to the last extremity, she raises all of her power from both her Staff and Covenant's ring, and commits those contradictory magicks to the *krill*. Doing so, she cuts through the Laws of Life and Death until she succeeds at resurrecting Covenant; drawing his spirit out of the Arch of Time; restoring his slain body.

Yet power on such a scale has vast consequences. Linden's actions also awaken the Worm of the World's End.

In addition, there are other problems. In *Against All Things Ending*, she finds that Covenant's leprosy is active again. And the stress of his return to mortality has fractured his mind. As a result, he is often unable to control his thoughts, his memories, or even his attention.

When the companions are informed that days will pass before the World's End is accomplished, Linden decides to accept the Harrow's bargain: one last attempt to rescue Jeremiah by surrendering her Staff and Covenant's ring. Then, however, another Insequent appears, the Ardent, who has come to ensure that the Harrow does not deal falsely with Linden. Under pressure, the Harrow—with the Ardent's support—transports Linden, Covenant, and all of their companions to the Lost Deep, elaborate caverns which were once the home of the Viles, creators of the Demondim. There Linden follows the Harrow to Jeremiah's hiding place.

The boy is still ruled by the *croyel*, and he has concealed himself even from the *Elohim* within one of his constructs. When Linden breaks the construct, Roger arrives to murder the Harrow, and to claim Covenant's ring. But Covenant opposes Roger with the *krill*, and while they struggle, Esmer suddenly takes Roger to safety. Esmer then announces that the company's actions have awakened an ancient bane, a sentient and eternal being called She Who Must Not Be Named. Now She is rising to devour the company.

Desperately Linden and her companions try to flee, bringing succubus-ridden

Jeremiah and a helpless Covenant, whose awareness of his circumstances has been blocked by Esmer. But while the company, led by ur-viles and Waynhim, scrambles to escape, Linden falls prey to the bane indirectly: believing herself to be invaded by worms and maggots, she collapses into unconsciousness. However, Covenant's love for her enables him to overcome Esmer's influence. With the aid of the Dead—who sacrifice the spectre of Elena, Covenant's daughter—he forestalls the bane until the Ardent is able to transport the company away.

On the Lower Land a considerable distance from Mount Thunder, the companions try to recover. All are exhausted, and Linden is trapped in nightmares, unable to regain consciousness. Dismayed by her condition, Covenant takes a desperate risk: he holds her underwater, hoping that the sensations of drowning will bring her back to herself. Fortunately his gamble succeeds.

The Ardent informs the company that he has caused his own death by interfering with the Harrow. Before he passes away, however, he supplies the company with food. Later he also transports the Ramen Cords, Pahni and Bhapa, to Revelstone so that they can try to win the support of the Masters.

When the companions have regained some of their strength, Linden attempts to free Jeremiah from the *croyel* by entering his mind: a graveyard where all of his thoughts and desires are buried. She fails; and before anyone can try a different approach, the company is attacked by *caesures*. In the confusion, Liand tries to use his *orcrest* stone against the *croyel*; but Anele—suddenly possessed by Kastenessen— kills the young villager.

A different attack soon follows: Roger and a host of Cavewights are joined by Esmer. Although the Swordmainnir and the *Haruchai* fight furiously, they are vastly outnumbered. But ur-viles and Waynhim respond by rendering Esmer helpless with their manacles. Now sane, Anele challenges the *croyel* with the *orcrest*. And when the Humbled Galt unexpectedly sacrifices himself to preserve Anele, Anele is able to destroy the succubus. The effort kills the old man, but not before he transfers his legacy of Earthpower to Jeremiah.

To save the company, Linden uses wild magic, wreaking terrible carnage even though she is not a rightful white gold wielder. In the aftermath, Esmer begs her to kill him. But she cannot: she has done too much killing. However, Stave—Galt's father—spares her by using the *krill* to end Esmer's life.

Later Covenant leaves the company, taking only the remaining Humbled, Clyme and Branl, with him. He intends to confront Joan in an effort to end her torment and stop the *caesures*; and he is unwilling to risk Linden against a rightful white gold wielder. Also he believes that Jeremiah still needs her. The boy is no longer possessed, but he remains buried in his long dissociation.

Stricken by Covenant's departure, Linden and her companions decide to let the

Ranyhyn choose their destination. After an encounter with the lurker of the Sarangrave, a wetland monster with terrifying appetites and strengths, the great horses run, taking Linden, Jeremiah, and Stave ahead of the exhausted Giants and Manethrall Mahrtiir. After many leagues, the three reach a crater full of the bones of ancient monsters. There Jeremiah begins to build one of his constructs while Linden defends him from *caesures*. But then Infelice arrives, intending to kill the boy because she believes that he will devise a prison for the *Elohim*—and because she knows that Lord Foul wants to use Jeremiah's talent to imprison the Creator. However, Stave's strength of will enables him to distract Infelice; and with Linden's help, Jeremiah completes his construct. When he enters it, he emerges with his mind restored.

Meanwhile Covenant and the Humbled travel toward Ridjeck Thome, where Covenant first defeated Lord Foul. Along the way, they encounter the Feroce, worshippers of the lurker, who offer Covenant a bargain: they will help him overcome Joan's defenders if he will try to preserve the lurker from the Worm. Knowing that he cannot protect the lurker except by saving the Earth, Covenant agrees.

True to their word, the Feroce sacrifice many lives; but their aid does not suffice. In order to reach Joan, Covenant and the Humbled enter a *caesure*: a doomed gamble from which Joan rescues Covenant so that she can kill him herself. And Joan is possessed by *turiya* Raver, who casts Covenant adrift in his memories. But before Joan can summon a killing blast, Covenant draws on her wild magic to heal his mind. When she is distracted by the Ranyhyn, he uses the *krill* to end her life.

A tsunami caused by the Worm follows. It nearly claims Covenant, Clyme, and Branl. And when it passes—when a new day begins—the sun no longer rises. The world has fallen into perpetual twilight: the onset of the last dark.

The
Last
Dark

Part One

ॐ

"to bear what must
be borne"

1.

Betimes Some Wonder

Linden Avery's fate may indeed have been written in water. It was certainly writ in tears. They blurred everything; redefined the foundations of her life.

Standing in Muirwin Delenoth, resting place of abhorrence, with Jeremiah clasped in her arms, she felt emotions as extreme as the dismay which had followed Thomas Covenant's resurrection and the rousing of the Worm of the World's End; as paralyzing and uncontainable as the knowledge that she had doomed all of her loves. But there, in Andelain, the scale of her distress had seemed too great to be called despair. Here, in the company of bones and old death, her glad shock at Jeremiah's restoration was too great and complex to be joy.

Stave of the *Haruchai* stood waiting with his arms folded, impassive as a man who had done nothing, and had never lost a son. Three Ranyhyn waited near him, watching Linden and Jeremiah with glory in their eyes. In the distant west, the sun drifted down shrouded in the hues of ash and dust, casting shadows like innominate auguries from the stone blades and plates which rimmed the hollow. Heaved aside by the deflagration of Jeremiah's construct, the skeletons of *quellvisks* sprawled against the far slope of Muirwin Delenoth as if they sought to disavow their role in his redemption—or as if they had drawn back in reverence.

Such things were the whole world, and the whole world waited. But Linden took no notice. She was unaware that she had dropped her Staff, or that Covenant's ring still hung on its chain around her neck, holding in its small circle the forged fate of all things. She regarded only Jeremiah, felt only him; knew only that he responded to her embrace. A miracle so vast—

I did it, Mom. For the first time in his life, he had spoken to her. *I made a door for my mind, and it opened.*

Joy was too small a word for her emotions. Happiness and gratitude and relief and even astonishment were trivial by comparison. A staggering confluence of valor and trust had restored her son. At that moment, she believed that if the Worm came for her now, or She Who Must Not Be Named, or even Lord Foul the Despiser, her only regret would be that she did not get to know who her son had become during his absence.

Somehow he had weathered his excruciating dissociation. In graves he had endured what the Despiser and Roger Covenant and the *croyel* had done to him.

She was murmuring his name without realizing it, trying to absorb the knowledge of him; trying to imprint his hug and his tangible legacy of Earthpower and his unmistakable awareness onto every neuron of her being. He was her adopted son. Physically she had known every inch of him for most of his life. But she had never met the underlying *him* until this moment: until he had arisen from his absence and looked at her and spoken.

The way in which she repeated his name was weeping; but that, too, she did not realize. She was no more aware of her tears than she was of Stave and the Ranyhyn and passing time and the ancient ruin of bones. Holding Jeremiah in her arms—and being held by him—was enough.

She had no better name for what she felt than exaltation.

Yet the exaltation was Jeremiah's, not hers. He had become transcendent, numinous: an icon of transfiguration. He seemed to glow with warmth and health in her arms as if he had become the Staff of Law: not *her* Staff, runed and ebony, transformed to blackness by her sins and failures, but rather the Staff of Law as it should have been, pure and beneficent, the Staff that Berek Halfhand had first created to serve the beauty of the Land.

The gift that Anele had given Jeremiah elevated him in ways that Linden could not define. He had not simply become responsive and aware. He appeared to dismiss the past ten years of his life as if they had no power over him.

Such things could not be dismissed.

"Chosen," Stave said as if he sought to call her back from an abyss. "Linden Avery." An uncharacteristic timbre of pleading or regret ached in his voice. "Will you not harken to me?"

She was not ready to hear him. She did not want to step back from Jeremiah. He vindicated everything that she had done and endured in his name. If she withdrew from exaltation, she would be forced to think—

And every thought led to fear and contradiction; to dilemmas for which she was unprepared. No one could endure what her son had suffered without emotional damage; without scars and scarification. Yet she could not discern damage. In her embrace, he felt more than physically well. He seemed entirely *whole*, mentally and spiritually intact.

That Linden could not believe. She knew better.

"Mom." Like hers, Jeremiah's voice wept gladly. "Mom, stop crying. You're getting me all wet."

For his sake, she tried.

Long ago under *Melenkurion* Skyweir, she had forgotten the sensations of being a healer. Although she had cared for her companions in various ways, she had responded to their injuries as if her own actions were those of a stranger. But she had not forgotten what she had learned during her years in Berenford Memorial, tending the wounded souls of the abused and broken.

Training and experience had taught her that an escape from unreactive passivity was a vital step, crucial to everything that it enabled—but it was only the *first* step. When a crippled spirit found the courage to emerge from its defenses, it then had to face the horrors which had originally driven it into hiding. Otherwise deeper forms of healing could not occur.

She realized now that she was expecting a rush of agony from Jeremiah: the remembered anguish of every cruelty which the Despiser and Roger and the *croyel* had inflicted. That prospect appalled her.

But when she considered her son clinically, she recognized that the outbreak which she dreaded was unlikely. Immediate firestorms of memory were rare. More commonly, a new form of dissociation intervened to protect the harmed mind while its new awareness was still fragile. Full recall came later—if it came at all. Jeremiah felt whole to her because his worst recollections had not arisen from their graves.

For all she knew, they might remain buried indefinitely.

Why, then, was she afraid? Why did she contemplate anything except her son's restoration? Why could she not be content with miracles, as any other mother might have been?

She could not because Lord Foul's prophecies might still prove true, if the Despiser contrived to recapture Jeremiah—

—or if events triggered more memories than he could withstand.

She had failed to resurrect Covenant without his leprosy. Other restorations might go awry. With or without Lord Foul's connivance, predatory pain lurked inside Jeremiah: she could not believe otherwise. Suffering as calamitous as his possession by the *croyel* might overtake him without presage.

For that reason, she needed to remain alert in spite of her gladness. But she did not know where to begin trying to identify the truths buried beneath her son's presence.

"Chosen," Stave repeated more sharply. "Linden Avery. I comprehend the force of your son's awakening, and of your reunion with him. Who will do so, if I do not? I, who have lost a son, and may only yearn bootlessly for his return to life? Nevertheless we cannot remain here.

"It appears that the Falls have ceased. Yet should the Unbeliever fail in his quest, they will surely return. And the wider perils of the world will not await the culmination of your release from sorrow. The last crisis of the Earth gathers against us. Also the Ranyhyn are restive. I deem that they are eager to rejoin our companions, and that they discern a need for haste."

Long before Linden was ready to release him, Jeremiah withdrew. For a moment, he gazed at her with gleaming in his eyes like the stars on the foreheads of the Ranyhyn. Then he turned toward Stave.

Linden was too full of other emotions to be surprised when Jeremiah reached out and hugged the *Haruchai*.

Although Stave did not respond, he suffered the boy's clasp until Jeremiah let him go. But when Jeremiah stepped back, the former Master lifted his eyebrow as if he were mildly perplexed.

"You are much altered," he remarked. "Is your condition such that you are able to remember Galt, who kept the fangs of the *croyel* from your neck?"

Jeremiah nodded. "I remember. He's your son. He let himself be killed so Anele could get that monster off my back. So Anele could give me all this power."

—the hope of the Land.

Linden watched the boy with a kind of awe. Some part of him must have remained conscious throughout the long years of his dissociation. Other aspects must have been evoked or informed by the *croyel*'s use of him. Otherwise he would not have been able to emerge so swiftly—or to know so much.

"Then," Stave said flatly, "I am content that you are indeed restored."

As if in confirmation, the Ranyhyn tossed their heads, and Hynyn trumpeted an imperious acknowledgment. From among them, Khelen came forward and nudged Jeremiah, apparently urging the boy to mount.

Jeremiah, Linden tried to say; but she had no voice. She did not know where to begin. Too many aspects of her relationship with her son had taken on new meanings.

Briefly the boy stroked the young stallion's muzzle: a small gesture of affection. Then he turned back to his mother.

"Mom." There were tears in his voice again, if not in his eyes. His grin fell away. With his halfhand, he pointed at the bullet hole over her heart. "I'm sorry. I never wanted you to get shot. But I'm glad, too. I needed you so bad—" For a moment, the color of his gaze darkened, hinting at black depths of pain. "I needed you to come after me. I was worse than dead."

His pajamas remained torn and stained. The horses ramping across the tops were almost indecipherable. And Liand's blood still soiled the tattered bottoms, in spite of Linden's efforts to wash them. She could barely remember that the fabric had once been sky-blue. It would never come clean.

But before she could reply, Jeremiah shook his head hard; blinked until his expression cleared. Gesturing around him, he snorted, "*Quellvisks*. They were good for something after all."

Something which Lord Foul had not foreseen. In a sense, the boy had reincarnated himself from the old bones of monsters.

Oh, my son. Linden needed to stop weeping. Really, she could not go on like this. When Stave said her name again, his tone had become more peremptory. And he was right. They could not linger here without food or water or their companions. The wonder of her son's emergence from his portal was a small detail compared to the threat of the Worm. The world's end would not pause for any instance of mere human exaltation and relief.

"Say something, Mom," Jeremiah prodded. His tone suggested a teenager's impatience. "Say anything. Tell me you heard Stave. He's right, we need to go." His next thought made him grin again. "And I want to see the Giants' faces when they see me. They are not going to believe it."

Linden tried to refuse. She wanted nothing except to concentrate on her son. Her thirst for the sound of his voice was acute. There was so much that she yearned to know about him. About what he had endured—and how he had endured it. It did not matter where she began, as long as she could search for the truth.

I never wanted you to get shot.

But there was something else— Something in Stave's tone nagged at the edges of her health-sense.

She absolutely had to stop crying.

When she rubbed at her eyes, the emptiness of her hands reminded her that she no longer held the Staff of Law.

She felt strangely reluctant to retrieve it. It represented responsibilities which were too great for her. Nevertheless she was capable now of many things that would have surpassed her less than an hour ago. She was still the same Linden Avery who had raged and failed and despaired; yet somehow she had also been made new. And watching over Jeremiah was a task to which she could commit herself without hesitation.

To meet that challenge, she might well need every conceivable resource.

Unsteadily she stooped to reclaim her Staff.

As her fingers closed on the engraved blackness of the wood, another faint pang touched her nerves: an evanescent breath of approaching *wrongness*. Frowning, she raised her head to scent the air, extend her health-sense.

The atmosphere had a brittle taste, as if it were compounded of a substance that might shatter. She knew that the season was spring; but that fact seemed to have no meaning on the Lower Land. Hideous theurgies and slaughter had made a wasteland of the entire region. Muirwin Delenoth was as desiccated as its bones: it had been shaped by death.

"Mom?" Jeremiah asked; but still she did not speak.

Drawing warmth and sensitivity from her Staff, Linden considered the slopes of the hollow, the ragged plates around the rim. Then she lifted her attention to the declining sun and the tainted hue of the sky. The pall of ash and dust overhead was wrong in its own fashion: it was unnatural, imposed by some force beyond the reach of her senses. But it was not malice; not evil or deliberate. The almost imperceptible frisson of *wrongness* rose from some other source.

"Stave—?" She had to swallow hard to clear her throat. "Do you feel it?"

The former Master's silence was answer enough.

Slowly she turned in a circle, pushing her percipience to its limits. She expected the disturbance to come from the vicinity of Foul's Creche; from Covenant's search for Joan. But she felt nothing there. When she faced northwest, however, she found what she sought.

It was faint, almost too subtle to be discerned. Yet it was thin with distance, not weakness. The fact that she could detect it at all across so many leagues bespoke tremendous power. As soon as she tuned her nerves to the pitch of this specific malevolence—and to the direction from which it spread—she knew what it was.

It was Kevin's Dirt, and it came from Mount Thunder.

For the first time, Kastenessen was extending his bale over the Lower Land.

Repeatedly he had tried to prevent Jeremiah's rescue from the *croyel*. Now he was sending the fug of Kevin's Dirt to hamper Linden and the Staff of Law. When it spread far enough, his theurgy would numb her senses, and Mahrtiir's, and perhaps Jeremiah's. And it would aggravate Covenant's leprosy. If Joan did not kill him first. With forces drawn from She Who Must Not Be Named, the mad *Elohim* strove to ensure that Linden and her companions would not survive.

A shudder like a chill ran through her. Her fingers clenched the Staff until her knuckles ached. Reflexively she confirmed that she still had Covenant's ring. An old comfort, it had steadied her for years, until he had refused her.

—*the last crisis of the Earth.*

"I understand," she told Stave abruptly. "We should go. Kevin's Dirt is coming. And maybe the *skurj*." Or Kastenessen might decide to challenge her himself now that he had lost Esmer. "We need to find the Giants and Mahrtiir. Then we'll have to decide what we're going to do."

Without Covenant—

She meant to mount Hyn and ride at once. But when she looked at her son again, she faltered. He seemed eager: too eager. Did she detect an undercurrent of alarm? If so, she suspected that he chafed to flee from his memories before they could emerge from their coverts and ravage him. He needed movement.

Stave waited for her impassively. Almost pleading, Linden asked him, "Do we have to ride hard? I need to talk to Jeremiah. There's so much—" Her son had become someone she did not know. "If the Ranyhyn run, I won't be able to hear him."

A quirk at the corner of Stave's mouth may have implied a smile. "Chosen," he answered, "the great horses have demonstrated that they are well acquainted with our straits. Mayhap they will moderate their haste for your sake, and for your son's."

"Then let's *go*," urged Jeremiah. "I can't wait to see the Giants. And Infelice gave me an idea. I want to try it."

He startled Linden. An idea? What could he possibly have gleaned from the interference of the *Elohim*? And how? Who had he become? Was he simply trying to pack down the earth that shielded him from his immured hurts? Or had he somehow learned strengths which she could not imagine?

If his instincts prompted him to seek safety by outrunning his wounds, surely she should trust him?

Pushing herself into motion, Linden turned toward Hyn.

At once, Stave came to help her mount. And when she was seated astride the familiar security of Hyn's back, he did the same for Jeremiah, boosting the boy effortlessly onto Khelen. Then he sprang for Hynyn.

Hynyn whinnied a command to the other horses. Together the three Ranyhyn flowed into motion so smoothly that Linden felt no need to cling. Urged by Jeremiah's shout of celebration, they accelerated at the slope of the caldera, pounding upward, flinging clots and plumes of dry dirt from their hooves. But once they had crested the rim, passed between the sandstone sentinels, and started down the long slope northward, they eased their pace to a light-footed canter. Their strides raised a low drum-roll from the baked ground; yet when Linden settled herself to Hyn's rhythm, she found that she would not need to shout in order to make herself heard.

Ahead of her, Kevin's Dirt expanded its maleficence by slow increments. Fortunately its peril was not exacerbated by *caesures*. Their absence troubled her on Covenant's behalf—they might now be aimed at him as he approached Ridjeck Thome—but it also reassured her. For the moment, at least, she, Jeremiah, and Stave were relatively safe.

Relying on the former Master and the Ranyhyn to warn her at need, she turned her attention entirely on her son.

"Jeremiah?" She resisted an impulse to raise her voice over the rattle of hooves. "Can you hear me all right?"

He flashed a grin at her. "Sure, Mom. I've been listening to you my whole life. I could probably hear you if you whispered half a mile away."

That simple answer was enough to stun her for a moment. Covenant had assured her, *None of the love you lavished on your son was wasted. That isn't even possible.* All those years of speaking her love to Jeremiah without any response—and yet he had heard her. More amazing still, he had believed her in spite of what the Despiser and his natural mother had done to him.

Until we know more about what's happened to him, just trust yourself.

A fresh rush of emotion made her awkward. "Then you've probably already figured out most of the questions I want to ask."

"Maybe." He cocked his head to one side, considering. "Let's see.

"That *croyel*"—he made a spitting noise—"used me to say all kinds of things. You want to know how many of them are true."

Linden nodded mutely. Everything about Jeremiah seemed to have the power to astound her.

"Well," he continued slowly, "a lot of them were. True, I mean." His voice held a note of caution, as if there were details that he wanted to avoid. "Mom, you tried hard to take care of me. I know that. It wasn't your fault you couldn't reach me. I just hurt too much. But giving me those racetrack pieces was like a miracle. I don't know how you came up with the idea, but it was perfect.

"Using those bones"—he gestured behind him—"was the second time I managed to make a—I don't know what else to call it—a door for my mind. That racetrack was the first. I couldn't do anything with my body except build. I wanted to. I just couldn't. But with my mind—

"Most of what the *croyel* said about that was true. When I went through my door, I was here. I mean, not *here*." He indicated the arid landscape. "I mean in the Land. In this world. But I was still just a mind. I was just kind of floating around. In one time or another. One place or another. I couldn't touch anything, or talk to anybody.

"But there were people that noticed me anyway. Powers. Beings. And if they noticed me, they could talk to me. The Vizard was one, like the *croyel* said. He wanted to use me. The Viles once, but they weren't interested. I think I met a Demimage, but he couldn't figure out what I was. A couple of Ravers. They *wanted* me." Jeremiah shuddered. "A few *Elohim*, but mostly they tried to convince me to go away and not come back." With a snort of derision, he added, "Like that was going to happen. It was the only escape I had. I couldn't give it up."

"And Covenant?" Linden asked carefully. "Did the *croyel* tell the truth about him?"

"As much as that monster could stand," Jeremiah replied without hesitation. She heard gratitude in his voice, saw affection in the brown warmth of his eyes. "I mean about the real Covenant. Not about Roger. The real Covenant talked to me more than all the rest put together.

"He talked like he actually cared about me."

Treading as cautiously as she could, Linden probed for more. "What did he say?"

The boy grinned at her again. "He told me I could count on you. Like I didn't know that already. If I needed you, you would do anything to help me, even if it was impossible. He said you have no idea how strong you really are. He said it makes you wonderful."

Wonderful—? That idea stunned Linden once more. It closed her throat; almost brought her back to tears. For long, terrible days, she had been tormented by the fear that her son secretly belonged to the Despiser; that he had acquiesced to the *croyel*; that he had been forever marked and marred by Lord Foul's bonfire, Lord Foul's malice. Yet Covenant had spent years of Jeremiah's childhood telling him that his mother was wonderful. And Jeremiah had believed the Unbeliever. Even in his dissociation, he had recognized something in Linden that she herself could not see—

While she tried to master her emotions, Jeremiah looked away. Frowning with concentration, he scanned the beaten terrain. "And he talked about the *Elohim*. I didn't really understand, but I think he was trying to explain why they're important. They're like a metaphor?" He sounded uncertain. "A symbol? They represent the stars. Or maybe they *are* the stars. Or maybe the stars and the *Elohim* are like shadows of each other. The shadows of the Creator's children."

He shrugged, flexing easily with the beat of Khelen's strides. "He wanted me to get it, but it didn't make much sense."

Linden, too, did not understand. But she did not care about the *Elohim*. At the moment, she cared only about the ineffable fact that Jeremiah was speaking to her; that her son had found his voice when he had recovered his mind. And he had recovered his will as well: oh, yes, his will beyond question. His years of self-protective absence had taught him unexpected resources of determination.

They encouraged her to keep him talking.

She avoided the most crucial issue because he avoided it. Instead she inquired further about his encounters with Covenant's spirit.

"I probably shouldn't admit this," she offered tentatively, "but I almost panicked when I saw Revelstone and Mount Thunder in the living room. I came close to taking you and running." She still believed that she should have done so. "Then neither of us would have been shot."

"And we wouldn't be here to fight for the Land," Jeremiah put in at once.

She conceded his point. She did not want to discuss the cost of trying to carry burdens which were too heavy for human arms to lift. "Of course," she continued, "I didn't know then that your mind was coming here at night, when I thought that you were asleep. But what I'm trying to ask is, what inspired you to build those models?" And to build them on the same day that Roger Covenant came to demand custody of his mother? "Was that Covenant's idea? Did he tell you to do it?"

Jeremiah thought for a moment. "Not exactly. He never *told* me to do anything. But he made sure I knew Revelstone and Mount Thunder were important. He said things could happen there that might frustrate Lord Foul." Suddenly vehement, he snapped, "I *hate* that bastard." Then, hunching his shoulders and knotting his fists, he calmed himself. "So I wanted to warn you. Legos were the only language I had."

The only language— Such things threatened Linden's composure. But Jeremiah had touched on his unspoken wounds, albeit obliquely. That demanded her full attention. Her own reactions could wait.

In the dirt ahead of her, she saw the marks of three Ranyhyn galloping toward Muirwin Delenoth: longer strides, deeper hoof-cuts in the ground, but the same track. Clearly Hyn, Hynyn, and Khelen were retracing their path away from the Swordmainnir and Manethrall Mahrtiir. They aimed to rejoin Linden's companions instead of pursuing some other purpose.

Instead of taking her to Covenant.

She told herself that she was glad. She wanted to be reunited with her friends. Wanted them, in effect, to meet Jeremiah for the first time. In addition, she needed their support, their comfort, their ready courage. And she felt that she could not afford to be distracted from her son: certainly not by her yearning for the only man whom she had ever truly loved.

As though he had caught the scent of her thoughts, Jeremiah asked abruptly, "Do you think he's dead? Covenant, I mean. When he left, he looked like he was going to die. Like he planned on dying."

Startled, Linden countered, "Why do you think that? What made you think he was going to die?"

The boy studied her. "Isn't that what *you* think? I must have picked up the idea from you."

Linden winced. She could easily believe that her reaction to Covenant's departure had conveyed the impression that she was bracing herself for his death.

While her son faced her with concern darkening in his eyes, she sighed, "No, Jeremiah. I don't think Covenant is dead. And I don't think he was planning to die. You've met him, but you haven't seen him in action. Practically everything he does is almost inconceivable, but he does it anyway. That's why the Land needs him. Why we need him." Her own needs were more complex. "Maybe he really does have an inherent relationship with wild magic. Or maybe he's just *more* than anyone else I've ever met. Either way, I don't believe that Joan can kill him. There isn't enough of her left, and that Raver can't make her into something she isn't."

After a moment, Linden forced herself to be honest. "But I do think something is dying. If it isn't already dead." Every word was bitter to her. It was gall on her tongue. She said it, and the next one, and the next, because she wanted to be worthy of her son. "That must be what you saw in me when he left. He doesn't love me anymore. Or he's afraid of me. I love him, but ever since the Ardent brought us out of the Lost Deep, I've been watching what Covenant and I had together die."

Jeremiah listened with an air of impatience; but he waited for her to finish. Then he said as if he were certain, "You're wrong, Mom. I've heard him. He still loves you. Whatever he's doing, it isn't about not loving you. That's what made me think he's planning to die. He left the way he did because he isn't sure he'll ever see you again."

Her son meant well: Linden knew that. He might even be right. Nevertheless she doubted him. Her awareness of the many ways in which she had failed ran too deep. After all, what had she done to enable Jeremiah's escape from his prison? Sure, she had resisted Infelice as much as she could. And she had extinguished Joan's *caesures*. But in the end, her only real contribution had been trust: trust in the Ranyhyn—and in Esmer's reasons for restoring Jeremiah's racecar.

She could not believe in Covenant's love because she did not know how to make peace with herself.

In self-defense, she reverted to her earlier questions. "We were talking about your models. You explained Revelstone and Mount Thunder. What about your Tinkertoy castle?" She had seen its original in the Lost Deep. "Were you trying to tell me something there, too? Was that another warning?"

Had Covenant nudged Jeremiah to prepare her in some fashion? If so, the effort had been wasted. It was too cryptic. Knowing nothing of the Lost Deep, she could not have interpreted her son's faery edifice.

This time, Jeremiah shook his head. "I was just practicing. I only visited the Lost Deep once. I mean, on my own." Without Roger and the *croyel*. "But while I was there, I saw what the Viles could do. I fell in love with that castle. Then later, when I started to get the idea I needed to warn you somehow, I didn't want to make a mistake. So I tried to copy the castle.

"I hadn't done anything like that before. Everything else I built I just sort of found. Even the racetrack. I don't know how to explain it. I didn't start out with an idea. The shapes came from whatever I was using. They all just *came*. But if I wanted to warn you, I had to choose the shapes for myself.

"The castle was my first try." Linden saw satisfaction in his mien: satisfaction— and a new surge of eagerness. "It was easier than I thought. Until then, I didn't know I can choose anything I want. Now I do. I just need the right pieces."

Now, Linden thought. While he was eager. While he felt sure of himself.

It was probably too soon. In her former life, she would have waited longer; perhaps much longer. But her son had so little time. The Earth had so little.

Her heart seemed to crowd her throat as she asked, "What was it like, having the *croyel* on your back? What did it do to you? What did Lord Foul do?"

At once, Jeremiah's manner changed as if he had slammed a door. He jerked his face away. "You know what it was like. I don't want to talk about it. I want to forget it ever happened."

Then he nudged Khelen away from Hyn. To Stave, he called, "Can we go faster? I want to reach the Giants."

"Chosen?" Stave inquired. His tone implied no opinion.

Cursing to herself, Linden muttered, "All right. They're probably worried about us."

The Swordmainnir had been left behind because they were too weary after their long struggles to run with the Ranyhyn. And Mahrtiir had stayed with them so that Narunal could guide them across the wide wilderland of the Spoiled Plains to rejoin the other horses.

Stave nodded. Briefly he stroked the side of Hynyn's neck.

With a whicker of command to Khelen and Hyn, the roan stallion gathered speed so fluidly that Linden could not discern the precise moment when he began to quicken his gait. He galloped slightly ahead of them, but they did not lose ground in spite of their smaller stature. Indeed, Hyn matched his pace with apparent ease. As she had done before, the mare cast the hard ground behind her as if she could equal Hynyn's thundering haste for hours or days.

Stave rode effortlessly, like a man who had become one with his mount. In Khelen's care, Jeremiah waved his arms and shouted encouragement. But Linden gripped her Staff and prayed that she had not driven her son to bury his wounds more deeply.

The quality of the light in the stained air told her that the sun was setting beyond the barrier of Landsdrop. In the distance ahead, still scores of leagues away, she felt the advance of Kevin's Dirt more strongly. After their fashion, the Ranyhyn were trying to outrace a doom for which she had no answer.

Linden's relief and joy at her son's restoration would have been greater if she had not been so afraid for him.

In your present state, Chosen, Desecration lies ahead of you. It does not crowd at your back.

It was entirely impossible that he had not been maimed in some way by Lord Foul's malice and the *croyel*'s cruelty.

2.

Nightfall

The sun set, casting darkness across the Spoiled Plains; shrouding everything except the sensory glower of Kevin's Dirt. But Kastenessen's oblique assault on Earthpower and Law was increasingly vivid to Linden's percipience. Soon it would begin to hamper her. Even Jeremiah's inherited theurgy might be tainted. And the resources of the Staff would be diminished.

In addition, Covenant's leprosy would worsen. He might go blind, or lose the use of his hands altogether. He might find it difficult to keep his balance because his feet were numb.

I need to be numb, he had insisted in Andelain. *It doesn't just make me who I am. It makes me who I can be.*

Linden did not understand that. The way in which he defined himself as a leper was like his relationship with wild magic, inherent, inexplicable—and too ambiguous to be measured.

Crossing terrain that made her feel numbed herself, Linden clung to the flowing reassurance of Hyn's back and prayed that some good would come of this long gallop through the threatened night.

Fortunately no *caesures* appeared. Joan's attention was focused elsewhere; or *turiya* Raver's was. Nevertheless Linden felt a growing disquiet across the region, an almost subliminal sense of disturbance that seemed separate from Kevin's Dirt. At first, she thought that she was tasting a nameless discomfiture in Hyn, a new anxiety that affected only the Ranyhyn. Yet when she pushed her percipience farther, she found a sensation of restiveness in the ground under Hyn's hooves. The foundations of the Lower Land appeared to be bracing themselves for an impact which they might not be able to withstand.

Across the leagues, Jeremiah's mood had changed. His eagerness had become impatience, frustration. He rode low over Khelen's neck, apparently urging the Ranyhyn to greater speed as if he fled from ghouls—or as if he were filled to bursting with an unspoken sense of purpose.

Stars sprinkled the firmament overhead: the only light on the Lower Land. Surely the moon would rise soon? Even a slim crescent would do more than the lorn stars to soften the dark. But there was no moon. In its absence, the stars seemed strangely closer, at once more distinct and more vulnerable, as if they were drawing near to witness the outcome of their long yearning.

The shadows of the Creator's children, for good or ill: come boon or bane. They glistened like weeping in the absolute black of the heavens.

With growing urgency, Linden tried to recognize some specific feature of the terrain. But she had not attended to her surroundings during the ride to Muirwin Delenoth. She did not know where she was, and could only guess where she was going.

Hyn's unfaltering strides spoke eloquently of trust. Linden heard them well enough. She knew what they meant. Nevertheless her anxieties harried her through the night. Galled by them, she traversed an unreadable landscape in darkness like the onset of a nightmare from which there could be no awakening.

How much time had passed? An hour since sunset? Surely no more than two? Nonetheless the star-strewn dark seemed complete, as if it were the last night of the world.

Abruptly Hynyn uttered a loud neigh like a blare of triumph in the face of oncoming evils. And a moment later, the stallion was answered. From the distance ahead came a welcoming whinny. Linden thought that she recognized Narunal's call.

"There, Chosen," Stave announced over the pounding of hooves. "Our companions await us where we last found water."

The Ranyhyn were running between low hillocks like mounds inadequately cloaked in scraps of grass. Vaguely Linden smelled water. But her attention was fixed elsewhere, straining to discern the presence of the Swordmainnir and the Manethrall.

"At *last!*" Jeremiah shouted. Then he began to halloo as if he expected everyone who could hear him to know his voice.

In moments, the Ranyhyn slowed their strides. Panting heavily, they dropped from a gallop to a canter, then to a jolting trot. Sure of their footing, they angled down into a gully where a small stream ran southward. As it muttered along its crooked path, it caught glints from the stars, a spangling of slight reflections which seemed to confirm that the lost lights were indeed becoming more distinct.

Silhouetted vague and fireless against the faint glisten of the water stood ten shapes that Linden knew instantly: eight Giants, Manethrall Mahrtiir, and Narunal.

At once, Rime Coldspray and her comrades raised a loud huzzah that startled the night, shivering in the air like a challenge to calamity. Jeremiah replied gladly, and all of the Ranyhyn whickered their approval. Only Mahrtiir voiced neither pleasure nor exultation. His reactions were more complex.

As Hynyn, Hyn, and Khelen halted, Frostheart Grueburn and Stormpast Gale-send surged forward to lift Linden and Jeremiah from their mounts. On Hyn's back, Linden almost felt equal to the exuberant relief of the Swordmainnir; but when Grueburn set her on her feet, the Giants towered over her, dwarfing her with their open hearts as much as with their size. She had more in common with Mahrtiir. While the Ironhand, Onyx Stonemage, and Cirrus Kindwind greeted Stave with claps on his back and shoulders that buffeted him in spite of his strength, Linden walked on legs stiff with riding toward the Manethrall. When she reached him, she dropped her Staff so that she could hug him with both arms.

Taken aback by her display of affection, he resisted momentarily. But then he returned her clasp. "Ringthane," he breathed softly. "Linden Avery. Though I trust the Ranyhyn in all things, I must acknowledge that I have been sorely afraid. Also I am much vexed that I was not permitted to stand at your side. I am diminished in my own estimation. I must remember that I am Ramen and human. I must not judge myself by the majesty of the Ranyhyn."

As if she were answering him, Linden murmured privately, "Jeremiah saved him-self. Now I don't know how to help him."

Like Mahrtiir, she would never be equal to miracles. She had to learn how to serve them, as he did.

But the Manethrall appeared not to understand her. "Help him?" he asked in a voice as low as hers. "His alteration is plain. He is transformed beyond all expectation or conception. What manner of aid does he require?"

Jeremiah was already talking to the Giants, practically babbling in his eagerness to tell his story. But *caesures* and Stave and Infelice and Linden and the Ranyhyn and his racecar and Anele's legacy and a construct of bone all tried to find words at the same time: they tripped over each other and fell and bounced back up like tumblers performing some implausible feat of dexterity. Laughing at his own happy incoherence, he repeated his verbal pratfalls until he occasionally achieved a complete sentence. And the Giants laughed with him, rapt and delighted.

Only Stave stood apart. His native dispassion did not waver. If he took note of Linden's exchange with Mahrtiir, he feigned otherwise.

Whispering so that she would not weep again, Linden told Mahrtiir, "He doesn't want to remember what he's been through. I can't think about anything else. No one suffers like that without being damaged."

The Manethrall stepped back to regard her with his bandaged gaze. Still softly, he replied, "That I comprehend, Ringthane. Who would if I do not, I who have lost eyes and use in a cause which exceeds my best strength? But I will speak once again of trust. Hear his vitality and joy. Hear him well. Far more than his wounds have been restored to him, and to you. If a lifetime of your love has not already wrought some healing, it will do so when its time is ripe."

Linden had no response. She recognized his effort to reassure her, but she was not comforted. Jeremiah was not her only concern: other anxieties were tightening around her. His emergence required her to shift how she thought of herself.

She had no idea what had happened to Thomas Covenant. League by league, Kevin's Dirt swelled closer, expanding the ambit of Kastenessen's wrath and pain. Her awareness of a visceral alarm in the earth was growing stronger. And the Worm of the World's End was at work. Where its power was concerned, she doubted nothing that Infelice had told her; nothing that she had heard from Anele.

The company's circumstances, and the Land's, implied an imperative need for action. Now that she had rejoined her friends, she felt the pressure of events mounting. Instinctively she believed that she and her companions had to make decisions and act on them. Now, while they still could.

Yet she restrained herself for the sake of her son's rambling tale; and also for the sake of the Giants, so that they could gauge him for themselves. Raising both of her hands, she bowed her thanks and respect to Mahrtiir in the Ramen fashion. Then she retrieved the Staff of Law and went to the stream to quench her thirst. The Giants still carried some portion of the Ardent's largesse. Surely she could afford to eat a meal and rest before she imposed her tension on her friends?

Yes, she could afford that—but she could not do it. When Jeremiah had given his audience a fairly complete description of what had occurred during his rescue or escape, she went in a gust of compulsion to join Rime Coldspray and Frostheart Grueburn and the rest of the Swordmainnir.

"Have you felt it?" she asked without preamble. "Kevin's Dirt is coming this way. Kastenessen knows where we are, and he intends to hurt us if he can. At this rate, Mahrtiir and I will start to lose our health-sense sometime around dawn. Even

Jeremiah may be affected. And Kevin's Dirt is going to limit what I can do with my Staff. I won't be able to fight the *skurj*. I may not even be able to fight the Sandgorgons.

"Can you feel it?"

One by one, the Giants turned toward her. She could not make out their expressions by starlight; but her nerves felt their enjoyment of Jeremiah subside, replaced by more somber emotions. The last of their laughter faded into the night. Standing with their Ironhand, the Swordmainnir regarded Linden gravely.

"Linden Giantfriend," Coldspray replied with an air of formality, "we have felt it. But it will not assail us until dawn, as you have observed. For that reason among others, it is not our immediate consideration.

"You have ridden long and long without food or rest or sufficient water. And Giant that I am, I confess that my weariness clings to me, though we have bathed as well as we are able, and have conserved our endurance. Will you not partake of our remaining food? Will you not sleep for a time? The trials of the morrow will not be made less by effort in darkness, when we are scarce able to discern where we set our feet."

Linden shook her head. Fears coerced her: she did not know how to relent.

"And there's some kind of distress in the ground," she countered. "Can you feel that, too? It's like the rock under this whole part of the Lower Land is afraid. The Worm must be getting close. What else can it mean?

"I don't regret anything that we've done since we lost Liand and Anele." Anything except Covenant's departure—and his desire to distance himself from her. "But we're running out of time. We need to decide what we're going to do, and then we need to do it."

The Ironhand regarded Linden for a moment, apparently searching for some clue to the turmoil which goaded her. Then the leader of the Swordmainnir said more gently, "You reveal a welcome alteration, Linden Giantfriend—as welcome as your son's restoration in mind and power. Heretofore you have given your concern chiefly to him, heedless of the Earth's doom.

"I do not fault you in this," she hastened to add. "We are Giants and adore children. Nonetheless other matters also weigh upon us. Your readiness now to challenge the foes of Land and life lifts our spirits."

Before Linden could find an appropriate response, Coldspray continued, "Yet your need for food and rest remains. Though you did not choose to be so, you are the rock on which we have anchored our own purposes. Since our first encounter in Salva Gildenbourne, we have claimed a place in your company at every turn of the winds and currents. This we have done because we see more in you than you see in yourself, and also because we seek to make amends for the follies which led to Lost-son Longwrath's *geas*. We will be guided by your heart.

"Still I must urge you to contain your apprehension for this one night. Much has transpired. Much has been asked of you—and much given in return." She nodded toward Jeremiah. "You would be more or less than mortal if you did not require time to absorb the gift of your son's restoration. And if you do not eat and rest now, you will be less able to withstand the coming storms.

"We will have need of you, Linden Giantfriend. You must grant to yourself some measure of kindness."

The Ironhand's consideration seemed to dissolve a barrier in Linden; to weaken or transform it. Her desire for decisions was as much an expression of incomprehension as it was of urgency. There were too many things that she did not understand. Covenant. Jeremiah. Lord Foul's plans for her son. And the *Elohim*, who could have done so much differently.

In bafflement, she nodded to Coldspray. "I'm sure you're right. Jeremiah must be hungry. And I could use a bath." The Ranyhyn had withdrawn into the night as if they had satisfied their own purposes; as if now they were content to wait until she determined hers. "Let's all get some rest. Maybe we'll be able to see what to do more clearly in the morning."

The Giants replied with murmurs of approval; and Jeremiah yawned unexpectedly. "I'm not just hungry," he announced. "I'm *sleepy*. I thought I was too excited to sleep, but maybe I'm not."

Linden nodded again. "All right." Feeling suddenly drained, she turned to Stave. "Will you guide me? I want to wash, but I'm not sure that I can find my way."

Without hesitation, the *Haruchai* took her arm and steered her into the darkness away from the company. Trusting his friendship and his certainty, she accompanied him downstream.

But she wanted more than a bath. She wanted to understand. Questions about Jeremiah led her to *quellvisks*, and to the *Elohim*. When she and Stave had gone beyond earshot of the Giants and her son, she asked him quietly, "Why do you think they did it?"

"Linden?" the former Master inquired with as much gentleness as his dispassion allowed.

"Why did the *Elohim* leave those bones where the Ranyhyn could find them? If they're so afraid of Jeremiah? They can move through time. The Theomach told me that. So did Esmer. They could have known that Jeremiah would need those bones. And they had the whole Earth to choose from. Why did they pick the Lower Land?"

Why did they make possible a fate that they abhorred and then try to prevent it?

Stave shrugged. "Mayhap they did not foresee him." Then he added, "Their belief that they are equal to all things deludes them. They cannot perceive their own misapprehensions. How otherwise did they fail to foresee that you would permit ur-Lord Covenant to retain his white gold ring when you had become the Sun-Sage? Their fear of the Unbeliever's power and resurrection blinded them to other paths."

By slow increments, Linden began to relax. Stave's answer sounded reasonable. If nothing else, it implied that comprehension was attainable.

As far as she was concerned, the *Elohim* had been wrong about her from the first.

Before long, the *Haruchai* brought her to a small pool among the mounded hillocks. It was too shallow to let her immerse herself, had no virtue to assoil her sins; but it offered her enough water to scrub at the worst of her dirt and doubt. When Stave had assured her that he would stand watch somewhere out of sight, he faded soundlessly into the night, and she was alone.

Kneeling among the stones and sand at the pool's edge, she placed the Staff of Law beside her; lowered her face into the cold tang of the water. As long as she could hold her breath, she dragged her fingers through her hair and rubbed hard at her scalp. After that, she unbuttoned and dropped her shirt, removed her boots and socks, took off her grass-marked jeans.

Alone with the stars, she did what she could to remove the stains of sweat and strain and dust and blood from her skin. With cold clean water, she tried to scour the soilure from her thoughts. Then she tossed her clothes into the pool and beat them like a woman who wanted to pound away every reminder that she was vulnerable to despair.

ᔕᗢᘓ

When she returned—sodden, dripping, and chilled—to her friends, she had not been made new. Her many taints had been ground too deeply into her to be simply washed away. Her runed Staff remained darkest black. If she raised fire from the wood, her flames of Earthpower and Law would be black as well, indistinguishable from the world's night. And there was an ache of apprehension in the ground that did not allow her to forget that her company and the Land and all of life were in peril. Nevertheless she had begun to feel the need for rest. And she knew that she was hungry.

"You look better," Jeremiah pronounced. "I know how you like being clean." Then he snorted a soft laugh. "I mean, I can guess. You sure gave me enough baths."

Linden answered by wrapping him in a long, wet hug. She had no other way to express what she felt.

In her absence, the Giants had set out a meal for her: cheese, dried fruit, a bit of stale bread and some cured meat. Embracing Jeremiah, her nerves assured her that he had already eaten. Now she felt a tide of drowsiness rising in him. While she held him, he stifled a yawn.

"Mom. You're shivering."

Cold and over-wrought nerves had that effect, in spite of the heat clinging to the Spoiled Plains.

"You're right." Reluctantly she released him. "Low blood sugar. I must be hungrier than I thought. Why don't you find a place to lie down while I eat something?" Smiling crookedly, she added, "If you're still awake when I'm done, you can tell me a bedtime story. I want to hear more about your visits to the Land." She particularly wished to hear more about Jeremiah's encounters with Covenant. "They're bound to be more interesting than 'Bomba the Jungle Boy.' "

He grinned, apparently remembering the books that she had read to him in another life. "But I don't want to sleep." He made a sweeping gesture that included Stave and the Giants. "This is too exciting."

"And it will still be exciting in the morning," Linden admonished him gently.

"Well—" He glanced around the floor of the gully. "Maybe if I get comfortable somewhere."

"You do that." Inexplicably she wanted to weep again; but she swallowed the impulse. "I really should eat." With a conscious effort, she turned to the meal that Frostheart Grueburn had left for her on a flat sheet of stone.

Night covered Grueburn's face, and Rime Coldspray's. Linden could not see their expressions, but she felt them grinning. As Jeremiah moved away, looking for a clear stretch of sand and dirt, Cabledarm remarked quietly, "Here Linden Giantfriend reveals yet another of her many selves. She is not merely the Sun-Sage, the Chosen, the indomitable seeker and guardian of her son. She is also the mother who provides care."

Linden might have protested, if she could have done so with the same light-hearted kindliness that filled Cabledarm's voice. Instead she began eating; and after her first bites of hard cheese and stale bread, she was preoccupied with hunger.

Mahrtiir responded on her behalf. "Are you taken aback, large ones?" he said with a gruff attempt at humor. "If so, I must chastise your lack of discernment. That she is a mother is plain."

Having spoken, however, he seemed disconcerted by the quiet laughter that greeted his gibe. Instead of laughing himself, he said more stiffly, "Some have journeyed hard and long. Others have walked when they were weary and heart-sore. I have merely ridden and rested. I will stand watch with the Ranyhyn. And perhaps Stave will consent to join me. I have heard young Jeremiah's tale of great events. I would hear how those events are interpreted by the long memories and acute judgments of the *Haruchai*."

Stave glanced at Linden, then gave the Manethrall a barely perceptible nod. Together they walked away along the stream until they found an easy ascent out of the erosion-cut. A moment later, they were gone into the night.

Still eating, Linden waited for the questions of the Giants.

But they did not question her. As if by common consent, they made themselves comfortable, some sitting against the walls of the gully, others half reclining beside the stream. Then in muted voices they began to tell old tales, stories which they all obviously knew well. None of their narratives went far: the Swordmainnir interrupted each constantly, sometimes with reminders of other tales, more often with good-natured jests. Nevertheless their interjections and ripostes had a soothing effect on Linden. That such strong warriors could be playful even now evoked an irrational sensation of safety. Indirectly they made light of their many perils and foes; and by doing so, they enabled Linden to relax further.

Surely she could afford to rest while Mahrtiir, Stave, and the Ranyhyn watched over her and Jeremiah, and the Swordmainnir were content to amuse themselves with tales and gibes?

When she had eaten everything that Grueburn had set out for her, she went to the stream for a long drink. Briefly she scanned the watercourse until her health-sense confirmed that Jeremiah was already asleep, sprawled unselfconsciously no more than a dozen steps away. Then she began to search for a place where she, too, could lie down.

The dampness and chill of her clothes were only vaguely unpleasant. She could have warmed them with her Staff, but she disliked the prospect of raising black fire here. It felt like a bad omen. And it might attract hazardous attention.

Recumbent on the sand with only a few rocks to discomfit her, Linden rode the current of low Giantish voices as if it were a tide that lifted her into the worlds of dreams.

They were many and confusing, fraught with cryptic auguries and possible havoc. Muirwin Delenoth. An unleashed avalanche of water in the depths of Gravin Threndor. Resurrections. She Who Must Not Be Named. But one vision had more power over her than the others. In it, she and Jeremiah sat together in the living room that she would never see again, he on the floor surrounded by boxes of Legos, she in an armchair watching him. He was building an image of Mount Thunder in elaborate detail; and she loved watching him, as she had always done. The best part of the dream, however, was that he talked while he worked, happily explaining why he had chosen that image, what it meant to him, and how he had become so familiar with it, all in words which made perfect sense to her—and which were forgotten as soon as they were uttered.

Once during the night, she was awakened by the visceral realization that a distant crisis had passed. Its aftershocks began to fade as soon as she became aware of them. Reassured by the knowledge that at least one cataclysm had kept its distance and run its course, she went back to sleep easily.

She yearned to return to Jeremiah and Legos, but that dream was gone. Instead, between one instant of consciousness and another, a hand touched her shoulder, and a low voice said her name. She recognized Stave before she knew that she was no longer asleep.

"Chosen," he said, still quietly, "dawn draws nigh. Though the disturbance in the Earth has subsided, the Giants surmise that it is but the first of many. Indeed, they deem that some alteration has come to the Land. Having rested, they judge that it is now time to arise."

In an instant, Linden was fully awake. Jeremiah was stirring, roused by Stormpast Galesend. Like Stave, Manethrall Mahrtiir had returned. He conferred in whispers with the Ironhand, perhaps sharing any impressions that he had received from the Ranyhyn, while the other Swordmainnir secured their armor, checked their weapons, tied the scant remnant of their supplies into bundles.

A low breeze drifted along the gully, touching Linden's nerves with an insidious sensation of change, not in the weather, but in something more fundamental, something in the nature of the air itself. The shift was not *wrongness* or malice, yet it seemed to imply that it could be as destructive as evil.

Gripping Stave's arm and the Staff of Law, she climbed to her feet. "Has anything happened? I mean, anything specific? Are the Ranyhyn worried?"

With his usual detachment, Stave reported, "The great horses appear restive. They snort at the air and toss their heads without any cause that I am able to discern. Nor do the Giants perceive any source of peril. Nonetheless—" He hesitated as if he were searching for contact with other *Haruchai* minds; with memories which were beyond his reach. Then he continued, "I share the apprehensions of the Swordmainnir. Some dire alteration approaches. We do well to meet it standing."

A moment later, he added, "It is in my heart that the Unbeliever has confronted his former mate, for good or ill." A hint of discomfort in his voice made him sound more formal. "He has quelled her, or she has slain him. But the import of either outcome lies beyond my ken. Do such events conduce to the Earth's salvation or to its damnation? It is said that there is hope in contradiction, yet that insight surpasses me. I am *Haruchai*, accustomed to clear sight or none.

"At your side, Chosen, I have made a study of uncertainty. Now I have learned that it is an abyss, no less unfathomable than the Lost Deep."

"Don't say that," Linden protested. She meant, *Don't remind me that Covenant may be dead. We need him. I need him.* "You understand more than you give yourself credit for."

Without uncertainty—without hope in contradiction—Stave would not have become her friend. He would not have stood with her against the united rejection of the Masters.

Stave appeared to raise an eyebrow. "Where is the harm? Have I not made my allegiance plain? And did we not escape both the Lost Deep and the bane, though *skest* and the *skurj* also assailed us? Chosen, I do not fear to name uncertainty an abyss."

Linden could have retorted, Sure, we escaped. After that bane nearly killed us. After we lost the Harrow, and the Ardent damned himself, and Covenant's hands were almost destroyed. After the Dead sacrificed Elena before I could ask her to forgive me. Don't you understand how *deep* those wounds are? But she kept her bitterness to herself. All of her protests came to the same thing.

She had no hope for Covenant.

Instead of responding, she left Stave and went to the stream. There she dropped her Staff, knelt, and plunged her face into the water, pulling her fingers through her hair while the cold stung her nerves.

Covenant had asked or ordered her not to touch him. He had spoken as if he believed that she feared his leprosy—or he feared it for her.

The Giants and now Mahrtiir conveyed the impression that they were waiting for her. When she glanced at the northwestern sky, she saw Kevin's Dirt glowering closer, riding the wind of Kastenessen's agony and virulence. In another hour at most, it would spread far enough to cover the company. Yet it remained hidden from mundane sight. It did not dull the stars. Indeed, it appeared to sharpen their brilliance and loss.

Linden wiped water from her face, dragged her tangled hair back behind her ears, and rose to her feet. When she had retrieved her Staff, she moved to greet Jeremiah.

"Mom." She could not read his face except with her health-sense, but he sounded implausibly cheerful. "Did you get some sleep? I sure did." He stretched his arms, rolled his head to loosen his neck. "Now I feel like I can conquer the world."

As if he were performing a parlor trick, he snapped his fingers, and a quick spark appeared in the air above his hand; a brief instant of flame. In itself, it was a small thing, almost trivial. But it implied—

He was already learning new uses for Anele's gift of Earthpower. Perhaps he was *becoming* Earthpower.

His momentary display caught the attention of the Giants; but he ignored them to concentrate on Linden. "What are we waiting for?" he asked in a tone of rising excitement. "We should go."

Infelice had given him an idea—

His manner troubled Linden. Instinctively she wanted to probe him again. She hungered to learn who he was in his new life. But she did not know what might happen if she interrupted his mood; his sense of purpose; his defenses. He might need such things more than he needed her understanding or sympathy.

Stave still stood nearby, a silent reminder of stoicism and rectitude. But he was more than that: he was also a reminder of trust. In the Hall of Gifts, she had confessed, *Roger said that Lord Foul has owned my son for a long time.* And Stave had replied, *I know naught of these matters. I do not know your son. Nor do I know all that he has suffered. But it is not so among the children of the* Haruchai. *They are born to strength, and it is their birthright to remain who they are.*

Are you certain that the same may not be said of your son?

If Linden asked him now, Stave might remark that Jeremiah had already proven himself in Muirwin Delenoth. The former Master might suggest that it would be better for her as well as for Jeremiah if she allowed him to discover his own path.

She was not ready for that. But the World's End would not wait for her to find enough courage. And when the Worm came, Jeremiah would share the Earth's fate no matter how hard she tried to save him.

She was responsible for the Worm's awakening. Now she needed to find better answers than the ones that had guided her here.

Sighing, Linden followed Jeremiah toward the Giants and the Manethrall. Sunrise would lift the darkness from the Lower Land. Perhaps it would shed some light into her as well.

When she reached Mahrtiir, she said quietly, "Kevin's Dirt is almost here. I hope that you'll let me know when it starts to blind you. I'll counteract it as much as I can. I don't like the way the air feels. We're going to need all the discernment we can get."

The Manethrall nodded. "Ringthane, I hear you. I cannot evade the approach of Kastenessen's malevolence." Bitterness whetted the edges of his voice. "It will make of me less than naught, a mere hindrance to my companions, as it did in the Lost Deep. Be assured that I will not scruple to seek your aid."

The promise appeared to cost him an effort of will or self-abnegation; but he spoke firmly, denying his pride.

Linden rested her hand on his shoulder for a moment: a gesture of empathy to which he did not respond. Then she sighed, "All right. We have a lot to talk about. Maybe it's time that we actually talked about it."

But she did not want to talk. She wanted to wait for the sun.

"Like you, Linden Giantfriend," Rime Coldspray offered, "we mislike the touch of this air. It speaks of forces which lie beyond our ken. Perils draw nigh which have heretofore remained distant.

"Also the beings and powers which seek the World's End remain unopposed. I am the Ironhand of the Swordmainnir. I speak for my comrades when I say that we must now choose a new heading. And we must not dally in doing so, lest forces which we cannot oppose overtake us."

Linden felt more than saw that night was ending. She smelled an easing of the dark. The first faint suggestion of daybreak drifted toward her from the east, riding the troubled breeze. But it did not dim the stars. Like the swift moil of Kevin's Dirt, the approach of dawn seemed to etch the profuse glitter overhead more precisely against the fathomless abyss of the heavens.

Still she wanted to see the sun. With her Staff, she was capable of much. At need, the ready wood would answer her call with fire and heat and even healing. But she could no longer summon illumination. Jeremiah might be able to do so, if his mastery of his new magicks continued to grow. Covenant's ring would cast silver and peril in all directions if she forced herself to use it. But the stark ebony of her own access to Earthpower and Law precluded light.

When the sun rose, the confused tangle of who she was and who she needed to be might begin to unravel like the recursive wards which had sealed the Lost Deep.

Stalling, she said uncertainly, "We've been trusting the Ranyhyn. They've brought us this far. Maybe we should keep doing that."

But Manethrall Mahrtiir shook his head. "Ringthane, they are Ranyhyn." She heard a note of finality or fatality in his voice. "They wield neither ancient lore nor mighty theurgies. They have borne many of our burdens. Doubtless they will bear more. But they cannot determine the Earth's doom. The deeds required of us they cannot perform.

"Also," he added more sadly, "I sense no clear purpose among them. They are restive, truly, and urgent to do what they may. But they neither command nor encourage us to ride. Rather they abide their discomfort, hoping—or so I deem—that we will soon determine our own intents."

Now, Linden thought. Now the sun would show itself. Surely the east had begun to lighten? Certainly the funereal bindings of night had loosened their grip on the landscape. A kind of vagueness eroded the dark. In hints, the contours of the watercourse and the stream unveiled themselves. She could make out the Giants more clearly, starker shapes in the enshrouding gloom.

"That's all right, Mom," Jeremiah put in, impatient for his chance to speak. "Like I told you, Infelice gave me an idea. I want to try it."

Linden avoided his gaze. "Can you wait a little longer, Jeremiah, honey? Just until sunrise?"

"But—" he began, then stopped himself. Turning to the east, he frowned at the blurred outlines of the horizon. "It should already be here. Why isn't it here?"

Kevin's Dirt was less than a league away, a cruel seethe spurred southward by rage. Night continued to fade from the Lower Land, giving way to a preternatural dusk, an imposed twilight. Nevertheless there was no clear daybreak, no sign of the sun.

"This is wrong," Linden breathed. "Something is wrong."

"Indeed," muttered Onyx Stonemage through her teeth. "Something comes. I know not what it may presage, but my heart speaks to me of dread."

The stars shone like distant cries. Somehow Kevin's Dirt and even the swell of gloaming made them brighter, louder. A change had come to the firmament of the heavens, a change that threatened the isolate gleams. A change that caused them pain.

Now? Linden thought. Now? Her sensitivity to organic truth assured her that the sun should appear *now*; that it should already have crested the crepuscular horizon. The absolute necessity of night and day required it, the life-giving sequence of rest and energy, relief and effort. The most fundamental implication of the Law of Time—

She was wrong. There was no sun. There would be no sun.

The nature of existence had become unreliable.

The dusk softened until she could discern the faces around her indistinctly; until she could almost see the details of their grimaces and fears, their clenched expectations. But then the greying of the world seemed to stabilize as though it had found a point of equilibrium between night and day. After that, there was no increase of light.

The sun was not going to rise because it could not. Forces beyond Linden's comprehension held the Land in a gloom like the onset of the last dark.

While Linden struggled to grasp the truth, several of the Giants gasped. Sharply Stave said, "Attend, Chosen."

She flicked a glance around her, saw that all of her companions were staring upward.

For an instant or two, a few heartbeats, startlement confused her. The sky was too full of stars; of lights that glittered like wailing. She could not understand the panoply. She felt the leading edge of Kevin's Dirt, tasted the shock and horror of her companions, recognized a jolt of vehemence from Jeremiah; but she did not see what her companions saw.

Then she did.

Oh, God—

Stars were going out.

One. Then another. A pause while realities reeled. Two together as if they had been swallowed simultaneously.

God in Heaven! The sun was not the only casualty. And the Worm of the World's End had not yet reached the Land.

The stars were vast in number, of course they were: numberless beyond counting. By the measure of their profusion, their losses were small; almost trivial. But by the measure of brief human lives—by any measure that included life and death—the scale of the carnage surpassed conception.

What kind of power could eat *stars*?

Who could hope to stand against it?

"Mom!" Jeremiah said urgently. "You need to listen. I've been waiting long enough."

She could not hear him; could not drag her gaze down to meet his. She was transfixed by the incremental ruin of beauty. She had to watch it because there was no sun.

"Maybe it's a good thing I waited." Jeremiah's voice was taut with restraint. "Maybe now you'll understand why my idea is important. Maybe now *I* understand what Covenant was trying to tell me." But then he could not hold back a yell. "*Mom!*"

His shout dragged at her attention. "Jeremiah—" His name caught in her throat. Hoarse as a woman who had spent the night howling, she asked, "What is it, honey? What's so important?"

Don't you see it? The stars are going out!

"You need to *listen*," he repeated. "I know what to do!"

Stave regarded the boy steadily. The former Master's gaze seemed full of the deaths of stars. Mahrtiir continued to peer blindly upward, but he appeared to be tracking the progress of Kevin's Dirt. Perhaps the stars were beyond the reach of his remaining senses.

Slowly the Giants forced themselves to lower their heads. Blinking as though they had been appalled, they turned their eyes on Jeremiah. None of them spoke. Rigid as women who had become stone, they were too full of horror to express it.

Without stars, every sailor on the seas of the world would be lost. Every Giant aboard a ship, every seafarer from all the peoples of the Earth: trackless and doomed.

"All right." Jeremiah sounded incongruously satisfied and eager, as if the heavens held nothing fearsome. Nothing except an opportunity. "I have an idea. I said that already. Infelice gave it to me. I mean, I got it from her. I'm sure she didn't mean what I heard."

Fortunately Kevin's Dirt had no immediate effect: it wrought its particular harm slowly. With her health-sense if not with her eyes, Linden watched her son. He no longer looked like a boy. He looked like a young man who did not need her.

The sight made her heart shiver as if she were feverish.

"You'll have to start from the beginning, Jeremiah. I don't know what you're talking about."

"You *do*, Mom," he replied without hesitation. "You were there. You just haven't thought about it enough.

"The stars going out." His assurance amazed Linden. It frightened her. "That's the Worm. It's eating the *Elohim*."

Too stricken to speak, everyone stared at Jeremiah. Beneath his familiar fierceness, Mahrtiir's visage betrayed an ashen dismay. The muscles of Rime Coldspray's jaws knotted and released like the hard beat of her heart. Latebirth had covered her eyes with her hands. Frostheart Grueburn gaped like a woman who had forgotten the meaning of her actions.

Every Giant—

"So what are they afraid of?" Jeremiah asked. "I mean, the *Elohim*. I'm just a kid. Why are they scared of me? What do they think I can do that's worse than being *eaten*?"

His purpose for us is an abomination, more so than our doom in the maw of the Worm.

"Infelice told us," he answered himself. "She thinks I'm going to *trap* them. And she knows I can do it. I can make a door they can't refuse. No matter how far they scatter, or how hard they try to hide. They can't refuse. That's part of who they are. They'll have to come if I make a door. I mean, the *right* door. The right size and shape. The right materials. I can construct a doorway that *forces* them. They'll have to pass through it.

"So of course she thinks I'll make a door they can't get out of." —*the Worm is mere extinction.* "That's what the Vizard wanted. It's what she would do if she were me." *The prison which the boy will devise is eternal helplessness, fully cognizant and forever futile.* "She thinks I'll trap the *Elohim* forever."

Caught in such a construct, Infelice and her people would *out-live the ending of suns and stars.*

Stave regarded Jeremiah without expression. Several of the Swordmainnir studied him as if he were changing in front of them, revealing unguessed aspects of horror or hope.

"But she doesn't know me, Mom." Jeremiah sounded almost smug. "She doesn't know what I've been learning all these years.

"I'm not crazy like the Harrow. I know I can't build anything big or strong enough to hold the Worm. But I can make a door that sucks the *Elohim* in. A door that takes them to a place where the Worm can't get at them. Only it won't be a prison because my door will let them leave whenever they want. I can keep them alive until they decide it's safe to come out.

"Then the stars will stop dying. And we'll have a better chance to stop the Worm."

He was moving too quickly for Linden. She scrambled to catch up with him; to untangle the significance of what he was saying. What had he told her about the *Elohim*? *They're like a metaphor? A symbol? They represent the stars. Or maybe they* are *the stars. Or maybe the stars and the* Elohim *are like shadows of each other.*

The idea made a weird kind of sense. Saving the *Elohim* might actually stop—or at least delay—the destruction of the stars.

Still Linden faltered. *His purpose for us is an abomination, more so than our doom in the maw of the Worm. But it is not the worst evil.*

Infelice believed that Lord Foul would eventually use Jeremiah to trap the Creator. Would that outcome be more or less likely if Linden's son contrived to preserve some of the *Elohim*?

Such questions were beyond her. She could not imagine their answers. She could hardly believe that they had answers.

She required an act of will to avoid looking up at the slow ravage of the heavens.

"I am exceeded," muttered Mahrtiir under his breath. "Here even a youth of new-born mind surpasses a Manethrall of the Ramen. Serving only the Ranyhyn, my people are too small to comprehend or equal such powers."

When no one else found a response, Linden asked tentatively, "But Jeremiah, honey, what will that accomplish? We can't stop the Worm. We just can't. It's too much for us."

"But I can *slow it down*!" Jeremiah crowed. "If I can build my door before it eats too many *Elohim*, I can buy us time!" With exaggerated patience, he explained, "The *Elohim* are its natural food. If it doesn't get enough to eat, it'll be weaker. It'll move more slowly."

"Then who knows?" He shrugged as though he knew nothing of uncertainty. "Maybe we'll think of something. Or Covenant will. He's like that."

If Covenant were still alive. If he had survived his encounter with Joan and *turiya* Raver. And if the Worm did not swallow Jeremiah's door whole. *By the measure of mountains, it is a small thing, no more than a range of hills.* It would dwarf anything that Jeremiah could build.

And still the Worm would get all of the nourishment that it needed from the EarthBlood under *Melenkurion* Skyweir. Anele had said as much. He had gleaned his knowledge from a stretch of veined malachite at the foot of the Hazard: stone lined with stains like Linden's jeans.

The prospect of acting on Jeremiah's desires scared her. She drew inferences from it that appalled her. If he did what he wanted to do, she would have to—

That thought she could not complete. It led her toward places which were too extreme to be contemplated.

The construct which he envisioned would be vulnerable. It would need protection. She would have to—

Against the *Worm*? She had never had that kind of strength. No one with her did. Perhaps even Covenant did not.

She would have to—

How could she make such choices? How could any mother put her son at risk and not stand ready to defend him?

And yet—

He was not the sum of her responsibilities. She had brought about the deaths of *Elohim* and stars. Liand, Anele, and Galt. Even Esmer. All of Lord Foul's victims. She had awakened the Worm: she bore the burden of a world's ruin.

Holding up a hand to ward off Jeremiah's eagerness, she said, "I'm sorry, honey." She could not meet his hot gaze. "I need to think about this. It puts a lot of pressure on you, and we can't be sure what the results will be." What materials would his construct require? And where in this blighted landscape could such things be found? "I want to talk to Rime Coldspray." She already knew what Stave and Mahrtiir would say. "Then I'll decide."

"Mom!" he protested. But almost at once he bit down on his frustration. Sounding truculent, he muttered, "Talk as much as you want. It won't change anything. I'm sure I'm right."

Linden glanced at Stave, asking him with her eyes to watch over her son. Then she raised her head to the Ironhand. "Do you mind if we talk alone?"

Coldspray acquiesced with a shrug. Her jaws continued to bunch arrhythmically, chewing prayers or curses, as she walked away along the stream.

Consumed by her own prayers, Linden followed.

They did not go far. Linden halted when Coldspray did, still within sight of their companions. Arms folded across her cataphract, the Ironhand stood rigid, waiting for Linden to speak.

Linden understood her attitude: she read it in the lines of Coldspray's visage, the set of her shoulders. The Ironhand was not reluctant to talk to Linden. Instead she was shaken to the core by the sight of stars dying; by the sheer scale of what was being lost.

"Here's my problem," Linden began. Reluctance and doubt made her brusque. "I don't know what to think of Jeremiah. He's my *son*. Seeing him like this is like seeing a new dawn. But I don't know what's happening to him—or in him. After what he's been through, I don't understand how he can be so eager. It doesn't seem natural.

"Mahrtiir thinks that I should trust him." *Far more than his wounds have been restored to him, and to you.* "That's hard for me. Where I come from, people who have been outrageously damaged don't suddenly become whole. I know that I haven't said much about my former life." She had been shot through the heart. Where she had been born—where she belonged—she had no life left. "But back then, I was a doctor. A healer." Such assertions felt false to her now. She claimed them only so that Coldspray would understand her. "I specialized in trying to help people with broken minds. And I never saw any of them recover completely without facing what happened to them. Not once.

"I'm afraid for him, Coldspray. I'm afraid of what might happen to him if he can do what he has in mind. I'm afraid of what might happen if he can't."

Either outcome might enable Lord Foul to claim him.

Brusque herself, Coldspray asked, "Is your health-sense now dulled?"

Linden shook her head. "Kevin's Dirt works slowly. It hasn't had time to affect me yet."

"Then I cannot counsel you as you wish to be counseled. Your son is closed to my discernment, as you are. Your perceptions exceed any that I am able to proffer."

More softly, the Ironhand admitted, "Yet I am able to conceive of no course more worthy of our hearts and lives than his. What greater deed can we attempt, few as we are, and friendless in this gloom? For that reason alone, I would follow him wheresoever his eagerness leads. But there is more.

"Linden Giantfriend, my spirit is wracked by the deaths of stars. In their name, my counsel is young Jeremiah's. We must do what lies within our strength to preserve the *Elohim*."

Before Linden could respond, Coldspray continued, "Nevertheless your son's purpose is perilous." Her tone tightened. "Indeed, its hazards are extreme. Should he succeed in his intent, he will draw every surviving *Elohim* to him. Doing so, he will also draw the Worm. They are its food. It will seek them out. Therefore his portal, his door, will require defense. It will require a defense greater than eight Swordmainnir, or eight score, or eight hundred can provide.

"For this reason, the choice must be yours. You alone among us wield true power." Sternly she concluded, "Knowing the plight of the heavens, you will not turn aside."

Perilous, Linden thought. Oh, Jeremiah! The same concern had occurred to her, although she had not gauged its implications so concretely. She dreaded what it might require of her.

Without realizing that she had lifted her eyes, she found herself staring skyward, transfixed by the calamity overhead. A gloom like bereavement covered the Lower Land. For all she knew, it covered the whole world. It would never be relieved.

Then she realized that Rime Coldspray was right. She would not turn aside. She could not.

Nevertheless the Giants clearly did not grasp all that Jeremiah's desires entailed. They were dangerous, yes; but there was more. They meant that Linden would have to leave him. Abandon him to his peril. So that she could find a way to ward his construct when it was complete. In spite of her Staff and Covenant's ring, she was too weak. She would have to go looking for greater power.

If such power existed anywhere, and could be found.

If Covenant did not return—

She saw no consolation in the gradual reaving of the stars. The heavens were an abyss of uncertainty. Stave did not fear such things. She did. She would have met a kinder fate in the maw of She Who Must Not Be Named.

Finally she forced herself to meet Rime Coldspray's gaze.

Because she could not bear to say what she was thinking, she murmured, "I would feel better about it if you were laughing. It's going to be hard." Earlier she had felt that the foundations of her life were shifting. Now they were being shattered. "We don't just have to find whatever it is that Jeremiah needs to make his door. And we don't just have to protect him. Somehow we have to live through it."

In response, Coldspray managed a wan chuckle. "Then I must concede that I have failed you. If joy is in the ears that hear, I have grown deaf. My hearing is whelmed by the clamor of an unrisen sun, and by the shrieking of slain stars."

"Don't worry about it," Linden answered as if she, too, were dying. "That makes two of us. I'm so deaf, I keep forgetting to be glad that my son is alive and eager."

"Come on." She gestured toward the waiting company. "Let's go find out what Jeremiah needs to save the *Elohim*."

The Ironhand nodded. "Well said, Linden Giantfriend." Now she made no effort to force a laugh. "Let us confront the challenge of these times together. While we do what we can, there is no fault in failure."

Confront the challenge, Linden mused as she and Coldspray began walking. What choice did they have? But if they succeeded in any fashion, they would not do so together. Eventually she would have to face her fears. And she would have to face them alone.

Her yearning for Covenant was so acute that it brought tears to her eyes.

Jeremiah seemed to swim through the blurring of her vision as he came to meet her. "Well, Mom?" he asked before she could say anything. "What did you decide?"

Instead of replying, she wrapped her arms around him and hugged him hard, mutely pleading for his forgiveness. Then she took him with her to rejoin the rest of their companions.

Stave regarded her return impassively, as if his resolve sufficed for both of them. But the Giants and Mahrtiir were more troubled. Grueburn, Cirrus Kindwind, and the others studied Linden with doubt in their eyes. Perhaps they worried that her desire for Covenant ruled her; that she would insist on waiting for him. But the Manethrall's disturbance was of another kind. His sense of his own uselessness galled him like an unhealed wound. In the risk that Jeremiah wanted to take, Mahrtiir would be able to contribute nothing except his service to the Ranyhyn. He would have been better content if the loss of his eyes had killed him.

Linden paused as though she wanted to be sure that all of her friends were paying attention. But in truth she was searching herself for courage, and trying to blink away her tears. She had always been vulnerable to the kind of paralysis that came from fear. From fear and despair.

"All right," she finally managed to say. "I'm willing to do this your way, Jeremiah. What do you need to make your door?"

She suspected that it could not be formed of bone. Bones implied mortality, and the *Elohim* did not die. They could only be devoured. Or sacrificed.

Jeremiah's instant enthusiasm seemed to fill the gully from wall to wall. Indeed, it seemed to urge the stars closer so that they could hear him. Nevertheless his eagerness made him appear strangely fragile to his mother. What would happen to him if his intentions failed? Or if the Worm simply ate his door after he had gathered all of the *Elohim* in one place? How would he bear it?

"Stone," he replied at once. "A lot of it. In big chunks. I mean, really big. I won't be able to handle some of them, even with Earthpower." He flashed a glance around the Swordmainnir. "I'm going to need all the help you can give me."

"Forsooth," Rime Coldspray responded in a noncommittal rumble. "If aid you require, aid you shall have. But of stone the Earth is a vast storehouse. Even this parched wasteland is rich in forms and substances and textures and indeed purities of stone. Surely, young Jeremiah, the portal which you propose cannot be composed of random fragments. Even the theurgies of stonework practiced by Giants demand rock of particular natures and qualities. We must ask you to name the stone which you deem needful."

Again Jeremiah did not hesitate. Where his constructs were concerned, he seemed incapable of doubt. "It's green. More like a deposit than actual rock. I don't know what it's called, but I saw some when you took me across the Hazard. Green like veins."

"Malachite," Onyx Stonemage pronounced; and Linden's stomach tightened as if the word were a prophecy.

Jeremiah nodded. "That's it. But there it was just veins. I need plenty of it. It doesn't have to be pure. As long as there's malachite in the stone, I can use it." After a flicker of thought, he added, "But if it isn't pure, I'll need more of it. I have to get the right amount. The less pure it is, the bigger the door has to be."

"Sadly," Cabledarm put in before Linden or the Ironhand could speak, "we have seen no malachite since our escape from the Lost Deep. We are Giants, certain of stone. Our course in these last days has encountered no malachite."

Now Jeremiah faltered. "But you must—" he began, then stopped. After a moment, he admitted, "I didn't see anything like it myself." His enthusiasm was crumbling. "The *croyel* controlled me, but it didn't control what I saw."

Caught in his emotions, Linden tried to help him. "Stave? The Masters scouted the whole Land. Did they find anything that resembled malachite around here?"

The *Haruchai* shook his head. "We are not Giants. Seeking signs of peril, we observe in a different fashion."

Jeremiah's consternation dominated the dusk. It demanded answers.

Linden faced him with disappointment in her eyes. "Jeremiah, honey. I'm sorry. I don't know what else we—"

He cut her off. Ferocity flared in him as if he had suddenly become someone else: a creature of savagery and suspicion. His hands curled into claws. "That's what you wanted to talk to Coldspray about," he snarled. "You wanted to be sure I couldn't get what I need before you said yes."

His transformation shocked Linden. Suffering had done this to him, *this*. But she was not prepared for it. While she reeled inwardly, she could not respond.

Around her, the Giants recoiled, as startled as she was, and full of disapproval. But Manethrall Mahrtiir's reaction was immediate anger. "It is *not*, boy," he snapped. "There is no particle of her which does not desire your well-being—aye, and the continuance of the Land. You speak now with the voice of the *croyel*, and will *be silent*."

Surprise stopped Jeremiah. For an instant, his vehemence faltered.

At once, Mahrtiir continued, "Behold!" With one arm, he flung a vehement gesture down the length of the watercourse.

As if by a flourish of magic, he dispelled Jeremiah's indignation. Instantaneously thrilled, Jeremiah wheeled to gaze where the Manethrall pointed.

The Ranyhyn were coming, four majestic horses bright with purpose. Prancing like pride made flesh, Hynyn led Hyn, Khelen, and Narunal along the stream toward the company.

"Their restiveness is answered," said the Manethrall. His tone was grim, but softer and more respectful, moderated by devotion. "Their uncertainty was ours. We have now determined our need. Thus their path is made plain.

"Mount," he urged Linden and Stave. Jeremiah was already running toward Khelen, unable to contain his eagerness. "Ride and hasten. The Ranyhyn have announced their will. Did they not discover bone when bone was needed? They will do as much for malachite. But we must not delay, lest the last *Elohim* be consumed ere we are able to attempt their preservation."

"Aye," Rime Coldspray assented. She and her comrades made a visible effort to set aside their discomfiture. "Make ready, Swordmainnir," she instructed. "We cannot estimate the leagues which lie ahead of us, but we must traverse them swiftly."

"Yet again," grumbled Frostheart Grueburn. "Must we run interminably?" Nevertheless she did not dally as she tightened her armor and checked her sword.

"These great beasts," the Ironhand replied sternly, "have given aid when we had no other. If they crave haste, they will learn that Giants comprehend its import."

Jeremiah had swarmed onto Khelen's back. Now he waved his arms like demands at the company. Hyn approached Linden, nudged her shoulder. For a moment, however, Linden did not react. Her heart was burning down to ash in her chest, and she did not know how to move.

She was sure now that Jeremiah's eagerness was his way of fleeing.

Without waiting for her consent, Stave boosted Linden astride the dappled mare. At the same time, Mahrtiir appeared to flow into his seat on Narunal. Mere heartbeats later, Stave mounted Hynyn; and the Giants announced their readiness.

With Khelen and Jeremiah in the lead, the company crossed out of the gully toward the northeast; toward the marge-land between the Shattered Hills and Sarangrave Flat.

Following her son, and surrounded by Giants, Linden wept again. She had been given her first glimpse of Jeremiah's immured pain. She knew now that he needed her—and that she was going to abandon him anyway.

That choice had been made for her. Acting on it would be worse.

3.

Not Dead to Life and Use

Barely able to hold himself upright, Thomas Covenant stood on the cooled flow of Hotash Slay at the headland or boundary of the promontory where Foul's Creche had once ruled the southeast. Beyond him and against the cliffs on either side, wild seas thrashed in the aftermath of the tsunami. He heard their turmoil, a thunderous seethe and crash like the frantic labor of the ocean's heart. But through the surly dusk of a dawnless day, he could hardly see the eruption and spray and retreat of the lashed waves. There was no sun. Distinct as murders, the stars were going out.

This was a consequence of the Worm's rousing, as it was of his resurrection. It heralded the world's ruin. Now every death pierced him. Joan's end felt like a knife in his own chest. Killing her, he had wounded himself—

He needed Linden. He did not know how to bear what he had become without her.

But he could not reach her. She was too far away—and he was too badly injured. A shard of stone at the edge of the Shattered Hills had restored the old gash on his forehead: an accusation confirmed during his confrontation with Joan. Blood still oozed into the drying crust around his eyes and down his cheeks. Falling on rocks and coral had gashed his ribs badly. Some of them were cracked or broken. Splinters of pain gouged every breath. His jeans and T-shirt had been shredded. A lattice-work of torn flesh and more blood marked his arms and chest and legs.

The *krill*'s heat must have burned his hands; his foreshortened fingers. But that damage, at least, he did not feel. Leprosy disguised his lesser hurts.

By comparison, the Humbled were almost whole. They, too, had been struck by scraps of flung rock. A cut marred the side of Branl's neck. Clyme's arms and tunic showed rents, contusions, small wounds. But they had not shared Covenant's floundering on the seabed, or felt Joan's blow. And they were *Haruchai*. They would be able to go on.

Now they appeared to be watching for some sign that the doomed sun would rise, or that the incremental extinction of the stars would cease. But perhaps they were waiting for the Ranyhyn. If they permitted themselves anything as human as prayer, they may have been praying that Mhornym and Naybahn had survived the tsunami.

Without mounts, there was nothing further that Covenant or the maimed Masters could do to defend the Land. The Shattered Hills were an indurated barricade thronging with *skest*, masterless and unpredictable. And the distance between him and Linden was impossible; scores of leagues—

His need for her was just one more wound that could not be healed.

The gloom lightened until it resembled mid-evening or the last paling before sunrise. But it grew no brighter. All of the illumination seemed to descend from the precise and imperiled stars. It was their lament.

The Worm was coming—and Covenant had no idea what to do. The light of the *krill*'s gem had gone out. There was no wild magic left in him. Simply staying on his feet required every shred of his remaining strength. He bore Joan's ring in the name of an unattainable dream.

Oh, he needed Linden. He needed to make things right with her before the end.

Such yearnings were as doomed as the stars. The *Elohim* had no hope of escaping the Worm's vast hunger.

Time may have passed, but he did not notice it. He did not notice that he was still bleeding. The stab of abused ribs when he breathed insisted that he was alive; but he ignored it. He did not think about anything except Joan and stars and Linden.

Long ago, he had promised that he would do no more killing. Now he was forsworn, as he had been in so many other ways.

Eventually Branl spoke. "Ur-Lord, we cannot remain as we are." Faithful as a grave, he carried Loric's *krill* clad in the remnants of Anele's apparel. "We will forfeit our lives to no purpose. If the *skest* do not assail us, privation and your wounds will bring death. We must delay no longer.

"If the Worm's advance may be measured by the fate of the stars, some few days will pass ere all time and life are extinguished. While they endure, a reunion with your companions—and with the Staff of Law—may yet be achieved. For that reason, we must abandon Naybahn and Mhornym. We must concede that they have perished. In their place, we must summon other Ranyhyn."

After a pause—a moment of hesitation?—he added, "And you must consent to ride. We cannot hope for your healing, except by the succor of the Staff."

Covenant meant to say, No. He meant to say, Never. He could not break more promises. But those words eluded him. Instead his knees folded, and he sank to the stone. Some other part of him croaked, "Here's another fine mess you've gotten me into."

He did not realize that he had spoken aloud until he tried to laugh. His chest hurt too much for laughter.

"Unbeliever?" Undercurrents of anger fretted Clyme's tone. He and Branl had followed Covenant into a *caesure*. They had saved him when he was lost. "Do you accuse us? These straits are not of our making."

For a while, Covenant could not imagine what Clyme was talking about. Then he managed to say, "Oh, you." He dismissed the notion. "I didn't mean you." Perhaps he should have laid the blame at the feet of the Creator; but he did not. "I meant Foamfollower. This is all his fault.

"If he hadn't insisted on keeping me alive. Making impossible things possible. Laughing in the Despiser's face. He was always the Pure One, even if he didn't think so himself. None of us would be here without him."

Even the Worm would not. Covenant would have died decades or millennia before Linden first met him.

Time was a Möbius strip. Every implication looped back on itself. Every *if* led to a *then* which in turn redefined the *if.* But his human mind could not comprehend causality and sequence in such terms.

The Humbled regarded him as if he were babbling. Their faces kept secrets. *Try to believe that you are pure.* Who had said that to him? Like his heart, his mind was failing. He could not remember. Then he could. It was one of the *jheherrin*; one of the creatures who had aided him after he had denied their prayer for salvation.

"Ur-Lord," Branl said finally. "Your hurts undermine your thoughts. Saltheart Foamfollower cannot be held to account for Corruption's deeds."

Baffled by the simplification of such reasoning, Covenant tried to shake his head. Instead the twilight seemed to waver as if it were dissolving; as if reality itself were in flux. "That's not the point." The point was that the *Haruchai* had no sense of humor. "The point is, I'm not going to ride the Ranyhyn." Foamfollower would not have known how to laugh if he had not been so open and honest in his grief. "I made a promise." A vow. "Promises are important. You know that at least as well as I do."

"We do," Clyme acknowledged. "We are the Humbled, avowed to your service. We comprehend given oaths. Yet yours contradicts ours. If you do not ride, your death becomes certain. This we will not permit while choice remains to us."

They had entered a *caesure* for Covenant's sake.

"Do you not comprehend the extremity of your straits? Weakened as you are, your oath cannot hold. Soon you will lapse from consciousness. Then we will summon the Ranyhyn and bear you away. This you can do naught to prevent. Where, then, is the harm in granting your consent?

"Did you not permit Mhornym and Naybahn to retrieve you from the path of the tsunami? Did their aid not violate your word?"

You don't understand. Covenant was too weak for this argument. He could not explain himself to the Humbled. Clyme and Branl had carried him; the Ranyhyn had not. The horses had only helped the Masters help him.

In various ways, the Ranyhyn had always aided him—but they did so because he did not ride.

He needed Linden. If nothing else, he had to ask her forgiveness. Express his love. Confess his sins. How else would he ever be able to put his ex-wife behind him? Nevertheless he could not face her like this. Not at the price of another broken promise.

Holding out his halfhand, he murmured, "Give me the *krill.*"

The Humbled looked uncertain in the preternatural twilight. Branl may have lifted an eyebrow. Clyme may have frowned. But apparently they could think of no reason to refuse. After a moment, Branl placed Loric's dagger in Covenant's grasp.

Trembling as though his burdens were too heavy for him, Covenant dropped the old cloth: Anele's last legacy. He did not need it now. The *krill* was cold. Briefly he steadied the forged metal, peered at the inert gem. Then he reached up to pull the chain that bore Joan's ring over his head.

"You know why the light went out. Joan was the only rightful white gold wielder here. The only one with a ring that belonged to her. The *krill*'s power died when she did.

"But I still have a claim on her ring. I married her with it." 'Til death do us part. "And I'm something more." He had become so in the inferno of the Banefire, and in the apotheosis of his death by wild magic at Lord Foul's hands. "I'm white gold." How else had he been able to transmute Joan's power, using it to heal his mind—and to refuse *turiya* Raver's malice? "Mhoram said so. Maybe I'm not the rightful wielder of *this* ring, but I can still use it."

Shaking, he pushed Joan's ring on its chain onto the little finger of his left hand. It stuck at the remaining knuckle, but he did not try to force it. He did not intend to wear it long.

With as much care as he could muster, he closed both hands around the haft of the *krill*. Then, suddenly desperate, he stabbed the blade at the stone under him.

The dagger was only sharp when it was vivified by the possibilities of wild magic. Lightless, it was dull. It could not pierce cooled lava.

But it did. As he struck, the scale of his need and the fundamental strictures of his nature brought forth a familiar blaze from the gem: familiar and absolute, as necessary as breath and blood. It shone into his eyes like the nova of a distant star. The power-whetted blade cut inward as though the stone were damp mud.

When he took his hands away, his fingers and palms felt no heat: the numbed skin of his cheeks felt none. Nevertheless he trusted the efficacy of wild magic; believed that the *krill* was already growing hot.

Blinking through dazzles, he squinted at Clyme and Branl. At first, they were bright with phosphorescence, as spectral as the Dead. Then they seemed to reacquire their mortality. But they were not diminished. Rather they looked as precise and cryptic as icons in the dagger's brilliance. Together they confronted Covenant's display of power as if they were prepared to decide the fate of worlds.

As distinctly as he could, Covenant said, "I forbid you to put me on the back of a Ranyhyn. Find some other answer."

Then he sagged. He thought that he had come to the end of himself. The Humbled were right: he could not hold out against his wounds. He had lost too much blood, and was in too much pain. If Branl and Clyme did not obey him, he would have to trust the great horses of Ra to forgive him.

When he felt certain that he was done, however, he found that he was not. A distant sensation of power seemed to call him back from the collapse craved by his ravaged body. Involuntarily he straightened his spine, sat more upright. He imagined that he heard either Clyme or Branl say, This delay will prove fatal. Then he saw them recoil like men who had been slapped. He felt their surprise.

Directly in front of him, the figure of a man stepped into the light as though he had been made manifest by wild magic and the eldritch puissance of Loric's *krill*.

The newcomer seemed to emanate imponderable age. Indeed, he appeared to be fraying at the edges as he arrived, blurring as though he took in years and released vitality or substance with every breath. Nevertheless he looked taller than the Humbled—taller and more real—although he was not. His apparent stature was an effect of the light and Covenant's astonishment and his own magicks. He wore the ancient robes, tattered and colorless, of a guardian who had remained at his post, rooted by duty, for an epoch. Yet his features were familiar; so familiar that Covenant wondered why he could not identify them. A man like that—

After two heartbeats, or perhaps three, he noticed that Branl and Clyme were preparing to defend him. Or they were—

Hellfire.

—bowing. *Bowing?*

Together they each dropped to one knee and lowered their heads as if they were in the presence of some august figure incarnated from the dreamstuff of *Haruchai* legends.

In Covenant, memories reopened like wounds, and he recognized Brinn.

The *ak-Haru*. Brinn of the *Haruchai*, who had outdone the Theomach in mortal combat to become the Guardian of the One Tree.

Here.

If Covenant had ever doubted that the Worm was coming, he believed it now. There could be no surer sign than Brinn's arrival. Even the absence of the sun, and the slow havoc spreading among the stars, did not announce the Earth's last days more clearly.

While Covenant stared, open-mouthed and helpless, the *ak-Haru* approached until he was no more than two strides from the *krill*. There he stopped, ignoring the obeisance of the Humbled. His gaze was fixed on Covenant.

In a voice rheumy with isolation and too much time, he said, "My old friend." Words seemed to scrape from his mouth as if they had grown jagged with disuse. The skin of his face had been seamed and lined until it resembled a mud-flat now baked and parched, webbed with cracks. "I perceive that your plight is dire, as it has ever been. The fact that I have come is cause for sorrow. Yet it is cause for joy that my coming proves timely. Once again, I learn that there is hope in contradiction."

Illumined by Loric's gem, Brinn's eyes shone among their wrinkles with a warmth of affection that Covenant had not seen in any other *Haruchai* face.

"It is well," Brinn continued, "that you have reawakened the Vilesilencer's *krill*." Strain complicated his tone, but not his gaze. "Lacking some beacon to guide me across the wide seas, my search for you might have been delayed. However, you have done what must be done, as you have done from the first. For that reason among many others, I swallow my sorrow and greet you gladly, ur-Lord and Unbeliever, Thomas Covenant, friend."

Still Covenant stared. Only the pervasive force of Brinn's acquired theurgy kept him from crumpling. Never in life had Brinn of the *Haruchai* called him *friend*.

Sudden woe and rue and gratitude clogged his throat. He had to choke them down before he was able to inquire hoarsely, "What are you doing here?"

At the Isle of the One Tree, Brinn had told him, *That is the grace which has been given to you, to bear what must be borne.* Surely now Covenant had reached the limit of what he could be expected to endure?

Still Brinn did not glance at either of the Humbled. His attention belonged to Covenant alone. Speaking more sternly, as if he were setting friendship aside, he replied, "All things exist organically. This you know, Unbeliever. As one swells, another dwindles. As the Worm of death rises, the Tree of life declines." A lift of his hand referred to the heavens. "After long ages of slumber, the Worm now draws nigh unto the Land, seeking its final sustenance. In natural consequence, the One Tree expires to its roots. Thus I am freed of my Guardianship.

"Alas, my powers diminish as the Tree fails. I am made less by the deaths of stars and *Elohim*. And it was never my task to preserve the Worm's sleep, except by protecting the One Tree. I have no virtue to oppose the World's End. Nor am I permitted to do so, regardless of the leanings of my heart. That burden is yours, Unbeliever, as it is the Chosen's as well, and also her son's. Together you must save or damn the Earth, as it was foretold in the time of the Old Lords."

Then the *ak-Haru*'s manner softened until it resembled his gaze. "Yet I will not disregard the leanings of my heart. When I had achieved the stewardship of the One Tree, and you were thereby grieved, I assured you that good would come of it, when there was need. That promise I fain would honor. Therefore have I journeyed hither while some small portion of my strength endures, bringing both gifts and counsel. Mayhap thereafter I will also be able to perform a service or grant a boon, if my life does not fray and fall in the attempt."

Covenant went on staring as though he had been made witless. Part of him heard hope in every word. Part of him had already fled toward Linden, thinking, Gifts? Counsel? A chance to make things right with her? And part of him remained stunned, too astonished to comprehend anything. Brinn had come like a figure in a dream. In another moment, he would depart in the same fashion, with the same effectlessness.

But the Guardian of the One Tree did not appear to take offense at Covenant's silence. His affection seemed to accept every facet of Covenant's condition. Nodding at what he saw, the *ak-Haru* took one step back from the *krill*. Then at last he looked at Branl and Clyme, still half kneeling, still bowing their heads in homage.

Now his mien darkened. Lines of anger tightened his visage.

"First, however," he pronounced severely, "I will deliver myself of a reprimand which has long festered within me, tainting my regard for those whom I must name my people.

"*Haruchai*, Masters, Humbled, I have come to reproach you."

At once, Clyme and Branl arose. The manner in which they surged to their feet and folded their arms conveyed surprise and indignation. In every line, their stances offered defiance.

Stolid as a graven image, Branl stated, "You are the *ak-Haru* who was once named *Kenaustin Ardenol*, though you are now Brinn of the *Haruchai*. We do not lightly gainsay you. If you have cause to reproach us, however, you discern some fault which we do not find in ourselves.

"The weakness of uncertainty we acknowledge. Failure we likewise acknowledge. Against our given word, we have permitted Desecration, upon occasion because we were opposed by those whom we esteem, and upon occasion because the ur-Lord Thomas Covenant commanded it. Yet we have stood as Halfhands at his side. For his sake, we have dared the Lost Deep and She Who Must Not Be Named and Esmer *mere*-son. We have confronted the *skurj* and Cavewights and the Unbeliever's own misbegotten scion. We have entered into a Fall, hazarding endless banishment from time and life, and have there given aid to the ur-Lord when he could not aid himself.

"You are the *ak-Haru*. Would you have done otherwise in our place? Wherefore will you reproach us?"

Brinn dismissed Branl's protest with a soft snort. "Your valor is beyond aspersion," he answered as if such things were trivial. Thunderclouds of ire seemed to gather about his head, contradicting the twilight and the clear stars. "Set aside your pride and hear me.

"Doubtless others have spoken of arrogance. I do not. Rather the fault with which I charge you is *simony*." He spat that word. His eyes flashed dangerously, echoing the *krill*'s radiance. "You have grown ungenerous of spirit, demeaning what would else have been a proud heritage. You have withheld knowledge from the folk of the Land when knowledge might have nurtured strength. And you have withheld trust from Linden Avery the Chosen, setting yourselves in opposition to her efforts and sacrifices because you were unable to share her love and passion. These are the deeds of misers. They do not become you.

"Upon a time, the *Haruchai* were not ungiving in this fashion. Had they not been ruled by open-handedness, they would have been less grievously stung by the Vizard's scorn. Yet open their hands were, and open they remained. The bonds among them were as vital as sun and snows, and as enduring as mountains. The wounds of scorn they sought to heal by open means, in direct challenge and honest combat. Thus it was that High Lord Kevin's generosity moved them to emulation. The Vow of the Bloodguard expressed an answering generosity, a desire to repay expansive welcome with expansive service until both welcome and service overflowed.

"Yet across the millennia of your Mastery you have allowed harsh times and cruel circumstances to bar the doors of your hearts. I will not cite your reasons for doing so, lest you deem yourselves thereby excused. Rather I say to you plainly that you have diminished yourselves until I am loath to acknowledge you as my people."

Instinctively Covenant wanted to defend Clyme and Branl. Oh, he agreed with the Guardian. How could he not? Nevertheless the Humbled had stood by him like the *Haruchai* of old. They had saved him again and again when he could not have saved himself.

But his companions did not turn to him for justification. They did not look at him at all. As if they were proud to be castigated, they faced Brinn squarely.

"*Ak-Haru*," Clyme replied, "this accusation is unjust." Tautness marred his flat tone. "We do not comprehend it. What deed of ours—or of any Master—has given rise to your wrath?"

At once, the Guardian retorted, "Are you truly so blind that you see no fault in naming yourselves 'the Masters of the Land'?" His voice had become a distant rattle of thunder. In spite of his diminishment, his words had the power to summon storms. "The Land is not a thing to be possessed as though it were a garment. It was not created for your use, that you might hazard it in a vain attempt to heal your ancient humiliation."

Unmoved, Branl countered, "Yet you yourself have done as we do. You are our exemplar. Our distrust of Linden Avery we learned first from you, who saw Corruption's hand at work in her, and who strove to preserve the Unbeliever from her errors."

Omens of lightning glared from Brinn's eyes. "I concede," he answered, "that I trod your path when I forsook the Unbeliever's service. What of it? Did Cail not return to speak of the Chosen's salvific efforts at the Isle of the One Tree? And if you did not heed him, did you also fail to heed the First of the Search and Pitchwife when they described the forming of a new Staff of Law, and the unmaking of the Sunbane?

"No," he said harshly. "Do not protest that you have endeavored to treat the Chosen with both restraint and respect. I am not swayed. Your restraint and your respect are as miserly as your deeds. Had you permitted them to do so, the Giants would have reminded you that open hands and open spirits were once valued among the *Haru-chai*. Yet for many centuries you have offered the kindred of the Unhomed naught but unwelcome.

"*Unwelcome*, forsooth!" The *ak-Haru*'s indignation was a thunderclap. "For the *Giants*, of all the peoples of the Earth. That is my reproach. Humbled, Masters, *Haru-chai*, I marvel that you are not shamed."

Now even Covenant's numbed nerves and blunt health-sense felt tension rising in the Humbled. Brinn's objurgation stirred millennia of suppressed passions, of ire and resentment and denied helplessness, into living flames.

Speaking softly, ominously, Clyme asked, "Do you seek to renew our humiliation? Is that the purpose which has brought you among us, the last purpose of your life?"

"Paugh!" The Guardian made a dismissive gesture with both hands. "I am done with you. You do not hear, and so you cannot be redeemed. From this moment, I speak only to the Unbeliever. He will not disregard the remnants of my life, as you have done."

His gesture seemed to dispel the sensation of storms seething around him. He was definitely growing weaker, but he did not act weakened. Simply by turning away from the Humbled, he thwarted their outrage; cast them into shadow. Now they stood silent, like men whose mouths had been sealed. When Brinn faced Covenant again, he was smiling with a hint of remorse—and also with an air of satisfaction.

On the far side of the *krill*, he seated himself cross-legged in front of Covenant. His eyes in their nests of seams and wrinkles glittered with refreshed affection. He sat with his elbows braced on his thighs and his chin propped on his fists; held himself leaning forward to study Covenant more closely. When Brinn was comfortably settled, however, he said nothing. Instead he gazed at Covenant as if he, the *ak-Haru*, had been made content by the sight of his old friend's face.

Covenant wanted to lie down. His forehead throbbed, and broken bones gnawed like teeth in his chest, biting deeper with every slight movement. Brinn's obscure intentions and the dammed fury of the Humbled and his own wounds exceeded him. He ached to close his eyes and slump backward and let everything go.

Yet he did not. His heart had not forgotten its stubborn litany of loves and needs. And the Guardian had come because he wanted to help in some fashion. Covenant could not allow himself to lapse while so much remained unresolved.

With an effort that nearly made him sob, he muttered, "You aren't exactly being fair. You know that, don't you?"

Brinn's smile grew warmer. "It is for this that I esteem you, Thomas Covenant—this among many other qualities. Regardless of your own plight, you do not neglect the hurts of your companions." Then his mien assumed more somber lines. "But now we must take counsel together. Your wounds are grave, my friend. Some healing you must have. Yet with healing will come sleep. It must, for your need is extreme. Therefore we must converse before I expend my waning strength. If you have not chosen your course, these Humbled will determine it on your behalf—and they will not determine wisely."

Covenant groaned. "You see me. You know what I've done. What's left? What can I possibly hope to accomplish?"

He meant, Take me to Linden. If you have that kind of power, use it. Before I'm too far gone to tell her I'm sorry.

The Guardian nodded. "Indeed, Unbeliever, I see you. Your desires are plain to me. You yearn to be reunited with Linden Avery the Chosen for the Land's sake, and for your own. Were these Humbled less parsimonious in their dealings, they would honor the passion which binds you to your loves. But I must urge you to reconsider the Land's peril.

"You have slain your former mate, a deed costly to you, and hurtful, yet nonetheless necessary. What then remains for you to attempt? Have you forgotten *turiya* Herem? He who reveled in your former mate's agony and abasement? He is not slain. Of that I need not assure you. You are already certain of it."

Oh, hell, Covenant thought. *Turiya*? But he did not have enough life left to curse aloud. On the fall of a shuddering breath, he asked, "You want me to go after *him*?"

Brinn's study did not waver. Instead of answering directly, he inquired, "He has failed Corruption's chief intent for him. What will he now essay in restitution?"

Hellfire. Covenant groaned again. He was in no shape to think, much less talk. Nevertheless he did what he could. Brinn had called him *friend*.

"He'll try to possess someone else. Or something else. He isn't good for much unless he's wearing a body."

The *ak-Haru* leaned closer. "Then whose flesh will he assume? Not yours, that is certain. He is not such a fool. Nor will he attempt the Humbled. Their intransigence has not waned. He cannot rule them. Among the *skest*, he may perchance strive to attain your death. But they are little, and by nature timorous, readily cowed. Also I deem that *turiya* Herem is too prideful to be contented by them."

Covenant peered past the actinic brightness of the *krill* as if he were going blind. "So—?" His former companion faded in and out of focus. Give me a hint. I can't keep doing this.

The Raver had a long head start.

Brinn watched as though his gaze could penetrate Covenant's soul. "I ask again. Whose flesh will he assume? Of those that fear the Worm's coming, which is comparatively near? Which is driven by hungers apt for possession?"

Covenant flinched at an intuitive leap. "What, the *lurker*?" He stared through a blur of argent and failing consciousness. "You want me to go after *turiya* before he can possess the *lurker*?"

So far, the monster had kept its word. True to the alliance, Horrim Carabal had sent the Feroce to rescue Covenant and the Humbled from the *skest*. But still— The lurker of the Sarangrave had been a tale of horror for millennia. In some sense, it was the Despiser's creation. Directly or indirectly, Lord Foul had invoked an immense and sentient atrocity from the poisons leaking out of Mount Thunder.

Now Brinn wanted Covenant to defend that—that thing—from *turiya* Herem?

The Guardian replied with a grin as poignant as the deaths of stars. "Name a better purpose, my friend, and I will honor it."

Covenant meant to say, No. That's insane. But then he thought, So what? The Worm was coming. He had killed Joan. Everything was insane. The idea of trying to track down and stop a Raver—in his condition—was probably no crazier than his desire to see Linden again.

Over the course of his life in the Land, he had caused or allowed terrible bloodshed. The Riders of the Clave whom he had killed personally were minor casualties compared to the uncounted villagers and *Haruchai* that he had forsaken to slaughter while he searched for the One Tree. Saltheart Foamfollower had died helping him. Inadvertently he had killed Elena, his own daughter. Then he had brought about the sacrifice of her spirit to She Who Must Not Be Named.

But he had never struck a blow against the Despiser's most fatal servants. And the lurker possessed by a Raver would be an appalling foe. More insidiously dangerous than Roger and a whole host of Cavewights. Conceivably more powerful than *skurj* and Sandgorgons. If that monster challenged Linden, she would have to face it without Covenant or love.

Thinking about her made his wounds burn. His damaged ribs were acid and remorse in his chest. He wanted—Oh, he *wanted*. Nevertheless he understood Brinn.

He rubbed at the crust around his eyes, touched the fresh accusation on his forehead. Eventually he managed to mutter, "Damnation, Brinn. I'm going to need a horse."

The *ak-Haru* beamed at him like Loric's gem. "And you will not ride the Ranyhyn. For this also I esteem you, ur-Lord. Yet a steed has been offered to you. You need only speak the beast's name."

Brinn's voice invoked memories. As if from a great distance, Covenant heard the dying croak of the Ardent's last gift.

"Ah." In spite of his satisfaction, Brinn's sigh conveyed a tinge of regret. "I see the recall in your gaze. My friend, you are indeed as I have remembered you. I am now content to provide those gifts which lie within my power."

His vigor seemed undimmed as he rose to his feet.

"Remain only a short while," he urged Covenant. "Your healing will be my second gift. Here is my first."

While Covenant watched, stupefied by too many hurts, Brinn raised a hand to his mouth and gave one sharp whistle as clear as a commandment.

Covenant was losing his grip on consciousness. The only *Haruchai* who had ever called him *friend* had asked too much of him. He was no longer sure of what he saw or heard. The Guardian's call may have echoed through the maze of the Shattered Hills. The stars appeared to draw closer. They seemed to cry out. Perhaps their wailing was underscored by a clatter of hooves, irregular and indefinite.

When the Ranyhyn arrived with their star-blazed foreheads shining like the emblems of *Elohim*, Covenant thought that he saw four of them.

Two must have been Mhornym and Naybahn. They looked worse than Covenant felt. Ripped flesh hung in strips from their sides, exposing the damaged gleam of bones, especially along their ribs and on their knees. Blood oozed everywhere as if they were coated in ruin. They limped on legs that should not have supported them, and their eyes were dull with mute agony.

But they were still alive. They had heard Brinn's call. Somehow they had found the resolve to answer.

Proudly the *ak-Haru* announced, "Here are heroes. They have participated bravely and well in the defense of the Earth. Such battles are not won at a single stroke. They must be fought incrementally, by one selfless act of valor following another in its necessary sequence. Now Naybahn and Mhornym have completed their task. Their part is done. Though my strength wanes, I will preserve them. Then I will release them. While the Earth endures, no further service will be asked of them."

Then he turned to the other horses, a palomino stallion and a black. "And here are Rallyn and Hooryl. They have come to bear the Humbled on a quest which will require much of them, and of their riders. That they do so fearfully is no fault in them. They are Ranyhyn. Fear will not hinder their service."

Briefly Covenant looked at Clyme and Branl. The sight of them made him wince. His senses were too blunt to discern anything except rigid indignation.

But Brinn ignored the Masters. Facing Covenant again, he said as if he were bidding farewell, "Now, Unbeliever, Illender, Prover of Life, you must speak the name. Only its name will summon the steed and obtain its compliance."

The stars were too close. Covenant had never seen them look so near. Yet their proximity only accentuated the voids between them, the immeasurable gulfs of their isolation. Vaguely he wondered whether the *Elohim* felt the same loneliness. Perhaps that explained their prideful self-absorption, their insistence that they were complete in themselves, *equal to all things*. Perhaps their surquedry was nothing more than compensation for prolonged sterility and sorrow.

But then the lamentation overhead and Brinn's kindness compelled him. Swallowing the taste of blood and woe, he did as the Guardian of the dying One Tree asked or commanded.

"Mishio Massima."

Brinn's smile was a confluence of hope and regret as he stepped past the *krill* to touch Covenant's blamed forehead lightly with one finger.

At the same time, he urged quietly, "Recall that the *krill* is capable of much. With use, it has become more than it was."

His touch seemed to light a star in Covenant's brain. Suddenly the dusk in all direction became a swirl of lights: the same swirl which had filled the Isle's cavern long ago when Covenant had tried to claim a branch of the One Tree. If Linden had not stopped him then, he might have brought about the world's end without realizing what he did.

He needed to make things right with her. He needed to tell her that he loved her—and that he had killed Joan.

Brinn had spoken of a service—a boon—but he had not revealed what it might be.

Then the stars took Covenant, and he went to sleep as if he were falling into the heavens.

4.

"Try to Believe"

Soreness and jostling finally roused Covenant. He had no idea where he was; but for a while, he did not care. If the flexing sensations of movement had not insisted on his attention, he would have tried to go back to sleep.

His whole body ached as though he had suffered a beating. A dull throb in his forehead matched the rhythm that carried him. But when he braced himself to draw a deeper breath, he found that the piercing hurt of broken ribs was gone. Bruises like groans had replaced the effects of sharp rocks and rending coral. His weakness felt more like convalescence than blood-loss.

A week, he thought to the cadence of hooves, the flow of stubborn muscles. Just let me rest for a week. Then I'll open my eyes. I promise.

He did not have a week. He doubted that he could afford hours.

Vaguely he deduced that he was mounted. But not bareback: not on a Ranyhyn. The saddle under him reminded him of the Harrow's fallen destrier. And he was not held upright. No, he was sprawled resting along a long neck. The saddle horn dug into his abdomen. His legs dangled free of stirrups. The jolts were the beat of a hard canter.

He remembered Mishio Massima, the Ardent's mangy, shovel-headed horse. Clyme and Branl must have boosted him onto the steed while he slept. And they must have secured his arms—perhaps with the reins—so that he would not fall.

Mishio Massima's jarring gait punished his recent wounds. Nonetheless he was grateful. At Brinn's insistence, no doubt, the Humbled had honored Covenant's promise to the Ranyhyn.

For a time, he was content to rest as he was in spite of the prod of the saddle horn. The mystery of Brinn's aid remained with him; the miracle of Brinn's friendship. Covenant was less alone in the world than he had believed himself to be. Less alone than he felt with the rigid companionship of the Humbled. The dying Guardian of the One Tree had given him a profound gift—

But it was not an unalloyed blessing. True, Brinn had mended the worst of his injuries. But the Guardian had also given him a task which he feared to contemplate.

Remembering *turiya* Raver, Covenant flinched. He needed to open his eyes. Hell, he needed to sit up. He had to know where he was. And where the Humbled were taking him. And how they had resolved their contention with their *ak-Haru*—if they had resolved it at all. And what the service or boon that Brinn had mentioned might be.

The possibility that *turiya* Herem might take possession of the lurker of the Sarangrave frightened Covenant as much as the idea that he might never see Linden again.

With an effort, he lifted his head; lowered it again. Blinking, he tried to clear his sight. Then he made an attempt to free his arms.

"A moment, ur-Lord," Clyme said over the steady rumble of hooves. "We will unbind you."

Now Covenant realized that the hoof-beats of the horses were muffled. The ground where they ran was too yielding to be stone; too soft for bare dirt.

Peering sideways through the gloom, he saw a shape veer toward him: a horse and rider. When Hooryl came near enough to brush his leg, Clyme bent down to undo the reins.

Briefly Covenant fought the blur that marred his vision. It seemed worse than it should have been. He could still see stars overhead, but his companion's features were a twilit smear. He had to squint in order to discern that the horses were cantering on thick turf.

Hell and blood. He should have been able to see better than this. Brinn had healed him, and leprosy did not progress so swiftly.

Unless—

Stung by an intuitive apprehension, he pulled his awkward arms under him; pushed himself off his mount's neck. Then he clutched at the saddle horn to keep his balance.

He could not feel the horn at all, except with the nerves of his elbows and shoulders. His hands were numb.

"What—?" he panted. He seemed to need all of his strength to keep his seat. Insensate in their boots, his feet floundered for the stirrups and did not find them. "What's going on?" His voice was as vague as his vision. He had slept too long. "What's happening to me? My eyes are going."

Around him, the aegis of the gloaming was complete. It ruled everything. It was leaking into his head; into his mind. Only the stars as they died were vivid to him.

Clyme draped the untied reins over Covenant's forearms. Hooryl moved away from Mishio Massima, perhaps so that Covenant could move his leg freely while he groped for the stirrup.

"Kevin's Dirt has overtaken us." Clyme sounded angry. No, it was more than that. He sounded like a man who had given up pretending that he was not angry. "It came upon us at midday. Clearly Kastenessen now directs his malice over the Lower Land, doubtless seeking to harm you, and also to hinder the Staff of Law. In this, he succeeds. To our sight, it is plain that Kevin's Dirt deepens your illness."

Covenant had guessed as much. But he had not expected the effects of Kastenessen's brume to be so swift. Came upon us at midday? How much time had he lost?

He turned his head to confirm that Branl also rode beside him. The motion and his mount's strides made his head pound and his ribs throb. But those pains were more bearable than his earlier hurts; somehow more human. He could imagine that they would fade.

Branl's visage wore a frown like a knot between his brows. It looked permanent, as if it had always been there; as if it had merely been masked by a learned and unnatural impassivity.

Slowly the vagueness faded from Covenant's thoughts. After a moment, he was able to ask Branl, "Where are we?"

"Ur-Lord," the Humbled answered, "the Ranyhyn are cunning. They eluded the snares of the *skest* and escaped the maze of the Shattered Hills well before the onset of Kevin's Dirt. Now we return along the path of our approach to Kurash Qwellinir. The cliff above the Sunbirth Sea lies there." He gestured eastward. "If your mount is able to sustain its pace, we will soon gain the region where we last found *aliantha*."

Covenant sighed his relief. This was not the most direct route to the Sarangrave, but it was the shortest path to food. If Branl and Clyme had over-ruled their *ak-Haru*'s counsel—if they had decided to seek Linden and the Giants instead of pursuing *turiya*—they would have headed northwest from the Shattered Hills.

Covenant looked around at the caliginous vista of the grass, the slope rising incrementally toward the east, the greying of the world. When he was ready, he announced, "I want to stop for a while. I ache everywhere. I need to walk around some. I'm sure this nag"—he indicated Mishio Massima with his chin—"can use a break." In fact, the Ardent's beast seemed preternaturally hardy. Unlike the Harrow's charger, apparently, this horse had been bred for endurance. "If nothing else, it probably wants grass. And we should talk."

He felt sure that the Humbled had much to tell him—if they chose to do so.

Clyme and Branl consented promptly: a bad sign. Had they trusted Brinn's advice, they would have argued that Covenant required haste. But they slowed their mounts without a word. Mishio Massima eased to a bone-rattling trot, then jerked to a walk like a thing formed of tree-limbs rather than flesh and bone.

Before the beast halted, Covenant slid out of the saddle. At first, his legs refused to hold him, and he dropped to his knees. Fortunately the turf cushioned the impact. Then he forced himself to his feet. Stifling a groan, he began to stamp in a circle, trying vainly to drive some sensation back into his ankles and feet. Their numbness affected him like imminent vertigo: he needed to rediscover balance. As he moved, he twisted his trunk from side to side, testing the condition of his ribs. Briefly he rolled his head and swung his arms. When he had assured himself that he was substantially intact, he took a few deep breaths and braced himself to confront the Humbled.

They had dismounted. Now they stood facing him, Branl with his clenched frown, Clyme with his hands curled into fists. But the mounts were moving away, trotting westward. Covenant guessed that they had caught the scent of water.

Alone with his companions, he rubbed at the crusted blood around his eyes; probed the new scar on his forehead with the nub-ends of his fingers. His fingers felt nothing, but the tenderness of the cut assured him that it needed more time to heal.

The Humbled had not endured their *ak-Haru*'s reproach gently: that was obvious. Groping for a tone of respect, Covenant said, "I'm not sure, of course. I was asleep. But I get the impression there are things you should tell me. Something happened while I was out—and I'm not talking about Kevin's Dirt. Did Brinn say anything else? Did he—?"

Clyme interrupted him curtly. "He did not. We were not heeded. No further speech was exchanged."

Covenant stared. "Are you sure? He said something about a boon. A service. He didn't tell you what it was?"

Brinn was *Haruchai*: he could have spoken to the Humbled mind to mind more fluently and thoroughly than aloud.

"He did not," Clyme repeated, rigid as metal. "He refused our mental communion, as only Stave has done heretofore. In his thoughts we found only silence."

Frowning like Branl, Covenant wavered on his feet. Keeping his balance was as difficult as he had feared. Too much had happened. He needed the feedback of nerves which no longer communicated with the rest of his body.

To that extent, at least, he knew how the Humbled felt. The Guardian had undermined their foundations.

"What does that mean to you?" he asked carefully. "Has he given up on us?"

After a moment, Clyme appeared to relent. His shoulders released some of their tension. Less stiffly, he replied, "When the *ak-Haru* had extended his strength for your healing, he was much reduced. Indeed, he resembled a man drawing the last breaths of extreme age. We deem that he did not speak again of a boon because he had come to the end of himself. He could not do more."

Ah, hell, Covenant sighed. He hated to think that Brinn had simply passed away. After so much time and devotion— He wanted to believe that his former companion would find some form of resolution or contentment; but Clyme gave him scant reason for hope.

However, he could not afford to dwell on grief. Other issues were more compulsory.

"Then tell me what's changed for you." He strained his eyes to study the faces of the Humbled. When neither of them spoke, he made an attempt to sound gentle. "Was being criticized by your *ak-Haru* that bad?"

Both men stiffened. Their anger made them vivid in the gloom. Branl's glower looked fierce enough to split his skull. Clyme knocked the knuckles of his fists together as if he were stifling an impulse to hit someone.

Like the cut of a blade, Clyme stated, "His words were hurtful to no purpose. He did not reproach what we have done. His reproach was that we are who we are. Is the wind to be faulted because it blows? Are the stones to be accused because they are not trees? We are *Haruchai*. We cannot be other than ourselves."

"Mayhap it was his right to speak as he did," Branl conceded. He was not less indignant than Clyme: he had merely assumed their shared burden of truthfulness. "He is the *ak-Haru*, Guardian of the One Tree. No other *Haruchai* has equaled his attainments."

"Nevertheless," Clyme snapped. "We care naught for his right to speak. Our true grievance, ur-Lord, is that he sought to counsel you, and his counsel was *false*."

He spat that word as if it were a curse.

"False?" Covenant nearly choked. "Hellfire! How do you get to a conclusion like that? You said it yourself. He's the *ak-Haru*, for God's sake! How can you even *think* a word like 'false,' never mind say it out loud?"

Now Clyme did not relent. His tone held an outrage so deep that it seemed to arise from the marrow of his bones.

"We do not charge him with malign intent, but rather with mistaken comprehension. As he has misesteemed us, so he has misjudged the Land's peril.

"The lurker's plight is of no consequence. That monstrous wight is an avatar of Corruption. A Raver's possession cannot increase its misbegotten appetites. It requires no urging to seek our ruin.

"Recall," he insisted as though Covenant had tried to interrupt him, "that the Soulsease has found new depths among the roots of Gravin Threndor. The Defiles Course will not resume its accustomed flow until the immeasurable abyss of the Lost Deep has been filled. Thus the poisons which supply the lurker's most necessary sustenance have been much reduced. Already its hungers swell. They must. Having grown so vast, they must be vastly fed. Such a creature will not long remember that it fears your magicks, or Linden Avery's. Your alliance was a thing of the moment. It cannot endure.

"To abandon all other needs in the lurker's name is madness."

Madness? Covenant wanted to protest. Is that what you think of Brinn? Is that what you think of *me*? But the Humbled were not done.

"That is reason enough to set aside the *ak-Haru*'s counsel," put in Branl. "Yet there are other reasons as well.

"Has not the Ardent cited the ravages of the *skurj* and the Sandgorgons in concert? Has not Kevin's Dirt been sent to weaken us? And is not Kastenessen the source of both evils? There lies your true path, ur-Lord. You must join with Linden Avery to challenge the mad *Elohim*'s malevolence. That task is paramount. An end to Kevin's Dirt must be accomplished.

"Doubtless Kastenessen is both spurred and guided by *moksha* Jehannum.

Certainly the Sandgorgons heed the Raver, seduced as they are by the remnants of *samadhi* Sheol's spirit. Yet the power is Kastenessen's. There can be no true defense of the Land while he stands in opposition."

Facing his companions, Covenant floundered. Anger he had expected. They were *Haruchai*, Masters and Humbled; proud. Naturally they had taken umbrage at Brinn's judgments. But he had not expected them to express their indignation like this.

Shaken and dismayed, he felt a reflexive desire to argue. He could have pointed out that Kastenessen was almost certainly positioned somewhere among the secrets of Mount Thunder, and that the distance was insurmountable. No doubt Linden was closer; but finding her would not take Covenant nearer to Kastenessen.

While he tried to assemble the necessary words, however, he realized that the distance was effectively irrelevant. *Turiya*'s head start was already insurmountable. Under the circumstances, one impossible distance was much like another.

In any case, no rational argument would sway the Humbled. They were too angry. Behind their masks, their attitude was based on a passion that Covenant did not understand.

Something had stung a primal nerve in them: primal and intimate. They had been hurt in a place at once carefully hidden and exquisitely raw. The pain of that singular wound drove them to extremes of emotion which Covenant had not witnessed before in any *Haruchai*.

Unsure of himself, he tried to be cautious. "The Feroce saved us." Still he winced at his own bleakness, his tone of confrontation. In his way, he was as irate as the Humbled. "Horrim Carabal held up his end. He didn't have to. He could have left us to the *skest*. After all, he hates wild magic. He hates the *krill*. But he kept his word anyway. We wouldn't be here talking about it if he hadn't honored his agreement. Maybe you can ignore that. I can't.

"First you wanted me to break my promise to the Ranyhyn. Now you want me to turn my back on an alliance. That doesn't sound like you. It doesn't sound like any *Haruchai* I've ever met." He had to grit his teeth to keep from shouting. "What's happened to you?"

Dark as incarnations of wrath, Clyme and Branl glared at Covenant. For a long moment, they did not reply. They did not move. Perhaps deliberately, they gave him a chance to fear that they would turn away from him. The Masters had spurned Stave—

But then, suddenly, Branl snatched the bundle of Loric's *krill* from inside his tunic. With a flick of his wrists, he spun the blade free of Anele's tattered heritage. As the gem's argence blazed out, he stabbed the dagger into the grass.

In the *krill*'s radiance, both Branl and Clyme looked hieratic, chthonic, as if they had already taken their places among the Dead. The reflections in their eyes gave them the authority of spirits unconstrained by the boundaries of life and time.

"Ur-Lord," Clyme announced, "we are the Humbled in all sooth, the Humbled triumphant and maimed. Have you forgotten so much that you do not recognize the men whom we have chosen to become?" His ire sounded more and more like lamentation. It sounded like fear. "Do you not recall that it is our task to embody you among our people? You are the purpose and substance of our lives.

"If you do not return to Linden Avery, and do so swiftly, you will perish. We cannot stem the harm which Kevin's Dirt wreaks within you. Nor can the lurker of the Sarangrave succor you. Without the balm of the Staff of Law, your end is certain.

"Come good or ill, boon or bane, you must not heed the counsel of the *ak-Haru*."

As Clyme spoke, Covenant finally heard what lay behind the frustrated fury of the Humbled. As though the insight had come to him from the lost expanse of the Arch of Time, he understood; and he found himself trying to laugh, although he wanted to weep. Oh, Clyme. Oh, Branl. Have you come to this? After so much fidelity and striving, is this the best you can do?

Their beliefs were too small to vindicate the race of the *Haruchai*. At the same time, they were too much for Covenant.

That was their tragedy. They had attached an almost metaphysical significance to a lone and lonely man who could not bear the burden. He was unequal to the task of meaning, not because he was sick and weak—although he was—but because he was just one man, nothing more. Even if he transcended his own inadequacies indefinitely, he could not provide transcendence for anybody else. The *Haruchai* needed to find it within themselves, not in him.

Nothing else would relieve the bereavement which had haunted them for millennia.

But they were not Giants: they would not respond to laughter; even to laughter as strained and loss-ridden as Covenant's. Their hearts spoke a different language.

As if he were translating alien precepts into pragmatic speech, he replied, "Did I ever tell you that I respect you? I hope I did. I've said as many hurtful things as Brinn did, but none of it would have been worth saying if I didn't respect you absolutely. You're the standard I use to measure myself—or you would be if I thought that highly of who I am. The idea that men like you care whether I live or die makes me want to prove you're right about me.

"But what's at stake here—what we're talking about—what we have to do—isn't about whether or not I live through it. It's about the Land, and the Worm, and Lord Foul. We can't let the fact that I'm sick choose our commitments for us.

"I've made promises. Now I have to take the risk of keeping them. I have to be willing to pay whatever they cost."

And his agreement with the lurker had been founded on a lie: the mistaken belief that he was the Pure One of *jheherrin* legend. He needed to redeem that falsehood.

Clyme and Branl watched him without saying anything; without any expression that he could interpret. Clyme braced his fists on his hips. Branl folded his arms like barriers across his chest. If they grasped that import of his affirmation, they gave no sign.

Nevertheless Covenant went on as if he had won their consent to continue. "But that cost— It may not be what you think. Which is my fault," he added quickly, "not yours.

"I don't say much about myself. I probably haven't told you or anybody that my disease—that leprosy—isn't fatal. Lepers can get worse for a long time without dying. Usually it's the things that happen to them *because* they're lepers that kill them.

"Kastenessen can make me a whole lot sicker without stopping me. Kevin's Dirt is nasty stuff, but it won't save him. He only imagines it will because he's crazy and desperate.

"Meanwhile leprosy is like most of the things we struggle with. It's a curse, but sometimes it can also be a blessing."

Cast back by the *krill*'s brilliance, the surrounding twilight seemed to deepen, drawing the stars ever closer to the world's doom. At the same time, the Humbled began to look both more substantial and more mundane; less like emblems from the realm of death. Unwillingly, perhaps, but irrefusably, they were being lured out of their moral reality into Covenant's.

More sure of himself now, the Unbeliever said, "Look at it this way. Have you never wondered why none of the Ravers has ever tried to possess me? They've had me helpless often enough. So why am I still here? Sure, Foul told them not to take me. He didn't want them to get my ring. But why did they obey?

"Well, they've been his servants so long, you might think they're incapable of independent thought. That's one theory. But it can't be true. If it were, they wouldn't be much use. He would have to spend all his time telling them what to do. No, he has to be able to give them orders and then leave them alone while they figure out how to accomplish what he wants. They have to be able think for themselves.

"And they're by God *Ravers*. It's their *nature* to be hungry for power and destruction." Just like Horrim Carabal. "So why have they never, not once in all these millennia, ever tried to possess me? Why haven't they tried to take my ring?"

Covenant spread his hands, his foreshortened fingers, showing the Humbled that they were empty—and that such appearances were as deceptive as the stoicism of the *Haruchai*.

"I think I know why. It's the same reason we can trust the lurker. And the same reason I have to do what I can to save him. Because they're afraid. They're all afraid. Horrim Carabal is afraid of the Worm. And the Ravers— Well, of course they're afraid of Lord Foul. But I'm guessing they're also afraid of leprosy. They're afraid of what it might be like to possess a body and a mind as sick as mine. They're afraid of all this numbness, and going blind, and feeling crippled not to mention impotent even when they have wild magic to play with."

He shrugged as if he were susceptible to contradiction; yet with every word he felt stronger. "Maybe being me would be too much like being the Despiser, trapped and helpless and full of despair even though he's too powerful and too damn eternal to be killed. Possessing other people, or other monsters, they can at least feel and hate and destroy. With me, they might not be able to do any of those things."

He was vaguely surprised to see Clyme and Branl blink in unison as if they were closing the shutters of their minds against illumination. But the moment was brief; no more than a flicker.

As if he were confessing an article of faith, Covenant concluded, "That's why I might be able to save the lurker. It's why I have to be a leper. *Turiya* won't even consider possessing me. Leprosy is my best defense. Even Lord Foul can't stop me if I'm numb enough."

Then he held his breath. He could not read his companions: he saw only anger and blankness and inflexibility. Argent lit them against the backdrop of the sunless day, but did not reveal their hearts.

They were slow to respond. They may have been sifting through their imponderable storehouse of memories, testing Covenant's asseveration against their entire history with him.

When Clyme finally answered, Covenant was not prepared for his response. Nothing in his manner, or in Branl's, hinted that the Humbled were capable of any reply except denial.

"How then," Clyme asked with the finality of a knell, "shall we pursue the Raver? He is no longer hampered by the limitations of flesh. Even the Ranyhyn cannot equal his fleetness, and your mount is no Ranyhyn. How can the lurker be spared if we cannot overtake *turiya* Herem?"

Dimly through the dusk, Covenant saw Rallyn and Hooryl returning, bringing Mishio Massima with them. They seemed to know that the time had come to bear their riders again.

He exhaled hard; panted briefly for air. "I have no idea," he admitted. "I'll have to think of something."

At that moment, he believed that he would succeed. Like Brinn, Clyme and Branl had given him what he needed. While the Humbled stood with him, he could imagine that anything was possible.

∽∾

But he put off thinking until he and his companions had ridden far enough to find *aliantha*. He needed time to absorb Clyme's and Branl's acquiescence. And he felt thin with hunger. He had eaten nothing since he and his companions had left their covert in the cliff early the previous morning. The streams that the Ranyhyn discovered now eased him somewhat; but water was not nourishment—and it was certainly not treasure-berries. He craved the rich benison of the Land's health and vitality. Without it, he could not reason clearly enough to untangle the riddle of *turiya* Herem's head start.

Fortunately Branl and Clyme knew where they had last seen *aliantha*. And Covenant did not doubt that the Ranyhyn could have located the holly-like shrubs even without the guidance of the Humbled. The way seemed long to him, but Clyme pointed toward the first bush well before the unbroken twilight became midafternoon.

There Covenant dismounted. At once, Mishio Massima lowered its head to the grass as if nothing mattered except food. Carrying the *krill* again, Branl remained with Covenant while Clyme rode ahead to gather more berries so that Covenant would not be required to waste time searching for a sufficient meal.

At the first tang of the fruit in his mouth, Covenant seemed to feel Brinn's hand reaching out to him across the leagues and hours; touching his sore forehead and damaged ribs and battered arms with renewal. In its own way, *aliantha* was as much a gift as the *ak-Haru*'s aid, and as precious. It answered questions which the Humbled had not asked.

It was for *this* that Covenant had to find and stop *turiya*, and then go on to the next battle, and the next. Not for the lurker. Not for the *Elohim*, in spite of their slow, inexorable decimation. Not even for Linden, although his ache for her resembled weeping. No, it was for *aliantha* that he had to fight: for treasure-berries, and for Wraiths; for hurtloam and Glimmermere and Salva Gildenbourne, Andelain and EarthBlood; for the Ranyhyn and their Ramen; for ur-viles and Waynhim; and for every mortal heart as valiant and treasurable as Liand's, or as Anele's. For their sake, he had to catch up with the Raver. He had to find a way.

When he had eaten enough to take the edge off his hunger, he began to pace slowly, chewing fruit, scattering seeds, and talking. The numbness of his feet made him feel that he walked a friable surface tipping him toward vertigo. Nevertheless he persevered. He needed to hear his thoughts aloud in order to believe in them. And he needed movement to loosen the knots that bound him to his limitations.

The Worm was coming. Lord Foul's triumph drew closer with every hesitation, every delay. The Land could not be saved by anything less than extravagant efforts and hope.

Hope did not come easily to lepers. But Covenant had learned that there were better answers than grim survival and despair. He had been taught by more friends and loves than he could count.

Unsteadily he ate, and marked out a circle on the giving ground with his steps, and talked.

"I keep thinking about Linden," he muttered as if he were speaking to Branl. With a wave of one hand, he dismissed a protest which his companion did not utter. "I was watching her. I remember her life almost as well as mine.

"She should have died when she first arrived on Kevin's Watch. A *caesure* broke the Watch right after she met Anele. All those tons of shattered granite collapsed like they fell from the sky. She should have been crushed. They both should have been reduced to pulp. But she kept them alive.

"I'm asking myself, how did she *do* that?"

Concentrating on other things, he lost his balance as if he had tripped. He almost fell. The deadening of his nerves was becoming extreme. Still he was familiar with such dilemmas. The loss of sensation was like Unbelief. It could be managed. Sometimes it could be set aside. And under the right circumstances, it could become a form of strength.

How else had he twice defeated the Despiser?

"I was watching," he repeated as he resumed his tread. "I saw what happened. I mean, what *literally* happened. She slipped outside time. And she took Anele with her. Somehow she bypassed cause and effect and even ordinary gravity so that she and Anele came down on top of the rubble instead of under it. Hell, she didn't even break bones.

"But *how*? That was a neat trick. How did she manage it?"

Peripherally Covenant noticed Clyme's return. But the Unbeliever did not interrupt the awkward whirl, the vertigo in slow motion, of his paced circle.

"It's obvious, really. She did it with wild magic. She used my ring, even though she had no idea what she was doing, and she certainly never did anything like that before. It must have been pure reflex. Raw instinct. But that part doesn't matter. What matters is, she *did* it. She proved it's possible.

"If wild magic is the keystone of the Arch of Time, it *participates* somehow." Those words raised echoes for him. They implied memories which eluded recognition.

"You could say Linden did the opposite of what Joan was doing. Instead of shattering pieces of time, she found her way around them."

The Humbled studied him in silence. Their faces remained as blank as age-worn carvings.

"Well." Unaware of what he did, Covenant spread gestures in all directions as if he were flinging out his arms for balance; as if he sought to encompass the world. "If she could do it, why can't we? After all, my poor son and that damned *croyel* did it. They slipped through time to take her into the past. Which the Mahdoubt also knew how to do. And they slipped past distance to reach *Melenkurion* Skyweir. Which both the Harrow and the Ardent knew how to do. So why don't we do the same thing?"

There was something that he needed to remember, but he did not try to force it. Instead he let the past reach him in its own way.

Clyme slid down from Hooryl's back. Lifting the hem of his tunic, he showed Covenant that he carried a feast of treasure-berries. But Covenant did not pause. He could not stop talking now, even for the Land's largesse.

"Ignorance, I suppose. We don't know what Roger and the *croyel* and at least some of the Insequent knew. If I ever understood how they did it, I sure as hell don't remember. And we probably haven't earned the knowledge. But when you can see a thing is possible, ignorance looks less irreducible. You can afford to try out theories or just plain guesswork because you know what you want to accomplish."

As if by an act of grace, the memory he sought came to him.

Time is the keystone of life, just as wild magic is the keystone of Time. Among the Dead, the Theomach had said that. *It is Time which is endangered.* His counsel had inspired Covenant to risk a *caesure* in order to confront Joan. *The path to its preservation lies through Time.*

That was cryptic at best; hardly comprehensible. Nevertheless it sufficed.

Abruptly Covenant stopped pacing, planted his legs for balance. His head continued its slow spin, but he faced the Humbled as squarely as he could.

"And Loric's *krill* isn't our only instrument of power. We have white gold." He tapped his sternum where Joan's wedding band hung under his tattered T-shirt. "If Linden can use my ring, I ought to be able to use Joan's."

You are the white gold.

Recall that the krill *is capable of much.*

Without transition, he told Clyme, "Give me some of that. I've got work to do, and I'm still hungry."

He had no real idea how to carry out his intentions. But he had found a place to start. And he could trust the Ranyhyn to help him.

He had suffered enough. Now he meant to surprise the hell out of *turiya* Herem.

ಬಲ

Before long, he had satisfied his hunger. The bounty of *aliantha* seemed to supply all of his immediate lacks. Each berry enriched his veins and muscles and even the fate written on his forehead until he was almost strong, almost steady. The threat of dizziness receded. His health-sense remained vague as a wisp, but he felt an unexpected tingle of renewed sensation in his ankles and wrists.

When he was ready, he thanked Clyme. He urged the Master to save as many treasure-berries as he could. Then he asked Branl for the *krill*.

"I'm not sure what I'm doing," he admitted. "But it's always helped me to have another source of power." The Staff of Law in Elena's hands. The Illearth Stone in Foul's Creche. Sunder's *orcrest*. Covenant had relied upon external catalysts or triggers until the Despiser's venom had eaten away his instinctive defenses, his visceral reluctance. "And this ring is Joan's, not mine. Using it won't be easy."

In contrast, he had earned the privilege of wielding Loric's eldritch dagger. He had paid for it with bloodshed.

Branl did not hesitate. Removing the wrapped blade from its place under his tunic, he delivered it to the Unbeliever.

Covenant hefted the dagger, felt its weight and its implied power. "Now what?" he asked, thinking aloud again. In spite of his millennia within the Arch of Time, the prospect of theurgy still disturbed him. Magic suited Linden. Her health-sense guided her: she could control herself. Covenant was only a leper. Nevertheless he had come too far to start shirking hazards that scared him.

How often had he told Linden to trust herself?

"Well, let's see. I don't understand *how* the Harrow and the Ardent did what they did. As far as I know, they just appeared and disappeared whenever they wanted. But Roger and the *croyel* are another matter.

"They faced each other with Linden between them. They raised their arms to make an arch over her head. An arch like a door." Instinctively he began to pace again. "A portal. But I can't do that. I can't stand in two places at once."

Could Clyme or Branl assist him? He rejected that idea. *Haruchai* did not wield magic. Whenever they could, they eschewed weapons of any kind. And Covenant had already required the Humbled to violate too many of their chosen prohibitions.

"Sounds like an impasse," he muttered. "But it can't be." He lifted his burden with a shrug. "So maybe I'm thinking about this the wrong way. Maybe Roger and the *croyel* weren't making a door. Maybe it just looked like a door. Maybe it was really something else.

"Like what?" For a moment, nothing occurred to him. Then he felt a surge of possibility. "How about an *enclosure*? A way to keep everybody together while Roger and the *croyel* combined their magicks?"

"*That* I can do."

"Ur-Lord?" asked Clyme. Another man might have sounded baffled. The Humbled's tone expressed only polite disinterest. "Your meaning is obscure to us. Speak more plainly."

Nourished by *aliantha*, a sensation like eagerness throbbed in Covenant's veins. Perhaps lepers were capable of hope after all.

"Watch," he said as if he were sure of himself. "Mount up." He took a few steps to increase his distance from the Humbled and the Ranyhyn. "Keep my horse with you. I'll join you when I'm ready.

"And concentrate on *turiya*. Rallyn and Hooryl can find him if they know that's what we want."

His companions may have hesitated. If so, he did not see it. He had already turned his attention to his task.

His arms still ached. The *krill* seemed too heavy to bear. In spite of Brinn's gifts, and the Land's, he remained weak. Nonetheless he used the stubs of his halfhand to pull out Joan's wedding band on its chain.

Ah, Joan—Her ring had encircled a world of promises, but none of them were kept. If he got the chance, he intended to make better promises before the end.

Drawing the chain over his head, he forced Joan's ring onto the truncated end of the little finger of his left hand. With the chain dangling, he unwrapped the remnants of Anele's raiment from the *krill*, carefully keeping fabric between the ring and any part of the dagger.

When the silver purity of the gem blazed out, defying the dusk in all directions, he paused. While his eyes adjusted to the shock of radiance, he tried to take stock of his condition; his fitness for what he meant to attempt.

At one time, he had feared white gold. He had been positively dependent on the idea that he was helpless; that he was capable of nothing, and that therefore nothing could be required of him. At another time, he had again feared wild magic, but for the opposite reason. Afflicted by Lord Foul's venom, he had raised fire from his ring too easily. He had become capable of appalling destruction and bloodshed at any provocation.

Now he felt like an amalgam of those two Covenants, an alloy: the leper who feared the responsibility of any power, and the poisoned man whose violence threatened to defy constraint. He could imagine himself accomplishing *everything and nothing,*

hero and fool
potent, helpless—
and with the one word of truth or treachery,
he will save or damn the Earth
because he is mad and sane,
cold and passionate,
lost and found.

Just like lepers everywhere, he reminded himself so that he would not falter. Just like all of us. Everybody who still cares. We're all in the same mess.

"Well, hell," he drawled unsteadily. "What's the point of dithering? Now's as good a time as any."

Damned if you do, damned if you don't. The Despiser's favorite game.

Wincing as though he expected to be struck down, Covenant released his left hand from the blade's haft and slapped Joan's ring against the shining gem.

In that instant, his whole body became fire.

He was burning, but he was not burned: he blazed unconsumed. He felt as incandescent as the torrent of wild magic with which Lord Foul had once slain and freed him, yet he was not harmed. All around him, the twilight became darkness, impenetrable, impermeable. But within the ambit of his theurgy, silver reigned. It made every blade of grass along the sloping turf look sacred; distinct and ineffable. Argent lit Branl and Clyme on their Ranyhyn, holding Mishio Massima between them: it etched them against the sunless world as if it had incarnated them from the numinous substance of Covenant's imagination. Emblazonry shone on Rallyn's forehead, and on Hooryl's. Even the Ardent's horse resembled reified sorcery, ready to run between realities. Power surged in Covenant's veins until he did not know how to contain it.

"Ur-Lord!" Branl called through the blare of light. "Be wary! Such might is perilous!"

But Covenant knew his limitations. He knew the difference between his puissance now and the immensely greater forces which he had wielded in his past life. In any case, he was still too frail to sustain so much power—and this ring was not his. The *krill* was probably burning his halfhand. For all he knew, Joan's ring was burning his finger. He simply could not feel the pain.

Deliberately he dropped his left hand to his side, gripped the dagger with only his right. As he did so, the fire left him. He no longer spread brightness and flame in all directions; no longer poured out light as though his flesh were wild magic. But the *krill*'s gem retained the radiance which he had summoned from it. Theurgy ran down the blade like water or blood.

At once, he stooped to touch the grass with the point of Loric's weapon. He let the blade's weight sink in as deeply as it wished, but he made no effort to drive the *krill* deeper. Then he watched as the rough turf became lambent as if it had been touched with ecstasy.

He feared to see that the *krill*'s touch had killed the grass, left it scorched and withered. But somehow he had invoked a form of power which was not destructive. Instead of dying, the turf continued to shine where he had cut through it.

Crouched and stumbling, he began to drag the dagger in a line through the grass.

His heart strained as he moved on. He intended to draw a circle around the Ranyhyn and Mishio Massima; to enclose them in wild magic. But of course such precision was impossible for him. Rather than a circle, he was creating a ragged imitation of one. Nevertheless he persisted; and his silver clung to the grass.

Now he could feel a throb of yearning from Joan's ring in his wrist and forearm. Her wedding band ached for more power. Perhaps it remembered the use which she had made of it, and craved ruin. But there was no wish for harm in Covenant's heart, and he was familiar with wild magic. His argent did no hurt.

Staggering, he looked around to get his bearings. Then he went on, pulling Loric's dagger through the grass; inscribing his crude and hopeful mockery of a circle.

His heart beat harder. He tottered from step to step in a cripple's stoop that cramped his lungs, exhausted his muscles. He wanted to stop. Wanted rest. An end to all this striving and inadequacy.

But he wanted other things more.

Gradually he passed behind the horses. Over his shoulder, he could see the place where he had begun. It still shone as though it fed on streams of his life-blood.

Come on, leper, he urged himself. Just take it one step at a time. One step. At a time.

Drawing argent with him as if it were alive in the grass, he went on.

"Hold to your purpose, ur-Lord," Clyme urged. "You near its completion."

Covenant did not glance at the Humbled. His attention was fixed on the end of his leper's circle, his lurching enclosure. For no better reason than exhaustion, he was holding his breath. His muscles sobbed in protest. He nearly fell through the last few steps.

The argent would fade quickly if he did not continue to feed it. He did not have time to straighten his back, or breathe, or run to his mount.

Somehow he had to do it.

But before he could decide to take the risk, Clyme snatched him from his feet. Cradled in Clyme's arms, Covenant was carried to his horse, tossed carefully into the saddle. At once, Branl caught Covenant's arm to steady him while Clyme sprang for Hooryl's back.

The world seemed to veer and yaw. There was not enough air, never enough air; or Covenant had forgotten how to inhale.

"Now, ur-Lord," Branl instructed him. "It must be now."

The enclosure was already starting to flicker and go out.

Covenant's companions raised his arms for him. They lifted Loric's *krill* and Joan's ring high over his head. Together they helped him strike the dagger's gem with white gold a second time.

Just for an instant, the Unbeliever became a conflagration again, a being of fire and theurgy. Then the Ranyhyn and Mishio Massima surged forward—and the world vanished as though it had been erased from existence.

ϾΟϽ

W hen his mount hit the ground at a full gallop, Covenant nearly lost his seat. His feet had not found the stirrups: he could not steady himself. And the after-flash of power filled his head. He flopped in the saddle like a loosely filled sack. Without the support of the Humbled, he would have fallen.

He had no idea where he was. The *krill*'s brightness effaced his surroundings. It made black night where there may only have been twilight. Illumined by silver, the horses pounded the turf: he recognized nothing else. For all he knew, he and his companions had only traveled a dozen strides.

But then the Ranyhyn and Mishio Massima began to slow their gallop to an easy canter. Although images of wild magic still spun like vertigo in Covenant's mind, his body began to recover its center. His extremities were numb: the nerves of his torso and hips and thighs were not. They reacted reflexively.

By slow increments, he became aware that he was holding the dagger dangerously close to his mount. For Mishio Massima's protection as well as his own, he flipped the fabric that shielded his hands over the blade; covered the gem.

At once, darkness swept over him. It felt strangely like solace.

He almost said, Have mercy on me. Instead he managed to pant, "What happened? Where are we?"

"It appears, ur-Lord," Branl replied, "that your efforts have succeeded." He took the *krill* from Covenant, wrapped it more securely in Anele's raiment. "We gauge that we have traversed some two score leagues, perhaps more. And our heading is to the northwest. The distance to Sarangrave Flat has been halved.

"In a sunless world, time is difficult to ascertain. Yet we are able to discern its passage. By our measure, an hour remains ere this gloom surrenders to true night. Our translation hither has not been altogether instant. Nevertheless we have been swift beyond comprehension.

"Ur-Lord"—for a moment, the Master appeared to hesitate—"if your strength suffices for a second exertion, we do not doubt that we will gain the marge of the Sarangrave. Mayhap we will do so ere *turiya* Herem threatens the lurker."

A second—? Covenant groaned to himself. Hellfire! Ask me to bring back the sun while you're at it. The dusk seemed to wheel around him as if it arose from his dizziness; as if he were the source of the enshrouding twilight. His legs and back would not suffer the strain.

If he staggered just once—if he pulled the *krill* out of the grass for any reason—he would have to start again from the beginning.

"Your weariness is plain," Clyme continued. "But *aliantha* will restore you." He showed Covenant his remaining treasure-berries. "Then we will aid you."

"Aid me?" Covenant asked. Mishio Massima cantered smoothly—and yet he felt that he was seated on rolling logs or a canted boulder. "How?"

Clyme faced him through the dulled grey of the air. "We will devise a means."

Covenant stared. "Well, damnation," he muttered after a few heartbeats. "Since you put it that way—"

When had any *Haruchai* ever failed him?

The Ranyhyn appeared to understand. With Mishio Massima, they dropped from a canter to a trot and then a walk. In a moment, they halted.

Clutching the saddle horn with one hand for balance, Covenant reached to Clyme for food.

His hunger surprised him. He had eaten enough earlier; more than enough. But as soon as he bit into the first berry, he found that he craved the Land's nurturance. Convalescence was a harsh taskmaster; and his first expenditure of wild magic had depleted his stamina. Careless of future needs, he ate eagerly.

It was entirely conceivable that he had no future.

Still the taste and efficacy of *aliantha* gave him their blessing. After a few swallows, the whirling in his head subsided as new energy anointed him with possibilities. As if he were choosing his fate, he devoured Clyme's supply of treasure-berries. Formally, like an act of contrition, he thanked both of the Humbled. Then he announced that he was ready.

His mount seemed oblivious to everything except the chance to crop grass. But the eyes of the Ranyhyn rolled fretfully, and long tremors ran through their muscles. He did not believe that they were exhausted: they were the great horses of Ra; and they had not lacked for forage and water. Rather he guessed that they were afraid. They knew where they were going.

Something about the lurker—Covenant had heard tales of their old trepidation, the only dread that they had never mastered. No doubt he had once known why they felt such fear. Now that memory was gone, lost when he had sealed the cracks in his flawed mind.

Thinking about the lurker, he felt a pang of his own. He had personal memories of Horrim Carabal; private reasons to be afraid. That the lurker of the Sarangrave feared white gold and the *krill* was no comfort. If *turiya* Raver managed to take possession of the monster, Horrim Carabal would resist Covenant with malice as well as terror.

Nevertheless he did not hesitate. "What now?" he asked his companions. "How are we going to do this?"

"I will bear you, ur-Lord," Clyme answered, "in such a way that you need only press the *krill* into the grass." He dropped from Hooryl's back, offered his arms to help Covenant dismount. "Thus supported, you will complete the enclosure more swiftly."

He did not add that any circle he fashioned would be more symmetrical than Covenant's.

"Ah, hell," Covenant sighed. "Why not?" As he let Clyme lift him down, he muttered, "But it's too bad you couldn't think of anything even less dignified. I should at least try to look as pitiful as I feel."

The Humbled gazed at him without expression. Neither of them replied. Calmly Branl surrendered Loric's blade.

Swearing under his breath, Covenant accompanied Clyme away from the horses. He had never accomplished anything without help; and yet he still had not learned how to accept assistance gracefully. Being a leper had taught him to think and act and live alone. He ought to act on his decisions without hazarding anyone else.

Unfortunately he could not pretend that he was strong enough for his task. When he and Clyme reached a safe distance, he said harshly, "Let's do this. I'm not getting any younger."

Vexed at himself, he unwound cloth from the *krill*'s gem. In the abrupt wash of radiance, he closed his left fist and punched the strange stone with Joan's ring.

Again he seemed to become argent delirancy. Power burned in his veins, flamed from his flesh, sprang toward the dying stars. In spite of his mortality, he felt that he had the resources of gods. The sensation was terrible and delicious, an exaltation of wild magic; capable of anything. But it was also brief. It forsook him as soon as he separated his hands.

Still the effects of that moment clung to him, vivid as vision or prophecy. He hardly felt Clyme scoop him from the ground. He was scarcely aware that Clyme bent low, holding him within easy reach of the turf.

As if of its own volition, the dagger's blade sank until it pierced grass and cut soil, pulling Covenant's clasp with it. Then Clyme began to move so that the *krill* sliced the earth with shining silver.

Secured against vertigo by Clyme's unyielding arms, Covenant watched as the flow of power which sustained his line in the grass emanated from Joan's ring aching on his finger. Indirectly, therefore, it came from the secret recesses of his heart. That was why he had been left so depleted—and so hungry. With wild magic, he expended his own spirit.

He wanted Clyme to hurry.

Clyme did not appear to make haste. Nevertheless he had already completed a perfect semicircle. From behind the horses, Covenant could see the spot where he had started. He would reach it in a score of heartbeats.

Perhaps because Clyme moved with such alacrity in spite of his crouched, crab-wise steps, or perhaps because his circle was so exact, Covenant's power shone more brightly, promising translation across a greater distance. With the help of the Humbled, he might have been able to travel the Lower Land from border to border in mere hours.

The thought of such imponderable speed made him dizzy again. If he could stop *turiya*—and if he could do at least *some*thing to help Horrim Carabal survive the Worm's arrival in the Land—he might actually have time to rejoin Linden. Wherever her own exigencies had taken her, he might be able to find her.

If.

Then the enclosure was done. It shone like the *krill*, defining itself against the gloom. At once, Clyme surged upright. Sprinting, he carried Covenant toward their mounts. Before Covenant could regain his balance, he sat in Mishio Massima's saddle. Branl steadied him while Clyme mounted Hooryl.

As if he were pitching himself over a precipice, Covenant brought the ring and the gem together above his head.

He became an instant of wild magic; and reality vanished as the horses sprang into a gallop.

He could not perceive time. He had no opportunity to draw a breath. His heart did not beat, or he did not feel it measure out his life. The disappearance of the world was as sudden as a blink, complete as soon as it began. Yet time must have passed. When the world reappeared, the horses were running hard, pounding along uneven slopes at the full extent of Mishio Massima's strength. And the half-light, the gloaming—

The dusk had deepened. The horses galloped in the core of the *krill*'s illumination; but beyond it, the darkness looked solid as a wall. Covenant and the Humbled had ridden into a realm of shadows, or night had fallen.

While he reeled, he tried to ask, Now where are we? But his throat was too tight to release words.

After a moment, however, the horses began to slow; and Branl urged him to cover the *krill*. "When you are no longer blinded by its light, you will perceive that the Sarangrave is nigh. It lies a stone's throw to the west."

"Here *turiya* Herem's spoor is strong," added Clyme. His tone was sharper than Branl's, whetted by anger or anticipation. "Nonetheless it appears that we are belated. The scent enters the wetlands ahead of us. Indeed—" The Master paused as if he were tasting the air. Then he stated, "We discern struggle, a contest of powers. Frenzy lashes the waters at some distance. We deem that a battle has begun."

Begun—? Alarm ran like acid along Covenant's nerves. In an instant, he forgot dizziness, fatigue, depletion. "Hellfire," he rasped. "This is my fault. I took too long." Recovering. Thinking. "Now I'm going to have to do this the hard way."

Instead of veiling Loric's dagger, he held it over his head. A beacon—

Spectral against the coming night, tangled brush and gnarled trees became visible off to Covenant's left: limbs and twigs that resembled bleached bones in the silver light; clumps of reeds like thickets of spears; dark floating pads with nacreous flowers; noxious scum; troubled waters so black that they refused lumination. The tenebrous air was thick with stagnation and rot, the putrid remains of corpses. The fetor made knots in Covenant's guts. Instinctively he wanted to shy away.

Nevertheless the Ranyhyn and Mishio Massima cantered toward the area where *turiya* Herem had entered Sarangrave Flat as if that were Covenant's truest desire.

Hell and *blood*. He was not ready for this. Not after everything that he had already endured.

Even his blunt nerves sensed the inherited dread that gathered in Rallyn and Hooryl.

"Ur-Lord." Branl held out his hand, asking for the *krill* as though he believed that he and Clyme could fight for the lurker in Covenant's stead.

But Covenant kept his only blade, his only light. He had no intention of risking his companions in the vile marshes of Horrim Carabal's demesne.

Far away through the scrub and trees, the scrannel brush and marshgrass, he caught flickers of a diseased silver that reminded him of his one confrontation with the lurker many centuries ago. Instinctively he believed that the monster was exerting its malevolent theurgies against the Raver. If Horrim Carabal had welcomed *turiya*'s possession, there would be no battle.

"Ur-Lord?" Branl asked again.

Bloody damnation! Covenant had to act. He was already late. He chose to believe that the lurker was fighting hard; but as the Raver mastered more and more of Horrim Carabal's imponderable bulk, the monster's resistance would weaken. Soon the lurker might begin to submit.

While the horses closed the distance, Covenant raised his voice. "We need the Feroce! I won't ride in that marsh. Some of those waters can strip flesh off bones." This decision, at least, his companions would approve. "And I don't know how else to communicate with the lurker!"

"We are come too late," countered Branl. "Already the Raver lays claim—"

"But he hasn't won yet," Covenant retorted. "Horrim Carabal is *huge*. *Turiya* can't overrun the whole lurker at once. Parts of that monster must be fighting back.

"I need to talk to it while it can still resist!"

If Lord Foul's servant triumphed, Horrim Carabal would be a horrific foe.

Clyme's passion grew stronger, feeding on a private repudiation. "We know not how to summon the lurker's acolytes."

"Then they'll just have to summon themselves," Covenant snapped. If they could discern his beacon. If their fear of white gold and Loric's *krill* alerted them to his presence. "If they don't, what good is an alliance?"

The wetland was close: too close for Rallyn and Hooryl. Their fright showed in their flaring eyes; in the tremors which marred their strides.

"Stop!" Covenant shouted to the horses. "I want to stop here!" Then he swung one leg over Mishio Massima's back; stood in the stirrup and braced himself to drop to the ground.

Hooryl and Rallyn complied. With the Ardent's mount between them, they slowed in sharp jerks, almost locking their knees. Within half a dozen strides, they halted, quivering as if they were feverish.

At once, Covenant let go and hit the grass, running toward the border of the Sarangrave, and waving the *krill*: a signal to any being or creature capable of noticing him.

Clyme and Branl accompanied Covenant as if they had expected his unpremeditated rush. In the sweeping wash of argent, they looked as ghostly as the wide wetland; as vulnerable to banishment as the Dead. Still they were *Haruchai*, as solid as their promises. Covenant did not doubt them.

But now he feared them. Their *ak-Haru* had judged them severely—and they bore an old grudge against Ravers. He shuddered to imagine how they would react when they learned that he meant to leave them behind.

"I'm here!" he yelled as he hit soggy ground, stopped at the water's edge. "We made an alliance! I want to keep it, but I can't if you *don't hear me!*"

He needed to know how far into the marsh *turiya*'s possession had spread. And he needed to get there; to the point of conflict, the heart of the struggle. Nothing that he tried would work if he did not first get ahead of the Raver.

He wanted the power to *forbid* Lord Foul's servant, the ancient puissance of the Colossus; but that knowledge was lost.

Thrashed by distant fighting, the water at Covenant's feet heaved against its scum and muck. Gouts of tiny plant life rose into the air like miniature geysers, then slumped back into the slime. He thought that he heard screaming, inarticulate fury like far-off thunder; but he could not be sure through the slosh and slap of the disturbed wetland. He strained his eyes for hints of the Feroce, but the *krill*'s radiance blinded him to everything beyond its reach. Again he yelled for attention—and still there was no sign that he had been heard.

"God *damn* it! What good is an alliance if you won't help me at least *try* to honor it?"

Nothing.

"Ur-Lord," Clyme offered, "we will bear you. We discern the conflict, though it is distant. We will convey you to a place where you may strike with some hope of effect."

"*How* distant?" snarled Covenant. "Is it leagues? Can you imagine what will happen to you if you try to carry me through *leagues* of this stuff?" He slapped a gesture at the marsh: bogs and quagmires; quicksand; depths and shallows; poisoned pools as harsh as vitriol. "And *turiya* is going to keep moving. What if he takes possession faster than you can travel? Our lives will be wasted."

Facing the Sarangrave again, he howled, "*I need the Feroce!*"

He had time to panic—and time as well to admit that behind his alarm lay a secret relief at the possibility that he might be spared.

Then Clyme nodded once. "Ur-Lord, you are answered."

Hell and blood— "Where? I don't see anything."

Covenant expected flickers of green like hints of the Illearth Stone, an approach of power the hue of sick and rotting chrysoprase. But though he searched until his temples ached, he found nothing except *krill*-light and darkness.

"On other occasions," Branl answered, "we beheld the Feroce bearing fires in their palms. Yet when the Masters observed them in centuries past, they moved within the Sarangrave without flames—indeed, without any evident magicks. We surmise that they require theurgy only when they are parted from the wetland.

"Nevertheless we discern them. Two now approach."

Two? Covenant stared and saw nothing. Only two?

Would two be enough?

At the limit of the light, he spotted a blur of movement. The creatures were stealthy, creeping behind clumps of scrub, stealing through pestilential grasses and mirkweed, crouching among trees that writhed as if they were in torment. He recalled the timidity of the lurker's acolytes during his earlier encounter with them. They had called him *the Pure One, wielder of metal and agony*, and they had feared him. Without their High God's command, they would not have dared to enter his presence.

But he had no time for their craven courage. "I'm *waiting*, dammit!" he shouted. "I made a promise, and I intend to keep it! Your High God *needs* me!"

Fronds rustled some distance away. Passing bodies contradicted the sluggish distress of the waters. At unexpected moments, the large round eyes of the Feroce caught reflections of silver. They were hardly tall enough to reach Covenant's chest. And they were desperately afraid. Naked and hairless, clad only in the commandments that ruled their fright, they slipped between patches of cover or ducked under pads and rushes as if they believed that Covenant could extinguish them with a glance.

But at last they emerged. At the boundary of the marsh, they risked the *krill*'s radiance.

Flinching, the Feroce brought forth guttering emerald from the palms of their hands. Then they crept onto the mud that marked the border of the Sarangrave. There they stood before Covenant, cowering in supplication.

"Be merciful!" they whimpered as if they shared one voice; one mind. "You are the Pure One. You wield abhorrent metal and deliver agony. Such agony! Yet you accepted our High God's alliance. The Feroce surrendered many and many lives to complete his offered service. Take pity upon us now. Become the Pure One who redeems, as you have done before.

"Our High God cannot withstand the horror that assails him."

Their tone was piteous, but Covenant felt too much pressure to respond gently. "I'm not the Pure One," he retorted. "I've never been the Pure One. But I try to keep my promises."

In truth, he had not committed himself to fight for the lurker. Deliberately he had withheld that reassurance. As far as he was concerned, however, Horrim Carabal had exceeded the terms of their agreement. And he believed that the lurker had a role to play in the Land's defense, although he could not name it.

"Right now," he continued without pausing, "I can't. I'm too far away. I'll fight for your High God, but first he has to help me. He has to take me where I'm needed."

"Not?" quavered the Feroce as if they had heard only his denial. "You are not the Pure One? We do not comprehend." Their protest sounded like the soughing of bogs, the suck of quicksand deprived of victims. "You wield vicious metal. You bring excruciation. You have delivered such agony to our High God that he quails to hear you. You are required to be the Pure One. There is no other."

"Stop!" Covenant demanded harshly. "Call me whatever you want. We don't have time for this.

"Here!"

Frantic to show his good faith, he swept cloth around the *krill*'s gem and blade. Instantly the light vanished. Night rushed over the region: it seemed to reel in its haste to fill the void left by covering the dagger. The fires of the Feroce revealed only themselves.

Urgent and awkward, Covenant thrust the wrapped knife into the waist of his jeans, then jerked Joan's ring from his finger, looped the chain over his head, dropped the band under his shirt; made himself appear defenseless.

"I'll need metal to fight." Fear made him savage. "And I'll have to hurt your High God. I'll have to hurt him *bad*. I need to cut off the infection," sever every portion possessed by *turiya*. "I don't know another way." He had no idea how to kill a Raver.

"But I can't do anything if he doesn't *take me where I'm needed!*"

The lurker was enormous. It could survive terrible damage.

As one, the creatures gave a quivering shriek as if he had appalled them to the core of their soft bodies. Their fires sprang high; dropped low. Flames dripped between their fingers like corroded flesh or spilth.

Covenant swore in frustration. He should have gotten here sooner. If he were not so easily wounded, so damn mortal—

"Ur-Lord," cautioned Branl. "Ready yourself. Again you are answered."

While Covenant strove to see, a dark shape arose from the waters.

Visible only as a starker blackness in the dark, a tentacle rose and rose as if it were reaching for the heavens. It was thick as a cedar, tall as an elm. Its surface squirmed with desperation. In spite of Kevin's Dirt, Covenant felt the lurker's strength, its bitter hunger. Reaching high above him, its arm seemed to search with inhuman senses for the taste of its prey.

Covenant had time to tell the tentacle or the Feroce, "Leave my companions here. They can't help me. I'll need them later."

Then the tentacle lashed down. Like a cracked whip, it snapped around him. Its fingers grasped every possible surface of his shirt, his jeans, his limbs. Coils clasped his arms hard to his sides. A heartbeat later, the tentacle sprang back; jerked him into the air with appalling ease.

He heard no response from the *Haruchai*. Only the voice of the Feroce scaled, frail and frantic, into the dark.

"Try to believe that you are the Pure One."

In a flicker as brief as a blink, he thought that he saw the Humbled take hold of

Horrim Carabal's acolytes. Then the lurker snatched him through the sky as though the monster intended to hurl him into the heart of Sarangrave Flat.

Hellfire! He could not move his arms; could hardly breathe. Black trees and obscured streams rushed below him as if they were plunging into an abyss. If the lurker did not fling him to his death, it was going to squeeze out his life.

Your alliance was a thing of the moment.

The Feroce would have reacted differently if their High God had been mastered by *turiya*. The Humbled would have tried to ward Covenant. But he could not be sure that the lurker understood his intentions—or knew how effortlessly he might be crushed.

He had no measure for direction or distance. The wetland seethed like a cataract below him. Night blinded every horizon. The roar of wind in his ears covered the stricken pound of his pulse. When he was thrown, he would soar for leagues before he hit and died.

Without warning, the coils wrenched him downward. Before he could even try to fill his lungs, Horrim Carabal slammed him into a pool, buried him in deep water acrid with poisons. His eyes would have been ruined in their sockets if he had not clenched them shut.

But the tentacle did not stop. It tore him through water and muck as easily as it had carried him above the marsh, as if he had no substance and did not need air.

The monster did not mean him harm. It had good reason to be terrified of white gold and Loric's *krill*. Good reason to fear wild magic. But it did not understand its own strength—or Covenant's weakness. He was dying for air. The corrupt water stung him like a swarm of ants, biting and endless. Apart from suffocation and dread and pain, he felt only nascent fire, as if his mere presence sufficed to set the toxic waters ablaze.

But he was well acquainted with pain. It was human and inevitable: he could ignore it. And dread was akin to fury. *You are the white gold.* When his fear became a form of rage, he could burn his way free.

Suffocation was altogether worse. Drowning was worse. He could more readily have endured the excoriation within a *caesure*. Drowning was desperation. It led only to unthinking frenzy.

He had to have air. *He had to have air.*

Or he had to have peace: the silence of the last dark, voiceless and blissful: the surrender of every demand and desire.

Air or peace: one or the other. He could not be given both.

But he wanted air.

He would never get it. He was already failing.

Still his given body remembered its own exigencies, its own compulsory striving. It locked itself against the impulse to inhale death—

—until the lurker suddenly ripped him upward.

He knew nothing; remembered nothing; could not interpret his changed rush through the fluid dark. But the flesh which Linden had fashioned for him was ruled by strictures that did not require conscious choices. As the tentacle heaved him out of the water and thrust him high, the pressure in his chest seemed to explode. Bursting, he found air.

For a time, nothing existed except wretched gasping and life. Blots like devoured stars swam across the void inside his eyelids, inside his head. Air and the wind of his blind movement exacerbated the sting of the waters until it felt feral, as fierce as wasps. Every breath was tumid and rank, difficult to take. The night tortured him with questions for which there were no answers.

Try to believe that you are pure.

Because he had to see, he slitted a glimpse outward and found ruptured dazzles there as well.

His eyes bled tears. Light smeared his vision. The shining was a noxious silver like and unlike the alloyed clarity of wild magic. And it was tainted by an underhue of emerald that resembled the virulence of the Illearth Stone. He did not understand it. The tentacle jerked him from side to side, asking its own febrile questions. The Sarangrave's fouled waters clung to his skin like scales. He felt blisters bubbling everywhere.

But tears washed away bitter minerals and evil. Blinking rapidly, he began to see.

Below him stretched a pool the size of a small lake. It veered one way and another as the tentacle squirmed. Its surface blazed with a nacreous lucence as dangerous as necrosis.

From the depths of the water rose two more tentacles. They were thick as towers, supple as serpents, mighty as siege-engines. And they were locked in battle. One struck at the other while the other writhed to avoid blows that would have toppled oaks. The ferocity of their movement churned the pool to froth. Their struggle cast shadows like screams across the wetland, but did not quench the light.

The attacking arm feinted to distract the other. An instant later, the attacker flung itself like a noose around its foe near the water-line. It tightened and strained, apparently trying to rip the other arm in half.

At first, Covenant did not recognize what was happening. Then he did. The lurker seemed to be fighting itself, but it was not. It was resisting the Raver. Covenant felt *turiya*'s loud malevolence in the caught tentacle. The Raver's mastery of the monster had reached this far along one arm. Now Horrim Carabal strove to tear off the possessed part of itself before *turiya* could claim more.

A doomed struggle: the lurker could not clench tightly enough, dismember itself swiftly enough. And it could not make the Raver flinch or shy because the Raver was not afraid. Moments after the monster grabbed its own arm, Covenant saw *turiya* Herem's evil slip past the constriction and spread farther.

The lurker released that arm, tried for a new grip. What else could the monster do? But it could not preserve itself by that means. The truth was plain. The Raver's viciousness moved too easily. Even if the lurker contrived to stop *turiya* in one place, Lord Foul's servant would simply shift his possession to another tentacle.

A timid shriek thronged into the dark sky. Around the pool were gathered the lurker's worshippers, hundreds of them. Some stood to their waists in the water: others crowded the verge. From all of their hands shone green fires, bright desperation. Their wailing was a ululation of terror. But their hands and flames moved in unison, dropping low and then rising high as one, swaying from side to side like an invocation.

In the distance behind them crouched tormented growth and lurid streams, helpless in spite of innumerable toxins. Beyond the light lay beleaguered darkness.

The Feroce were trying to save their High God. Surely that was what they were doing? But Covenant had no idea what they sought to accomplish.

Then he understood.

Two nights ago, in his cave above the Sunbirth Sea, the lurker's creatures had given him unexpected aid. Wielding their peculiar theurgy, they had caused the Harrow's prostrate destrier to recover its captious nature. *We have not given it strength. We cannot. But we have caused it to remember what it is.* That gift had enabled the beast to bear Covenant farther than he would have thought possible.

Now the Feroce were fighting for the spirit of their High God with the only power they had: the power to impose memories. Frantically they struggled to help the lurker recall freedom.

That effort, too, was doomed. *Turiya* Herem was stronger.

Nevertheless the effects of emerald worship and panic granted Covenant a little time to gather himself.

He could not help the lurker as he was, trapped in the tentacle's coils. But he had only one way to communicate with the monster, to explain his needs and intentions; and the turgid atmosphere resisted every breath. His gasping did not bring in enough good air to support a shout that the Feroce might hear.

He tried anyway.

"Listen," he croaked: a sound too small to pierce the forlorn shrieking; the savage slash and pound of tentacles; the turmoil of bright water. "I want to fight, but I can't move my arms. I have to reach the *krill*. And your High God has to work with me. We have to fight together."

His flawed sight detected no sign that any of the creatures had heard him.

Still the lurker of the Sarangrave feared possession more than pain. Doubtless the monster did not understand what Covenant had said. Yet it recognized that he had spoken. Perhaps it had felt his resistance as he squirmed against its coils.

Abruptly a fourth arm reached out of the scourged pool. It snatched up a cluster of the Feroce. Wrapping them like Covenant, the massive appendage lifted them until he could look straight into their appalled eyes.

"Listen," he panted again. "I need my arms. I have to reach my knife." It was likely that the Feroce did not know Loric's dagger by name. "And your High God has to carry me to the right place. The place where I can cut off the horror, all of it."

"Make him understand. We have to do this *now*."

Turiya did not fear the lurker, but he would fear the *krill*. He would fear wild magic.

Round eyes gaped at Covenant as if they had been blinded. The creatures had been crying out continuously. They did not stop. And there was no difference between the wailing in front of Covenant and the shrieks from below. All of the Feroce had one voice, the same voice. They uttered only anguish.

Yet the grip of the lurker's arm loosened. Its fingers shifted the coils lower on Covenant's chest.

Still he could hardly breathe. The air was too damn thick—

With all of his insignificant strength, he tried to grasp the *krill*.

The tentacle moved farther. After a moment that made dots of weakness dance across his sight, his halfhand found the dagger.

Now, he thought. Hellfire! *Now.*

Holding his weapon for his life, he drew it free. Dropped its covering. Raised it over his head in both hands.

"I'm ready," he gasped. "Do it!"

With actions as plain as language, Horrim Carabal chose agony. Any maiming was better than possession. In an instant, the monster stopped fighting itself. With a ponderous heave of its possessed tentacle, it extended the boundary between itself and *turiya* Herem's mastery higher and then higher; away from the corrosive waters; closer to Covenant's elevation.

As if Covenant were an axe, the lurker swung him at a section of the massive arm which *turiya* had not yet claimed.

In every limb, Horrim Carabal had the strength of half a dozen Giants. It struck with the force of frenzy. Covenant whipped forward like the crack of a flail. When his blade bit flesh, any ordinary weapon would have been ripped from his clutch. But wild magic whetted the edges of Loric's *krill*. Spitting flames, the dagger cut. Covenant hardly felt the impact.

His blow sliced partway through the tentacle. Vile blood fountained from the wound. It stank like distilled corruption. The whole of the Sarangrave seemed to erupt in an excruciated howl as if every leaf and stem and bog, every current, every swath of scum gave voice to the lurker's pain: a howl so vast that it effaced the thin shrieking of the Feroce.

But the tentacle was not severed. It was far too thick to be lopped off by a single slash. Through the gush of blood and the yowling, Covenant felt *turiya* hesitate in alarm; draw back. In another moment, however, the Raver would surely control his fear. He would rush to pass beyond the cut deeper into Horrim Carabal.

"Again!" Covenant rasped, although he could not hope to be heard. He could not hear himself. He needed the lurker to understand that if it did not ignore its hurt—

Like the Raver, the monster hesitated.

Then it recovered its fury. Still howling like myriad ghouls, like the immeasurable torment of the damned, the lurker swung Covenant again.

The second slash cut through more of the appendage. Torrents of blood stained the waters, and were swallowed by shining. The lurker's roar seemed to batter Covenant's bones. Dazed by conflicting brightnesses, he could no longer see. The *krill*'s heat ached in his wrists. Soon he would be too badly burned to hold on.

But now the monster did not hesitate. Savagely it swung yet again.

Flopping like a doll in Horrim Carabal's coils, Covenant delivered a third cut.

The possessed arm was toppling. Still it had not been entirely severed. And while it fell, the Raver's lust to rule the lurker overcame his fear of Covenant's power. Vicious as a striking asp, *turiya* Herem surged forward.

As if the monster's pain and rage had become his, Covenant thought, Over my dead body.

In a rush like delirium or exaltation, the Unbeliever and his ally hacked once more—

—and the slain tentacle crashed down into the pool.

Stunned by howling and hot blood, Covenant struggled to retain his grip on the *krill*; his grip on himself. Cutting off the claimed limb was a temporary victory at best. The Raver had not been harmed. If Covenant did not strike again instantly—if he did not force *turiya* to defend against him—Lord Foul's servant would escape. At need, the Raver could claim one or more of the Feroce. He might feel demeaned by their littleness, but he could conceal himself among them nonetheless. And if Covenant failed to locate him before he rallied his strength, he could make another attempt on the lurker.

Covenant felt like a toy in the hands of an insane juggler, utterly disoriented, impotent with vertigo. Up and down had become the same thing. He could not distinguish any of his horizons. The violence of the monster's movements seemed to have dismembered him.

Still he refused to accept a victory that might become defeat at any moment.

The lurker had done its part. The rest was Covenant's problem. He had to do something.

Now or never.

With as much haste as Horrim Carabal's thrashing allowed, he tugged the chain holding Joan's ring over his head, clasped the hard circle in his left hand. Then he slapped the ring and the dagger's gem against each other.

Without transition, conflagration erupted in him as if his living flesh were tinder.

Sudden power anchored him. Disarticulated pieces of his surroundings were flung back into their natural relationships. But he did not care about his horizons, or his position in the air, or the lambent waters. The strange voice of the Feroce meant nothing to him. He needed—

There, in the pummeled pool; in the corpse of the cut tentacle subsiding toward the depths: *turiya* Herem. He felt the Raver's presence as if it were louder than the monster's roar.

—needed the lurker to drop him.

His fierce fire succeeded. It made the monster's coils flinch, loosen. Voluntarily or involuntarily, Horrim Carabal let go of him directly above his target; and he fell.

For an instant, he tumbled helplessly, out of control. But he was far from the waters when the lurker released him; and his fire made everything clear. Wild magic lit his nerves as if it were percipience. He had a sharp shard of time in which to master his limbs, twist his posture into a dive.

Still holding white gold against Loric's gem, he struck the turbulence head first and plunged deep.

At the last moment, he remembered to shut his eyes. This water would blind him. It would scald his skin until it fell from his bones. But he was too frantic and furious to care. And here he did not need sight: there was nothing to see. He only had to sink faster than the tentacle. He had to reach it before *turiya* could escape.

He sensed the Raver's terror. It filled the pool, as bright and bitter as the waters. But he also felt the slain appendage below him. It was close.

As he hit the still-squirming arm, he hammered the *krill* into it and sent a blast of passion along its length, striving with his last breath, his last strength, to shred the Raver. If he accomplished nothing else with his life, he would at least give Linden the lurker of the Sarangrave as a potent ally rather than a lethal foe.

—*writ in water.*

Delirious and resolved, he poured out his heart until he felt *turiya* Herem's spirit begin to fray.

Torrents of wild magic ripped through the Raver. *Turiya* was ancient and enduring, single-minded in his malevolence. He withstood more force than Covenant could have survived. But he was going to die.

If Covenant did not falter first.

Badly burned, and dying for air, he grew weaker. He was human, after all, heir to every inadequacy that made life precious. No matter what his determination demanded of it, his body could not absorb unlimited quantities of damage. There were prices to be paid for the feats which he asked of himself. Collapse and unconsciousness were only the beginning.

Without the lore of forbidding—

Before the end, however—the Raver's end, or Covenant's—the *krill* was snatched away. Covenant almost dropped Joan's ring, but its chain was tangled in his fingers. Strong arms closed around him, bore him surging toward the surface. He had no time to remember that he was not done; that the Raver was still alive. His head was lifted into the air. Of its own volition, his defeated body fought for life.

Stentorian as a Giant, Branl shouted, "These waters harm the Pure One! He must be relieved!"

The Master supported Covenant with one arm. In his other hand, he clasped High Lord Loric's dagger.

Deprived of theurgy, Covenant's head reeled. He could not understand what was happening, could not think, could hardly suffer the burns that ravaged his skin. Confused and thwarted, sick with vertigo, he did not recognize it when the tip of a tentacle slipped between him and Branl; when it curled around him and pulled him out of Branl's embrace. He only knew that now he hung in the air close to the seethe and lash of the pool. He did not know how or why.

Below him, Branl sculled as if he were waiting. In fragments of residual clarity, Covenant saw a fretwork of fine blisters on the Humbled's arms. The fabric of Branl's tunic appeared to be rotting on his shoulders. The gem of the *krill* blazed with power that seemed purposeless, devoid of meaning.

Hellfire, Covenant groaned as his mind wandered among his defeats. Hell and blood. What have you done?

Then he felt *turiya* Herem rising. The viciousness of the Raver's aura pierced Covenant's bewilderment.

With the slow deliberation of a torturer, Clyme of the Humbled broke the surface in front of Branl. They were no more than two arm spans apart.

At the sight, Covenant's confusion became keening. That was not Clyme: it was *turiya*. The Raver's presence was too fierce to be mistaken for anything else.

The light of the acrid waters reflected in Clyme's eyes like the eagerness of depravity. The grin baring his teeth anticipated bloodshed and triumph.

Oh, hell. Hell and damnation. Clyme was possessed. *Turiya* Herem had taken him.

That should have been impossible. Covenant had said as much. He knew it to be true. The *Haruchai* could not be mastered by anything less than the concentrated evil of the Illearth Stone. They were too strong.

Nevertheless *turiya* wore Clyme's body like a cloak. It was his to use or discard.

Covenant's heart struck blows like knells inside his chest. His mind staggered, clutching at implications, inferences.

Turiya Herem could not have mastered Clyme. That was entirely impossible. It defied reality.

Therefore—

God in Heaven!

Therefore—

Covenant wanted to wail.

Clyme must have *admitted* the Raver. He *must* have. No other explanation sufficed. Branl had interrupted Covenant, and Clyme had acquiesced to *turiya*, so that the brother of *samadhi* and *moksha* would not perish.

So that Covenant would not sacrifice himself trying to destroy the Raver.

Sweet Christ! What have you *done*?

If Horrim Carabal had dropped Covenant again, he would have flung himself at Clyme in pure panic. But the lurker's coils held, and Covenant was too weak to break free.

Swimming with his head and shoulders above the surface, Clyme glared delight at Covenant.

"Do you behold me, groveler?" the Raver panted as if words were an unfamiliar exertion. "You have attempted my end, yet you have not overcome me. Now your companion is mine.

"Will you slay him to assail me? I judge that you will not. Your heart is flawed. It cannot sustain such deeds."

Groveler. That ancient epithet suited Covenant. He deserved it. He had become an avatar of abjection in the flagrant depths of the Sarangrave.

But *turiya* Herem was not done. His malice demanded taunts which he spat out with extravagant glee. Only the effort, the obvious difficulty, with which he fought to speak hinted that his exultation was marred.

"The killing of your mate I acknowledge. There you surpassed my expectations. But her death bore the stench of mercy. That reek will not arise from the fate of Clyme *Haruchai*, Master and Humbled. His execution at your hands will be purest murder." Clyme gnashed his teeth as if he were rending flesh. "You lack the *belief* necessary to the task."

Covenant thought that he heard Branl say, "Trust in us, ur-Lord." An echo of earlier promises. But he could not drag his attention away from *turiya*'s scorn and Clyme's surrender. And the turmoil of the pool was loud. It masked every voice except the Raver's. Horrim Carabal's hurt and trepidation seemed to make no sound. Even the Feroce appeared to have fallen silent.

"Nonetheless," *turiya* gasped savagely, "I desire you to surpass yourself yet again. I crave the pleasure of your efforts to extinguish me. Should you discover within yourself the valor which you lack, you will learn its futility. Blithely I will disencumber myself of this mad *Haruchai*. While you expend your despair upon your companion's husk, I will possess myself of other lives"—he gestured around him—"which attend upon us in abundance. And if you seek me among these timorous wights, I will renew my mastery of their High God.

"Your death is thereby made certain. If I do not compel the lurker to slay you, the Sarangrave itself will do so. Already your passing has been too long delayed."

Clyme's grin stretched. He seemed to be screaming. Then he bit down on his lips until his teeth drew blood. The muscles at the corners of his jaw knotted like fists. For a moment, he squeezed the reflections out of his eyes. Anguish and resistance twisted across his visage like noisome creatures crawling under his skin. Blisters burst. They leaked dire fluids. His arms flailed.

When he opened his eyes again, the light in them had changed. They caught the *krill*'s radiance rather than the shining of the waters.

"This Raver lies." Clyme's voice was torment—but it was *Clyme's*. "He does not hold me. I hold him. I contain him as Grimmand Honninscrave once contained his brother. His mockery and struggles I disdain. He cannot flee. I will hold him while his ruin is achieved."

Again the Master's eyes were forced shut. In spite of *turiya*'s opposition, however, he reopened them almost immediately. Ignoring the involuntary contortions which complicated his mien, he made his purpose clear.

"But his end must come swiftly. Though I am *Haruchai* withal, and potent in my fashion, his malice undermines me.

"I will hold him." He looked, not at Covenant, but at Branl. "The *krill* must accomplish his death."

And Branl did not hesitate. His people did not forgive. Because they did not mourn, they did not know mercy. Nor did they count the cost.

One swimming stroke took him close enough. Without a heartbeat's pause, he plunged the dagger into Clyme's chest.

Turiya's shriek exceeded hearing. It scaled higher as though it had the power to make the whole of the Sarangrave tremble. The sound ripped along Covenant's nerves until they seemed to bleed.

Clyme's features looked like they were being torn apart. Still he retained the iron intransigence of the *Haruchai*. At the end of his life, he lifted his head to Covenant. While blood gushed from his mouth, he pronounced distinctly, "Thus I answer the objurgations of the *ak-Haru*."

Branl disagreed—or his approval was so great that he could not contain it. Clyme's affirmation unleashed a kind of madness. Violence which had simmered beneath the impassivity of the *Haruchai* for millennia exploded in the last of the Humbled.

Gripping Clyme's shoulder with one hand, Branl cut open the whole of Clyme's torso in a single slash. When the *krill* found the friable barrier of bone between Clyme's hips, Branl dragged the blade in a circle through the Master's abdomen, disemboweling him. Then Covenant's companion drew back the dagger and began to hack—

Covenant tried to look away. In that attempt also, he failed.

Flesh was soft to the *krill*'s keenness. Bone meant nothing. In a convulsion of movements so swift that no part of Clyme had time to sink, Branl severed his comrade piece from piece until only gobbets and shards remained. Then finally they drifted away like stains upon the water; and the pool fed on them like a beast devouring tidbits. Moments after Branl ceased his butchery, they were gone, all of them.

Oh, Clyme! Is this what you think Brinn wanted?

When he was done, Branl swam below Covenant, squinting upward with galled eyes.

"Are you content, ur-Lord?" Grief clenched his visage. "*Turiya* Raver is unmade. Naught of him endures."

But the same was true of Clyme.

Covenant had no answer. He wanted to weep; but he was in too much pain for tears. The Feroce called him the Pure One. They had asked him to *believe*. But he had not redeemed them, just as he not redeemed their distant ancestors, the *jheherrin*.

The Humbled had proven themselves. Nevertheless the difference between Saltheart Foamfollower's example and that of Branl and Clyme was more than Covenant knew how to bear.

5.

Coming

Fury and thrashing were gone from the Sarangrave. By increments, the astringent light subsided from the pool. Breathing became marginally easier. With elaborate care, the lurker lifted Thomas Covenant high into the air. Another tentacle arose to bear Branl of the Humbled and High Lord Loric's *krill*.

Stately as a procession, at once celebratory and funereal, Horrim Carabal carried its saviors eastward above the writhen trees of the Flat.

Scores of the Feroce accompanied them. Scurrying around copses, sinking and then rising in quagmires, drifting like mist across streams and backwaters, the creatures went ahead of their High God's allies. And as they moved, they kept their emerald fires bright in their hands. Like the Wraiths of Andelain, the Feroce thronged forward in homage, escorting Covenant and Branl through the contortions and perils of the lurker's demesne.

But Covenant ignored the monster's acolytes. With the last of his scant endurance, he clung to Joan's ring and tried to stifle images of butchery. The manner in which Branl had destroyed Clyme burned in his mind. The sight seemed acid-etched inside his lids: whenever he closed his eyes, he saw it. The world had become a visceral dismay that refused utterance.

Around him the fires of the Feroce shed little insight: a gleam of green across scum and mirkweed here, a brief flash on scrub and branches there. But the *krill* still shone, casting its spectral light through the Sarangrave. The waters had destroyed the dagger's protective fabric covering. The haft's heat must have hurt Branl's hand; but if it did, he gave no sign. His true wounds ran deeper. His countenance was a fist which he could not unclench, and he did not glance at Covenant.

In the gem's echo of wild magic, tree limbs and marsh reeds as ghostly as spirits bobbed as if they were bowing. Harsh grasses swayed from side to side in consternation or awe.

Then the tentacles paused above a small pond as clear and dark as the ravaged heavens: an eyot of starker blackness in the crowding mass of the Flat. There the damp voice of the Feroce rose. "Our High God loathes the touch of such water," the creatures intoned. "You will fall. But we have caused the water to recall its ancient purity. It will soothe you while we prepare a more worthy consolation."

Soothe you, Covenant thought dully. That would be nice. His body was covered in blisters that stung like the tears which he could not shed. Anything cool—anything that was not gall and bitter lamentation—

The arms of the lurker sank close to the lightless pond. Briefly they hovered as if they were considering their options. Then they uncoiled.

With Branl beside him, Covenant dropped into cleanliness that resembled bliss.

The Feroce had spoken truly. Their magicks had made this water pure. He could drink from it, and drink, without any aftertaste of the seepages and rot which polluted the wetland. Nevertheless it did not heal. It was not Glimmermere. It did not wash away hurts or cleanse souls.

He needed something more. Untenable weeping filled his chest. He could not shut his mind's eyes against the brutal slash of the *krill* in Branl's hand.

The *Haruchai* swam at Covenant's back, supporting him. That was well. Covenant was too weak to move. And he did not want to look at Clyme's killer.

Perhaps to ease his burned hands, Branl held Loric's knife underwater. That, too, was well. Darkness was another kind of balm. It eased Covenant's aggrieved nerves.

After a time, he remembered to replace the chain of Joan's ring around his neck. Then he asked the dusk, "Did you have to do that? Couldn't you just kill him and be done with it?"

He had seen *Haruchai* fight on any number of occasions, but he had never seen such an abandoned frenzy of violence.

Branl's answer ached across the water. "It was agreed between us. We remember Grimmand Honninscrave, and the Sandgorgon Nom, and *samadhi* Sheol. By Grimmand Honninscrave's death, Nom rent the Raver. Yet shreds of that dark spirit endured within the Sandgorgon. They endure still, and cling to malice.

"We knew no other means by which *turiya* Herem might be altogether unmade."

Covenant nodded to himself. He accepted Branl's justification. What choice did he have? The Humbled had argued against pursuing *turiya*, or considering the lurker's plight—and still they had accomplished something that Covenant could not have achieved alone.

Later he suggested like an offer of forgiveness, although he did not know how to forgive anything that had occurred, "Then maybe you'd better explain how you did it. I told the Feroce to leave you behind."

Silence held the gloaming for a while before Branl replied, "It was not difficult to persuade the Feroce that you would have need of us." He sounded like the stars, forlorn and doomed. "Our lives are memory. The creatures have no power to disturb or alter us. And their fear for their High God was extreme. Regardless of your command, they could not reject any form of aid. They summoned the arms of the lurker, that we might follow behind you.

"Thereafter Clyme and I determined our course together. I chose the task of your life, deeming that purpose paramount. Freely Clyme assumed the burden of the Raver.

"The *ak-Haru* spoke of simony. We are"—his sudden pause had the force of a stab—"we were the Humbled. We could descry no other means by which we might correct our fault. How otherwise might we have become worthy of the Guardian, and of ourselves?"

In a voice thick with woe, he concluded, "I must believe that good may be gained by evil means."

And now you're alone, Covenant sighed. This far from any of your people, you're cut off from everything that makes you who you are.

As isolated as a leper.

Simony, by hell! Covenant breathed faint curses to himself. Branl's people had never been as open-hearted as the Giants. But they had always been generous with their lives.

Eventually Covenant began to think that forgiveness might be possible after all.

Then a shiver of anticipation or effort ran through the burning green around the pond. Sharing one voice, the Feroce announced, "Consolation has been made ready. We are the Feroce. Our High God speaks in us. But you must remove yourselves from the water. To sustain its purity demands much of us, and our High God will not touch it."

With Covenant's consent, Branl swam toward the pond's edge. And when they were able to stand in the muck of the bottom, two tentacles snaked out of the surrounding marsh. As before, the lurker's arms closed carefully around Covenant and Branl, and lifted them high to avoid the trees.

Again the *krill* shone silver in all directions, but its light revealed nothing that might be *consolation*.

Side by side, Covenant and Branl arced upward, still moving eastward, into the accumulated dark of night in a sunless world.

Horrim Carabal bore Covenant and his companion so lightly that he had no sense of duration or distance. He only knew that he was moving because the Sarangrave squirmed below him and the air felt like a rasp on his raw skin.

Soon, however, the tentacles descended again. Then the lurker halted once more. This time, the monster held Covenant and Branl over a vaguely shimmering swath of dampness like a pit of quicksand eight or ten paces wide. Here, also, Feroce surrounded the lurker's destination. But now their numbers had become a multitude.

Hundreds of the creatures waved their small fires, making the wetland garish, and chanted like worshippers in the presence of divinity.

Horrim Carabal poised Covenant and Branl over the center of the quag, but did not drop them. The Feroce did not speak.

"Ur-Lord." Branl's tone changed. Surprise—or something more than surprise—penetrated his distress. "Here is a great wonder. I would have avowed that such a—I have no name for it—that such astonishment could not exist in Sarangrave Flat. Surely it is precluded by the manifold illnesses and evils of the lurker's demesne. Yet it is unmistakable. It is—"

He stopped as though what he beheld had sealed his throat.

Covenant peered downward, but he saw nothing that did not resemble quicksand or some other mire. He smelled only the cloying scents of rancid plants and putrefaction. The tumid exudation of the lurker's presence made breathing difficult.

"What is it?" he murmured. "What do you see?"

The Humbled appeared to wrestle words past an obstruction. "Ur-Lord, it is hurtloam. *Here*, where no clean thing grows, and no health flourishes. It cannot be, yet it is."

Hurtloam. The word sent conflicted squalls through Covenant in spite of his near-prostration and his complex pains. Hurtloam would heal his wounds; but it might also cure his leprosy. It had done so before. It could restore his crippled health-sense. It could make him potent and capable in ways which were denied to lepers.

It was life and ruin. It would rescue and damn him—

—because his illness was essential to him. *I don't expect you to understand*, he had told Linden's company in Andelain. *But I need this. I need to be numb.* He had believed it then: he believed it now. *It doesn't just make me who I am. It makes me who I can be.*

His leprosy was all that enabled him to hold the *krill*. In some sense, it was a defense against the Ravers. And he was not done. He had to remain as he was until the end.

And yet he wanted to be healed. Oh, he *wanted* it. He had become so much less than he needed to be. Wounds and weakness made him useless. He had nothing left to offer Linden. He would not be able to fight for the Land.

Inadvertently cruel, the Feroce and their High God proffered a gift which might also be a curse.

And while hurtloam healed him, it would make him sleep. He would miss his chance to redefine his alliance with the lurker; perhaps his only chance. After everything that he and the Humbled had done to secure the terms of the bargain—

Fearing the worst, he croaked, "Wait!" If the tentacle dropped him now— "Hellfire! Just wait!"

At once, the Feroce stilled their chanting. Horrim Carabal did not let go.

Together the creatures spoke. "Memory is a potent magic. We are the Feroce. We serve our High God. We have caused this small portion of his vast realm to remember what it was. The task has been arduous. We have expended much to complete it. But we are unworthy of the majesty which we worship. We have prepared this consolation because our High God has commanded it, and because we have failed in our service."

Impassive now, Branl asked, "How have you failed?"

A shudder passed through the throng. Emerald guttered in every hand. But the Feroce did not refuse to answer.

"We hazarded much, fearing the Pure One's wrath. Yet we are the Feroce. We serve our High God. For his life, we strove to awaken recall in the Pure One."

With those words, the small creatures drew Covenant's attention away from the conundrum of hurtloam.

"Our High God has not forgotten," they explained. "He is vast in all things. He recalls a time when a strange force forbade the horror which you have slain from venturing beyond the great cliff in the west. We cannot conceive such might. But the Pure One knows forbidding. He has forgotten it.

"For our High God's sake, we sought to awaken memory. Forbidding would have served him better. It would have inflicted less agony. He would not have suffered abhorred metal and fire.

"Alas, the Pure One has sealed himself against recall. We could not elicit his knowledge. In that, we failed our High God. Our shame is great."

"Wait," Covenant demanded again. "You mean you weren't fighting for your High God? You were trying to make me remember?"

That accounted for his wasted regret that he had no lore to forbid *turiya* Herem.

The creatures wailed. They cowered. "Now you are wroth. Forgive, Pure One. Our High God is himself, great in wonder and sovereignty. He has no need of our small magicks. If you will not forgive our attempt, forgive our failure."

"Wait," Covenant insisted for the third time. "You don't need my forgiveness. That's not important. But forbidding—"

He could not think. A fretwork of blisters covered his whole body. They seemed to cover his mind. Pain burst and bled wherever he turned. Whether or not he accepted hurtloam and healing, the Feroce were right: he had sealed himself against recall. For him, the strength of the Colossus was lost; irrecoverable.

But Linden—

She was capable of surprises that appalled and delighted him. She might—

Struggling to articulate ideas as they formed, he said urgently, "A message. I need you to carry a message for me. As fast as you can. To Lin"—he stumbled momentarily—"to the woman with the stick of power. The woman you tried to hurt. Tell her to remember forbidding."

"We're going to need it." *Without forbidding, there is too little time.* "And she has resources we don't. If nothing else, she's met Caerroil Wildwood. He knows a thing or two about forbidding." In an ancient age, he had participated in the formation of the Colossus as an interdict against the Ravers. "Why else did he give her those runes?"

The end must be opposed by the truth of stone and wood, orcrest *and refusal.*

"*Tell* her," Covenant ordered; pleaded. "Remember forbidding. Promise me you'll tell her."

Now the Feroce appeared to grow stronger. They stood straighter. Their fires burned more brightly. "It is done," they announced. "Be assured, Pure One. Even now, your words hasten. We are little, but we are also many. We inhabit our High God's realm from verge to verge. Your command will be fulfilled."

Like a sigh made flesh, Covenant sagged in Horrim Carabal's coils. He had done what he could. Now there was only one dilemma left to consider. One intolerable choice to make.

—*save or damn*—

His frailty blurred such distinctions. The Lords had misremembered their prophecy about the wielder of white gold; or they had misunderstood it. The words should have been "save *and* damn." If he let himself die now, his end would be wasted. And if he let himself be healed, his life would be wasted later.

Therefore he ought to choose life. While he lived, he could hope that something might change, for good or ill. *And betimes some wonder is wrought to redeem us.* Preferring death when life was offered was just despair by another name.

But, God, he was tired! He had already endured too much. In his present state, he imagined that the final darkness would be a kinder fate than hurtloam and more striving.

And he was a leper. For a man like him, nothing undermined his foundations more than being cured. Because he was who he was, he did not know how to bear the moral contradiction of being spared.

Like the *Haruchai*—

By that reasoning, he should have refused Brinn's succor.

But he had always been weak. Time and again, he had turned away from the strictures of his illness because he loved the Land. And Linden. In his own way, he also loved being human.

And he had always needed help.

Under the right circumstances, weakness was a form of strength.

While he wandered in his personal gyre, circling its edges like trapped flotsam, the Feroce renewed their thetic chant. The arms of the lurker held firm, waiting. But Branl grew restive. He, too, was in pain. The damage to his body he would doubtless survive. Certainly he would ignore it. The damage to his spirit was another matter.

"Ur-Lord," he said at last. "Hurtloam awaits you. Will you not accept its benison? Alone, I cannot preserve your life. The lurker and the Feroce cannot. Kevin's Dirt will make corruption of your scalds until no recovery is possible.

"It was not for this that the *ak-Haru* healed your earlier hurts. That he saw worth in the lurker's preservation does not entail that he desired your death."

Covenant lifted his head, stared at the Humbled. With two words, Branl had shown him a way out of his confusion: Kevin's Dirt. Hurtloam would heal him as completely as his various maimings permitted. But it had never altered his essential nature. And some of its effects might be transient. His illness might thrive again under the bale of Kevin's Dirt.

Was that not the underlying purpose of Kastenessen's curse? To thwart the deepest needs of those who loved the Land? In Linden's case, to limit her access to Earthpower? In Covenant's, to deny his fitness to be loved in return?

Save and damn.

Finally he faced the last of the Humbled. So that he would not be misunderstood, he told Branl, "Only if you join me."

Once before, he had required the Master to accept healing. Now Branl needed it as much as he did, if for different reasons.

He had no idea what he would do if Branl refused. But the Humbled did not. Nodding once, Branl said, "If that is your wish. I have traveled too far from myself to gainsay you."

Then he announced to the Feroce, "The Pure One has prepared himself. We accept your consolation, deeming it well-meant."

In response, the chant of the creatures became a shout. Green that shed too little light flared and danced on all sides. The arms of the lurker let go.

When Covenant fell into the mud, his whole world became spangles of gold like the rising of little suns.

ʊʘʚ

L ater Branl drew him out of the hurtloam. Tentacles lifted Covenant and the Master again; carried them away. At the eastern edge of the Sarangrave, the lurker lowered them onto a swath of grass on a hillside unspoiled by ancient wars or poisons. Then the arms withdrew, leaving only a few of the Feroce to watch and wait.

But Covenant knew none of this. He was deeply asleep, resting as though he had received an act of grace.

🙰

W hen he awoke, he came from the depths of dreams which he did not know how to interpret. He had sojourned among the Dead: they had given him obscure counsel. But they had stood, not in Andelain, but on the friable span of the Hazard, speaking of doom while below them raved the many maws of She Who Must Not Be Named, as ruinous as the Worm. Behind them, Branl had slain Clyme again and again; but the Dead had paid no heed. With infinite relish, the bane had devoured Elena and Linden and the future of the Forestals, making them participants in an eternal scream.

In dreams, time blurred and ran, as chaotic and rife with death as the mingled perils of the Sarangrave.

Forbidding, the Dead had urged. Forgotten truths.

The Chosen's son.

Kastenessen.

A-Jeroth of the Seven Hells, who desires all things unmade.

Repeatedly Branl hacked at Clyme and *turiya* until only gobbets and blood remained.

Baffled and thwarted, Thomas Covenant opened his eyes to the grey murk of dawn in a world where the sun did not rise.

But his own condition seemed to repudiate Branl's ferocity and Clyme's death. He had slept deeply and long. God, he had *slept*. On this open grass, he had slept the sleep of renewed health, fathomless as the growing gaps between the stars. It was an anodyne that he had not expected, as salvific as hurtloam, and as necessary.

No doubt he had slept too long. Every hour counted against him. But he could not regret losing the night.

When he opened his eyes and looked at the sky, he saw the stars clearly. Those that remained were as bright as gems of Time, and as disconsolate as condemned children. One after another, they went on dying.

Their slow plight grieved him. Yet it was countered by the sheer freshness of his physical sensations. Every burn and blister had been replaced by a tingling that resembled eagerness. His heart beat with a vigor which he did not recognize, as though it had been unshackled after a lifetime of imprisonment. His fingers flexed as if they had never known excruciation. Potential smiles twitched in the muscles of his face. And his feet— By hell! He could feel his toes, actually *feel his toes*. They told him that his socks and boots were still sodden.

Hurtloam was a miracle: there was no other word for it.

And like his body, his health-sense had become stronger. It assured him that his new life would be temporary. Kevin's Dirt shrouded the region, wreaking its incremental havoc; working against his restoration. Nevertheless he was grateful for any reprieve. The strange alchemy of hurtloam made even Clyme's death seem less bitter. At least for a little while, the future did not look as bleak as this day, the second without true sunlight. When numbness returned to his fingers and toes—when his sight began to fail again—he would be able to bear it.

Propping his elbows on the thick grass of his bed, he raised his head and shoulders to gauge his circumstances.

He lay on a gradual slope that he did not remember, cushioned by turf like luxuriance. Therefore he was somewhere north of Lord Foul's many battlefields; somewhere in the long wedge of hale ground between Sarangrave Flat and the Sunbirth Sea. The lurker must have carried him here.

Shaking his head in surprise at such consideration, he regarded his companion standing like a sentinel a score of paces past his feet. Branl appeared to be keeping watch on the rank mass of the wetland. Or he may have been—

Beyond the *Haruchai*, Covenant finally noticed a small cluster of emerald fires burning in the hands of four, no, five Feroce. They waited a few steps outside the border of their native waters. Branl may have been guarding Covenant against them; refusing them in some fashion.

Apparently their High God was not done with the Pure One.

Covenant was reluctant to face them. He did not want to recall Horrim Carabal's peril, or to think about what the Humbled had sacrificed. But time was precious—and the Feroce had blessed him with hurtloam. They had promised to speak to Linden for him. They had earned his attention.

Sighing at the ache of memories as cruel as Joan's suffering, Covenant pushed himself to stand.

Around him, murk veiled every feature of the landscape, turned hills and grass and marsh and sky to an indeterminate, irredeemable smudge. Only the wavering fires of the Feroce contradicted the universal twilight; and they cast too little illumination.

Awkwardly, as if he had forgotten how to walk, he went to join Branl.

Like him, the Master still wore a second skin of mud. A trivial concern: it would flake away as it dried; and in the meantime, it provided a measure of protection against the increasing coolness of the air. But under the mud, Branl's tunic hung in tatters, eaten by the Flat's corrosive waters. Indeed, Covenant's own clothes were badly damaged. His jeans looked like they had been mauled, and his T-shirt was little more than scraps. Yet that, too, was trivial. Ruined attire suited the Unbeliever and his guardian.

Looking more closely, Covenant was relieved to find that Branl also had been healed. In more ways than one— A portion of the distress clenched and hidden behind his *Haruchai* stoicism had been eased. He looked like a man who had finally come to terms with an amputation, or with some other old wound.

Resting his halfhand on the Master's shoulder, Covenant said, "I'm sorry." Perhaps he would learn how to forgive Branl if he first asked forgiveness for himself. "I can only guess what killing that Raver cost you. But I regret it. I wish I hadn't needed you to save me."

Again.

Branl's gaze did not waver. "You sought to spare us, ur-Lord," he replied as though every human tone had been hammered out of his voice. "That you have ever done, though you have long known that no *Haruchai* wishes to be spared. To be denied the outcome of our deeds implies a judgment of unworth. Yet you are the ur-Lord, the Unbeliever. As we are known to you, so you are known to us. By long travail, we have learned that your choices are indeed a judgment of unworth. But it is yourself that you judge, yourself and no other. Therefore we found no insult in your wish to confront *turiya* Herem alone."

Involuntarily Covenant winced. The Humbled certainly knew him too well. But he did not like to think of his personal strictures in such terms.

Sighing again, he changed the subject. "Do you still have the *krill*?"

Branl nodded. From the remains of his tunic, he drew out a bundle of broad leaves. "Do you require its light, ur-Lord? I have covered it to appease the timidity of these Feroce." After a moment, he added, "They crave speech with you yet again. For that reason, they have awaited your return from slumber."

Covenant dropped his hand. "Never mind. They're already scared enough. They've waited this long for me. I can wait a little longer to see where I'm going."

He had decisions to make, but he was not ready for them. He wanted Linden's forgiveness more than Branl's—or his own.

Standing at his companion's side as if he and the Humbled carried the same stigma, he addressed the Feroce.

"So far, you've honored your part of our agreement." That the lurker wanted something else from him made him brusque. "I expect your High God to keep doing that. We've done more than I promised. You should do the same."

The Feroce flinched. Their flames guttered and spat. "You are the Pure One," they answered, quavering, "though you deny yourself. So it was at the time of the *jheherrin*. So it remains.

"You have exceeded the terms. This our High God acknowledges. The alliance is sealed."

Covenant nodded; but he did not relax. "And my message? Did you deliver it?"

"We are the Feroce," the creatures replied. Their single voice sounded like mire forced to assume the shapes of language. "We serve our High God in every pond and stream and quag of his glory. Your words have been conveyed. Their import we have striven to convey also."

Covenant bowed his head in relief. Linden would understand. He had to believe that she would understand. And she would know what to do. *Something unexpected.* Something that he could not imagine.

But the Feroce were still speaking. "If we have failed," they said, "or if we are not heeded, our High God commands contrition. Our lives are forfeit. Should you wish to slay us, still the alliance is sealed. It will not be unsealed."

Then the creatures stood and waited as if they were resisting an impulse to cower.

Their unrelenting fears troubled Covenant. "Well, gosh," he drawled to disguise his dismay. "That's magnanimous of him. Is everybody in this bloody mess trying to make amends for sins they haven't committed?"

The fires of the Feroce quailed. Their large eyes reflected emerald alarm. They had tried to help him remember *forbidding*—they had given him hurtloam—and still they expected to be punished.

Swearing to himself, Covenant tried to soften the edges of his voice. "You did what you could. If we exceeded the terms, so did you. What happens next isn't your fault."

He meant, You don't need to be afraid of me.

"So what does your High God want now?" he continued. "He's already sacrificed enough of you for my sake. I don't want more. What does *he* want?"

"He is our High God," the descendants of the soft ones replied. "His greatness commands us. We do not refuse. We—"

Abruptly they flinched like children at the first touch of a flail. Facing each other, they crowded closer together. Their flames seemed to gibber.

From their circle of fire and fear, their voice arose like muffled wailing. "Our High God commands. The alliance is sealed. It will not be unsealed. But he asks—"

For a moment, they appeared to lose control of themselves. Their green faded to flickers in their palms. Their voice became a thin cry like an echo of their earlier shrieking. Their bodies jerked as if they were appalled by what they had to say.

But then they mastered themselves—or they were mastered. Their fires sprang back to life. The flames strained upward, striving toward the heavens. Garish emerald glared like malevolence on their weak features. Their wailing became words.

"Our High God craves a boon."

Covenant stared at their chagrin. He required a moment to grasp that the Feroce were distressed by the notion that their High God had needs which could not be met by commands or alliances or raw power; that the lurker's tremendous size and strength could be reduced to pleading. In effect, Horrim Carabal had confessed an inadequacy that struck at the roots of their devotion.

Shaken on their behalf, Covenant said, "You don't need to be afraid. There's no harm in asking. I'm not offended. Just say it. What does your High God want me to do?"

He could not tell whether the Feroce understood him. They did not unclench their circle, or lower their fires, or cease their wounded cries. After a moment, however, their wailing became speech again.

"You are the Pure One. The Pure One redeems. Now havoc comes, a great and terrible hunger. It draws near. It is death. Utter death. Our High God cannot stand against it. He does not know what he must do. Will you heed him? Will you answer?

"Our High God must not perish!"

Ah. Covenant nodded again. The lurker wanted to survive, and it did not know how.

But he was loath to suggest a course of action. "That depends," he said carefully. He could not guess what the implications might be. "I don't know exactly what you're asking. First tell me this. The havoc is coming. That's a fact. But *where*? Where is it coming?"

Would it head straight toward *Melenkurion* Skyweir? Was it ready to end the world? Or did it want more food? More *Elohim*? Or something else—?

The possibility that the Worm was hungry for *something else* made Covenant's stomach twist.

"You are the Pure One," the Feroce replied in consternation. "Do you not know that the havoc nears the heart of our High God's realm, the deepest waters? How is it that you do not know?"

The deepest waters? Covenant frowned. That must mean Lifeswallower, the Great Swamp: the delta of the Defiles Course. He groaned at the idea. The ground on which he stood seemed to cant as if realities were shifting. Hellfire! The Worm was approaching Lifeswallower.

But it could have no interest in the lurker's demesne. It would find no sustenance in that polluted swampland. And certainly the Worm had no appetite for a monster like Horrim Carabal, a living corruption of Earthpower. Which meant—

Covenant dragged his hands through his hair, trying to steady his thoughts.

—that Lifeswallower was simply in the way. The Worm would merely pass through it. The instrument of the world's end had a different goal.

Perhaps the Worm was coming from the north. Perhaps its path toward *Melenku-rion* Skyweir ran through the Great Swamp by chance.

Or—

Damnation!

—it was going toward Mount Thunder.

To Kastenessen. Or to She Who Must Not Be Named.

Hell and *blood*!

Both explanations seemed plausible. Kastenessen was *Elohim*. He might be the nearest source of food. But he was tainted. He had merged a portion of himself with the *skurj*. Their sulfurous scent might make him unpalatable. In his own fashion, he was as corrupted as the lurker.

She Who Must Not Be Named was another matter. She was—Covenant had no apt language for Her—a gaoled god. She was not Earthpower. Nevertheless She was *power*. If the Worm sought to feed on Her—

The battle between such beings would stagger the Arch of Time to its foundations. It might accomplish the purpose for which the Worm had been created.

Lord Foul had planned well. Oh, he had planned well! Here was another conceivable reason why Roger had hidden Jeremiah in the Lost Deep. To conceal the boy, of course. To preserve him for Roger's use—and for the Despiser's. But also to arouse She Who Must Not Be Named if Linden discovered Jeremiah's covert.

It boots nothing to avoid his snares, for they are ever beset with other snares—

"You are the Pure One," repeated the Feroce in trepidation. "Will you not answer?"

With an effort, Covenant shook aside a whirl of sickening speculations. "Oh, I'll answer." He did not know what he would say until he heard himself say it. "But you still haven't told me what your High God wants. He can't believe *I'm* going to stop the Worm. That havoc, as you call it, will swat me like I'm nothing. What does your High God think I *can* do?"

Straining to respond, the voice of the Feroce scaled higher. The lurker's reply was naked supplication. "Will you counsel?" they asked as if they wanted to weep and had no tears. "Will you reveal what must be done? For the alliance? For our High God's life?"

"*Damn* it," Covenant muttered to himself. His impulse to speculate was too strong. His mind wheeled. "I can't." Even if the Worm hunted only Kastenessen, it was certain to encounter She Who Must Not Be Named. "Not until I know where it's going."

Before the lurker's servants could muster more words, Covenant turned to Branl. "What do you think? Maybe coming to Lifeswallower is an accident. Maybe the Worm is just passing through. But maybe it's aiming for Mount Thunder. Don't we have to know?"

The gloom masked Branl's features; but the Humbled faced Covenant with a firmness that resembled certainty. "Ur-Lord, hear me. You contemplate a journey to the last boundary of hills between Lifeswallower and the Sunbirth Sea. Such a quest will bear us many leagues farther from our companions, wherever they may be."

Covenant braced himself to argue; but Branl was not done.

"Understand, ur-Lord, that I do not protest. Your task is mine. I am alone and have no path other than my chosen service. Yet I must observe that our need for an end to Kevin's Dirt is absolute. Your straits confirm this. Already your illness regains its force. The Worm in Mount Thunder may perchance bring about the cessation of Kevin's Dirt. Perchance it may not. Is it not therefore plain that our surest road to Kastenessen's defeat lies toward Linden Avery and her company? Your powers and hers together are more certain of success than any chance or mischance of the Worm."

Covenant shook his head. Studying Branl while memories of Clyme's end scarified his thoughts, he said slowly, feeling his way, "That makes sense, as far as it goes. But what if the Worm runs into She Who Must Not Be Named?"

Realizations seemed to swarm in Branl's gaze. Apparently he had not considered the bane. "That outcome," he said slowly, "must be prevented." Then he asked, "Yet how can it be forestalled?"

Covenant grimaced. "That's the problem. We have to know where the Worm is going. We might need the lurker against it."

When his companion acquiesced, Covenant turned back to the Feroce.

Swallowing a clot of apprehension, he said, "Tell your High God this. I want him alive. I'll give him counsel, if I can think of anything. But not until I know more.

"I have to see this havoc for myself. Then we'll talk."

The idea that he would be moving farther from Linden made him ache; but he ignored that pang as well as he could.

The creatures fluttered their fires in alarm, but they did not protest. For a moment longer, they crowded together, mewling wordlessly while their theurgy pulsed in the twilight. Then they answered, "You are the Pure One. The Feroce will await you. Our High God commands us. The alliance is sealed."

At once, they broke away from each other and hastened toward the wetland. As soon as their feet entered the waters of the Sarangrave, their flames went out. Covenant lost sight of them as if the marsh had swallowed them whole.

His mouth was suddenly dry, and his heart pumped dread. The enormity of what he meant to do seemed to thicken the murk. It made the air difficult to breathe. He had no real comprehension of the Worm's puissance. For all he knew, its power was too destructive to be gazed upon. The sight alone might scald his eyes in their sockets.

Fiercely he told himself, Or it might not. He would learn nothing if he did not take the risk.

Stop dithering. Just do it.

There was no other way to earn the necessary knowledge.

"We need the horses," he muttered to Branl. He would probably never see Hooryl again. He had to hope that Rallyn would be able to command Mishio Massima without help. "And food. Water. From here on, everything is only going to get harder. I don't doubt that you can hang on indefinitely, but I have to keep up my strength."

The Humbled nodded. He did not speak of trust in the Ranyhyn, or in himself.

That was well. Memories of *turiya* and butchery clung to Covenant. When the *Haruchai* invoked *trust*, the word meant too much. Long centuries ago, Covenant had asked the ancestors of the Humbled to preserve Revelstone. Clyme's death was only one of the results.

ﾚﾘﾊ

But trust was still trust. It was earned, or it was not. As faithful as the *Haruchai*, who remembered everything, Rallyn cantered out of the dusk in Naybahn's place, answering Branl's summons. And the palomino stallion brought the Ardent's mulish beast with him. When the Humbled had checked Mishio Massima's tack, he announced that the horses were ready.

With leaves to protect his hands, Covenant uncovered the *krill*. Then he removed Joan's ring from around his neck. As he had done before, he pushed the ring onto the stub-end of the last finger of his left hand; closed his fist around the chain to secure the band. As before, he struck the dagger's gem with the ring until his body blazed with wild magic. After that, he concentrated on pressing the point of the blade into the grass while Branl carried him around Rallyn and Mishio Massima.

When Branl lifted him into his saddle, he nearly fell off the far side. A second Humbled should have been there to catch him. But he managed to steady himself on the saddle horn.

While his line of silver lingered in the turf, the horses surged into motion, bearing him farther from his heart's desire.

ﾚﾘﾊ

After a blink of darkness which seemed to deny any possible passage, either through time or across distance, Covenant and Branl arrived galloping in a region that looked indistinguishable from the place which they had left. The hillside may have leaned at a slightly different angle. The slope ahead may have been less even. Conceivably Sarangrave Flat had receded to the west. But Covenant could not be sure. Beyond the *krill*'s reach, the unnatural dusk masked details, and his vision was fading.

Branl took Loric's dagger and covered it, giving Covenant's eyes a chance to adjust to the universal grey. The horses ran on as if they were determined to reach the edge of the world.

Before Covenant could swallow enough of his vertigo to frame a question, the Humbled pointed ahead. After a few moments, Covenant made out a deeper gloom like a clump of shadows in the rumpled ground: a small copse in a hollow. Soon he caught the faint glint of water. A stream purled over the contours of the hillside, hastening in the direction of the Sarangrave.

As the horses slowed, Branl stated with quiet satisfaction, "The Land is provident— as is Rallyn. Here we will find both water and sustenance. Corruption's wars did not extend into this region. Nor do the blights of Sarangrave Flat."

Covenant did not doubt his companion, but he had other concerns. While he scrambled for balance, he asked, "How far have we come?"

"A score of leagues, ur-Lord. Perhaps somewhat more."

Covenant winced. Only a score?

"Did we lose much time?"

"No other mount could have borne us so swiftly," Branl replied with uncharacteristic asperity. He seemed to hear a complaint in Covenant's tone. But then he continued more flatly, "Yet it is plain that our passages are not immediate. Though the sun no longer measures the day, I gauge that mid-morning is nigh."

Covenant frowned, thinking hard. To some extent, at least, the distances that he and Branl could cover appeared to be controlled as much by Rallyn's instincts as by the size or even the precision of his argent enclosures. Nevertheless the abilities of the Ranyhyn clearly had limits. Otherwise they would not have needed two attempts to reach the Sarangrave the previous day.

Still he was losing chunks of time. Where did the hours go? Where—if anywhere— did he and Branl and their horses exist during the interval?

The lag may have been inherent to his specific use of wild magic; or it may have been an outcome of his relationship with Joan's ring, a ring which was not his. After all, Linden had experienced something similar. When she had saved herself and Anele from the collapse of Kevin's Watch, she had done more than pass from one place to another. She had also moved through time: in effect, she had fallen more slowly than the broken remains of the Watch.

As soon as the horses halted near the stream, Mishio Massima jerked the reins away from Covenant and began cropping grass. Branl slid down from Rallyn's back; offered to help Covenant. But Covenant dismounted on his own. For a few moments, he braced himself against the Ardent's steed while the last sensations of vertigo faded, giving himself a chance to accept the returning numbness of his feet and the loss of sensation in his finger-tips. Kevin's damn Dirt— Then he left the beast's side.

With Branl, he considered the nearby trees.

They were wattle, fast-growing and resilient. In sunlight, they would have been a verdant green, fresh and promising. Now they resembled shadows cast by a different version of reality, although they swayed in the tumble of a growing breeze. Certainly they appeared to offer nothing that Covenant could eat.

Nevertheless the Humbled seemed sure of his own perceptions. Firmly he beckoned Covenant to accompany him among the trees.

The copse was thick. Pushing his way between the trunks, Covenant soon tripped. When he looked down, he found that he had caught one of his boots on the thick stem of a vine.

In fact, vines twisted all over the ground among the trees. The whole stand was tangled with them.

"Do you recall this, ur-Lord?" Branl sounded subtly amused. "You were once familiar with it."

"Huh?" Covenant had lost ages of memories, but he was sure that he had never heard one of the *Haruchai* sound amused. "When?"

"During the time of the Sunbane," answered Branl, "it provided nourishment when Corruption's evil spawned no edible growth, and *aliantha* were scarce. It is *ussusimiel*."

For a moment, Covenant groped inwardly. Then he spotted the darker knob of a melon in the gloom; and he remembered. Long ago under a desert sun, Sunder had invoked vines and their fruit from parched, barren dirt. *At need it will sustain life—*

It did not taste as piquant as treasure-berries. And it lacked their extraordinary vitality. But it would be enough.

"Well, damn," Covenant muttered. "If that isn't providence, I don't know what is." He felt unexpectedly cheered, as if an old friend had taken him by surprise. "Hell, I don't even know what the word means."

"Then, ur-Lord"—Branl held up the wrapped *krill*—"if you do not deem it an incondign use, I will harvest melons. While you break your fast, I will weave a net of smaller vines to carry a supply of the fruit."

Covenant found that he was too hungry to argue. "Do it. Somehow I'm sure Loric wouldn't object, even if he did spend damn decades sweating over that knife."

But he did not stay to watch Branl work. Instead he turned away, sparing his eyes the stab of the gem's shining. Lit by slashes of silver, he withdrew from the copse and went to the stream to drink.

Providence in all sooth. Even here, so many leagues away from the wonders of the Land that he had known in life, there were still gifts—

Now he prayed that food and water would sustain him well enough for what lay ahead.

಄

A second self-contained violation of time or space took him and Branl nearly thirty leagues closer to their destination. As Rallyn and Mishio Massima galloped out of theurgy onto a long facet of exposed rock, Covenant clung frantically to his saddle horn, straining to contain a gyre of dizziness. But Branl rode as though he and Rallyn were more dependable than stone. Over one shoulder, the Humbled carried a net sack filled with enough melons to keep Covenant fed for a day or two.

A wind out of the east buffeted the riders like the presage of a gale, but it was useless to Covenant. It did not stop the spin that sickened him, or lessen the blurring of his sight.

According to Branl, one more passage of comparable length would convey them to the bluffs between the Sunbirth Sea and Lifeswallower, the headland which bordered the delta of the Great Swamp. From that vantage, they would be able to watch for the Worm without precluding contact with the Feroce.

Unfortunately noon had already passed. Each translation by wild magic washed away time as well as balance. In some sense, the linear certainty of causality and sequence formed the ground on which Covenant's mind stood. His thoughts were moments; bits of bedrock. When he blinked from one location to the next, the change staggered him as if every nerve in his body had misfired.

For that reason, and because each exertion of Joan's ring drained him, he had to rest in spite of an accumulating sense of urgency. When the horses had slowed to a halt, he half fell out of Mishio Massima's saddle and lurched away like a wounded animal looking for a place to hide.

He yearned to be alone, at least for a little while; to soothe his vulnerability in isolation. But Branl followed him. After a silence, the Humbled pronounced, "This frailty is an effect of Kevin's Dirt, ur-Lord."

Instead of speaking, Covenant gritted his teeth and waited.

Inflexibly Branl added, "The distress which results will fade more readily if I am permitted to hold High Lord Loric's *krill*."

Covenant blinked at the knife bright in his grasp. Damnation. It's getting worse. Like the encroaching deadness of leprosy, vertigo was tightening its noose around him. In his confusion, the injured whirl of disorientation, he had not realized that he was still holding the dagger. He had not felt its heat—

With a jerk of his arm, he surrendered the *krill*.

As Branl covered the gem, dusk flooded over the region. Under other circumstances, the sun's absence would have galled Covenant. Now, however, it felt like an act of kindness. Twilight was a kind of privacy. He needed it to recover his balance.

The lurker wanted counsel, but he had no idea what he could possibly say. If the Worm caught Kastenessen's scent, it would head toward Mount Thunder—and toward She Who Must Not Be Named. Nothing would survive that encounter.

To prevent that outcome, Covenant might have to ask Horrim Carabal to sacrifice itself. But the monster would surely refuse. No alliance would persuade it to surrender its life voluntarily.

He had to hope that the Worm's approach to Lifeswallower was a coincidence; that it would ignore Mount Thunder. Otherwise he would have to think of a better answer for the lurker.

Hampered by Kevin's Dirt and vertigo, he could hardly think at all.

ꙮ

F ortunately a third passage brought him to the headland. His mount hammered up a slope of saw-edged grass between bare juts of granite and basalt: a narrowing wedge of rising ground. To the north stood the bluffs which restricted the spread of Lifeswallower. In the east were the low cliffs bordering the Sunbirth Sea. Beyond the gap-toothed horizon ahead was nothing except grey sky and stars. They seemed to mark the edge of existence.

This time, the wind hit Covenant hard. Heavy as a torrent, it knocked him askew. When he tried to dismount, he toppled backward; landed on the grass with a jolt that stopped his breathing. The ground tilted from side to side, forward and back, in a sequence devoid of reason, as unpredictable and dangerous as dreaming. Gusts swept past him, sucking air out of his mouth. Blots marred his vision like the mottling of disease.

But then Branl took the *krill*. With a suddenness that resembled fainting, Covenant began to breathe again.

While the stains faded from his sight, and the canting of the horizons eased, he was content to lie still and let the impact of his fall ebb. The troubled labor of his heart suggested that he had undergone an obscure ordeal. Nevertheless it reassured him. It confirmed that time endured, unbroken; that one thing led to another. The Law that constrained and enabled life held true.

When he felt ready, he rolled onto one side, forced his arms and knees under him, pushed himself upright.

God, the wind—He could barely stand against it; had to squint at the sting of tears. Without Branl's support, he might not have been able to move.

Blinking, he scanned his surroundings. He had the visceral impression that he was standing on the highest peak of the world. But of course that was nonsense: this was not a mountain. Rather he had arrived downhill from the wedge-tip of the headland. To the east, the sea thrashed at the Land's last rock. He smelled salt on the blast. If he could find the vantage he sought, he would be able to see the surge of waves.

Around him, the headland was a jumble of protruding stone, granite and basalt weathered smooth; gnawed across the millennia into shapes that resembled anguish and intransigence. Some of the rocks wore fringes of moss in the lee of the wind. Others had acquired threadbare cloaks of lichen.

Peering behind him, he thought at first that the slope sank lower indefinitely. But when he squeezed the wind from his eyes and looked harder, he realized that the westward hillside was cut off by a line of darkness in the distance. There lay the Great Swamp, sweeping around the headland toward the sea. He could not smell Lifeswallower. The wind tore away the swampland's complex fetors. But below him the waters of the delta reflected a faint shimmer.

After a moment, he spotted the horses. They were cantering down the slope, keeping their distance from the wetland as they descended. Apparently Rallyn believed that the riders had no immediate need of their mounts. And naturally both Rallyn and Mishio Massima wanted water as well as forage.

Then Covenant noticed the emerald fires, small as dots, ascending slowly toward him.

He watched the creatures briefly. But they were still far away; and he had nothing to say to them. Turning back toward the tip of the promontory, he went upward with Branl's aid until he glimpsed the darker grey of the sea beyond the headland's rim. There he stopped.

The waves heaved frantically against their own weight, hacking across each other, rising into sudden breakers, erupting in spume. Some mighty pressure disrupted the normal scend and recession of tides. The seas were flung in frenzy at the cliffs, where they rebounded, smashed together, became chaos. The wind assailed Covenant's ears with their clamor as if the headland were under siege.

Gripping his companion's arm, he asked, "Can you see anything?"

Branl studied the sea. "I do not doubt that the Worm comes, as the Feroce have declared. In turmoil, the waves contradict themselves. Some cataclysm goads these waters. But its source is too distant for my discernment."

"How much time did we lose?"

A slight frown of concentration or surprise disturbed Branl's mien. After a moment, he replied, "It appears that our final passage was prolonged. Mayhap the

Worm's approach misleads my senses. Nonetheless I gauge that evening is nigh. Ere long, this dusk will turn toward true night."

The coming of night after a second sunless day felt like a bad omen. Covenant had no power against the World's End.

Nonetheless he had made promises—

"In that case," he told Branl, "I need to get out of this wind. Can you find a place where I can watch the sea and Lifeswallower? A place with some shelter?"

Nodding, Branl drew him toward the stones which cluttered the corner of the headland. In the lee of a blunted fang as tall as Covenant, the Humbled urged him to sit and rest. Then Branl left. Still bearing his net of melons as well as Loric's *krill*, he disappeared among the twisted shapes of basalt and granite, the motley of lichen and moss.

Covenant sagged against the fang; rubbed his stiff cheeks with his insensate fingers; wiped away residual tears. Reflexively he confirmed that Joan's ring still hung under his T-shirt. The wind moaned miserably past the rocks, a raw sound like keening, but he tried to ignore it. Tried to think. Wind was only air in motion, he told himself. It merely reacted to forces beyond its control. If he heard lamentation in it, or auguries of havoc, he was misleading himself. The world did not *care*: the natural order of things did not grieve or grow glad. Only the sentient beings who inhabited time wept and struggled and loved.

There was a kind of comfort in the notion that the Earth neither understood nor feared its own peril. Its life was not a reflection of himself. But such consolation was too abstract to touch him—or his dying nerves did not feel it. Ultimately nothing ever mattered, except to the people who cared about it. To them, however, the import of the stakes was absolute.

Covenant grimaced ruefully at his thoughts. Long ago, he had insisted that the Land did not exist, except as a form of self-contained delirium. In that sense, it *was* a reflection of himself. And he was powerless in it because he could not change his own image in the mirror: it only showed him who he was. Therefore he could not be blamed for his actions; or for the Land's fate. Now he found himself arguing that the world was really nothing more than an impersonal mechanism inhabited by self-referential beings. Therefore no failure, here or anywhere, could be held against him.

After so many years, he had changed very little. He was still looking for a way to forgive himself for being human and afraid.

But in fact he did not believe that the Land and its world were simply parts of a mechanism. They formed a living creation. And like all living things, they yearned for continuance. If he failed them, the world's woe would be as vast as the heavens.

While it lasted.

There were hints of travail in the wind; suggestions of iniquity. But he did not know how to interpret them—or he was not ready.

He was still wrestling with himself when Branl returned, no longer carrying his supply of *ussusimiel.*

"By good fortune, ur-Lord," the Humbled announced, "there is a covert which I deem apt for your purpose. The wind is obstructed, yet views to the east and north are accessible. Will you accompany me?"

Briefly Covenant considered what he could see of his companion. Then he muttered, "Well, hell. Why else are we here?" Extending his arm, he asked for help.

True to his commitments, the Master lifted Covenant upright. And he kept his hand on Covenant's arm for support and guidance. His grasp may have been meant as reassurance.

Covenant glanced downhill to check on the progress of the Feroce. Their noxious fires shone more clearly now; but they were still no more than halfway up the slope. Trusting their uncanny ability to find him wherever he was, he turned away.

As Branl drew him among the stones, the Humbled asked, "Ur-Lord, have you determined how you will counsel the lurker?"

Bracing himself on contorted plinths and tall slabs, Covenant picked his way forward. "It's like I said. I need to know where the Worm is headed. If it comes from the north, or the northeast, and doesn't turn, it's probably going straight for *Melenkurion* Skyweir. In that case, the lurker isn't in danger. It doesn't need advice. But if the Worm comes from anywhere south of us, it's ignoring its direct line to the Earth-Blood. That means it wants Kastenessen—or She Who Must Not Be Named. Then I'll have to tell Horrim Carabal *some*thing."

"To what purpose?" countered Branl. "That you desire to determine the Worm's immediate path, I comprehend. But what will any counsel avail? The lurker will not hazard its life at your word."

Covenant stumbled to the left around one thrust of basalt, to the right past another. The cry of the wind was louder here. It pummeled him in forlorn gusts. But as he went farther among the stones, he was spared more and more of the wind's force.

"I'm still thinking," he answered through his teeth. "There has to be something we can do." To accomplish what? Slow the Worm? *Stop* it? He told himself not to be absurd. "I just don't know what it is."

The Humbled may have shrugged. He did not argue.

His path twisted like a maze. It seemed long. But eventually Covenant came to a small patch of grass just wide enough to sit in. Branl's net of melons rested there in a notch between stones the size of Giants. Standing in the center of the grass, Covenant found that he had a clear line of sight northward. Through a gap in the jumble, he could see the rim of the bluffs perhaps ten paces away. And beyond the precipice—

There the Sunbirth Sea assailed Lifeswallower with the mindless fury of a berserker.

At one time, perhaps only a few hours earlier, the waters of the Great Swamp had drained eastward in ramified channels like the branches of an immense tree. Among them had stood islands of unpalatable grass, tormented eyots of brush, clusters of hoary cypresses and other marsh-trees like sentinels watching over a sargasso. But such things were gone now. Indeed, every feature of the delta had been inundated or swept away. The mounting seas flailed in all directions, tearing apart or dragging under everything that defined this region of Horrim Carabal's realm. The portion of Lifeswallower that Covenant could see had become indistinguishable from the ocean's violence.

The sight made him shiver as if vertigo had already wrapped its cold fingers around his heart. Grinding his teeth, he turned to the east.

At first, he could not gain a view of the sea. Too many protruding rocks rose too high. But when he leaned to one side of his covert, he found an opening. There ages of wind and weather had scalloped the sides of several stones. And one slab of basalt had lost a substantial section of its center: it resembled a cripple hunching over a collapsed chest. The result was a window like an oriel, a gap that revealed an arc of the Sunbirth Sea.

Through the window came flicks and slaps of wind, occasional stings of spray; but Covenant was able to endure them for a few moments at a time.

At that distance, he could not discern any specific swell or cross-current. The whole ocean looked like a darker and more troubled iteration of the sunless sky. Even the horizon was no more than a smear of grey. If the Worm were coming from that direction, he saw no sign of it.

Blinking hard, he moved back into shelter. With a gesture, he asked Branl to watch for him. Then he lowered himself to the grass and tried to believe that he had not come so far for nothing: that when the Worm arrived, he would know what to say.

Branl scrutinized the east for a while; turned his attention briefly to the ruined delta in the north. Then he shook his head.

"Ur-Lord, I judge that the Worm is not imminent. I know nothing of its speed, but I will believe that a span of time remains to us. We are granted a respite." He removed the *krill* from his tunic. "Should you wish it, I will prepare *ussusimiel*."

Covenant nodded. "Sure. Why not?" He needed strength. When the Worm came, he would have to flee, whatever happened. If he and Branl died here, their lives would be truly wasted.

Uncovering only the dagger's blade, the Humbled deftly took a melon, sliced it into sections, cut out the seeds. The pieces he handed to Covenant one at a time.

Covenant ate until only rinds remained; but he did not notice the taste, or attend to what he was doing. He was listening to the unsteady ululation of the wind, trying to decipher its oblique message. Its salt tang and its keening were auguries that he did not know how to interpret.

Branl offered to prepare another melon. Vaguely Covenant declined. He was not conscious of hunger; or he was not hungry for that kind of sustenance. He wanted the richer nourishment of an *answer*.

After cleaning the blade, Branl put the *krill* away and resumed his study of the east.

Wind and salt. The ravage of the delta. The Worm of the World's End. Kastenessen. She Who Must Not Be Named.

And Linden, who was so far away that only Rallyn would know how to find her. The thought that he might not see her again before the end made Covenant's chest ache like a wound to the heart.

Branl stepped back to gaze around the stones. After a moment, he said, "Attend, ur-Lord. The Feroce approach."

Jerking up his head, Covenant spotted glints of emerald on the rocks. Fires guttered; flared more brightly; receded. Soon two of the creatures brought their flames and their timidity to the border of the grass. Two or three more Feroce followed behind them. Their eyes cast echoes of their theurgy into his shelter.

In their damp, squeezed voice, they asked, "Pure One?"

Covenant faced them until he was sure that they did not mean to say more; that the two words of their question sufficed for them. Then he looked at Branl. "What time is it?"

The Humbled was a thicker shadow in the gathering murk. "Evening becomes night," he answered. Responding to Covenant's underlying query, he added, "I do not yet descry the Worm. Though its coming is plain, it remains beyond my discernment."

And mine, Covenant sighed. Tightening his grip on himself, he turned back to the Feroce. "Is the havoc close? The Worm? Do you know? Can your High God feel it?"

The creatures replied with a thin wail, quickly cut off. Almost gibbering, they forced themselves to say, "It is near. How do you not know that it is near? Our High God asks what he must do. He asks with desperation. His alarm is terrible."

Near? Covenant muttered to himself. Hellfire!

"I'm sorry," he told the Feroce gruffly. "You'll just have to wait. I won't know what to say until I see it." Almost at once, he went on, "And I won't see anything until you get rid of those fires." They blinded him to everything else; cast a pall of memories over his mind. He remembered the Illearth Stone too well. "If you can't survive without them outside the Sarangrave, hide them somewhere. I won't abandon you. I'll tell you as soon as I have something."

The creatures quailed. They moaned like the wind. But they did not protest. One by one, they retreated among the stones. For a while, their emerald lingered on rims of granite and basalt. Then Covenant lost sight of them.

"Branl?" he asked anxiously. "Anything?"

"Perhaps," replied the Humbled. "I am uncertain."

Cursing, Covenant surged to his feet. The wind seemed to blow darkness into his covert. Branl was little more than an outline against the rocks.

If the Master's acute senses were uncertain, Covenant would be effectively eyeless; but he had to look. Pressing himself against his companion, he stared through the eastward oriel until the strain of trying to see made his forehead throb as if he had bruised it. Still he found nothing.

Or something.

A hint of light at the boundary between sea and sky.

"There." He pointed. "Did you see it?"

At first, he thought that it was heat-lightning: a storm brewing. Almost immediately, however, he realized that he was wrong. The light did not flicker and glare. Instead it appeared to float on the distant turmoil of the seas.

Wind lashed at his eyes. It had become a gale.

"It resembles fog." The last of the Humbled sounded utterly dispassionate. "A luminous fog, lit from within. Storms which arise nowhere else clash within it." After a moment, he remarked, "The fog and its storms shroud an immense power. It brings havoc in all sooth, such havoc as no *Haruchai* has ever witnessed. Yet the power does not harm the seas. It merely disturbs them."

Waves hammered harder at the base of the cliffs. In spite of his numbness, Covenant felt the ground under his boots trembling.

Hell and blood. "That's the Worm?"

Coming from the east? Straight for the Great Swamp?

"I deem that it is. And it is swift. Yet the fog—and indeed the storms—run some distance ahead of their source." Branl turned to Covenant. "Ur-Lord, I must speak of this. Time remains to us. If you wish it, we may flee in safety. Wild magic will enable us to traverse many leagues ere this peril achieves landfall."

Covenant clenched his teeth until his jaws ached. "Who do you think you're kidding? We can't leave now. Not until we see what that thing does."

The eerie glow expanded on the horizon. Already it was distinct even to his marred vision. He felt its force in the wind on his face. Its teeth seemed to gnash at his cheeks. The luminescence did indeed resemble fog, vapor filled with lightning. But the lightning did not waver or strike: it *endured*, a convulsion of bolts without beginning and without end.

And the fog did not flow toward the southwest. Rather it sent tendrils like arms ahead of the storms, questing over an area as wide as the delta. Soon, however, even the most distant streamers began curving inward, reaching for Lifeswallower.

Reaching as if they had found the spoor of the Worm's prey.

Oh, bloody hell!

Bands of fog drifted over the seas. They drew closer with every harsh thud of Covenant's heart. Wild winds hurt his eyes, but he could not look away. Now he saw that the actinic glare within the brume was not truly constant. Instead of jumping and crackling, it swelled and receded incrementally, a slow seethe which belied the speed of its advance; a gradual rhythm like the undulating heave of a tremendous body. And every surge flung the vehemence of the waves harder against the cliffs. Collisions and crashes sounded like thunder; like the blare of steerhorns announcing ruin.

"Ur-Lord," Branl stated, "we must not delay. These forces threaten the headland. We cannot withstand them."

Damn it! The wind was trying to tell Covenant something. It urged him to *think*—

The inundation of Lifeswallower's delta. The bitter lash of salt.

If he judged only by smell, he would believe that the whole of the Great Swamp had already been ripped out of existence. Uncounted millennia of poisons no longer reeked; no longer spread their nauseating odors into the air. The fury of wind and water effaced every other perception.

Surely that *meant* something?

Streamers full of fatal light swept closer, riding the blasts. One of them poured up the precipice in front of Covenant and Branl. Squirming like a serpent of moisture, it writhed among the stones. A ribbon as luminous as the enchanted stone of the Lost Deep brushed Covenant's cheek before he could jump back. For an instant like a heartbeat, it appeared to curl around Branl. Its touch was damp and gelid, bitterly cold, as fierce as the caress of a *caesure*. But the fog did not react to Covenant and his companion; to Joan's ring or Loric's *krill*. Oblivious to anything that was not food for the Worm, it ran on along the wind, gusting westward.

Now Covenant saw a shape within the hermetic mass of the storms, a dark form limned by the heavy rise and fall of the lightning. Infelice had described the Worm as *no more than a range of hills* in size. *An earthquake might swallow it.* But to him, it looked more like a chain of mountains breasting inexorably through the seas. Its power was staggering: he was barely able to keep his feet. Perhaps his appalled senses exaggerated the Worm's physical bulk; but nothing could measure its sheer *force*. He was too human to look at it for more than a moment at a time.

By comparison, the lurker was trivial in spite of its polluted mass. It could do nothing to thwart the Worm's passage. It could only die.

And the World's End was definitely heading west. Toward Mount Thunder.

Hellfire! Hell and damnation! Covenant was thinking about the problem backward. The wind carried away the rancid effluviums of Lifeswallower and the Sarangrave. Of course it did. But considered from a different perspective, the gale *blocked* the fetor.

And how did the Worm find its prey? How did it locate the *Elohim* in their myriad hiding places? By scent. It smelled them out. Not in any ordinary sense, no. They did not emit a mundane aroma. But their magicks, the mystical essence of who they were: *that* the Worm could detect.

If those emanations could be detected, perhaps they could also be blocked. By a different kind of power. A force that was inherently *wrong* for the Worm, antithetical to its appetites.

More urgently, Branl insisted, "Ur-Lord."

The Worm's puissance had become explicit, even to Covenant's blunted nerves. Its might shone through the rigid rocks of the headland as if they were transparent.

He guessed that it was still two or three leagues out to sea. But at that speed— He had no time to doubt himself. Practically reeling, he wheeled away from the oriel; away from the heedless band of fog.

And as he moved, he yelled, "Feroce! I need you!"

Glints of green showed in the jumble. They were too far away.

"I need your High God! I need him *now*!"

The wind snatched words from his mouth. They disappeared among the stones, meaningless. Nevertheless the fires came closer. Gleams flashed from place to place, apparently running.

As the first creature emerged from the maze, the voice of the Feroce moaned urgently, "Pure One? What must our High God do? He must not perish!"

Streamers searched the turmoil of the delta. Lightning pulsed with every heave of the Worm's bulk. Seas hurled chaos at the cliffs. The silent shout of storms constrained by the Worm's aura made the ground under Covenant lurch as if the foundations of the promontory were in spasm.

An earthquake might swallow it. Under the right circumstances, Linden could trigger an earthquake. She and the Staff of Law had that kind of strength. Covenant did not: not with Joan's ring.

Haste and frenzy gripped him. "Listen fast." He was hardly coherent. "Try to understand. I don't want your High God dead. He can't fight the Worm. But he has to *act* like he's going to fight. He has to rear up. Make himself as big as he can. Right *there*." Covenant pointed at the drowned stretch of Lifeswallower to the north. "I need him to block the way," confuse the Worm's instincts, fill the Worm's senses with corrupt emanations; mask the powers hidden in Mount Thunder.

"*Ur-Lord*," protested Branl.

"Pure One?" The voice of the Feroce was a cry, a groan, a prayer. Their fires shuddered like the cliffs' bedrock. "We are little. Our minds are small. We do not—"

Covenant cut them off. "Just *tell* him!" He wanted to tear his hair. "I can't explain. I don't have time. I need him to *do it*. Rear up. Make himself *huge*. Pretend he's a barrier."

If the lurker did not panic—if the monster kept its word—

Frantically Covenant strove to impose comprehension on Horrim Carabal's acolytes. "The Worm doesn't want him. If he doesn't fight, it won't hurt him. But he has to look *big* enough to fight.

"*Tell* him! He can get out of the way if the Worm doesn't stop. But first he has to try to make it *pause*! He has to make it look somewhere else for food!"

Would that work? Of course not. Or not for long. But it might distract the Worm for a while. Slow it down. Buy a little time. Until the World's End found a different scent.

The Feroce could do what he asked of them. They could communicate swiftly enough. And the deeper waters of Lifeswallower were the lurker's true home. The core of the monster's mass and muscle lived there. If Horrim Carabal chose to do so, it could respond immediately.

Already the Worm had seethed a league closer.

Wind scattered the wailing of the Feroce among the stones. Their fires rose like screams. The gale did not touch their emerald theurgy, but the mounting convulsions beneath them did. The Worm's hunger made the flames flinch and bend.

Instead of answering, they turned and fled.

"Ur-Lord!" Branl demanded. He stood in the path of a glowing tendril, but it flowed around him as if he were nothing more than granite or basalt. "We must depart!"

Shaking his head, Covenant turned to peer down at the delta. "I just need a minute! I have to see if this is going to work!"

Please, God damn it! he begged the lurker. I almost killed myself against *turiya*. Clyme died for you. I know you're terrified. But you made a promise.

Why would Horrim Carabal comply? Covenant was asking the monster to dare its own extinction.

The lash of seas over Lifeswallower had become an undifferentiated flood.

Incoming waters tried to withdraw and could not: the imponderable forces of the Worm's approach drove them farther into the Great Swamp. Night had overtaken the Lower Land, but it changed nothing. The fog shed its own light. Its radiance made the hard stone of the headland seem as insubstantial as dreams. Through obstructions of rock, Covenant felt every rise and dip of the Worm's heaving. The rhythm of its undulations was slow. It seemed almost casual. Or perhaps it was sluggish yet. Nevertheless its speed—or its power—filled him with dismay. His chest felt ready to burst.

Desperately he stared past the rim of precipice, praying.

Branl put a hand on his shoulder. "Rallyn comes. We must ride."

The Humbled could have coerced Covenant; but Covenant ignored his companion. "Look!" Flailing one arm, he indicated the delta. "*Look!* Tell me what you see!"

Instead of pulling Covenant away, Branl moved to stand at the Unbeliever's side. *Your task is mine.* Leaning forward, he studied the thrash and clash of the flood. *I am alone and have no path other than my chosen service.* For a moment, he did not speak. Then he announced through the gale, "Ur-Lord, you are answered."

Answered?

"The lurker gathers beneath the waters. Its bulk is immense. I cannot gauge its full extent. At present, it does not rise. It merely gathers. Yet I deem that it will heed your wishes. Its presence serves no purpose else."

"Tell me," Covenant panted. "Tell me when it moves." The growing might of the Worm's aura snatched the air from his lungs. He struggled for every breath. "I can't *see*."

Luminescence shone through the stones, but it did not affect the Humbled. He seemed impervious to fog and catastrophe. He sounded more stolid than granite.

"Ur-Lord, there is more."

"More?" Hellfire! "Tell me!"

The Worm was coming closer. In all the world, only a few moments remained; a handful of heartbeats. If the Worm passed the lurker toward Mount Thunder, nothing would stop it.

"The lurker begins its rise," reported Branl impassively. "It is not alone."

Covenant fought to see; fought to breathe. At first, he could only discern the tumultuous scourge and moil of seas, the accumulating pressure of the Worm's advance. But then he thought that he saw darkness swell near the boundary between the delta and the ocean. The waters there piled higher as if they were surmounting an obstacle.

"Do you descry them, ur-Lord? They cling to the lurker's sides."

Covenant shook his head. He was sure of the monster now. In the center of his vista, it burst above the waves. Like a tectonic plate thrusting upward, the lurker jutted into the air. Breakers slammed against Horrim Carabal and were flung aside.

Brandishing scores of tentacles like threats, it stretched higher, taller than any Giant-ship. Its central mass was a match for the Worm's. And it spread itself wide, wider than the coming catastrophe: a barricade against havoc. Clearly the monster under-stood its task.

But *them*? Clinging to the lurker anywhere? No. His eyes were too weak.

The lurker was too weak as well. In spite of its size and muscle, its emanations did not reach Covenant. He felt every surge of the Worm's approach; felt the harsh chill of the fog and the static charge of lightnings. But Horrim Carabal was nothing more than a shape in the distance, scarcely visible: too mortal to hinder the World's End.

Nevertheless the Worm slowed. Apparently it could sense the lurker's presence, although Covenant could not. A wall of malign toxins had arisen from the waters. The Worm slackened its haste as if it had become uncertain.

Them?

Covenant tried to plead for an explanation, but he had no air and no words.

Yet clearly Branl had not forgotten the effects of Kevin's Dirt on Covenant. The Humbled answered Covenant's soundless query. "Ur-Lord, they are ur-viles. They are Waynhim."

Covenant stared, and panted, and could not think. Ur-viles and Waynhim? Here? Why?

Branl pitched his voice to pierce the blast's lurid wail. "I gauge that every surviv-ing creation of the Demondim has come to oppose the Worm. Holding to the lurker's flesh, they wield their lore. Black theurgies with the appearance of corrosion spread from hand to hand among them. These magicks are not liquid. Rather they resemble strands of incantation. As they expand, they take the form of a web."

Covenant cursed his inadequate sight. He ignored the shudders rising through the headland. Fervently he concentrated on Branl; listened as if he were counting every word.

"This web the creatures extend across the monster where it fronts the Worm. The sorcery of the web is fierce and bitter, rife with the unnatural fury of the Demondim, and of the Viles. I do not doubt that Linden Avery would name it *wrongness*. Yet the lurker takes no notice. Clearly the web does not pain the High God of the Feroce."

Covenant groaned and swore because he could not *see* it. He recognized only Hor-rim Carabal's bulk rising like midnight in the Worm's path. If the glow of the Worm's lurid aura glistened on the lurker's exposed flesh, or on the weird theurgy of the ur-viles and Waynhim, those sights lay beyond his reach.

Like the world at the mercy of its own death, he was mostly helpless, yet not help-less enough to be spared the burden of bearing witness. And he was not blind to the Worm. Its power shone, vivid as etch-work, through every crouched or yearning menhir around him. It shone through the flesh of his arms and chest, lit every bone.

He was as vague to himself as mist. Without Branl's solidity at his side, Branl's uncompromising substance, he might have been torn apart and scattered by the gale.

If he could not see the lurker distinctly—and could not see the creatures or their lore at all—he could still watch the approach of the World's End.

"It appears," Branl said, "that your ploy may accomplish its intent. The lurker and the Demondim-spawn present a barricade of ill and evil, of ancient poisons and unnatural knowledge. It does not bar wind and storm and seas, though the lurker's form does so. Yet it disturbs perception. It would offend Linden Avery's percipience. It defies my efforts to name its essence."

And it was working. Covenant felt that in every nerve of his disease-ridden body. It was *working*.

Like the lurker itself, the strange theurgy of the web confused the Worm's senses. In spite of their fluid shapes and their arrogance, the *Elohim* were beings of Law. They existed in accordance with the strictures of the Earth's creation. But Horrim Carabal was a perversion of Law. And the weird powers and comprehensions which the ur-viles and Waynhim had inherited or gleaned from their makers seemed to render Law meaningless. Together, the monster and the Demondim-spawn masked the scent of food.

Baffled, the Worm slowed again. Gradually it heaved to a halt.

A small tsunami pounded against the lurker, slashed at the web of sorcery. From border to border, the delta convulsed as if its foundations were vomiting. But Horrim Carabal withstood the assault. And the Demondim-spawn knew what they were doing. Their lore did not falter.

The Worm's storms and streamers searched to one side, explored the other. But the lurker had made itself *wide*. And the net of dark magicks covered Horrim Carabal from edge to edge. The webbing throbbed with acrid implications. The Worm's hunger hunted—and did not find.

This eerie equipoise between ruin and darkness would not last: Covenant knew that. The Worm was too powerful to be stymied indefinitely. The lurker or the Demondim-spawn might flinch at any moment. They might all die. But they were holding *now*. If they could stand until the Worm detected the spoor of some other *Elohim*—or until its primal needs urged it toward *Melenkurion* Skyweir—

A turn in the direction of the EarthBlood would bring the Worm straight at Covenant and Branl.

Clutching his companion, Covenant gasped, "Let's go! While we still can!"

His unlikely allies had achieved a tenuous pause. If the Land needed more time, Linden or some other power would have to provide it. Thomas Covenant had come to the end of what he could attempt as he was.

6.

Promises Old and New

The twilight did not change as Linden's company rode. A harsh grey held the landscape, a half-light without the softening of dawn or the soothing after sunset. It might have been the gloom before the onslaught of a storm, but there were no clouds. Despite the intrusion of Kevin's Dirt, the sky remained clear, fretted with doom, drawing the bright plaint of the stars closer, etching their deaths vividly against the fathomless abyss of their firmament. Linden could have believed that the Arch already trembled on the verge of collapse; but her health-sense insisted otherwise. The long strides of the Ranyhyn and the hoarse panting of the Giants insisted. Even in the absence of natural day, her pulse continued to measure out her life. And the blurred terrain continued to modulate around the company: a sign of movement that was also an affirmation that Time endured.

Riding with the Staff of Law and Covenant's white gold ring into the last dusk of the world, Linden tried to think of the unrisen sun in terms that did not terrify her. After all, the sun was simply another star. The Worm's power to affect or even extinguish it made a kind of sense. And did not the gloom itself assert that the sun was not altogether destroyed? The final dark had not yet claimed the Earth. Even in this crepuscular blight, hope might be possible.

Kevin's Dirt asserted the contrary. Indeed, it seemed stronger here than it had on the Upper Land. Even now, no more than an hour or two after the failed dawn, the vile fug had begun leeching the sensitivity from Linden's nerves, blunting her ability to discern the conditions of her companions and even the nature of the terrain; promising failure.

Accentuated by the dull light, the bloodstains that darkened the bottoms of Jeremiah's pajamas seemed to creep higher, opening like jaws to swallow him.

But the Ranyhyn ignored Kevin's Dirt. Running at a canter that accommodated the ragged endurance of the Giants, the horses had left behind the mounds surrounding the gully and the stream. Now they measured out the leagues across a hammered plain that appeared to stretch endlessly into an obscured future. Gloaming effaced the details of the landscape, rendered it effectively featureless in every

direction. Still the eaten chart of the stars and Linden's tarnished health-sense confirmed that the horses had not altered their heading. They reached for the northeast
with every stride, never hesitating.

Yet they did not neglect the needs of the Giants or their riders. In spite of Jeremiah's impatience, they paused at every clump of *aliantha*, every thin rill and brackish
pool. At such times, the boy refused to dismount. Instead he sat chafing until the
company was ready to run again.

By mute agreement, Linden, Stave, and Mahrtiir drank little and ate none of the
treasure-berries, leaving them for Coldspray and her comrades. Nonetheless it was
clear that the Swordmainnir were suffering. Linden heard an ominous wheeze in
Latebirth's respiration, and in Cirrus Kindwind's, and occasionally in Stormpast
Galesend's. The others heaved for breath against the weight of their armor and weapons. Their faces were grey with exertion.

At a time that should have been mid-morning, Manethrall Mahrtiir brought
Narunal to Hyn's side. "Ringthane," he called over the clatter of hooves, "we must
consider what we do. If we do not soon gain our aim, the Giants will be too weary to
aid your son. That they have come so far at such a pace bespeaks both great strength
and great valor. Yet they are mortal withal. Ere long, even they must falter."

"What do you suggest?" Linden could sustain the Swordmainnir with Earthpower
for a while. But repeated infusions of imposed energy would exact a price. The
women might well be left utterly prostrate when her assistance finally lost its efficacy.
Earthpower and Law were only Earthpower and Law: they could not counteract the
organic need for food and water and rest indefinitely. And Linden was reluctant for
other reasons as well. Speed might be Jeremiah's only defense. "Of course they need
rest. We all do. But the Worm is coming. You said it yourself. We have to hurry."

Mahrtiir faced her with disgust in his mien, but it was not directed at her. "For
that reason, Ringthane, I deem that we must part again. While you accompany your
son with Stave, I will remain to guide the Giants at a slower pace. Their aid may be
much delayed, but they will rejoin you *capable* of aid."

As if he expected Linden to demur, he added harshly, "I serve no other purpose in
this company. But I am able to ride brave Narunal, and to obey him—aye, and also to
comprehend his wishes. Therefore I await your consent."

Linden saw that Jeremiah was listening; felt protests rise in him. She phrased her
reply for his sake as much as for Mahrtiir's.

"That makes sense. Exhaustion won't help any of us." She forced a wry smile. "And
if anyone can convince Coldspray to be reasonable, you can. Maybe Stave and I can
help Jeremiah make a start without you."

Jeremiah brandished a fist in approval.

But Mahrtiir hesitated. "Then I crave a boon of you, Ringthane," he said after a moment. "Restore my discernment to its fullest, that my use to the Swordmainnir may be prolonged. It will not endure. Of that I am aware. But I yearn to postpone the return of complete futility."

In spite of herself, Linden was loath to comply. She did not want to raise black fire in a lightless world. The prospect felt like a violation. Yet she could not refuse the Manethrall. Had her fears been his, he would have faced them at once, eager for struggle and combat.

Adjusting her grip on the Staff of Law, she reached for Earthpower.

As she had expected or dreaded, her flames were barely visible. Their force was palpable enough, and to an extent comforting. But they were the hue of Jeremiah's fouled pajamas, the color of deepest night, and they seemed to thicken the gloom around them.

Nevertheless her magic was an expression of Law. Its inherent beneficence had not been altered. She had turned the wood to ebony in battle under *Melenkurion* Skyweir. In the graveyard of Jeremiah's mind, she had become a form of blackness herself. If her power disturbed her now, it did so because it told the truth about her.

As if she were abasing herself, she covered first Mahrtiir and then herself in cleansing theurgy. And when her senses had recovered their acuity, she extended fire to the Giants, gifting them with all of the vitality that she could provide.

Then Linden quenched her Staff. Slumping on Hyn's back, she told Mahrtiir weakly, "Be safe. Catch up with us when you can. We'll need you."

Clarion as a whinny, the Manethrall replied, "Fear nothing, Ringthane. We will come." Then he drew Narunal back from Linden's side so that he could speak to Rime Coldspray.

Hyn, Hynyn, and Khelen seemed to understand what had been decided without any word from Linden or Mahrtiir—or indeed from Stave. Running like water on a smooth slope, they extended their strides into a full gallop. In the lead, Jeremiah yelled his excitement at the heavens. Then he settled himself along Khelen's neck as if he sought to increase the young stallion's speed.

In moments, the Giants were no longer visible behind Linden. For a short time, she continued to feel their presence. Then the Ranyhyn outran the range of her health-sense, and she was alone with Stave and Jeremiah once again.

ᴕᴖᴕ

F rom the plain, the riders entered a region of jagged stones piled against each other like the detritus of a mountain broken by earthquake or cataclysm. Some of them resembled the riven limbs and torsos of megalithic titans. Others were towers about to topple, or raw chunks of granite and obsidian the size of Giantships, or splinters as sharp as spears. Among them, the footing was treacherous, and the horses were compelled to pick their way at a gait little quicker than a trot. As if in compensation, however, springs and streams became more plentiful. Most were too thick with minerals and old rot to drink; but a fair number were merely brackish, and a few ran clear, gurgling untainted from some buried source. As before, Linden and her companions had left all of their supplies with the Giants and Mahrtiir; but they found more than enough good water to appease their thirst.

Pausing at a stream where the Ranyhyn drank as though they did not expect to discover more water for a long time, Linden asked Stave where they were. Sure of himself, he replied that they were approaching a region like an isthmus of the Spoiled Plains between Sarangrave Flat to the north and the Shattered Hills in the southeast. She had guessed as much; but she was relieved to hear that the marge-land was ten leagues wide or more, and that beyond it the Spoiled Plains expanded to fill the Lower Land between the Sarangrave and the Sunbirth Sea. If the horses kept to their present heading, they would have nothing to fear from the lurker.

"Come on," Jeremiah muttered. "Come *on*." Then he sighed. "I'm hungry. I hope we find *aliantha* soon."

Sternly Stave remarked, "In the ages of the Lords, there were no *aliantha* on the Lower Land to the south of Lifeswallower. We are fortunate that they have taken root here during more recent millennia, sparse though they may be. But we cannot know how they were spread, or by whom. If we have ridden beyond their extent, we have no redress for their absence."

"That's easy for you to say," Jeremiah retorted; but he sounded impatient rather than irked. "You're *Haruchai*. I'm not. If we don't find treasure-berries, I hope you can think of something else for us to eat."

Stave's only reply was a shrug.

Soon the Ranyhyn were in motion again; and shortly after midday, they left that wrecked region behind. Now they ran, fleet as coursers, along a comparative flatland that lay at the foot of a long incline like the rim of a tectonic upheaval. There the running was easy, and the strides of the horses overcame distance as though the leagues were trivial.

Still the stars died overhead. Like Jeremiah, Linden was hungry. But in addition, she was beginning to share his frustration. A part of her did not want to discover malachite. It did not. Her reluctance was a thin whimper in the background of every thought. More would be required of her than she could bear to contemplate. Nevertheless the plight of the stars—and of the *Elohim*—infected her with urgency. The prospect of a lightless sky appalled her. Much as she disliked or even loathed the *Elohim*, their peril seemed more important than her personal fears.

The grey gloom wore on her like an old sore, immedicable, weeping vital fluids. While Hyn's muscles flexed under her, and the mare's sweat soaked into her jeans, irritating her legs, Linden began to wonder whether night would ever come again— and if it did, whether the Ranyhyn would allow themselves and their riders to rest. If Time remained essentially intact, surely some form of circadian cycle continued to rule the world? What would it mean if night did not come?

Her private dread seemed to grow more petty with every surmounted league, every troubled thought. Now she wondered how anyone could refuse to take the innominate risks that lay ahead of her. How could she? If she ever hoped to hold up her head in front of Jeremiah and Covenant again?

Gradually the incline swung away, surrendering to erosion. Beyond it, Stave called Linden's attention to the fact that the Ranyhyn were adjusting their course. "The northeast remains accessible," he informed her, "yet now our path tends toward the Sarangrave."

"Do you know why?" Memories of the marshland's fetor and the lurker's malevolence ached in her guts. She never wanted to approach the Flat again.

"I do not. *Haruchai* cannot commune with Ranyhyn as the Ramen do. However, I surmise that the horses require fodder. Among the wetlands on the verges of Sarangrave Flat, they may find grasses to sustain them."

"Can't the lurker reach them if they do that?"

"Indeed," Stave acknowledged. "Yet sustenance they must have, and there is none in this region. Nearer to the coastline, the devastation of Corruption's wars and workings eases. There forage may be found. But the distance is too great, even for the endurance of the Ranyhyn. If they would continue to run as they do, they must dare their ancient foe."

Oh, good, Linden muttered to herself. Perfect. Just what we need. Another fight with that monster. But she could feel a new trembling in Hyn's muscles, hear hints of frenzy in Hyn's respiration. Stave was probably right.

"Then we'll have to protect them." She meant herself. Her companions could not oppose the lurker—and the monster craved her Staff.

"Maybe we'll find *aliantha*," called Jeremiah. "If the ground grows other plants, it can grow treasure-berries."

"Maybe," Linden conceded. To Stave, she added, "If I get in trouble," if the Feroce cast their glamour over her mind again, "take the Staff. I don't care if you have to hit me to get it. Just don't let that monster have it."

"I hear you, Chosen." The former Master sounded as passionless as marble.

She trusted him. Nevertheless he eased none of her trepidations.

Still Khelen, Hynyn, and Hyn ran, defying their tangible exhaustion: the froth on their nostrils, the sweat on their coats, the ominous rattle in their mighty chests. At intervals, Linden refreshed them with brief blooms of Earthpower. But she did not use magic to extend her percipience. She did not want to know how near the Sarangrave might be.

Heading more north than east, the riders rushed down into a wide lowland like an ancient caldera. There the Ranyhyn found a few patches of scrannel grass, only a few mouthfuls apiece, hardly enough to blunt the keenest edges of their need. Then they resumed their stubborn race against the reaving of stars. Laboring painfully, they pounded up the slight slope at the far rim of the lowland; and still they ran.

In this direction, they would certainly encounter the Sarangrave. Linden tried to tell herself that they might find what they sought at any time; that their ordeal might end beyond the next rise, or somewhere in the next shallow vale. But she did not believe it.

Again and again, she came back to *trust*. She had given the Ranyhyn the only gift that was hers to grant; but neither she nor they could afford to rely upon it. She would have to simply trust that they could accomplish what they had asked of themselves.

A long time later, when her bestowed Earthpower had drained out of the horses entirely, the twilight began to thicken, become more viscid. A tumid dark crept out of the east to mask the contours of the landscape, deepen the bitter doom of the heavens. For a while, the dull light faded by minor increments, barely detectible: then it was gone altogether. Linden could not imagine how the Ranyhyn knew where to set their hooves. Nevertheless they did not falter. Perhaps they saw or felt the stars as clearly as she did. Perhaps they could hear the undefended lights pleading for redemption.

Absorbed by worries, she was slow to notice that she could smell water. It was dank and stagnant enough to be Sarangrave Flat, pervasive enough, fraught with implications of rot and dire corpses—but it was water nonetheless. And where there was water, there might be provender for the Ranyhyn.

As if to answer her, Khelen whickered weakly; and Stave said, "The Sarangrave is nigh, Chosen. It is shallow in this region. A fool who did not fear bogs and quags might wade for a league without encountering deeper streams. Yet I do not doubt that we are now within the ambit of the lurker's awareness."

He paused to let Linden respond. When she found nothing to say, he asked, "Will you now surrender the Staff? I cannot wield it. Yet its absence from your hands may serve to ward you."

"Not yet." She was shivering at the cooler air as though she shared the extremity of the horses. Her memories of the Feroce and the lurker were too recent. And yet the Ranyhyn appeared to be on the verge of stumbling to their knees. They had to have food and rest. "Not until we see the Feroce. They're the real danger." The theurgy of green fires cupped like instances of the Illearth Stone in their palms enabled them to enter her mind. They could erase the distinction between reality and memory. "The lurker can't reach us if we don't get too close."

"I don't care about that," Jeremiah put in. His voice seemed to come from the bottom of an abyss. "The Ranyhyn are desperate.

"I don't think I have the kind of power that's good for fighting. But I can be a distraction. I mean, since the lurker is so hungry for Earthpower. Maybe I can get its attention."

"Then stay back," Linden ordered hoarsely. "If you're going to distract anything, do it from a safe distance. Let Stave and me protect you."

As she spoke, Hyn's strides began to slow. Just for an instant, Linden thought that the mare had come to the end of her endurance. But the smell of water was so thick that it hurt Linden's sinuses; and she recognized almost at once that Hyn was slackening her gait deliberately.

Stave responded by urging Linden to dismount. "The littoral of the marsh is nigh. We must remain beyond the lurker's reach."

When Linden nodded her consent, Hyn staggered to a halt. While Linden slid to the ground, Stave sprang down from Hynyn's back. Lurching, Khelen brought Jeremiah to Linden's side. In spite of his impatience, Jeremiah did not complain as he dismounted. Instead he patted Khelen's neck, muttering, "Don't worry about me. I'll be all right."

The young stallion whickered thinly. Shambling into the darkness with Hyn and Hynyn, he headed toward water and forage.

While Linden watched the horses, Stave spoke again. "Await me, Chosen. I will attempt to discover *aliantha*. If I discern water which we may drink without harm, I will guide you to it."

At once, he followed the Ranyhyn. Like them, he disappeared as if he had been swallowed by the tenebrous air.

He may conceivably have wished to let Linden talk to Jeremiah alone. Beneath his *Haruchai* dispassion lay a familiar capacity for solicitude.

But what could she say to her son? In certain respects, she understood him too well. Trapped deep within him, a terrible storm was brewing. He needed his defenses, his urgent focus on a vital task, to contain the violence of his refused memories. And he was altogether too young for his years. Lost in dissociation, he had not had time to learn how to live with himself.

As gently as she could, she murmured, "You told Khelen not to worry, but I can't help it." Feeling him stiffen, she continued, "Oh, I'm not worried about the waiting. You can do that when you have to. You've had plenty of practice.

"No, it's what you want to do for the *Elohim* that scares me. A door like that— You'll have to make it so *big*. It's going to take time. And when you're done, it's going to be vulnerable. If we can't protect it—"

She would need help. She could no longer ignore that truth. More help than any of her friends could supply. Covenant himself had said it. *We're too weak the way we are. We need power.* More power than Loric's *krill* could summon, or the Staff of Law diminished by Kevin's Dirt, or a woman who was not a rightful white gold wielder.

At her side, Jeremiah relaxed a bit. "I know," he admitted grimly. "If we go through all that—I mean, if we find enough malachite, and the Giants help me build what I want, and it pulls the *Elohim* in, at least all the ones who're left—and then the Worm just swallows my door—" He shuddered. "That'll be worse than anything."

Hearing him reminded Linden of Kevin Landwaster and her own despair. Before she could respond, however, he said, "But, Mom." He sounded as harsh as the night. "I have to try. I don't know what else to do."

That, too, she understood. "Then listen to me," she returned more sharply than she intended. "Building your door— That's your part. And it's enough. It's *enough*. The rest is up to us." It was up to her. "We'll figure out a way to protect it. And if we can't, you'll just have to keep reminding yourself that *you did your part*. You aren't responsible for what happens after that."

"But it'll all be wasted!" he protested. "They'll all die."

High Lord Kevin must have felt the same before the Ritual of Desecration. Nevertheless his ancestors among the Dead had forgiven him. And Linden had missed her chance to take pity on Elena. From She Who Must Not Be Named, Linden had learned how much her self-absorption had cost Covenant's daughter.

"No," she replied carefully, "it won't be wasted. I can only imagine how bad it might feel to see something that you built destroyed. Especially something like *that*. But *listen* to me. In a way, I've only known you for a day and a half, and already I'm so proud of you that I don't have any words big enough for it. Now I understand what parents mean when they talk about their hearts bursting."

She gathered passion as she spoke. Her own parents had never felt that way about her. Not once. The bitter legacies of her childhood filled her voice. Trying to sway her son, she was pleading for herself.

"For all of those years when I was taking care of you, do you know how many times I wondered if it was all wasted?" If she had opened her heart and lavished her love for nothing? "I'll tell you. I *never* wondered. It was always worth doing, all of it.

"Of *course* I cared about what might happen. Of *course* I wanted you to find your way out. I wanted you with me. But I didn't adopt you and love you because of what *might* happen. I did it because you were *always* precious to me, every minute of every day. You were enough. I didn't need to know the future to know that you were worth everything."

She felt frustration from him, a rising denial; but she over-rode it.

"So maybe you won't be able to build your door after all. Maybe we won't be able to protect it after you make it. Maybe the *Elohim* and the stars and all of us are doomed. So what? Right here, right now, you want to do everything you can to help, and that's wonderful. If the Worm eats your door, and you feel so hurt and angry and useless that you can't stand it, remember that I'm *proud* of you."

"Stop it, Mom." He was crying, and trying not to show it. "*Nobody's* proud of a failure."

"That's nonsense." Instinctively she responded as if he were a normal boy, able to hear her. "Failure isn't something you *are*. It's something you *do*." She needed to hear what she was saying. With every word, she pleaded for an answer to her mute dread. "Having the courage to escape your prison is who you are. Wanting to help the *Elohim* because the world needs them is who you are. My son is who you are. Everything else is just making mistakes, or not having the right materials or enough help, or not knowing enough, or trying to do something that's actually impossible. It just *happens*. It isn't who you are."

With her whole heart, she asked, "How do you suppose Covenant managed to save the world *twice*? It isn't because he's stronger or smarter or greater than Lord Foul. He's just stronger and smarter and greater than Lord Foul *thinks* he is. He's had the right kind of help. And he isn't afraid to take the chance that he's going to fail."

"Mom." Jeremiah was crying openly now. "Mom, stop. Please. I need— I need—"

She understood that as well. Who would, if she did not? Remembering Anele— remembering *Must* and *Cannot* and the old man's last valor, an act of self-confrontation that humbled her—she dropped her Staff and swept her son into her arms. Hugging him tightly, she murmured his name to him as if it confirmed his worth.

Like a young boy, he sobbed hard for a moment—and like a teenager, he suppressed his pain quickly. For a heartbeat or two, he held his mother as she held him. Then he let go of her, stepped back from her clasp. Snuffling loudly, he rubbed his face with both hands, wiped his nose on his forearm. In a congested voice, he asked, "What's taking Stave so long? The Flat is right over there." He gestured uselessly in the darkness. "I'm hungry. He should be back by now."

Well, he was a fifteen-year-old boy, embarrassed by what he considered a show of weakness. For his sake, Linden smiled ruefully. Her sigh of regret she kept to herself.

"I'm sure—" she began. But before she completed the sentence, she felt the former Master's severe aura returning.

"It's about time," Jeremiah muttered. Then he called to Stave, "Did you find *alian-tha*? Are we that lucky?"

Almost immediately, Stave arrived, a darker shape condensed from the raw stuff of night. His hands were full of damp plants. "I did not," he answered. "However, I have discovered tubers which I deem edible. They resemble the roots from which the Ramen prepare *rhee*. Cooked, they will provide sustenance."

Linden smiled again. As warmly as she could, she thanked the former Master. Then she asked her son, "What do you think? Can you use your Earthpower for cooking?" Had he gained that much control over his inheritance? She hoped so. He needed a chance to recover his sense of competence. "I can do it, but I'm more likely to attract attention that we don't want."

She did not doubt that the lurker would devour Jeremiah avidly. But she also felt sure that the monster would find her Staff better suited to its particular hunger.

Eager to put aside his distress, Jeremiah extended his halfhand, accepted a root. "I'll give it a try."

As he did so, Linden retrieved the Staff, braced herself on its possibilities. Then she turned every dimension of her remaining discernment toward Sarangrave Flat, searching for some sign of the lurker—or of the Feroce.

After a moment, she located the Ranyhyn. They stood along the verge of a stagnant pool, cropping bitter grasses and vaguely pernicious shrubs with apparent unconcern. Clearly no hint of the lurker disturbed them. Nor did what they ate.

The wetland beyond them looked shallow. Its waters ran in sluggish streams or sat in rancid ponds interrupted by small eyots of grass or twisted brush; by occasional trees gnarled and stunted in putrefying mud; by brief swaths of reeds that nodded back and forth like conspirators in the currents and the breeze. Everything within the range of Linden's percipience reeked of age and decomposition and ancient malice. Darkness covered the Flat, as funereal as a grave-cloth. Nevertheless nothing suggested the presence of the lurker or its acolytes.

At her back, she felt a short burst of fire. At once, it winked out. Jeremiah snorted in quick disgust, but his concentration did not waver.

A moment later, she sensed heat. It flickered, shrank, threatened to die out, then swelled more strongly. "Ha!" Jeremiah panted. "So *that's* how—"

Soon he was able to hold his magic steady. The smells of cooking joined the thick odors of the Sarangrave.

Somewhere in the depths of the wetland, a night bird cried: a wail of fright. Linden heard a sharp splash, a sucking sound. She may have heard the clamp of teeth. The cry was cut off. More distant birds squalled as they took flight. From other directions came the rustle of disturbed roosting; the squirm of thick bodies in mud; the plash of creatures that may have been fish. After its fashion, Sarangrave Flat was thick with life.

Still nothing resembled the lurker. Nothing warned of the Feroce.

Before long, Jeremiah let his Earthpower dissipate. "Ow!" he muttered cheerfully. "That's hot." Then he bit into the tuber. Through a mouthful of crunching, he announced, "Tastes like dirt." But he did not stop eating.

By degrees, Linden began to relax.

Jeremiah took another root from Stave, summoned fresh theurgy. "Your turn, Mom," he murmured as he worked. "It's actually pretty good, if you pretend you can't taste it."

"Stave?" Linden asked over her shoulder.

"I keep watch, Chosen." The *Haruchai*'s tone hinted at reproof. She should have known that he was always alert. "Doubtless the Ranyhyn also will give warning at need. Eat while you may." A beat later, he added, "I have yet to discover clean water."

Linden hesitated to lower her guard. She had encountered the lurker more than once—and once was too often. But hunger overcame her uncertainty. With an effort, she turned her back on the Sarangrave.

Jeremiah had nearly finished cooking a second tuber. He held it in his halfhand with his left cupped over it. A faint glow of heat radiated between his palms. When he judged that root was ready to eat, he handed it to Linden.

"Just remember. Pretend you can't taste it."

Stave was right, of course: when Linden studied the steaming tuber, she saw that it was safe to eat. More than that, it would strengthen her if she ate enough of it. Swallowing hard to clear the discomfiture from her throat, she took a bite.

"Dirt," she answered Jeremiah's expectant gaze. "Just like dirt." In fact, the crisp plant was bland at first; but it had a sour after-taste that made her yearn for the cleanliness of *aliantha*. Nevertheless she ate it while Jeremiah cooked another root for himself. She had no choice. She was facing a future which might never contain another meal.

ℭ

After Jeremiah had finished preparing all of the roots, and he and Linden had eaten as much as their stomachs could tolerate, Stave left again to search farther for water.

He was gone for what seemed like a long time. While he was absent, the Ranyhyn withdrew from the edge of the wetland, putting a little distance between themselves and the disturbing seethe of the waters. But they did not go far. Linden felt them clearly enough, resting between her and the Sarangrave.

When the former Master returned, he announced that he had located safe water in an eddy cast by the turbid seethe of the Flat. It was admittedly brackish and tainted, but not so foul that it would make Linden and Jeremiah ill. There they were able to quench their thirst before the impulse to gag became too strong to suppress.

Returning to the place where they had eaten, Linden urged her son to get some sleep while he could. Then she searched out a relatively level patch of ground for herself. With the Staff clasped across her chest, and her eyes closed against the dying of the stars, she tried to take her own advice.

But her fears nagged at her. They seemed to crawl over her skin under her clothes. Soon, she knew, events might compel her to forsake her son. She had it in her to imagine a source of malachite, and the aid of the Giants, and a portal which would summon the *Elohim*. Those ideas only asked her to believe in the Ranyhyn and her friends and Jeremiah. But guarding the portal against the Worm would require a miracle, and she had none to offer. Therefore—

Ah, God. Therefore she would have to go in search of a power great enough to accomplish what she could not. She would have to leave Jeremiah to the care of her friends. If she did not, everything that he hoped to accomplish would indeed be wasted.

The fact that she lacked the courage was no longer relevant. Like Jeremiah, she would have to try.

Only Covenant's return might spare her. She yearned for that. But she could not suppose that he would come. The task which he had undertaken was too dangerous, and he was too far away. No, the burden of preserving Jeremiah's construct was hers to bear in spite of her weakness. She could not hope to be spared. The Worm of the World's End was coming. Nothing that lived would be spared.

Gradually she found a kind of resignation. It felt like defeat, but it allowed her to drift into a sleep too stunned and shallow for dreams.

∞

Hynyn's shrill whinny awakened her with the suddenness of a knife. Even before Stave said her name, she began drawing black fire from her Staff.

Reflexively she glanced at the sky to gauge the time. Dawn was near, although it did not promise a sunrise. Nevertheless a certain amount of light was coming. Without it, the air would have been colder. Soon the darkness would become gloaming.

Then she felt the Ranyhyn running. Urgently they fled from the vicinity of the Sarangrave.

Why did they not pause for their riders? They could have taken her and her companions to safety.

But she had no time to think about such things. At Stave's command, she surged to her feet.

Jeremiah was ahead of her. He stood squinting in the direction of the Sarangrave. Before she could speak, he pointed.

"The Feroce. They're coming this way." A heartbeat later, he added, "I can practically smell the lurker."

"Indeed, Chosen." Stave sounded as calm as a clear day. "Now you must release the Staff of Law to me. I will ward it."

Like her son, Linden stared at the crouching malevolence of the wetland. At first, she discerned nothing except the movement of small bodies. As they bobbed past obstructions, they appeared to fade in and out of existence. But then they passed the last islets of trees and brush, and emerald flames the precise hue of the Illearth Stone opened in the darkness. At the same time, the air became thicker: more humid, rank with moisture.

"How many?" She wanted confirmation. She counted six flames, therefore only three Feroce. But somewhere behind them she felt the bitter aura of the lurker. Surely the monster would not challenge her without more support?

"Three," Stave stated as if he could not be mistaken. "Also I sense but one tentacle. More may come, but the one lingers a stone's throw behind its minions."

"Mom?" Jeremiah asked anxiously. "Shouldn't you give Stave the Staff? You said those things can mess with your mind."

Linden ignored him. "This doesn't make sense," she muttered. "The last time, there were a lot more. And now I'm braced for them. What does that monster think three Feroce can do?"

"Who can declare the lurker's thoughts?" Stave responded. "Yet the peril remains. And it will be directed at you, Chosen. The monster covets the Staff of Law."

"Then be ready." Linden tightened her grip on the ebon wood. "If they're going to say anything, I want to hear it while I can still defend myself."

"Mom!" Jeremiah protested. But Stave did not remonstrate.

Leaving the marsh, the creatures approached with an air of hesitation or timidity. They were still some distance away, but her nerves read them clearly. They were hairless and naked, apparently frail. In their large round eyes, green glints reflected like threats. Only their flames implied any force. But their magicks were strange to her, nameless and unrecognizable. The capering fires could have been desecrated Wraiths, captured and cruelly transformed. Or—

Hell, they could have been anything.

Why had the Ranyhyn fled without their riders?

The question suggested possibilities that nearly staggered her. Perhaps it was deliberate. Perhaps the horses had taken her close to Sarangrave Flat once before precisely so that the lurker's acolytes could draw her into the monster's reach—

The Ranyhyn feared the lurker: she knew that. Mahrtiir had accounted for their terror clearly enough. But she could not believe that they had betrayed their own devotion. So maybe they had risked attracting their ancient foe—then and now—for a reason. A reason that had nothing to do with shelter or weariness.

What reason? she asked herself wildly. Did they *want* her to lose her Staff? Did they want the lurker to have it?

They were the *Ranyhyn*. They would not forsake their riders without a compelling reason.

The Feroce were drawing near, still timorously, but still coming—and Linden was out of her depth; foundering.

"Chosen," Stave said like the night. "If you do not attend, I must claim the Staff without your consent."

"Give it to him, Mom!" Jeremiah demanded. "Do it *now*. You aren't paying attention!"

She gripped the Staff as though her life depended on it. She was paying attention to too many things at once.

The Feroce stopped ten paces away. Instead of spreading out, they stood close together. "We are the Feroce," they announced as if Linden had never faced them before. They all spoke, yet they seemed to share one voice: a voice as moist and malleable as mud. But they did not continue. In silence, they awaited a response.

"What is it this time?" retorted Linden. "You've already attacked us once. Isn't that enough? What do you want now?"

The creatures flinched. Their voice quavered. "Our High God commands. We must speak."

Again they fell silent.

Linden trembled with remembered distress and pain. Covenant's farmhouse erupting in flame around her. Recursive memories looping back on themselves, blocking her escape. She Who Must Not Be Named. "Then speak," she snapped. "But don't think that you can hurt me again. I know you now. I won't leave any of you alive."

The Feroce recoiled a step. They needed a moment to rally their resolve. When they replied, their voice was faint, squeezed out of them by pressures which they could not refuse.

"We speak for our High God. We bear a message from the Pure One."

The Pure One? Where had Linden heard that term before?

"I'm listening."

Her manner must have appalled the creatures. They quailed as though they might dissolve at any moment.

"Our High God has offered an alliance with the Pure One. It has been accepted. No harm will come to you that our High God or the Feroce can prevent. You will be given aid at need."

Linden stared, reeling inwardly. She could hardly understand what she heard. Who would form an alliance with the lurker? Who was that crazy?

Given aid—?

Panting at the viscid air, she asked involuntarily, "The Pure One?"

In a tone like a sheet of basalt, Stave said, "The *sur-jheherrin* spoke of the ur-Lord as the Pure One. They esteemed him by that title, though he deemed the Pure One to be Saltheart Foamfollower."

"Covenant!" Jeremiah crowed. "He must have done something to that monster. It's afraid of him!"

Now Linden remembered. In the Sarangrave with Covenant, Sunder, and Hollian. A few *Haruchai*. Her first meeting with the Giants. The lurker's attack. Then the rescue by the *sur-jheherrin*.

The Pure One.

Covenant was alive? Alive?

The Feroce reacted as though Jeremiah had offended them. Their posture stiffened. The fires in their hands grew brighter, shedding green light like malice. Their voice gained strength.

"Afraid? Our High God fears the cruel metal. He does not fear the Pure One. Nor does he fear the wielder of the stick of power. Blades and burning he withstands. Yet a havoc which he cannot withstand approaches. He must live. Failing to obtain the stick of power, he sought alliance with the Pure One. The terms were agreed."

Then the creatures appeared to remember that they were little and frightened. They shrank within themselves. Their tone suggested awe or dismay. It may have held gratitude.

"The Pure One has exceeded the terms. This our High God acknowledges. The alliance is sealed."

"All right!" Jeremiah exulted. "All *right*!"

Covenant was *alive*. He had to be. Linden clung to that. She had only encountered the Feroce two nights ago, and Covenant had turned away from her two days before that, rushing to meet the crisis of *caesures* and *turiya* Raver and Joan. But he had so far to go—He must have met with the lurker, or the Feroce, after Linden did, but before he found his ex-wife. Indirectly Infelice had confirmed it. In Muirwin Delenoth, she had said that the lurker's minions were aiding him. Yet when could he have fulfilled—exceeded—his promises to the lurker? He would not have allowed any agreement to distract him from Joan. Therefore he must have sealed his incomprehensible alliance *after* that confrontation. He must have survived it.

But Stave's demeanor did not soften. "Continue," he said, implacable as a force of nature. "You bear a message from the Pure One. When was it given to you? Where was it given?"

The Feroce made placating gestures. "The Pure One named his wishes in the early hours of this same night. Our High God was lost. Then he was redeemed. Far to the east, the Pure One made his desires known."

This same night? Covenant had stopped Joan. He had lived through the ordeal. There was no other explanation. Linden wanted to fling herself at the creatures; hug them in gratitude. Covenant had *redeemed* the lurker? But she could not move. The extremity of her relief held her.

This was what the Ranyhyn had done to her. For her. For the Earth. They had exposed her to their worst nightmares and fled so that she might inspire an alliance with the evil which had slain great *Kelenbhrabanal*, Father of Horses.

From the first, they had *trusted* her—

"Then deliver his message," Stave commanded.

Bobbing and cowering, the creatures complied. "The Pure One has exceeded the terms," they repeated. "Therefore our High God commands us to convey words from the Pure One. They are meant for the wielder of the stick of power. The words are these."

Waved flames left emerald cuts across the darkness. "Remember forbidding."

Like a sovereign enchantment, that utterance altered the conditions of Linden's existence. Realities veered around her or within her, effacing the tangible world where she gripped her Staff; transforming the causes and sequences which ruled her known life. The night and the Feroce vanished. Stave and Jeremiah were gone. Every vestige of Sarangrave Flat passed away.

For one sickening instant, she understood that the creatures had done it to her again. They had imposed their glamour on her memories. Her belief that she was ready to resist was an illusion.

Then that knowledge was swept away in a moil of altered revelations. It was forgotten as if it had no meaning.

Without transition, she stood on a fan of obsidian marked like her jeans with green stains; with streaks of malachite crooked as veins. The light of Liand's *orcrest* defined the stone. Utter darkness filled the rest of the world. Imponderable leagues of stone stretched overhead, held in place by their preserved recollections. Other figures clustered nearby, but she could not see them. Before her, Anele lay prone on the fan with his arms splayed as if in crucifixion. Grief and enduring pain marked every line of his emaciated form, the mute woe of Mount Thunder's foundations.

"It is here." The words were etched in Linden's mind. "The wood of the world has forgotten. It cannot reclaim itself. It requires aid. Yet this stone remembers. There must be forbidding." His voice sounded harsh as rock. In Salva Gildenbourne, he had referred to *the necessary forbidding of evils*. Now he insisted, "If it is not forbidden, it will have Earthpower. If it is not opposed by the forgotten truths of stone and wood, *orcrest* and refusal, it will have life.

"When the Worm of the World's End drinks the Blood of the Earth, its puissance will consume the Arch of Time."

The forgotten truths? Linden wanted to ask. What truths? But Anele's distress kept her silent.

Then he lifted his head, looked directly at her with his blind eyes. As if he were speaking for someone else, he said precisely, "Everybody concentrates on stone, but that's not the whole story. Wood is important, too."

Forgotten, she thought. Forbidding.

It requires aid.

Like an affirmation or a denial, reality veered again. In silence that battered her like the clamor of mighty bells, she was driven deeper, farther. Anele and stone vanished. Mount Thunder's betrayed sorrow evaporated as though it had never existed.

Linden feared the bitterness of killing her mother, the horror of watching her father's suicide. Instead she felt the barren dirt of Gallows Howe under her feet, bereft by the knowledge of endless slaughter, and crowded with wrath; avid to repay the cost of so much death. She sensed recrimination and the long butchery of trees. Music had brought her here, the fraught melody of Caerroil Wildwood's singing. Again she was not alone, but she could not see her companion. She saw only the Forestal.

He stood beside the dead trunks of his gibbet with song streaming from his robe as if the fabric were woven from threnodies and dirges. The silver vivid in his eyes hinted at wild magic, although he had no white gold. His beard had the luster of age and vigor and unending travail.

"While humans and monsters remain to murder trees," he mused, angry and doleful, "there can be no hope for any Forestal. Each death lessens me."

Showing more restraint than Linden had any right to expect, he sang, "I have granted boons, and may do so again. But you have not requested that which you most require. Therefore I will exact no recompense. Rather I ask only that you accept the burden of a question for which you have no answer."

He enthralled and terrified her. Her own anger was fresh from her failure to rescue Jeremiah; from the carnage of stone under *Melenkurion* Skyweir. Her heart was as hard as the mountain's, and as flawed.

"How may life endure in the Land," inquired Caerroil Wildwood, "if the Forestals fail and perish, as they must, and naught remains to ward its most vulnerable treasures? Must it transpire that beauty and truth shall pass utterly when we are gone?"

"I don't know." What else could she say?

Another voice, the voice of her companion, said, "He does not require that which the lady cannot possess. He asks only that she seek out knowledge, for its lack torments him. The fear that no answer exists multiplies his long sorrow."

And because she stood on Gallows Howe—and because her spirit burned for Thomas Covenant after her failure to redeem her son—and because Caerroil Wildwood could still wring her heart in spite of all that she had endured—she made a promise that she did not know how to keep.

"I will."

Then the Forestal took the Staff of Law, black as fuligin after her battle—and she lay on her back on the hard ground with the night sky above her like the abyss that awaited all striving. A sensation of impact throbbed in her forehead, a shock too sudden to bring instant pain. The hurt would come later; soon. Her neck felt wrenched and torn. Dying stars filled her eyes, consumed one after another in slow sequence by the Worm's unappeasable hunger.

"Damn it, Stave!" Jeremiah yelped. He plunged to his knees beside her. "Did you have to hit her so hard?"

Stave replied without inflection. "She fell under the glamour of the Feroce. I could not scry what might transpire. And her grip on the Staff was urgent."

Linden thought, You hit me?

She had told him to do so.

She could not look away from the ruin of the heavens; the inexorable depredations. Too many things had been made clear to her. The actions of the Ranyhyn were only the most immediate of her new insights—and the least cruel.

"Mom!" Jeremiah urged, tugging at her shoulders. "Are you all right? Can you move? Stave is too strong."

Because he was her son, she dragged her gaze down from the sky. His face was a smear of darkness. Dawn was coming, but it did not ease the night. Without her health-sense, she would not have been able to trace the outlines of Jeremiah's alarm.

What—? she tried to ask; but she made no sound. Lingering comprehensions clogged her throat. And her neck was starting to ache. She might not be able to lift her head. The throb in her forehead became a rusty blade. Soon it would cut.

Somehow she forced herself to ask aloud, "What—?"

Quick with concern, Jeremiah told her, "The Feroce did—whatever it was. You went blank. When you didn't come back, Stave hit you to take the Staff. I guess that broke you loose. Now they're leaving.

"But, Mom," he added, hurrying. "The lurker— You've got to see this. If you can stand. If Stave didn't break your neck."

Percipience assured Linden that her neck was not broken. Raising her head would hurt; but it would only hurt.

"I," she breathed through a rising pulse of pain. "Can. Try."

In one smooth motion, Stave scooped her from the ground. Cradling her neck, he held her in his arms for a moment. Then he lowered her legs gently. When her boots were settled on the dirt, he offered the Staff of Law to her weak grasp.

"It is yours, Chosen. I have no virtue to wield its healing, but you are able to relieve the harm of my blow."

Her hands were numb. She could not feel the warm wood. Stave had hit her too hard. Nevertheless her Staff was there. She seemed to hear it murmuring to her, urging her to call on its benign strength.

Instinctively she summoned black flames to lave her as if they were the waters of Glimmermere.

Her heart seemed to stagger in its beat. Then Earthpower and Law took hold. Her shock and hurt began to ease. She recognized her surroundings more clearly, identified Jeremiah and Stave as if their substance had been affirmed by fire. In the distance, she discerned the Ranyhyn. They appeared to be waiting, watching; perhaps praying. When she turned her head hesitantly in the opposite direction, she saw Sarangrave Flat crouching along the horizon, a starker and more telic dark within the enshrouding night.

"Look, Mom," Jeremiah insisted. "You won't believe it."

No proffered or sealed alliance could soften her fear of the lurker. But when she looked—when she focused her health-sense as well as her inadequate sight—she saw a single tentacle rising from the disturbed muck of the wetland. It stood taller than any Giant, far taller, and as erect as a sentinel. All of its many fingers, hundreds of them, were curled and clenched as though they feared an attack. Yet the lurker's arm did not flinch or waver.

Horrim Carabal. The Ardent had told Linden the monster's name.

She gripped her Staff more tightly, absorbed more fire.

When it was certain of her attention, the tentacle dipped as if in acknowledgment or homage.

"See that?" Jeremiah breathed. "Did you see that?" He sounded proud. "It bowed to you, Mom. The lurker *bowed* to you."

Before Linden could reply, the tentacle slipped back into its fouled waters. At first, it appeared to leave no ripples in its domain. But then she saw the massive arm squirm away, a crooked seethe through the stagnant pools and mud. As it retreated, the air became easier to breathe. In moments, Horrim Carabal had withdrawn beyond the reach of her perceptions.

"Amazing," Jeremiah proclaimed more strongly. "I don't know what Covenant did, but he sure got that thing's attention."

"Be wary, young Jeremiah," Stave advised. "The lurker of the Sarangrave is malevolence incarnate. The actions of the Ranyhyn speak of this, if your own discernment does not."

Then he turned to Linden. "By your earlier account, Chosen, the glamour of the Feroce inspires you to relive events and perils belonging to your former world. We cannot interpret the lurker's intent until you speak of this new visitation."

Carefully Linden leaned her head from side to side, tested the effects of Earthpower. Joints popped: stiffness lingered in her neck: pain still throbbed in her forehead. But she was essentially intact.

And dawn was near. There was an unmistakable paling in the east.

"Well, I know one thing, anyway." Anele's prophecy and Gallows Howe left her hoarse. "This is what the Ranyhyn were hoping for.

"The last time, they did it on purpose. They took us close enough to the Sarangrave for the Feroce to find us. They wanted us to meet the lurker and beat it so that it would know we were too strong for it. It already knew that it couldn't fight Covenant. Not when he has the *krill*." Clearly Horrim Carabal had not forgotten the agony of Covenant's power millennia ago. "The Ranyhyn wanted it to understand that it can't fight us, either.

"After that, I'm guessing. But I think that the Feroce must have approached Covenant. Infelice said something—"

Stave would remember. Jeremiah might not. He had been absorbed in his construct.

"The Feroce must have talked to him about an alliance. Whatever he said, it must have satisfied them." And he had done more: that was obvious. She simply could not imagine what it might have been. "In any case, the Ranyhyn brought us here tonight because"—she shrugged awkwardly—"well, because they needed fodder, of course. But they also wanted to know where the lurker stands now. Or they wanted us to know."

And they had trusted both her companions to take care of her however the lurker reacted.

With a subtle air of satisfaction, Stave asserted, "The Unbeliever has exceeded the terms, as is his wont. The alliance is sealed. It is my thought that the lurker fears the Worm. Therefore it craves power. And therefore it seeks allies.

"Yet, Chosen," he continued, "you have said naught of your experience within this new glamour. Your interpretation of the Ranyhyn I accept. I have none better. Will you now speak of the visions imposed upon you?"

Linden did not want to reply. What she had learned or deduced was too great for her. She did not know where she would find the courage to bear it.

I will. She had promised that she would seek out an answer for Caerroil Wildwood. An answer which she could not possibly possess. For that reason, and because her company did not suffice for its task, she would have to forsake her son.

"It wasn't like the last time," she said, striving for a steadiness that she could not feel. "It wasn't terrifying. First I was down in the Lost Deep. Before we crossed the Hazard. I heard Anele reading that fan of obsidian and malachite. Then I was back on Gallows Howe with Caerroil Wildwood. The Feroce reminded me that I made a promise then. I told him that I would find out how the world could survive without Forestals."

Now she felt certain that the world could not.

"But why?" Jeremiah asked quickly. "I mean, why did they want to remind you? It's not like you were ever going to forget things like that."

Linden believed that she understood the point of Covenant's message. And she surmised that the Feroce had tried to ensure that she did not misinterpret it. But she did not say so. Instead she deflected Jeremiah's query.

"Maybe the lurker doesn't really understand alliances. It's used to having worshippers. Alliances are new. Sure, I was never going to forget. But the lurker can't know that. It's just choosing between powers that can hurt it. The Worm is going to destroy everything. The lurker is bargaining for its life."

After a moment, Jeremiah conceded, "That makes sense, I guess."

Stave regarded her with his customary lack of expression. Briefly he lifted his head as if he were scenting the air. Then he said, "Dawn begins. It appears that the coming day will resemble the one past. And the Ranyhyn return. Doubtless they will feed again. Then we must hasten once more."

Linden nodded to escape more inquiries. Unlike the horses, she was not hungry. The roots that she had eaten still lay in her stomach, a fibrous mass difficult to digest. At uncomfortable moments, its taste returned to the back of her throat. But water was a necessity.

"In that case," she told the *Haruchai*, "we should get something to drink while we still can."

He flicked a glance toward her, but did not demur. And Jeremiah agreed at once. Already he was eager again; impatient.

In the rising gloom of a new day—the second since the sun had failed—Linden and her son followed the former Master back to the eddy where they had risked the water the previous evening.

The possibility that they might not find the like again did not trouble her as much as the prospect of her own intentions. They were too much for her: one appalling risk piled on another until their sheer scale threatened to overwhelm her.

7.

Taking the Risk

Soon Linden, Jeremiah, and Stave were mounted and running again, heading away from the Sarangrave directly into the northeast. Hyn's straining betrayed that the mare had not recovered her full strength. Both Hynyn and Khelen labored over the barren terrain. Still they had reserves of stamina. Linden understood their physical prowess no better than she comprehended their ability to find their way within *caesures*, or their strange insight into the mind of Horrim Carabal. She knew only that Earthpower flowed richly in their veins. They seemed to draw their vitality from the Land itself, regardless of its blasted condition.

Kevin's Dirt loomed overhead, but she banished its effects almost reflexively. The threat of the lurker was behind her, and she no longer feared to exert her Staff.

Gradually the darker gloom of night became a kind of twilight over the region. Ahead of her, the ground undulated in slow dips and gradual rises toward its dulled horizons. Then the terrain became rougher—the hollows deeper, the sides steeper—until the horses appeared to traverse a protracted series of impact craters: the ancient outcome of fallen meteors, or of terrible bolts of theurgy. But the Ranyhyn were not daunted. Instead they seemed to gain fresh resolve from the difficulties, as if they were nearing their obscure destination.

And eventually the terrain on Linden's right began rising. Along a line parallel to the path of the mounts, southwest to northeast, the stricken ground piled higher until it formed a ridge with a front as sheer as a cliff and a more gradual slope at its back. To her left were only more hollows or craters; but opposite them, the ridge jutted with its gutrock exposed as if a range of higher hills had been cleft.

Approaching the highest point of the ridge, the Ranyhyn slowed. Rubble, boulders, and other detritus cluttered the base of the cliff, but did not extend far enough to obstruct the horses. Hyn, Hynyn, and Khelen had a different reason for easing their pace.

In the lead, Jeremiah rose on Khelen's back as if he were standing in stirrups. He punched his fists at the sky, defying the reaving of the stars. "This is *it!*" he shouted. "Malachite! That cliff is *riddled* with it!"

While Hyn jolted to a trot, Linden tried to spot what Jeremiah had seen.

At first, the profile of the ridge held her. From her perspective, it cut off perhaps a third of the heavens. Irrationally she hoped that she would not see more stars dying. But the slow carnage continued overhead. She could only spare herself that vista by lowering her gaze.

Even then, she could not locate the source of Jeremiah's exultation.

Fortunately the Feroce had renewed her recollection of black rock elucidated by green veins. When she concentrated inward, tuned her senses to the hue and pitch and timbre of memory, and then studied the cliff-face once more, she began to discern flakes and small seams of the mineral she sought. They were difficult to detect, in part because they felt miniscule, too trivial for her son's needs, and in part because they were crowded among streaks of verdigris, knobs of blunt granite, porous patches of sandstone; masked by reflective facets of quartz, mica, feldspar, other crystalline stones. But there *was* malachite.

It did not look like enough.

Yet Jeremiah's excitement was undaunted. As his mount halted, he vaulted to the ground; ran a few strides toward the ridge. "There!" he called as though he wanted the world to hear him. "It isn't much. I mean, on the surface. But deeper—! If we dig into the cliff far enough"—his hands sketched dimensions in the air—"some of it is practically pure!"

Pointing, he indicated a section of the ridgefront a long stone's throw above his head.

Oh, God. Linden would have asked, How can we get at it? But a different problem had already occurred to her. Assuming that the cliff could be excavated, surely the stone above it would collapse? Anyone digging there would be crushed and buried.

The Ranyhyn had found what Jeremiah needed.

It was effectively inaccessible.

Hyn had stopped. Her breathing wheezed faintly as she waited for Linden to dismount. But Linden was too shaken to move.

Like her, Stave remained mounted. His mien revealed nothing as he asked, "Will not these boulders suffice, young Jeremiah?" He nodded toward the debris at the foot of the cliff. "They also contain portions of malachite."

Jeremiah turned to glare at the *Haruchai*. "Sure," he snorted with the inadvertent disdain of a boy. "If I wanted to build a door for mice. One that didn't go anywhere. But the *Elohim* are bigger." He must have meant in personality and puissance. "And the door has to take them someplace safe.

"No," he asserted. "We need to get into that cliff."

"Then this is labor for Giants." Smoothly Stave slid down from Hynyn's back. "While we await them, however, I will commence. Inform me when I have climbed to the place where you wish me to begin. I will discover what the strength of the *Haruchai* can accomplish against such stone."

In response, Jeremiah laughed: delight, not derision. Flourishing his arms, he cast arcs of yellow flame across the gloom. "I knew I could count on you. While you're doing that, I'll look at a few boulders. Maybe some of them have enough malachite. I'll need as much as I can find."

Stave nodded. Instead of approaching the ridge, however, he faced Linden. "Chosen, you also must dismount. The Ranyhyn require rest. Indeed, they must depart in search of water and forage. And I will be unable to ward your son while I ascend the rock. That task falls to you." After a brief hesitation, he added, "I do not dream that our foes have forgotten their craving for your son's gifts."

Roger had an uncanny ability to appear out of nowhere. Distance was no obstacle to Kastenessen. And Lord Foul's powers—even those of the Ravers—were beyond estimation.

Falls, Linden echoed; but she was not listening to Stave. Her mind followed other paths. The Masters called *caesures* Falls. She could not conceive of any other way to keep her promises. But there were many kinds of falling. She could too easily imagine Stave crawling spider-like up the cliff—until some hand- or toe-hold failed.

What choice did he have? What choice did anyone have? Jeremiah needed malachite.

She shook her head, resisted an impulse to slap herself. She could not afford to sit on Hyn's back feeling stupid and defeated. Her son needed more than malachite. The whole Earth needed more.

When your deeds have come to doom—

She had to think.

Staring vacantly at the ridge, she told herself that the question was one of power. Surely it was a question of power? Even if Stave lived, what could he hope to achieve?

And when the Giants came—if they came—they would be in as much danger as he, with as little chance of success.

Therefore—

Well, obviously, the cliff would have to be broken open from a safe distance. What else? And that was a task for theurgy. Even if the stonewise Giants could devise an alternative, they were only eight—and they were already weary. The work would take time. Not hours: days.

Power was the only answer.

But what could she do? Fire she understood: black flame and burning. Yet merely scorching the face of the cliff would be a waste of effort. Heat alone would have no effect. In the Lost Deep as well as under *Melenkurion* Skyweir, she had shattered stone; shaped it instinctively. If she could summon that form of strength or desperation again, she might be able to tear apart the ridgefront. But the malachite would be torn apart as well. Tons of mineral-seamed rock blasted to gravel would not serve Jeremiah's purposes.

Doubtless the Staff of Law had other uses—many of them—but she was not lorewise enough to know what they were, or how they were done. And anything that she attempted with Covenant's ring would be worse. Wild magic resisted control. In that respect, it resembled the *caesures* it created.

How could she open that ridge without risking lives?

"Chosen," said Stave more sharply. "We cannot delay."

But then another possibility occurred to her. She had been given hints enough—

Men commonly find their fates graven within the rock, but yours is written in water. The lady's fate is writ in water.

"Wait." Scrambling to catch up her ideas, she slipped down from Hyn's back. "Before you do anything rash. Do you know if there are any streams on the far side of this ridge? Any water at all?"

"Mom," Jeremiah protested. "We don't need water. We need to get started."

She and Stave ignored him. The *Haruchai* met her gaze squarely. "No, Chosen. This region is unknown to me. The Masters have found no cause to scout it. And I have discerned neither streams nor springs." After a flicker of thought, he said, "Yet the Ranyhyn may discover what you desire. Doubtless their path lies toward water."

"Mom," Jeremiah objected again. "What's so important about water?"

The three mounts were already trotting back the way they had come. Eventually they would come to the place where the declining slope of the ridge met lower ground.

"I'm not sure yet," Linden answered. "Maybe there isn't any. And if there is, I might not be able to use it."

Impatiently Jeremiah came to join her and Stave. "I don't get it. Sure, I'm thirsty, but it isn't bad yet. If you aren't going to drink it, what do you want it for?"

Life, Linden could have said. Hope. Fate. Doom. But she felt too uncertain to describe what she had in mind.

"Just wait," she urged her son. "Watch the Ranyhn. We'll know soon enough." To ease his frustration, she added, "I don't want to risk Stave if we don't have to."

"But—" Jeremiah began, then clamped his mouth shut.

Dim as shadows, the Ranyhn were only trotting. Nevertheless they appeared to cover distance rapidly. And as Linden watched, they began angling closer to the ridge.

She gripped the Staff hard; tried not to hold her breath.

Before long, the horses quickened their pace. Rushing at the slope, they ascended the dwindling silhouette of the ridge. For a moment, they labored upward. Then they gained the ridgeline and disappeared from sight.

Linden sighed. She could assume that the Ranyhn were seeking water; but that did not necessarily imply that it arose from a source within the ridge. The horses might have to search to the south or east beyond the thrust of the cliff.

Still she could hope—

"All right," she said finally. "So maybe there's water. I won't know for sure until I find it."

Jeremiah had reached the end of his restraint. "But *why*?"

Impelled by the pressure of yet another burden which she might not be able to carry, Linden started toward the ridge. "The Lords," she replied over her shoulder, "back when there were Lords— They must have known how to do lots of things with a Staff of Law. But I can only guess what those things were. I don't know how to do any of them. I only know fire and healing." And brute force.

While Jeremiah caught up with her, and Stave followed in silence, she continued, "I can't heal anything here. But fire makes heat—and heat makes water expand." Trapped water would be ideal, or water that could only rise to the surface in trickles. But buried springs and even pockets of moisture might conceivably suffice. "Heat water fast enough and hard enough, and it explodes into steam. Maybe I can break part of the cliff."

For an instant, Jeremiah seemed stunned. Then he burst out, "That's *brilliant*!"

"It is a tenuous prospect," remarked Stave. "The obstacles are many. I name only the site and quantity of water required, if indeed water exists within such a formation. Nonetheless the deed cannot succeed if it is not attempted."

Linden was not listening. As she walked, she summoned Earthpower to sharpen her percipience, bathed her nerves in fire like condensed midnight. Then she began to explore the ridgefront. Concentrating on the section that Jeremiah had indicated, she felt her way inward, searching into and through multitudes of rock as if she were probing for wounds hidden deep within living flesh.

At the nearest obstruction, a boulder the size of a hut, she halted momentarily. But then she realized that she needed to be closer: close enough to study the face of the cliff with her hands. Cursing under her breath, she passed around the boulder and mounted a stretch of lesser rubble, the fallen residue of the cliff's severance. When she stumbled, she caught herself on the Staff and climbed higher.

Finally she reached the main wall. From far above her, it loomed as if it were glowering in suppressed wrath. But she ignored its impending bulk, its ire, its enduring intractability. She needed nothing from it except water.

In one approximate location.

In sufficient quantity.

After all, it was only a cliff. It was not the cunning subterfuge and malice of the Demondim, seething to mask the *caesure* which gave them access to the Illearth Stone. Nor was it the recursive wards of the Viles, coiling themselves into a mad tangle to prevent intruders from entering the Lost Deep. It was only pieces and shards and spills and plates and torsos and veins and thews of the world's rock compressed by their own weight until they formed a front which had outlasted millennia. It had no defense against her health-sense.

But it was so *much* rock. Of so many different kinds. In so many different shapes and structures. And it supported a mass which would have squeezed ironwood to pulp. Its secrets resisted discovery as if it had set its will against her.

Leaning her Staff against her shoulder, Linden closed her eyes. Hesitantly at first, then more firmly, she placed her hands on the wall and began to insinuate her touch inward.

Stave had followed her as far as the rubble. There he kept watch. Jeremiah stood a bit behind her, but he did nothing to interrupt her concentration. At first, she felt his attention focused on her. Then she closed her mind. Deliberately she thought only about water.

Now that she was not seeking them, she found streaks and facets of malachite everywhere. Crystalline deposits reflected her probing. Heavy granite ground against flows of basalt, reducing them to powder across the eons. Compacted dirt filled every crevice and crack. Schist blocked her search as though its memories and therefore its anger were more recent or more extreme than the rest of the rock.

But Jeremiah needed her. The *Elohim* needed her. The Earth required its panoply of stars. And her friends would be at risk if she failed. They would have to hazard their lives if she could not open the cliff.

Water, that was all she wanted: the most ordinary, necessary stuff of life. And it was everywhere in the created world. It rose from springs among the deepest roots of mountains. Beneath the desiccated purity of the Great Desert, it oozed and ran. The shores of every continent and island felt its surge and lash. From the sky it gave nourishment. And it could be violent. Oh, it could be violent! Linden had felt its force often enough to know what water could do with fury and turbulence.

Yet no Law required it to emerge where she could reach it.

Then Jeremiah's halfhand clasped her shoulder; and for an instant, her concentration faltered. Almost immediately, however, she felt vitality flow into her from his touch. He was giving her Earthpower as the ur-viles had given her blood, so that she might be able to exceed herself.

Riding the energy of his aid, she sensed a damp patch of dirt between a crumbling granite monolith and a writhen vein of sandstone.

It was small, little more than a suggestion of moisture; perhaps only a few drops. But it was water.

Galvanized by hope and her son's support, she marked the dampness in her memory and pushed her senses farther.

She forgot hunger and thirst and weariness. Deeper in the ridgefront, higher, she found a second hint of water. By oblique implication, it led her to another pocket of moisture, and another. Another. There bits of damp marl and pumice were strung together like beads along a fissure between incompatible sheets of granite and obsidian. Linden marked them all, and followed them.

The detritus in the fissure became dense gravel. More water seeped in the gaps, fine droplets acrid with minerals. Carefully she extended her perceptions among them. The vein of gravel became a wedge, wetter and looser. Then it was plugged by schist. She stumbled within herself; leaned her forehead against the face of the cliff. That damn schist— She did not understand how it obstructed her. But she could not spare the energy to study it. Insidiously, as if she sought to possess the rock without being noticed, she slipped her senses past the plug.

Beyond it, she found what she sought.

Water. A space like a bubble in the compressed flesh of the ridge. A cavity filled with water.

It was no larger than her head. And the water had not moved for an age of the Earth: it was cut off from its original source. But flaws packed with more gravel guided her to a pocket of water the size of her body. Farther in, she found a space big enough to hold a Giant's chest; then two more—no, three—each little more than a trapped fist; then, finally, a gap as large as the chamber where she and Anele had been imprisoned in Mithil Stonedown.

After that, there was no more, or she had reached the limit of her reach, or her strength was failing.

Had she located enough? Taken altogether, it was only a drop within the inland sea of the ridge. Nevertheless it would have to suffice. She would have to make it suffice.

She took moments or hours to ascertain that she could remember precisely where and what she had discovered. Then warily, as if she feared the cliff's animosity, she withdrew.

God, she could barely stand— How had she become so tired?

She had no time for weakness. The marks in her memory would fray and fade. Reeling against Jeremiah, she took up the Staff again. His aid vanished, but she ignored its absence. Her eyes stared at nothing. She saw only the places that she needed to remember.

"Mom?" he asked anxiously.

She staggered past him, nearly falling down the rubble toward Stave. When the *Haruchai* caught her, she panted, "Don't say anything. I have to concentrate. Just get me away."

If she succeeded, and they were too close—

Stave seemed to understand. With an arm around her waist, he half carried her toward the hollows or craters in the northwest.

Have mercy, she groaned as she stumbled along. I can't do this.

She had to do it.

A long stone's throw from the ridge, Stave stopped; turned Linden to face the cliff. Jeremiah caught up with her there. He must have been able to see her fatigue. Standing behind her, he clasped her shoulders with both hands.

Fresh theurgy set fire to her blood. Flame ran in her veins. Her heartbeats were conflagration. Blackness bloomed from her Staff as if Jeremiah had invoked it without her volition. Fuligin etched everything that she saw and remembered against the tarnished grey daylight.

She told herself to start small. Begin with the tiniest bits of moisture. Try to force a few new cracks. Weaken the cliff.

If she could find them from this distance.

A troubled wind out of the east tumbled over the ridgecrest, skirling in plumes and dust devils out across the wasteland of craters. It chilled the unnoticed sweat on her forehead, tugged loose a few strands of hair that were not matted to her cheeks and scalp. But it did not soothe her whetted senses; her urgency. In this season, the Land's prevailing winds were from the west.

Straining, Linden Avery reached out to the cliff and tried to prove herself worthy.

A damp patch between granite and sandstone. For a heartbeat or two, she focused her intentions there. Then she sent a dark burst of power to boil that small instance of moisture.

She almost felt the dampness swell; almost felt microfissures mar the surrounding rock. Almost. But she had expected nothing more. She was only trying to create a slight frailty.

With as much care as she could muster, she moved inward, upward.

Pieces of wet marl and pumice strung together like beads: a thin crack separating granite and obsidian: a more difficult challenge. If she failed to heat all of the beads at the same time, her efforts would lose some of their effect. Force would dissipate along the string.

It was too much for her.

It had to be done.

Gathering her resolve, she murmured the Seven Words. Her Staff became a scourge in her hands. Magic struck the string of moisture like a barbed flail. Black fire filled even the most miniscule hints of fluid with passion. For an instant, she thought that she heard the scream of over-heated water, the groan of stressed rock. Then the sound was gone.

Involuntarily she sagged as if she had been overcome. Blots swam and burst across her vision, stars and small suns, stains like abysms.

But Stave upheld her. Jeremiah gripped her shoulders, sharing the strength which Anele had concealed. Earthpower burned in her vessels and nerves, in the channels of her brain and the secret recesses of her heart.

She could not afford to fail.

The wind flicked grit into her eyes. She blinked rapidly, then shut them tight. Ordinary sight was a distraction. Looming huge and unmoved, the rock mocked her inadequacy. Only percipience would enable her to make her last attempt.

She had found six spaces filled with water. She meant to superheat all of them at once. Then larger cracks might join with minor flaws. They might trigger any inherent instability which the immense bulk of the cliff suppressed. They might cause seams and plates to slip—

If one puny human being, exhausted and trembling, could induce something that size to shift.

The Staff shook in her hands as though it had become a burden too great for her to bear. Aching for puissance and accuracy, she invoked the Seven Words again. "*Melenkurion abatha.*" Her voice rose in desperation. "*Duroc minas mill!*" The invocation became a wailing cry. "*Harad KHABAAL!*"

When she unleashed her fire, its blackness seemed to efface the world.

Intense heat constricted by immutable mass created pressures which would have torn mere flesh to shreds. Pockets of water tried to expand. Granite and schist and a mountain's weight refused to move. The ridge had endured for millennia. Linden poured out power as if she were expending her soul. Given a voice, the stone would have laughed.

Then it found a voice. Through the harsh beat of the Seven Words and her own gasping, she heard the cliff groan.

A short sound, little more than a sigh; but it was enough to break her concentration. Unaware of herself, she dropped her Staff. Fighting a giddy swirl of phosphenes and oxygen deprivation, she opened her eyes; tried to see what was happening.

In two or three places across the ridgefront, dust puffed outward. Almost at once, wind dismissed the small exhalations as if they had never occurred.

After that—

—nothing. The cliff stood glowering in the gloom. It had not been touched, and did not care.

"Oh, Mom," Jeremiah moaned. "No. That can't be right. I saw—I felt—"

Linden saw nothing. She felt nothing.

"Indeed," Stave pronounced. Abruptly he released Linden; left her to Jeremiah. Without explanation, the former Master strode toward the mountain.

Perhaps he had decided to act on his original suggestion. Climb the ridge. Try to break loose pieces with his fingers.

But he stopped before he had crossed half the distance. From the ground, he picked up a rock. For a moment, he hefted it in his hand, tested its weight. Then, fluid as water, he flung it.

It struck the cliff-face above the places where Linden had seen puffs of dust. Three heartbeats passed. Four. Without her son's support, she would have collapsed.

Then a grinding shriek appalled the air. The earth under her trembled. Tremors kicked up spouts of grit like gusts of pain everywhere between her and the ridge.

With the massive inevitability of a calving iceberg, a wide section of the wall shifted. For a moment, it seemed to hang on the edge of itself, clinging to its long stubbornness. But it could not hold against its own weight.

When it fell in thunder, Linden fell with it. She had nothing left that might have enabled her to remain conscious.

ᔕᓂ

S he did not know how much time had passed when a glad halloo awakened her. Only moments, she thought at first. But her head felt too heavy to lift, burdened by sleep. And when she tried to gauge the condition of her surroundings, estimate the effects of plunging rock, she found that her reality had contracted. She recognized only the pressure of the hard ground against her body, the leaden weariness of her limbs, the ragged effort of her breathing, the parched ache of dust in her throat and lungs.

Eventually she realized that Kevin's Dirt had reclaimed her. Her health-sense was gone.

Not moments, then. She must have slept for hours. Kevin's Dirt did not erode percipience so suddenly.

Without opening her eyes, she fumbled around her for the Staff of Law.

"It is here, Chosen," said Stave. The warm wood of the shaft was pressed into her hand. "And now the Giants come. Manethrall Mahrtiir leads them. Soon the true labor of your son's purpose must begin."

Linden hardly heard him. She had no attention to spare for anything except her Staff. Without her health-sense, she was less than useless.

Fortunately Liand—lost Liand—had taught her how to find the possibilities beneath the written surface of the wood, even when she had no enhanced discernment to guide her. He had given her more gifts than she could count. Pulling the Staff toward her, she held it close until its natural beneficence began to enlighten her nerves. After that, she was able to absorb Earthpower more quickly.

Stave had said something about the Giants—and Mahrtiir—

Softly through the dirt, she felt the tread of heavy feet: distant yet, but closing. Within that staggered beat, she detected the sharper impact of hooves. As her health-sense expanded, she identified Narunal.

Then she located Jeremiah. He was closer than the Giants, but in a different direction. He must have been scrambling over the wreckage of the ridgefront; but now he stood waving his arms eagerly at the Swordmainnir.

Coughing, Linden tasted the air. Between what should have been sunrise and sunset, the grey half-light remained uniform, undefined by any obvious passage. Nevertheless the flavor of the gloaming modulated incrementally, measuring time. Its faint savor told her that she had slept past midafternoon. A more natural twilight was only a few hours away.

Apparently Stave had kept watch over her for quite a while.

Now the Giants and Mahrtiir had come. Soon she would have to face the fears which had harried her ever since Jeremiah had explained his intentions.

She did not need to raise her head to know that the stars were still going out one by one.

Perhaps she should have been afraid; but she was too tired. She required more than mere sleep to restore her. She needed good food and drink, long rest—and an easing of her ache for Thomas Covenant.

Instead of thinking about what she meant to do, she turned to the question of keeping Jeremiah safe.

In spite of their shouted greetings, the Swordmainnir and the Manethrall did not hasten. Rime Coldspray and her comrades were profoundly weary. A little more time would pass before they came close enough to require Linden's attention.

She could at least try to talk to Stave.

With a muffled groan, she pulled her knees under her, pushed herself up with her arms. Her own fatigue felt as heavy as the ridge. She had to rest for a while before she shifted into a sitting position.

Mutely Stave extended his hand to help her rise.

She shook her head. She needed an entirely different form of aid from him—and she had to talk to him about it alone. He deserved that.

"Stave," she said or coughed. Her throat was as dry as the wilderland. Deliberately she did not regard her son, or her approaching friends, or what she had done to the cliff. "There's something that I want you to do for me."

Cruel days ago, the Mahdoubt had said of the former Master, *He has named his pain. By it he may be invoked.* That had been her last gift before she was lost to use and name and life. But Linden did not want to insist. She suspected that she would damage their friendship if she pressed him.

"Then speak of it, Chosen." His tone was uncharacteristically wry. "Have you not learned that there need be no constraint between us?"

Responding to a question about Kevin Landwaster, he had once told her, *In your present state, Chosen, Desecration lies ahead of you. It does not crowd at your back.* She knew now that he was right. Nonetheless she hoped that he was also wrong.

"All right." She tried to clear her throat. Then she gave up. Coughing intermittently, she said, "I have to go away, and you can't come with me. I want you to stay with Jeremiah."

Stave's silence seemed louder than curses. Was he not her friend? Had he not endured the spurning of the Masters for her? Had he not stood by her in every crisis? The ferocity with which he could have protested, and did not, made her flinch.

"Covenant said it," she explained hoarsely. "It's all about power. I have to assume that Jeremiah has enough malachite. If he does, the Giants will find a way to help him. He'll be able to build his door. And it will work. The *Elohim* will come. I have to assume all of that.

"So he's going to draw the Worm. I have to assume that, too. And when he does, he'll be in danger. He has too many enemies. I might be able to hold off Roger, but I can't fight Kastenessen. No matter how careful we are, a Raver might slip past us." If *moksha* Jehannum took possession of Jeremiah— "I can't even imagine what Lord Foul is going to do. And we don't have a prayer of resisting the Worm.

"We need more power." She was pleading. "I'm going to go look for it. But I can't bear to do that if you don't stay here for Jeremiah."

Stave's flat mien concealed his reactions. His aura seemed to assert that he had no emotions. Yet Linden had seen him grieve over Galt. And she knew his concern as well as his fidelity. Surely he had other human feelings as well, in spite of his stoicism and his vast memories? Surely he could understand her?

He sounded as ungiving as schist as he asked, "Where will you go?"

"I'll tell you." She was done coughing. "Everyone has to know." She no longer flinched. "But I'm not brave enough to say it more than once. This part is between us. It doesn't involve anyone else."

Again Stave was silent. Linden folded her arms over the Staff, held it against her heart, and tried to match him.

After some consideration, he said, "Do not mistake me, Chosen." His tone was like the dusk, unrelieved from horizon to horizon. "I await only some mention of the Mahdoubt—or perhaps of the Vizard. Were you not offered the means to command me?"

Clinging to her weariness as if it were courage, Linden replied, "I won't do that. I'm just asking. I'll beg if that's what you want. If Covenant were here, things would be different. But he isn't. I'm the one who has to go. I'm the only one who can. If I know that you'll protect my son."

Stave's manner conceded nothing. Nevertheless his response seemed to imply that a concession was possible. "Yet some companion you must have."

In Muirwin Delenoth, he had argued that the participation of *the natural inhabitants of the Earth* was a necessary condition for the world's survival, just as the presence of *beings from beyond Time* was essential to Lord Foul's designs. And Linden knew that she needed help.

"I'll take Hyn," she answered weakly. "And Mahrtiir, if he's willing."

He, too, could not assist Jeremiah. Nor could he fight Roger or Kastenessen or Ravers or—

"Then, Linden," Stave said as if he were merely offering to help her stand, "I will do as you request." A heartbeat later, he added, "But do not doubt that my heart is torn within me. I will know neither certainty nor peace until your return."

Linden's eyes were too dry for tears, but a sob twisted in her chest. "All right." Bracing herself on the Staff of Law, she climbed to her feet. Then she dropped the wood so that she could wrap her arms around the former Master. "Thank you."

He called her by her name so rarely—

She would not have been surprised if he had stood rigidly passive in her clasp. But he answered her hug with his own. Almost gently, he murmured, "You will not fail. Come good or ill, boon or bane, you are Linden Avery the Chosen. You will suffice."

When he let her go and stepped back, he had done enough. As he had from the first, he had given her more than she had any right to expect.

She offered him a wrenched smile. "If you say so."

In spite of her weariness, she stooped to retrieve her Staff. Then she turned to face Jeremiah and the Giants and Mahrtiir and the meaning of her life.

While her attention had been fixed on Stave, Jeremiah had descended from the rubble which she had gouged out of the ridge. Now he was running toward the Iron-hand, Mahrtiir, and the rest of their companions. Rime Coldspray quickened her pace slightly to meet him; and Linden thought that he would leap into the Ironhand's arms. But at the last moment, he restrained himself. Stopping suddenly, he braced his fists on his hips.

"What kept you?" he demanded cheerfully. "We've been waiting for *ages*."

"Alas," the Ironhand replied with a wan smile, "we are Giants and perforce lag-gardly. Yet at last we have come." She kept on walking. With the boy trotting at her side to match her strides, she asked more soberly, "What are your tidings, young Jeremiah? Malachite we see. And we see that it has been but recently torn from the thrust of yon ridge. A prodigious feat, and unexpected. Your tale must be equally prodigious."

Stooping under her burdens, Linden moved to intercept her friends. The exhaus-tion of the Giants was plain at any distance. To arrive so promptly, they must have marched through the night. Nevertheless her heart was drawn to Manethrall Mahrtiir.

His condition seemed as explicit as iconography. Uselessness and the loss of his health-sense had marked his mien until he looked haggard, too downtrodden to endure more: as deprived as he had been in the Lost Deep. But there he had been almost continuously active, and occasional gifts of Earthpower had eased his sense of futility. Here he had received no relief from the grinding depression wrought by Kevin's Dirt. Now his misery ached like an unhealed wound.

To ease his plight, Linden uncurled tendrils of flame from her Staff and stretched them over him. It was the least that she could do.

Fortunately this effort was within her strength. When her fire touched the Mane-thrall, he reacted as if he had been struck. For an instant, his misery seemed to spread its wings and become joy. Almost at once, however, he reassumed the glower which had become habitual during the past few days. But now his scowl had recovered its familiar combativeness.

While Linden wielded Earthpower, some of the Giants paused to stare at her. Oth-ers cheered for her sake, or for Mahrtiir's. And Frostheart Grueburn called, "Prodi-gious tidings, in all sooth! Here surely is a tale worthy to be told at length, and to be heard with laughter!"

"It was all Mom," said Jeremiah proudly. "She was brilliant! She found pockets of water in the cliff and made them explode. Now we have malachite." Then he made a visible effort to contain his eagerness. "We can get started when you've had a chance to rest."

Through the twilight, Linden studied the faces of the Swordmainnir. Like Mahrtiir, they needed the Staff's gifts. Yet she could see that rest and refreshment were not their primary concerns. They were hungry for some reason to believe that they had not expended themselves in a futile cause.

"Alas," repeated Rime Coldspray, speaking to Linden rather to Jeremiah, "our small store of viands we have consumed, lest we falter in our trek. Now I find that I am grieved by our failure of foresight. Your need for sustenance is clear."

Linden started to say, Don't worry about it, but the Ironhand continued without pausing, "In truth, we knew not how to measure your need against our own. And we did not imagine that we would encounter no *aliantha* along our course." Then she grinned grimly. "However, great Narunal is provident. We do not lack for water."

Wearily Grueburn, Latebirth, and Onyx Stonemage held up bulging waterskins.

Linden wanted to express her thanks, but her throat was too dry for speech.

"Well, all *right!*" Jeremiah answered for her. "We haven't eaten since we cooked some roots near the Sarangrave. But it was like chewing mud. My stomach still isn't happy. And you have no idea how bad water tastes there. I could drink a gallon."

The Giants exchanged quick glances. Stonemage promptly lowered a waterskin, untied its neck, and held it for Jeremiah.

At the same time, Coldspray faced Linden with danger in her eyes. "Beyond question, there are tidings here. What mischance or peril guided you within the lurker's reach? At no time did our own course approach the noisome banes of Sarangrave Flat."

Struggling to moisten her throat, Linden admitted in an awkward rasp, "That's a story. We have a lot to talk about." She looked around. "Maybe we can find a place to sit down. I'm thirsty too," and so tired that her knees quivered. "I can try to explain while we're resting."

Coldspray agreed with a nod. Pointing toward an area where several large chunks of the ridge formed an arc with a clear space among them, she said, "There we may sit at our ease. When you have relieved your thirst, we will hear your tale."

Linden nodded in turn. That place would be as good as any. It was far enough from the scar to be safe from late-falling stones and slides. And she wanted something to lean against: support for her back, if not for her raw heart.

Sighing, she accompanied Rime Coldspray.

The rest of the Giants followed with Stave and Jeremiah; but Mahrtiir brought Narunal to Linden's side. Dismounting, he bowed his homage to the stallion; watched briefly as the Ranyhyn cantered away in the direction taken by Hyn, Hynyn, and Khelen. Then he turned to Linden.

"Ringthane," he began gruffly, "I have no speech adequate to my gratitude—aye, or to my bitterness. It is my greatest wish to prove worthy of this company, and of the peril of these times, yet Kevin's Dirt renders me effectless. Having naught of merit to say on such matters, I will not speak of them again. Know only that I am avid for use—and that my thoughts are clamorous with concern for the Swordmainnir. Giants they are in good sooth. Yet they have walked without respite for nigh unto two days and a night, and now an immense labor awaits them. Some succor they must have.

"Ringthane, I ask this of you. When you have rested, extend to the Ironhand and her comrades the same benison which you have bestowed upon me. They will have need of it."

Oh, Mahrtiir. Linden dragged her free hand through her hair, tugging to untangle emotions as complex and self-referential as the wards which had guarded the Lost Deep. "As soon as I get some rest," she assured him. "After what they've been through, I'm surprised that they're still on their feet."

"That is well," the Manethrall replied more quietly.

Watching him sidelong, Linden saw that his spirit required more substantial nourishment. But she was not ready to speak of that.

He would get his chance to be of use.

As she and her friends reached the stones that Coldspray had indicated, several of the Swordmainnir groaned with relief. Cirrus Kindwind, Cabledarm, and Hale-whole Bluntfist began loosening their armor. Latebirth, Stonemage, and Galesend handed their water skins to Grueburn. Then they, too, unclasped their cataphracts. When they had shrugged the shaped stone off their shoulders, they slumped to the ground.

Before seating herself, Frostheart Grueburn handed a waterskin to Linden, and another to Mahrtiir. Stave she did not neglect in spite of his ability to convey the impression that he had no physical needs. Then she joined her comrades, leaving only Rime Coldspray upright.

Jeremiah was too excited to sit. With his thirst satisfied, he began to pace as if he were already measuring out the dimensions of his construct. And Stave remained on his feet. But Linden sank gratefully to rest against a rough curve of rock. Fumbling, she untied the neck of her waterskin, lifted it to her mouth. For a long moment, she let the simple bliss of untainted water pour down her throat.

As she drank, fresh beads of sweat gathered on her forehead and were cooled by ragged winds. Tears stung her eyes; but on this occasion, she was glad to be a woman who could weep. Briefly she paused to let her flesh absorb the blessing which the Giants had brought. Then she swallowed more water.

Mahrtiir studied her closely. When he was satisfied with what he saw, he seated himself cross-legged near Latebirth: a position that allowed him to face Linden directly.

While she could, Linden unfurled her power and spread it around the company as Mahrtiir had requested, sharing her only resource. But she did not heed the reactions of the Giants. Whatever she did for them would not be enough.

Grateful for any relief, Coldspray removed her own armor, placed it near her feet so that her stone glaive was within easy reach. Rolling her shoulders and neck, she loosened her sore muscles. Then she folded her arms across her chest and waited for Linden's tale.

Before long, Jeremiah's impatience overcame him. "Mom," he prompted. "You said we have a lot to talk about. And I want to get started. The sooner we can build my door, the more *Elohim* we can save."

Linden sighed; set her half-empty waterskin beside her. "I know. This isn't easy to talk about. We could discuss it for a long time. But I'm going to keep it short. If you want to argue, you'll just be wasting effort. I've already made up my mind."

Eventually she would have to call upon the strength of the Staff for herself. But not yet. Later she would need all of the energy that she could impose on herself.

Around the arc, her friends and her son waited, watching her as though they heard omens in her tone; tocsins of dismay.

"Going to the Sarangrave wasn't our idea," she began. Wind twisted around her. She smelled dust from the wilderland of craters; dust and old death from the wound that she had torn in the cliff. In the sun's absence, the air had acquired a chill edge. "The Ranyhyn made that decision."

In a few words, she described what had happened just before dawn. She recited the message that the Feroce had delivered. Even more tersely, she outlined the memories which the lurker's worshippers had invoked. While her companions considered her tidings, she drew her conclusions.

"So now I think that the Ranyhyn got what they wanted. Somehow they gave the lurker a reason to form an alliance with Covenant. An alliance with us." *No harm will come to you*— "What that means, I don't know—except that Covenant is alive. And he wanted me to remember *forbidding*. He wanted to remind me that it's necessary.

"I've thought about it, and as far as I'm concerned, we can only get what we need from wood. I don't mean the Staff of Law. I mean the forests. From the One Forest. From a time when the Forestals knew how to *forbid* Ravers."

She felt Mahrtiir's reverent awe at the motives which she ascribed to the Ranyhyn. In the eyes of the Giants, she saw speculations and chagrin. Stave's mien revealed nothing; but Jeremiah stared at her as though he did not know whether to feel amazed or appalled.

The wind was growing stronger. Unexpected gusts brought tears to Linden's eyes again. She let them fall, careless of the streaks of dust with which they marked her cheeks.

Resisting an impulse to hurry, she drank again. Then she continued.

"We need power." Her tone was steady. Fatigue had the effect of calm. "You all know that. We aren't enough. I'm not a rightful white gold wielder, and Kevin's Dirt limits what I can do with Earthpower. If we have to fight off Roger and Kastenessen and God knows who else—if we want to protect Jeremiah's door—if we want to save the *Elohim* and the stars—we aren't enough." Not without Covenant. "We have to have more power.

"So—" Briefly the consternation mounting in Jeremiah's gaze undermined her, and she faltered. But she had prepared herself for this. And she had done as much as she could for him. The time had come to confront other concerns.

Everything would have been different if she had known how to help him. But his needs were too deep for her to reach—and she had too little time.

"So," she began again, "I'm going to open a *caesure* and force my way into the past. Hyn can take me where I need to go. She won't get lost. And I have Caerroil Wildwood's runes. They should be good for something more than bringing Covenant back to life. Maybe they can guide me.

"I'm not just too weak the way I am. I'm too ignorant. I don't have any lore. All I have is emotion," despair and love, joy and grief and dread, "and it isn't enough. I want to find the Forestals and get them to teach me *forbidding*. There's no one else I can ask—except the *Elohim,* and they won't tell me." They considered Jeremiah's purpose abominable. "If I want an answer, I have to get it from the Forestals. Then maybe I can use that kind of magic to stop our enemies. Maybe I can even use it to keep the Worm away from Jeremiah's door."

"Mom!" Jeremiah protested hotly. "You *can't. Caesures* are *dangerous.*" In a smaller voice, he said, "And I need you. I need help."

Linden avoided looking at him. The sight might break her. Leaving him felt like committing a crime; but she could not make any other choice.

"You'll have help. You've always had help. But you can do what you have to do. I'm not worried about that."

She wanted to be able to say the same of herself.

She had expected vehement objections from the Giants and even Mahrtiir; indignation and arguments; angry pleading. What she received was harder to bear. Her friends were shocked: that was obvious. But they did not react like people who believed that she had proposed a Desecration. Their emotions were vivid to her health-sense.

What they felt after the initial jolt was hope.

For a long moment, none of the Giants looked at her. Stave appeared to regard some private vista which was visible to no one else. Only Mahrtiir and Jeremiah kept their attention fixed on Linden. The Manethrall watched her as if he were probing her defenses, looking for an opening. Jeremiah stared with dismay gathering like stormclouds in his darkened gaze.

Frostheart Grueburn was the first to speak. As if to herself, she mused, "Extreme straits require extreme responses. It cannot be otherwise."

"No!" Jeremiah snapped immediately. "Mom, you can't *do* this!" He seemed to keep himself from howling by an effort of will that made Linden's heart quake. "Maybe you can go away. Maybe you can make a *caesure* do what you want." When he clenched his fists, flames dripped between his fingers like blood. "But you won't be able to *get back*!"

At that moment, he sounded unutterably forlorn.

Dust bit at Linden's eyes. She blinked furiously to clear them. Don't say that, she wanted to plead. Don't make this harder than it already is. But she demanded a sterner reply from herself. The Land required more from her. Jeremiah himself required more.

God, she was tired—

Meeting her son's gaze with wind and dust and tears in her sight, she said, "I made a promise to Caerroil Wildwood. I don't know how else to keep it. I don't know how else to save any of us. I'll find a way to get back."

Stave had turned his unyielding gaze toward Jeremiah. Manethrall Mahrtiir appeared to be suppressing a desire to speak. Tension mounted among the Giants, as restless as the wind. But the Ironhand still stood with her head bowed, studying the ground at her feet, saying nothing.

"And I'm talking about moving through time," Linden added before Jeremiah could respond. "Remember that. How long it takes for me won't have any effect on you. If I can do anything that even remotely resembles what I have in mind, there's no reason to think that I won't get back before the Worm comes."

"But you won't *get* back," Jeremiah insisted. His voice shook. Nevertheless he made a palpable effort to reason cogently. "You can make a *caesure* now because the Law is already weak. I mean Time and Life and Death. It's all been damaged. But back *then*, when there are still Forestals, everything is intact. How can you make another *caesure* that long ago? Just trying, you'll change the Land's history. Even if that doesn't break the Arch, you'll hurt it."

Desperately he finished, "We'll never see you again."

His wounds were so close to the surface that Linden could almost name them.

And she understood his objection. It was apt in more ways than he appeared to recognize. If she reached the Forestals, her arrival would inevitably afflict them with knowledge—or at least questions—which they should not possess. That alone might do irreparable harm to the Arch.

Yet she had an answer. "Then I won't go back to the oldest Forestals. I'll try to reach Caer-Caveral." Hile Troy. "He was the last. Meeting me won't affect any of the others. And in his time, the Law of Death was already broken. He's about to break the Law of Life himself. I won't change his history."

Surely Hyn could find her way through a *caesure* to Caer-Caveral?

"In any case," she said, "what else do you want me to do? I'm useless here. I'm useless to you. I don't understand your talent, and I can't carry boulders. My only alternative is to supply the Giants with strength until they work themselves to death—and *that* I can't bear.

"I know it's dangerous," she concluded. She was running out of words. "But I'll get back somehow. Hyn will bring me."

Neither her manner nor her appeal comforted her son: she saw that. He felt threatened, rejected. Forsaken when he finally had a chance to prove himself. He no longer looked at his mother. One finger at a time, he unclosed his fists. Then he spread his hands to reveal small gusts of fire cupped in his palms.

"You can say what you want." In the gloom, the stains on his pajama bottoms seemed to devour his legs. "Talking won't help. I have more important things to do."

Lit by Earthpower, he turned away.

The sight twisted a knife in Linden's heart. She needed the kind of courage that Thomas Covenant had tried to teach her. But she did not have it, and he was not here.

Grueburn and the other Swordmainnir squirmed. Rime Coldspray scowled thunderous disapproval at the dirt. The Manethrall's bandaged attention did not leave Linden's face.

Leaning against her boulder, she waited for their reactions. She had chosen this crisis for herself. Come good or ill—

How often had she heard those words?

They were better than despair.

Finally the Ironhand raised her head. Gloaming veiled her mien, but it did not conceal the set of her jaw or the lines of her shoulders. Without preamble, she asked, "Swordmainnir, will you gainsay me?"

Her tone was like the edge of her glaive.

As if they knew her mind, Latebirth, Onyx Stonemage, and Halewhole Bluntfist muttered, "Nay." The others shook their heads. With both fists, Frostheart Grueburn punched lightly at the earth to emphasize her answer.

"Then," Coldspray announced harshly, "I say to you, Linden Avery, Giantfriend, that you are a wonderment. I speak with respect—aye, and with admiration as well, though my manner belies the fullness of my heart. That your intent is foolhardy beyond all reckoning cannot be doubted. Indeed, it appears to be as extreme as a leap into the abyss of She Who Must Not Be Named. Nonetheless you raise my spirits. In such times, all deeds must be extreme. The Earth's need requires it.

"Therefore my word to you is this. My comrades will give of their utmost to aid young Jeremiah, for his purpose is likewise admirable. Stave of the *Haruchai* and I will accompany you, doing what we may in your service."

The other Giants nodded their approbation. Some of them started to applaud. But Stave cut them off. Peremptory as a challenge, he stated, "I will not. My place is with the Chosen-son. And he will have need of your aid, Rime Coldspray, your labor and stonelore. You cannot be spared."

Quick protests gathered in the Swordmainnir. Before any of them could speak, Stave declared, "Yet some companion she must have. Should she attempt this quest alone, she will not return. In the absence of High Lord Loric's *krill*, she cannot wield white gold while she holds the Staff of Law. The conflict of such theurgies must prove fatal."

At once, Manethrall Mahrtiir surged like a shout to his feet. "Then this task is mine. It was foretold for me by the Timewarden himself while his spirit remained within the Arch."

Linden had not forgotten. *You'll have to go a long way to find your heart's desire. Just be sure you come back.*

"In Andelain," the Manethrall continued, gathering force as he spoke, "Covenant Timewarden avowed, 'There is no doom so black or deep that courage and clear sight may not find another truth beyond it.' For that reason, and in the name of prophecy, and because I must, I will accompany Linden Avery, Chosen and Ringthane, Wildwielder.

"In the endeavor which young Jeremiah contemplates, I have no part. Yet I am Ramen, attuned to the Ranyhyn, and also acquainted with the perils of passages within Falls. Where I am weak, *amanibhavam* will sustain me. I will not fail the Ringthane."

Jaw jutting, he averred, "I speak for my people. We must become more than we have been, lest we prove unworthy of the Ranyhyn. The tale of the Ramen is too small to justify the service which defines us."

Coldspray and her people studied him with darkness in their faces. Some of them still wished to protest, especially Latebirth, who had often carried the Manethrall. Others showed resignation or grief, or waited uncertainly for their Ironhand's reply. But Linden bowed her head and let new gratitude flow through her. Although she wanted Mahrtiir with her, she had been loath to ask so much of him. His unrequested willingness eased her reluctance.

After a long moment, Rime Coldspray raised her voice into the twilight. "Manethrall of the Ramen, I am abashed." Her tone was gentler now, and more sorrowful. "I confess it, Giant though I am. Eyeless, your sight is clear where mine is clouded. We must accede to your counsel."

"Then," Mahrtiir returned, "I bid you farewell for a time. May our absence be brief. For my part, I am certain of you. When you have set your hearts to any purpose, you will accomplish it. So it was said of the Unhomed, and so it is with you. But where their tale has grown dim with age, yours will shine out, illuminating the last days of the Earth."

Hurrying as if he feared that Linden might object, the Manethrall turned to her. While she sat with her head lowered and a dull ache in her chest, he asked, "Ringthane, shall we depart?" An eagle's eagerness sharpened his voice. "That you are sorely weary is plain. Yet delay will not restore you. Doubtless you desire to be reconciled with your son. Yet delay will not comfort him. He spoke thoughtlessly, and will recant when he is calmer. I do not doubt that he will greet your return with joy."

"All right." Linden did not raise her head. "All right." Carefully she took a last drink from her waterskin. Then she rested her hands on the blackness of her Staff. "We should go while I'm too tired to be terrified."

Still without looking at her friends, she said, "Coldspray, Grueburn, all of you—I'm not worried about you." Instead of facing anyone, she studied Caerroil Wildwood's runes as if they might suddenly reveal their meaning. "You're *Giants*. If it can be done, you'll do it."

Her weakness and dread were a sickness in the pit of her stomach, a foretaste of nausea and hornets and gelid emptiness as cruel as a chasm. They seemed bottomless.

"But, Stave—" she added unnecessarily. "Be sharp." She could not meet his gaze. "At some point, someone is going to try to stop Jeremiah. I hope that Mahrtiir and I can come back before that happens. If we don't, Jeremiah and the Giants will need everything that you have in you."

The former Master regarded her with no expression that her nerves could interpret. "Linden Avery, I have said that uncertainty is an abyss." His flat voice contradicted the gust and swirl of the wind; the plumes of dust. "Nevertheless I do not fear it. Only your self-doubt troubles me. You esteem yourself too slightly. For that reason, you are prone to darkness—and for that reason alone. Forget such concerns. You are not Kevin Landwaster. Remember, rather, that you are loved by those who know you well.

"Go blessed by the goodwill of your companions here, and by the stalwart aid of the Manethrall, and by the prowess of the Ranyhyn. It may chance that you will accomplish something other than your intent. Yet good will come of it ere the end."

"All right," Linden repeated. What else could she say? But still she did not lift her head or rise to her feet. Her mortality was too heavy for her to carry.

She felt Frostheart Grueburn moving toward her; but she did not know why until Grueburn scooped her from the ground. Clasping her under her arms, Grueburn held her high, extending her into the grey light as if she were the standard around which all of the Swordmainnir rallied; and as Grueburn did so, the other Giants called Linden's name softly, celebrating her with murmurs. Then Grueburn set Linden on her feet.

There Mahrtiir took her arm. Baring his teeth like a hunter who had finally found the spoor of his prey, he said, "Come, Ringthane. Lean upon me while you may. In a moment, Stave will summon the Ranyhyn. To spare our companions, we must gain a wary distance ere you attempt the creation of a Fall. We will walk while we await great Narunal and valiant Hyn."

Linden accompanied him because he drew her with him. Her attention was contracting. Already the Giants were becoming dim. Stave had begun to fade. Jeremiah was little more than a will-o'-the-wisp bobbing among the boulders and shards. But she was not growing faint with fatigue and fear; not sinking back into the blankness which had overcome her in front of She Who Must Not Be Named. Rather she was concentrating inward, seeking the private door, secret and familiar, that opened on wild magic; the learned impulse which allowed her to invoke rampant argent.

Its imperfection is the very paradox of which the Earth is made, and with it a master may form perfect works and fear nothing. Kasreyn of the Gyre had said that. But he may have been wrong. And she was not a master.

Still she persisted. In recent days, she had surrendered any number of things. The time had come to surrender hesitation and doubt. Like a derelict, she limped over the cratered ground. Step by step, the stains mapped into her jeans and the runes which defined her Staff led her away from her son. Without the Manethrall's help, she could have fallen.

Vaguely she heard Stave whistling. Soon the Ranyhyn would come: yet another reason for gratitude. It impelled her to turn her mind outward once more.

Resting on Mahrtiir's support, she asked, "You do understand, don't you? You can let Hyn and Narunal know what we want?"

"Aye, Ringthane," Mahrtiir answered steadily. "I comprehend. And that which I comprehend, our mounts will grasp as well. Are they not Ranyhyn, the great horses of Ra, Tail of the Sky, Mane of the World? Their devoir will both serve and preserve us."

Linden nodded, but she was not listening. He had said enough. Now she needed wild magic, and it did not come naturally.

Perhaps she managed a hundred paces. The scuff of her boots cast small plumes of dust into the swirling wind, the increasing chill. Then she heard or felt the approach of hooves.

Gratitude, she thought. Maybe that was the answer. Gratitude and trust. Jeremiah was alive and free. So was Covenant, in spite of Joan. And Covenant had urged Linden to take this risk. Hyn and Narunal would make it possible. Maybe if she remembered to be grateful and have faith, she would be able to avoid High Lord Kevin's tragic arrogance.

When the mare and the stallion joined her, Mahrtiir spent only a moment in homage. Then he boosted Linden onto Hyn's capable back. A heartbeat later, he mounted Narunal. In the half-light, he looked to Linden like all of the Land's bounty incarnated in one mere human as frail and fallible as herself.

Prompted by Narunal's imperious whinny, Linden passed the Staff of Law to the Manethrall. Covenant's ring she lifted from its hiding place under her shirt. Pressing the wedding band between both of her hands, she brought forth silver flame as if she had the courage to defy the Earth's doom.

As if she believed that good could be accomplished by Desecration.

In the distance, Jeremiah seemed to call her name. Overhead Kevin's Dirt appeared to catch fire and burn, lit by wild magic. But she paid no heed. Taking the risk, she created a disruption of Time and history that might destroy the world.

8.

The Right Materials

 Jeremiah was only a boy, but in some ways he knew too much. In others, he knew too little.

Dissociation had denied him the normal processes of growing up; the gradually acquired experience of passions and denials, of joys and disappointments. Even in the most practical matters, his development—his acquisition of earned knowledge— had been stunted. At the age of fifteen, he had never so much as changed his own clothes. Certainly he had never learned the most mundane social interactions. In that respect, he was younger than his years; unfamiliar with himself.

Yet he had learned other lessons too well. The flames of Lord Foul's bonfire had taught him that some pains were unendurable. And the moral rape of possession— the manner in which he had been used by the *croyel* to betray Linden's trust—had shown him that hating what was done to him both aided and harmed him. It gave him the desire to fight back—and yet it also convinced him that he would not have been so hurt if he did not deserve it. Hate cut both ways. If he had not been such a coward—if he had not hidden himself away to escape his wounds—Lord Foul and the *croyel* would not have been able to possess him, use him. He had brought his worst suffering on himself.

He did not understand why that was true. Nevertheless he yearned to *pay back* what had happened to him. At the same time, he hated what he felt. He hated himself for feeling it.

But there had been other forces at work in him as well. His mother's love and devotion had kept him alive. With Tinkertoys and Legos, Lincoln Logs and racetrack sections, he had constructed a sense of possibility and worth that might have eluded a less abused youth. And during his visits to the Land, Covenant's spirit in the Arch had offered him a one-sided friendship, compassionate and respectful.

The result was a conflicting moil of emotions which he did not know how to manage.

And now Linden had abandoned him; actually *abandoned* him in order to enter a *caesure* with Mahrtiir. The fact that she had explained her actions did not ease him. It did not muffle the beat of indignation and fear in his veins. He had *counted* on her. She had *taught* him to count on her.

And yet, strangely, he could hardly contain his excitement. Right here, right now, he had a chance to make his whole life worthwhile. If he succeeded, he would save some of the *Elohim*, some of the stars. He would prove that Lord Foul and the *croyel* and his natural mother were wrong about him. From head to foot, he trembled with eagerness to begin.

That contradiction was confusing enough; but he had more.

He had inherited Anele's legacy of Earthpower. It belonged to him now: the Land's living energy had become as much a part of him as the blood in his veins. He was inured against the vagaries of heat and cold, wind and wet. His bare feet endured sharp rocks and the ancient shards of weapons or armor without discomfort. His health-sense sloughed off Kevin's Dirt. He could fuse bones to make marrowmeld sculptures. He could even summon fire from his hands. And there might be more possibilities.

For him, Earthpower had become a piercing pleasure. It had enabled him to rescue himself from his prison.

But he had received other things from Anele as well. The old man had given him inarticulate scraps of knowledge, and horrific vulnerabilities, and an instinct for moral dread. Much as he treasured Anele's gifts, their implications appalled him.

And because he had never learned how to manage among his emotions, he tried to ignore the worst of them. Nevertheless they clung to him. He was like his pajamas. His mother had dressed him in them and tucked him lovingly into bed. The horses rearing across their faded blue might have been Ranyhn. Now they were torn and tattered; soiled with grime and dirt; defined by bullets. From the waist down, their innocence bore the stains of Liand's death. The *croyel*'s gore marked the shirt.

So he had turned his back on Linden when she had insisted on throwing her life away in the Land's past. What else could he have done? He did not know who he was without her. He hardly seemed to exist. When her *caesure* collapsed into itself and vanished, taking her and Mahrtiir and their Ranyhn to a place and time from which they might never return, Jeremiah dissociated them in his mind, buried them away. Then he chose the excitement of building. It was his only escape.

"Come on!" he called down to the Giants and Stave. "Let's get started. The longer we wait, the more *Elohim* we'll lose."

Elohim and stars.

That was why he was here, after all: to save things that could not save themselves. To delay the Worm's feeding, slow its progress toward the Blood of the Earth. To buy time until somebody came up with a better answer.

But the Giants ignored his shout. None of them glanced up at him. Even Stave did not. With the Swordmainnir, the former Master watched the place where Linden and Mahrtiir had disappeared as if he hoped or feared that she would return almost immediately. They were all acting like there was no need to hurry. Like Jeremiah did not need them—or like the *Elohim* and the stars and the whole world did not need *him*.

Wind skirled like travail around him, tugged at his pajamas. It carried dust from the gouged cliff, the fallen debris. Perhaps it would have stung his eyes if he had not been so full of Earthpower. Somewhere inside him was a small boy who wanted to cry because his mother had left him. But he refused to be that boy. The structure that he wanted to make both goaded and protected him.

Somehow he swallowed the impulse to yell at the Giants in frustration. Here was another aspect of his confusion, his inability to resolve his own contradictions. The Giants were ignoring him—but they were *Giants*, and he had loved them ever since he had first seen them. When he and Linden and Stave had ridden to rejoin the

Ironhand and her comrades, his response to the sheer size and wonder of who and what the Swordmainnir were had opened like a flower in his heart. They were Giants in every sense: he had no other word for them. And he had seen the delight in their eyes when they had gazed at him, the relief and welcome. They had made him feel that he was capable of putting his past behind him. Of cutting it off entirely. Under their influence, he had believed that he could accomplish something wonderful.

If they rebuffed him now—

Abruptly his frustration became chagrin. His health-sense was precise: he could see that he had offended the Swordmainnir. There was anxiety in the slump of their shoulders, worries aggravated by a great weight of weariness. And they carried griefs which Jeremiah did not recognize. But there was also anger. Their refusal to acknowledge his call was deliberate.

He had to talk to them—and he was afraid of what they would say.

Hesitating, he took a moment to scan his surroundings. Above him hung the gouge which his mother had made in the ridgefront. It and its slope of rubble faced the north, or a bit west of north. At odd intervals, chunks of rock and clumps of dirt still fell from the upper surfaces of the gouge; but they clattered harmlessly to the sides. Buffets of wind scattered the dust before it could settle.

The ridge filled that side of the landscape. In every other direction, an almost featureless plain stretched out to the horizons, a beaten flat pocked with hollows like craters left behind by a barrage of huge stones or heavy iron, or of bolts of magic. In the cloying dusk, these hollows or craters gave the terrain a mottled appearance, as if it were stippled with shadows or omens.

As far as Jeremiah could see, nothing grew or moved. Nothing lived at all. And no springs or streams nourished the plain. In this region, the foundations of the Lower Land wore only a thin mantle of dirt, soil so barren that it refused even *aliantha*.

And over it all lay the pall of the sunless murk, an augury of the last dark. As Jeremiah gazed around, he noticed that the afternoon was waning. Evening was not far off. Then would come full darkness, the second night since the sun had failed.

Even now, the stars were visible, as bright as cries overhead. He could have watched them wink out of existence, had he been willing to face them. But at night—

At night, the Giants would have more difficulty doing what he wanted from them.

The situation was urgent—and still the Swordmainnir rested against their boulders. They had promised to help him. Now they acted like they had changed their minds.

He had to talk to them.

His private turmoil made him awkward as he began to descend from the rubble. Whenever he was working on one of his constructs, he was deft and graceful, full of confidence. But when he felt stymied, his muscles forgot what they were doing. He fumbled at the rocks, jerked downward, lost his balance and caught himself like a child half his age.

He hated being clumsy. He hated himself when he was clumsy.

The curve of boulders where the Giants sat faced away from him. Like Stave, they were not affected by Kevin's Dirt: they must have been aware of Jeremiah. Still they did not look in his direction. Earlier they had shed their armor and swords. Now they all rested against thrusts of stone. Only Stave remained on his feet, still watching the place where Linden and Mahrtiir had disappeared.

Biting his lower lip, Jeremiah resisted a desire to start protesting before he reached his companions. Fortunately Rime Coldspray turned toward him while he was still a short distance away. Although her disapproval was obvious, her gaze steadied him. Clearly she did not intend to keep ignoring him.

Troubled gusts stirred up dust, carried it away. Clad in twilight, the Giants resembled shadows or stones. Like shadows or stones, they looked deaf to persuasion. Still Jeremiah walked closer until he stood near Coldspray at the edge of the arc.

None of the Giants spoke. Stave did not. But they were all looking at him now.

For a moment, Jeremiah clamped his teeth down on his lip. Then he tried to say something that would not make his mother's friends angrier.

"I know you're tired." He was whining: he heard it in his tone. That, too, he hated. "I know you need rest. But I can't tell how long this is going to take"—he gestured at the slope of rocks—"or how much time we have, or how many *Elohim* we can save. And it'll be harder at night.

"I want to get started. Why is that wrong?"

He felt the attention of the Swordmainnir. Nevertheless they conveyed the impression that they wanted him to go away.

The Ironhand shifted her shoulder so that she faced Jeremiah more squarely. Even seated, she was taller than he was. She seemed to glare down at him in the gloom.

"Young Jeremiah," she sighed, "we are Giants. Children are more than our joy and our delight. They are our future—if the notion of any future has meaning in these fraught times. We are endlessly indulgent."

Before Jeremiah could ask, Then why are you mad at me? she said more sternly, "But by the measure of your kind, you are not a child. Much has been given to you. Therefore much is expected in return."

Wincing, Jeremiah retorted, "I know that." The sound of his own truculence disgusted him. It sharpened the vexation of the Giants. But he did not know how to control it.

"Do you, forsooth?" drawled Frostheart Grueburn. "You conceal your wisdom well."

Latebirth and Cabledarm offered their own ripostes; but the Ironhand gestured them to silence. On their behalf, she asked Jeremiah, "Do you indeed comprehend what Linden Giantfriend has done for love of you?" Her tone was a bared blade. "Your manner suggests that you do not.

"I do not speak of her search for you across many centuries and uncounted leagues. Other mothers have done as much, if in differing times by different means. Nor do I speak of her surrender to the machinations of the Harrow, or of her perilous descent into the Lost Deep, or of her many efforts to relieve your absent mind. These things might other mothers have done as well. We ourselves have done much in Lostson Longwrath's name, and we are not his mothers.

"Now, however, Linden Giantfriend has exceeded our conceptions of love and fidelity." Rime Coldspray's voice cut. "She has surpassed the hearts of Giants. Knowing that you have need of her, she yet prizes your worth so highly that she has hazarded more than her own extinction. She has dared the end of all Time and life. This she has done for the Land's sake, aye, but also for yours, that your endeavors here may accomplish their intended purpose.

"Does her attempt not express her devotion? Does it not merit your esteem?"

Remember that I'm proud of you.

Jeremiah's immediate reaction was a flare of anger. "She *left* me." But then tears burned his eyes, and he wanted to weep. He understood what his mother was trying to do—and yet he had treated her courage like a betrayal. Winds swirled around him like misery. Abruptly he sank to the ground; sat cross-legged with his elbows braced on his thighs and his head down.

Come on, he commanded himself bitterly. Don't be a baby. If you start crying now, I'll never forgive you.

In a small voice, he asked the scoured dirt, "What do you want me to do?"

Gradually the Ironhand's aura lost its irate flavor. "Attempt patience, young Jeremiah," she replied as if she had exhausted her reprimands. "Grant to us an hour of rest. Linden Giantfriend's fire is a rare gift, but it cannot efface the cost of all that we have endured. When we have rested, two of us will commence the labor which your purpose requires. The others will sleep while they may. When the two must pause, they will awaken two others in turn. By twos, we will achieve what we can until all have slept. With the return of day, we will arise together to serve you."

After a moment, she added, "If need compels you, make use of the night. Doubtless there are preparations which will serve to hasten the morrow's labors."

Attempt patience? That seemed impossible to Jeremiah. Patience was for people who were incapable of anything else. He had spent ten passive years exhausting his ability to *wait*. But when Coldspray suggested preparations, his heart veered. That he understood: identifying his materials; setting them out so that he would not have to search for them when the time came to put them in place. And he knew that he would have to spend a lot of time searching for the right sizes and shapes and quantities of malachite. While he did that, two Giants might be able to give him as much help as he could use.

Thinking hard, he grew calmer.

A flurry of gusts out of the northeast slapped at the company. They tumbled against the ridgefront, scurried out across the plain. To Jeremiah's nerves, they felt like the leading edge of a gale. But the forces driving the wind were still distant. The full strength of the blast might not reach so far.

A part of his mind was making calculations: measuring the mass of rocks against their hidden seams of malachite; estimating sizes and dimensions and positions. But that part of him was instinctive. It did not require his conscious attention. Instead of focusing on it, he tried to think of a way to make amends.

He did love Giants.

Groping, he said tentatively, "You've talked about Longwrath before. Lostson Longwrath. I heard you"—in spite of himself, he winced—"when the *croyel* had me. But I don't know who he is.

"What happened to him? Where is he?"

At once, Jeremiah felt a pang spread among the Giants, and he feared that he had made a stupid mistake. They looked at each other or turned away; shifted uncomfortably where they sat; touched their weapons. But then he saw that he had not irritated them again. Instead he had reminded them of a pain which they did not know how to relieve.

"Ah, young Jeremiah." The Ironhand sighed once more. "You request a tale—"

Abruptly Frostheart Grueburn heaved herself to her feet. Towering against the dimming sky and the lucid stars, she announced to her comrades, "It is a tale which need not delay young Jeremiah's task. If Latebirth will consent to join me, we two will be the first to aid him. And while we do so, we will speak of Longwrath.

"I have borne Linden Giantfriend across many arduous leagues. In her name, I will bear this burden also."

"You are harsh, Grueburn," Latebirth retorted. "You ask much. Scend Wavegift's death clings unkindly to me. Should Longwrath appear before us here, I would wish both to embrace him and to strike him down."

"As would we all," muttered Coldspray. "Nonetheless Frostheart Grueburn's offer is a gift. Should you prefer to rest, Latebirth, I will join her."

"Nay, Ironhand." Groaning lugubriously, Latebirth pushed herself upright. "I merely complain, as is my wont. Grueburn's thought is worthy of her—"

"A jest of two edges," remarked Onyx Stonemage. "It both gives and takes."

"—and I will endeavor to prove worthy as well," Latebirth finished without pausing.

Ducking his head, Jeremiah mustered the grace to say, "Thanks. I know this is hard. But I really can't do it without your help."

Grueburn swung her hand at his shoulder, a comradely clap that nearly knocked him off his feet. "Waste no heed on us, young Jeremiah. We are Giants. We revel in bewailing our lot.

"Come." Followed by Latebirth, she steered him back toward the sloping rockfall. "You will describe what is required, and we will speak of Lostson Longwrath while we attempt your desires."

"In that case"—with a nudge of his shoulder, Jeremiah redirected her toward a stretch of open ground at the foot of the rubble—"let's start there." Within three steps, his distress became excitement again. Wind slapped grit and portents at his face, but he ignored it. The preparations for his construct seemed to spring into focus of their own volition. "I'll show you where I want to build."

Grueburn nodded her approval; and Latebirth said, "That is well thought, young Jeremiah. In the absence of plain commands, we would doubtless cause ourselves much unnecessary labor."

"And we would moan," Grueburn stated, feigning pride. "Even among Giants, I am prized for the purity and pathos of my moans."

"I don't believe you," snorted Jeremiah. Carried on a rise of anticipation, he tried to emulate his companions. With gibes, the Swordmainnir refreshed their spirits: he saw that. Now he wanted to participate. "You've probably never moaned in your whole life."

"Latebirth has not," Grueburn asserted while the other Swordmain chuckled. "She is entirely dour. But I am capable, I do assure you, of the most extravagant and heart-rending moans."

"Enough, I implore you!" pleaded Latebirth. "Young Jeremiah's ears will bleed if you proceed to a demonstration." More soberly, she added, "And we have consented to speak of Longwrath."

"Yet time remains to us," Frostheart Grueburn countered. "When I regard the approach of the Worm, the hours appear as brief as heartbeats. But when I contemplate the exertions before us, mere moments are protracted to the horizons and beyond. If we lack time sufficient to speak at leisure, we also lack time for our task. Haste will gain naught."

Latebirth grunted glum acquiescence. In silence, the two Giants accompanied Jeremiah to the span of ground where he proposed to build.

"Here," he announced at the edge of his goal. With a gesture, he asked Grueburn and Latebirth to halt. "I'll mark out dimensions. If we don't pile rocks inside that space, they won't be in the way later."

Latebirth scanned the area, muttered something that he did not hear. His attention had shifted. Images flared in his mind, becoming more explicit as he estimated shapes and masses, ratios of malachite, necessary boundaries. Stooping, he selected a fragment of basalt with a sharp point. For a moment longer, he studied the ground. When he was sure, he began gouging lines in the dirt.

Four paces for a Giant straight toward the ridgefront. Five parallel to the spill of rubble. Four more to form the third side of a precise rectangle. And a line along the northwest to close the space. There he interrupted his marks to suggest a gap. Eventually that gap would become an entryway.

While Jeremiah outlined his construct, Frostheart Grueburn began.

"Speaking of Lostson Longwrath is hurtful to us," she said gruffly. "The fault of his plight lies with our forebears. From them, we inherit a shame which we do not bear lightly. For that reason, and because your kind is born to brevity, and because we must conserve our strength, I will be concise."

"Concise, forsooth," scoffed Latebirth. "Already you falter in your intent."

Grueburn ignored her comrade. "Young Jeremiah," she went on, "Longwrath's plight shares much with your former state."

Jeremiah flicked a startled glance toward her. But his task held him, and he did not pause.

"He is possessed," she explained. "Forces which he did not choose and could not refuse have deprived him of himself. In the name of a foolish and unheeding bargain with the *Elohim*, he is ruled by a *geas* both cruel and minatory. Where he was once a Swordmain honored among us, he has become a madman bent on murder.

"And he is lost in another sense as well." Grueburn's tone was as personal as a plea. "Though we were his guardians and caretakers, he was separated from us. Now we know not where he wanders, or indeed whether he yet lives. Nor do we know what form his *geas* has taken. He failed in his first compulsion. Has he now been released? Is some new atrocity required of him? It is possible that Infelice might have answered us, had we inquired of her in Andelain. But we were consumed by our shame—aye, and also by our wrath. We did not think to inquire.

"Whatever the burden he now bears may be, he was consigned to it by our thoughtlessness as much as by the *Elohim*."

Jeremiah tried not to listen. Grueburn raised too many echoes. They were as insistent as the erratic buffeting of the wind. But unlike the wind, they did not hurry past him. Instead they squirmed like crimes in the background of his mind.

He should not have asked about Longwrath.

Nevertheless he surprised himself by demanding when he meant to remain silent, "What's your point?"

Some denied part of him wanted an answer.

His companions regarded him gravely. After a moment, Grueburn replied, "My point, young Jeremiah, is that Longwrath's madness and pain do not foretell your doom. There is this difference between you. You were taken. He was bartered in a witless exchange."

Jeremiah flinched. Before he could stop himself, he retorted, "It's the same thing." He did not want to say this. The words were compelled from him by pressures which he yearned to defy. "My mother gave us away." He remembered it vividly. The *croyel* had delighted in raising such spectres from their graves. "I mean my natural mother, not Mom. She must have thought she was getting something. She sacrificed my sisters and me when she handed herself to Lord Foul." The bonfire had cost him two fingers. If he had not hidden from them, eyes as hungry as fangs would have claimed him. "We were too young to know what she was doing."

But he had not been too young to be terrified—

Grueburn's shoulders slumped. "Then I will grieve for you. And I will hold out hope for Lostson Longwrath, that he may evade his *geas* as you have foiled your imprisonment."

Jeremiah poked at his leg with the tip of his rock, trying to suppress a residue of agony. Dust had already begun to fill his lines. In any case, they were shrouded in twilight, almost imperceptible. Resisting the unspoken appeal in Grueburn's voice, he asked roughly, "Can you still see where I want to build?"

"We are Giants," Latebirth replied as if she were certain of herself. "We will not forget."

"Good for you," Jeremiah muttered under his breath: a sour whisper. Then he turned toward the rubble. "Come on. We've wasted enough time."

Almost immediately, however, he regretted his tone. It sounded too much like petulance, the whining of a boy who did not want to grow up. As an apology, he clenched his hands into fists, then opened them with cornflower flames in his palms.

Lighting the way, he led Frostheart Grueburn and Latebirth onto the rockfall to search for malachite.

♾

Some of the stones with their secret deposits of minerals and hope were small enough that he could manage them without help. Those he ignored temporarily. Instead he probed the rubble until he located two or three rocks that required

Giants. These he indicated to Grueburn and Latebirth. When they assured him that they would be able to wrestle the stones from the slope without causing it to shift, he quenched his fires. In darkness softened only by the half-light of evening, he returned to the smaller pieces of granite and basalt, and began hurrying them downward.

He was going to need a lot of them. And dozens or scores of bigger chunks. The proportions of malachite were meager. With purer, richer deposits, he could have contrived a structure no taller than himself, its walls closer together: little more than a shrine. But with these rocks, his construct would have to be the size of an impoverished temple, crudely raised by people too poor to afford a better place of worship. And even then, he could not be sure that he would find enough malachite for his purpose.

The right materials in the right amounts with the right shapes. If he succeeded, the *Elohim* would come. They would have no choice. But if he failed to locate enough malachite—or to build his temple before every *Elohim* perished, or before the Worm came—then everything would be wasted. His own life would have no meaning. Mom would have saved him and then left him for nothing.

While he fretted, however, other facets of who he was made their preparations with a confidence that seemed almost autonomic. Hardly thinking about his choices, he set the stones he carried where they would be readily accessible. As Grueburn and Latebirth struggled down the slope, supporting between them a massive boulder, and gasping stertorously, he estimated its shape in relation to its freight of malachite, then directed them to place it like a cornerstone where two of his lines met. When they dropped it where he indicated, and leaned on it to ease their trembling, he instructed them to turn it slightly. And as soon as they complied to his satisfaction, he followed flurries of wind back onto the rockfall to retrieve more fragments of his intent.

In moments, he found a chunk of a size that threatened to exceed him. But before he could pry the rock out of the slope, he felt Stave coming toward him.

"Permit me," the former Master offered. "There is little else that I can do to aid you. I lack the stonelore of Giants. Nor, it appears, do my senses equal yours. Yet strength I have.

"Also I am not needed to stand guard. In the absence of such glamour as the Unbeliever's son has wielded, any force potent to endanger Swordmainnir will be perceived at some distance." With a gesture, he indicated the open plain. "So far from the foes gathered in the region of Mount Thunder, I deem that we are in no imminent peril of attack. And I do not doubt that Hynyn and Khelen watch over us in their fashion.

"Therefore permit me, Chosen-son. Carry lesser stones as you have need of them. Provide guidance to the Giants. Permit me to make use of my strength."

Stave's voice conveyed an oblique impression of appeal. He seemed to want more than he asked. Apparently being separated from Linden was hard on him. He needed distractions while he waited for her return.

Nodding, Jeremiah stepped aside. When he had remembered to say, "Thanks," he added, "I'll show you more as soon as you're ready." Then he turned away to check on the Giants.

Latebirth had a lump in her arms that she could barely lift alone. Tortuous with caution, she picked her way downward. At the same time, Grueburn strained to loosen a boulder which was too heavy for her—and which might let the rockfall above her slip. Sure of himself in at least this one respect, Jeremiah told her to leave it. "I'll need it"—it was veined with too much green to ignore—"but we can move it later. For now, we should look higher up."

Grueburn gasped a sigh as she straightened her back. For a moment, she raised her face to the stars, groaned unfamiliar curses. "Even among Giants," she admitted, "I am proven foolish. Clearly movement here will weaken the slope. This I should have discerned without your counsel."

Jeremiah felt her weariness. It slapped at him like the wind. But he could think of nothing reassuring to say except, "We still have plenty to choose from."

Unsteady as an invalid, she accompanied him upward.

He studied her sidelong for a moment, remembering his mother and the Staff of Law. Then he slapped his hands together, lifted fire into the night. His flames were more than light and warmth. They were Earthpower. He wanted to believe that their uses were not limited to fusing marrowmeld structures and cooking sour tubers; but he had no one to teach him. He could only learn by trying.

"When Mom does this," he said more to himself than to the Swordmain, "it helps." Reaching out, he grasped Grueburn's forearm.

While he concentrated, trying to send his inherited magic into her, she watched him with a glint of hope in her eyes. After a few heartbeats, however, she murmured, "A worthy attempt, young Jeremiah. Alas, it is not the Staff of Law. It warms and soothes. It does not restore."

As if he were flinching, he let her go. His failure was obvious. He did not need to hear it named.

Failure isn't something you are. His mother had told him that. *It's something you* do. She had said it as if she believed it. But it did not feel like the truth. His inability to help Grueburn felt like just another demonstration that he was not *good enough* to deserve success.

Without warning, he saw Lord Foul's eyes in the bonfire that had maimed him. Unbidden and compulsory, the memory cut him like the flick of a lash. It cut deep enough to draw blood.

In that instant, he wanted to hit back. He needed a lash of his own. He saw the *croyel*'s neck gripped in his strangling hands; saw himself pounding the Despiser's head to pulp with a stone. His eagerness to *hurt them* was so swift and unexpected that he was unable to control it. It snatched a snarl past his teeth before he could restrain himself.

At once, he slapped his halfhand over his mouth. But he was too late. Frostheart Grueburn had heard him.

She studied him anxiously. For a while, she seemed to flounder, uncertain of her course. But then she summoned her frayed strength. With elaborate care, softly, she said, "Heed me, young Jeremiah. Linden Giantfriend fears for you. She fears that both the *croyel* and the Despiser have wrought untold harm. Now I discern that she has good cause. But I do not perceive the form or substance of your distress.

"Will you not reveal yourself to me? There is much to be gained by the setting aside of such concealments. And I remind you that I am a Giant. The burden of joy is mine. It belongs to the ears that hear, not to the mouth that speaks."

I don't believe you, Jeremiah retorted in silence. Hear joy? That's not even possible. People judge. The *croyel* taught me that. *Mom* taught me that. She judges herself all the time.

But his secrets were too dark for him. They implied too much vulnerability, too much helplessness. They would reduce him to a whimpering child. They might send him back to the safety of graves.

Seething, he filled his hands with fire again. Then he scrubbed it across his rough cheeks, ran flames through his tangled hair. While light like dishonesty shone in his eyes, he avoided Grueburn's gaze.

"I don't know what you're talking about." Deliberately he tried to sound callous. "Look for malachite higher up." He waved a dismissal. "Find a piece you can lift. I see a few rocks I can manage."

Bitterly he turned away. He told himself that he was angry at Frostheart Grueburn because she had tainted the pure excitement of his talents and his task, but that was not the truth.

Like the wind, the truth thronged with omens.

∽∞∾

A t intervals, Grueburn and Latebirth asked for Jeremiah's opinion of one ponderous fragment or another. Most of the time, they labored without him. And before long, Latebirth limped away to rejoin her resting comrades. After rolling one more boulder down the slope, Grueburn followed her. Eventually the Ironhand and Halewhole Bluntfist came to toil in their turn.

Stave needed more of Jeremiah's guidance, but he gave no sign that he required any respite. He worked steadily, moving chunks and slabs that would have tested the thick muscles of Giants.

And Jeremiah also did not tire. He considered that he had already spent ten years effectively asleep. That was enough. In addition, Anele's gift of Earthpower provided reserves that seemed boundless. Occasionally he paused to measure his growing collection of fragments against his temple's requirements. From time to time, he asked Rime Coldspray and Bluntfist—or, later, Cabledarm and Onyx Stonemage—to position their burdens on one of his structure's boundary-lines. But those interruptions were brief. Between them, he moved up and down the rockfall with the assurance of inspiration. Hidden deposits and delicate veins held his attention as if they made him complete.

Displayed against the fathomless velvet of the heavens, the stars continued their gradual dance of death. And with every loss, the lights that remained seemed to shine more brightly, like beacons pleading for rescue. Only their vast profusion, and the immeasurable distances between them, suggested that the Earth's demise was not imminent.

For a while, Cirrus Kindwind with one maimed arm and Stormpast Galesend relieved Cabledarm and Stonemage. But soon, too soon, they wore themselves to the fringes of prostration. Then only Jeremiah and Stave were left to carry on the task.

Midnight had come. It had not passed. Dawn and more help seemed impossibly distant.

The wind gathered force through the darkness, rushing from nowhere to nowhere, and contradicting its own impulses incessantly. Dust and grit driven away in one direction flailed the ridge from another. Sudden blasts strong enough to stagger Jeremiah righted him in an instant. Nevertheless the gusts did him one service: they scoured away the dirt between the stones. As a result, he was able to locate portions of malachite more quickly. Chunks no bigger than his head and ragged menhirs the size of Giants revealed their secrets as if they were etched in possibilities.

Still there was too little that he and Stave could accomplish alone. Long before dawn, they had gathered all of the lesser shards that the edifice required. Some pieces they put in place: others they could not. For the heavier labor, only Giants working together would suffice. And even when Jeremiah had identified every fragment that he would ask the Swordmainnir to move, he lacked one crucial element.

Eventually he would need a capstone, a culminating lump of malachite. Not a large one: nothing bigger than his two fists together, or perhaps his goaded heart. And its precise contours were not critical. Any approximation would serve his purpose. But it had to be pure—

Well, not absolutely pure. He could tolerate some slight admixture of other substances. But not much. Not much at all.

Where in or under this rubble was he going to find enough unadulterated green? So far, everything had been veins, tracery, small nodes; threads deposited in trickles across centuries or millennia. Otherwise he would have needed rocks of lesser bulk.

Without its capstone, his edifice would have no power over the *Elohim*.

While the Giants rested, there was nothing more that Jeremiah could do to prepare or build. He could only search. And dawn was still three hours away.

Increasingly alarmed, he scrambled up and down the rockfall, moving with less assurance and more haste; gripped by a fever of trepidation. Over and over again, he told himself to slow down. He could not probe the slope deeply or accurately while he was hurrying. But he seemed to feel jaws snapping at his back, fangs wet with venom and malice, rabid agony. Memories— At any moment, they might catch him.

If he failed now, he would not deserve anything that Linden had done for him.

A slap of wind caught him rushing from one boulder to another. His foot missed its step as if the solidity of the world had faded. Without warning, the entire rockfall seemed to stand on its side. Then he plunged.

In an instant, realities transposed their definitions. Through the darkness, he saw as clearly as prescience that all of his conflicts and confusions would be resolved when his head smashed itself open on that looming jut of granite, *that* one. He was falling too hard to twist aside. But now he understood that being overtaken by his fears was not the worst possible outcome. Even a retreat to his graves was not the worst. Anything could be destroyed, anything at all, by a senseless, childish accident.

Then Stave caught his arm, swung him out of danger so suddenly that Jeremiah did not recognize Stave's grasp until Stave had settled him on a canting shelf of basalt. He did not feel the tight hurt of Stave's fingers until the first wildness of his heartbeat began to subside.

He was panting as though he had lost a race.

"Chosen-son," Stave said like a man who had seen nothing, done nothing, "you appear troubled to my sight. Do not take it amiss that I say so. I am *Haruchai*. Your silence I deem condign. I gauge that you have concealed naught which may alter the choices of your companions. What purpose, then, is served by speech? Nonetheless you are mortal, as I am. And at the side of the Chosen your mother, I have learned that it is not shameful to request or receive aid. Therefore I will hear if you wish to speak."

Jeremiah was breathing too hard to think clearly. Mom wanted him to talk. Grueburn wanted him to talk. They wanted to probe horrible memories, expose parts of him that bore the marks of the *croyel* and the Despiser. Of course he refused. But now he knew that there were worse things than failure.

He had in fact concealed something that might have affected Linden's choices. She did not understand the dark core of Anele's legacy.

The former Master had promised to watch over him. To keep him safe.

"Stave—" he began thickly. "They don't know. I'm so afraid—"

But he could not continue. The words stuck in his throat.

What purpose, then, is served—? His mother was already gone.

While Stave waited impassively, Jeremiah wrestled his demons into their familiar shapes.

"I'm afraid this is all wasted." He gestured awkwardly around him. "There's a piece I need, and I can't find it. Without it, nothing else counts."

Stave lifted an eyebrow. "What is it that you require, Chosen-son?"

Jeremiah swallowed a groan. "A lump of malachite. About this big." He put his fists together. "And it pretty much has to be pure. But all I've got are traces. That whole ridge probably doesn't have any pure malachite big enough to save the *Elohim*."

Stave scanned the slope as though it did not interest him. "Perchance it does not," he remarked. "We cannot be certain until we have searched with greater care. Also it may be that the surface of the rockfall conceals its depths. I will accompany you until you are confident of your perceptions. If no hope is found, then mayhap we would do well to delve within the rubble.

"I see no cause for concern"—he may have meant despair—"until we have done our utmost. And even then, the lore of our companions may devise possibilities which elude us."

Jeremiah stifled a protest. He wanted to say, That isn't going to work. All of us together can't move this many rocks fast enough. But Stave's uninflected calm seemed to refuse objections.

How could he be right? He did not share Jeremiah's fears.

He was *Haruchai*. He had sacrificed his place among his people to stand with Linden. How could he be wrong?

After a moment, Jeremiah nodded reluctantly. "Sure. Why not? What else are we going to do?"

Bracing himself on the former Master's dispassion, he filled his hands with fire. Earthpower might serve to sharpen his health-sense. And if it did not, it might comfort him anyway.

Together Jeremiah Chosen-son and Stave of the *Haruchai* began the tedious task of scrutinizing the rockfall from every angle.

ℜ

F or Jeremiah, time crept by in an ocean surge of frustration, inexorable as a tide, rising and falling from one moment to the next, but always climbing higher. An accumulating sense of futility lured his attention into darker places. His flames changed nothing, and he let them go; immersed himself once more in the world's darkness. Occasionally his heart rose at the glimpse of a deposit. When he saw that the amount of malachite was too small, his spirit sank again.

But Stave was always at his side, always calm—and steadier than Jeremiah's pulse. Over and over again, Jeremiah swallowed his alarm and kept going for no better reason than because Stave was with him.

Stealthy as betrayal, dawn came closer; and still Jeremiah could not find what he sought. An hour before the moment when the sun should have risen, he and the *Haruchai* completed the first stage of their search. They had looked everywhere. They had looked at everything. Now nothing remained except the imponderable labor of digging into the rockfall.

High up on the slope, Jeremiah collapsed on a slab of granite with his elbows propped on his knees and his face hidden in his hands. He was tired now, worn out by defeat. Everything that felt like excitement or hope had drained out of him. No doubt Stave would go on searching. Jeremiah could not.

The *Haruchai* remained standing nearby, glancing here and there with apparent unconcern. He may have been waiting for Jeremiah to recover. After a few moments, however, he said, "Set aside discouragement, Chosen-son. Hope remains."

The flatness of his tone made him sound reproachful.

Jeremiah jerked up his head. As aggrieved as a child, he burst out, "It does not! We've looked everywhere! And I don't care what you say about taking this rubble apart. Sure, we can look deeper that way. But we only have eight Giants—and *they* don't have any food. They'll have to shove rocks out of the way for *days* while they starve. The world is going to end, and it'll break Mom's heart, and we'll still be here just digging!"

"Softly, Chosen-son," Stave replied as if he were commenting on the condition of Jeremiah's pajamas. "The time has not come to rouse the Swordmainnir. Doubtless they would answer your urging, but we have no cause to summon them. In one respect, you are mistaken. We have not extended our search to its boundaries."

Jeremiah stared. He wanted to shout something vicious, but Stave's manner stopped him. Briefly his mouth and throat worked without producing a sound. Then he asked hoarsely, "What're you talking about?"

"Chosen-son," Stave stated without hesitation, "you have not turned your gaze upward."

Still Jeremiah stared. What, upward? At the stars?

"Consider the ridge," explained his companion. "Consider the wound which the Chosen has made. Your discernment exceeds my senses, but to my sight it appears that there is a source of malachite above us."

Jeremiah sprang to his feet as if he had been stung, flung his gaze at the source of the rockfall.

At first, he found nothing except blunt granite, blind basalt. Apparently every bit of green had already fallen.

But Stave was looking higher, studying the hollow near its ragged upper rim.

A tall slab stood there, a monolith heavy enough to resist Linden's detonation. To a quick glance, the stone resembled granite or schist. But when Jeremiah looked harder, he saw that the slab was actually a flawed mix of igneous rock and more porous sandstone supported by rigid shafts of flint.

And enclosed within the monolith were signs—

"Really?" he breathed. "Are you sure?"

Was that his capstone? Exactly what his temple needed?

If so, it was inaccessible. Completely out of reach. Perhaps Linden could have used her Staff, caused the slab to topple somehow. Her son could not.

With enough rope—

The Giants had no rope.

Scowling, Jeremiah clenched his fists until his fingers ached. "I can't tell. It's too far away." Then he beat his knuckles against his thighs so that his frustration would not erupt into the night. The monolith appeared to lean as if it were taunting him; daring him to believe that it would topple. "But even if it's enough, it's useless. We can't get at it."

"Chosen-son." Now Stave's tone was unmistakably a reprimand. He regarded Jeremiah as if the tugging of the fractured gale did not touch him. "You judge in haste. Therefore you judge falsely. Have you come so far in Linden Avery's care and failed to learn that despair gives poor counsel? If the needed stone lies beyond your grasp, withdraw. Retreat to the foot of the rockfall. Acknowledge this truth, that you are not alone."

Jeremiah opened his mouth; closed it. A mordant voice inside him snarled, What're you going to do? Fly up there? I dare you. But that reaction arose from memories which he strained to suppress. He would have pulled down the ridge gladly to bury them. And Stave was impervious to Jeremiah's galled incredulity. Withdraw. Fighting himself, Jeremiah moved backward under the pressure of Stave's severe gaze. Retreat.

Mom! Where are you? I don't know what's going on.

Retreat from *what*?

Awkward as a youth who had never been sure of anything, Jeremiah went down the rubble as quickly as he could manage.

When he reached bare dirt, he peered upward. Just for a moment, he could not locate Stave. But then a suggestion of movement snagged his attention. Squinting, he spotted a hard shape like a piece of condensed midnight untouched by starlight. Stave had already climbed beyond the top of the rockfall. Now he hung splayed against the ridgefront, searching with his fingers and toes for holds which would enable him to lift himself toward the immense hollow cut by Linden and Earthpower.

He must have been creeping: he hardly seemed to move at all. Jeremiah could not imagine how he found cracks and rims still solid enough to support him. Yet Stave did move. Sudden jerks conveyed the impression that a grip had failed, or a toehold. He appeared to swing from side to side, hanging by one hand; perhaps by one finger. Uncertain as hallucinations, bits of debris dropped away. But he did not fall.

He was *Haruchai*, born to the crags and precipices and flensing winds of the Westron Mountains.

If he gained the gouge, he would be able to climb more easily, at least for a while. Its lower surface was not vertical. He would be halfway to the monolith.

The monolith itself was three times his height, many times heavier. It could have served as a monument for a Giant. He would not be able to dislodge it by simply throwing rocks at it. His only choice would be to work his way higher.

But toward the back of the hollow, the ascent would become steeper. Then the harmed stone above him would tilt outward. There the slab he strove to reach stood on a crude protrusion like a snout. That formation multiplied the hazards. He would have to climb beneath it, hanging precariously in the air—

Jeremiah heard one of the Swordmainnir moving toward him, but he could not look away from the small flutter of darkness that represented Stave. Over and over again, he held his breath as if he believed that his own tension might protect the former Master. The whole night had come to this: the little increments, barely perceptible, of Stave's efforts.

Wrapped in winds, Rime Coldspray towered out of the night to stand beside Jeremiah. The Ironhand had left her armor and sword behind, but she moved as if she still carried them—and had another Giant sitting on her shoulders. That she had slept was plain. But she needed more than rest. She needed sustenance. Above all, she needed relief. She and her comrades had known little except struggle and strife since they had first approached the Land.

Briefly she regarded Jeremiah. Then she lifted her gaze toward the ridge and Stave.

He had almost reached the hollow. Holds broke in his hands; but he cast those shards away and hunted for better grips. Occasionally Jeremiah heard the clatter as rocks hit the slope. At other times, gusts carried the sounds away, and Stave seemed to climb in a preternatural silence, fraught as a clenched breath.

"Stone and Sea," murmured Coldspray. "If this is not madness incarnate, it serves some purpose which I do not discern."

Jeremiah pointed. "He's trying to reach that slab. It has malachite I need. But I don't think he can even get there. He won't be able to break it loose."

"Ah." The Ironhand released a sigh. "Now I comprehend. The malachite itself is vague to my sight. But consider the stone within which it is concealed." She stared hard under her heavy brows. "If distance and darkness do not mislead me, the stone stands somewhat apart. A cleft or flaw has detached it from the ridge.

"Stave Rockbrother will endeavor to dislodge it."

Jeremiah did not believe that Stave could do it.

As if to herself, Coldspray added, "When it falls, he will also. Then he must perish. Though he is *Haruchai*, his flesh is not iron. His bones are not. They will not withstand an impact from that height."

While pressure mounted in Jeremiah's chest, Stave's unyielding shape crossed into the gouge. There he rose to his feet and paused, secure against the battering of the wind. For a few moments, he appeared to study the challenge ahead of him. Then Jeremiah saw the former Master wave one arm: a gesture of reassurance so unconvincing that it made Jeremiah wince.

This was impossible. It was all impossible. What Stave had done was already insane—and there was worse ahead of him. When it falls, he will also. Jeremiah had not thought that far ahead.

Then he must perish.

Abruptly Jeremiah wheeled on Rime Coldspray, clutched at her arm. "Do something," he panted. "He's *Stave*. Mom will never forgive me if he dies." Because he was pleading with a Giant, the Ironhand of the Swordmainnir, he tried to tell the truth. "I'll never forgive myself."

Without turning her head, Coldspray answered, "This choice was not yours to make, young Jeremiah. It belonged to Stave Rockbrother. It remains his. He will suffer the cost because he chooses to do so.

"At present, his peril is diminished. Later it will become extreme. Should he fall within the hollow, we can do naught to aid him. We must trust his skill and agility to preserve him.

"The achievement of his purpose is another matter."

Still watching Stave's wary ascent, she called, "Ho, Swordmainnir! Bestir yourselves! You will wish to witness Stave Rockbrother's valor. And he will have need of you!"

At first, there was no response.

"Frostheart Grueburn!" shouted the Ironhand. "Latebirth!" She sounded more relaxed than Jeremiah felt; far more confident. "Cabledarm! Onyx Stonemage! Hear me! Hear and come!"

After a moment, a bleary voice answered, "We hear you." Grueburn. "The very stars hear you."

If she said more, gusts carried the words away.

For a while, Stave moved more easily. But soon he reached the steeper recesses of the wound, where the stone had more cracks. He was forced to resume his earlier care, testing each handhold, each support for his feet, each small ledge and crack and bulge, before he committed his weight to it.

Yawning, Giants approached Jeremiah and Coldspray. He recognized them without glancing at them. Only Stormpast Galesend and Halewhole Bluntfist lagged behind—or they were still asleep.

While Stave crawled up the back of the hollow and began to creep toward the granite jut which supported the monolith, often hanging by his hands alone until he found places to anchor his feet, Coldspray explained his intentions to her comrades. Then she said, "He is Stave Rockbrother, able and stalwart as the *Haruchai* of old. He will not fail."

"When he succeeds," muttered Grueburn, "he will fall. He must."

"And he will perish," Stonemage added grimly.

"Therefore," concluded the Ironhand, "we must intervene."

Considering the problem, her comrades nodded.

Jeremiah wanted to ask, Intervene *how*? But Grueburn, Latebirth, Stonemage, and Cabledarm were already moving away. Apparently they did not need Coldspray's instructions. As they started up the rockfall, they separated. Grueburn and Latebirth on one side, Cabledarm and Stonemage on the other, they labored toward the ridgefront.

At first, Jeremiah could not imagine what they had in mind. Then he understood. They aimed to bracket the slab's likely path when it toppled. Clearly they meant to position themselves on either side of that path. If they could avoid being struck, they might have some chance of catching Stave.

If he did not fall first. If he managed to shift the monolith. If loosened rocks did not hit anybody. If just one of the Giants was quick enough to intercept his plunge. If his impact in her arms did not kill him as surely as the jagged rubble. If it did not break or kill her—

Jeremiah was holding his breath again. He thought that he saw Stave's arms flailing. Dislodged debris spattered like rain into the hollow.

But Stave's indistinct form still clung to the rock. One grip at a time, he eased upward.

Cirrus Kindwind left the Ironhand's side, strode some distance up the rockfall. When she had climbed atop an especially tall boulder, she stopped to study the ridgefront. Then she raised her voice in a shout.

"Grueburn! Latebirth! Alter your heading!" She waved her arms, directing her comrades to the left. "You will be struck!"

The two women did not respond to Kindwind's hail; but they must have heard her. They shifted their course.

Unfortunately now they were no longer clambering up the rockfall's spine. Instead they were forced to straggle along the side of the slope. If Stave came down toward the crest of the rubble, they would not be able to reach him without sprinting upward—and they were fatally weary.

Still Stave made his way by undetectable increments. Only the erratic spatter of stones and the wind-torn fall of dirt showed that he was still moving. But he *was* moving. One hand or foot or finger or toe at a time, he worked his way closer to the bulbous rock supporting the slab.

Jeremiah hardly dared to estimate the distance. Involuntarily he imagined Stave's fingers bleeding, his muscles trembling—

Rime Coldspray rested a gentle hand on Jeremiah's shoulder. "Remember that he is *Haruchai*," she murmured. "He has performed wonders ere now. Mayhap he will surpass our fears yet again."

"But he's in trouble either way." If Stave failed to shift the slab, he would never be able to climb back down. "Can they"—Jeremiah meant Grueburn and Latebirth, Stonemage and Cabledarm—"actually catch him?"

"We are Giants." The Ironhand's reply was softer than the wind. "Often we have been tested. Often we have prevailed."

For a time, Stave seemed to vanish. Hidden by the shape of the bulge, he had become indistinguishable from the stone.

In alarm, Jeremiah blurted, "Where is he? What's happened?"

"Gaze more closely," Coldspray advised. "You will perceive that he is safe for a time. One arm he has wedged into the cleft between the monolith and the cliff. While he remains thus secured, his peril is diminished. Now the uncertain balance of the stone is the gravest threat. Should it tilt suddenly, catching him unprepared—" She allowed herself a sigh. "In that event, opportunities to affect his fate will be slight. Far better for him if he must exert his full strength to shift the stone. Then his efforts will carry him outward, away from the precipice and ruin."

As she spoke, Jeremiah caught an image of Stave dropping like more rubble. Spinning out of control. Hitting the ridgefront over and over again until he was mangled beyond recognition.

The former Master had made his own choices—but Jeremiah had inspired them. His whole body ached with a futile desire to keep Stave safe.

Still resting her hand on Jeremiah's shoulder, Rime Coldspray continued, "For the moment, I am primarily concerned by the width and depth of the cleft." She sounded deliberately casual. "At this distance, I cannot gauge it. If the stone does not stand free of the cliff, it is unlikely to fall. And if the cleft will admit no more than Stave's arm, he will have scant leverage. Then the bulk of muscle which he will require might exceed even a Giant.

"No, we must hope that he will contrive to force his arms and chest—indeed, his body entire—into the cleft. For him as for us, that will be the most favorable circumstance."

She may have been trying to soothe Jeremiah by focusing his attention on practical details.

To an extent, she succeeded. As if involuntarily, he found himself imagining Stave squeezed behind the slab; Stave straining to shift the monolith. While Stave did such things—if he did them—he would not fall.

Wind stung Jeremiah's eyes. His pajamas fluttered around him in tatters. He ignored Stormpast Galesend and Halewhole Bluntfist as they drew near. Instead he watched Grueburn and Latebirth, Stonemage and Cabledarm. They had reached the places where they meant to wait for Stave. Now they stood motionless in the night. They were not immediately below the slab, but they were close enough to be struck by debris—or by the slab itself if it bounced crookedly against the ridgefront. Still Jeremiah thought that they were too far from the cliff—and too far from each other. He could not believe that they had a prayer of saving Stave.

The three Swordmainnir with Jeremiah studied the monolith and its pediment. From her boulder, Cirrus Kindwind did the same. Winds flailed like indignation in all directions, outraged by affronts too distant to be answered.

Without warning, Kindwind shouted, "Ware, Frostheart Grueburn! The stone shifts toward you!"

It might move in that direction if Stave could use only one arm. Or perhaps the rim of the bulge above Grueburn's position was simply weaker.

Faintly through the tumult in his heart, Jeremiah heard Grueburn reply, "I have seen it."

She did not step back. Nor did Latebirth.

Onyx Stonemage and Cabledarm readied themselves to spring forward.

Under her breath, Coldspray murmured, "Be swift, comrades. You must be watchful and wary, but above all you must be swift. We can ill endure any loss of life."

"Or indeed any injury," muttered Galesend, "worn and weakened as we are."

Jeremiah beat bruises onto his thighs and strove to see.

There. He had lost sight of Stave. The *Haruchai* had thrust his way into the cleft; or the shape of the jut masked his presence. But the monolith had moved: Jeremiah was sure of it.

It did not move again.

Then it did.

At first, it appeared to lean back toward the cliff as though it sought to crush the force which had disturbed it. For moments as long as heartbeats, as urgent as cries, it hung in place, scattering scree from its base.

With the suddenness of a calving glacier, the slab slid away.

Silent as a cast-off leaf, it appeared to drift through the darkness until one end collided with the ridgefront. Instantly it broke apart, became half a dozen pieces. They rebounded from the impact, falling like a barrage toward the waiting Swordmainnir.

Grueburn, Latebirth, Cabledarm, and Stonemage were all in danger; but the threat to Grueburn and Latebirth was greater.

"He is yours, Cabledarm!" Grueburn yelled. Jeremiah saw her and then Latebirth leaping down the jagged slope of the rockfall.

Granite thunder boomed. Heavy shards pounded the rubble where the two women had been standing.

At the same time, Cabledarm dodged a fragment which would have slain her. She surged upward. Unscathed, Onyx Stonemage braced herself; remained where she was.

Above them, Stave also struck the cliff. But he twisted as he dropped so that he hit with his feet. Somehow he planted himself long enough to flex his legs and spring away. His great strength transformed his plummet into an outward leap.

Arms spread like wings, he cast himself soaring into the mad roil of the winds.

Cabledarm was there when he came down.

In spite of his splayed posture, he was falling too hard, plunging like a chunk of the slab. Even a Giant could not hope to catch him safely. His weight and momentum would shatter bones, Cabledarm's as well as his.

But she did not try to catch him. She had other intentions. During the quick instants of his descent, she crouched low. Then she sprang to meet him, arching away as she did so; already pitching herself backward.

Her huge hands found his hips. Her arms bent to absorb the collision. Then she gave him a prodigious heave.

His force and hers flung her, helpless, down the side of the slope. She tumbled like a piece of the ridge.

But she had redirected his fall. He was soaring again.

Toward Onyx Stonemage—

—who caught him in both arms.

Like Cabledarm, she did not try to hold him. Instead she swung him in an arc and released him so that she seemed to throw him in the direction of open ground beyond the rockfall.

He landed on his feet; dove and rolled to dissipate the last of his momentum. Then he rose to stand upright in the thick dusk.

Jeremiah began running before the *Haruchai* came to a halt.

The monolith was broken. Its burden of malachite may have been shattered, made useless. Everything may have been wasted. Even Linden's ride into the chaos of a *caesure*—

But Jeremiah was not racing to locate the outcome of his only hope. He was running as if his heart might burst to find out if Stave and Cabledarm were all right.

In the east, a dull dawn announced the third sunless day.

9.

An Impoverished Temple

The company gathered around Stave and Cabledarm. Jeremiah fought down an impulse to babble. *I can't believe it! That was amazing! Are you all right?* But he could hardly speak in any case. He was panting as though he had run an inconceivable distance, and had witnessed wonders.

Stave's arms and feet were latticed with scratches. His palms and fingers, his toes, the soles of his feet: all oozed blood. But those injuries were trivial. The effects of his impact with Cabledarm's hands were another matter. His whole body had struck and recoiled like a cracked whip. Now every joint looked torn; every muscle. His internal organs appeared to throb as if they had been beaten with clubs. Blood gathered at the corners of his mouth: he had bitten into his tongue. In spite of his *Haruchai* stoicism, he was trembling.

He stood, but he seemed unable to speak. Like a man who had been blinded, he stared at nothing. If he felt the presence of his companions, he did not react to it.

Rime Coldspray studied him for a grim moment. Then she sent Cirrus Kindwind to retrieve a waterskin. She had nothing else to offer him.

Cabledarm's wounds were more obvious. They looked worse. Pitching Stave to Stonemage, she had flung herself down the raw edges and fanged splinters of the rubble. Like Stave, she had regained her feet beyond the slope. Unlike him, she stood hunched in pain, hugging her left arm against her chest. Giantish obscenities bubbled like froth past her lips. She was bleeding from half a dozen gashes, at least two of them deep enough to expose bone. Contusions covered her from shoulder to ankle. But her worst injury was to her left shoulder.

The force of Stave's plummet had ripped her arm out of his socket. It was dislocated so badly that Jeremiah could hardly bear to look at it.

"Only you, Cabledarm," the Ironhand muttered through her teeth. "Only you could emerge so harmed from such a rescue."

"It is my gift," Cabledarm rasped. Then she groaned a curse. "Stone and Sea! Am I not a Giant? And have I not vaunted myself the mightiest of the Swordmainnir? How am I thus humbled by mere falling?"

"We need Mom," Jeremiah breathed miserably. "We can't help her. And Stave looks like he's going to pass out."

But the Giants did not respond. Cabledarm's dislocation, at least, was hurt which they knew how to address. At a nod from Coldspray, Halewhole Bluntfist moved to stand behind Cabledarm. With one arm on Cabledarm's left shoulder near her neck, and the other across her chest under her right arm, Bluntfist grasped Cabledarm tightly enough to wring a moan from her comrade. Without a moment's consideration, Coldspray gripped Cabledarm's damaged limb and heaved; twisted.

The sound as the arm slipped back into place hit Jeremiah like a jab to the stomach.

Cabledarm roared. Briefly she wobbled as if she were losing consciousness. But Bluntfist held her until her faintness passed, and she began to curse again.

Grimacing, Cabledarm moved the fingers of her left hand, managed a fist. When she was done swearing, she muttered, "It is much and naught, Ironhand. It will hamper me, but it will mend. Only stanch some few of my rents, and I will name myself blessed. Stave Rockbrother lives"—she glanced quickly around—"does he not?" Seeing the answer in the eyes of her comrades, she finished, "Then will I name myself blessed in all sooth."

"For the present, however," the Ironhand commanded, "you will conserve yourself, Cabledarm. Cirrus Kindwind brings water. While you drink and rest, we will contrive bindings for your wounds. You have earned the tales which we will tell of you. Now we will contrive to earn those which you will tell."

"Aye," Cabledarm assented: another groan. With Bluntfist's help, she lowered herself to the dirt. There she extended one gashed leg so that Bluntfist could try to stop the bleeding.

Jeremiah saw her injuries too clearly: the rich pulse of her blood and pain made him feel sick. About some things he knew too much. About this he knew too little. He could too easily believe that Cabledarm would bleed to death. That Stave was dying inside.

Fortunately Kindwind soon returned with several waterskins. Two she tossed to Bluntfist. A third she took directly to Stave.

Fleeing the sight of Cabledarm's torn flesh, Jeremiah joined Kindwind.

Stave did not react to their presence. He remained standing; continued to stare at nothing as though his whole world had become the abyss of the Lost Deep. Tremors ran through him like waves of fever. His hands shook. Even his lips quivered.

Jeremiah did not know what to say or do. Stave had promised to protect him. This was the result.

Frowning, Cirrus Kindwind rested her hand on Stave's shoulder. "You are not alone, Rockbrother," she assured him. "Rest you need. So much is certain. But first you must drink. Your flesh has been much abused. It requires refreshment. And see?" She unbound the neck of her waterskin, held it in front of him. "Here is water."

Stave did not move. He did not appear to hear her. But when she touched his mouth with the lip of the waterskin, he raised his arms, accepted it from her. Trembling, he drank.

Jeremiah had never seen any *Haruchai* do more than sip from the cup of one hand. Now Stave swallowed long gulps as though more lives than his depended on them; drank until he had emptied half of the waterskin. Then, slowly, he sank to his knees, settled back to sit on his heels. The waterskin he placed on the ground. His hands he rested, open palms upward, on his thighs. He seemed to nod.

After that, he resumed gazing sightlessly at the twilight of the new day.

Beckoning for Jeremiah to accompany her, Kindwind stepped away. When they had withdrawn a few paces, she said, "We must trust, Chosen-son, that his folk restore themselves in this manner. It appears that his spirit has turned inward. But I will believe that a man who has performed his feats must soon heal himself and return to us."

Jeremiah swallowed against the dryness in his throat. "I hope so. He doesn't deserve this."

"Ah, deserve," sighed Kindwind. "The notion of deserved and undeserved is a fancy. Knowing both life and death, we endeavor to impose worth and meaning upon our deeds, and thereby to comfort our fear of impermanence. We choose to imagine that our lives merit continuance. Mayhap all sentience shares a similar fancy. Mayhap the Earth itself, being sentient in its fashion, shares it. Nonetheless it is a fancy. A wider gaze does not regard us in that wise. The stars do not. Perhaps the Creator does not. The larger truth is merely that all things end. By that measure, our fancies cannot be distinguished from dust.

"For this reason, Giants love tales. Our iteration of past deeds and desires and discoveries provides the only form of permanence to which mortal life can aspire. That such permanence is a chimera does not lessen its power to console. Joy is in the ears that hear."

Her assertion startled Jeremiah. It seemed to question his foundations. If he closed his eyes, he could still see the extremity of Stave's fall. The hard throb of Cabledarm's bleeding and the excrucation of her shoulder cried out to his senses. Awkwardly he reached for Kindwind's last waterskin. When she released it, he drank as if his thirst—his dismay—had the force of a moral convulsion.

"So you're saying," he protested or pleaded, "what Stave did is worthless? What Cabledarm did is worthless? It's all dust?"

"Aye," Cirrus Kindwind assented, "if that is how you choose to hear the tale." Her tone was mild. "For myself, I will honor the effort and the intent. Doing so, I will be comforted."

Jeremiah wanted to shout. Instead he fumed, "You sound like the *croyel*." Was joy in the ears that hear? Then so were agony and horror. So was despair. "It was forever telling me everything Mom did was useless. Nothing matters. It's all dust. That's why Lord Foul laughs—and Roger—and those Ravers. They agree with you. In the end, they're the only ones who get what they want."

Kindwind looked at him sharply. Like the flick of a blade, she retorted, "Then hear me, Chosen-son. Hear me well. There is another truth which you must grasp.

"Mortal lives are not stones. They are not seas. For impermanence to judge itself by the standards of permanence is folly. Or it is arrogance. Life merely is what it is, neither more nor less. To deem it less because it is not more is to heed the counsels of the Despiser.

"We do what we must so that we may find worth in ourselves. We do not hope vainly that we will put an end to pain, or to loss, or to death."

Failure isn't something you are. *It's something you* do.

Without warning, Jeremiah found that he ached to share Kindwind's beliefs, and Linden's. Perhaps the monolith had never contained enough malachite. Perhaps the deposit had shattered. Perhaps Stave and even Cabledarm would die. Perhaps Mom would never come back. Perhaps futility was the only truth. Still Jeremiah would have to find a way to live with it.

To himself, he muttered, "It's not that easy."

Cirrus Kindwind had never been possessed.

Her response was a snort. "We were not promised ease. The purpose of life—if it may be said to have purpose—is not ease. It is to choose, and to act upon the choice. In that task, we are not measured by outcomes. We are measured only by daring and effort and resolve."

Jeremiah wanted to insist, It's not that easy. It's *not*. But the words died in his mouth. Kindwind had already turned away. Several of the Giants around Cabledarm had turned away. They were gazing up at the spine of the rockfall.

At Frostheart Grueburn and Latebirth. As Jeremiah caught sight of them, they labored past the crest and began their descent. Between them, they carried a large chunk of stone.

It resembled a fragment of the monolith. He detected distinct signs of malachite.

Not seams or veins, delicate trickles. A concentrated lode.

In an instant, he forgot everything else. Leaving Kindwind, he ran at the slope.

That was a piece of the slab: it had to be. And its mineral deposit was still intact.

How big was that sealed lump of green?

The two Giants came a little way to meet him. Then they set down their burden and straightened their backs, loosened their arms. Before he reached them, he felt their emotions.

In spite of the gloom, they were bright with vindication.

"By good fortune," Grueburn called to her comrades, "the object of Stave Rock-brother's extravagance contained an admixture of sandstone. When it struck, it broke along its less durable seams. The malachite of its heart was preserved."

Jeremiah needed to see for himself. Filling his hands with Earthpower, he clapped them to the surface of the rock; probed inward with all of his senses.

Then he wheeled away, flung his gaze down the slope toward Stave.

"You did it! Stave, you *did* it!"

The former Master knelt with his back to the rockfall. He did not lift his head or turn. He may have sunk so far down into himself that he did not hear.

Nevertheless he had succeeded.

Some things were too easy. Accepting failure was one of them.

ᔕᗄᔭ

For a time, Jeremiah was content to confirm the various locations of his materials, study their shapes, and plan. While he did so, the Giants finished tending Cabledarm's wounds. Then they rested.

Eventually Stave stirred. With an air of caution, as if he feared that he might break bones, he looked around at the cratered plain, the crepuscular day. Then he rose to his feet.

The relieved shouts of the Giants elicited no response. Jeremiah's gladness he acknowledged with no more than a nod. He gave the impression that he had forgotten speech, or gone beyond it. When he had surveyed the company and the rockfall, the beginnings of Jeremiah's construct, and perhaps the passage of time, he put a hand to his mouth and whistled.

While Jeremiah and the Swordmainnir watched him, wondering, Stave waited for Hynyn.

The stallion came promptly. Although Jeremiah had seen no sign of the star-browed roan earlier, Hynyn appeared as if he had reincarnated himself from the substance of the gloaming. At Stave's side, he halted; stood patiently while Stave welcomed him by stroking his neck and shoulder. Then, together, they approached the Giants.

At once, Jeremiah hurried to join Rime Coldspray and her comrades.

Wavering on his feet, Stave stopped. He seemed to have achieved an unstable victory over his private wounds, one which might become defeat at any unexpected action, any unpremeditated word.

"You did it," Jeremiah said again, but hesitantly, unsure of himself in Stave's presence. "You saved us."

You saved me.

Stave glanced at Jeremiah, then away. He did not meet Coldspray's gaze. With obvious difficulty, as if language required skills which he had forgotten or misplaced, he said, "Hynyn will guide you to water. The way is long." His voice began to fade. "But there is water."

In a husky whisper, he added, "My thanks to Cabledarm. Also to Onyx Stonemage." He made an effort to gather himself. "And to Cirrus Kindwind."

Still cautiously, he turned his back. With the elaborate care of a man who feared falling, he walked out onto the plain until he was barely visible. There he knelt again, facing the northwest like a diminished sentinel.

Hynyn remained with the Giants. Clearly the great stallion understood the promise that Stave had made in his name. He waited for the women to act on it.

After a brief consultation, Kindwind announced, "With your consent, Ironhand, this task is mine. In the shifting of stones, I am hampered, but the bearing of water-skins will test only my dexterity."

Rime Coldspray nodded. "Go with my thanks. Return as swiftly as you are able. Water we must have. The tasks remaining to us will be arduous."

Nodding to her comrades, Cirrus Kindwind left with Hynyn. The imperious arch of the stallion's neck seemed to assert that he could not be humbled by such mundane service.

When they were gone, Rime Coldspray said, "Now, Chosen-son. We have delayed too long. There is death in every lost moment. Instruct us, that we may begin."

Jeremiah's heart beat eagerly. At last— "I've found everything I need," he answered. "But some of it still has to be moved. Then I'll need help putting the pieces in place."

"Indeed." Coldspray scanned her comrades. "For the present, we are only six. But six are more than five, or three, or one. We must suffice.

"Instruct us," she said to Jeremiah again. "Come good or ill, boon or bane, we will strive to do as you ask."

Urged by relief and gratitude, Jeremiah tried to cheer. Then he turned to lead the Giants. With every step, he recovered more of his necessary excitement.

ॐ

By midday, the women had finished moving green-veined rocks to open ground. Before they were done, they were all trembling on the verge of exhaustion. But earlier Cirrus Kindwind had returned with every bulging waterskin that she could carry. The Swordmainnir had been able to continue working because they had enough to drink.

Now they were sprawled in the dirt, resting as though they had been felled. The fraught rasp of their respiration sawed at Jeremiah's nerves until he felt as raw as their lungs; as desperate to be done. But they still had a lot to do.

For him, actually assembling his temple would be comparatively easy. It required no thought at all. His talents were certain, as instinctive as breath. He could have completed the structure without hesitation—if he could have raised the heavier rocks alone.

But for his companions—

The work ahead of them would demand more effort, not less. As the walls rose, massive chunks and boulders would have to be lifted higher. And the roof would be more difficult than the walls. The Giants would have to hold the stones in place at the height of their own shoulders until he could brace the construct with his last hunk of granite, his capstone of malachite. Only then would the temple stand without support.

At some point, Cabledarm had climbed upright. Walking stiffly, she had come to watch her comrades. But she was still too weak to stay on her feet. She had nothing to offer except the encouragement of her presence.

Stave had not moved. At some distance, he knelt facing the northwest as if he sought to ward off threats by nothing more than force of will. Or perhaps he was praying for Linden's return.

Standing near the Ironhand, Jeremiah said uncomfortably, "When you're ready." Erratic bursts of wind slapped at him. Grit stung his cheeks. Beyond his horizons, a fierce storm was brewing. The air was growing cooler. "I know where everything goes. I can do this fast." *Elohim* were dying. "But you should take your time. We can't afford mistakes."

Infelice had tried to prevent his escape from his graves. She should have known better. She should have trusted Linden.

"Yet it must be done," Coldspray replied in a low growl. "Much depends upon it. When we are beset by storms as we sail the world's seas, we do not rest merely because we are weary. Rather we cling to our tasks, and to our lives." She seemed to be trying to convince herself. "Matters do not stand otherwise now."

"Sooth," groaned Frostheart Grueburn. "All that you say is sooth, Ironhand. We must—yet I cannot. In the Lost Deep, I deemed that I had measured the depths of exhaustion. Now I learn that our flight from She Who Must Not Be Named was no more than a child's game by comparison."

"Nay, Grueburn," Stormpast Galesend countered like a pale imitation of herself. "You misesteem us. Exertion alone does not justify our weariness. In addition, we lack viands. Do not discount that deprivation."

"Indeed!" exclaimed Onyx Stonemage. "I will give my oath that I am dwindling. Hunger diminishes me. My garments hang loosely, and my cataphract has become an encumbrance, and I fear that my sword has grown too long for easy use."

For a moment, the Giants were silent. Then Coldspray said like a sigh, "You forget to whom you speak, Stonemage. All here know that in your care every sword grows too long for easy use."

Another silence followed while Jeremiah fretted. The Ironhand's comment may have been a jest. If so, he did not understand it.

Apparently the other Giants did. After a moment, they started laughing.

At first, their laughter was as weak as their limbs: a sound like moaning amid the confusion of the winds. But then Stonemage retorted, "Mockery is ignorance. Occasions there have been in abundance, yet none have inspired complaint," and her comrades began to laugh harder. Soon they were laughing with such abandon that they could not lie still. Latebirth and Galesend tossed from side to side. Grueburn pulled her knees to her chest, hugged them. Even Cabledarm chuckled in spite of her wounds.

"I don't get it," Jeremiah protested; but the women went on laughing.

Joy is in the ears that hear. Clearly the Swordmainnir lived by that creed. Jeremiah did not understand at all. They sounded hysterical. Yet when they subsided, they were stronger. Somehow laughing had restored them.

That was enough for him: he could accept it. When he was able to believe that the Giants were ready, he moved away toward the scant beginnings of his construct, beckoning as he went.

The rectangle that he had marked in the dirt was still vivid in his mind, although its visible lines had been erased. A few heavy stones had already been put in place for him. He had added a number of small rocks himself. But that was barely a start. Most of the building remained to be done.

However, all of his materials were waiting for him. He could imagine their eventual positions precisely, as if they were lit by sunshine rather than masked by dusk. His part of the work that remained was simple.

Followed by the Giants, he thrust his way through the wind to select rocks in their proper sequence: a sequence that would allow him to prop each one securely before the next was lifted.

That the women were more willing than able was painfully obvious. Stones that one Swordmain had managed alone earlier now required the strength of two or three, or even four. Nevertheless their willingness did not waver. To spare themselves, they rolled rather than carried rocks to the edges of the nascent temple. Together they heaved the shards into position. Then Jeremiah scrambled to insert the chunks of granite and basalt that would brace the bigger pieces in place.

The Giants took turns, resting as much as they could. When their waterskins were empty, the Ironhand sent Kindwind to fill them again. And the women watched over each other. Whenever one of them faltered or stumbled, others moved to help.

By slow increments, the walls of the temple rose.

Every now and then, Jeremiah remembered to glance at Stave. Indistinct in the distance, the former Master still knelt with his back to the construct, motionless as a tombstone. He gave no sign that he was aware of his companions' efforts.

They could have used his help.

By the time that Kindwind returned, the walls were nearly complete. A crude slab had been set to form the lintel of the entrance. Without counting, Jeremiah knew that a dozen heavy rocks and twice that many smaller ones remained before the capstone could be wedged into place. He knew exactly where the pieces would go. But he did not know how his companions would be able to finish the work. They seemed entirely spent. He was not confident that their hearts would continue to beat much longer.

While Kindwind handed around waterskins and her comrades rested, Jeremiah went to plead with Stave.

But when he reached the *Haruchai*, he did not know what to say. He could see that Stave was healing. The former Master knew how to provide for his own recovery. Nevertheless his heart beat with palpable reluctance, the pulse in his veins was as thin as a thread, and his breathing barely lifted his chest. In spite of his native toughness, he looked like a man who might not stand again.

Jeremiah's appeal for help turned to dust in his mouth. Winds seemed to drive it back down his throat.

Stave did not turn his head, but his shoulders stiffened slightly at Jeremiah's approach. After a moment, he answered the supplication of Jeremiah's silence.

"Chosen-son." His voice was a wisp of its familiar inflexibility. "Say what you must. I hear you."

"I don't know why you're still alive," Jeremiah blurted. "But I don't know why the

Giants are still alive either. They're way beyond exhausted. They can hardly lift their arms. And we still haven't done the hardest part."

Abruptly he stopped. He had no idea how to continue.

"The hardest part?" Stave inquired: a mere breath of sound.

"The roof. I'm making a temple. I mean, that's how I think of it. It has to have a roof. But it won't stay up until I brace it. That's what your lump of malachite is for. They'll have to lift the rocks and stand—" Simply thinking about such things hurt. "They'll have to just stand there holding up the roof. And even if they can do that, I don't know how they're going to set the capstone. I can't imagine—

"It has to be just right, or it won't work." He struggled to devise scenarios. They were all cruel. "So even if four of them can hold up the roof, that only leaves two to lift the last piece because at least one of them has to climb up there," adding her weight to the rocks on the shoulders of the other Giants, "and put that piece in place. I'll probably have to be there myself to make sure it's right."

Without warning, sobs crowded into his chest. If he let himself, he would wail like a child. He was tired to the bone, and all of his talents and excitements were useless now. He did not have the strength to complete his construct.

"It's terrible." He restrained himself by gritting his teeth. "It's all terrible. I don't know how to make it better."

Stave did not react. For a time, he knelt motionless and said nothing, as if he had no interest in Jeremiah's distress. Eventually, however, he bowed his head in submission.

"Yet the attempt must be made." He spoke as if the wind tugged the words out of him. "I will remain as I am for a time. Then I will come."

With that, Jeremiah had to be content.

As suddenly as it had arrived, his impulse to sob faded. He had reached the end of his emotions. Now he felt emptied. Matters were out of his hands. He had done what he could. Anele's gift of Earthpower did not make him mighty. It only made him vulnerable.

Sagging into himself, he left Stave and stumbled across the wind back toward the Giants.

But he did not go to them. He had nothing to tell them that they did not already know. Under kinder circumstances, they probably could have finished the task without him.

Instead he made his way to his crude edifice. For a while, he studied the four walls and the northwest-facing entrance. Then he set to work.

With negligent, futile ease, he tossed small stones into their necessary positions along the tops of the walls. Doing so did not require thought: it required only certainty. But soon he had done what he could. Then he had to wait for the Giants.

Around him, the day grew darker. That was wrong: his senses were sure. The time was early afternoon, no later. Yet the vague illumination was fading. He had become little more than a shadow to himself, a wraith in a distorted dream. His construct crouched in the gloom like the base of a tower broken by siege.

Carried by baffled gusts and blasts, the darkness gathered from the east, or perhaps somewhat north of east. It advanced in tatters like the wind, moiling and routed, then surging ahead. And its source was still distant, scores of leagues away. Nonetheless the fading of the light was a warning.

"Ho, Swordmainnir." Rime Coldspray sounded improbably far away. "Now or never. Behold! Night gathers against us prematurely. I know not how to interpret this augury, but I do not doubt that it promises ill. We must complete our purpose."

A chorus of groans arose: protests and curses. Across the distance, Jeremiah felt the Giants climbing to their feet as if they were struggling out of an abyss. Even Cabledarm stood.

Leaning against each other, the Ironhand and her women came to stand with Jeremiah.

He heard their exhaustion, their frailty. He seemed to taste it like charcoal on his tongue. He did not know how to bear it—or how to ask them to bear it.

Because he was concentrating on them, a moment passed before he realized that Stave also had joined him.

Several of the Giants greeted the *Haruchai*, but he did not reply. Instead he regarded the walls of the construct. After a pause, he announced thinly, "This is *suru-pa-maerl*. The folk of the Stonedowns formed such sculptures balancing and fitting stones to each other. In Muirwin Delenoth, Chosen-son, you devised a structure of marrowmeld. Now you have restored *suru-pa-maerl* to the Land, or perhaps created it anew. Perhaps it gives cause for hope."

Then he turned to Rime Coldspray. "I have recovered strength enough for one effort. I will expend it here. Afterward I will pray that we have no more need of it.

"You must fashion the roof. When it lacks only its capstone, I will ascend. Receiving the stone from those below, I will place it as the Chosen-son instructs. That I will be able to do, that and no more."

Jeremiah winced. In her weariness, the Ironhand herself flinched. "Will you?" she asked, stern and anxious. "Stave Rockbrother, the prospect troubles me. The monolith which you dislodged is broken. The portion containing malachite is small by comparison. Still it outweighs you.

"Your prowess is ever a cause for wonder. Nevertheless I fear that no *Haruchai* could lift and settle that fragment."

Gloom masked Stave's visage. Even his lone eye was shrouded as if it had fallen into shadow. "Yet the choice is mine," he answered. "The strength is mine. The life is mine.

"If I am not needed, I will stand aside."

Coldspray rubbed her face like a woman disguising another flinch. First with one hand, then with the other, she slapped her cheeks. She seemed to dig deep into herself for a response.

"Certainly you are needed," she rasped.

"Thus in the end," one of her comrades muttered, "even Giants may be reduced to brevity."

Stave nodded. "Then have done with delay."

Jeremiah opened his mouth to argue; closed it again. How could he object? His construct was impotent without its capstone. Everything that he and the Giants and Stave had done here hung in the balance. If he wanted to spare the former Master, he would have to suggest an alternative; and he had none.

Sighing, the Ironhand said, "Come, Swordmainnir. The task exceeds only our muscles and thews. It does not lie beyond our comprehension. We must believe that a feat which may be understood may also be achieved."

In response, Cabledarm lifted her head, flexed her arms. "I will join you," she announced grimly. "I am less than I was. What of it? I am able to stand. Therefore I will be able to stand under some weight of stone."

Coldspray nodded. "That is well. You also are needed."

Like a woman walking to an execution, she went to the nearest roof stone. There she told her comrades, "Some will lift. Others will serve as pillars. The first pillar will be Kindwind. Cabledarm will be the last. When the roof is complete, Bluntfist and I will pass the final fragment to Stave. Thereafter we, too, will become pillars until the capstone is set."

The other Swordmainnir nodded their assent. When Cirrus Kindwind had entered the temple, Rime Coldspray and Stormpast Galesend rolled a chunk of granite inside. There they heaved it upward until Kindwind could crouch under it, accept its weight with her back and shoulders.

At the same time, Latebirth and Grueburn began shifting another stone. Onyx Stonemage joined Kindwind: a second support. Halewhole Bluntfist and Cabledarm readied themselves.

Jeremiah, too, was needed: he knew that. The sections of the roof had to be positioned exactly. Otherwise they would not remain in place when they were wedged by the capstone. Yet he did not move. He had lost every resource of excitement. Now he felt only a sickening apprehension.

How much more would his companions have to suffer because he had suggested building a sanctuary for the *Elohim*?

∽∞∾

For a while, he sank into a kind of paralysis. Matters of scale overwhelmed him: the extremity of the Giants; the consequences of failure. Possible deaths drained the volition from his limbs. But then his fears were thrust aside by a summons which he could not refuse.

The straining women did not call out to him. Stave did not. His construct did.

It was crude in every detail, and so tenuously balanced that a nudge might knock it down. At the same time, it was ineffable, capable of mysteries. Eloquent as a paean, it spoke the language of his talents, his deepest needs. He had to finish it.

Compelled, he followed a Swordmain into the temple.

Now he seemed calm to himself, although his voice shook and his hands trembled. Fervid and sure, he told the Giants, the pillars, where they had gone wrong; urged subtle corrections of tilt and fit; encouraged them to stand taller under their burdens. While darkness mounted across the plain, he guided the placement of his materials.

Soon only Halewhole Bluntfist and Rime Coldspray remained to move the last stones. Cabledarm had already taken her place inside the temple. Blood seeped from her bound wounds, but she ignored it. With her comrades, she did what she could to keep the roof steady. But there were still two slabs to raise. One would have to rest entirely on the injured woman and the wall. The other she would be able to share with Cirrus Kindwind.

The gasping of the Giants sounded like anguish. They had to stand as rigid as foundations, but they could not stand straight. The finished walls around them were no higher than their shoulders. They had to lower their heads and bow their backs in order to balance the roof stones. That posture constricted their breathing. Their heavy muscles quivered on the verge of collapse. Any sudden shift might scatter them like dying leaves. Sweat streaming from their faces spattered the dirt, made marks like cries. Their staring eyes showed white like terror in the enclosed gloom.

Nevertheless Coldspray and Bluntfist forced the remaining stones upward. Somehow Cabledarm and Kindwind bore those added loads. Somehow they managed to turn and twist—lowering one shoulder, raising another, shifting their feet incrementally—so that the slabs fit where they had to be.

Jeremiah supervised all of this without thinking about it. He could not afford to regard the sufferings of the Giants, and nothing else required his consideration. As soon as Cabledarm and Kindwind achieved the right positions, he dashed out of the temple with the Ironhand and Halewhole Bluntfist at his back.

Stave waited there as if he were deaf to the desperation of the Giants. Shredded gales as fragmentary as the rocks of the construct gusted around him and away, but did not move him.

Fighting for breath, Coldspray and Bluntfist paused briefly; braced their trembling hands on their hips; straightened the cramps out of their backs and legs. Then Rime Coldspray nodded to Jeremiah and the *Haruchai*.

"Ready yourselves," she warned the other Swordmainnir as if she wanted to scream and did not have the strength. "The end is near. One exertion remains, the last and the worst."

At once, she grasped Stave and wrenched him into the air. He landed on the roof as if he were as weightless as dust.

Then it was Jeremiah's turn. He held his breath while Bluntfist lifted him; placed him beside Stave.

With his bare feet, he felt the ordeal of the Giants. The surface of the roof resembled strewn rubble. It shifted under him when he moved. The women were only moments from absolute exhaustion. The roof might yet cave inward. And there was one more rock—

If Coldspray and Bluntfist could even raise that piece. If Stave could manage it alone in spite of his wounds.

If.

Entire realities rested on one small word.

"Hang on," Jeremiah croaked. "We're moving as fast as we can."

He was sure only of himself. The temple had been built correctly: it was exactly what it needed to be. When the capstone sat in its proper position, the whole edifice would become secure. Even rested Giants might not be able to knock it down.

Stone was not bone: he could not fuse it. Nevertheless there was power in shapes: the right shapes, the right materials, the right fit. The right words. The right talent. Even the right Earthpower. Such things could change the world.

Praying, Jeremiah watched Stave at the edge of the roof. Coldspray and Bluntfist would have to do more than lift the last stone. They would have to hold it over their heads for the *Haruchai*. If he had to reach down for it—if he could not crouch under it—even his great strength would not suffice.

Groaning like women whose hearts were about to burst, the Ironhand and Halewhole Bluntfist heaved. In their extremity, they half threw their burden at Stave.

Jeremiah did not understand how Stave caught it. He did not know why Stave's bones did not break; why Stave's muscles and heart did not rupture. The former Master was not breathing. He had no pulse. A convulsion seemed to stop his life.

The roof where he stood tilted. The stones on either side of him swayed fatally. Giants groaned in dismay.

He stayed upright, but he did not move. He looked like he could not. Every sudden thrash of wind threatened his balance.

Then Coldspray and Bluntfist reentered the temple to help their comrades. Together they steadied the roof.

Slowly, as if he thought that he could live forever without air or blood, Stave turned away from the edge. He took one abused step toward the hole in the center of the roof. Then he took another.

And another, ascending the slope of the stones.

Still his heart did not beat. He did not breathe.

A sensation like terror gripped Jeremiah. He moved toward the *Haruchai*. He could not help Stave carry the stone, but he could guide it. As firmly as he dared, he placed his hands on the rock. By touch, he urged Stave to accommodate a subtle rotation: a shift of inches so that the rock would fit its intended seat.

Stave did not appear to look at his target. His eye seemed sightless. No part of him reacted to the pressure of Jeremiah's hands: no part except his feet. At his next step, he angled his failing stance slightly to match Jeremiah's wishes.

With the slowness of hindered time, one instant forced to pause for the next, he sagged to his knees. By rending increments, he extended his arms. Beyond the limits of his strength, he dropped his treasure of malachite into place.

In almost the same motion, he thrust himself away. From his knees, he fell onto his back. Soundless as a figure in a dream, he rolled down the slant of the roof, fell over the edge.

The jolt when he hit the ground restarted his heart. He began to breathe again. With a gasp that no one heard, he fought air into his lungs.

Jeremiah did not see him. Suddenly faint, the Chosen-son crumpled as if his own heart had stopped.

⋙⋘

ut he was only unconscious for a moment. Then he jerked up his head like a swimmer who had been underwater too long.

The roof under him felt as solid as the cliff looming across the southeast. It looked like an accidental spill of stone too heavy to hang in the air; but it was not. It had become something more. Delicate strands and small deposits of malachite held the roof and the walls together as if they had become one with each other. The hidden green was now a mesh of theurgy able to withstand shocks which would have broken a house.

And the whole edifice thrummed with power. It sent a thrill of summons along the winds, out into the twilight and the rising dark.

They had done it, the Giants and Stave and Jeremiah himself. Somehow they had vindicated Linden's faith in them.

But he did not know how many of his companions had survived.

Then he did. As soon as he cast his health-sense farther, he located Stave. The *Haruchai* lay prone in the dirt. Respiration barely lifted his chest. His heart straggled from beat to beat. Nevertheless he lived.

Apart from Cabledarm, the women were in no worse condition than Stave. Rime Coldspray, Cirrus Kindwind, and three others had managed to stagger out of the temple before they collapsed. Now they sprawled on the ground like invalids in the last stages of a wasting illness.

Felled by their efforts, the remaining Swordmainnir lay like debris on the floor of the construct. Frostheart Grueburn and Onyx Stonemage were there. Their prostration resembled Coldspray's, and Kindwind's. Still Jeremiah could hope that they would recover. But Cabledarm's plight was more severe. She had lost too much blood. He had no idea how much longer her heart would be able to sustain its beat.

Yet she had succeeded. The whole company had succeeded. The construct was complete. It was exact. In some sense, it lived. That achievement counted. It may have been as costly as a defeat, but it was a victory nonetheless.

Jeremiah wanted to hear a song of praise. He should have sung it himself, but he did not know how.

Unaware that he was hurrying, he gained his feet, went to the edge of the roof, dropped to the ground beside Stave. "We did it," he told the *Haruchai*. "You did it." Then he trotted around the corner to the front of the structure.

There he announced to the Swordmainnir, "You did it. All of you *did* it. You were *amazing!*"

The Ironhand turned her head. She was too weak to lift it. Wan as a whisper, she asked, "Do the *Elohim* come?"

Jeremiah looked up into a hard slap of wind, scanned his surroundings. Mottled by craters, the hardpan plain stretched away into the gloom. It looked as empty as a wasteland. Toward the east, darkness continued to swell, dimming the unnatural day, obscuring even the ravaged heavens. But full dark was still hours away.

"Don't worry about it," he answered Coldspray. "They'll come. They have to."

They could not refuse without ceasing to be themselves.

His purpose for us is an abomination, more so than our doom in the maw of the Worm. But it is not the worst evil.

Infelice believed that Lord Foul would use Jeremiah's gifts to form a prison for the

Creator. *The eternal end of Creation is shadow enough to darken the heart of any being.* For that reason alone, her people had no choice. While any of them lived, they would make one last attempt to stop Jeremiah.

But the prospect did not scare him. He was looking forward to it. Infelice thought that she knew him. She was wrong.

"Then, Chosen-son," murmured Coldspray, "I ask that you bring water. Cabledarm must drink. Water may ease her."

"Of course." Quickly Jeremiah looked around for the waterskins. All of the Giants needed to drink. Stave did. Jeremiah was thirsty himself. But Cabledarm— "I'll be right back."

Fortunately Kindwind's last trek to the distant spring or stream had delivered seven full waterskins: as many as she could manage. Several had been emptied, but Jeremiah found three that still bulged. With the strength of his inheritance, he carried two. One he left within Coldspray's reach. The other he took into the temple.

He did not want to look at Cabledarm. Her injuries still seeped blood, in spite of makeshift tourniquets and bandages. Her spirit had been reduced to embers. The idea that those sparks might fade twisted his heart.

But he could not both lift her head and hold the waterskin. She was too big for him, too heavy. After a moment's hesitation, he knelt beside Frostheart Grueburn, nudged her gently.

"I need you. Please. Cabledarm is dying. I've got water, but I'm not strong enough to help her drink."

With a strangled groan, Grueburn tried to raise her head. Her eyes opened, but at first she did not appear to see. Then her gaze focused on the waterskin. Groaning again, she flung out an arm. Her hand found the waterskin. She dragged it to her.

While she drank, Jeremiah insisted, "Cabledarm needs that. Did you hear me? She's dying."

Wearily Grueburn nodded. After a few swallows, she wedged her elbows under her, forced herself to rise to her knees. There she paused while she tried to remember strength or balance or at least determination.

"Chosen-son." Her voice was an exhausted rasp. "Does your edifice stand?"

Jeremiah was too anxious to answer. "Cabledarm," he pleaded. "Water." Grueburn would recognize the truth for herself when her mind cleared. "I'll get another waterskin."

In a rush, he left the construct.

Outside, he saw that Coldspray had managed to sit up and drink. In spite of her frailty, however, she was sparing with her own needs. Two swallows, or three: no more. Then she began to rouse her comrades.

Jeremiah allowed himself a quick drink from the third waterskin before he carried it into the temple.

He found Grueburn and Stonemage beside Cabledarm. Grueburn supported Cabledarm's head and shoulders while Stonemage held the waterskin to Cabledarm's mouth.

Grueburn glanced up as he entered. "Our thanks, Chosen-son," she said hoarsely. "Cabledarm will perish, or she will not. In large part, the choice is hers. For the present, this must suffice." With a twitch of her head, Grueburn indicated the waterskin Jeremiah held. "Succor to our comrades."

Glad to be spared the sight of Cabledarm's peril, he turned away.

In the gloom beyond the entrance, Rime Coldspray was no longer the only Giant conscious. Halewhole Bluntfist sat nearby, rocking from side to side and holding her head. Latebirth had begun the arduous chore of prying herself out of the dirt. Stormpast Galesend was stirring. And Cirrus Kindwind was already on her feet. She had labored less than her comrades: she rallied with less difficulty. Now she was readying herself to go for more water.

She gave Jeremiah a grimace that almost became a grin. "We live, Chosen-son. And we have accomplished our purpose. I have said that I honor effort and intent. Now I also honor their outcome. Few in life are given such gifts."

Then she nodded in Stave's direction. "How fares Stave Rockbrother?"

Before Jeremiah could reply, he heard a sound in the wind.

He was expecting the chimes that announced the sovereign of the *Elohim*, waiting for it: the crystalline clear ringing of small bells, lovely and delicate. Instead he heard a sharp clatter like the ruin of gongs; like a welter of huge iron crashing down. It was not loud. Indeed, it seemed imponderably distant, as if it had reached him from the far side of the world. Yet its tone and timbre were unmistakable. They spoke of shattering and calamity and irreparable loss.

He tried to call a warning to the Giants inside the temple, but the words stuck in his throat.

Instinctively he believed that Infelice was coming to prevent *the worst evil*. To kill him before he could be reclaimed by the Despiser.

If so, none of his companions would be able to defend him. No Giant could stand against any one of Infelice's people. And the Swordmainnir were too weak to don their armor or swing their swords. Stave was not even conscious.

But Jeremiah did not flinch. He knew that Infelice was wrong about him. She would see the truth when she arrived.

Forgetting Stave and Kindwind and water, he went to stand at the entrance to his temple as if he had become its guardian.

The metallic clamor continued. It acquired intensity and ire. It was as sharp as knives forged to flense and flay. In spite of the distance, it cut. And it was coming closer. The Giants heard it now. The Ironhand and Bluntfist struggled upright, stood wavering with their fists clenched. Latebirth was at Galesend's side, rousing her comrade. Cirrus Kindwind moved to join her.

As Jeremiah reached the entryway, Grueburn and Stonemage emerged, supporting Cabledarm between them. They bore her a few paces to one side, lowered her carefully to the dirt. Then they stood over her as though they meant to fight for her.

But the wrath and repudiation of the *Elohim* would not be directed at her, or at any of Jeremiah's companions.

He folded his arms across his chest; across the fouled blue and horses of his pajamas. He did not know how else to contain his trembling.

Rime Coldspray took a position on his left. Halewhole Bluntfist matched her on his right. Together they waited.

He expected to see forces gathering in the eastern darkness, anger as fierce as lightning, an army of eldritch beings. The shredded winds seemed to promise multitudes and violence. But when Infelice came, she came alone. And she did not arrive from any direction. Instead she incarnated herself in front of him like a star plucked out of the heavens. She was no more than five steps away.

Involuntarily he blinked. Her brightness stung his eyes. She was clad in light: an elegant profusion of gemstones—emeralds and rubies, sapphires and garnets—all shining with their own radiance, all arrayed like garments woven of glory. Only the iron clangor and desperation of her bells contradicted her deliberate loveliness, her stubborn will to believe that she was the crown of Creation.

Across the plain behind her, the wind fashioned illusions of movement in the hollows, illusions that made the ground look like it was squirming.

Her vehemence seemed to appall the dusk. It buffeted Jeremiah's bones. Now he saw that her many jewels resembled tears, incandescent woe. Her wrath was weeping. The suzerain *Elohim*'s form and raiment articulated fury indistinguishable from grief.

"*Abomination!*" she cried. "Malign child! Thus you complete our despair! Better for us to be devoured by the Worm. Better had you never been given birth.

"I am able to decline entrance only because I am Infelice. I cannot continue to do so. My people have not come only because I prevent them. I cannot continue to do so. Soon we must accept eternal absence and futility, eternal continuance in a void in which we can do nothing, and from which we cannot return.

"This evil you have performed, though I have both striven and pleaded to avert it. In your heedlessness, you are a-Jeroth's servant, and all of your deeds conduce to his designs."

Coldspray and Bluntfist glowered uselessly. Farther away, Stormpast Galesend tottered to her feet between Latebirth and Kindwind. Grueburn and Stonemage knelt like shields on either side of Cabledarm.

Jeremiah should have been terrified. On some level, he was. Infelice had not given rise to the darkness mounting in the east. Her ire and lamentation had not caused the turmoil of winds. Something else was coming—

Nevertheless his fears only made his hands tremble, only caused his heart to stutter. His crossed arms closed a door on that part of himself. Behind his façade, memories of the *croyel* barked in derision. Outwardly he faced Infelice as if he could not be daunted.

In spite of her supernal powers, she did not know him. He was exactly what she believed him to be. At the same time, he was something entirely different.

He raised his halfhand as if he expected her to respect it; to recognize that it did not resemble Covenant's. "You're wrong," he said in a fevered voice. "You don't know what you're talking about.

"Your people are dying. You need to get them here." Then he gestured behind him. "But first you need to *look*." He wanted to shout in the *Elohim*'s face. "You've been wrong about me all along."

"Do you think to mislead me, boy?" Infelice retorted imperiously. "Do you believe that *I* may be deceived?"

Nonetheless she glanced past him.

Then she stared. Confusion made chaos of her clangor and radiance. Her apparel thrashed around her like the storms of desire and misery which had haunted Esmer. Her visage modulated: it seemed to become scores of different faces in quick succession, as if all of her people were suddenly manifested in her. As if the entire meaning of their existence had been called into question.

An instant later, the clatter of falling metal ceased. Every wind dropped. Silence closed like a lid over the plain. The gems of Infelice's raiment corrected themselves, resumed their accustomed grace. When she spoke again, her voice was little more than a whisper.

"It is not a gaol. It is a fane."

Like an antiphony, her bells chimed relief. They implied awe.

"That's right!" Jeremiah crowed. Vindication rose in him. It felt like scorn for the ways in which the *Elohim* had misjudged him. "You have to go in, but you can come out whenever you want. If you want. If I were you, I would stay inside. Let the rest of us worry about the Worm. As long as you're in there, it can't reach you."

For a moment or two, Infelice looked so lovely that every aspect of her seemed to sing: every line of her face and form, every implication of her demeanor, every glad jewel. She was lucent with melody. But then she appeared to recall herself from a vision of hope. It had almost seduced her. Now she returned, unwilling, to the implications of her plight.

Frowning, angry again, and strangely uncertain, she said as if she were asking a question, "Yet the Worm will destroy the fane. Though we will not be consumed, we will be denied our place in life. That you cannot prevent.

"You have wrought a surpassing wonder. I acknowledge it. I acknowledge that we have misesteemed you. And your theurgy is—" Bells described her astonishment. "Child, it is vast. My strengths are many, yet I cannot unmake what you have formed. Against any threat other than the Worm, this fane would stand.

"But you do not comprehend the Worm's power. It *transcends*. Sensing our presence, the Worm will devour the fane without thought or effort. Then it will continue its search for the EarthBlood and doom. Deprived of egress, we will be eternally lost."

"Mom is working on that," Jeremiah replied without hesitation. "Sure, what we've done is vulnerable." Roger had smashed Jeremiah's Tinkertoy castle with the ease of contempt. "And we don't have enough power to stop the Worm. But Mom went looking for somebody who can teach her how to do what we need.

"As long as she gets back—"

"Madness!" Infelice cried at once. "Utter madness!" Apparently her fears had blinded her to other things. Preoccupied by carnage, she had focused on Jeremiah rather than Linden. Now she reached for arcane sources of knowledge. Revelations struck her like blows. "The Wildwielder hazards the world's past. She seeks a Forestal forged from the substance of an *Elohim*. She seeks *forbidding*.

"It is madness." Infelice seemed to be speaking to herself. Arguing with her own instincts. "Should she fail, she will destroy all Time and life ere the Worm achieves its culmination." But then her attention focused on Jeremiah again. Softer hues flowed through her raiment. "Yet I see valor also in her, as we have from the first. Therefore we sought to forestall her darkest desires, and to serve her in defiance of her own wishes. Should she succeed—"

"That's right," Jeremiah said again. "You'll still have a chance. You'll be safe, at least until the Worm gets to the EarthBlood. And it'll be slow. I mean, slower than if it ate you. We'll have more time."

Time for Linden or even Covenant to come up with a better answer.

"A worthy effort," murmured the Ironhand, "regardless of its hazards."

The other Giants remained silent.

Infelice appeared to consider Jeremiah's assertion. Instead of contradicting or challenging him, she consulted the ineffable ramifications of her bells and Linden's daring and his construct.

He bit his lip; tried not to hold his breath. He had done what he could. If Infelice turned her thoughts now to what she had called *the worst evil*, nothing that he had done—nothing that he might say—would satisfy her.

Abrupt gusts broke free around the *Elohim*. Winds like the discarded scraps of a hurricane, tattered and imminent, gusted at the Giants, the fane, Jeremiah. Fretted with new grit, they rebounded from the ridge. The plain blurred and ran like a landscape in a mirage. Driven air did not touch Infelice, but it pulled like thorns at Jeremiah's pajamas, moaned in the gaps between the stones of his construct.

It was possible that Jeremiah had built hope for everyone else, and had left none for himself.

Finally Infelice looked at him again. For the first time, he heard regret in her voice.

"You have exceeded our conceptions of you. This I confess freely, though it humbles me. Yet one threat remains unaddressed. Your companions have named you Chosen-son. I do so also. Yet you are chosen of a-Jeroth as you are of the Wildwielder. I have spoken of his desire to accomplish absolute evil. Chiefly for that reason, he has endeavored to possess you. He will do so again.

"You have completed your fane." The music of her bells became sharper. It cut against the winds. "Your part in the world's doom is done. For the Earth's sake, and for Creation's, I must now slay you."

Her words shocked the Giants. They hit Jeremiah hard even though he had expected them. He had no defense.

"I am loath to do so," admitted Infelice. "Yet I cannot otherwise forestall a-Jeroth. The Worm will feed, or it will not. The Arch of Time will fall, or it will not. Still the Despiser will make use of your gifts. From your heart and passion and youth and weakness, he will devise imprisonment for the Creator. He will put an end to the very possibility of Creation. Only your death will prevent his eternal triumph."

Jeremiah stared at her; said nothing. Simply standing his ground required everything within him, his most intense love and his bitterest darkness.

He had inherited too much from Anele.

But Cirrus Kindwind rose to her feet. She spoke for him. With gems reflecting in her eyes, she said, "You forget, *Elohim*, though you are the highest of your kind. The Chosen-son is not alone."

"He is not," Rime Coldspray affirmed. She sounded as hard as a fist. "Doubtless you discount his companions. And in this you are perchance correct. Our striving in your name has weakened us. We cannot oppose you." In spite of her weariness, her voice hit and tore as if its knuckles were studded with spurs. "Nor do I name the Timewarden, whose deeds and purposes remain unknown to us. But having misesteemed young Jeremiah, will you now compound your error? Have you forgotten that Linden Avery, Giantfriend and Wildwielder, has proven herself capable of much? Have you forgotten that there is hope in contradiction?

"No. I will not credit it. You are *Elohim*. You do not forget. Yet one matter lies beyond your comprehension. Being who you are, you have no experience of it. Therefore I will say *this* in the teeth of all who meditate ill toward the Chosen-son. He has *friends*. The Despiser may well attempt to possess him. If so, that evil will fail. No possession can hold one who does not stand alone."

She seemed to mean, One who is loved.

"Why otherwise," she concluded, punching home her avowal, "is he now free of the monster which once ruled him? Doubtless foes who relied upon the *croyel* were certain of their designs. Yet here he stands, relieved from mastery, and dedicated to the preservation of beings who abhorred him."

Conflicting responses appeared to twist Infelice's mien. Her raiment fluttered in disarray. At first, Jeremiah thought that she had taken offense; that she would react with wrath and violence. But then he saw her more clearly.

The sovereign *Elohim* was diminished. Her assurance, her contentment in herself, had received a blow from which she did not know how to recover. The notion of *friends* perplexed her; undermined her. Winds gyred around her like relief and dismay: a conundrum which she appeared unable to resolve.

But she did not hesitate long. Pressures that surpassed Jeremiah compelled her to a decision. Her voice wore discordant chiming like a funeral wreath. Though she was the highest of her kind, she had been wrong too often.

"I can delay no longer. I must acknowledge that I am answered, as the summons must be answered. You have spoken truly. We are *Elohim*. We have no knowledge of *friends*.

"This, then, is my word. Come what may, we who are great must now place our faith in you who are small."

Then she found a brief severity. "Be wary, Chosen-son. Your deeds bring perils which you do not foresee. We have given of our utmost, according to our Würd. Now we can do naught. If your companions fail you, you are undone."

Turning away, Infelice lifted a cry into the heavens: a resounding clang like a hammer-stroke on an immense gong.

At once, other *Elohim* began to appear as if they had been brought by the winds; as if they had found their substance among the oneiric seethings that troubled the plain.

One after another, they flowed like liquid light toward the fane, so many of them that Jeremiah was astonished. He had seen stars dying: he had not considered the number that still lived. Perhaps the relationship between these beings and stars was more symbolic than literal. Nevertheless the heavens had not been entirely decimated. Those *Elohim* that answered the call of Jeremiah's construct resembled a multitude.

The sight enchanted him. They were so beautiful—! One and all, they were lovely beyond description. To his human eyes, they were men and women clad in elegance, and accustomed to glory: innocent of mortality; untainted by the dross of inadequacy and the burden of suffering; immune to the woes and protests that could only be stilled by death.

They were the *Elohim*, eldritch and fey: as cryptic as prophecies in a foreign tongue, and as ineffable as the beauties of Andelain, or the melodies of Wraiths. An uncounted host of them had already perished: a throng remained, craving life.

They sanctified the unnatural twilight as if their coming were a sacrament.

Instinctively Stormpast Galesend and Latebirth forced themselves to their feet. Even Cabledarm found the strength to stand. All of the Giants endeavored to square their shoulders, straighten their backs. In spite of their troubled history with the *Elohim*, they set aside their exhaustion.

Graceful as willows, stately as Gilden, each faery individual paused only to exchange a nod with Infelice, who stood aside for her people. Each glided into the fane and vanished from sight. And Jeremiah watched them stream past like a boy who had become magnificent in his own estimation, full of pride. He had caused this: *he*. He had justified Linden's highest hopes for him. Yet the swelling of his heart was not pride. At that moment, at least, it was gratitude. The success of his temple was not something that he had accomplished: it was a gift that he had been given. He did not waste himself on pride.

For that moment, while it lasted, he soared above his secrets as if he had been lifted into the heavens.

Exalted and transfixed, he could not brace himself against the convulsion that shook the ground like the onset of an earthquake. He had no answer for the blast of heat as fierce as an eruption of magma, or for the blare of savagery that seemed to repudiate the world. He did not understand the sudden cries of the *Elohim*, or the haunted look that filled Infelice's eyes, or the frantic shouts of the Giants. He did not know what was happening until Kastenessen entered him, and all of his thoughts became anguish and slaughter.

Ecstatic agony. Rage so great that it could not be contained. Pain too extreme to be called insanity.

The mad *Elohim* struck the plain like a fireball flung by a titan. At the impact, the very ground under his feet seemed to ripple and clench like water, liquefied by ferocity. He came roaring with triumph and lunacy and hate: a monster who no longer resembled the people who had imprisoned him; damned him. He was not lovely, not graceful. His visage was a contortion of suffering. Interminable pains gnarled his limbs. His vestments were fire. His eyes blazed like the fangs of the *skurj*. From his kraken teeth, slaver splashed the dirt and smoldered. And he dominated the horizon; cast back the gloom until even the darkness in the east appeared to wither and fade. He had made himself taller than a Giant, as tall as one of the avid worms which he had once restrained.

His right fist he held above his head, ready to hurl ruin at the fane.

It was not an *Elohim*'s fist. It was Roger's, human and fatal. With it, Kastenessen could deliver devastations that no other being of his race might attempt or condone.

But he did not strike. He was not ready—or he saw no need.

He had already taken Jeremiah, who stood on bare dirt. The boy had inherited this vulnerability from Anele.

In an instant, less than an instant, a particle of time infinitely prolonged, Jeremiah passed through the eager malice and sadism of the *croyel* into pure fire, the catastrophic frenzy of bonfires. During that interminable flicker, his spirit was split. He seemed to become several separate selves, all simultaneous or superimposed, all cruelly distinct.

Now he knew why Anele had chosen madness.

One Jeremiah realized that he had been possessed—again!—and tried to scream. One stood in the white core of a furnace, while another interpreted every form of pain as delight, as agony perfected to ecstasy. One watched the Giants, who should have scattered, saved themselves. But they did not. Doomed and determined, they placed themselves in the path of Kastenessen's savagery. And another Jeremiah relished the knowledge that he had become incarnate lava. The idea that his companions were about to die glorified him. It was for this that the Despiser had marked him. It was for this that he lived.

Swift with glee, he moved to do his ruler's bidding.

Still another self remembered every horror which the *croyel* had inflicted upon him. He experienced again the misery of deluding Linden in Roger's company, cringed at what he had done under *Melenkurion* Skyweir. Another aspect of his shredded identity fled for the safety of sepulchres. Another gibbered for the godhood of eternity. In that manifestation, he knew the keen pain of the *krill* against his throat.

And one—

One of the many Jeremiahs *understood*.

This Jeremiah recognized the extremity of Kastenessen's need for ruin. He remembered the forbidden love, potent as delirium, and altogether delicious, which had drawn Kastenessen to mortal Emereau Vrai, daughter of kings. He felt Kastenessen's rage and dismay while he fought for his love against Infelice and others of the *Elohim*, who should have valued him more highly. This Jeremiah knew intimately the unconscionable hurt of Kastenessen's Durance, his imprisonment against and among the *skurj*. This Jeremiah recalled in every detail the torment which had driven Kastenessen to begin merging himself with monsters.

This Jeremiah understood why Kastenessen cared only for the utter destruction of the *Elohim*. More, he knew why Kastenessen had not acted directly against Linden, or indeed against Jeremiah himself, until now; until all of his surviving people were gathered in one place. Although Kastenessen had used Esmer with remorseless brutality, he had not delivered his fury in person because any absence from the proximity of She Who Must Not Be Named would have put an end to Kevin's Dirt. His presence was required to channel and shape and direct the bane's fearsome energies. And he had believed, or *moksha* Raver had persuaded him, that only the dire brume which hampered Earthpower and Law would make his revenge possible.

Now Kastenessen had no more need for such stratagems. He had come in response to the fane's call, but he was not mastered by it. He was part *skurj* and part human: he was in enough pain to refuse any coercion. No, he was here because he had achieved his desires. One of the Jeremiahs would carry out the last preparations.

That in turn was why Kastenessen raised Roger's fist, but did not strike. He had the power to shatter the fane, render it back to rubble. Nevertheless he withheld his blow, waiting for the certainty that every one of the *Elohim* would be destroyed.

Nothing that happened in or to Jeremiah took any time at all. Part of him regretted that. He loved what he had become. He reveled in the purity of his given hate.

Incandescent or incinerated in each of his separated selves, he flung himself at Infelice.

It was for this that he—that Kastenessen—had planned and waited and endured: so that the highest and mightiest and most dangerous of the *Elohim* would be slain with the rest when he delivered his retribution.

Three swift strides would be enough. Then Kastenessen in Jeremiah would wrap hate like molten stone around Infelice. He would hurl her through the fane's portal, the entryway to extinction. After that, only heartbeats would remain until the summons was complete; until every *Elohim* was inside.

Until Kastenessen could unleash uncounted millennia of torment.

Jeremiah was sudden. He was quick.

Stave was faster.

The former Master was scarcely conscious. He could barely stand. Nevertheless he kept his promise to Linden. Lunging, he grasped Jeremiah's arm.

Heat as fierce as brimstone savaged his hand, but he did not let go. Desperate and already failing, he delivered Jeremiah to the only protection that lay within his reach.

As Rime Coldspray had done to Stave himself earlier, the *Haruchai* wrenched

Jeremiah into the air. Off the bare dirt that exposed him to Kastenessen. Onto the stone roof of the temple.

Into the direct line of Kastenessen's intended attack.

Then Stave collapsed again. He did not rise.

But Infelice remained untouched outside the fane.

Kastenessen howled rage at the heavens, but Jeremiah no longer heeded him. As Jeremiah's feet left the ground, he crashed inwardly. His many selves seemed to smash against each other like projectiles, like bullets.

The force of their impact stunned him. It numbed his mind. He no longer thought or moved: he hardly breathed. Instead he lay still, wracked by revulsion; as weak as Stave. He could do nothing except watch and dread.

Kastenessen roared, but he did not strike. He wanted his full triumph. In moments, even Infelice would answer the fane's call. Then—

Already the last of the *Elohim* were passing inward. Their hope had become horror, and their features were written with dismay, but they had no power to reject their own natures. Two heartbeats, or perhaps three, no more than that, and Infelice would stand alone. Then she, too, would enter—and Kastenessen would strike.

No, he would not. Not with Roger's hand. Never again.

While Kastenessen readied his blast, a Giant surged out of a crater behind him. Jeremiah would not have known who the newcomer was if Frostheart Grueburn had not shouted, "Longwrath!"

Swift as a bolt of lightning, the man reared high behind the deranged *Elohim*. In both fists, he gripped a long flamberge with a wicked blade. It edges gleamed against Kastenessen's lurid radiance as if starlight had been forged into its iron.

One stroke severed Roger's hand from Kastenessen's wrist.

Kastenessen screamed like an exploding sun. He staggered.

Longwrath followed him to strike again.

But Kastenessen caught his balance. Blood pulsed from his wrist, the tainted ichor of Earthpower and lava. He did not heed it. Wheeling, he swung at his attacker with his good arm.

Power erupted in Longwrath's chest. His armor had been damaged, torn apart at one shoulder: it could not withstand Kastenessen's virulence. The wrought stone sprang apart, spitting splinters as piercing as knives. But the shards evaporated or melted at the touch of Kastenessen's lava. Longwrath was flung backward, hurled away like a handful of scree. When he fell, he did not move again. Smoke gusted out of his chest as if his heart and lungs were on fire.

Roaring once more, Kastenessen turned back to Infelice and the fane. Obscene heat mounted within him. He grew taller, blazed brighter. Acrid flames swirled higher, spinning about him like the birth-pangs of a cyclone. His sick brilliance stung Jeremiah's eyes, but the boy could not look away.

"Hear me, treacher!" the mad *Elohim* howled. "I am more than you deem! Yon puerile fane cannot compel me! Still am I Kastenessen! Still my pain suffices to destroy you!"

Raving, he stoked his lethal energies, Earthpower and magma, *Elohim* and *skurj*, until they looked fierce enough to consume every life that had ever walked the plain. They were far more than he needed them to be. They would level Jeremiah's crude edifice as if it had no substance and no meaning.

Infelice had been appalled earlier. Now, strangely, she was calm. She did not answer Kastenessen. Instead she remarked to Rime Coldspray, "You think ill of us, Giant, and you have cause. But we are not as dark as you deem. For this also we laid our *geas* upon your kinsman. For this also he acquired his blade. Failing one purpose, he has served another.

"He has not redeemed us, but he has weakened our lost brother. Now comes one who may achieve our salvation, however briefly. We cannot ask more of any who oppose the Worm.

"You will forgive your kinsman's passing," she added sadly. "Alive, he would not lightly bear the recall of his deeds."

Then the bedizened *Elohim* faced Kastenessen across the gulf that separated their thoughts and desires, hers and his.

"I have heard you, doomed one." She did not raise her voice, yet it rang out, clarion and clear. "Now you will hear me. Cease your striving. Enter among your people. Permit your hurt to be assuaged. We have dealt cruelly with you, but we are also kind. While life endures to us, we will provide a surcease from all that you have suffered."

She may have been telling the truth.

Now comes one—

But Kastenessen had spent long ages in his Durance. He had made choices which exacerbated his fury. Infelice's appeal could not reach him. For him, it may have been the final affront.

He gathered flames until they burst from his eyes and his mouth, from every limb and line of his towering form. He was becoming a holocaust, devastation personified: a bonfire high and hot enough to ravage the plain. His reply was one word:

"*Never!*"

Yet he was not given time to release his accumulated hate.

From the northeast, a burst of extravagant argent opened the twilight. It cast back the darkness, dismissed the sunless gloom. It was as bright as Kastenessen, and as complex, but immeasurably cleaner. And it was brief, little more than a blink. Nevertheless it was long enough.

Out of it came riding Thomas Covenant and Branl *Haruchai* of the Humbled. Covenant held Loric's *krill*.

The shock of their arrival snatched Kastenessen away from his victims.

Covenant rode a shovel-headed horse as ungainly and muscular as a mule. Branl was mounted on a Ranyhyn that Jeremiah had never seen before. And they were in a desperate hurry. Froth snorted from the nostrils of Covenant's horse, the muzzle of Branl's palomino stallion. Sweat reflected brimstone on their coats. They looked like they had galloped for leagues or days. Covenant lurched in his seat as if he were falling.

As soon as his mount's hooves struck the dirt, he pitched from his saddle. But he did not sprawl. Staggering like a holed ship in a storm, he managed to stay on his feet. Awkward and urgent, he confronted Kastenessen as if he had forgotten that the *Elohim* could reduce his bones to ash.

In his maimed hands, the gem of the *krill* shone like a kept promise in an abandoned world.

"You—!" Kastenessen began: a strangled howl. Rage clenched his throat, choked off his protest.

"*Try* me," Covenant panted as if he were on the verge of prostration. "Do your worst." He looked too weak to withstand a slap. Streaked by conflicting illuminations, his face had the pallor of a wasting disease. Still he was Thomas Covenant. He did not falter. "See what happens.

"I killed my ex-wife. I helped destroy a Raver. And I've seen the Worm of the World's End. I am *done with restraint!*" His teeth gnashed. "I used to care how much you've suffered. I don't anymore. If you think you can beat me, go ahead. I'm *wild magic*, you crazy bastard. I'll cut you apart where you stand."

Jeremiah stared and stared, and could not name his astonishment, when Kastenessen flinched—

—and took an alarmed step backward.

Covenant advanced, holding up the *krill*. It blazed like havoc, unmitigated and unanswerable. Its argent covered him with majesty. The silver of his hair resembled a crown.

Branl came behind him, but did not intrude.

Kastenessen retreated another step, and another. Another. The passion in Covenant's eyes drove him. He must have realized that he was being forced toward Infelice and the fane; but he did not stop. Perhaps he could not. Perhaps he saw something in Covenant, or in Loric's numinous dagger, that cowed him.

With every step, he dwindled. Retreating, he became smaller. Lava seemed to leak out of him and fade, denatured like water by his own thwarted heat.

Covenant stumbled and wavered, and kept coming. Kastenessen shrank away from him.

Giants let him pass. They watched as if they were as stricken as Jeremiah; as transfixed.

Then Infelice spoke Kastenessen's name like a command, and Kastenessen turned from Covenant to face her.

Terror and loathing contorted his features. He conveyed the impression that he wanted to scream and could not because he feared that he might sob. Through his teeth, he spat words like fragments of torment.

"You have earned my abhorrence."

Infelice's calm had become irrefusable. Placid as Glimmermere, she answered, "We have. We will not ask you to set it aside. We ask only that you allow us to soothe your pain."

Her response appeared to horrify him. "It is what I am."

"It is not," she countered, undismayed. "When it is gone, you will remember that you and you alone among the *Elohim* have both loved and been loved."

To that assertion, he had no reply.

She did not repeat her invitation. Instead she reached out one hand to clasp his severed wrist. With chiming and mercy, she stanched his bleeding. If the pollution of the *skurj* within him caused her any hurt, she accepted it.

His eyes bled anguish. He made no attempt to pull away.

Briefly Infelice glanced at the Giants, at the Ironhand. "Be warned," she told them. "*Moksha* Jehannum now rules the *skurj*. He will wield them with cunning and malice. And do not forget that the Chosen-son is precious to a-Jeroth."

Then she surrendered at last to the imperative of Jeremiah's construct. Drawing Kastenessen with her, she entered the fane. In an instant, they were gone as if they had stepped out of the world altogether.

"Damnation," Covenant gasped. "I wasn't sure I could do that."

Lowering his arms as if he had been beaten, he tried to approach the Swordmainnir. But his legs failed, and he dropped to his knees.

Overhead Kevin's Dirt had already begun to dissipate. If more stars perished, they did so beyond the horizons. Jeremiah did not see them die.

10.

But While I Can

As if they were each entirely alone, Linden Avery and Manethrall Mahrtiir rode through hell to save or damn the Earth.

They did not exist for each other. They were mounted on Ranyhyn that did not exist. Immersed in a cyclone of rent instants, they were consumed by the kind of hiving that drove men and women mad. Every nerve was stung beyond endurance, assailed by bitter particles of reality. At the same time, every perception had become white ice, gelid as the gulfs between the stars. Linden and her companion inhabited a frozen wilderland eternally unrelieved in all directions. They had entered a realm in which excruciation defined them. It was all they knew because it was all that they had ever known. It was all that they would ever know. One moment did not lead to the next, and so there was nothing to see or do or understand.

In that perfection of agony, Linden may once have imagined that she and Mahrtiir would be defended by experience. They had endured *caesures* twice before, and had survived. Surely they would be sustained by the knowledge that what they were trying to do was possible? But she was wrong. Memory was meaningless in a place that contained all time and none simultaneously. One instant, *this* instant, was the whole truth of who and what they were.

Yet it was not the whole truth of their plight. The *caesure* imposed other dimensions of torment as well, other forms of futility. She had asked the Ranyhyn to take her and Mahrtiir backward in time, against the current of the Fall's wild rush; and that effort had consequences. While hornets burrowed into her flesh, and she occupied a bitter wasteland as if it were the summation of all her needs and desires, she also floated inside herself like a spectator, helpless amid the chaos, watching her own desecration as if she were dissociated from it.

Days and days ago, she had once hung suspended like this inside Joan's mind, observing ruin through Joan's eyes because she had entered a *caesure* of Joan's making. But now Linden was the cause of her own suffering. While other tortures failed to tear her apart only because their duration had no meaning, she also bore witness to herself.

She watched the Linden Avery who had always been inadequate to what her life required of her. The Linden who had allowed herself to be misled by Roger Covenant and the *croyel*. The Linden who had defied every Law by resurrecting Thomas Covenant, *compelled by rage*—and had nonetheless failed to resurrect him whole. The Linden who had been consumed by She Who Must Not Be Named, and had not sufficed to raise her precious son from his graves.

The Linden Avery who had roused the Worm of the World's End.

But there was more. Observing, she was able to recall things which the storm of time denied.

There is no doom so black or deep that courage and clear sight may not find another truth beyond it.

Covenant had told her that. In the aspect of her anguish that resembled a shadow cast by her own flawed self, she yearned to believe him.

Trust yourself.

Oh, she ached for the ability to believe. But he had also said, *Don't touch me*, as if he feared that her love would corrupt some essential part of him. She did not know how to trust herself. She was the daughter of her parents, a mother and father who had feared every hurt of living, and had raised her for death. That knowledge endured in her bones. A Raver had confirmed it. Unforgotten and unredeemed, it ruled her even now, in spite of Covenant and Jeremiah and the Land.

In your present state, Chosen, Desecration lies ahead of you. It does not crowd at your back.

It was here. Was it not?

But because she was watching herself as if she were someone else, she was able to recognize that there were other ways to think. Her many friends had been trying to teach her that lesson ever since Liand had first introduced himself in Mithil Stonedown. By their devotion, they had assured her that she did not need to judge herself as if she were defined by her sins. In spite of her concealments and dishonesties, her fury *contemptuous of consequence*, she was not alone.

If *courage and clear sight* exceeded her, they did not surpass her companions. From the first, she had been supported by people whose hearts were bigger than hers; by loyalties more unselfish than hers. *Every essential step along the path*, Stave had assured Infelice, *has been taken by the natural inhabitants of the Earth*. Linden's friends had urged *trust* until even she had heard them.

Trapped in the savagery of the *caesure*, she found that desperation was indistinguishable from faith.

Attempts must be made—

Hyn had carried her willingly into the Fall. Mahrtiir on Narunal had accompanied her willingly. She could believe in them.

—even when there can be no hope.

And she had done some things right. Witnessing herself with the detachment of a spectator, she could acknowledge those deeds. She had fought her way through the machinations of Roger and the *croyel*. She had provided for her son's rescue from the *croyel*'s covert in the Lost Deep. And when every other action had been denied to her, she had given Jeremiah his racecar: the last piece of the portal which had enabled him to step out of his prison.

In those moments, no one else could have taken her place. To that extent, Anele had told the truth about her, as he had about so many things. *The world will not see her like again.*

And there was more.

Nothing ameliorated the extravagant burrow and sting of dismembered moments. Nothing eased the cruelty of the frigid wasteland which would arise from Desecrations like hers. Nothing could. Nevertheless she still held Covenant's wedding band clasped in her hands. Silver fire still shone from the metal even though she was not a rightful wielder of white gold. It was as vivid to her as Covenant himself. It could be an anchor for her foundering spirit.

Then she was no longer alone. She had always and never been alone. Manethrall Mahrtiir was at her side, holding the Staff of Law for her and looking ahead as if he had nothing to fear; as if he had finally identified the import of his life.

And she was seated on Hyn's back, as she had always been. Narunal was at her side. The horses were not moving. Movement required causality: it depended on sequence. Yet they ran. Stride for stride, dappled Hyn matched Narunal's strength, Narunal's certainty, as the palomino stallion raced from nowhere to nowhere across the white wilderness.

In spite of the *caesure*'s excoriation, Linden clung to Covenant's ring and endured.

She did not have to wait long. She had been waiting forever, and did not have to wait at all. This moment did not move on to the next because it could not, or because there was no *next*. Nevertheless the hard circle between her hands flared suddenly; and Hyn carried her out of chaos into sunshine under a summer sky.

Sunshine. A slow hillside clad in brittle grey-green grass as thick as bracken. A summer sky as lenitive as hurtloam.

Without transition, Linden was released.

The shock of change made her muscles spasm, made the world reel. Her stomach hurt as if she needed to spend hours puking. Blots of black confusion wheeled around her as though she were under assault by crows or vultures. The continuity of her personal world had been severed from itself. Unable to determine her position in time and space, she tumbled from Hyn's back, landed hard on the grass.

For a moment, she could not breathe; could not think. While her nerves floundered, she clung to the kind earth and wrestled with her impulse to vomit. She had arrived somewhere. Some when. Hyn had brought her here. She smelled summer in the air, felt an insistence on life in the stiff grass in spite of a prolonged paucity of rain. Straining to inhale, she caught a whiff of distant desiccation, as if she had arrived too close to a desert. The sky held too much dust. She had expected Andelain and lushness. She was unprepared for this baked hillside, this heat, this—

Something had gone wrong.

"Ringthane," Mahrtiir croaked as if he were retching. "Release the white gold. You must. Accept your Staff."

She heard him, but the words did not make sense. He sounded like an ur-vile, barking incomprehensibly. Something had gone wrong. The world was wrong: the grass, the sky, the sunshine. Only the writhing ruin of the Fall as it drifted away felt familiar. Narunal trumpeted a warning that she did not know how to interpret. Alarm fretted Hyn's answering whinny.

"Chosen!" insisted the Manethrall. "Linden Avery! Your *Staff*. You must quench the *caesure*! If it enters among the trees, it will wreak harm which no Forestal will pardon. We will not be heeded if you do not first spare the forest!"

Linden recognized a few sounds. The sigh of an arid breeze. The consternation of birds somewhere in the distance. A few words.

When she remembered to let go of Covenant's ring, she began to breathe again.

Mahrtiir stumbled to her side. Roughly he rolled her onto her back. "*Ringthane!*" Crouched against a glare of sunlight, he dropped the Staff of Law onto her chest. Then he fumbled at the dried remains of his garland, pinched off one of the last nubs of an *amanibhavam* bloom. Scrubbing the nub between his palms to powder it, he slapped one hand to his nose, clamped the other over Linden's nose and mouth.

Too many sensations. *Amanibhavam* stung her sinuses as if she had inhaled acid. She had no time to notice that it dispelled her nausea. The sunshine wore a faint patina of dust. Shadows blurred Mahrtiir's visage.

Then Earthpower flowed into her from the black shaft of the Staff; and she thought, Trees? A Forestal?

Oh, God.

You must quench the *caesure*!

Caesures destroyed stone. They would tear any forest to shreds. Even a forest defended by a Forestal—

Where *was* she?

Mahrtiir knew Andelain. Surely he would have called that woodland by name?

Reflexively she clutched the Staff. Then she heaved herself into a sitting position; staggered to her feet.

The Fall was already thirty paces away, forty. And it was big, as virulent as a tornado; a rip in the fabric of reality. Seething, it lurched toward a scatter of trees:

Gilden, ash, sycamores, thirsty willows. They stood alone and in loose copses, punctuating the browning grass like the out-riders of an army in retreat. Like the grass, they looked parched, stricken by a persistent lack of rain, a dwindling watershed. She could not see past them to the forest itself, but she knew instantly that the forest was there. It seemed to glower in the distance, defying an inexorable drought.

The *caesure* savaged the ground as it moved. It was going to plow a furrow of devastation into the heart of the woods.

"*Melenkurion abatha*," she gasped as if she were cursing. The burn of *amanibhavam* sent flames like tendrils along the channels of her brain. "*Duroc minas mill.*" She felt as blighted as the trees, wan with thirst.

Where am I?

What have I done?

"*Harad khabaal.*"

One fire led to another; enabled another. As if she were turning her mind inside out, she drew ebon conflagration from the Staff and flung it like outrage into the core of the Fall.

Earthpower and Law, the salvific antitheses of the time-storm. Her flames were as stark as fuligin, as black as the immedicable gulf of a night sky after every star had been devoured. But the darkness was hers: it was not inherent to the Staff's magicks. And here—wherever *here* might be—she was not hampered by Kevin's Dirt. Riding the invocative force of the Seven Words, she hit the *caesure* with a deluge of extinction as if she were pouring a lake onto an inferno.

The Fall could not withstand her. As she had done before, she caused the violent miasma to implode. With a sound like thunder, the *caesure* swallowed itself as if it sought to suck her with it into nothingness. Then it was gone.

Its passage had galled the earth—a bitter wound—but the nearest trees had not been touched.

"Mane and Tail, Ringthane!" breathed Mahrtiir. Already he sounded steadier, stronger. Even withered, *amanibhavam* retained the potency to restore him. "That was well done. Another moment, and our quest would have failed. No tale of Forestals told among the Ramen makes mention of forbearance. They do not countenance the ravage of their woods."

Trembling, Linden extinguished her flames. Well done? she wondered. Really? Mahrtiir was right, of course. She could not expect any Forestal to grant her desires after she had damaged his trees. But now she had no idea how she and her companion would return to their proper time. Too tired to think clearly, she had assumed that she would use the same *caesure*. An impossible idea. It had brought her to the brink of a terrible mistake. Yet the result was that she and Mahrtiir were trapped.

She could not imagine an escape that did not require another *caesure*, another

Desecration. And she could not guess what would happen if she violated Time in this era. Thousands of years separated her from Jeremiah, Stave, and the Giants; from any conceivable reconciliation with Thomas Covenant. The Law of Life had not yet been violated. A time-storm created here might consume every possible future.

She bit her lower lip in an effort to control herself; but she could not stop trembling. These trees did not belong to Andelain: she was sure now. The forest beyond them was too dark, too angry. And she knew of no time in which the heart of the Land had been gripped by a drought like this. Clearly Hyn and Narunal had ignored her desire to reach Caer-Caveral. So when *was* she?

Why did the mood of the woodland seem familiar?

Nagged by the same concerns, Mahrtiir continued, "Yet I confess that I am troubled. Was it not your intent to seek out the Forestal Caer-Caveral? That I conveyed to great Narunal. But this is not Andelain. Plainly it is not. Rather we have come to a place and time unknown to me." He muttered a Ramen curse. "I cannot account for it. I am certain only that the gifts of the Ranyhyn are unerring. They have turned aside from your wishes for some good purpose."

Linden nodded in bafflement. The presence of the great horses nearby offered an oblique solace. Still she could not keep the tremor from her voice as she asked, "Do you recognize anything? Anything at all? Can you guess where we are?"

The Manethrall scowled above his bandage. "In these straits, Ringthane, blindness hinders me, though I am not constrained by Kevin's Dirt. I am able to assure you only that I have never stood in this region of the Land." After a moment of hesitation, he added, "Among the Ramen, however, there are tales—"

His voice trailed away. Before Linden could prod him, however, he asked, "The trees lie to the north, yes?"

She nodded automatically, trusting his awareness of her.

"Are there hills in the east?" he continued. "Do they mount toward mountains?"

She looked in that direction, summoned Earthpower to increase the range of her senses. "If I'm not mistaken."

"And in the west? Do mountains also arise there?"

Squinting into the distance, she murmured, "I think so."

Mahrtiir's manner became sharper. "One question more, Ringthane. Does a waste extend at our backs? I perceive barrenness. Does it spread to the horizon and beyond?"

"As far as I can tell. It looks like the edge of a desert."

The Manethrall stood taller, straightened his shoulders as if he had found himself in the presence of majesty. "Then I must surmise," he announced so that the trees and even the wide sky might hear him, "that we stand in the gap of Cravenhaw.

Before us lies dire Garroting Deep. Narunal and Hyn have delivered us, not to Caer-Caveral, but to Caerroil Wildwood. If you would speak with him, Ringthane, we must dare his demesne."

He sounded almost eager.

But his words gave Linden a jolt. Details came together, formed connections.

Caerroil Wildwood. Garroting Deep.

No wonder the darkness seemed familiar.

She had encountered Caerroil Wildwood when Roger and the *croyel* had stranded her deep in the Land's past. At that point in his long life, the Forestal's puissance was undiminished. He had given her gifts: her life as well as runes for her Staff. In some sense, he had made possible Covenant's resurrection. And he had charged her with a question.

How may life endure in the Land, if the Forestals fail and perish, as they must, and naught remains to ward its most vulnerable treasures? We were formed to stand as guardians in the Creator's stead. Must it transpire that beauty and truth shall pass utterly when we are gone?

He had understood that she had no reply. Nevertheless he had spared her. He had seen something in her, *the mark of fecundity and long grass. And the sigil of the Land's need has been placed upon her.* What sigil? For all she knew, then or now, he had referred to the bullet hole in her shirt. Or to the healed wound in her hand where the *croyel* had stabbed her. Still she had felt compelled to promise an answer.

But long ago—millennia later in the Land's life, a decade earlier in Linden's—when she and Covenant had first met Caer-Caveral in Andelain—when the guardian who had once been Hile Troy had sacrificed himself against the Law of Life—he had been the last Forestal. By that time, Caerroil Wildwood had passed away. All of the Upper Land's ancient forests had been destroyed by the Sunbane.

"My God, Mahrtiir." Inferences linked themselves into language as rapidly as she could speak. "This must be hundreds of years after I met Caerroil Wildwood," after the Mahdoubt had saved her. "It must be before the Clave. Before the Sunbane."

The kingdom against which Berek Halfhand had waged his war was not a desert.

Hyn and Narunal had known what they were doing. Here she was in no danger of confronting the Forestal before her first encounter with him.

"That is well," averred Mahrtiir. "Alas, to their shame the Ramen have no tales of events in the Land after the onset of the Sunbane. I must believe that Caerroil Wildwood perished striving against that abomination."

"No," Linden said at once. Covenant had learned the truth from the Clave. He had told her. "He passed earlier. Before the Sunbane."

The Manethrall's surprise was plain. "Then how was he brought to his end?"

She bit her lip again. "I'm not sure. It had something to do with the destruction of the first Staff of Law." Then she hurried on. "But at least now we know *when* we are—approximately, anyway. Caerroil Wildwood is still alive. He may recognize me. If he doesn't, he'll recognize his runes. We have a chance."

She had intended to address her appeal to Caer-Caveral; but she saw now that Hyn and Narunal understood her needs, and the Land's, better than she did. What had she expected of Andelain's Forestal? Had she truly imagined that meeting her before her proper time would not affect his later decisions?

In *this* time, here and now, she was in no danger of burdening Caer-Caveral with knowledge which he had not earned. The Ranyhyn had spared her a potentially catastrophic miscalculation.

"Thus," the Manethrall observed proudly, "Hyn and Narunal vindicate their wisdom once again." Then he admitted, "Yet queries remain. Are you able to summon the Forestal? To attract his notice is both perilous and necessary. And will he heed your desires? If the tales are sooth, Caerroil Wildwood will not grant a kindly hearing. Even in the days of dark Grimmerdhore, Garroting Deep was deemed the most wrathful of the forests. You have encountered this Forestal and lived—aye, and were given ambiguous boons. Do you conclude therefore that he will bestow the knowledge you seek, though you wish to preserve a world in which he does not exist? Neither he nor any Forestal?

"Ringthane, if you are able to gain his heed, how will you sway him?"

How may life endure in the Land—?

Linden watched birds soar like questions among the trees. Beyond them, Garroting Deep brooded over its innumerable wounds and grievances, its savage hungers. Winds from the mountains which walled Cravenhaw on both sides did nothing to soften the heat swelling from the south. Already sweat gathered at the corners of her eyes. Dampness trickled down her spine.

"I don't know," she admitted. "Caerroil Wildwood gave me his runes for a reason, and I don't think that it was just because I needed help. It had something to do with the question he asked me. He knew that I couldn't answer it, but he wanted an answer anyway. Maybe his runes were part of the question. Or he hoped that they might be part of the answer."

Mahrtiir considered her for a moment. Then he nodded with an air of renewed anticipation. "For us, then, only the simpler query remains. How will you attract the Forestal's notice? He is said to be an imperious being, mighty and impatient withal, having good cause to loathe humankind. Also Garroting Deep is vast. He may be many leagues distant, unaware of our approach. Or he may be unwilling to acknowledge beings whose like have butchered trees beyond all counting."

Linden frowned, shook her head. "Hyn and Narunal got his attention for us. They brought us so close—I almost let that *caesure* hurt his forest. I don't care how far away he is. He must have felt that kind of violence. He'll come, even if all he wants to do is to kill us."

The Manethrall nodded again. "Indeed, Ringthane. I cannot gainsay you. Thus my query becomes, how will you forestall his ire? Our tales assure us that the Forestals were mighty beyond comprehension. How otherwise did their puissance suffice to forbid the Ravers from the Upper Land?"

She shrugged. "I'm not exactly helpless myself." She had different concerns: fears that baffled her. *How may life endure in the Land—?* They were laden with doom. *Just be sure you come back.* "But I won't fight him." She, too, loved trees. And she had not forgotten the lessons of Gallows Howe. "I won't have to." Again she said, "He'll recognize his runes."

For another moment, Mahrtiir scrutinized her as if he sought to gauge her resolve. Then he nodded once more. "As you say, Ringthane. As ever, the deeds of the great horses conduce to hope. I grasp now that there is a fitness to your purpose. My own desires are thereby justified. Come good or ill, boon or bane, I will regret no moment of our quest."

"All right," Linden murmured. Gradually her attention shifted away from her companion. "Then all we have to do right now is wait. And try not to go crazy."

What choice did she have? She did not want to think about Jeremiah; about people and loves that she had left behind and might never see again. In one respect, her presence in a time where she did not belong was no different than any other crisis. In fact, it was no different than ordinary life. The only way out was forward. While Time endured, there was no going back.

Gripping her Staff for courage, she tried to put everything else out of her mind. At her side, Mahrtiir folded his arms across his chest like a man who knew how to contain his impatience. In the service of the Ranyhyn, he had learned the discipline of setting himself aside. He knew how to accommodate his frustration.

Her former world had taught Linden similar skills. She had acquired a professional detachment in medical school and emergency rooms and Berenford Memorial. But she had lost that resource, or had left it behind with Jeremiah and the Giants, Stave and Covenant. She did not know how to stop fretting. Instead she gnawed on her fears as if she hungered for them; as if at the marrow she would find sustenance.

She needed her son and Covenant. She had to do what she could to keep them alive in spite of the intervening millennia.

"Oh, hell," she muttered abruptly. "Who am I kidding? I can't just wait around. Let's at least get closer."

Holding her Staff ready, she moved toward the nearest trees.

Their suffering without sufficient water was palpable. The willows in particular ached with distress, and the grass crackled under her boots. As the ground sloped down behind her toward the wasteland, moisture was wicked away from the woods. Apparently Caerroil Wildwood's music could no longer protect the outlying trees from the effects of the diminished watershed. Even if Garroting Deep faced no other perils, it was under assault by the perpetual drought in the south.

Tensely Linden crossed through stippled shade to bypass the forest's first fringes. Unaware that she was holding her breath, she approached the ragged edge of the Deep. At her shoulder, Mahrtiir matched her pace. A short distance away, Hyn whickered softly, and Narunal stamped his hooves; but the Ranyhyn did not follow.

Linden passed a stunted copse, then a magisterial Gilden with leaves like scraps of clawed fabric, an oak mottled with brown stains like blights. The low rustle of breezes among their branches seemed to sound her name until she reached a stretch of open ground like a clearing. With enough water, it might have been a glade surrounded by verdure and consolation. Here it was simply earth that nourished little more than grass. Nevertheless the grass was healthier than it was beyond the trees.

In the center of the clearing, she stopped. Surely the Forestal was close? Surely he had felt her presence? But he was needed everywhere in Garroting Deep. He might turn away when he saw that the danger of the *caesure* had passed. And she could only call out to him in one language: the speech of fire.

Unsure of herself, she turned to Mahrtiir.

The Manethrall considered the forest for a moment. Then he offered gruffly, "Here I am reminded of a tale concerning Lord Mhoram at a time when the forces of the Lords were threatened by an army commanded by a Raver. It is the same tale which relates the doom of Hile Troy. Risking much, the Lord approached Garroting Deep from Cravenhaw and raised fire in supplication. But he also dared to speak words of power, words which belonged to the Forestal. Therefore Caerroil Wildwood came.

"But those words were not repeated to the Ramen. The tale is known to us only because it was shared by Bannor and others after the *Haruchai* had withdrawn from their service as the Bloodguard. They are a reticent people, as you know"—Mahrtiir sounded grimly amused—"and did not tell the tale fully."

"I wonder what they were," Linden mused absently. Her ears strained for hints of Caerroil Wildwood's singing: the poignant and feral melody of the Forestal's strength.

A *caesure* should have been inconceivable in this time. How could any lover of trees ignore such a threat?

Apparently Caerroil Wildwood could not. When Mahrtiir had been silent for a while, and Linden's trepidation seemed ready to burst out of her chest, she heard the first notes of a song that rent her heart.

It seemed to arch from tree to tree as if it were setting every leaf alight. Its power was unmistakable, a force as fraught as wild magic. But its potential ferocity was muted, held in abeyance: perhaps because its full might was not needed to rid the Deep of two mere humans; or perhaps because the Forestal was curious in spite of his unrelieved wrath; or perhaps because he recognized—

Breezes and tuned ire made the woods appear to waver like a mirage. Scraps of song more audible to percipience than to ordinary hearing spread like ripples. Boughs and roots added notes which should have been discordant, but which instead wove a dire counterpoint through the lamentation of leaves, the grief and objurgation of sap. Words that almost formed verses skirled through the grass at Linden's feet: *days before the Earth*, and *its walk to doom*, and *forbidding dusty waste*.

Wearing an aura of embattled music, Caerroil Wildwood appeared far back among the trees.

His steps were instances of a dirge, ancient and unreconciled; irreconcilable. Lucent melody rather than light cloaked him in lordship. A penumbra of sorrow etched with gall and despair surrounded him as he advanced; and he seemed to waft rather than walk, as if he were carried along by the chords of his puissance. He was as tall as a king; his flowing hair and beard and his long robe were white with antiquity; the silver authority of his eyes judged all things harshly. He commanded homage from the trees as he passed, but it was an obeisance of appreciation and reverence, not of servility. The service here was his: the forest did not serve him. In the crook of one elbow, he cradled a gnarled wooden scepter as if it were the symbol and manifestation of every trunk and shrub and seed-born wonder that he had ever loved. Loved and lost.

At her first glimpse of him, Linden bowed her head. Carefully she displayed the Staff of Law in front of her, lying like an offering across her hands.

Please, she breathed in silence. Just look. Don't decide anything until you look. I abandoned my son for this. If you don't help me, I've abandoned the whole world.

Beside her, Manethrall Mahrtiir stood straighter. He held up his head as if he wanted to emphasize his bandage, the ruined sockets of his eyes; wanted the Forestal to see that he was unafraid in spite of his blindness.

At the edge of the clearing, Caerroil Wildwood stopped. He did not deign to come closer. He did not speak. His tune in its myriad voices spoke for him.

My leaves grow green and seedlings bloom.
I inhale all expiring breath,
  And breathe out life to bind and heal.
My hate knows neither rest nor weal.

Linden ached to sing with him. If she could have replied with melody, he would have known that she had no wish for harm: not here; not in any forest. But she did not know the rites and cadences of his lore. Even her own magicks were mysteries to her. She could not address the Forestal in his natural tongue.

Still she had to try. Singing, he seemed to become higher and mightier, exalted by the inadequacy of her silence.

"Great One—" she began. But then her littleness caught in her throat, and she faltered.

"Ringthane," Mahrtiir urged privately, "you must. It is as you have said. He is aware of his doom. There lies the true heart of his torment. With every leaf and sprout of his realm, he cries out in bitterness and supplication. I hear now that he cannot decline to heed you. Some hope he must have. Is it not for this that he has clung to his devoir? Is it not for this that we have come, to proffer hope? Or, if not hope itself, then our striving in the name of hope?"

Linden feared the guardian of the Deep. Oh, she feared him! *From border to border, my demesne thirsts for the recompense of blood.* Now more than ever, that was true. He had known for millennia that he could not prevail over heedlessness and malice. His trees were too vulnerable—

Vulnerable and precious.

Yet his insights when she had met him before had surpassed her comprehension. They might do so again.

She made another attempt. "Great One. You know me."

She wanted to raise her voice even though she had no music to match Caerroil Wildwood's. But she could not be peremptory in his presence. She had to speak softly.

"You gave me a gift." She insisted on her Staff as if it were a pledge. "And you asked me a question that I couldn't answer. I need your help."

Vexation spread through the trees. "What is that to me?" the Forestal countered: raw tatters of sound that seemed to arise from the woods at his back. "In a bygone age, my heart was wrath. I was avid for bloodshed, and my ire suffused every leaf and twig and branch and trunk and root of my demesne. Yet now I recall that time as a halcyon era. Though I knew myself and all forests doomed, I remained capable of much, potent for both killing and nurturance in the name of trees and green. As you foretold, I feasted on the flesh of a Raver. But the years have become an age of the Earth, and the time of my power has passed. My strength withers in my veins. I cannot restore it.

"Do you ask my aid? I have none to give. My every effort is required to slow the ruin of all that I have held dear."

He fell silent, although his music went on weeping.

"You're right," Linden replied, forcing herself. Such honesty was difficult for her, but she had no other response. "You've always been doomed. But soon it's going to get worse. Much worse." She meant the Sunbane. "The Clave is going to create an evil like nothing that the Land has ever seen before, and it won't stop even when it has destroyed every last fragment of the One Forest. Eventually even Caer-Caveral will be gone. He'll reach the end of himself and let go.

"But long ago I told you that you would have a chance to make a Raver suffer. Now I tell you that the coming evil *will* be stopped. White gold and Law and love will cast it out. A new forest will grow," Salva Gildenbourne, "and it will be vast. The world will keep on turning, Great One.

"But that's not the end of what I know. Eventually there will be new evils. Worse evils. That's why I'm here. I can't offer you hope. I have to ask for it. I need *forbidding*. I need to know how to *forbid*. Otherwise my time will be as doomed as yours. Where I come from, the world won't keep on turning. The evil has gone too far. Nothing except forbidding can save it."

"What is that to me?" the august figure asked again. "The end of my days crowds close around me. I cannot forbid the waning of my own strength. My trees must perish. What will you forbid that I have not already failed to prevent? Soon or late, all things come to dust. I have no other purpose than sorrow."

"Now, Ringthane," Mahrtiir breathed like the breeze. "You are acquainted with despair. Harken to his, and he will heed you. His song speaks to my heart. In this, he and I are one."

Linden winced. She understood the Manethrall. She feared that she understood him too well. She had been given hints enough. But she could not afford to falter in her purpose.

"Great one, look at me," she implored. "Look at my Staff." *This blackness is lamentable—* "Look at your runes. You know what they mean. You gave them to me long ago, but even then you saw what was coming. You could already feel the hopelessness that eats at you now. You were so angry then because you were fighting your own futility. That's why you asked me a question." *How may life endure—?* "Now I've come back. You've been waiting for millennia, and I'm finally here. Let me try to answer you."

Let me tell you why I need you.

The Forestal did not reply at once. For a time that strained Linden's nerves, he sang to himself as if he were considering her plea, or her death; debating the many cruelties of his plight. Small winds carried plaints through the struggling grass.

When he spoke at last, his melody sounded sharp enough to draw blood.

"Then come, human woman." He gestured imperiously with his scepter. "Bring your companion if you must. If you would dare my scrutiny, you must stand upon

Gallows Howe. In the presence of my doom and denunciation, you will speak. There you will live or be slain."

Before Linden could give her assent, Mahrtiir's voice rang out, pealing against the chime of the Wildwood's music. "What of proud Narunal, Great One? What of Hyn, loyal and loving? They are Ranyhyn, as revered as trees. Without them, we are lost."

For the third time, Caerroil Wildwood demanded, "What is that to me?"

Then Linden no longer stood on open ground. Ripples altered the surface of her senses, and she drifted among the trees where the Forestal had waited. The Forestal himself was gone: his song remained. It summoned her like a *geas* from the depths of the dark Deep.

While she staggered within herself, the fringes of the forest wavered like disturbed water. She stepped without transition onto a thin track like a path for deer wending crookedly among monarchs thick with age. She had no sensation of movement, but she had already come far. Aching branches swathed her in shadows defined by sunlight falling cleanly between the leaves. Caerroil Wildwood was drawing her toward the heart of his demesne. Doing so, he seemed to call her in the direction of her own past, and the Land's. With every stride, she crossed decades and leagues as if they were seamless, woven together by the fecund mutter of music from a thousand thousand voices.

Vaguely she was aware that Manethrall Mahrtiir walked at her side, passing farther and farther into Garroting Deep and time. He did not speak, and she did not. Like her, he appeared ensorcelled by the counterpoint of the Forestal's ubiquitous song.

Together she and her companion traveled among changes in the terrain: hills and streams; low stone buttresses grey with age and clad in moss; complex trails like a web of welcome for the animals that enriched the woodland. Variations among the trees themselves measured the progression of leagues: stands of new growth interrupted by the magisterial contemplation of ripe oaks; thickets crowded with orchids and *aliantha*; vibrant tracts of aspen and cottonwood on higher ground in the west, draped cypress and willow in lowlands and swales to the east. If the sun moved at all in the distant heavens, Linden did not notice it.

How far had they come? How far were Gallows Howe and the Black River from Cravenhaw? She did not know—and could not care. While Caerroil Wildwood's trance carried her, compelled her, she only took one step after another, and filled her lungs with the woodland's wealth of scents, and marveled that so much largesse had withstood the depredations of centuries and humankind and malevolence.

The woods seemed as timeless as the chaos of a *caesure*; but Garroting Deep was not Desecration. In spite of its enduring bitterness, its galls of woe and ire, it had been formed for peace. The lost nature of the One Forest was irenic, as rapt as *Elohim*, and as self-absorbed. Perhaps that similarity, that kinship, explained the willingness of the *Elohim* to take action for the preservation of woodlands. The result was an anodyne for travail even when the trees were stiff with outrage. If Linden had ever been afraid, or desperate, or appalled, she had forgotten it; or the Forestal's music warded her from herself.

For her, the way was not long. Denser shade cut out more and more sunlight. Darker trees gathered gloom beneath their branches: their roots fed on shadows. Vines like hawsers tangled the underbrush on both sides of the trail where she and Mahrtiir walked. Swaths of leaves looked as black as dying blood except when brief glimpses of the sun revealed their true green. After unremarked moments or hours, she found herself approaching the barren slope of Gallows Howe.

The hill seemed higher than she remembered it: higher and more cruel, as if it had absorbed a terrible increase of savagery from the killing of a Raver's physical form, the destruction of a fragment of the Illearth Stone. The very dirt radiated hunger, thirst, desire, as though every clod and pebble craved the taste of blood; of slaughter enough to drench the soul of the forest. Here the Deep had no language for its bereavement except rage. Utterly dead, the Howe piled darkness upward as if it were impervious to sunshine; as if no light from the heavens could touch it. And near the crest arose the two dead trunks which supported the Forestal's gibbet.

From the branches of the crossbar hung two nooses, ready and willing.

Beside his gibbet, Caerroil Wildwood stood with his arms folded over his scepter as if he had been waiting for an age of the Earth. Around his neck he wore a garland braided from the stems and blooms of accusations. The song he spread around him had once been a dirge, but it had become as harsh and heavy as drumbeats announcing judgment.

His presence stopped Linden and Mahrtiir at the foot of the slope.

"Ringthane," the Manethrall breathed, suddenly aghast. "This place— Mane and Tail! Tales name it, but no Raman has beheld it. It is the Forestal's heart. It cannot be answered."

"I know," Linden said hoarsely. The labor of her pulse seemed to clog her throat. "But he has a right to it. I felt like that, and all I lost was my son. What he's suffered is worse.

"The *Elohim* made this possible." One of them had planted the seeds of power and lore which had germinated to become Forestals. "But they don't die, so they don't grieve. They had no idea what his life would be like."

A handful of Forestals had not sufficed to save the woods. As benign as Gilden and oaks, Caerroil Wildwood and his kind had been slow to recognize hate and heedlessness. They had taken too long to learn anger, too long to summon their strength. As a result, they had been forced to watch millions of living things in their care perish.

"But you said it yourself," Linden went on. "He'll hear us anyway. He needs something to hope for."

She had to believe that.

Touching Mahrtiir's shoulder, she urged him to join her as she began her ascent of Gallows Howe.

He may have faltered for a moment—but only for a moment. Then he found his resolve, and his features seemed to become sharper. *You'll have to go a long way to find your heart's desire.* With his chin jutting, he moved upward at Linden's side.

Death accumulated under her boots at every step. The dirt heeded no appeal and would never be appeased: it had lost too much. On this hill in another era, she had found the granite rage which had carried or driven her from her battle with Roger and the *croyel* to Thomas Covenant's resurrection. She understood the Howe's ire in the deepest channels of her heart.

As she climbed the hill's accreted hunger, however, she recognized other emotions as well. Listening with her nerves, her health-sense, she heard more. The passion of Gallows Howe was for revenge, retribution: the ground burned to repay its ancient pain. But that trenchant yearning arose from a foundation of unannealed bereavement. Trees beyond counting had been destroyed before the woods had awakened to anger. Grief came first. Without woe and protest, there would have been no wrath.

Then inchoate perceptions which had tugged at the edges of her thoughts for days shifted toward clarity, and she heard still more. In spite of their avid bitterness, the songs sung by Caerroil Wildwood beside his gibbet were more complex than they appeared to be. First came grief. Yes. It led inexorably to rage. But it did so only because a different need had been denied. Between the underlying loss and the accumulated gall lay a yearning of another kind altogether: a vast, sorrowing, stymied desire, not for revenge, but for *restitution*. The forests, and the emblem of Gallows Howe, would not have grown so dark if they had not first failed to reclaim what they had lost. If the Forestals had not failed at restitution, they would not have succumbed to ire and viciousness.

That unbidden insight humbled Linden. It daunted her when she could not afford to flinch or turn away. It had too many personal implications.

She, too, had gone from loss to rage when her first efforts to find her son had failed. Nevertheless Jeremiah had been restored to her. Even though she had refused to forgive.

She could not ask Caerroil Wildwood to pardon the foes and forces which had ravaged his demesne. His vehemence was necessary. It was just. It was—

But the Forestal did not wait for her to sort through her confusions. His music demanded more of her. While she and Mahrtiir neared his gibbet, the tall figure commanded, "Speak, then." Melodies sawed across her hearing as if they sought to cut away subterfuge and falseness. "I am done with forbearance."

Because she did not know what else to do, Linden lifted her Staff once more.

"Great One."

Every word required an effort of will. Inwardly she slogged through a quagmire. How could she ask Caerroil Wildwood for anything? He was doing what she would have done in his place; what she had already done. Nevertheless she made the attempt for Jeremiah's sake, and for the Land's, and for Covenant's—and perhaps even for her own.

"A long time ago, you asked me a question. I think that I can answer it now. Or a piece of it, anyway.

"That isn't why I came. I've tried to imagine an answer for you ever since you spared my life, but I couldn't think of one. I wasn't even trying to reach you. But now that I am here, I see things differently.

"Great One, I need your help. If I'm right, that's your answer. You can help me." *Must it transpire that beauty and truth shall pass utterly when we are gone?* "And you're the only one who can. If you don't, beauty and truth will be just the first casualties." She meant the *Elohim.* "Eventually the whole world is going to die."

The Forestal studied her. In a voice as low as a hum, and as piercing as an auger, he commanded her again. "Set aside your blackness. I well recall the craving which inspired me to carve my will upon it. It has no virtue to preserve you."

He may have been asking for a show of good faith.

As if the written wood had burned her hands, Linden dropped her Staff.

Caerroil Wildwood allowed the limbs of his trees a brief flourish of approval. But he did not dwell on it. Still stringently, he sang, "You acknowledge that it was not your intent to seek me out. To that extent, I discern sooth. Now you will speak further. Do you ask me to credit that the desires of one human, or of two, or of a myriad myriad, suffice to determine the doom of the Earth? Justify your need, woman. Sway me or perish."

Linden shook her head. "You already know the truth." She had come too far to hold back. And she understood the peril of revealing things which might affect the Wildwood's role in the Land's history. "You've known it for a long time. If you didn't, you wouldn't have given me your runes."

He would not have prevented Hile Troy from accepting Covenant's ring.

"You asked me how life can go on without Forestals. It can't. Thousands of years from now, it won't. Evil doesn't die. It doesn't stop. And where I come from, it's finally found a way to end everything. Unless you teach me how to *forbid* it."

There must be forbidding.

"If I can do that, maybe I can save something." *Without forbidding, there is too little time.* "I'll start with the *Elohim*," what was left of them. "If that works, I'll do more. With my Staff and white gold and what you know, I'll stop as much evil as I can." *If it is not opposed by the forgotten truths of stone and wood*— "But I can't do anything without the power to say *no*.

"You blocked the Ravers from the Upper Land. I need to learn how you did that. I need to be able to do the same thing. If you don't teach me, you might as well give up." From her perspective, his surrender had already happened. Something had driven Caerroil Wildwood to abandon his devoir long before she had first entered the Land with Covenant. "There won't be any hope for any of us.

"Do you need a future for trees, Great One? This is your only chance. Without your help, I'm as lost as you are."

Silver flared in the Forestal's eyes. It limned his gibbet and the surrounding trees, gave them a spectral cast as if they were etched with presentiments of ruin. The music of the woods became a threnody, forlorn and irredeemable. Leaves rose and sank like sobbing on their twigs. Song fell like tears on all sides.

"Then you are lost indeed. You speak words which you deem sooth. That I acknowledge. And you have striven to satisfy my query. That, also, I acknowledge. Therefore I will not require your heart's blood to repay the hurt inflicted by your plea.

"But I cannot grant your desire. You are human and ignorant, incognizant of deeper truths. You do not grasp that the forbidding which you seek is not lore. It is neither knowledge nor skill. It is essence. It is both my nature and my task. I cannot impart it."

His response was as simple as a sigh—and as fatal as an earthquake. Linden staggered as if the Howe itself had shuddered under her; refused her. Cannot? She wanted to wail in chagrin. You *cannot*? After what she had done?

But he was Caerroil Wildwood, the Forestal of Garroting Deep. His grandeur and grief silenced her protests. Instead of yelling, she floundered for arguments.

"Then how did you make your Interdict against the Ravers?" Her voice trembled on the verge of breaking. "If you can't impart what you are, how did the Colossus of the Fall keep Ravers away from the Upper Land?"

Abruptly Mahrtiir took a step forward. Like the woods around the Howe, like the gallows, he looked sharp with intensity, whetted by the Forestal's shining. His eyeless visage seemed to yearn. His hands were ready for his garrote; for some demand that required death. But the Wildwood did not regard him.

"By transformation," the Forestal told Linden severely. "By the alteration of essence. There is no other means. The *Elohim* who became the Colossus of the Fall

ceased to be who she was. She was made stone and could not unmake herself. Therefore her refusal endured. It did not wane until the forests dwindled, too grievously
diminished to sustain her."

While Linden cried out inwardly, unable to articulate her sudden despair,
Mahrtiir took another step forward; upward. Then he stopped, holding himself
poised as if for battle.

"Great One," he said, insisting on Caerroil Wildwood's attention. "The world of
our time requires forbidding—and the forest of our time requires a Forestal to wield
that stricture." His tone defied contradiction. "You have it within you to create
another of your kind, as you did with Caer-Caveral. Do so again with me. Make of
me a Forestal for the woodland which will arise when its time has come, and for the
preservation of the world. Permit me to carry on your labors. Share with me your
mighty purpose, for I have none of my own, except to stand with those who shed
their lives for the Land's sake."

He was certainly as blind as Hile Troy had been: as blind and as valiant. Like Troy,
he had already chosen his doom.

Linden tried to object; but the Manethrall's willingness and the Wildwood's singing closed her throat. *No*, she pleaded, *no*, but her voice made no sound, or no one
heard her.

The guardian of the trees was going to refuse. Of course he was. His own fate
was sealed, whatever happened. She had offered him only abstractions, vague predic-
tions empty of substance. He had no reason to care about a world that did not exist
for him.

Yet he seemed to stand taller, towering over the Manethrall. The multiplicity of
songs around him acquired a new tune that vied against the woods' immedicable
sorrow and ire. He raised his scepter. From its gnarled length sprouted notes woven
to form harmonies which Linden had never heard before.

"That gift," he pronounced as if it were a sentence of death, "is mine to grant."

Oh, Mahrtiir—

Were *all* of her friends going to sacrifice themselves?

If she had snatched up her Staff, she might have been able to intervene. She could
at least have made the effort. *And betimes some wonder is wrought to redeem us.* But
she did not move. Perhaps she could not. Or perhaps she simply understood.

I seek a tale which will remain—

Still she had to say something. "Mahrtiir—"

"No, Ringthane," the Manethrall replied at once. "You are the Chosen, but this
choice is mine." He knew her too well. "In this, Anele spoke wisely, as he did on other
matters. To you, he said, 'All who live share the Land's plight. Its cost will be borne by

all who live. This you cannot alter. In the attempt, you may achieve only ruin.'" Then he gave her a fierce grin. "It is done. The Forestal of Garroting Deep has heard me. His heart and his pain are great. He will not refuse."

"Indeed," Caerroil Wildwood hummed in harmony with his trees. "I do not recant my gifts."

A sharp skirl of music seemed to snatch her Staff from the dirt, carry it toward him. Holding his scepter in one hand, he caught the Staff in the other. The lines of his runes began to burn like his eyes, silver and severe.

"Yet I am grievously diminished. My strength falters. Therefore I will make use of your blackness to sustain me, as I have written that I must."

With the Staff and his scepter held high, he brandished gleaming like certainty over the Howe. "Harken now. Hear my answer to your need."

Extremes contradicted each other in Linden's heart, a turmoil of unexpected hope and dread. Possibilities that she had failed to foresee daunted and exalted her. In the dirt under her boots, complex emotions thrummed as if Gallows Howe had forgotten or surrendered none of its desires. Ahead of her, Mahrtiir stood with his hands open as if he were waiting for the weapon which would give them meaning at last: an import which no mere garrote could supply. Higher on the hill, and wreathed in compulsions which appeared to draw only purity from the Staff of Law, Caerroil Wildwood made his music louder, more encompassing, until it became a hymn chorused by the entire woodland. At the same time, he tuned his singing to a pitch that resembled language. Perhaps with her ears, or perhaps only with her health-sense, Linden listened to an arboreal melody more numinous than speech.

> "It is my heart I give to you,
> My blood and sap and bone and root,
> To serve the woods with what we are
> While what we are endures to serve.

> "I guard and grow the world's deep love.
> Its loveliness must justify
> The sterner truths of rock and sea,
> For they persist but do not grow
> And so their life is only Law:
> It is not melody or joy.
> Their substance, substanceless, is woe
> Unless it is redeemed by green,
> By growth and verdure that relieve
> The world from stone's commanding cold.

"If rock does not erode it does
Not feed the trees that give it worth.
If sea does not give way to rain
It does not vindicate its surge.
Such passage is Creation's pulse:
Its transformation brings forth love
From Law's unending rest and flood,
For only life which passes on
Can glorify remaining life.

"For loving's sake I guard the green:
Its steward I became and am—
And you as well, for by my song
It is my soul I give to you
To serve the woods until we die."

And while the Forestal's invocation swelled across tree and hill, Manethrall Mahrtiir of the Ramen began to change. Ineffable magicks wrapped him in their cocoon until he was barely visible. Swathed in Caerroil Wildwood's power, his bandage was burned away, and his raiment fell from him like dross. His lean form with its scars of struggle and its ropes of muscle was robed in samite that shone like incarnate cleanliness. An unalloyed argent too rare and refined to be wild magic transformed his visage. As if he had brought it forth from within him, a twig grew in his grasp until it became a sapling nearly as tall as himself: a child-tree crowned with new leaves, its roots clinging to a ball of rich loam, which he held with the ease of supernal strength.

The end of his human life had come upon him. When he emerged from the Forestal's theurgy, the man who had been steadfast in the face of every peril would be gone. Like the *Elohim* of the Colossus, he would not be able to revoke his transubstantiation. Nevertheless his gladness aspired among the harmonies of Garroting Deep, and his eagerness for strife contributed a peal of joy.

Watching him, Linden wanted to cry; but she had no tears for a friend who had found his heart's desire.

11.

Back from the Brink

Thomas Covenant could hardly stand. He felt like wreckage. Certainly he looked like a derelict, with his tattered jeans and T-shirt, and his silver hair wild. Only his boots had come intact through his immersions in Sarangrave Flat. If Rallyn had not led Mishio Massima through an arduous series of translations by wild magic, he would not have arrived anywhere. He and Branl would still be trudging along the edges of the lurker's wetland an impossible distance from where he was needed. Traveling through argent circles drawn on grass and stone and dirt with Loric's *krill*, he had exceeded his image of himself.

But he had not done so without help. He was not as weak as he should have been, or as numb. Some of the effects of hurtloam lingered deep within him. He had drunk water made clean for him by the Feroce, and had eaten *ussusimiel* melons. Aided beyond any reasonable expectation, he had been able to traverse the leagues.

With Kastenessen gone, Kevin's Dirt may have begun to dissipate; but if so, that was a victory which Covenant could neither confirm nor measure. Instead he was torn inside, frantic and grieving. Clyme's death remained as vivid as scars, as harsh as Joan's. The Worm was coming: it had already reached the Land. And Linden was not here.

She was not here.

In the instant of his arrival, he had seen things that deserved celebration. Jeremiah had escaped from his mental prison, or had been freed: that was obvious. Otherwise he would not have been able to design the crude structure at the foot of the rubble and the ridge. The Giants would not have known how to build it. And the edifice had succeeded. Infelice's presence at the portal, and Kastenessen's raging opposition, demonstrated that Jeremiah's efforts had achieved their strange purpose—whatever that might be.

But the boy sprawled on the roof of the construct as if he had been felled. Stave lay motionless in the dirt near Infelice. None of the Giants wore their armor. They had no weapons. And there was no sign of Mahrtiir. Like Linden, the Manethrall had gone somewhere else—or had been left behind—or—

Covenant was stretched too thin to appreciate what the Land's defenders had accomplished.

Without any flicker of hesitation or pause for thought, he had flung himself toward Kastenessen armed only with Loric's eldritch dagger and his own extremity. *I killed my ex-wife.* Joan's ring seemed trivial against a being of Earthpower merged with brimstone and lava. *I helped destroy a Raver.* Yet Kastenessen had believed him. *And I've seen the Worm of the World's End.* Perhaps the *krill* was capable of killing greater foes than Joan and *turiya* Herem. *I am* done with restraint! Or perhaps Kastenessen had secretly wished to be swayed.

Beyond the construct where Infelice and Emereau Vrai's lover had vanished, the gouged ridge rose like a barricade against the southeast; against memories of Joan. Covenant had sacrificed his own daughter. More than once. He had raped her mother. Ignored Triock's death. Permitted Clyme's. And he was Roger's father. He was responsible for that lost soul as well. In Morinmoss long ago, he may have killed the woman who had healed his mind. Hell, he had even ridden the Harrow's destrier to its death. He had committed wrongs enough to mark him as an acolyte of the Despiser.

Now Linden was not *here.* He could not confess himself to her, or seek absolution.

Stave had said of her that she did not forgive. If that were true—

The aftermath of Kastenessen's surrender left Covenant reeling with needs and ignorance. To defeat Joan, he had sealed the fracturing of his mind, but he had not rid himself of vertigo. Even the comparatively level plain felt like a precipice in the doom-clogged twilight. Slaps of wind raised dust on all sides as if every step altered the ground itself. He hardly noticed when Branl took the *krill* to spare him at least that one burden.

Unheeded or unneeded, Rallyn and Mishio Massima trotted away, presumably seeking water and forage.

"Unbeliever," Giants murmured or panted. "Timewarden." Wan with exhaustion, Rime Coldspray called, "You are timely come." And Frostheart Grueburn, "Have you accomplished your purpose?" And Cirrus Kindwind, "Some ill end has befallen Clyme *Haruchai.*" Other Swordmainnir repeated like groans, "Longwrath," and, "Lostson." They sighed the names of the *geas*-damned man's parents, and ached for Moire Squareset and Scend Wavegift, both of whom were dead because of Longwrath.

Too many questions. Too many contradictions to absorb. Covenant only knew that Jeremiah was still alive because the boy was looking at him; staring as if he were stunned, barely conscious. Stave lay like Longwrath. Like Longwrath's, Stave's flesh smoked as if Kastenessen had scoured his heart with scoria.

It was all too much. As if he were being ripped open, Covenant released a cry that seemed to come from the marrow of his bones.

"*What happened to Linden?*"

Then he stood wavering as if he could not take another step without the woman whom he had loved for all of the Earth's ages.

Swordmainnir hung their heads, too weary or overwhelmed to answer. But after a moment, Rime Coldspray summoned a vestige of resolve. She leaned into motion, came unsteadily toward Covenant. Tears that might have been relief or chagrin or sorrow—that might have been anger—made runnels through the dust on her face. When she was near enough to speak in a hoarse whisper and be heard, she stopped.

Like Saltheart Foamfollower, the Ironhand towered over Covenant. The Giants had always been too much for him, more than he deserved. Trying to meet her gaze, he staggered until Branl steadied him.

"Timewarden," Coldspray breathed, "our need is great. We have expended our last strength, Lostson Longwrath lies before us, slain for our salvation, and Stave Rock-brother is much harmed. For these ills, we have no anodyne. We must— Ah, Stone and Sea. We must be more than we are.

"Yet I discern that your need is also great. Indeed, I fear that it exceeds comprehension. Therefore I will speak when I fain would hear."

She looked like she might collapse, but she did not. Even now, she met the challenge he represented.

"We deem that an alteration in Linden Giantfriend began when she was borne to the verge of the Sarangrave a second time."

Gloom held the plain. Beyond the stark brilliance of the *krill*'s gem, the preternatural twilight seemed to defy every sentence. A second time? When was the first? Was that when she had hurt the lurker enough to inspire an alliance?

"There the Feroce conveyed a message, citing your command. They urged her to *Remember forbidding*. For that reason, she parted from us."

The Feroce had done Covenant's bidding. He had no one else to blame.

"Here we have fashioned a fane for the *Elohim*. It compelled them to come, and to enter, drawing Kastenessen with them. There its magicks will ward them from the Worm's feeding."

Covenant stared up at her. Silver etched the lines of her visage, cut them into shapes that he feared to recognize. He believed the Ironhand, of course he did. Vast spans of time and knowledge were gone from him; but he remembered Jeremiah's importance, Jeremiah's talent. In some nameless sense, every future depended on Linden's son.

Chosen-son. The Giants had given the boy an epithet to call his own.

Exhaustion abraded the Ironhand's voice. "All remaining *Elohim* are now here.

Therefore the Worm also must come. Preserved within the fane, they cannot be consumed. When the Worm destroys our edifice, however, they will have no egress. They will be eternally lost. For this reason, Linden Giantfriend determined that the Worm must be turned aside."

That, at least, Covenant understood. The Worm would come. It was coming. He wanted to ask, Then why gather all the *Elohim* in one place? But he knew the answer: to give them a chance. They were helpless otherwise. And their presence here would not hasten the Earth's demise. Having reached the Land—and having been blocked from Mount Thunder—the Worm was bound to sense the location, the comparative proximity, of its final food. It would have come this way no matter what Jeremiah and the Giants did.

But it was not here now. The crazy turmoil of winds might mean anything. The clotted darkness on the northeastern horizon had more than one possible interpretation.

"Therefore Linden Giantfriend has invoked and entered a *caesure*. Accepting only Manethrall Mahrtiir as her companion, she seeks the deep past of the Land, where it is her hope that a Forestal will impart to her the forbidding which the world's peril demands."

Without Branl's support, Covenant might not have been able to stay on his feet. The deep past—Oh, hell. Joan's death had not put an end to *caesures*. In spite of everything, Linden was still exceeding his expectations.

Branl's expression was unreadable, as inarticulate as a mask of marble. However, his gaze was fixed, not on Rime Coldspray, but on Stave. Mind to mind, the Humbled may have been asking the former Master for confirmation.

How had Linden persuaded Stave to let her go without him?

At the end of her determination, the Ironhand said, "If she succeeds—and if the Arch does not fall—and if she is able to return—she will endeavor to refuse the Worm from this place."

Covenant groaned aloud. Linden's absence was his doing. He had pushed her toward a risk so extreme that merely hearing it described made his pulse falter in his veins. He had been pushing her ever since she had returned to the Land, even though every stricture of Law and Time had screamed against such intervention. If she failed, the fault would be his.

But what else could he have done? He could not have acted differently without ceasing to be who he was.

Rime Coldspray was waiting. Her comrades were waiting. He had to say *something*: something that was not more self-recrimination. He had done enough of that. It served no purpose.

And Linden was not here to heal or curse him.

Goading himself, he rasped, "You already know some of my story." The Sword-mainnir had heard his challenge to Kastenessen. "Joan is dead. I rode the Harrow's horse until I killed it. We almost lost Mhornym and Naybahn. But they saved me. Then we went after *turiya*. Branl and me. And Clyme."

Now that he had made a start, he meant to continue. But Coldspray held up her hand, asking him to pause. Other Giants were coming closer. Limping arduously, Frostheart Grueburn led the way with Latebirth and Cirrus Kindwind at her back. Onyx Stonemage and Stormpast Galesend moved like cripples, supporting Cabledarm between them. Wheezing, Halewhole Bluntfist labored after them.

As the women gathered beside the Ironhand, Covenant went on.

"Some things I have to guess," he admitted, "but I gather Linden had a run-in with the lurker. You were probably there. Whatever happened, it got that monster's attention. Apparently Horrim Carabal can feel the Worm coming. It doesn't want to die. It needs more power. But it couldn't beat Linden—or you and Linden. So the Feroce found me." They had accused him of being the Pure One. "They offered us an alliance." *In pain and desperation*—"Mutual help, safe passage, that sort of thing." *Already he suffers the presence of one who wanders lost within his realm*—"That must be how Longwrath got here. The lurker let him through. And dozens of those little creatures died helping us get to Joan."

His listeners nodded again. Silver reflected like keening in their eyes. Longwrath's attack on Kastenessen must have astonished or appalled them. They had tried so hard to follow his *geas* with him until he found peace. But they did not interrupt.

"After that," Covenant said, fierce and quavering, "I wanted an alliance myself." He dreaded memories like this one. They were as piercing as images of Joan. "It isn't hard to imagine we're going to need all the help we can get. And I was afraid *turiya* would take the lurker." He did not mention the former Guardian of the One Tree. The Sword-mainnir would recognize Brinn's name; but Covenant had no courage to spare for that explanation. "Once I learned how to jump across leagues, we went after the Raver.

"We didn't catch up with him until he was in the Sarangrave. I tried to kill him, but I couldn't. Clyme and Branl did it." In spite of his private horror, he could not gloss over this detail. The Giants needed to hear it. They would understand. And the Humbled deserved at least that much homage. "Clyme let *turiya* possess him." Like Honninscrave in Revelstone. "Then he held the Raver while Branl cut him to pieces." Covenant remembered hacked flesh, severed bones, blood. "*Turiya* wasn't just rent. He's gone. There isn't anything left."

The distress of the Giants showed in the way they looked at Branl; in glances teary with compassion and dismay. Perhaps more than any other living people, Coldspray and her comrades knew the cost of causing a Raver's end. Yet Branl's gaze gave them nothing. He was *Haruchai* and did not accept grief.

Covenant considered that rigidity a weakness, not a strength. He believed that forgiveness began with sorrow. But perhaps he was wrong. Perhaps a man who grieved would have spared Clyme. Then *turiya* Herem would have lived. Eventually Horrim Carabal would have been lost—and the Worm might have made its way, unresisted, to Mount Thunder.

Grinding his teeth, Covenant went on.

"When Branl and I got out of the Sarangrave, we probably weren't all that far from where we are now. But the Feroce told us the Worm was getting close. That's when I sent my message. Then I wanted to see it for myself. We went to look.

"Now the Worm is here." He bit down on his voice to hold it steady. "I can't describe it. I'm not going to try. But I can tell you this." Facing the clenched apprehension of his audience, he said, "It wasn't headed *here*," toward Jeremiah's fane and the sealed *Elohim*. "It was going west. Straight at Mount Thunder. At She Who Must Not Be Named.

"That scared me," he growled. "Lord Foul likes convoluted plots. Every trap you face has another one hidden inside. If the Worm and that bane went after each other, we wouldn't have to worry about the *Elohim*, or anything else for that matter, because we would already be dead."

He spread his hands; his truncated fingers. "We're not, so I have to assume—"

Rime Coldspray looked like she wanted to interrupt then; but Covenant did not pause. As concisely as he could, he explained how the lurker and the Demondim-spawn had striven to deflect the Worm from Mount Thunder. Then he finished, "I didn't wait around to see how long they could hold. Branl and I just ran. But they must have held long enough." Somehow. "I can't imagine it would take this long for the Worm to get through Lifeswallower. Now I just have to hope we didn't lose them in the process."

He expected Coldspray or the others to question him. He had questions of his own. What had happened to Jeremiah and Stave? How had Jeremiah been retrieved from his dissociation? But before anyone spoke, Branl moved.

Without ceremony, as if the action did not require comment, the Humbled handed Loric's *krill* to Rime Coldspray.

She accepted it reflexively, her eyes wide, as Branl strode past her toward Stave.

With Handir and the other Humbled, Branl had participated in punishing—in excommunicating—Stave for his defiance of his kinsmen; his devotion to Linden. The Masters had refused to acknowledge Stave's mental voice. Like Clyme and even Galt, Branl had treated Stave with disdain. Like them, Branl had challenged Stave more than once, tried to strike him down.

Now the last of the Humbled approached Stave's prone form like a man who proposed to deliver judgment.

Covenant should have stopped him; should have said something, anything. Clyme's death was only one example of the severity with which the *Haruchai* judged themselves. But at that moment, Covenant was like the Giants. He had come to the end of what he could do.

A darkening storm made omens in the northeast. Winds whipped Branl's legs, tugged at the tears in his tunic. But he ignored them. Implacable as a fanatic, he strode through the gusts.

At Stave's side, he stopped, braced his fists on his hips. For a moment, he bowed his head over Stave, apparently searching Stave's slack form for some sign of awareness. Stave's hand and forearm, his right, no longer smoked. Still he lay helpless, as if his mind or his heart had been as badly charred as his skin.

"I have named Stave 'Rockbrother,'" Coldspray announced. She may have been warning Branl; but she seemed unable to raise her voice.

Abruptly Branl stooped over the fallen *Haruchai*. With both hands, he lifted Stave upright.

Stave's head lolled to one side, then sagged until his chin rested on his chest. He dangled emptily in Branl's grasp.

In a blink of motion so swift that Covenant barely understood it, Branl released one hand and slapped the side of Stave's head. The blow made no sound that Covenant could hear through the wind.

Frostheart Grueburn winced. Coldspray lurched toward the *Haruchai*, going too late to Stave's defense.

As if the movement were full of pain, Stave slowly raised his head. His lone eye opened. Blinking, he fixed his gaze on Branl.

Branl did not strike again. Unsure of herself, the Ironhand halted. Covenant watched with his pulse trapped like a cry in his throat.

For a few heartbeats, Branl met Stave's gaze. Then Stave's head sagged again; and the Humbled nodded once. Shifting his grip, he wrapped his arms around Stave.

With Stave hugged against his chest, Branl informed Covenant, "The tale of the Giants is incomplete. We do not fault them. Their heed was consumed by Kastenessen and great weariness. It may be that they did not recognize the plight of Linden Avery's son. To Stave, however, it was evident that the boy received more than Earthpower at Anele's hands. The gift included Anele's openness to possession.

"Arriving in his fury, Kastenessen entered the boy. His apparent purpose was to drive Infelice into the fane, that he might destroy her with the other *Elohim*. But Stave intervened. By removing the boy from dirt underfoot, he severed the possession. Hence his burns, and his unconsciousness, and the boy's presence atop the fane, where he is warded by stone.

"There he might readily have been slain. Only Longwrath's coming, and yours, ur-Lord, preserved him. Yet more Stave could not have done. Without aspersion to the Swordmainnir, I assert that no other could have done as much."

Fresh vertigo sucked at Covenant. Realities shifted into new alignments: their implications veered like the world. Somehow Jeremiah had been rescued from his dissociation, or had saved himself. A mixed blessing: the Earthpower with which Anele had invested Jeremiah had made the boy vulnerable. No wonder Anele had hidden himself in madness; made himself blind. How else could he have concealed his true abilities, his secret purpose, from the Despiser? But Jeremiah did not have the old man's cunning. Lord Foul would be able to claim the boy whenever Jeremiah chanced to stand on the right surface, the right rough grass.

The ridge seemed to wobble from side to side, mocking Covenant. There were other inferences—

Branl had said *we*. He had addressed Stave in the fashion of the *Haruchai*—and he had listened to Stave's reply. Now he had reaffirmed his kinship with Linden's friend as if he felt pride in it. He spoke for Stave as well as himself.

A profound change. If the Humbled had ever needed or desired Covenant's forgiveness, he earned it now.

Apparently the Ironhand also had heard and understood Branl's *we*. She raised the *krill* so that its gem lit the *Haruchai*. Striving for formality, she replied, "There is no aspersion, Branl Humbled. There is only praise, both for Stave and for you—and for Clyme as well. At a better time, we will tell the full tale of Stave Rockbrother's deeds. We will honor your own. For the present, be assured that we esteem your courage and devoir."

Indirectly she steadied Covenant. Breathing deeply to calm his private reel, he muttered, "Then I guess Linden did the right thing when she made Stave stay behind."

"Indeed," assented Coldspray. And Branl said unexpectedly, "In this, the Chosen has shown foresight. I am reminded of matters which Stave has not forgotten concerning her former service to the Land."

Another surprise. Covenant frowned through the silver light, and found that he had no response. For a moment, he almost wept.

None of the Humbled had ever called Linden by her title.

"And Stave Rockbrother himself?" asked Cirrus Kindwind. "How does he fare? He is closed to our discernment, as you are, Branl Humbled. We fear for him."

Branl shrugged to indicate Stave. "This state is not unknown among the *Haruchai*. More commonly, we have recourse to it when we are snared by storms among the high peaks of our homeland. When both passage and shelter cannot be attained, we withdraw as Stave has done to preserve the essence of our lives. Thus we endure the gales, emerging when they are spent. Upon occasion, however, we withdraw similarly to heal otherwise mortal wounds, or mayhap to weather such shocks and virulence as Stave has received. When he has restored himself, he will stand among us once more."

Carefully he lowered Stave to the earth, then stepped back to resume his place with Covenant. He may have thought that he had said enough.

But Covenant had not entirely regained his balance. "Wait a minute," he objected. "There has to be more to it than that. Stave has touched Kastenessen before, and he wasn't hurt like this. Something is different now."

"It is, ur-Lord," admitted Branl. But he did not elaborate. Perhaps Stave had not remained conscious long enough to share those memories.

Rime Coldspray sighed heavily, a gust torn away by the moiling winds. "I am too worn to bear the burden of Stave's tale. I will say only that he was gravely injured in the raising of young Jeremiah's fane. We will speak further when we have rested. I cannot remain upon my feet."

In fact, Covenant suspected that she was close to fainting. And the condition of her comrades was no better. Cabledarm's was worse. Even to his blunted sight, it was obvious that the injured Giant could not stand without support.

"Then don't worry about it," he said unsteadily. "We'll have plenty of time for tales"—a grimace jerked across his face—"unless we don't, in which case it won't matter anyway.

"Is there any shelter around here? We should try to get out of this wind."

Grueburn glanced at Jeremiah's construct. "Can we not find calm within the fane?" She sounded wistful. "I am not so chary of *Elohim*—or indeed of Kastenessen—that I would decline to ease my weariness in their presence."

When Covenant followed her gaze, he saw Jeremiah lower himself to the ground. A moment later, the boy came running, waving his arms for attention. His ragged pajamas—soiled with grime and stained by blood—made him look destitute and desperate. Nevertheless he was recovering from Kastenessen's violation.

Together, the Giants turned to watch him. Rime Coldspray held up the *krill*.

He reached the company, jerked to a halt. "You won't see them," he panted. Apparently he had heard Grueburn. "It's just stones. The magic only works on them."

A heartbeat later, he flung himself at Covenant, wrapped his arms around the Unbeliever. Suddenly he was crying—and fighting to deny it.

"I'm sorry. I didn't have a chance. Mom left, and Stave was hurt, and Kastenessen—he—out of nowhere—The *croyel* was bad. He's worse. Much worse.

"I am *so* glad to see you."

Covenant returned Jeremiah's hug without hesitation. He ached for that himself; for any embrace if he could not have Linden's. And he, too, loved the boy.

He, too, feared for Linden's son.

As carefully as he could, he asked, "What did Kastenessen do to you?"

Jeremiah swallowed a sob; clung harder. "He broke me."

Sudden compassion stung Covenant. Deliberately he eased his own clasp until Jeremiah did the same. Then he held the boy at arm's length, studied every detail of Jeremiah's mien: the rich brown of his eyes, the passionate mouth, the fine stubble on his cheeks; the lines cut by too much suffering. But he could not discern how deeply Jeremiah's hurts ran, or how badly he had been marred.

"How did he do that? What was it like?"

The question seemed to transform Jeremiah. Ferocity darkened his eyes to the color of rot-laden silt. His mouth stretched, baring his teeth. The lines of his face assumed predatory angles. In an instant, he was no longer a boy confused by his wounds. He had become a young man crowded with bitterness.

Almost spitting, he snapped, "I'm sorry Infelice let him inside. I'm sorry you didn't kill him. I want him *dead*. I hate being used, and *I don't want to talk about it.*"

His vehemence shocked Covenant. A similar reaction twisted Coldspray's visage, and Grueburn's. Branl took a subtle step closer as if he sensed that Covenant was in danger.

But Covenant stood taller in front of Jeremiah. With a portion of his own ferocity, his rage for the damaged and the outcast, he retorted, "Then hang on to feeling broken. Hang on to the pain. It can be useful. I should know."

Then he lowered his voice. "In any case, Kastenessen is different now. Without Kevin's Dirt, he's just another victim."

Jeremiah looked like he wanted to sink his teeth into Covenant's throat. "I don't care."

"Chosen-son," the Ironhand murmured: a reprimand that lacked the strength to insist.

To himself, Covenant groaned, Oh, Linden. I'm so sorry. Nevertheless he held the boy's glare without flinching. Severe as a judge, he demanded, "Then tell me something else. Is that temple a prison?"

He already knew the truth, but he wanted to hear it from Jeremiah. He wanted Jeremiah to acknowledge it. It might help.

At once, Jeremiah's fury became chagrin. Without transition, he seemed altogether young and vulnerable. "No!" he cried as if Covenant had slapped him. "I wouldn't do that. They can get out whenever they want."

Ah, hell. Covenant's relief was so swift that he sagged against Branl. Hell and blood. A host of fears drained out of him before he had managed to name them all. Sure, the boy was in pain. His rage revealed the depth of his wounds. But his distress now was as true as his desire for harm. And he had done what he could to forestall the world's end.

As soon as Covenant recovered his balance, he moved to hug Jeremiah again.

"Thanks," he breathed like a sigh at Jeremiah's ear. "I knew that about you. I just needed to hear you say it."

"Linden will be so proud we won't know what to do with her."

Jeremiah sobbed again, a small sound like a plea. But he did not stiffen or pull away. Surrendering to Covenant's hold, he asked fearfully, "Will she make it? Will she come back?"

He seemed to say, I don't know who I am without her.

Covenant knew how he felt. Striving for confidence, he countered, "She's *your* mother. Has she ever *not* come back?"

Centuries ago among the Dead in Andelain, High Lord Elena had urged Covenant to take care of Linden, *that in the end she may heal us all.*

Before Jeremiah could reply, the Ironhand wavered on her feet: she nearly fell. Blinking as if she could no longer focus her eyes, she croaked, "For mercy's sake, have done with contention. We must rest."

"Hellfire," Covenant growled. During his many experiences with Giants, he had seen them in every extreme of peril and pain; but he had never known them to be utterly exhausted. "What're we waiting for? You don't just look tired. You must be half starved." Where could they have replenished the Ardent's supplies? "Let's go lie down."

Instead of responding, the Swordmainnir simply turned and trudged toward the fane like women who had come to the end of every desire except the wish for relief. Longwrath they left where he had fallen. After everything that they had done and endured, they were too weak to lament his end.

ᛤ

Inside the edifice, the company found better shelter than Covenant had expected. Though the walls were punctuated with gaps, and the ceiling looked precariously balanced, the winds outside were reduced to a confusion of mild breezes. In addition, the stones retained a suggestion of warmth: an aftereffect of theurgy. There Rime Coldspray returned the *krill* to Branl, and the Giants stretched themselves out like dead women. But they did not sleep immediately. In low voices, wan and necessary, they began to talk, first Cirrus Kindwind, then Latebirth, then Onyx Stonemage. They told Covenant how Linden had broken open the ridge to uncover malachite. Passing the story from one to another, they described the building of Jeremiah's fane, and the extravagance of Stave's efforts, and the narrowness of his survival. And when their voices trailed away at last, Jeremiah gave Covenant a condensed version of his escape from his mental ensepulture.

Among his companions, Covenant sat with his knees hugged to his chest and tried not to rock from side to side like a child in need of solace. He wanted Linden, and had no way to reach her.

Cabledarm lay shivering as if she were feverish. Shock, Covenant thought. She had fallen hard and badly after deflecting Stave's plummet. Not for the first time, he felt bewildered by the abilities of the Giants. Saltheart Foamfollower had once walked through lava: a kind of *caamora*, terrible pain and cleansing. Such deeds had come to appear almost normal for Foamfollower's people. Now Covenant wondered whether the Swordmainnir would be able to leave their present straits behind if they did not first find fire in which to release their sorrow.

A comparable extravagance seemed normal for the *Haruchai* as well. Covenant could hardly bear to contemplate what Stave had done to help complete Jeremiah's construct. And the sheer strength of will with which Stave had resisted Infelice for Jeremiah's sake, and for Linden's, left Covenant gaping inwardly.

How was it possible for any ordinary man—or woman—or boy—to live up to the example set by the Land's other defenders, the natural inhabitants of this world?

Nonetheless Linden had taken Mahrtiir into the Land's past for a purpose as extreme as anything that the Giants and Stave had attempted. Covenant yearned to believe that she would succeed. And he had one tentative reason to think that she would not fail—or had not failed yet. The Arch of Time still held. One moment led to the next. Covenant inhaled and then exhaled. He heard words arranged in comprehensible sequences. Therefore Law endured. Linden had not caused a fatal rupture—or its ripples had not yet reached him.

Perhaps that inference was an illusion. Perhaps he only experienced time chronologically because he was human, too mortal to perceive any other reality. Perhaps nothing truly existed outside the confines of his own perceptions.

He had considered such ideas before. At one time, he had trusted himself to them. Now he discarded them with a private shrug. They changed nothing. He was responsible for the meaning of his life, as he had always been: for his loves, and for his rejections. While he remained able to think and feel, he could not set such burdens down without betraying himself.

No doubt Linden believed something similar. How otherwise could she have hazarded a *caesure*? Without some kind of faith in the necessity of her commitments, how could she have ridden away from her son?

No wonder Covenant loved her.

Eventually the voices of his companions fell into silence. With the suddenness of a child, Jeremiah collapsed into slumber: an aftereffect of effort and Kastenessen's touch. Cabledarm stared wide-eyed at the ceiling, in too much pain to sleep, or to hear. But Bluntfist's eyelids closed, and she sank away. Onyx Stonemage resisted yawns—briefly, briefly—until they overcame her. Then Latebirth and Galesend slept as well. Soon only Coldspray, Grueburn, and Kindwind remained awake with Covenant and Branl.

The three women regarded Covenant, obviously waiting to hear more of his own tale.

As much for his own sake as for theirs, he began to speak. But he did not talk about what he had done and endured. He had no language adequate to Joan and the Ranyhyn, or to *turiya* Herem and Clyme, or to the Worm of the World's End. Instead he spoke of Linden and Horrim Carabal.

"At least now we know what the Ardent meant when he said her fate is *writ in water*. Or part of it, anyway. She gave us an alliance with the actual lurker," who was nothing if not a creature born of water, made great by water. "Hellfire! How improbable was *that*? But there's more. If she hadn't brought down that flood above the Lost Deep, none of us would have escaped. If she hadn't gone back to the Sarangrave, the Feroce might not have been able to give her my message."

She had used water to provide malachite for Jeremiah. And Covenant himself had broken her free from memories of She Who Must Not Be Named by holding her underwater. In retrospect, he trembled at his own daring.

"Long ago," he finished hoarsely, "I told her to *Do something they don't expect*. If we ever find a way to stop Lord Foul, it'll be because she's taken him by surprise over and over again."

After a long pause, Rime Coldspray mused, "It indeed appears that many unforeseen outcomes were enabled by Linden Giantfriend's last effort among the caverns. But the same may be said of any deed. If she had not retrieved the Staff of Law. If she had not accompanied your false son and her possessed boy into the Land's past. If she had not dared all things to create a place for you among the living. Life is ever thus. One step enables another. For that reason, auguries are an ill guide. They tread perilously upon the borders of unearned knowledge.

"Still we are Giants. We crave an understanding of your own deeds. Will you not tell their tale more fully?" She spread her hands in the light of the *krill* as if she wanted to convince Covenant that they were empty and needed to be filled. "Ignorance haunts us. It hinders rest."

Instead of saying, No, or, Have mercy, or, I can't bear it, Covenant countered, "I'm not sure that's true. I think it's Longwrath who haunts you." The Giants may have felt that they had failed him. "You need a *caamora*, and you don't know how to get one. It eats at you."

The Ironhand did not contradict him. Instead she asked, "Are our hearts so plain to you?"

Covenant shook his head. "I only think you need to grieve because I've known Giants for a long time. I can't *see* you. And Kevin's Dirt just makes me blinder."

Numbness was eroding his ability to *hold on*. When he could no longer grip, he would be effectively impotent.

"Then it will comfort you," interposed Frostheart Grueburn, "to hear that Kastenessen's vile brume has faded from the heavens. His entry to the Chosen-son's fane has unbound his theurgies. Also the decimation of the stars has ceased. While the remaining *Elohim* are preserved, it will not be resumed."

Faded—Covenant released his legs, sat up straighter. "Well, damn." He had assumed that Kevin's Dirt was gone—that its bale required Kastenessen's constant attention—but he had not had an opportunity to ask for confirmation. "*Thank* you. If you hadn't built this place"—he gestured around him—"I might be useless by now."

He had always been useless without friends.

But the Giants were not deflected from their concerns. "Nonetheless," Cirrus Kindwind remarked, still probing, "your ailment has gained force. And we fear that you will refuse Linden Giantfriend's succor, as you once refused hurtloam in Andelain. It is your resolve that you must not be healed which most drives our desire to comprehend you."

Reflexively Covenant grimaced. In a quiet rasp, he said, "I don't know how to explain it. Leprosy protects me somehow." If Lena had not given him hurtloam when he first came to the Land, he would not have been able to rape her. "Sure, it costs me a lot. But it's also a kind of strength. It makes some things possible that I couldn't do without it."

Then, to forestall more questions, he urged, "You should get some sleep. We all need rest. Later I'll figure out some way to give poor Longwrath a *caamora*." Once before, he had done something similar. "I have Joan's ring. And the *krill*. I should be able to manage a fire."

"Very well," the Ironhand murmured. She was already drifting. "Though the burden of our woe is great, it is surpassed by weariness."

In another moment, her head sagged, and she was asleep.

Frostheart Grueburn tried to swallow a cavernous yawn. Then she did what she could to make herself comfortable on the bare dirt.

For a while, Cirrus Kindwind continued to study Covenant through the *krill*'s silver. But she did not prod him further. Nodding as if she were content, she said, "Earlier I had occasion to remind Stave Rockbrother that he is not alone. I would proffer a similar assurance now. Whatever the substance of your fears or pains may be, you will not be required to confront it alone. We are merely weakened. We are not inclined to forsake you." She hesitated briefly, then added, "And Linden Giantfriend has not forgotten her love for you."

Before Covenant could decide whether to weep or smile, Kindwind turned away and settled herself for sleep.

⤫

Covenant dozed for a while himself. Most of his efforts since the struggle with *turiya* Herem had been mental and emotional rather than physical, but they had drained him nonetheless. He did not mean to sleep while he hoped for Linden; but drowsiness overcame him, and he sank into a shallow slumber.

Later some preterite instinct roused him, and he jerked up his head to look around. Squinting against the blur that marred his sight, he saw Stave enter the fane.

The former Master moved cautiously, as if he had become unsure of his balance. His right hand and forearm gave the impression that they ached. But his single eye as it caught the *krill*'s shining was clear. It flashed argent at Covenant as if Stave had gained the ability to see into the Unbeliever's soul.

Perhaps he had. He had allowed himself to grieve for Galt, his son. And he had let Linden convince him to remain with Jeremiah. To Covenant, those were astonishing changes. Of the *Haruchai* whom he had known, only Cail had revealed a comparable willingness to go beyond rigid stoicism. Even men like Bannor and Brinn, Branl and Clyme, had measured themselves by standards which any other *Haruchai* would have approved.

Carefully Stave eased himself to the ground in front of Covenant. There he sat cross-legged, upright as a spear driven into the dirt, with the backs of his hands resting on his thighs. His eye seemed to transfix Covenant.

Without preamble, as if he were resuming a conversation, Stave said, "I did not part willingly from the Chosen."

His manner rather than his tone suggested that he wanted to be understood.

"I know," Covenant answered quietly. "But you let yourself be persuaded anyway. She asked, and you agreed."

"I did," the former Master admitted. "I have found that I am no longer able to refuse her."

Covenant's mouth twisted. "I know the feeling."

Stave flexed the fingers of his right hand, testing them for residual damage. "*Haruchai* do not indulge in regret. Yet I am"—he appeared to search for a word—"unsettled. If she does not return, Timewarden, I will be unable to quench my sense of loss, or my remorse that I did not stand at her side."

Now Covenant winced. "I know that feeling, too." He had not simply turned away from Linden. He had told her not to touch him. More harshly than he intended, he said, "But sometimes things like that have to be done anyway."

Stave nodded. "Necessity demands. It does not countenance denial." Then, unexpectedly, he looked away, as if he rather than Covenant had cause to feel shame. "Thus I am compelled to inquire of myself what purpose is served by regret—or indeed by grief."

Without pausing to consider his reply, Covenant countered, "How else do we know we're alive?"

"By our deeds," Stave answered. "By striving and service. By—"

Abruptly he froze. His gaze sprang back to Covenant's. Nothing else moved.

After a moment, he released a long breath. "Ah." His regard did not waver, but his rigidity eased. "Now I begin to grasp how it transpires that you and the Chosen have failed to comprehend the Masters—and how the Masters have been misled in their apprehension of you. You and the Chosen—those of your world— The Chosen-son. Hile Troy. You judge by your hearts. It is by grief and regret that you know yourselves, rather than by deeds and effort and service."

In his turn, Covenant nodded. "Well, yes." More than once, he had tried to explain himself to the *Haruchai*; but somehow he had failed to grasp the question implicit in their notions of service. "Grief and regret. What else is there? Those are just other names for love. You can't feel bad about losing something if you don't love it first. And if you don't love, why else would you bother to *do* anything at all?"

Of course, love was not so simple. He knew that as well as anyone; perhaps better than most. It spawned complications faster than it clarified them. It could be misguided or selfish. It could close its eyes. It could curdle until it became hate. And it implied rejection. Stepping in one direction required moving away from another. But at its core—

At its core, love was the only answer that made sense to him.

There is hope in contradiction.

From where Branl stood, the *krill* left Stave's features in shadow. Covenant could barely discern the outlines of the former Master's mien. Only Stave's eye pierced the dusk.

Impassive as any *Haruchai*, he said, "It is a terrible burden, Timewarden."

Covenant shrugged. "Look at Branl. Look at the Masters. Look at yourself." Briefly his old rage for the abused of the world rose up in him. "Hellfire, Stave! Look at the *Elohim*." Then he subsided. Almost whispering, he asked, "Is what you see any less terrible?"

"It is not," Stave replied as if he were sure. "It is more so."

A moment later, something that may have been a smile tugged at the corner of his mouth. "Were I inclined to the homage of mutilation—which I am not—I would now claim a place among the Humbled. Though they have aspired to emulation, they have not grasped the full import of their desires.

"Until now," he added in Branl's direction, acknowledging what Branl had done and endured.

Branl lifted a shoulder slightly. "Should the world endure," he promised, "and the Masters with it, I will undertake to instruct our people."

Finally Covenant bowed his head. The Humbled had made it surprisingly easy to forgive the manner of Clyme's death.

ΙΟΟΙ

Gradually the gloom within the temple became the more ominous twilight of late afternoon. By degrees, it thickened toward evening and full night. Branl remained standing, so motionless that he did not appear to breathe; holding Loric's dagger steady as a beacon. Stave still sat in front of Covenant, resting while his strength returned.

In the gathering darkness, the Giants began to wake.

Frostheart Grueburn was the first. Muttering Giantish expletives, she rolled onto her side and struggled upright. Without a word, she left the fane. When she returned, she brought several waterskins. One she passed to Covenant.

As Covenant drank, Halewhole Bluntfist raised her head. After gazing blearily around her for a moment, she nudged Onyx Stonemage. Stonemage responded by ascribing a list of offenses to Bluntfist's parents; but she did not refuse to be roused.

One after another, the Swordmainnir arose. In the stark illumination of the *krill*, they looked garish, like women who had become fiends while they slept—or had been tormented by fiends.

Among them, Jeremiah woke up suddenly. His eyes seemed to give off glints of panic as he looked around for some sign of his mother. When he realized that she was still absent, he slumped back to the ground, covered his face with his hands. But then he practically flung himself to his feet. Ignoring his companions, he hurried out of the fane.

The Ironhand shrugged. No one said anything.

By turns, the Giants studied Cabledarm's condition, offered her what encouragement they could. Stormpast Galesend urged a little water into her mouth. They had no other help to give her.

All of them drank until they had emptied the waterskins. To no one in particular, Latebirth sighed, "I would barter my sword—aye, and my arm with it—for a handful of *aliantha*, and count myself fortunate in the exchange." Her comrades nodded mutely.

While Covenant watched, Rime Coldspray stretched her arms and back, loosened her neck. Then she looked at him. "Longwrath," she said curtly, reminding him of his promise.

Fire, he thought. Lamentation for the dead. The pain that consoles. In his own fashion, he understood how Giants grieved. Still he was reluctant to move. He had spent hours waiting for Linden: waiting and aching. Now he felt too heavy to stand, as if he were wrapped in iron chains. He would have preferred to go on waiting.

But he might not get another chance to keep his word. For all he knew, Cabledarm was dying.

"We need Linden," he muttered to no one in particular. "I need her." Then he extended a hand to Branl, let the Humbled lift him upright.

After sitting against the wall for so long, his muscles had stiffened. He felt like an assemblage of mismatched parts as he accepted the *krill*. But he was accustomed to that. And the gem of Loric's weapon shone steadily, answering the presence of white gold. With its magicks, he had already accomplished things which he had considered impossible. Why not more?

You are the white gold.

Holding the dagger by its wrapped hilt, he led his companions from the shelter of the fane.

Outside he found that night had almost claimed the plain. Beyond the reach of the *krill*'s gem lay only blackness. Harsh buffets of wind seemed to hit him from every direction simultaneously. The chill pang of the air augured days of deeper cold. He had hoped for a moon; but it had not risen—or it was left in darkness by the sun's absence from the world.

Here even his blunted senses felt the violence glowering in the northeast: a crouched impression of storm as fierce as a predator, and as absolute as fuligin. He wanted to ask how far away it was, and how quickly it was moving, but the words caught in his throat.

"It is the Worm, ur-Lord," Branl stated like a man who could read minds. "Yet it is many and many leagues distant. Also the fury of its coming outruns the Worm itself. It is not imminent."

Covenant forced himself to breathe. After a moment, he managed to ask, "How much time do we have?"

The Humbled looked at Stave. Something silent passed between them. Then Branl said, "If it does not increase its haste, it will not strike this region until the morrow, perhaps some hours after dawn."

In a low growl, the Ironhand confirmed Branl's estimate. "Beyond question, the lurker and the Demondim-spawn have accomplished the wonders which were asked of them."

The force and confusion of the winds affected Covenant like vertigo. Lurching like a holed ship in an uneven gale, he moved toward Longwrath's corpse.

The two *Haruchai* accompanied him, and behind them came the Swordmainnir. Cabledarm the Giants supported between them, although her mind wandered the borderland between consciousness and delirium. Maybe they hoped that fire would cauterize her internal bleeding.

Eventually Covenant spotted Jeremiah. The boy had climbed back onto the roof of the fane. Vague in the darkness, he stood there as if the crude edifice were a watchtower. Restlessly he scanned the plain from horizon to horizon, searching for some sign of his mother's return.

Covenant felt a pang for the boy, but he did not allow himself to pause. Winds slapped at his face. They came at him from one direction and then another as if they were trying to nudge him aside from his purpose. The Worm was a condensed apocalypse: it pushed turmoil ahead of it like a bow-wave. He kept moving so that he would not relapse to waiting for Linden.

Lostson Longwrath lay where he had fallen, charred and lifeless: a darker shape like an omen outstretched on the benighted ground. Beside the *geas*-doomed Swordmain, Covenant stopped. Too many lives had already been lost. No doubt the Worm had left tens or hundreds of thousands of deaths in its wake, perhaps millions—and the carnage was just beginning. The *Elohim* would not be the only casualties of Lord Foul's quest for freedom; his obsessive denial of his own despair. As it always did, Despite littered the world with victims.

Covenant had to do what he could.

While he secured his numbed grip on the *krill*, however, Rime Coldspray said, "A moment, Timewarden. One matter remains to be resolved. It concerns Longwrath's flamberge." She indicated the wave-bladed longsword where it lay near the man's burned fingers. "He appeared to acquire it at the behest of his *geas*, and therefore of the *Elohim*, though we saw no clear purpose in it. Now, however, it appears in an altered light. The Harrow said of it that it was forged by theurgy to be potent against Sandgorgons. Its puissance has faded with disuse, he informed us. But those monsters have come to assail the Land, and we are too few and worn to oppose them. Therefore it is my hope that the blade's force has not altogether waned.

"If this weapon retains any virtue, one among us must wield it."

A good point, Covenant thought. No matter what happened, the Land's defenders would need every conceivable weapon. But while the Giants looked at each other and frowned, weighing possibilities, Branl spoke.

"The ur-Lord will have need of the *krill*, and I have no sword. A Giant's blade is an inconvenient length in my hands, but its weight does not exceed my strength, or my skill.

"The *Haruchai* have ever eschewed weaponry. Nevertheless weapons we must have. If our people do not elect to reinterpret their service, they will render their lives effectless in the last crisis. Fists and feet suffice to oppose Cavewights, but they will not harm Sandgorgons or hinder *skurj*."

Standing over the flamberge, he watched the women for their reactions.

Hesitating, the Ironhand asked, "Timewarden?" She seemed loath to let a man who was not a Giant take up Longwrath's only legacy. She faulted her ancestors for Longwrath's *geas*. It was the responsibility of the Swordmainnir to attempt amends.

But Covenant was sure. "Why not?" he returned. "One way or another, we all have to reinterpret our notions of service. That's what Linden is doing. Stave did it a long time ago. Now Branl is doing the same. Why not let him keep going?"

Coldspray gave her comrades a chance to object. Some of them scowled or looked away, shifted their feet uncomfortably; but no one contradicted Covenant.

Finally their leader nodded. "Let it be so. Branl of the *Haruchai*, accept Lostson Longwrath's flamberge in the name of ancient friendship and faith. May you find worth in it—aye, and give it worth as well—to redeem the tale of a loved Giant thoughtlessly betrayed."

Branl's reply was to take the longsword in both hands. Briefly he swung it around his head as if to demonstrate that he was equal to its heft. Then he stepped back from Longwrath's corpse, making room for Covenant.

Stave watched, expressionless as any of his kinsmen. Nevertheless he conveyed the impression that he approved.

It was time. Covenant had made a promise. Trembling, he drew out Joan's ring on its chain. With the ring's uncompromising circle in one hand, he raised High Lord Loric's *krill* over the dead.

"Lostson Longwrath," he began. For the sake of the Giants, he strove to speak formally. "Parents who cherished you named you Exalt Widenedworld, but they couldn't protect you from being hurt. Forgive one more wound. What you've suffered tears the hearts of your people, and I don't know another way to help them.

"A natural fire would be better for them, maybe even for you. I know that." Long ago, he had summoned the Dead of The Grieve into flames to find their release. "But we don't have any wood. This is the best I can do.

"Whatever happens, remember that you saved the Giants who knew you best. None of them wanted this to happen. All of them are grieving."

Deliberately Covenant put restraint out of his mind; pushed away his old fears of wild magic that refused control. Kneeling at Longwrath's side, he hammered the *krill* through armor and raiment into Longwrath's chest.

At once, the gem blazed with such brightness that it seemed to erupt. Silver incandescence poured over the Giants and the *Haruchai*. It flooded the plain and the temple, drenched Jeremiah, ran up the slope of rubble to the ridge; denied the night. It was not fire, although Covenant thought of it as conflagration, saw it as flame. But it was capable of anything. In the hands of its rightful wielder—sane or deranged, driven by love or *contemptuous of consequence*—it could shatter the foundations of Time. It made Longwrath's flesh and even his armor burn like kindling.

And from the heart of the coruscation, Linden Avery came galloping on Hyn's back with the Staff of Law black as midnight in her hands.

12.

After Too Long

The flare of power from the gem resembled a scream. It struck Covenant as if it were tangible, a physical impact. He reeled backward. Quick as gusts, Branl and Stave dodged. The Giants scrambled aside from Linden's wild rush. They barely hauled Cabledarm out of the way in time.

In full career, Hyn pounded among them, past them, a prow of force cleaving a path for a second rider, a second Ranyhyn. They were halfway to the fane before Linden and her companion could bring their straining mounts to a halt.

From atop the construct, Jeremiah flailed his arms with Earthpower blazing in each hand. If he yelled something, anything, Covenant did not hear it. A shock like vertigo seemed to unmoor his mind. He stood on a shattered world—on fragments of comprehension—and did not know what was happening.

Linden—? How—?

Linden hardly appeared to see her son; or she absorbed the sight of him in an instant, recognized that he was safe and whole. Wildly she wheeled as if she had arrived with furies and woe on her heels. The *krill*'s shining glared like a crisis in her eyes.

But not alone. Covenant stared after her. Not alone?

He should have been able to identify that second Ranyhyn, that stallion. But he had no mind and could not think.

The stranger was singing—or he emanated complex melodies like an aura. And he was not chasing Linden: he was her companion. Together they turned their mounts to confront the Giants and the *Haruchai* and Covenant.

Then Rime Coldspray called, "Linden Giantfriend!" and parts of Covenant's reality fell back into place. When she added, "Manethrall Mahrtiir, most valiant of Ramen!" Covenant began to regain his footing.

Mahrtiir? No. Impossible. *That* was not—

Oh, God. Blood and damnation.

Narunal. The second horse was Narunal.

Now Covenant recognized Mahrtiir's eyelessness, Mahrtiir's fierce visage. But the Manethrall was altogether changed; fraught with music and theurgy. His bandage was gone. In its place, the ravage which had cost him his eyes had become whole skin, seamless and new. He wore a robe of samite so white and pure that it might have been woven of starlight. Garlands of harmony draped his neck: a wreath of counterpoint adorned his head. And his mien— His familiar combative frown had become radiance. It had become eagerness. Reflecting the *krill*'s gem, he looked like wild magic cleansed of its extravagance and peril.

In his hand he carried a sapling—a *sapling*—as if it were weightless in spite of its root-ball thick with loam and its wealth of new leaves like a gift of verdure to the barren plain.

His mere presence shed hymns like promises in all directions, and Narunal bore him as if the stallion had been exalted.

"No," Linden answered. She sounded hoarse and ragged, as if she had spent hours yelling—or perhaps sobbing. "Not Mahrtiir. Not anymore. This is Caerwood ur-Mahrtiir. If he ever gets the chance, he's going to be the Forestal of Andelain and Salva Gildenbourne."

The figure beside her nodded gravely. He may have been humming. Then he turned away as though Linden had introduced him to people who did not interest him. Guiding Narunal with his knees or his music, he rode, stately and ineffable, toward Jeremiah's temple.

Linden remained where she was. Her eyes were full of frenzy. Too much had happened to her. Too much had happened while she was gone.

"You did—" She appeared to grope for words as if she had no names for what she saw and felt. "Covenant, you—"

Yet Covenant faced her like the man who had chosen to forsake her days ago. He should have said something, *wanted* to speak. Goading himself with curses, he strained to break the logjam of his emotions. But he was still stunned, still floundering.

A *Forestal*? Of course. He had urged her to *Remember forbidding*. How else could she have done it? *Without forbidding, there is too little time.* The magicks of the ancient woodland guardians were not instruments which could be passed from one hand to another. They were inherent. So she had decided—or Mahrtiir had decided for her. The Manethrall of the Ramen had been sacrificed.

And Covenant had no idea where she had found the power to transform Mahrtiir; how far into the Land's past she had been forced to travel. Hellfire! It was no wonder that she looked wild, frantic. She had done and endured things which had shaken her heart to its foundations.

He wanted to ask, Who was it? Who did you find? He had the question ready; but he gritted his teeth against it. She needed something more from him. Something better.

While Covenant stood paralyzed, silent and useless, Jeremiah came running from his construct. His hands burned like shouts as he sprinted toward Linden.

"Mom! You came back!"

Linden hardly glanced at him. Other concerns already gripped her. Her attention shifted from Covenant to the Giants. Her eyes widened in shock.

"God!" she panted. "What have you done?"

Abruptly she flung herself from Hyn's back. Unfurling fire as black as the distant storm, she strode toward the Swordmainnir. Toward Cabledarm.

In that instant, Covenant saw that the grass stains were gone from her jeans. She no longer needed them. And she looked clean, as if she had been refined by fire. Even her hair and clothes— But the tatters of her shirt remained: the tearing of thorns, the bullet hole, the rent hem.

She ignored his scrutiny, his surprise. Focused on the dying Giant, she advanced as if she meant to hurl an attack.

Onyx Stonemage and Stormpast Galesend flinched reflexively, then stood their ground, upholding Cabledarm between them. The other Giants stepped away to make room.

"God *damn* it." Linden's voice was a raw mutter, barely audible, as if she did not expect to be heard. "What happened to you? What have you done to yourself?"

Then she sent a torrent of flame at the damaged woman. Swift as empathy, she inundated Cabledarm with Earthpower.

She remained a healer, Covenant told himself, no matter how she judged herself. Wounds came first, pains and afflictions which she was able to treat. She had been through an ordeal: that was obvious. She must have been desperate to do *some*thing that felt like restitution.

Her effect on Cabledarm was not gentle. It was too urgent, too full of need. And perhaps she had not yet realized that the hindrance of Kevin's Dirt was gone. She seemed to scourge Cabledarm with healing.

The woman's head jerked back. Twisting against the grasp of her comrades, she gave a groan like a throttled scream. But she was not being harmed. Her pain was the hurt of internal organs violently mended, of bones roughly reset and sealed, of bleeding stanched as if it were being cauterized. When she fainted, her slackness—and the new ease of her respiration—suggested that she had already begun to recuperate.

Watching, Covenant leaned on Branl as if he needed the comfort of the Humbled. He wanted to tell Linden that she was wonderful—that he had been terrified for her—that he was sorry—that the world would *not see her like again*. But still he could not speak. He had no language for the extremity of his heart.

"That is well done, Linden Giantfriend," murmured Coldspray. "Well done in all sooth. Now only Stave Rockbrother requires similar care."

Unsteadily, as if she had assumed Cabledarm's fever, Linden looked around for Stave, who stood on the far side of Covenant's aborted fire. For a moment, she appeared to fix her senses and her bewilderment on the ashen remains of Longwrath's corpse. Her mouth opened for a cry of protest.

Then she must have felt Jeremiah rushing toward her. She spun away from the fallen Giant and the wounded *Haruchai* to catch her son in her arms.

"Jeremiah," she breathed. "Oh, Jeremiah. I'm so sorry. I'm sorry that I had to leave you. I'm sorry that you had to do everything without me. You must have felt so abandoned—"

"Mom, stop." Jeremiah gripping her with flames. "*I'm* sorry. I acted like a kid. You did what you had to do, and I didn't even tell you I love you. I didn't tell you I understand."

Some distance beyond the gathered company, Caerwood ur-Mahrtiir had paused in front of the fane, singing softly, rapt in contemplation.

"And we did it," Jeremiah added. Linden's return appeared to galvanize him. Abruptly he pulled away from her and gestured at the temple. "We did it right. I mean, the Giants and Stave did it. They were amazing. And they came. The *Elohim* came. They're inside. Even—"

There he faltered. His whole body seemed to clench at the memory of Kastenessen.

"I believe you," Linden assured him. "I can't see them, but they left traces. They must have gone in to somewhere else, just like you said that they would. It must have been extraordinary."

She was making an effort to affirm her son. Nevertheless her tone was thick with tension.

"But are you all right? Did anything happen to you?"

She must have been able to see farther into Jeremiah than Covenant could. *I'm sorry you didn't kill him. I want him* dead.

Jeremiah ducked his head. "There are worse things than being afraid, Mom. Being useless is worse." He indicated the fane again. "The Giants did that. Stave did it. He and Cabledarm got hurt doing it. All I did was tell them what I wanted. Without them—"

Helpless as a spectre, Covenant watched and listened. He loathed his silence, but did not know how to break it. Jeremiah did not mention Kastenessen or being possessed. And Covenant had no intention of telling the boy's story for him; betraying the boy's secrets. But he had so many other things to say.

"I know the feeling," Linden replied harshly. "I've taken terrible chances because I felt that way. You've seen me. But it happens to all of us. We can't do everything alone. Or we can't do enough. Without help, we're all useless."

She was speaking to Jeremiah, but her words—or her anger—may have been directed at Covenant. How often had he said, *Don't touch me*? How badly had he hurt her by leaving her behind?

He, too, would have failed at everything without help.

He could almost see Jeremiah's needs aching in Linden's eyes as she turned away from her son. Innominate tensions and uncertainties ruled her. She seemed unable to stop moving.

Apparently she was trying to focus her attention on Stave.

The music emanating from the Forestal had changed. It had assumed a more telic mode, as if he were done with study. He had set his sapling upright directly before the fane's portal. Now he withdrew his hand—and the sapling did not fall. He had already sung its roots into the hard dirt.

Stonemage and Galesend continued to support Cabledarm. The rest of the Giants gathered closer to Linden. Cirrus Kindwind rested her hand on Jeremiah's shoulder as if to soothe him until Linden could attend to him again.

When Linden looked toward Stave, her gaze snagged on Branl. On the flamberge—

For an instant, she froze. Fright flared in her gaze. Then her features knotted. From the Staff, she summoned a curling flame; sent fire licking up and down the rune-carved surface.

Bitter as bloodshed, she demanded, "What're you doing with Longwrath's sword? Is that how you're going to kill me?"

What else could she think? Longwrath had tried more than once to cut her down. She had not seen him since the Wraiths had repulsed his desire for her death from Andelain. And the Humbled had distrusted her from the first, in spite of her history. They had threatened and opposed and judged her.

Nevertheless Covenant blurted, "Linden, no." Distress broke through the blockade of his silence. Her reaction was too much for him. "It's not like that."

"Why not?" She did not glance away from Branl, or quench her power. "He's wanted me dead ever since I resurrected you. What's changed?"

While she spoke, Covenant seemed to hear her crying, I woke up the Worm! Is no one *ever* going to forgive me?

Yet Branl faced her without expression, without moving. He gave no sign that he regarded her as a threat.

"He killed Clyme," Covenant said in a frayed croak. "Clyme let *turiya* possess him. Then Branl killed Clyme. The Raver is gone. Everything's changed."

Again Linden froze. He could not read her.

She would not have forgotten Honninscrave's sacrifice against *samadhi* Sheol, *turiya*'s brother.

Now Covenant felt driven to talk. He yearned to tell her about his alliance with the lurker. He wanted to convince her that she had made the lurker's efforts against the Worm possible. *Writ in water.* When she had eluded the snares of the Feroce, she had saved him and enabled Joan's end and given the Land precious days of life.

But he restrained himself. He needed to say such things—but explanations of that kind were not what *she* needed. She had been through too much: her nerves and her heart were too raw. An abstract alliance would not console her.

Near the fane, Caerwood ur-Mahrtiir's sapling spread new branches and put forth fresh leaves and grew as if the Forestal had compressed years of rain and sun and rich soil into brief stanzas of hymnody.

Linden seemed unable to move. Covenant's revelation must have shaken her conception of the Humbled. But he was not given time to continue. While he groped for better words, words that might ease her, Stave came to stand between Linden and Branl.

Impassive as polished stone, he said, "Chosen, I am here. I have done as you asked of me." Nothing in his gaze or his mien hinted at his intent. "Now I am in need."

Deliberately he showed her his savaged forearm and hand.

One of the *Haruchai*. Asking for help.

At the sight, something inside Linden snapped. Stave was her friend, one of the first. He had supported her against the combined repudiation of the Masters—and had paid a cruel price. Her eyes filled with tears: she called up more fire as if her Staff's flames were sobs. But she did not reach out as she had to Bluntfist. Instead she cocooned herself in conflagration. Then she carried the dark blaze of her pain to Stave and wrapped her arms around him.

And he returned her embrace as though he had grown accustomed to such familiarity. Accustomed to setting aside his native stoicism.

A sigh of relief passed among the Giants. Jeremiah whispered, "Mom. Mom," as if she made him proud.

When she finally let Stave go, she was calmer. Quenching her power, she made the *krill*'s illumination brighter in contrast. Still her eyes were full of darkness, as if her Staff's stain lingered in them. Trying to imagine how she had gained Mahrtiir's transformation—and how she had managed her return—Covenant shivered. He could only be sure that the cost had been high. But now at last she looked *present*, as if she had been reclaimed by the time where she belonged.

That was well. The barriers inside him had broken. He could no longer remain silent.

He wanted to fall to his knees before her, abase himself somehow, plead with her. But self-recrimination was an expensive indulgence: he could not afford it. Controlling himself, he held her gaze until he was sure that he had her attention.

Caerwood ur-Mahrtiir's sapling had become a young tree. Its leaves were spangled with melody as if the notes of his song were stars. And beneath the expanding spread of the branches, a furze of grass sprouted from the barren ground, punctuated by undefined clumps that might grow into shrubs. A liquid sound ran faintly through his singing like a promise of water.

To Linden, Covenant said, "I killed her," as if the words burned his mouth, raised blisters on his tongue. "I killed Joan. I promised myself I would give up killing. Now I hardly do anything else."

Like the voice of the night, Branl asserted, "It was not murder." Like an echo. "It was mercy."

Stave nodded his assent.

Covenant ignored the *Haruchai*. He concentrated on Linden's frown, and her eyes, and the tightness of her mouth.

"The Feroce cleared the way. Dozens of them died against the *skest*. Branl and Clyme helped me through a *caesure* so I could reach her. She was going to finish me, but Mhornym and Naybahn distracted her. I killed her with the *krill*. I didn't know what else to do."

Linden seemed to gather darkness where she stood, as if she were pulling the night around her, wrapping herself in shadows. "Good!" she snapped: a flare of vehemence like a reiteration of Jeremiah's rage at Kastenessen.

Abrupt anger swelled in Covenant. "There was a tsunami." Joan had suffered too much. "It could have crushed us." Her weakness had not merited the use which Lord Foul had made of her. His voice rose, impelled higher by fury or supplication. "Branl and Clyme and the Ranyhyn saved me.

"Hell*fire*, Linden." His own heart was as raw as hers. "Do you remember Brinn?

Now that the Worm's awake, he doesn't have anything else to do. He showed up after the tsunami to tell us *turiya* was going to possess the lurker. We went to try to stop that from happening."

Then he forced himself to stop. In spite of his ire and numbness, he felt Linden withdrawing. She did not step back, but her frown became a scowl as her features closed against him.

"Why are you angry at me?" Her voice shook. "I haven't touched you. I wasn't even here."

Covenant swore at his clumsiness, his difficult, stymied honesty. He bit down on his wrath hard enough to draw blood.

"I'm not angry at you. I'm ashamed. It's not the same thing."

Jeremiah may have tried to intervene. If so, the Giants kept him quiet.

"What are you ashamed of?" Linden sounded impossibly distant, as if she had retreated to a redoubt where he could not hope to reach her. "You put Joan out of her misery. She wasn't just in terrible pain. She was possessed. Death was the only way to give her any relief. And you stopped her *caesures*. Why is that something to be ashamed of?"

"Because I failed!" Covenant wanted to hit someone, anyone. If he could have felt what he was doing, he would have torn at his hair. Instead he knotted his insensate fingers together and twisted until his wrists ached. "I wasn't strong enough to handle *turiya* myself. That's why Branl had to kill Clyme. They both had to compensate for me.

"And because—"

Suddenly awkward, he faltered. How could he say what was in his heart? To Linden? Like this? Beyond question, he was not strong enough. If he had ever been brave enough, he no longer remembered how that much courage felt.

The glittering among the leaves of the ur-Mahrtiir's tree had become a silver penumbra, purer that the brightness of Loric's *krill*, and more melodious. The tree was a willow, graceful and arching. Soon it would be tall enough to spread its branches in a wide circle that included the fane. Its limbs drooped like weeping, though they grew like gladness. And under its shade, the thin grass was now turf, as lush as the greenswards of Andelain. Bushes grew like adornments under the dangling leaves around the verge of the grass. A delicate rill rippled argent past the Forestal's feet and chuckled away beyond the rubble, wending harmoniously toward the distant Sarangrave.

"Because?" Linden prompted like a woman hiding behind a shield.

He was losing her. He did not know how to bear it.

"Because I hate the way I treated you! I hate the way I *left* you. I had to go. I had to go alone. I couldn't risk you against Joan. And you had other things to do."

Finally he managed to lower his voice. If he meant to tell the truth, he had to set aside the luxury of shouting; of judging himself.

"Linden, do you understand that *Kastenessen* is in that temple? Have you realized yet that Kevin's Dirt is gone? If I hadn't left you behind, none of that would have happened."

She did not react. She had no attention to spare for victories.

Groaning inwardly, Covenant confessed, "But I shouldn't have treated you the way I did. I was just afraid. I was broken," maimed by fissured memories, "and I didn't know how to live with it. I couldn't ask you to trust me," love me, "because I didn't trust myself, or what I was becoming, or what I had to do. I wasn't sure I would have anything left when I was done. I couldn't say what I really meant."

Loric's gem lit a subtle shift in Linden's gaze, a modulation in the darkness. Small black flames coiled like tendrils around her hand on the Staff. Covenant thought that he saw tremors in her shoulders.

"You told me not to touch you," she said as if the words were splinters of glass, sharp enough to pierce and rend. "Isn't that what you meant?"

"*No.*" He gritted his teeth so that he would not cry out. "It's what I needed. It's what I knew how to say. I'm a leper, for God's sake. It's how I cope with practically everything. But it is not the truth."

Not the whole truth.

She appeared to be floundering: a drowning woman who nonetheless struggled against her desire to clutch at rescue. So softly that he barely heard her over the labor of his heart, she asked, "Then what is the truth? What would you have said if you weren't broken or scared?"

Obviously bewildered, Jeremiah watched his mother and his earliest friend. The *Haruchai* betrayed no reaction; but the Giants gave the impression that they were holding their breath.

Damn you, Covenant snarled at himself. Say it. *Do* it. She can't read your mind.

What did he gain by being a leper if numbness did not dull the edges of his fears?

His hands shook as he reached up to his neck. Fumbling, he grasped the chain that held Joan's ring under his T-shirt, pulled the chain over his head. For a panicked moment, his eyes failed him: he could not find the clasp. Then his fingers were too awkward to unclose it.

But he remembered who he was, and why he was here, and what was at stake; and a strange certainty came over him. The clasp seemed to open by itself, as if he had been given a blessing. *Attempts must be made—* How else could he believe in anything?

He dropped the chain. Holding the ring between the remnants of his thumb and forefinger, he extended it toward Linden.

"Linden Avery." His voice was hoarse, congested with emotions straining for release. "I think I've earned the right to give this to anybody I want. But there's nobody else. I love *you*. That's all. I *love* you. Will you marry me?"

She flinched as if he had slapped her. For an instant, she recoiled, startled and uncomprehending.

But while she froze, caught in a maelstrom of surprise and consternation, disbelief and repudiation and self-doubt, the Forestal's song came clearly through the silence.

"It is my heart I give to you,
My blood and sap and bone and root."

In an instant, her turmoil was transfigured. Out of confusion and pain, she gathered herself. Her eyes reflected argent and recognition in patterns that spoke to Covenant. Without glancing at Stave, she tossed her Staff to the former Master. Its fire vanished before he caught it.

Her gaze clung to Covenant's as she drew out his ring, freed it from its chain, discarded the strand as if it had become meaningless. For a few heartbeats, she closed the ring in her fist. Then she opened her hand, held the ring out on her palm.

"*Yes*." That one word seemed to contain her whole heart. "Thomas Covenant, yes. I don't care what you've done, or what you're afraid of, or what you said days ago. I don't care how broken you were, or what's going to happen to us later. I only care about *now*. I love you."

As if she had summoned him past restrictions more personal than life and death, he started toward her. When he reached her, he took her left hand, lifted it to his lips, then slipped Joan's ring—no, *Linden's* wedding band—onto her ring finger.

With this ring I thee wed.

And betimes some wonder is wrought—

He thought that she would offer his ring to the index finger of his halfhand, where he had worn it ever since he had grown gaunt. But instead she claimed his left. To his surprise, his ring finger accepted the band as if damage and scars had made him strong enough to wear white gold where it belonged.

"I'm yours," she murmured through a blur of tears. "You're the only man I've ever really loved. You're the father Jeremiah should have had. As long as you wear this ring, I'm yours."

He knew what she meant. Long ago, he had surrendered his wedding band to the Despiser.

He was not going to do that again.

When he took her in his arms and kissed her, he was trying to assure her that he would keep this promise.

Her arms were around his neck. She returned his kiss as if she were opening her whole self.

And slowly their embrace was transformed. It became a glow of wild magic. Alloyed argent expanded around them, wrapped them in light. Gentle as a caress, it swelled into the night, swirling warmly as it scaled higher and higher until they appeared to stand at the source of a gyre which might reach the stars. The gem of the *krill* gave answer, as if High Lord Loric's ancient theurgy approved; but the effulgence of Thomas Covenant and Linden Avery out-shone it. Their power lit the battered plain to the horizons, reveled on the faces of the Giants and the *Haruchai* and Jeremiah, emblazoned the outlines of the fane beneath the willow. Even Caerwood ur-Mahrtiir paused in his fertile labors to contribute a paean like a benediction.

If Covenant had been inclined to heed them, he would have heard the Giants cheering. He would have seen Jeremiah waving flares of Earthpower and grinning. He might have noticed Stave's brief, unconflicted smile.

But Covenant was kissing Linden. At that moment, nothing else mattered.

hen he was finally able to look around, he saw that the Forestal had fashioned a bower.

The willow had grown as tall as a Gilden. Spangles of song lingered on its leaves, bedecked its branches with bright silver like the glimmering of unendangered stars. Illumination under the canopy of the boughs seemed to hold the memory of wild magic made tender by acquiescence. The tree stood directly before the fane's portal: its drooping arch almost concealed the construct. In the tree's shade, luxuriant grass cushioned the ground like a profusion of pillows.

The plashing runnel was now a grateful brook. It seemed to carry light and music with it as it chimed out across the plain. And near the edges of the circle, where the leaves trailed along the grass, Caerwood ur-Mahrtiir had invoked *aliantha*. A score or more of the holly-like shrubs with their viridian berries ripe surrounded the greensward, abundant as a feast.

The relative privacy of the bower suggested a form of sustenance that Covenant needed more than food. Perhaps that was the Forestal's intent. The heat in Linden's eyes affirmed that she felt as Covenant did. He was in a trembling hurry.

But the company had other needs: those took precedence. The privation of the

Giants was extreme. They had given their last strength—and then had given more. Covenant himself wanted more than the unsatisfying aliment of *ussusimiel*. Linden had probably gone longer without food. And Jeremiah was avid for treasure-berries.

For the sake of everyone with him, Covenant schooled himself to eat and drink and wait. When Linden smiled ruefully, he tried to match her.

Speaking for her comrades, the Ironhand gave thanks to the Forestal. They all bowed as if they declined to prostrate themselves only because they lacked the strength to rise again. Then they picked their fill of *aliantha*. The seeds they scattered around the plain and in the hollows like prayers for the Land's future. More boisterously, Jeremiah followed their example. As for the *Haruchai*, Branl stood apart from the company as if all of his lacks had been satisfied by Longwrath's flamberge; but Stave ate without hesitation and offered the former Manethrall his gratitude.

Considering that they were Giants, inclined to relish the bounty of their own relief, Rime Coldspray, Frostheart Grueburn, and the others finished their meal quickly. They spent only a few moments thanking Caerwood ur-Mahrtiir. Then they passed beyond the thick willow-trunk to reenter the fane, taking Jeremiah with them so that Covenant and Linden would have some semblance of privacy.

Stave also went into the construct, bowing first to Caerwood ur-Mahrtiir, then to Covenant, finally and most deeply to Linden. However, Branl remained. "Ur-Lord," the Humbled said with his usual absence of inflection, "the return of the Chosen is a cause for gladness in itself, and is more so because she has restored a Forestal to the Land. Yet in one respect, it is misfortune. The Giants have been denied their *caamora*."

To the sudden inquiry of Linden's expression, he explained, "The ur-Lord sought to relieve their sorrow by drawing flame from Longwrath's remains. Your arrival interrupted his efforts. Now Longwrath is naught but ash, and we have no wood."

While Linden winced in regret, Branl addressed Covenant once more. "Among Giants, denied lamentation is an enduring distress. Other tasks we have in abundance. And doubtless the Swordmainnir will be prompt to set aside their needs. Nonetheless I urge you to seek some blaze in which they may ease their loss.

"I am a Master of the Land," he said as if he were merely reciting a formula rather than acknowledging a profound change. "I bear the taint of the unwelcome which the Giants have received at our hands. I would make amends, but have no means to do so."

"Oh, stop," Covenant protested. "I forgot about that. We all had too much going on. But of course you're right. I"—he glanced at Linden—"we won't forget again."

"We won't," Linden affirmed. "And I won't forget what you've done. I haven't been fair to you. I should have known better."

Instead of nodding to her, as he had done so often in the past, Branl bowed. And when he had shown the same respect to both Covenant and Caerwood ur-Mahrtiir, he left the bower between the hanging branches to stand guard outside.

Alone with the Forestal, Covenant and Linden faced each other as if they had lost the ability to look anywhere else; but they did not move.

Briefly Caerwood ur-Mahrtiir sang words that Covenant recognized.

"I am the Land's Creator's hold:
I inhale all expiring breath,
And breathe out life to bind and heal."

Then he faded into his music as if he had made himself one with the willow and the boughs, the leaves and the bedizening melody. In a moment, he was gone.

"Covenant—" Linden bit her lip, twisted the ring on her finger. "I have too much to tell you. And there are so many things I—"

He interrupted her with a grin that felt like a grimace. "Don't you think it's about time you stopped calling me 'Covenant'?"

"Thomas, then," she offered. "Thomas. Thomas of my heart."

He would have accepted anything, but he was grateful that she did not choose to call him *Tom*.

When he opened his arms, she came to him like an act of grace.

ᘺᗘᘯ

When they were done, they lay relaxed on billows of grass, covered by the soft radiance of the bower. For a time, they talked casually, softly, reminding themselves of each other. But then they turned to more serious concerns.

Covenant had his own questions, but Linden spoke first. Somber with doubt, she asked him what he thought about Jeremiah.

He sighed to himself. "You mean, not counting the fact he's actually *with* us? After what he's been through? It's amazing he can so much as speak, never mind design that sanctuary for the *Elohim*. He's already done a world of good. If you want more, you should talk to him."

She certainly needed to know how much her son had inherited from Anele. She needed to know about Kastenessen.

She cuffed him lightly. "That's not an answer."

"I know. But I'm serious. He should tell his own story. He doesn't want to, but he should. Maybe you'll have better luck than I did."

Linden gnawed at her lower lip for a moment. "I'm not sure that I have the right to pry. He's already pushed me away more than once. I might do more harm than good."

Covenant shrugged against her head on his shoulder. "I'm not sure anybody has the right. Maybe prying does more harm than good. But look at it this way. He's too young for his years. He's had experiences that could cripple an adult, and he's never had a chance to grow into them. Parts of him are still a kid." And parts of him remembered the *croyel*.

"Sometimes kids need their parents to pry. Sometimes I think Roger wouldn't be such a mess if his mother ever took an interest in him."

Covenant himself had never been given an opportunity with his son.

Luminous in the warmth of Caerwood ur-Mahrtiir's music, Linden rolled over to rest her hands on Covenant's chest, prop her chin there and study his face.

"Thomas, what happened to you? What did you do after you left? How did you do it? What healed your mind? How did you change how Branl thinks?"

He winced reflexively. But he did not refuse to answer. Eased by her love, he was able to describe the days that he had spent away from her.

When he was done, she hugged him hard and wordlessly. For a time, she seemed to take his anguish and dread from him; and he thought about nothing except her.

Afterward they rested. But neither of them slept.

In a more playful mood, she asked, "So why aren't you growing a beard? You're human now. All the way human. As far as I can tell, the Arch of Time has lost its hold on you. Why isn't your beard growing?"

"I don't know," he admitted. "If I ever did, it's gone. But if I had to guess—"

Briefly he rubbed at his cheeks, pushed his fingers through his transformed hair. "You didn't have access to my physical self. That part of me died so long ago there was nothing left. And yet here I am. You must have created me out of my self-image." He spread his maimed hands. "Apparently that includes leprosy, but it doesn't include whiskers."

Long ago, shaving had been a form of self-abnegation for him, a punitive discipline. He was glad to be rid of the necessity.

Stroking her, he said, "Now it's your turn. Linden, you're a mystery to me. And I don't just mean—" He gestured to indicate her adored body. "I don't think I've ever been as surprised as I was when the Feroce offered me an alliance." Surprised and dismayed. "Somehow you did that. Somehow you saved me." He would not have reached Joan, or survived his attempt on *turiya* Herem, without the aid of Feroce. "But you did more than that. You also rescued Jeremiah." When she shook her head, he amended, "I mean, you gave him what he needed to rescue himself.

"That would have been enough for anybody else, but not for you." Not for a woman who thought so little of herself. "After you brought Jeremiah here, you went to find the only possible source of forbidding." The only hope for the *Elohim*, and perhaps for the Earth. "Then you did something even more miraculous. You came back. Without using a *caesure*.

"Linden"—he kissed her eyelids, her nose, her mouth—"you amaze me. I want to know how you did it."

He saw her reluctance. It showed in the way she shifted to nestle against his shoulder so that he could not look into her eyes or watch her face. For a moment, he was afraid again. But then she began to answer, and his fear left him.

Because he knew the outcome, he listened calmly as she described how the Feroce had tried to lure her into the grasp of the lurker, and how Infelice had striven to prevent Jeremiah from freeing himself in Muirwin Delenoth. Jeremiah's desire to build a construct that might preserve the *Elohim*. The message of the Feroce. Her own decision to enter a *caesure*. Her arms tightened like grief around Covenant as she talked about her second meeting with Caerroil Wildwood, and about Manethrall Mahrtiir's transformation.

"But I still didn't know how to get back. After what Caerroil Wildwood did for us, the idea of making another Fall horrified me. I would have had to ruin an unconscionable amount of Garroting Deep. But I was desperate to return, and I couldn't wait until we left the forest. I didn't know what to do."

Covenant heard the force of that emotional snare in her voice, the intolerable conundrum of being caught between mutually exclusive commitments. He recognized it.

"Mahrtiir"—she corrected herself—"no, Caerwood ur-Mahrtiir helped me. You should have seen him, Thomas. He stood here like a king, as if he had earned the right, and he sang things that I couldn't understand until Caerroil Wildwood nodded. Then Wildwood gave me another gift."

Like suppressed weeping, she said, "Oh, Thomas. Caerroil Wildwood said that he was tired of living. Tired of trying. Worn out by losing trees to people and wars. Law was getting weaker, and he knew that he was doomed. He'd faced too much evil. That was why he created Caer-Caveral, and why he made Caerwood ur-Mahrtiir. So that he could finally rest.

"He told me"—her voice broke—"that he still had no answer for the deaths of trees." Then she hurried to finish.

"Every leaf and branch all around the Howe sounded like it was sobbing, but he had made up his mind. He brought Hyn and Narunal to us. He gave us time to mount. 'By wild magic you came,' he said. 'Wild magic must guide your return.' When we were ready, he did something like what the Mahdoubt did for me. He didn't violate Time, he used everything he was to make an opening." Covenant felt her tears on the soft skin of his shoulder. "Then he pushed us through so that Hyn and Narunal could find the way back.

"It killed him, just like it killed Caer-Caveral. All of his music and glory and anger and effort seemed to wail. The whole Howe was like a shriek. When we rode away, there was nothing left except screaming."

Trying to comfort her, Covenant murmured, "I wish I could remember." He did not care what he said: he only sought to acknowledge her distress. "While I was still part of the Arch, I probably knew why Caerroil Wildwood decided to let go. Now that's gone. As far as I can tell, you found the only—I don't know what to call it—the only clean way to do what we need. The only safe way. The only way that doesn't change the Land's history."

Linden wiped her eyes and nose. Under his caresses, her tension and remorse eased. "I've been so scared. I didn't know what I was doing. Half of the time, I felt terrified. Otherwise I was just frantic. Jeremiah and the Land and even you needed more from me than I knew how to give. I only did what I did because I couldn't think of anything else."

"Hellfire, Linden," Covenant snorted. "Don't sell yourself short. Miracles are becoming practically normal around here, and most of them are your doing."

When she felt less troubled in his arms, he asked a different question. "So how did you get rid of those stains on your jeans?"

She lifted her head in surprise. After a moment, she sat up, snatched at her jeans, studied them. "Oh my God. They're gone. I've had them for so long, I stopped seeing them. They must have faded when Caerroil Wildwood—"

Eyes wide, she faced Covenant. "What does it mean?"

He smiled crookedly. Still hungry for her, he said, "Maybe Caerroil Wildwood took away those stains because you don't need them anymore. They were a map, and now you've found your way." She had found him—or they had found each other. "Maybe it just means we should try to take advantage of every minute we have left."

For a moment, she appeared to struggle against her uncertainty—or against the particular intensity of his regard. But then she seemed to find that he had said enough. That his response sufficed. Dropping her clothes, she moved to put her arms around his neck.

That response sufficed for him as well.

ΩΩΩ

Eventually Linden asked a more difficult question. "After Lord Foul killed you, you left your ring for me. You wanted me to have it, didn't you? So why haven't I been a 'rightful white gold wielder' all along?"

"I'm not entirely sure," Covenant admitted. "Sure, I wanted you to have my ring. But I didn't *give* it to you. Lord Foul just dropped it. And I was in the same situation with Joan. I only got her ring"—he stifled a wince—"because she couldn't hold it any longer. That didn't make me a rightful wielder either."

He had experienced *rightfulness*. He knew what it meant.

"Now that's changed." With a gesture that felt effortless, he drew a brief streak of argent through the air, instantly ready, instantly quenched. "So here's what I think. It isn't the getting that makes the difference. It's the giving. The choice. And the *kind* of choice matters. Surrender is one kind. A vow is another. I didn't just give you a white gold ring. I gave you *me*. That's something the almighty Despiser is never going to understand. He's clever as all hell, but he's too self-obsessed or frustrated or maybe too damn miserable to figure out why he keeps losing."

Then Covenant thought that he ought to warn Linden. "But we still have to be careful. I don't have enough health-sense to feel the effects of what I'm doing. And you have the Staff of Law." It lay on the greensward beyond their clothes, its black shaft runed with auguries. "I don't want to say wild magic and Law are antithetical. That's too simplistic. But the energies are incompatible. Wild magic refuses boundaries, and Law is all about boundaries. If you hadn't used the *krill* when you resurrected me, you would have torn yourself apart. That's the *krill*'s real power. It mediates contradictions."

For a moment, he thought that he heard the wind outside the bower blustering bitterly against the willow. But the blast did not trouble Caerwood ur-Mahrtiir's irenic singing, or ruffle his healing lumination.

Still Covenant did not relax, in spite of his satiation. He sensed something unresolved in Linden—or he knew that in her place he would not be at peace.

At last, she said, "Thomas, I love you. I *love* you. But I did a terrible thing when I forced you back to life. Waking up the Worm was bad enough. The Humbled were right about me. That was a Desecration. But I'm afraid that I did something worse at the same time. Do you remember what Berek said? I've made it impossible to stop Lord Foul."

Covenant tightened his embrace as if he imagined that he could protect her. He remembered Berek's assertion perfectly. *He may be freed only by one who is compelled by rage, and contemptuous of consequence.* He recognized her fear.

"Now we can't save the world. We can't stop the Worm. We can only try to slow it down. Before long, Lord Foul will get his chance to escape."

"Thomas," she insisted, "I *did* that." In spite of all that she had done, she still found cause to accuse herself. "*I* did it." Then she admitted, "But it didn't feel that way. Oh, I didn't care about the consequences. I can't deny that. But was I 'compelled by rage'? I don't think so. I was just desperate. Desperate for you. Desperate for Jeremiah. Desperate for *help*. I didn't know where else to get it.

"Is that all it takes to ruin everything? Is Lord Foul going to get free because of me? Is the whole Earth going to die because of me?"

At that moment, Covenant would have given the remains of his fingers to reassure her. But he did not respond immediately. He had good reason to be cautious. During his early visits to the Land, he had justified himself falsely too often, and the cost of his obfuscations had been too high. And her needs were not his. Her desperation was not the same as his. It was more intimate, or more personal, or simply more consequential. He had only raped Lena and betrayed Elena and destroyed the first Staff of Law. He had not awakened the Worm. In an earlier age, Linden herself had prevented him—

Now he suspected that Jeremiah was more likely to be *compelled by rage*.

He wanted to say, Maybe you're right. Any one of us can destroy the whole world— if it's *our* world. All we have to do is destroy ourselves. But he demanded more of himself.

"Sometimes 'desperate,'" he began, "is just a convenient name for being so angry you can't stand it. After everything you went through—after Roger and the *croyel* and Esmer and Kastenessen and the Harrow and even Longwrath—you finally got to Andelain"—he winced at the memory—"and I refused to talk to you. Hellfire, Linden! Only a dead woman wouldn't have been sick with fury."

She hid her face as if she were cowering; as if he had poured acid on her heart. "Then I've done it. I've doomed—"

If she had pulled away from him, he might have cried out. He had hurt her enough to maim the bond which they had only begun to renew. But she still clung to him as if he were all that she had left. She still thought that he had a better answer—or that he *was* a better answer.

As gently as he could, he said, "It's tempting to think that way. It lets us off the hook. If we've already made the only mistakes that matter—or if somehow we just *are* the only mistakes that matter—we can't be expected to do anything else. But it's not that simple.

"For one thing, we aren't alone. We're all in this mess together. We're all making decisions and trying to justify the consequences. Whatever you've done, good or bad, you didn't do it in a vacuum. You've been reacting to people with their own agendas and situations you didn't cause. From the start, the Despiser has been pushing you where he wants you to go. And you've had help along the way.

"And for another—" Goaded by his own necessary passions, Covenant's voice rose. "Linden, I just don't *believe* it. I don't believe Lord Foul can't be stopped. I don't even believe the world can't be saved. Freeing Lord Foul wasn't the only thing Berek talked about. He also said there's *another truth* on the far side of despair and doom. All we have to do is find it."

She did not react. He could not be sure that she was listening. He might have been speaking to the leaves and boughs, the harmony of gleams, rather than to the woman in his arms.

Nevertheless she continued to hold on to him.

You will not fail, however he may assail you. There is also love in the world.

Because she did not let go, he said more.

"And for another— Oh, hell. I've written entire novels about this. 'Guilt is power. Only the damned can be saved.' Maybe that sounds cynical. Maybe it is. But who else *needs* to be saved? Who else *can* be? Not the innocent. They have their own problems." He was thinking of the Masters, who thought that rigid purity of service would relieve their ancient humiliation. "They don't need anything as gracious or just plain kind as forgiveness.

"So maybe blaming ourselves is a waste of time. Maybe we should just admit that everybody goes wrong. Everybody does damage. That's what being human enough to make mistakes means. And if that's what being human means, then there's really only one question we have to answer. Is making mistakes *all* it means?

"If it isn't, then *everything* counts. Resurrecting me and waking up the Worm. Making love together and killing Cavewights. Hell and blood, Linden! I let my own daughter be sacrificed against She Who Must Not Be Named. And I didn't stop there. I went right up to the most pitiful woman I've ever known and stuck a knife in her chest. If you think I don't feel *bad* about things like that, you haven't been paying attention. But if everything counts, then guilt is no reason to stop trying for something better."

Somewhere among the music of his lights, Caerwood ur-Mahrtiir sang, "It is my heart I give to you—"

Finally Linden stirred. With small movements, she shifted the position of her arms, adjusted her head on Covenant's shoulder. For a time, she conveyed the impression that she was listening to the Forestal, or to the rebuffed thrash of the winds beyond the bower, or to the restless concern of Covenant's pulse. Then she brushed a delicate kiss across his chest.

"Here's the funny part," she murmured. "I tried to say practically the same thing to Jeremiah. I used different words, but the point was the same. Maybe I should listen to myself every once in a while. You shouldn't have to make a speech whenever I think that I've done something wrong."

Suddenly she yawned. "If I weren't so sleepy, I would ask you to make love again."

Entirely to himself, Covenant released a deep sigh of relief. There were any number of questions for which he had no answer; but for the time being, he was content with the one that she had given him.

You do not forgive.

Perhaps she did.

Part Two

⚭

"the abyss and
the peak"

1.

A Tale Which Will Remain

Weary to the core, and yet eased in more ways than she knew how to name, Linden Avery dozed in Covenant's arms, *Thomas of my heart*. But she did not sleep deeply or long. After a time, a rustle among the willow branches plucked at her attention. She felt the pressure of hooves on the sumptuous grass, followed by the sounds of feeding. Casting a bleary glance over her shoulder, she found horses in the bower.

Hyn and Hynyn. Khelen. Rallyn. And the Ardent's mulish steed, Mishio Massima. In this lifeless region, their need for fodder had become imperative.

Linden closed her eyes again, nestled against the anodyne of Covenant's shoulder. Her only true lover— He had never stopped loving her: she believed that now. To some extent, she understood why he had seemed to spurn her days ago. And those aspects of his singular straits that still baffled her did not mar her gratitude. The sensation that he had vindicated her, body and soul, was more profound than her fatigue. It felt numinous and ineffable: a homecoming of the spirit. Every part of him had become as precious to her as a sunrise.

The ring on her finger resembled certainty. She could have spent days with her husband in the balm of Caerwood ur-Mahrtiir's bower, and done so gladly.

But eventually the snorts and snuffles of horses cropping grass prodded her to wonder how much time had passed. Motionless so she would not disturb Covenant, she extended her senses beyond the Forestal's bedizened canopy, and was surprised to discern that dawn was near: the feigned dawn of a sunless day. The fourth day— was it really the fourth?—since the sun had failed to rise.

Her companions had left her alone with Covenant for most of the night. Even Jeremiah—

Curious now, Linden raised her head to look around.

Melodies gemmed the leaves overhead as if they had been set in place to watch over her and Covenant; but of Caerwood ur-Mahrtiir there was no sign. He had hidden himself in the fecund intricacies of his hymns. Apart from the horses, she saw only the broad trunk of the tree, and beyond it the fane of the *Elohim*.

Groaning softly, Covenant blinked his eyes open. When his gaze found Linden, he tried to smile: an awkward twist of his mouth. In the delicate light of the Forestal's music, the pale scar on his forehead seemed to glow. It might have been a nascent anadem, an old wound that was slowly becoming a crown. The stark silver of his hair promised flames.

Remembering his ardor, she felt a delicious shiver like an intimation of the life that she wanted to have with him.

An impossible life while the Worm stalked the World's End, and Lord Foul plotted to reclaim Jeremiah.

Covenant propped himself up on his elbows and looked her over with yearning in his eyes. He seemed to desire every contour. Then he frowned ruefully. Nodding toward the Ranyhyn and Mishio Massima, he muttered in mock-disgust, "I probably shouldn't say this, Linden, but I don't really like horses."

She laughed softly. "Neither do I." He made her name sound like a cherished endearment. "But I'm very fond of Hyn," she added in case the mare understood her. "And Khelen, of course."

How could she feel anything other than affection for them?

As if her response were a cue, Jeremiah called from within the fane, "Mom? Can we come out? We're hungry. You have all the *aliantha*."

She was on the verge of saying, Sure, honey, when she remembered that she was naked.

Stifling a giggle, she answered, "Give us a minute." She looked at Covenant, offered him a lop-sided smile, kissed him swiftly. Then she reached for her clothes.

"Hellfire," he growled under his breath. "Bloody damnation."

He had not had enough of peace and privacy, or of her.

She pulled up her jeans, buttoned her shirt without regarding its tears and snags, its neat hole over her heart. Leaving her feet bare to enjoy the lush grass a little longer, she retrieved her Staff. Then she paused to study Covenant.

His leprosy had worsened in recent days. A slight haze occluded his vision. She suspected that he could not see clearly past twenty or thirty paces. And the numbness of his fingers stretched into his palms toward his wrists. His toes, and patches on the soles of his feet, had no sensation. Now the end of Kevin's Dirt had halted his deterioration. She found no indication that his symptoms were still spreading. Nevertheless he was farther from health than he had been when she had first resurrected him.

He fumbled into his jeans, worked his T-shirt over his head. While he tugged at the laces of his boots, she asked tentatively, "Do you want any help, Thomas? I can heal—"

He hesitated for a moment, scowled, then shook his head. "Thanks anyway. I can see well enough." He seemed to mean, Well enough for what I have to do. "And I need my hands like this. The *krill* gets hot. If I'm in too much pain, I won't be able to hold it."

She considered asking, Why is that important? How much do you know about what we have to do? But she rejected the idea. She did not want an answer: not really. She was in no hurry to think about the Despiser and the World's End.

Covenant gave her a look full of hunger. Then he shrugged and nodded his readiness.

Holding his gaze, she raised her voice. "Come on out, Jeremiah. All of you. It's time."

At once, Jeremiah emerged from the temple. The sight of him both lifted and soured Linden's spirit. The emotions clenched inside him showed in his aura. He could smile because she had come back for him, and because she and Covenant were finally united—and because he had been able to sleep. But the effects of Kastenessen's possession persisted: he did not know how to relieve them. And he had accomplished his one purpose. In the aftermath, he had lost the eagerness of his talent, the excitement which had driven and protected him. His ruined pajamas and his muddy gaze made him look haunted.

Behind him loomed the Swordmainnir, grinning. Sleep and gladness had refreshed them, and their eyes as they regarded Linden and Covenant seemed to glow with warmth.

Rime Coldspray approached first, followed by Cirrus Kindwind, and then by Cabledarm brimming with restored wholeness. The other women carried their depleted waterskins. Among them, Stave walked like a man who had never been harmed.

Covenant rose from the grass to greet them. With a mixture of pleasure and regret, he said gruffly, "I should probably thank you. But I'm sure you can understand that one night just isn't enough." He touched Linden's shoulder briefly. "I feel like I've been waiting for this my whole life, and now it's over"—he grimaced—"unless we can do things that are even more unlikely than what we've already done." Glowering like a man who did not know how to smile, he finished, "Just once, I would like to face a challenge that turns out to be easy."

Linden smiled for him. He had given her another gift to counterbalance the night's passing. Indirectly, perhaps, but unmistakably, he had already reassumed his rightful place as the leader of the Land's defenders.

"Yet betimes, Timewarden," replied the Ironhand, "we are granted ease. To behold you and Linden Giantfriend as you are does not test my heart. It gives only joy."

Covenant ducked his head. "Maybe that's why I've always loved Giants. You remind me—" He spread his hands as if he had run out of words.

Linden guessed that he was recalling Saltheart Foamfollower; or perhaps Pitchwife and the First of the Search.

But other matters quickly claimed the attention of the Swordmainnir. They were hungry, of course. And they knew as well as Linden did, or Covenant, that all of the company's deeds so far were only stopgaps. Branl outside the bower would have given warning of any imminent threat; but every peril was growing, and time was running out. With both pleasure and rue, the Ironhand and her comrades turned to Caerwood ur-Mahrtiir's abundance of *aliantha* and clean water.

Before Jeremiah could join them, Linden stopped him with a hug. "Can we talk, honey?" she asked privately. "I haven't had a chance to hear how you're handling what you've been through."

He avoided her gaze. "There isn't much to tell, Mom. The Giants and Stave did everything. I mean, pretty much. All I did was organize the pieces and make sure they fit."

She recognized the deflection in his voice, but she did not question it. Instead she insisted mildly, "I still want to hear about it. This may sound strange, but you probably know me better than I know you. You've been my son for years, but I feel like we've just met. I want to understand how you think. Just give me a minute to finish getting dressed."

The boy acceded with a glum nod.

Covenant left her with Jeremiah, but he did not follow the example of the Giants. While she pulled on her socks and boots, he asked Stave abruptly, "Is Branl saying anything?"

Stave faced the Unbeliever with his customary lack of expression. "Ur-Lord, the storm of the Worm's coming approaches. He gauges that an hour remains ere we must flee its ravages." The former Master glanced away briefly before adding, "Should the Worm quicken its rush, we will receive warning."

"Well, damn," Covenant muttered. "I should probably be glad. At least that thing isn't heading for Mount Thunder. But it's *hungry*. It's going to hit hard when it gets here."

Scowling, he went to the brook for water. Then he moved toward the nearest shrub and began to eat.

Linden winced to herself. Covenant had seen the Worm before: she had not. But she imagined that it was huge and virulent—and she had no idea whether the Forestal would be able to stand against it. The fact that the *Elohim* were no longer physically present in this manifestation of reality might lessen the Worm's impulse to overwhelm Caerwood ur-Mahrtiir. Or deprivation might make the instrument of the World's End savage.

More savage than it was already.

She swallowed an urge to look outside the willow, confirm Branl's perceptions for herself. The Humbled was not likely to be mistaken. And her concern for her son was more immediate.

There are worse things than being afraid, Mom. Being useless is worse.

As far as she knew, a sense of purpose was all that had defended him against the cost of his emotional wounds. Now he had nothing to build—and perhaps nothing to hope for.

If so, she knew the feeling. But she had her faith in Covenant to steady her. And long ago, she had been assured, *You will not fail*—She wanted to share those gifts with Jeremiah if she could. They were better than despair.

Praying that she would be able to give him what he needed, she beckoned. "Come on, Jeremiah, honey. Let's go into your temple. We can be alone there."

He flinched. He seemed to hide behind the silted hue of his eyes. His manner said, No, although he did not refuse aloud.

"I know that you don't want to talk," she offered patiently. "I don't mean to make you uncomfortable. But I'm your mother. Worrying about their children is what mothers do.

"Come on," she repeated. "If you help me understand, you might find that you feel less alone."

Jeremiah opened his mouth, closed it again. He looked around at the Giants, and then at Covenant, as if he hoped that one of them would intervene. But the women only nodded encouragement; and Covenant's attention was elsewhere.

The boy avoided Linden's gaze. Looking truculent and defensive, he joined her. When she turned past the willow trunk toward the fane's opening, he followed, scuffing his feet in protest.

Inside the construct, she found bare dirt between crooked walls supporting a ceiling that looked like it might fall on her at any moment. Gaps among the stones let patches of Caerwood ur-Mahrtiir's shining into the gloom, but that glow did not lift the shadows from Jeremiah's mien. He might have been little more than an emblem of the deeper night awaiting the Earth.

Facing him, she put the Worm out of her mind; braced herself to concentrate on her son. He could not rid himself of his demons if he did not acknowledge them.

He began before she could choose a question. "I don't know what you think we have to talk about. I already told you. The Giants and Stave did practically everything. After that—" A scowl concentrated his features. Its tightness reminded her of the twitch at the corner of his eye when Roger and the *croyel* had lured her into the past. "They must have said what happened. The *Elohim* came. So did Kastenessen. Then Covenant showed up. Infelice took Kastenessen with her.

"That's *it*. That's all there is. The rest was just waiting for you and trying not to think you were dead." From his fists, small flames squeezed between his fingers. A caper of yellow light and shadows up and down his body made him look lurid. As if he were pleading, he added, "Nothing else matters."

Linden waited until he started to squirm under the pressure of her regard. Then she folded her arms over the Staff of Law, held it against her heart, and tried to be gentle.

"Jeremiah, honey. This isn't doing you any good. I'm your mother. I know that there's more. But there's something that you don't know about me."

Her years at Berenford Memorial had taught her more than one way to probe the people who needed her.

"I'm more like you than you think. There were a lot of things that I refused to talk about. I kept them secret. That hurt me, of course, but I could live with it. The part that I didn't understand"—the part that she had been fatally slow to recognize—"was that I hurt my friends at the same time.

"Now I don't want any more secrets. I kept mine too long, and I finally learned something about them."

While he stared at her, she told him the truth as if she were tearing away the scab from an unhealed wound.

"They feel like they protect us—like we don't have to be ashamed of our secrets, or ashamed of ourselves, as long as no one knows about them. We tell ourselves that we're doing the right thing by keeping them. But that isn't true. Mostly we keep them because we don't trust the people who love us. And *that's* just another way of saying that we don't trust ourselves. We really *are* ashamed. We think that we're at fault and we're going to be condemned, or that we're weak when everyone else is strong, or that we actually deserve to be in pain and alone.

"My secrets were different than yours," she confessed. "Of course they were. They're probably even more shameful. And they hurt everything and everyone that I love."

Every death caused by the Worm, every instance of destruction, was her doing: the loss of the sun; the reaving of the heavens. She was only able to live with that fact because Covenant loved her—and because her son's mind had been restored—and because she had friends. And because she did not know what else she could have done.

In spite of Jeremiah's defenses, she reached him. She felt his sudden uncertainty—

his alarm—as if it were physically solid. In some ways, he was indeed younger than his years. Hearing his mother accuse herself made him feel threatened. For years, she had been his foundation. Now he could not be sure of her.

"Like what?" he asked in a taut voice. "What did you keep secret?"

From his perspective, there were too many possibilities. Most of them had the power to undermine him.

Linden did not hesitate; but she could not keep the harshness out of her voice, the implied savagery.

"Resurrecting Thomas. I knew that I was going to break every Law the Earth absolutely needs to survive, but I kept what I had in mind to myself." —*compelled by rage, and contemptuous of consequence.* "I made sure that no one had a chance to stop me. Now it isn't just the world that's doomed. As soon as the Worm gets to the Earth-Blood, Lord Foul will be able to escape.

"*I* did that, Jeremiah.

"But I didn't keep what I was going to do secret because I wanted those things to happen. I didn't think about the danger at all. I kept it secret because I was afraid that my friends would interfere. I didn't trust them enough to believe that they would understand, or that they would still be my friends if they knew the truth. And I felt that way because I was ashamed. I was ashamed of not protecting you from Roger in the first place. I was ashamed of letting him and the *croyel* trick me.

"We're in this mess right now because I kept secrets."

Jeremiah nodded, but he seemed unaware of his own response. His eyes were full of dismay. He sounded small and inexpressibly forlorn as he admitted, "I hate what's happened to me. I hate how *dirty* the *croyel* made me feel. I could hide from the pain. I knew how to do that." He had concealed himself for most of his life. "But I couldn't hide from all that sneering.

"And I hated the way it made me hurt you. I couldn't prevent anything. I hated being too weak to stop it. I wanted to hurt myself, not you." Under *Melenkurion* Sky-weir, he had stabbed her hand— "But I couldn't. I just couldn't."

Facing his unshielded need, Linden fought down her yearning to put her arms around him. He was both a child and a young man; but it was the young man who most needed her succor. The child understood too well how to bury himself away. The young man was the Jeremiah who would have to face what was coming. And that Jeremiah would not be consoled by hugs.

But he was not done. As if he were cutting himself, he said, "Then Kastenessen took me, and I was helpless again. He reached out and *took* me like I was nothing. Good for nothing. Useless. And I felt how he felt. He burned every nerve in my whole body until I thought I loved it. I thought it made sense.

"I'm ashamed of *that*. I *should* be. I wanted him *dead*—I want Lord Foul *dead*—so I don't have to be ashamed anymore. And I don't want to talk about it because talking just makes it more real. It just tells everybody how useless I am."

For a moment, Linden could not respond. Kastenessen had taken him? She nearly cried out. Covenant had not told her. No one had warned her.

Her son must have inherited more than Earthpower from Anele.

I want Lord Foul *dead*. How else did she expect him to feel? She had once been possessed herself. The force of her own desire to see the Despiser's end made her tremble.

Nevertheless she had to offer Jeremiah something. She had to try.

Hoarse with empathy and suppressed outrage, she asked, "Don't you think that maybe we all feel that way? He's the Despiser. He's spent eons doing as much harm as he can to the whole world. Don't you think that maybe everyone you know wishes he could be destroyed?"

Quick as a slash, Jeremiah retorted, "But you aren't useless! Covenant isn't. The Giants are strong. Stave and Branl are strong. Covenant has his ring. You have a ring and the Staff of Law. I've already used up everything I know how to do. Now I'm just nothing."

It was too much. Without pausing to consider what she said, Linden snapped, "That's how *I* feel. *I've* already used up everything I know how to do." Before he could protest or withdraw, she explained, "Oh, I understand what you're saying. And you're right. Of course you are. There are probably all kinds of things I can do that you can't. But, Jeremiah, *I don't know what they are.* I've done everything I can think of. It doesn't matter how much power I have because I have no idea what to do with it." Her son also had power. "Compared to the Worm—hell, compared to the *Despiser*— I'm as useless as you feel." Deliberately she made her heart as naked as his. "We have the same problem. What's happening is too big for us. It's just too big."

Jeremiah did not look at her. He stood half turned away like a boy who wanted to run and hide; a boy who already knew where he could go to feel safe. But he did not go. She felt his attention cling to her while his fears and his pain urged him to flee.

"Then how?" he asked like a waif too lonely to wail. "How do you go on?"

Linden did not hesitate. "I've been here before." She had come too far to falter now. "That's the advantage of being older. I've been here before. With Thomas. I've seen what he can do. Maybe *I've* come to the end of what I can do, but *he* hasn't. And he doesn't believe Lord Foul can't be stopped. He doesn't even believe the world can't be saved."

Thinking, Listen to me, Jeremiah. *Hear* me, she finished, "As long as that's true, I won't give up. I will not give up."

After a long moment, she added, "And I certainly won't give up on you."

His struggle was terrible to watch. He knew how to protect himself. His craving for the sanctuary of graves was visible in the way he stood, in the clench of his fists and the hunch of his shoulders. Sharing herself, Linden had not reassured him: she had precipitated a crisis which he had been fighting to avoid. But he also had reason to know that safety was a trap; that every sanctuary was also a prison. On some deep level, he had chosen to free himself from his long dissociation. More consciously, he had chosen to do what he could for the *Elohim*. He understood the choice that his mother wanted him to make now.

In the same tone—forlorn and frail and alone—he told her, "I'll try."

Then he let Linden hug him.

With that she had to be content. Perhaps it was enough.

hen she and Jeremiah left the temple to rejoin their companions, Caerwood ur-Mahrtiir stood among them.

As before, he wore an aura of isolation, of harmonized and hermetic concentration, as if he were essentially alone. His eyeless visage did not regard the Giants or the horses. He appeared to ignore the *Haruchai* and the Unbeliever. Nevertheless something in his stance or his singing conveyed the impression that he was aware of Linden. Melodies seemed to skirl around her like promises or compulsions.

Under the gemmed leaves and boughs of the willow, his music sounded like wrath.

Covenant came to her at once, kissed her quickly, studied her with anxiety in his eyes. But she only returned his kiss and nodded: she did not answer his unspoken question. What he wanted to know would have to come from Jeremiah—and at that moment, Jeremiah clearly did not mean to say anything. His face wore a sullen glower which masked his heart.

The Giants greeted her and Jeremiah with wry smiles and troubled frowns. Instead of asking questions, however, they busied themselves with necessary tasks. They had refilled most of their waterskins. Now they moved among the shrubs, gathering treasure-berries which they placed in the last two waterskins so that the company would not go hungry for a while.

To Linden, Stave bowed without any visible stiffness. After a moment's consideration—or consultation—he announced, "Chosen, the storm of the Worm draws nigh. And its course lies directly toward us. We must depart."

Ah, God. Linden tightened her grip on the Staff until her hands ached. She was not ready—and she had not eaten. Jeremiah had not.

But Hyn gave a soft whinny as if to confirm Stave's assertion. Facing Jeremiah,

Khelen tossed his head and stamped one hoof. Restive and proud, Hynyn waited behind Stave.

In contrast, the Ardent's spavined horse, with its distinct ribs and slumped back, paid no heed to anything except grass. And Rallyn had already left the bower, presumably to join Branl.

Studying Jeremiah, Covenant's expression settled into its familiar strictness, as exigent as a prophet's. "I'm sorry, Linden," he said, muted and grim. "We have to get out of here."

Before she could force herself to move, however, the Forestal spoke. He did not change his stance or gaze at anyone; but his song became words, as peremptory as commands. As if he were encouraging haste, he said, "I have no staff."

He startled Linden; perplexed her. Fortunately Rime Coldspray seemed to understand him instinctively. Without hesitation, she replied, "Great one, your lack is plain. If you will condone it, I will sever a branch to serve you, though I am loath to harm the loveliness and shelter which you have provided."

Caerwood ur-Mahrtiir hummed to himself. After a brief pause, he answered, "Do so. All of the world's woods know that boughs must fall like leaves—aye, and the grandest of monarchs also—when there is need."

The Ironhand bowed. Hurrying, she thrust her way between the hanging branches and lights to retrieve her stone glaive.

Would a staff be enough? Would the ur-Mahrtiir himself suffice? Linden wanted to believe that. Long ago, the forbidding of the Forestals had blocked the Ravers along the whole length of Landsdrop. But the Worm was immeasurably greater than Lord Foul's most potent servants.

Her hands on the Staff were suddenly damp. Sweat ran like spiders down her spine; like centipedes and maggots. Her flesh had not forgotten She Who Must Not Be Named. Nevertheless the Land's peril compelled her.

Her voice shook as she asked the Forestal, "Do you need any help?" She had assured Jeremiah that she would not give up. "Is there anything that I can do?"

"There is." Caerwood ur-Mahrtiir's music gathered around her. "The approaching puissance is vast. As I am, I cannot withstand it. I require your strength."

Involuntarily she quailed. Her old friend might need more from her than she knew how to give. But Caerwood ur-Mahrtiir wove the many strands of his music into a soothing counterpoint. He stood directly in front of her now. And as she regarded him, another face seemed to emerge within his, softening his unanswerable visage. Like shadows, blurred and tenuous, the former Manethrall's features joined those of the Forestal.

Humming in a more human voice, he said, "Yet I have not forgotten you, Linden

Avery, Ringthane and Chosen. You bear dooms greater than the fate of the *Elohim*, or indeed of the world's remaining trees. You must not perish in my aid. I ask only your blessing."

My blessing? She mouthed the words, but made no sound. Oh, Mahrtiir! My *blessing*?

Caerwood ur-Mahrtiir unfurled ancient tunes around him, verse and refrain. "This invoked bourne of verdure and health is small. By the measure of the world's end, it is little more than vainglory. But I will not have it so. I will not. Here stands the forgotten truth of wood, just as the fane which preserves the *Elohim* expresses another truth also forgotten. While my bourne endures, it affirms that the Worm and death are not the sum of all things.

"Linden Avery, Ringthane, friend. Bless this beauty with your strength. Nourish it, that I may suffice in its defense."

Now she understood. Relief and sorrow clogged her throat as if she had inherited them from Caerroil Wildwood and his gibbet. She could not speak. But she understood. At one time—a time as forgotten as other truths—she had been a healer. Behind the wrath of the olden Forestals, and the barrenness of Gallows Howe, lay passions of another kind altogether.

While her companions waited, staring, Linden stepped back from the Forestal; cleared enough space to wield her Staff. Then she reached into herself, reached into the black shaft defined by runes between bands of High Lord Berek's iron lore, and brought forth Earthpower and Law for their intended purpose: not for battle and killing, but for sustenance and restoration.

This might be her last chance to use her Staff condignly. From this moment on, she foresaw only strife and carnage; possible Desecrations. With her whole heart, she sought to give her best to Caerwood ur-Mahrtiir's bower.

Her health-sense guided her, first into recognition of the thetic nature of the Forestal's harmonies, then into awareness of their interplay, then into sensitivity to their tones and timbres. Her power was as black as the coming storm of the Worm, but it was made for this, God, it was *made for this*. Perhaps her magicks were flames. Perhaps she only imagined them as flames. Nevertheless they suited her purpose. When she had refined her fire to suit the chords and lines of the music which inspired the lush grass and the rushing brook, the willow with its limbs and leaves and glimmerings, the bedizened shade of the sanctuary, she poured out fuligin in the form of vitality.

She went deep into the dirt to fill it with Earthpower, feed every questing root. Baked and beaten earth she enriched until it became loam. From the soil, she brought Law and energy upward, encouraging sluggish sap, enhancing the hardiness of bark, suffusing boughs and twigs and leaves with anticipation. Among the branches, she added luster to the Forestal's gleams until they shone like refined stars.

Everything that Caerwood ur-Mahrtiir had brought into being, she increased. The willow stretched taller, spread its shelter wider. Bursting from the ground, the brook became a stream gurgling with gladness. Grasses grew like dancing until they twined around the feet and ankles of the company. The faces poised before Linden were lit with spangles like epiphanies.

In response, the Giants bowed low, too entranced for speech. Covenant's eyes reflected the shining of leaves. Moved in spite of his mood, Jeremiah brought forth gentle flames the color of sunshine from his hands and forearms. Only Stave did not react. He stood with his arms folded as if the sole task required of him was to bear witness.

And as Linden worked, the Forestal himself seemed to grow taller. His aura of exaltation and severity expanded until the nearest Giants and even Jeremiah backed away, giving themselves room for wonder. The promise of his mien became a cynosure, as compelling as a demand. Soon his fierce vigor filled the bower.

He needed only an instrument to wield his will against the Worm.

Then the Ironhand returned, harried by winds, to give Caerwood ur-Mahrtiir what he lacked. While Linden withdrew her power and stepped aside, Rime Coldspray bowed deeply, showing her blade naked in her hands. When the Forestal nodded his consent, she moved to the edge of the bower, readied her glaive.

With one stroke, she lopped off a limb as tall as she was. As she did so, a sting of pain shot through the music, and the lights of the Forestal's theurgy glittered furiously. But the willow's distress soon passed, leaving a renewed tranquility under the canopy.

Leaves and twigs and all, Coldspray brought the bough to Caerwood ur-Mahrtiir.

Though it was twice his height, he accepted it easily; held it high as if it were the chorus of a hymn. For an instant, all of its leaves quivered. Then they began to glisten as if they were dewed with power.

"I am armed," he sang. "Let every force and foe which disdains the glory of wood and green be warned. Though I have no forest to sustain me, I will not be thwarted while one tree stands at my back."

Through a quick blur of tears, Linden watched him as if he had been transformed again; as if he had surpassed his given exaltation.

"Linden," Covenant murmured as if he had no other language for what he felt. "Linden. Hellfire."

"Nonetheless, ur-Lord," Stave put in brusquely, "we must depart. If we do not attain a considerable distance, we will not survive the Worm."

Covenant shook himself. He seemed to struggle for words. "I know. We should go." His tone said, *Now.*

"Aye, Timewarden," the Ironhand sighed. "Doom crowds close upon us. We dare the Worm at our peril. We must trust that the Forestal who was once our friend and companion will not fail."

More firmly, she ordered her Swordmainnir to reclaim their armor and weapons. While Linden tried to break free of the spell which Caerwood ur-Mahrtiir had cast on her, the Giants gathered up their stores of water and *aliantha.* Then they ran from the bower.

Covenant came to her with pride in his eyes. Wrapping his arms around her, he assured her softly, "We can do this. Somehow we can do it. We just have to get started. As long as we're together—"

He steadied her. Somehow we can— If the Forestal was strong enough.

After a moment, she nodded.

With an air of regret, Covenant released her.

A heartbeat later, Stave put his hands on Linden's waist and boosted her unceremoniously onto Hyn's back. As her muscles settled into their familiar places astride the mare, the former Master went to help Jeremiah mount. Covenant heaved himself into Mishio Massima's saddle. Stave sprang for Hynyn.

Before Linden was ready—before she could possibly be ready—the riders surged into motion.

An alteration in the Forestal's music parted the canopy to the northwest, opening a path out of the bower. Together Covenant and Linden, Jeremiah and Stave rode from shelter and solace into the bleak dawn of a sunless world.

✇

L eaving the protection of the willow and Caerwood ur-Mahrtiir was like passing from Andelain into the virulence of the Sunbane. Linden and her companions staggered to a halt. The Ranyhyn flinched; rolled their eyes. Mishio Massima shied and crabbed, nearly unhorsed Covenant. Caerwood ur-Mahrtiir's music had concealed the extent of the peril. Outside the bower, the storm's scale was unveiled.

It was enormous.

During the night, the blast of presage had reconciled its confusion. Instead of writhing from one direction to another like a beast in agony, it had become a stiff assault from the northeast; a gale arising from the heart of the utter blackness that now loomed into the heavens like the front of an atmospheric tsunami. Eerie ululations like the anguish of ghouls sounded in the distance. Scourged gusts scooped groans from the craters that littered the ground; scaled into wailing on the ragged edges of the belabored ridge. If the Forestal's theurgy had not protected the willow, its leaves would have been torn away, scattered like debris. Boughs would have split like screams.

That was bad enough; but there was worse—

The core of the storm was a blare of *might* that defied perception: too loud to be heard, too dark for vision; too savage to register as anything except horror. But at the fringes of the Worm's approach, thunder crashed, a wild barrage like a convulsion that would never end. It seethed like the collapse of cliffs. Within it, armies of lightning stalked the plain, hammering the earth until the very dirt seemed to erupt and burn. Sudden and erratic, flashes lurid as bruises punctuated the blackness. On either side of the advance, desolations writhed like orgies, articulating the Worm's hunger.

God in Heaven! Linden had never—

Instinctively she snatched fire from her Staff. The sheer force of the blast threatened to extinguish her mind. But Earthpower sharpened her senses, made her more vulnerable. It seemed to *expose* her, as if the magnitude of the storm served to measure her inadequacy.

She had unleashed this doom.

Her strength left her. Her power became dust and ashes in her veins. Her heart lurched to a halt.

Cowering into herself, she did not feel the Giants running toward her. She hardly noticed them as they joined her. Their cataphracts would not protect them. Their swords were useless. She could not hear herself gasping, "Oh, God. Oh, God."

In size, the Worm may have been *no more than a range of hills*, but it had enough raw force to rive the world.

How close was it? Two leagues? Three?

Distance meant nothing to such a creature. It was already too near. It would arrive more swiftly than any Ranyhyn.

Then one of the Swordmainnir shouted, "Behold the Forestal!"

Like a strike on an anvil, Linden's heart beat again. It began racing.

Mahrtiir!

Behind her, Caerwood ur-Mahrtiir emerged from his bourne. Bearing his staff like an emblem of defiance, he strode to meet the gale.

He did not go far. Less than a stone's throw from the battered drape of the willow, he stopped; prepared to make his stand. He must have been singing, but the wind's thrash and groan and howl tore the sound away.

Linden reached out for Jeremiah; caught his arm as if her mere grip had the ability to protect him. When he glanced at her, she saw a wasteland of shock in his eyes. Nothing in his life had prepared him for the magnitude of the Worm's violence.

While she held her son, Stave held her. The Giants stared wildly, like women caught in the toils of the Soulbiter.

Covenant struggled to keep his seat until Branl came to his side, helped him control the Ardent's horse. Then the Unbeliever panted hoarsely, "Run! Hellfire! We have to *run*!"

Transfixed by Caerwood ur-Mahrtiir's daring, Linden could not drag herself away; but Hyn chose for her by surging into motion. Swordmainnir slapped themselves and each other, forced their limbs to move. Branl hauled on Mishio Massima's reins until the horse sprang forward. A stentorian peal from Hynyn seemed to take Khelen by the throat.

The company broke and ran as if it had been routed.

On some level, Linden recognized that she and her companions had to do more than simply evade the Worm itself. They had to get beyond the Worm's cloak of power. Those lightnings would sear the flesh from their bones. The winds would rip the riders from their mounts, knock even Giants to the ground. Yet she did not heed such things. Unregarded, her hand lost its hold on Jeremiah. She could not look away from the Forestal.

Small against the background of the bright willow, Caerwood ur-Mahrtiir stood before the blast. It wrenched at him, tried to shred his robe. Shafts of lightning marched closer with every heartbeat. Gales tore the branches of his staff. Still the leaves clung to their twigs: the glitter of song clung to the leaves. With music and wood, he opposed the dark as if he had within him the authority to deny annihilation.

Linden could not believe that he was strong enough. He was a Forestal, transformed scion of a lineage potent against armies and Ravers. His puissance surpassed the Lords of old with all their lore. But the Worm exceeded every other living force. It dwarfed the exertion of wild magic and Law which had plucked the huge creature from its slumber. And Caerwood ur-Mahrtiir could not draw on the spirit of a spanning woodland, the will and energy of trees in their millions. He had only the willow at his back.

The willow—and the fane with its treasure of *Elohim*.

Still the company ran. Urgent and frantic, straining to their limits, the horses and the Giants ran. Branl warded Covenant. Stave brought Hynyn between Hyn and Khelen, watched over Linden and Jeremiah with his lone eye. Rime Coldspray and her comrades stretched their strides and raced for the horizon, running heavy as boulders, and yet fleet as driven seas.

Too frightened to shout, Jeremiah flailed his arms, flinging streams of Earth-power in all directions as if he sought to haul his companions forward. The storm brushed his theurgy aside like dust.

Holding her breath, Linden watched the Forestal.

He dwindled with distance, shrank in proportion to the Worm's vastness. As the storm towered over him, an ebon and unanswerable tsunami, his staff's gleaming and the willow's seemed smaller and smaller. They became puny things, ineffable and frail. At any moment, they would be extinguished. In its hunger, the Worm would swat them out of existence and take no notice.

Yet Caerwood ur-Mahrtiir stood. He sang, and refused to be silenced. The Worm's tumult was less than a league away, less than half a league; and still he stood. He was more than Caerwood ur-Mahrtiir. He was also Manethrall Mahrtiir, Raman, given to service. He refused as if his *No* could sway even the unthinking appetite of the World's End.

Thunder shook the ground. When Linden risked a glance at the nearest light-nings, the boil of blackness, she saw that the company was too slow. The Giants and the horses were sprinting hard enough to burst the hearts of weaker beings, but they could not run fast enough. The storm was too wide: they had not begun their flight in time to avoid it.

And yet the argent of Caerwood ur-Mahrtiir's forbidding endured.

"Linden Avery!" Somehow Stave made himself heard through the chaos of run-ning and winds, lightning and thunder. "Chosen, attend! The Forestal succeeds! The Worm slows!"

Impossible! She stared in disbelief. The Forestal could not—

He could. Caerroil Wildwood and Linden herself had given him enough.

The storm inundated her senses. Its might blotted out the heavens. Caerwood ur-Mahrtiir's light had become tiny in the face of the tremendous black. Nevertheless she saw the change of pace, not at the storm's core, but at its near edge.

Stave was right. The Worm was slowing down. It was actually *slowing down*.

And slowing more and more as the Forestal's denial stiffened.

"Hell and blood!" Covenant yelled. "He's doing it! He's by God *doing it*!"

Manethrall Mahrtiir, who had found his heart's desire—and had come back.

It was not enough. Running as they were, Linden and her companions might escape the storm. If the Worm came to a complete halt—if it paused to confront the Forestal, however briefly—they might evade the lightning; the worst of the vehe-mence. But that alone would not save them. The World's End might then turn from Caerwood ur-Mahrtiir to follow the scent of EarthBlood. If it did, the storm would leave the bower and the fane intact. Instead it would swing in *this* direction, away from the ridge. With one lunge, the Worm would send its ferocity raving toward the riders and the Giants. They would die like Joan in her former world, burned by blasts which no mortal flesh could withstand.

Still the Worm *was* halting. For this one moment, at least, the Forestal sufficed.

Without warning, Covenant also halted. Wrestling with the reins, he forced Mishio Massima to obey him. While the rest of the company wheeled in confusion, he swung out of the saddle, snatched at the bundled *krill*, uncovered the blaze of the gem.

Waving his arms, he shouted, "Get together! As close as you can! I don't know how long Mahrtiir can forbid that thing! We have to get *out* of here!"

Linden gaped at him. She felt snared by the Worm and the storm and Caerwood ur-Mahrtiir; unable to break free. But Hyn heeded Hynyn's whinny, or Rallyn's. In a rush, the mare crowded close to Hynyn and Khelen. Frantically the Ironhand and her comrades formed a tight cordon around Linden, Stave, and Jeremiah. Only Covenant and Branl, Mishio Massima and Rallyn stood apart.

Branl had dismounted beside Covenant. With negligent ease, the Humbled tossed Longwrath's flamberge to the nearest Giant. At once, Covenant pitched himself into Branl's arms. As Branl crouched low, Covenant stabbed the *krill*'s blade into the dirt.

Bright silver bloomed from the cut. Sustained by white gold and will, it clung to the ground as though it fed from a trough of oil.

Swift as only the *Haruchai* could be, Branl carried Covenant around the company while Covenant dragged the point of High Lord Loric's dagger through the earth. And as they moved, the *krill* gouged a shining line in the earth, a curve becoming a circle.

Dirt was not tinder. It was not wood or oil. Nonetheless it held Covenant's power, undaunted by the gale, while the curve extended to enclose the company.

More quickly than Linden would have thought possible, Covenant and Branl completed their circle.

Immediately the Humbled surged upright. Still carrying Covenant, he sprinted for the horses. Tossing Covenant deftly into Mishio Massima's saddle, Branl leapt for Rallyn's back.

Now the line of light began to gutter and fade. But Covenant did not hesitate. With his left hand, he slapped his wedding band against the dagger's jewel.

Sudden incandescence surrounded the company. Without transition, the world vanished.

Linden heard herself cry out for Mahrtiir, but there was nothing that she could do.

2.

Toward Confrontation

Linden Avery had passed through *caesures*. She had been taken out of her time by Roger Covenant and the *croyel*, and had been returned by the compassionate lore of the Mahdoubt. The arcane abilities of the Harrow and the Ardent had conveyed her to and from the Lost Deep. Most recently, Caerroil Wildwood's last deed in life had restored her to her present.

Nevertheless she was not prepared for the sensations of being rushed out of time and space within a circle of wild magic.

If she could have stood apart from herself and watched, she might have noted the similarity between this translation and the reflexive evasion of linear time which had preserved her and Anele from the collapse of Kevin's Watch. She might have recognized that she and her companions occupied a void like a bubble in the blood of reality, an embolism that floated on its own currents, ignoring the natural pulse and flood of life. She might have realized that she herself was alight; that Covenant's use of the *krill* and his wedding band drew a response from her own ring. She might have become aware that she was being reincarnated as much as translocated.

But she could not stand apart or think. Instead she simply went blank. And after an eternity or an instant, she returned to her mortality with a visceral crash while Hyn pounded beneath her, galloping back into the darkened world.

She felt blind, blinded, yet she saw everything at once; saw it limned in argent, distinct as a cut against the gloom, as if each detail had been etched in her brain.

Led by Branl on Rallyn and Covenant on Mishio Massima, the company hammered the ground. They had been stationary: now they ran like panic. Fleet and certain, Hynyn kept his position between Hyn and Khelen, Linden and Jeremiah. Stave's flat visage showed no surprise. But Jeremiah reeled on his mount's back, caught off balance: only Khelen's care kept him from falling. Around him, the Giants staggered on the sudden surface. Their eyes rolled: they gasped and gaped. Yet they ran.

Together they followed the bottom of a wide depression which may once have been a swale, before it was baked dry. Patches of scrannel grass still clung to the dirt, rough-edged and stubborn. Between them, the ground was erratically cobbled with worn stones. Pummeled winds brought whiffs of dampness and rot from Linden's right: a direction which she instinctively knew was north. Ahead of the company, the terrain rose gradually toward a rumpled landscape a league or more distant.

Covenant lurched in his saddle. He had dropped the reins to strike Loric's dagger with his ring. His boots had lost the stirrups. In another instant, he might fall. But then Branl caught Mishio Massima's halter to slow the beast. A heartbeat later, he snatched the *krill* from Covenant. Covenant slumped forward, clutched at his mount's mane to keep his seat.

The Humbled had done such things before. He must have done them often.

The *krill*'s brightness shrouded the heavens, made night of the twilit morning beyond its ambit. Everything outside its illumination had a look of fatality, of waiting, as if the unnatural dusk masked an ambush.

As Rallyn and Mishio Massima eased their pace, the other Ranyhyn shortened their strides. Around the riders, Rime Coldspray and her comrades relaxed their haste. Running became trotting; became walking. Covenant pushed himself upright, prodded his boots unsteadily into the stirrups.

Winds boiled among the companions, tangled hair, flicked grit at faces. Here, however, the disturbance in the air was only a faint echo of the Worm's harsh turmoil. As Linden struggled to recover from the shock of translation, her first coherent thought was that the company must have crossed a considerable distance: far enough to pass beyond sight or sense of the Worm's storm. Whatever happened—or had already happened—to Caerwood ur-Mahrtiir and the fane, Linden and her companions had escaped.

But they had not done so instantaneously. She felt in her nerves that a portion of the morning was gone, perhaps an hour, perhaps more.

Her ring still burned in response to Covenant's burst of wild magic, but its power was fading.

"Oh, wow!" Jeremiah panted as if he rather than Khelen had galloped. "How did he do that? Where are we?"

Eager for solid ground, he leaned forward, swung one leg to slide off his mount.

Silver-edged images lingered in Linden's mind, after-flashes of vision. Darkness clotted the surrounding twilight. Ahead of the company, the slope out of the depression or swale was still a stone's throw for a Giant away. Half buried stones staggered like the remnants of a broken road among stretches of rough grass. The grass blades were more grey than green, a hue like a memory—

Long ago, days or lifetimes in the past, Anele had stood on grass outside Mithil Stonedown. In a rancid voice, he had said, *There is more, but of my deeper purpose I will not speak.*

On grass that resembled this.

Abrupt connections snapped into focus. Too late, Linden cried out, "Jeremiah! *No!*"

He reached out and took me like I was nothing.

But Stave was faster. He seemed to know her thoughts; or he had his own fears. As she began to shout, he vaulted from Hynyn's back. Swift as thought, he caught Jeremiah before the boy's bare feet touched the ground and the grass. With a heave, Stave returned Jeremiah to Khelen.

"Mom?" Jeremiah yelped. "What—?"

Now a different kind of shock reeled through Linden. Kastenessen was gone—but he had not been Anele's only vulnerability. More than once, another being had possessed the old man.

"This grass," Stave stated flatly, "is of another kind. That which cloaks the hills about Mithil Stonedown grows more thickly, and remains shorter."

And nothing had harmed Anele among the lush verdure of the Verge of Wandering. Still—

Linden studied the grass, probed it with her health-sense. "But it's similar. I'm not sure that it's safe."

"*Mom?*" Jeremiah insisted.

The Giants stared. Some of them gathered nearby. The others seemed content to stand and breathe. None of them interrupted Linden's concentration.

Covenant turned his horse to face her. He watched her as though he knew what was in her heart.

"I'm sorry, Jeremiah," she said, thinking furiously; trying to calm herself. "I didn't mean to startle you. But I don't know how much you've inherited from Anele. Kastenessen wasn't the only one who could use him. Lord Foul—" The memory of the Despiser's voice in Anele's mouth ached like a bruise too deep to heal. "Whenever his feet touched a certain kind of grass, Lord Foul could take him."

Whenever the Despiser had felt like taunting her.

Even his aid had been manipulation. True, he had led her to hurtloam. Indirectly he had enabled her to avoid recapture by the Masters. But that ploy had served his purposes as much as hers. If the Masters had been able to prevent her from reaching the comparative sanctuary of the Ramen and the Verge of Wandering—prevent Hyn from choosing her—prevent her from retrieving the Staff of Law—she would never have been able to find Loric's *krill* and resurrect Covenant. But she also would not have awakened the Worm.

"I don't want that to happen to you," she told her son. "It was agony for Anele, but at least he knew how to mask himself. There were parts of him that Lord Foul and Kastenessen didn't recognize or couldn't reach. If you have to defend yourself that way—if you go back into hiding—I'm afraid that you won't be able to get out again."

He had no bones with which he might devise another portal. His racecar was gone.

The troubled silt of Jeremiah's eyes held more than surprise; more than chagrin. Their sullen smolder looked like fury.

"That doesn't make sense," he protested. *I want Lord Foul dead.* "I stood on grass when we went to the Sarangrave. When we drank at the edge of the marsh. Nothing happened."

"I know," Linden admitted. She had not known then that he was vulnerable. "But maybe that was the wrong kind of grass. And Lord Foul isn't Kastenessen," *compelled by rage, and contemptuous of consequence.* "He only shows himself when it suits him.

"We know that he wants you. At some point, he's going to try to take you."

She ached to protect her son; but her warning seemed to miss its target. His expression grew darker.

"Fine," he muttered. "Let him try. I don't care. Kastenessen surprised me. Lord Foul won't."

His attitude stung her. For the first time in their lives together, she wanted to slap him; to get his attention somehow. But she held back. In spite of her alarm, she could see that he would not heed her: not on this subject, at this moment. His bitterness was too strong. And she knew how he felt. His manner reminded her of herself when she had been about his age, at her mother's abject bedside. If anyone then had told her not to end her mother's life, she would not have listened. Her own distress had ruled her, and she had already chosen her path.

"Then don't rush into it," she replied unsteadily. "It's going to happen whether you're ready for it or not. And the Despiser is stronger than Kastenessen." A lot stronger. "Give yourself as much time as you can."

Jeremiah glared at her for a moment. Then he turned his head away. "Fine," he snorted again: a response that gave her nothing.

Linden winced. She did not know what to say. She had been possessed once herself. More than once, she had fled within herself in terror and dismay. She knew at least that much about what he had endured—and what lay ahead of him. But she could not simply *tell* him what those experiences had taught her, or what they had cost. No description would suffice.

Aching for him, she sighed, "All right. As long as you know what might happen."

Still Jeremiah kept his head turned away as if he were thinking about something else; as if in his mind he had left her behind.

Kindwind opened her mouth to say something, then reconsidered and remained silent.

Now Covenant came closer, steering Mishio Massima among the Giants. The comprehension in his eyes made Linden want to hide in his arms as if he had the power to spare her; as if his embrace might heal the wound of her son's straits. But when he reached her side, he said nothing about Jeremiah. Instead he announced, "That was easier than I expected."

He may have been trying to deflect her from her fears.

"Those translations are draining. I can't even begin to tell you how tired I've been since I went after *turiya*. Branl had to carry me. By the time I got to Kastenessen, I was so exhausted I didn't think I could stay on my feet. But this time—"

"Hellfire, Linden. This time I had help. I felt it. With so many of us, it still should have been difficult, even for a rightful wielder. But you helped me."

Then he changed the subject. Without transition, he asked, "Can you see the stars? My eyes aren't that good anymore."

The stars—?

For no apparent reason, the Swordmainnir began to relax. The Ironhand nodded. Frostheart Grueburn chuckled softly. Onyx Stonemage, Cirrus Kindwind, and the others looked bewildered for a moment. Then they smiled. They seemed to understand Covenant better than Linden did.

"The stars, Linden," he insisted patiently. "Are they dying? Are they all dead?"

After an instant like another translocation, she caught up with him. The Giants were shaking their heads, but they let her answer Covenant.

The stars. When she looked at the sky, she saw that they were fewer than they had been mere days ago. The gaps between them were wider. Nevertheless no more of the forlorn lights were winking out. From horizon to horizon, they remained as bright as supplications in the black heavens.

"All right," she breathed as if she had forgotten to be afraid. "All *right*. He did it. He's doing it. My God, he's *doing* it."

Mahrtiir.

"No." Covenant spoke softly, but he sounded like he was crowing. "You did that. You. You took Mahrtiir into a *caesure* and brought back a Forestal. You made him strong enough to forbid the actual Worm of the World's End. Sure, *he's* saving the *Elohim*. But *you* made it possible."

He was looking, not at her, but at Jeremiah. He was trying to tell Jeremiah something—

But he did not wait for some sign that the boy had heard him. Glancing around the cluster of Giants, he pointed at Linden with one foreshortened finger.

"My wife," he pronounced as if those two words were a celebration. "Anele was right. The world won't see her like again."

He took her by surprise. For a moment, her eyes filled with tears. She could hardly remember being a woman who wept too easily.

Wiping her cheeks, she missed Jeremiah's immediate reaction. When she turned to him again, his shoulders were hunched, strangling emotions. "Fine," he rasped yet again. He was talking to Covenant. "I saved the *Elohim*. Stave did. The Giants did. You did. Mom did. Caerwood ur-Mahrtiir did. That's great.

"What do we do now?"

Several of the Giants grimaced at his tone. Scowling, Covenant showed his teeth as if he wanted to take a bite out of the boy. But it was Stave who answered.

"We have shared an abundance of *aliantha*," he remarked with particular dispassion. "You and the Chosen have not."

The Ironhand nodded gravely. "Indeed, Stave Rockbrother." At the same time, Cabledarm and Halewhole Bluntfist raised their waterskins.

"Fortuitously," Cabledarm proclaimed to Linden, "we are Giants, and provident. In addition to water, we bear treasure-berries. They will feed us well enough for the present, and perhaps for the morrow as well."

For a moment, Linden simply stared while her emotions tried to go in too many directions at once. Then she murmured an inadequate thanks.

Yet she could not leave Jeremiah as he was, not without offering him some form of acknowledgment. In the act of reaching for Bluntfist's waterskin, she paused. "But Jeremiah is right. What *are* we going to do? Saving the *Elohim* is just a delay. We have to do more." With a quick glance at Covenant, she suggested, "Maybe we can talk about that while Jeremiah and I eat."

Jeremiah accepted treasure-berries from Cabledarm as if he were turning away. Nevertheless his gaze followed every shift and flicker of Covenant's reaction.

Frowning, Covenant considered Linden's suggestion. After a moment, he muttered uncomfortably, "We probably should."

At once, the Giants gathered around him. Stave remounted Hynyn, and Branl nudged Rallyn closer. In their disparate fashions, they all needed a sense of purpose as badly as Jeremiah did. A chance to live—or to give the end of their days meaning.

Sitting Mishio Massima in the center of the company, Covenant asked Branl, "How far have we come?"

The last of the Humbled shifted his grip on Longwrath's flamberge. "Not less than a score of leagues, ur-Lord, else we would be able to discern the storm of the Worm."

"Northwest, right?"

"Our heading has been chiefly to the west. We stand some small distance from the southmost verge of the Sarangrave. We must pass the wetland to gain Landsdrop and the Upper Land."

Covenant nodded. "And how much time did we lose?"

Branl glanced at Stave. "We gauge that our passage has consumed little more than an hour."

"Aye," Rime Coldspray assented. "So it appears to me also."

Linden did not bother to concur. While she listened, she concentrated on shaking out berries from the waterskin and tossing them into her mouth; relishing the abrupt tang of energy and health. The seeds she discarded as she ate.

Covenant nodded again. "Good. Since the Forestal has held on this long, we can at least hope he won't fail. The Worm will move on eventually, if it hasn't already. It's fast, and it'll go faster when it gets closer to *Melenkurion* Skyweir. But we can be pretty fast ourselves now. Maybe we can get where we're going faster than Lord Foul expects."

The Giants watched him in silence, waiting for an explanation. Like Jeremiah—like Linden—they had come to the end of what they knew how to do. Now they sailed chartless seas and needed a heading.

"So." Covenant seemed to be reasoning aloud, speaking primarily to himself. "Landsdrop. The Upper Land. Mount Thunder. That's where Lord Foul is. He has to be. He needs to be close enough to She Who Must Not Be Named to take advantage of whatever She does, but not close enough to be in danger himself. And he has to be able to organize his forces, all of which are somewhere inside or near Mount Thunder." Then he shook his head. "Hell and blood. I think that's a mistake."

Linden agreed. Of course it would be a mistake to approach Mount Thunder. She did not doubt Covenant, and Jeremiah had to be protected.

But the Giants passed puzzled glances back and forth; and Rime Coldspray held up her hands. "A moment, Timewarden, I implore you. Your thoughts out-pace ours. Are you certain of our destination? Have you determined our purpose?

"Surely it would be folly to hazard Mount Thunder. You speak of She Who Must Not Be Named and other forces. I must also name your fell son, whose command of the Cavewights appears complete. I deem it unwise to trust that his puissance has been diminished by the severing of Kastenessen's human hand.

"Yet these are lesser concerns. Of greater import is the Worm, a threat to pale all other perils. I know not how we may oppose it, but we can accomplish naught if we do not make the attempt. Therefore surely we must follow, hoping to forestall the Worm from *Melenkurion* Skyweir. How otherwise may the Land and the Earth and life be preserved?"

Her comrades murmured their agreement; but both Stave and Branl frowned as if they wanted to challenge the Ironhand's assessment. Jeremiah watched Covenant with an intensity that resembled nausea. His mouth shaped words that Linden could not interpret. They may have been protests.

"Well," Covenant said gruffly. For a moment, he appeared to wrestle with himself. Then he announced with an air of defiance, "I disagree.

"I won't try to make your decisions for you. Even Linden and Jeremiah—you all have to do what you think is right. But *I'm* going to Mount Thunder. I have to try to stop Lord Foul. And I need you with me. I need you all.

"It's not just that I have no earthly idea what to do about the Worm. That thing is part of the created world. It's inherent to the way this world works. There isn't enough power anywhere to get in its way. But on top of that, I think the Despiser is more important. He's absolutely more important to *me*." Passion mounted in him. He did not raise his voice, but it thrummed with intensity nonetheless, with the authority of earned conviction. His whole body seemed to imply imminent wild magic. "Ever since I first came here—ever since he and the Creator picked me—my life has been about Lord Foul. He scares me worse than any ordinary death, even if the people I love most are the ones who do the dying. I have to face that. I have to do something about it.

"Sure, if we could stop the Worm, Foul would be stuck in his prison. But we can't, and he won't. Think about that. Think about setting Despite loose in eternity, where it can pollute every new creation just like it's polluted this one. That's bad enough. Hellfire, *that's bad enough*! But it could become even worse. If he gets his hands on Jeremiah, he'll try to trade places with the Creator. He'll try to make a prison that will put an end to the very *possibility* of creation. He'll wipe out everything that has ever lived, everything that ever might live, every conceivable world.

"If he can do that, *eternity* will become the kind of wasteland we've only seen in *caesures*. Then there won't be anything anywhere ever again. Nothing except scorn until even Lord Foul's heart breaks."

Amid the shocked silence of the company and Linden's dismay, Jeremiah asked like sneering, "So your solution is to take me *closer* to him?"

Covenant wheeled his mount to face the boy. "Hell, Jeremiah, he can get you anywhere. All he needs is the right kind of grass and one mistake. Then you'll give him whatever he wants. That won't change if we're a hundred leagues from here fighting the Worm. And you'll never get a chance to find out what how you feel and what you can do are good for."

Then he turned Mishio Massima toward Linden. His eyes blazed with need. "Linden, I'm sorry. I have to do this. Eventually we all have to face the things that scare us most. And I'm not actually convinced that the Worm can't be stopped. I just don't think *we* can stop it. There's more going on here than just the Worm and Lord Foul and Jeremiah and more enemies than we can count. I don't know what it is, but I don't believe—I don't choose to believe—that the way things look to us right now is the whole story. We have two white gold rings and the Staff of Law and Jeremiah's talent. We have friends who have never let us down. All of that has to be good for something."

He might as well have added, *And betimes some wonder is wrought to redeem us.*

But he did not wait for a reply. The naked chagrin on Linden's face seemed to drive him away. Again he turned his mount.

To the Ironhand and her Swordmainnir, he said, "So, yes. I do want to go to Mount Thunder. In spite of, or maybe because of, all the obstacles you mentioned. That's not the mistake I was talking about. The mistake would be to go there the way damn Foul expects."

In spite of their deliberate dispassion, the approval of the *Haruchai* was plain.

Rime Coldspray held up her hands again. "Enough, Timewarden." She and her comrades studied him with a mixture of rue and wonder. Cabledarm and Latebirth grinned openly. "We cannot protest such passion. For us, any deed which can be attempted is preferable to one which cannot. If your purpose is clear to you, it will suffice for us. Unless," she added, "Linden Giantfriend reasons against it. Then we will heed her as we have heeded you, and will await the outcome between you."

Linden hardly noticed that everyone was looking at her now. She hardly recognized the confusion of dread and hope in Jeremiah's eyes. The light of the *krill* and Covenant's extravagance filled her mind with gibbering.

No. Gibbering and carrion-eaters. Not She Who Must Not Be Named. I can't.

And not Lord Foul. Not Jeremiah. *His worth to the Despiser is beyond measure.* I can't take that chance.

Nevertheless the bright gem of the dagger held her. Covenant's gaze held her. She had never been able to refuse him. From the moment of their first meeting on Haven Farm, he had compelled her by simply being who he was.

Feeling bitter and beaten, she said slowly, "Don't stop now. Tell us how you think we can get into Mount Thunder. Tell us how you think that's even possible."

He was still her husband.

A sigh passed among the Giants.

"Mom," Jeremiah groaned: a low sound that did not distinguish between protest and relief.

Covenant's eyes did not let Linden go. He spoke to the company as if he were answering only her.

"I've been inside Mount Thunder twice, and both times I went in by the front door. From the Upper Land along Treacher's Gorge to Warrenbridge, then into the catacombs. *That's* the mistake. Foul is bound to be expecting us. We need another way in."

"Indeed, ur-Lord," remarked Branl. "It is certain that other passages exist. One enabled the quest for the Staff of Law to evade Drool Rockworm. Another brought Cavewights and your son to assail us. But such paths are known only to the Cavewights. Also they are perilously small, ill-suited to Giants."

"Right." Covenant did not glance at the Humbled. All of his attention was fixed on Linden. "We'll have to try a different approach.

"Forget the Upper Land. If the Sandgorgons and the *skurj* were cutting into Salva Gildenbourne back when the Ardent brought us out of the Lost Deep, they'll be near Treacher's Gorge by now. Even if we get into the Wightwarrens ahead of them, they'll be right behind us.

"I think we should try climbing up from the Defiles Course."

No, Linden repeated. She could not stop herself—and could not find her voice to tell him that he was wrong about her. *No.* What he said made sense. Nothing made sense. She Who Must Not Be Named was too strong for her.

"The waters are corrupt," objected Branl.

"Well, sure," Covenant countered. Every word was addressed to Linden. "But they must have receded by now. The Soulsease has been pouring into the Lost Deep for days. Until all those chasms and caverns fill up, there won't be any water coming out. Or not much," he amended. "There are probably other sources, but they're nothing like the Soulsease."

Branl was not deflected. "Also the path is unknown. Uncounted millennia of slime and filth and dire poisons will clog the channel. The inhalation of the vapors will cause sickness and death. The Giants will not be spared. The *Haruchai* will not."

At last Covenant turned away as if Linden's silence and dismay had defeated him. He sounded sour and forlorn as he retorted, "I'm not worried about the damn *vapors*. Linden has her Staff. We'll be fine. And we'll have another advantage. We'll be close to water.

"Hellfire!" The scar on his forehead seemed to bleed silver. It squeezed out of his old wound like sweat. "We'll be close to the lurker. If we need help, we'll get it. That monster has already staked its life on the alliance. We can do the same.

"Linden's fate is 'writ in water.' The Ardent told us that. What the hell else do you think he meant? The lurker can't reach the Upper Land, but the Defiles Course opens into Lifeswallower. That's where Horrim Carabal *thrives*."

But Branl did not relent. He and Stave had already shown their approval. Now the last of the Humbled seemed determined to judge Covenant's intentions accurately, as if he agreed with Linden.

"And also there is the matter of the Cords. They have been conveyed to Revelstone to seek the aid of the Masters. Should they succeed, that aid will not find us at the Defiles Course."

"Don't you think I know that?" Covenant snapped. "But they can't help us. If Bhapa and Pahni succeed, the Masters will head for Treacher's Gorge—where they'll be slaughtered. They can't do anything against *skurj* and Sandgorgons. For their sakes, we have to hope the Cords don't convince them.

"Whatever happens, we'll have to find the way by ourselves."

Writ in water. Finally those words reached Linden. She remembered how Covenant had rescued her from her terror of She Who Must Not Be Named. He had gone to that extreme for her: her husband who loved her. How could she fault him for still being a man who went to extremes? When extremes were needed? And she knew that he was right about Jeremiah, although the truth appalled her. Lord Foul could reach him anywhere. The Despiser did not need proximity.

While Covenant faced the company with his needs and his pain and his severe convictions, Linden found her voice. But she did not speak to him: she spoke to her son.

"What do you think, Jeremiah?" Her voice shook. "This has got to be harder for you than anyone else." He had said as much himself. He had no instrument of power. No weapon, no prowess, no great strength. "Are you willing to go to Mount Thunder and take your chances?"

Jeremiah's attention seemed to leap at her. "Sure," he returned as if he had never questioned himself. "Why not? Otherwise we're all just dead. If it's too much for me, I can always hide again. Lord Foul will still be able to use me, but I won't have to feel it. Not like I did with Kastenessen, and he only got me because I didn't expect it."

He gave the impression that he meant, Maybe I don't have to be useless. Covenant said he needs us. But Linden heard more. As if Jeremiah had spoken to her like the *Haruchai*, mind to mind, she heard him say, I want Lord Foul *dead*.

Oh, my son—

"Linden?" Covenant asked. Now he sounded deliberately neutral, as if he thought that he had already put too much pressure on her. "It's up to you."

From him also, she heard more than he said.

I know what I have to do.

I can't do it without you.

She recognized the knots that defined his face, the lines like cuts, the clench of understanding and regret. How often had he regarded her like that? When he knew what the Land's need required, and regretted it for her sake rather than his own?

Eventually we all have to face the things that scare us most.

A flick of grit forced her to shut her eyes for a moment. She felt suddenly parched in spite of the lingering taste of treasure-berries; scorched by the heat of Covenant's gaze. She had ashes in her veins instead of blood. God, he was a cruel man some-times. Cruel and terrible and irrefusable.

Barely able to clear her throat, she said, "You aren't just my husband," Thomas of my heart. "You're Thomas Covenant the Unbeliever. And Jeremiah is willing. I'll go with you as far as I can."

At that moment, the sudden lift of relief and hope and even love in Covenant's gaze did not touch her. And she ignored the reactions of the Giants. Their Ironhand had already given her assent. Instead she remembered Berek Halfhand among the Dead.

He may be freed only by one who is compelled by rage, and contemptuous of consequence.

The Lord-Fatherer's pronouncement made her want to weep. He may have been trying to warn Covenant rather than her. He may have been describing Jeremiah.

Or he may have seen the Land's doom in all three of them.

ಞ

A second circle of wild magic. A second rush of disorientation. A second reflexive response from Linden's wedding band. Then the horses and the Giants pounded as if they were deranged down the bottom of a ravine that Linden almost recognized.

Weathered hills rose on either side. The cut between them was comparatively shallow, a crooked trough wide enough for the company. The sand and age-smoothed stones of the bottom provided an easy surface for the mounts and the Swordmainnir as they pounded along, slowing with every stride. And ahead of them—

Black in the unnatural twilight of midday, a stream slid past a widening fan of sand punctuated by the jut of a few boulders. Complaining against rock on the far side, the water flowed down a small canyon that arced around the swath of sand.

As Hyn's gait eased, and Linden's nerves began to recover from the mad reel of translation, she realized that she did indeed know this place. Here the company had rested days ago. Here she had rejoined her companions after Covenant had retrieved her from nightmares of She Who Must Not Be Named. Here the Ardent had deliv-ered a feast, and had lost his grip on name and use and life. And back there, behind her now, lay the ridge of fouled gypsum where Liand and then Galt had been slain, and Anele had perished; where Esmer had passed away: the crest crowned by cairns. In this low canyon, Covenant had ridden away with Branl and Clyme as if he did not want her love. It was a place of loss and struggle and butchery, a black omen.

The Ranyhyn must have chosen this destination. As far as she knew, Covenant did not have such control over his translations.

Fortunately the company had arrived in a region of calmer winds. The Worm seemed far away, as if it had lapsed back into abstraction.

As Mishio Massima slowed, Branl took the *krill* from Covenant, held it up to light the way. Near the water's edge, the horses stamped to a halt. Heaving for air as if they had run for hours instead of moments, the Ironhand and her comrades stopped. Briefly silver glared like frenzy in their eyes. But within moments they began to breathe more easily. As they looked around, they nodded their recognition.

At the forefront of the company, Covenant practically fell out of his saddle, tottering like a man on the verge of prostration. But his unsteadiness was vertigo, not fatigue. He began to look stronger as he recovered his balance.

Still mounted, Linden did not meet his gaze. She was not ready. She still felt stricken by his intentions and her own acquiescence—and by her son's peril.

An awkward shrug clenched his shoulders. He left her to herself. Scanning the Giants, he drawled, "Don't take this the wrong way, but you all look like you need a bath."

Coldspray gave him a lugubrious frown. "We are clogged with grime, Timewarden, made filthy by long exertion. Indeed, we are altogether unlovely. How might your observation be interpreted wrongly?"

He blinked at her as if he could not think of a response. Then he muttered in feigned disgust, "Giants." More loudly, he remarked, "God knows *I* need one. Maybe my eyes are going, but I can still smell myself." To Jeremiah, he added, "Come on. Let's at least try to get clean. Maybe we'll feel better."

Jeremiah had kept his seat on Khelen as if he were impatient to continue the journey. He avoided Linden's eyes as she avoided Covenant's. But he did not refuse. After only a moment's hesitation, he dropped to the sand. Together he and Covenant splashed into the stream.

Linden held her breath until she saw that Covenant did not take Jeremiah beyond his depth. When could her son have learned how to swim? Then she looked away and made an effort to come to terms with her dismay.

It rose in her, a pressure that felt too strong to be contained. Covenant was taking Jeremiah to Mount Thunder. To Lord Foul. The hills crouched like threats on either side of the ravine, and on the far bank of the watercourse. The sunless stream looked more like vitriol than water. Beneath its vexed surface, it seemed to imply malice. Overhead the stars glittered as if they were trying to warn her.

If Jeremiah thought that anger and bitterness would preserve him, he was wrong.

Around Linden, the Giants set aside their swords, then began loosening their cataphracts, shrugging the armor off their shoulders. Of no one in particular, Latebirth asked, "Does the Timewarden mislike his odor? I cannot discern it. My own aroma precludes other scents."

"Aroma, forsooth," snorted Halewhole Bluntfist amid a chorus of muted chor-tling. "If that is aroma, I am the suzerain of the *Elohim*. For my part, I do not scruple to name it 'reek.' "

While the other Swordmainnir jested, Frostheart Grueburn came to stand beside Linden. From Hyn's back, Linden only had to lift her head a little to regard Grue-burn.

In contrast to her comrades, Grueburn looked grave, almost somber. Softly she said, "Linden Giantfriend, perhaps you will consent to speak with me apart from these coistrels. A matter weighs upon my heart. You will do a kindness if you allow me to unburden it."

"All right." Linden's clothes were still clean, scrubbed by the benison of Caerroil Wildwood's power. Even her hair was clean. And she welcomed any distraction from herself. "Let's talk."

As she slipped down from Hyn's back, Stave and Branl also dismounted. At once, the four Ranyhyn turned away from the stream and followed the ravine, taking Cov-enant's steed with them. No doubt they sought forage.

Frostheart Grueburn loomed above Linden. With her back to the *krill*, the Sword-main looked benighted, mired in shadows. A lift of her arm suggested the direction taken by the horses.

Linden glanced at Stave. "Keep an eye on Jeremiah?"

Stave shook his head. "Branl will do so."

The Humbled was headed toward the stream. There he stopped, watching Cove-nant and Jeremiah.

"All right," Linden said again. To Grueburn, she added, "If you don't mind Stave's company."

"My concern is private," replied the woman. "It is not secret. Stave Rockbrother's companionship is welcome at all times."

Linden nodded. With Stave a few paces behind her, she accompanied Frostheart Grueburn up the ravine. At every step, she had to resist an impulse to stamp at the sand with her Staff. Did Covenant expect her to face the things that scared her most? She did not know how.

Perhaps a dozen Giantish strides from her comrades, Grueburn halted. For sev-eral moments, she stood with her face raised to the sky as if she were studying the stars, or listening to them. When she lowered her head to look at Linden—and past Linden at Stave—her aura was troubled.

"Linden Giantfriend," she said quietly, "my thoughts are awkward. I am uncertain how to speak of them."

"You're a Giant," Linden murmured. "You'll find a way."

Grueburn offered a strained smile. She seemed to shake herself. "Toward you," she confessed, "I feel more than friendship. Amid the perils of the Lost Deep, and at other times, I have cared for you, as you know. For that reason among many others, your place in my heart is great."

When the woman paused, Linden said nothing. Grueburn was not waiting for a response. Rather she was hunting for a way to broach her concern.

Finally Grueburn began. "Some days past, while we traveled together after the Timewarden had parted from us, I chanced to stand with you while you and Stave Rockbrother spoke. Together you considered questions of Desecration."

Like a slap of wind, Stave observed, "Our words were intended for each other alone, Frostheart Grueburn."

"Yet I heard them. From that time to this, I have respected that they were not for me. Nevertheless my thoughts have turned often to matters of Desecration."

Linden swallowed a groan. She did not want to talk about such things.

To Stave, Grueburn continued, "Here I do not ask you to reveal what you have foreseen, or indeed what your insights may be. I do not seek to probe your heart. I wish to unveil my own."

Her response seemed to satisfy Stave.

Frostheart Grueburn returned her attention to Linden. Silver from the *krill* caught the lines of the Giant's mien. With an edge in her voice, she said, "You stand at the center of all that has transpired. I do not deem it unlikely that you will continue to do so. Your deeds are potent to cause some futures while ending others. And I say again that you are dear to me. Therefore my spirits were lifted to soaring by the outcome of your union with Covenant Timewarden. I saw gladness in you, the gladness and relief which dismiss Desecration. But now—

"Ah, now, Linden Giantfriend, some new darkness hovers in you. For that reason, I am troubled. If you will consent to speak of your concerns, you will ease my own. Comprehension will open my ears so that I am again able to hear joy."

In your present state, Chosen, Desecration lies ahead of you. It does not crowd at your back.

Linden bit down on her lip; steadied herself on that small pain. Then she countered, "What are you afraid of?"

Grueburn sighed. "Chiefly I fear that you sail a course which leads to the desecration of yourself. To my sight, it appears that you confront an impossible conundrum. You are a mother. You must preserve your son. Yet you cannot. You cannot ward him from the Despiser's malice. Nor can you ward him from the world's end. His doom—if he is doomed—lies beyond your intervention. His despair—if he falls into despair—is not yours to relieve. And in these straits, it may be that your distress is increased by your union with Covenant Timewarden, for how can a mother know gladness with her husband when her son is in peril? I fear the effect of this conundrum. Linden Giantfriend, I fear it acutely."

While the woman spoke, Linden turned away. Beat after beat, she thudded one end of her Staff into the sand. She wanted to rebuff Grueburn. The Giant saw her too clearly. Perhaps they all did. But she had talked about *trust* with Jeremiah; about the implications of withholding the truth. And the Swordmainnir were her friends. They were in as much danger, and had as much to lose.

Facing the darkness, Linden replied, "I don't know what to tell you. I don't know how to explain it, even to myself." Her horror at the idea of approaching Mount Thunder was too intimate to be named. "But I can tell you this much. Thomas wants to walk right up to his worst fear and look it in the eye, but I'm not like that. Lord Foul isn't my worst fear," no matter how much she loved Jeremiah. "And the Worm isn't. Even having to watch while everyone and everything I care about dies isn't. As long as Thomas is still alive, none of that is inevitable.

"My *worst* fear"—this was as close as she could come to complete honesty—"is that there may actually be something I could do, and I won't be brave enough to do it."

When her father had killed himself, she had been too young and little to stop him; but years later, when her mother had begged for death, Linden had done what her mother asked of her. Eventually she had learned to believe that there were worse things than Desecration. Letting the pain *go on* was worse. It had to be healed. If it could not be healed, it had to be extirpated. And if it could not be healed or cut out, it had to be ended in some other way.

That "some other way" was her real conundrum. And her greatest fear was that she did not have it in her to resolve the contradiction.

She knew how Kevin Landwaster must have felt.

For a time, Frostheart Grueburn and Stave answered her with silence. What could they have said? She was who she was. Her fears were her own. But then Stave said like a man who had never known a moment's doubt, "It is written in water, Linden. Deeds are not stones. Fears are not. And even stone may fail. No outcome is certain."

Before Linden could think of a response, Grueburn began to chuckle. "Well said, Stave Rockbrother. As ever, Linden Giantfriend misesteems herself. She has restored joy to my ears, though she does not hear it."

Then she added, "Accept my thanks, Linden Giantfriend. You have comforted me. I regret only that you are not likewise comforted."

At once, the woman turned away. Perhaps she sensed that Linden wanted to be alone; that Linden needed time to accept what she had heard and said. Still chuckling, Grueburn went to rejoin her comrades. But Stave remained.

He said nothing further. For that, Linden was grateful. His presence was enough to remind her that she was not alone. No other answer would suffice unless she found it for herself.

ᔕᗢᑐ

T ime brought her no clarity; but after a while, she felt steady enough to return to the company. While the stars were dying, they had called to her nerves like keening; like bright supplications. But now they were not vanishing from the heavens. Perhaps as a result, they looked less forlorn to her. They seemed to gaze down almost hopefully, as if they had found something to believe in.

Sighing, Linden rested a hand on Stave's shoulder to thank him. Then she began to make her way back to her companions.

Before she reached them, Covenant came to meet her, still dripping from his immersion. His face was full of shadows because the light of the *krill* had shifted: Branl had taken the dagger to a nearby hillcrest upstream. Spectral as the elucidation of dreams, argent shone on Covenant's silver hair but left his features in darkness.

At once, the Swordmainnir withdrew. Some splashed into the water to bathe. Others moved away as if they were making room for Linden and her husband.

While she wondered what she could say to him, he took her in his arms. Holding her close, he murmured, "I'm sorry, Linden." His voice was little more than a husky rasp. "I feel like I've hurt you, but I'm not sure how.

"I expected you to argue."

She let him hug her for a moment. Then she returned his clasp. "I've been arguing with myself."

He stepped back enough to look into her eyes. "What about?"

She tried to meet his scrutiny, but her gaze slid away as if she were ashamed. "I understand what you want to do," she told him with a rasp of her own. "I don't have any better ideas. But you didn't explain what you want from me."

Or from Jeremiah.

Covenant's manner said, I don't want anything from you. I just want you. I just need you. But aloud he admitted, "I know. I couldn't. I can't. It's all so *vague*." He rapped his forehead with his knuckles. "I'm clear about what I have to do. What I have to try to do. But everything else is just impressions, instincts. It's not an accident that you and Jeremiah are here. It's not an accident that we're here together. Hell," he snorted, "I wouldn't be here at all without you. But I have no idea what it means."

He hesitated for a moment. Then he squared his shoulders, shook Linden gently.

"The only thing I'm sure of is that *this*—the three of us together, with friends to help us—is not what Lord Foul wants. We've already done things he couldn't have foreseen. Now I think we *are* something he can't foresee."

He almost eased her. She believed in him: now she could almost believe him. But she was still afraid—and she had not told him what she feared. She had not named it to herself.

"That's not enough," she said awkwardly.

I'm not enough.

His voice hardened. "Then I'll say something else." It set like cooling iron. "If none of this works out—if everything goes to hell no matter what we do—if the worst turns out to be worse than we can imagine—you might want to remember that we didn't *start* it. It's the Despiser's doing. We couldn't have prevented anything. All we've ever done is react to what he does.

"Even if this whole world only exists in our minds—even if damn Foul is just an expression of a part of ourselves we don't like—we can't be blamed for it. We didn't *make* ourselves. We were born into lives we didn't choose, parents we didn't choose, problems we didn't choose. We aren't responsible for that. We're only responsible for what we do about it.

"If what we do isn't enough, too bad. Let the Creator worry about what happens next. If he doesn't care, at least he can't accuse us of anything."

Gentle as a caress, Covenant cupped his palm to the side of Linden's neck and offered to kiss her.

For a moment, she resisted. He had not given her enough. Nothing would ever be enough. But he had given her what he had. And he was Thomas Covenant, her husband and lover. As much as possible, he was even her protector. And he would do what he could for Jeremiah. She could not refuse him. She did not want to refuse him.

While she kissed him, she thought, Thomas of my heart. I can't do this.

But she imagined that perhaps she could. As long as he never let her go.

⟨∞⟩

L ong moments passed before she found the strength to step back. She was not done with Covenant. She needed his touch, his arms, his mouth. She could have held him, and been held, as long as time remained in the world. But she was also Jeremiah's mother. Her heart was divided.

In this, she knew, she was not alone. All hearts were divided, Covenant's as much as hers. She would not have been surprised to learn that his desire for her and his concern for the Land and his need to confront Lord Foul threatened to tear him apart whenever he faltered. But her divisions were more personal. And when she scanned the company—the Giants washing in the stream and those waiting nearby—she saw no sign of her son.

Her stomach tightened reflexively. At once, she turned to Stave. "Where's Jeremiah? You said that Branl would watch him."

"He does so." Stave nodded stolidly toward the shining on the rise beyond Linden. "The Chosen-son parted from the company to wend upstream. Branl followed at a slight distance. He does not neglect his charge."

Linden flung a glance at Covenant; but he shook his head. "He didn't say anything. I tried to get him talking, but he had too much on his mind."

If something had happened to her son, she would have felt it. Surely she would have felt it?

"Beyond the hillside," Stave continued, "the boy has discovered a stretch of grass among sheltered stones. It bears some resemblance to that which Anele had cause to fear. There he stands, offering demands and imprecations. Yet naught transpires. For that reason, Branl does not intervene.

"It appears that your son does not partake of the vulnerability or flaw which exposed Anele to Corruption. We conclude that the boy has inherited only Anele's openness to Kastenessen—a peril which no longer threatens him. His wish to encounter evil is foolhardy, but it does not endanger him."

"Or," Linden countered over her shoulder, "Lord Foul just hasn't taken advantage of it yet."

She was already running.

Boulders like raised fists complicated her path. Possibilities reeled through her. Stave might be right. The gifts and curses which Jeremiah had received from Anele might have strict limits. She was not lorewise enough to know. But she could imagine other explanations.

Kastenessen could have used his ability to take Jeremiah at any time, whenever the boy stood on bare dirt. Yet the *Elohim* had not done so, despite his driving pain and fury. Instead he had waited, bided his time until the opportunity he desired presented itself.

If he could exercise such restraint, Lord Foul could do so with ease. His malice was colder than Kastenessen's—and far more calculating. The Despiser had allowed Anele to walk on rough grass unpossessed for a considerable distance during Linden's flight from Mithil Stonedown.

Yet naught transpires. Linden did not doubt Stave—or Branl. Nevertheless the danger was real. It was always real.

And Jeremiah did not understand it. He thought that he would be able to defend himself as long as he was not taken by surprise.

The slope ahead of her was not steep. And she was too frightened to feel tired. She should have been able to ascend easily, swiftly. Yet she grew weaker as she scrambled upward. Something profound within her had shifted. Her surrender to Covenant's intentions had diminished her. The strength drained from her limbs at every step. Her breathing was a hoarse gasp as she gained the crest.

Branl stood there, gazing at her with only argent in his flat eyes. He might have said something if she had given him a chance, but she forced herself to hasten past him; downward.

She felt Stave only a few strides behind her. Covenant followed more slowly, accompanied by Rime Coldspray and Frostheart Grueburn. But Linden ignored them. Her attention was fixed on Jeremiah.

He stood in a hollow between hills too old and worn to glower down at him. And he had indeed found grass: a patch of saw-edged grey-green blades growing stubbornly where a cluster of rocks had collected soil from the erosion of the surrounding slopes. In the ghost-light of Loric's gem, those blades looked sharp enough to cut. Everything around Jeremiah was blades: the etched hillsides, the ragged edges of the rocks, the black lift and slice of the stream. To Linden, he resembled a child in the midst of shattered glass, heedless of the danger, about to take a step which would shred his soles.

He did not see her. She had come from the south, and he was facing the northward crease where the hills slumped to close the hollow. His head was bowed in concentration. Waves of tension made his shoulders twitch: the muscles of his back bunched and released. Between his teeth, he muttered words which did not reach Linden.

She forced herself to slow down. Yet naught transpires. Stave was right. Branl had seen no reason to take action because there was no reason. Jeremiah was only himself: taut with anger and dread, desperate to prove his worth, but untouched.

She stopped a few steps away. "Jeremiah," she panted. "Honey." God, she felt so *weak*— Unmade. As if her refusal to name her greatest fear had been her only source of strength. "That's enough. You tried. You can stop now."

Stave arrived at her side. Covenant, the Ironhand, and Grueburn crossed the rise toward her. Coming to bear witness—

Branl trailed behind them, spreading the *krill*'s light as far as possible.

Jeremiah lifted his head. Keeping his back to his mother, he made a scything gesture with his halfhand.

Without warning, a silent shock jolted the hills. For one small splinter of time, the world's Laws seemed to pause. Linden's heart did not beat. Her lungs did not stretch for air. The stream hesitated in its course, poised and motionless. Stave became one more stone in the hollow. Covenant hung between one downward step and the next. Coldspray and Grueburn froze.

Then a second shock released the hollow. Linden's pulse hit like a blow on an anvil. Covenant lurched for balance. Stave readied himself.

Instantly the air became attar, thick as the smoke of burning flesh, cloying as an inferno of incense. The heavens leaned down on Linden as if they had become lead. Even Stave flinched. Coldspray or Grueburn stumbled. One of them caught Covenant. Branl started downward with the *krill* raised.

In Lord Foul's voice, Jeremiah announced like a grinding millstone, "It may interest you to know, fools and servants, that your ploy has achieved its purpose. Your edifice stands, a worthy emblem of your wish to oppose me. Yet even there, your deeds work against you. Deprived of *Elohim*, the Worm hastens onward. It *hastens*, fools! The hour of my many triumphs approaches. You cannot thwart it."

"Branl!" Covenant gasped. "The *krill*. Give me the *krill*!"

The Despiser and Jeremiah ignored him. They spoke only to Linden.

"Nonetheless," the crushing voice continued, "this callow whelp thinks to challenge me. *Me!* As guerdon for his puerile valor, I have given him a gift which will make him wise in the subtleties of despair. When I have need of him, I will claim him, and no endeavor of yours will suffice to redeem him."

If your son serves me, he will do so in your presence.

"And you, frail woman—" Lord Foul's mirth filled the vale. "You have become the daughter of my heart. In you, I am well pleased. Ere the end, you also will serve me.

"Thus all things conduce to my desires."

Covenant snatched the dagger from Branl. "Is that what you think, Foul? Have you forgotten what we can do to you? Have you forgotten we're *coming* for you?"

"Forgotten, wretch?" retorted the Despiser, bitter and gleeful. "I rely upon it. I forget nothing. I am prepared for you. If you think to confront me, you will discover that your efforts harm only yourself."

Covenant did not reply. With the *krill* gripped in both fists, he advanced like an incarnation of wrath.

Instinctively Linden barred his way. She had no idea what his intentions might be. If she had taken time to think, she would have realized that he would not hurt Jeremiah. He was bluffing again. But she did not think. Jeremiah was her *son*. And she was capable of responses which Covenant could not match.

Whatever you do to my son, she had promised the Despiser long ago, *I'm going to tear your heart out.* Now she knew that she would not. She was not the woman she had once been. Events since her arrival in the Land had taught her expensive lessons. Covenant was still teaching her.

Like Gallows Howe, the world had more important needs than retribution.

Nevertheless she did not hesitate. She had made other promises as well, ones that she knew how to keep. With a sweep of her Staff, she unveiled Earthpower and Law.

Her health-sense was precise. Her fire could be equally precise: as refined as a scalpel in spite of its blackness. Just for an instant, she sent it gyring skyward while she prepared it for her purpose; confirmed that it was exact. Then she swung it like the crack of a whip at her son.

It poured through Jeremiah without touching him. She had tuned her theurgy to the pitch and timbre of Lord Foul's malice rather than of Jeremiah's body, Jeremiah's appalled mind. Her dark flame struck only the Despiser.

She could do so because Lord Foul's mastery was of an entirely different kind than the *croyel*'s. That monster had merely reached into Jeremiah; fed on him; used him: it had not existed within him. And his defenses—his dissociation—had protected him. But now he had arisen from his graves. He inhabited himself. That change enabled Linden to distinguish between his reclaimed self and the force which ruled him.

She may have been as frail as Lord Foul believed. She may indeed have become his daughter in despair. Still she was Linden Avery the Chosen, Jeremiah's mother and Covenant's wife.

In a burst of conflagration, she banished the Despiser. His malevolence burst and vanished like a punctured bubble. Intangible gales swept away the stench of attar. The laughter of broken rocks dissipated until it was entirely gone.

Like a discarded puppet, Jeremiah collapsed to his hands and knees.

Linden reached him a heartbeat later, dropped her Staff, flung her arms around him. Through his skin, she felt his warmth and dismay, his wholeness, his horror. He strained to breathe as if his lungs were clogged with the sweet, sick odor of a body arrayed for burial.

"Mom," he croaked. "Oh, Mom. I can feel the Worm. I can *feel* it. It's going up a cliff. A cliff! And it's going fast. Like the cliff was nothing."

The Despiser's gift.

Shivers that began in the marrow of Jeremiah's bones spread through him. Linden hugged him tightly, but could not still his trembling.

Lord Foul had taught her son to fear him.

3.

Summoned to Oppose

Another race through the interstices between instants and leagues brought the company to a twisted heave of hills that Linden had never seen before.

She had no idea how far Covenant's eldritch circle had carried the riders and the Giants. She could be sure only that she and her companions were still on the Lower Land. As Hyn slowed her wild gallop, following Rallyn's lead with Hynyn and Khelen, Linden saw Landsdrop massive on her left, thrusting its crooked rims thousands of feet above its foothills. And in the distance on her right, she caught troubled glimpses of water, grey and dim as tarnished silver: Sarangrave Flat between the barricade of the cliffs and deeper mire of Lifeswallower, the Great Swamp.

Overhead the stars were no longer visible. Thunderheads like clenched fists battered each other back and forth between the cramped horizons, occluding the sky. The weather tumbled in confusion, affronted by the Worm's passing far away. With every sunless hour, the air grew cooler.

Abruptly the company plunged down a steep hillside. Skidding on loose shale, the Giants floundered to keep their balance. Hyn locked her knees for a moment and slid. Then she lifted into a light-footed prance that carried Linden safely.

Jeremiah reeled on Khelen, but not because the young stallion had jostled him. Ever since he had regained his feet after his encounter with Lord Foul, the boy had wobbled as if some of his sinews had been cut. His eyes, always changeable, had acquired a nauseated hue. If they reflected his mind, his thoughts were a spew of vomit.

Covenant also reeled. As Mishio Massima lurched to a halt, he pitched from the saddle. But that was an effect of vertigo. Every exertion of wild magic seemed to cast him into a whirlwind.

On more level ground at the foot of the slope, the company gathered among a few patches of scrub oak clinging to the thin soil between stubborn tufts of grass and weeds. A more gentle hillside lay ahead; yet no one proposed to hurry onward. Covenant had already returned the *krill* to Branl. Now he folded cross-legged to the dirt, holding his head like a man trying to remember who he was. As before, the Swordmainnir labored for air as if they had been carrying monoliths on their backs.

Almost at once, heavy raindrops struck Linden's face. Spatters hit randomly around the area, raising small bursts of dust where they found dirt. Soon there would be more. Torrents were coming, a monsoon downpour entirely out of place in this season of the Lower Land.

Wincing in anticipation, she nudged Hyn closer to Khelen.

At the same time, Covenant heaved himself upright. Unsteady on his numb feet, he made his way among the Giants toward Linden and Jeremiah. Droplets ran down his cheeks like sweat.

Carefully he asked, "How are you doing, Jeremiah?"

The boy glared past Covenant. He avoided Linden's concern. "Stop worrying about me," he muttered. "I'm fine. You can't do anything about it."

His hands still trembled as if he were feverish.

Covenant looked questions at Linden.

She studied her son. Superficially he was undamaged: that was plain. The distress that appeared to disarticulate him was emotional, not physical. Only his spirit had been harmed.

He had spent too much of his life hidden: a powerful defense which had both shielded and hampered him. Crouching in his graves had preserved him in some ways, but had not taught him how to weather the Despiser's virulence. Possession and vicious scorn had withered his attempt at defiance.

From Hyn's back, Linden reached out to touch Jeremiah's arm, get his attention. "Is it that bad, honey? Can you talk about it?"

She wanted to ask what had impelled him to risk exposing himself to the Despiser, but she suspected that she already knew the answer. He felt useless: he needed to do something that would help him believe in himself again. And Covenant had given him an oblique form of permission or encouragement.

Eventually we all have to face the things that scare us most.

Jeremiah glared at her for a moment, then turned his head away. To the coming storm, he muttered, "You don't understand. You don't see it. I can't stop. All that power— It isn't just terrible. It's more *real* than we are. We're all going to die, and I get to watch."

Scattered raindrops struck at Linden like pebbles. Fiercely she wiped her face.

"You're right, Jeremiah. I *don't* understand. But I still know how it feels. I'm not any braver than you are, or stronger, or better. My *God*, Jeremiah. I let a crazy man stick a knife in Thomas because I couldn't make myself try to stop him. *Turiya* Raver touched me, just *touched* me, and I got so scared that I was gone for days. And *moksha* actually possessed me. I know what that *feels* like."

How much of her life had she spent ashamed? Despising herself?

"But I'm still here for the same reason you are. We aren't alone. We are not alone."

"Indeed," Cirrus Kindwind confirmed softly. "We have spoken of this, Chosenson. Giants affirm that joy is in the ears that hear because the telling of our tales binds us one to another. Speaking and hearing, we share our efforts to give our lives meaning."

The rain was falling harder. Soon it would be falling too hard to hear anything; say anything.

Through a slash of water, Jeremiah whispered, "But you don't *see* it. I don't mean anything."

His misery closed Linden's throat. She had no answer for him. She believed in Covenant, but she was afraid to believe in herself. Her greatest fear—

While she stumbled inwardly, Covenant put his hand on her thigh. "We should get out of here." Slapping raindrops obscured the severity of his mien, the lines of his willing compassion. "Maybe we can escape the worst of this storm."

As if he had triggered it, lightning shrieked overhead. Thunder made the air shudder.

"To my sight," Rime Coldspray remarked, pitching her voice to carry, "the coming downpour does not appear extensive. Nonetheless it will be extreme. The Timewarden counsels wisely."

"Branl!" Covenant barked over his shoulder. "How far have we come?"

The Humbled sat Rallyn with the *krill* raised in one hand and Longwrath's sword leaning on his shoulder. "Our translations have increased, ur-Lord," he replied. "We have traversed nigh unto thirty leagues, and have lost but a portion of the afternoon."

Stave nodded in confirmation.

Linden tried to remember how much ground the Ardent had covered when he had conveyed the company out of the Lost Deep. Another glare and shout among the clouds distracted her. The rain was becoming a deluge.

Cursing, Covenant started back toward the head of the company. Incipient torrents belabored his head and shoulders.

At once, Branl dismounted. The flamberge he handed to Onyx Stonemage. With Covenant and Loric's dagger, he strode beyond the company.

Rain hammered the ground. It beat the dirt to mud. Clotted rills squirmed past the feet of the Giants. Linden felt herself sinking under the weight of the downpour, hunching over her heart. Her son needed help, and she had nothing to give him.

The Giants braced themselves for a sprint which would have no perceptible beginning: it would simply come over them somewhere within the blank space created by wild magic and Loric's blade. Hyn tossed her head, repositioned her hooves. Khelen snorted a warning at Jeremiah. Lightning ripped through the gloom. Thunder roared against the cliff like the wrath of mountains.

Branl moved swiftly, carrying Covenant. Covenant's line of fire defied the torrents as if dirt and rain were fuel. Flames danced like Wraiths on Linden's wedding band. Reflexively she held the Staff as far away from her ring as she could.

When the world vanished, her heart plunged into darkness. She and her companions were taking Jeremiah to Mount Thunder.

To the Despiser.

He would relish her son.

ﾛﾛ

W ithout transition, the horses and the Giants were running as if their lungs would burst. They strained at a steep slope, labored forward against the obstructions of their mortality. Then they pitched down a hillside, plummeting like a landslide.

There was no rain. The dusk of late afternoon held the world under a sparse sprinkle of stars. Every breath sucked at a humid miasma of putrefaction and worse poisons.

On the left some distance away rose a high cliff sheer as a cut slab. And water lay *there*, on the right: the rank wetland of the Sarangrave, brandishing its tortured trees and twisted scrub and fetor. Branches writhed like the beckoning limbs of demons. The companions hurtled toward the Flat as if they aimed to cast themselves headlong into its reek.

Then Covenant heaved on Mishio Massima's reins, yelled at the beast to stop. Rallyn braced his legs against the descent: the Ironhand and her comrades dug in their heels. Stride by stride, the company slowed.

A tree flashed past, and another. Ironwood? Hyn splashed through a stream. A glowering cluster of cypress reached out from the edge of the marsh. Following Rallyn and Covenant's mount, the companions veered away, angling closer to the cliff.

As Hyn mastered her momentum, Linden realized where she was. Although she had never seen the mountain from this perspective before, she recognized Mount Thunder. In profile, it resembled a titan kneeling against or within Landsdrop with its forearms and torso braced on the Upper Land, facing west. The nearby cliff was a side of the mountain rather than an extension of the great precipice which divided the Land. The hillside down which Hyn moved, trotting now, was one of the titan's calves. The other formed the far side of a valley leading from the base of the cliff into the Sarangrave.

The valley was wide enough to hold a large herd of Ranyhyn, long enough to accommodate several hundred Masters fighting Cavewights or *kresh*. On the lower slopes and in the bottom grew scattered ironwood trees nourished by streams of fresh water tumbling downward on both sides, north and south. Marsh grasses climbing out of the Flat wrestled for room to grow with bindweed and more noxious plants.

But the spine of the valley bottom was a riverbed that stank like a sewer.

Black water viscid as oil, putrid as excrement, ran from a gaping wound in the cliff between the mountain's knees. At one time, the river had thundered from that wound, flushing the bowels of Mount Thunder with the combined waters of the Upper Land, emptying the effluvium of banes and charnels, of disused Wightwarrens and discarded corpses and lakes of acid, into the welcome of the Great Swamp. But now the level had fallen far below the bed's rims. Even augmented by the streams, the Defiles Course barely carried enough water to cover the slimed rocks of its bottom. The wound in the cliff gaped like a waiting maw.

Insects hummed with hunger past Linden's head. Some of them stung. Swarms of midges swirled here and there as if they fed on the odor of excreted toxins. As she rode downward, the cypresses appeared to rise up until they towered above her, avid and polluted. The ironwoods looked mighty, although they would surely have grown taller and broader in a kinder setting. Above them, the cliff extended itself to giddy heights.

Even from lower ground, she could see that the exposed gutrock of the cliff was little wider than the valley between the mountain's calves. Slopes spread up at awkward angles from Mount Thunder's thighs into its back. There the mountainsides were rugged and threatening, riddling with clefts and flaws as if they had been hacked by gargantuan blades: they looked impassable. Nevertheless she suspected that Rime Coldspray and her comrades might be able to climb there, given time— and perhaps rope. Stave and Branl could certainly do so. But Linden herself could not. For her, the higher sides of Mount Thunder were unattainable.

Here she had no choice except to follow Covenant, unless she turned Hyn and fled, taking Jeremiah with her.

In the valley bottom near the trunk of an ironwood, Covenant finally halted. He handed the *krill* to Branl; but he did not dismount. Instead he waited, peering into the gullet of the mountain, for the rest of the company to close around him. The tension in his shoulders, and the clutch of his hands on the saddle horn, told Linden that he was holding himself in his seat by force of will. His eyes bled tears as if the stink of the Defiles Course burned them; as if the fetor were remorse.

While their respiration eased, the Swordmainnir scanned their surroundings anxiously, considering possible attacks or escapes. In contrast, the *Haruchai* gauged the terrain with their characteristic dispassion. Alone among their companions, they remembered this place. No doubt their communal memories included recollections of the Defiles Course at its torrential height, when the flood in the lower end of the valley would have reached at least partway up the trunks of the cypresses. But Jeremiah did not lift his head or look around. Muttering to himself, he studied his hands and scowled as if their emptiness angered him.

When he had regained his balance, Covenant announced, "This is it. I guess that's obvious. We should rest while we can. I'm not sure we'll get another chance." Coming here had been his decision. Nevertheless his tone was thick with doubt. "And we should send the horses away. They can't help us now.

"When we're ready, I'll try to get the attention of the Feroce. I'm hoping they can guide us at least part of the way."

Forestalling an objection which no one expressed, he added, "Not that I think they've ever been *in* Mount Thunder. But they're creatures of water. And not just any water." He gestured at the river. "They thrive in this stuff. Plus they don't need light. Maybe they can lead us far enough to find the Wightwarrens.

"After that," he finished trenchantly, "we won't need to know where we're going. We'll just have to fight. Eventually the way Foul defends himself will show us where he is."

He may have meant, Show us or herd us.

While Linden tried to gather herself, Jeremiah glared at Covenant under his eyebrows. "It's a waste of time," the boy rasped. "I'm starting to recognize some of the landscape. The Worm is on the Upper Land. Beside a river. We'll still be groping around like we're lost when it reaches *Melenkurion* Skyweir.

"And what makes you think you can trust the Feroce?" He clenched his fists, apparently trying to muster flames. But his access to Earthpower eluded him. Perhaps visions of the Worm blocked it. "You had an alliance while the lurker was scared. Now the Worm is moving away. Maybe the lurker thinks it doesn't need you anymore."

Covenant shrugged. He faced Jeremiah squarely, but did not respond.

Feeling helpless and dismal, Linden asked, "Thomas, are you sure you want to do this?"

"What else are we going to do?" Leprosy blurred Covenant's eyes like pain or empathy. "We're here now. If that's a mistake, it won't be my first. Most of what I do in life is just trying to make amends for things I've done wrong.

"Anyway you heard Jeremiah. We don't have time to try anything different."

Linden did not respond. She had already lost this argument.

But Jeremiah was not done. "But why bother? I thought I understood. I mean, before I could see the Worm. Now I don't. What's the point? We're all going to die anyway."

I have given him a gift, oh, Jeremiah, *which will make him wise in the subtleties of despair.*

Linden might have tried to reassure him. Covenant might have. But the Giants silenced them by the simple expedient of bursting into laughter.

Their loud mirth filled the valley. It seemed to startle the insects. Midges fled for the safety of the wetland's mire. Horseflies and mosquitoes skirled away, whining. Just for a moment, even the stinks of the Defiles Course and the Sarangrave became less daunting.

"Bravely said, young Jeremiah," Grueburn guffawed. "A fine riposte."

Latebirth and Halewhole Bluntfist doubled over, gasping for breath.

"'But why bother?'" echoed Cirrus Kindwind. "Why, indeed? You make sport of our fears, Chosen-son."

Stormpast Galesend slapped Cabledarm's back. Cabledarm aimed an elbow at Galesend's ribs.

Expecting Jeremiah to take offense, Linden flinched. At the same time, however, she felt a rush of gratitude. Too much had happened since she had last heard laughter.

While Jeremiah fumed, the Ironhand struggled for gravity. She scrubbed at her eyes until her humor receded to chuckling bursts. "All paths lead to death," she said when she found her voice. "This the Worm merely hastens. Nonetheless we must strive. How otherwise will we hold up our heads at the end of our days?"

Linden watched Jeremiah wrestle with himself. He must have felt mocked. Surely he felt that? But he also loved the Giants. And their mirth was too open-hearted to sound like ridicule. Briefly his mouth twisted: he almost smiled in spite of himself. Then he mustered a conflicted glower.

"Never mind. I wasn't serious. Have it your way."

That may have been as much grace as he could muster. If so, it was enough for Linden.

"Well, hell," Covenant drawled as the Giants subsided. "Hellfire." Then he fell silent as if he had run out of words.

As if by mute agreement, Stave and Branl slipped down from their Ranyhyn. If the *Haruchai* were capable of laughter, Linden had never heard it. Here, however, she caught a glint that looked like amusement from Stave's eye. Branl's manner as he leaned Longwrath's blade against the trunk of the ironwood hinted at the easing of subtle tensions.

When Jeremiah dropped, dour and distant, to the ground, and Covenant dismounted, Linden joined them. The unfamiliarity of her wedding band or the aftereffects of wild magic made her finger itch. Holding the Staff in the crook of her elbow, she rubbed absently at the itch while she tried to think of a way to thank Rime Coldspray and her comrades.

Twisting the kinks out of his back, Covenant made his way toward the nearest stream. The Ardent's steed cantered past him to thrust its muzzle into the water, blowing bubbles as it drank. The four Ranyhyn followed more sedately. Hynyn's wonted imperial air was subdued, and Hyn's head drooped as if she were weighted down with farewells. Khelen cast anxious looks at Jeremiah, but did not hang back.

After the Swordmainnir had loosened their armor, Onyx Stonemage passed around the remaining waterskins of *aliantha*: the last meal that Linden expected to eat. Covenant accepted treasure-berries. Even the *Haruchai* did so. Then Kindwind and Grueburn carried the emptied sacks to another stream.

The valley's insects had forgotten their fright. A few flying things with stingers found Linden. One raised a welt on the back of her hand: another, on the side of her neck. Irritated by those pangs, and by the region's renewed fetor, she found herself remembering carrion. She remembered *being* carrion; remembered the howling anguish and condemnation of She Who Must Not Be Named. Remembered Elena—

Entering the maw at the base of the cliff would resemble falling from the Hazard.

Swearing to herself, she called Earthpower from her Staff to heal her little hurts, chase away the insects and the worst of the stenches; cleanse the recall of maggots and lice from her nerves. Then she extended the same small benison to her companions.

Jeremiah ignored her gift. Trapped in his own thoughts, he did not appear to feel any physical discomfort. Perhaps the same inheritance which protected him from cold and preserved his bare feet also warded him from stings. Whenever Linden thought that she should talk to him, she discovered that she was not ready. What could she have said? His ability to watch the Worm's progress was a wound for which she had no salve.

Like her companions, she refreshed herself at the stream, ate her portion of the treasure-berries. Then she shared a hug with Covenant; leaned against the stubborn bones of his chest while his stubbed fingers ran awkward reassurance through her hair.

As the tenuous afternoon dwindled toward evening, vapors began to rise from the waters of the Sarangrave. At first, they were vague, visible only when they caught the light of the *krill*. But gradually they thickened into blots and tendrils of fog. By degrees, opaque arms and sheets found their way into the valley, traced the Defiles Course toward the sides of the mountain. Before long, the fog was a softly roiling wall that veiled the Flat. If it continued to expand, it would soon fill the valley.

As strands of fog coiled among the sparse ironwoods, the horses took their departure. Mishio Massima simply trotted away, tossing its head as if it had exhausted its patience for riders. The Ranyhyn were more formal. First they gathered around

Covenant. As one, they reared, pawing the air as if he had won their approval. Then they separated, Hynyn toward Stave, Rallyn to Branl, Hyn and Khelen to Linden and Jeremiah. Hynyn nuzzled Stave while Stave stroked the stallion's nose. Khelen offered the same gesture of affection to Jeremiah. For a moment, Jeremiah appeared to rebuff the Ranyhyn. Abruptly, however, he flung his arms around Khelen's neck: a boy who did not want to be forsaken.

Branl answered Rallyn's whinny with a salutation as old as the Lords. To Linden, Hyn lowered her head to the ground, bending one foreleg like a curtsey. "No," Linden breathed as she hugged the mare, "please. We're past that. I should be bowing to you."

Hyn replied with a soft nicker. The look in her gentle eyes implied sadness, pride, affection, regret, even an atavistic alarm. Nonetheless it seemed to aver that she had not lost faith.

In homage, the Giants drew their swords. Holding their blades high, they saluted the fidelity and service of the great horses.

As one, the Ranyhyn turned away. Together they followed Mishio Massima into the fog. If they neighed any last farewells, their calls were swallowed by the brume.

The stars were gone; masked. Damp vapors blurred the shape of the watercourse. The cliff lost its definition, its implacable rigidity. Around the companions, the *krill*'s argent reflected back from the fog until they seemed to stand within a cynosure. A beacon. Beyond the light, the rest of the world was reduced to a slow seethe of blankness, moist and clinging.

Linden regarded the fog with fresh apprehension. It seemed to imply perils which would strike without warning.

"What does it mean?" demanded Jeremiah hoarsely.

"It means," Covenant replied, a low growl from the back of his throat, "we've waited long enough."

Suddenly brusque, he claimed the *krill*. With Branl at his side, he headed down the valley toward the Sarangrave. Loric's dagger thrust illumination ahead of him. At his back, fog crowded in to enclose the company. Where he stopped, the outermost twigs and boughs of cypresses were visible; but Linden could barely distinguish her companions.

"I'm here." Covenant appeared to shout, but the fog muffled some sounds while it accentuated others. The distant plash of water carried more distinctly than his voice. "You called me the Pure One. We made an alliance. I've been keeping my part. Now we need to talk. I want the Feroce."

Wrapped in that fug, Linden found it impossible to believe that any of the Sarangrave's ears would hear him.

Droplets beaded on her skin. The damp seeped through the flaws in her shirt.

With her nerves rather than her eyes, she located her son's aura. His emanations conveyed the impression that he was crouching down inside himself; that he feared the touch of the vapors; that he wanted to flee.

"I discern no cause for alarm," Grueburn stated. "Do our foes deem that mere fog will affright us? We have endured the toils of the Soulbiter, and have emerged scatheless. We are not so blithely overcome."

She may have been trying to comfort Jeremiah.

"Aye," answered the Ironhand. "Yet fog occludes here as it does in the Soulbiter. Ready yourselves, Swordmainnir. Mayhap this brume is a natural exudation of the wetland. Or mayhap—"

Around her, Giants tightened their cataphracts, loosened their arms and shoulders.

"Jeremiah?" Linden felt an instinctive impulse to whisper. "Listen to me. Are you listening?"

Stave stood at her back, impassive and silent.

Covenant may have been yelling at the Flat, but his words were lost. The *krill*'s light did not penetrate the shroud over the Sarangrave.

"There's no stopping it, Mom," Jeremiah replied like a groan. "You should see what it's doing to the plains."

Linden grasped his arm. When he tried to pull away, she tightened her hold. "I said, *listen*. Maybe there's a way out of what you're feeling. Maybe Foul gave you those visions to distract you. Maybe he doesn't want you thinking about other possibilities. Maybe your real problem is that you don't know how to defend yourself."

Jeremiah's tone changed. "Mom?"

"You have Earthpower," she explained, "but it isn't a weapon. It's like *orcrest*." Or like Anele himself. "It doesn't protect you. Maybe you wouldn't feel so hopeless if you had a way to fight."

"But I don't." In spite of her grip on his arm, he sounded as remote as Covenant. "I'm useless." He may have meant broken. He had learned that his desire to repay the Despiser's malice was a foolish fantasy. "All I can do is watch."

"No." Simply because her son's distress hurt her, Linden wanted to raise her voice. She had to force herself to speak quietly. "Listen to me, honey. There's always something we can do, even if it's just changing the way we look at what's happening, or the way we look at ourselves.

"I think I know how you can defend yourself."

With her fingers, she felt his shock. "How?"

"Linden Giantfriend." The fog muted Rime Coldspray's tension. "My heart misgives me. The Timewarden's hopes fail. The Feroce do not come. And this fog—" She made a spitting sound. "Stone and Sea! I cannot persuade myself that it is natural. Some evil summons it."

Linden closed her ears to the Ironhand. "Try this." She pulled Jeremiah closer. "Fill your hands with fire. You can do that. I know you can."

"Why?" He tried to draw back. He had failed earlier. "What good will that do? You just said—"

She cut him off. "Just *do* it. Then touch my Staff."

"Mom!" he protested. "I can't use your Staff!"

"We don't know that yet." She strove to sound calm, but she trembled in spite of her efforts. "We haven't tried it.

"First your Earthpower. Then my Staff. After that, I'll help you figure out what comes next."

Through her teeth, Coldspray muttered warnings which her comrades did not require.

"Hellfire," Covenant raged in the distance. The *krill*'s shining throbbed ineffectually. "I saved you from *turiya* by God Raver. And I told you not to sacrifice yourself against the Worm. If you got hurt, it wasn't my doing. I kept my part of the deal. I've been keeping it. Now it's your turn."

Linden felt his vehemence, but she did not hear an answer. Fog eddied around her head. She could barely make out Jeremiah's features.

He floundered in her grasp as if he wanted to resist and comply simultaneously. "Mom—?" His distress came in bursts. "I don't— How can—? Don't make me. I—"

Just for a moment, she feared that she had pushed him too far. He was only a boy. And he had spent most of his life hiding. In effect, he had only known himself for a few days.

But then he stopped trying to pull away. Flames appeared in his palms as if his skin had caught fire.

They danced and fluttered, leaned raggedly from side to side like fires in a harsh wind. But they grew stronger as he gained confidence in them. By the measure of his needs, they were little things, no bigger than his hands. The sun-yellow of Earthpower did not push back the fog. Still these flames were *his*. They had been given freely.

Yes, Linden thought. If he could do that, he could do more. She would teach him somehow. His own health-sense would guide him if hers did not suffice.

"Giantfriend," the Ironhand insisted. "Linden Avery."

"Now the Staff," Linden instructed Jeremiah, whispering again. "It's full of possibilities." The runes. The iron heels as old as Berek Halfhand. The combined essences of Vain and Findail. Her own love. "Try to feel them. Maybe they'll answer," Earthpower to Earthpower.

She had her wedding band. Covenant had made her a rightful white gold wielder. Surely she could fend for herself without the Staff of Law?

"It might not respond right away," she admitted. "It isn't yours. I made it. I have a kind of symbiotic relationship with it. But if you keep trying, you should—"

"*Attend*, Giantfriend!"

The Ironhand's shout snatched at Linden. Involuntarily she wheeled away from her son's guttering hands.

At once, the distinctive reek of gangrene stung her nose. Impressions of necrosis seemed to hit all of her nerves, her whole body. She recognized that smell, those emanations; but for a confused instant, she could not identify them.

Then she saw a lurid swelling of brimstone, a fierce gnash of lava. It was some distance away on the far side of the Defiles Course. Nevertheless it was hot enough to pierce the fog. She remembered roaring ferocity, fangs like scimitars in long rows, terrible jaws.

Oh, God—

Beyond her, the Swordmainnir strode down the slope to intercept the attack, spreading out so that they would each have room to strike and dodge. Stave stood a few paces in front of Linden as if he imagined that he could counter one of the *skurj*.

Covenant may have been unaware of the threat behind him. He continued hurling his demands into the shrouded Sarangrave. The *krill* slashed back and forth: cuts that had no effect. But now he was alone. Apparently Branl trusted that the lurker would not assail the Pure One, even if the monster had withdrawn its aid. With calm haste, the Humbled came back up the valley, gripping Longwrath's flamberge in both hands.

"Mom?" Jeremiah called: a small sound like a whimper. "Mom? What's happening?"

Abruptly a monster surged up from the eaten ground.

Now Linden saw it clearly. The unthinking creature had devoured its way through the earth to emerge among the roots of an ironwood. Almost immediately, the tree exploded into flames. Bright as a bonfire, and hot as the ravaging of Covenant's home on Haven Farm, it heralded hunger and scoria.

Tall and thick as a Giant, the *skurj* stood in conflagration with half of its full length braced underground. Roaring like an eruption, it twisted from side to side, apparently seeking the scent of its prey. Then it began its rush toward the company, drawing its whole body out of the dirt as it snaked into the valley bottom.

Under other circumstances, the river might have forced the monster to pause; perhaps to chew its way beneath the watercourse. But the Defiles Course was much diminished. The *skurj* did not hesitate. Coiling its strength, it launched itself in a brimstone arc above the waters.

Its fury dismissed the fog around it. Even at that distance, Linden felt waves of heat beat against her face.

Covenant's shouting was hoarse and doomed. Still he persisted.

Linden did not think. She had no time. Raising her Staff, she left Jeremiah's side. Black flames like the tails of a scourge pulled free of the wood and whipped around her as she hurried toward the Giants.

Stave accompanied her without question. He seemed to have no questions left.

"Don't move," she urged as she passed between Coldspray and Frostheart Grueburn. "I can do this." She hardly heard herself. "Take care of Jeremiah." In the back of her mind, she had already begun to pronounce the Seven Words. "Lord Foul doesn't want him dead, but that monster probably doesn't care."

The *skurj* was only one.

In Salva Gildenbourne, one alone had overwhelmed her in spite of her Staff. And during the company's flight toward Andelain, Kastenessen's monsters had been too strong for her. She could not have fought them in the Lost Deep.

Since then, everything had changed. Kevin's Dirt was gone. Kastenessen's passing into the fane of the *Elohim* had struck manacles from her wrists. While Covenant still believed that the lurker might heed him, she meant to guard his back.

"*Melenkurion abatha,*" she promised softly while the *skurj* arose from the riverbank and swept toward her. "*Duroc minas mill. Harad khabaal.*"

Down the valley from her, Branl did not quicken his pace. He advanced with the remorseless inevitability of a breaking wave.

"Help her!" Jeremiah panted at the Swordmainnir. "That thing is going to *eat* her!"

If the Ironhand or any of her comrades replied, Linden did not hear them.

Now! she told herself. Do it *now*.

Get away from me, you overgrown slug. You cannot have my son! Or my friends. Or my *husband*.

With the Staff of Law alive and lurid in her grasp, she flung an ebon torrent of Earthpower and Law between the jaws of the *skurj*.

The creature's body radiated heat, but it did not emit light. All of the monster's radiance came from the cruelty of its fangs. They were lambent and infernal, curved for ripping: they blazed with havoc. Looking into that wide maw was like staring down the gullet of a living cremation.

But Linden was as ready as she would ever be. Her power was ready. And she was sick of frustration and fear, more profoundly infuriated that she had allowed herself to realize. She felt that she had not struck an effective blow since the day of horror when she had slaughtered uncounted Cavewights with wild magic: sentient creatures whose massacre at her hands still filled her with revulsion. She was by God *ready* to oppose a monster which sought destruction merely to feed its own worst appetites—and to satisfy a Raver's commands.

Moksha Jehannum had once possessed her. She remembered him vividly. Like Covenant, if only with her Staff, she was done with restraint.

Her dark torrent tore a howl from the throat of the *skurj*. The monster reared back, balancing like a cobra on its length. For a moment or two, long enough for her to shout the Seven Words, it tried to swallow her power; gulp it down as if it were the natural drink of *skurj*. But it could not. Her power shredded its gullet, sent agony inward. Thrashing its head, it clamped shut its mouth, closed its jaws on its horrid lumination. Then it whirled away before she could inflict more pain.

Branl intercepted the *skurj* smoothly, as if he had foreseen the timing of his strike as soon as he had left Covenant's side. The flamberge was a streak of theurgy in his hands. One stroke cut halfway through the monster's neck.

Then he sprang aside as the *skurj* became a flailing fountain of blood as bitter as acid. Convulsions writhed through the monster: it seemed to snarl itself in knots. But it could not survive its wounds. While it gaped and snapped at the air, the light of its fangs faded into the fog.

Still Linden did not stop. She had endured too much, and yearned to repay it. Branl had killed the *skurj* for her: she turned her fire to quench the virulence of the monster's blood.

Even when she had eradicated every spot and spatter from the dirt, she wanted to continue until she had reduced the corpse to ash. But she felt Stave's hand on her shoulder, heard him say, "Enough, Linden. The monster is slain. Now you must conserve your magicks. Where one *skurj* arrives, others will surely come."

"No," Jeremiah breathed, apparently to himself. "Not more of those things. I can't stand it. How did it find us?"

If he sought reassurance, no one offered it.

"Aye, Linden Giantfriend," rumbled the Ironhand. "Your prowess raises a paean in our hearts. Yet Stave Rockbrother counsels wisely. In Kastenessen's absence, the *skurj* are doubtless ruled by *moksha* Raver. We must believe that a greater force follows this lone creature. We must spare our strength while we may."

Someone should have said that to Covenant. He was still trying to coerce a response from the Sarangrave, hacking at the fog with Loric's *krill*, and yelling intermittently. The gem's argent spread out until the wetland smothered it. His voice made no sound that Linden could hear.

"In that case," she said as if she had only now begun to understand Rime Coldspray's warning, "we need to *see*. We can't let whatever comes take us by surprise.

"Watch for me. I'm going to get rid of this damn fog."

The vapors baffled percipience. Like the Ironhand, Linden did not know whether they were natural or invoked. But she did not care. The fog itself was just suspended moisture. Earthpower and Law would dispel it.

"That would be a benison in all sooth," answered Coldspray. "Make the attempt, Giantfriend. The Swordmainnir will ward your son."

Linden nodded, but she had stopped listening. Again she prepared the Seven Words in her mind. Instinctively she moved away from her companions so that she would have space to work. With only Stave nearby, she tuned her senses to the pitch and timbre of mist. Then she lifted new flames from the Staff and sent them skirling upward.

She regretted the blackness of her fire. She would always regret it. But she had no idea how to relieve it. The fog was a simpler problem. And her stained theurgy was still Earthpower.

With her eyes closed, she summoned more and more of her Staff's potential. Her health-sense recognized and measured the vapors: their specific dampness on her skin; their distinctive currents and flavors. As if she were musing to herself, she murmured the Seven Words.

The only substantial obstacle to her intent was the extent of the fug. It arose continuously from the Flat, curled up into the valley without ceasing. To be rid of it, she had to dismiss it faster than it came.

Melenkurion abatha.

Obliquely she wondered whether it had been invoked by the lurker, perhaps so that the High God of the Feroce would have an excuse for ignoring Covenant's appeal. On a deeper level, she chewed the gristle of Jeremiah's question. She feared that she knew the answer.

Duroc minas mill.

But she had work to do and could not afford to distract herself. If more *skurj* were coming—

Harad khabaal.

Behind her, the Giants muttered their approval. Stalwart as any of his kinsmen, Stave guarded her back.

When she had cleared the air directly overhead, unveiled the stars and the onset of evening, she sent her fire toward the cliff above the Defiles Course; toward the steep slopes on either side of the exposed gutrock.

"How did it find us?" Jeremiah repeated. He raised his voice, tried to make his question a demand. "We can't get away if we don't know how it found us."

The *skurj* were able to sense exertions of Earthpower; but Linden did not know how far their perceptions reached. Could they detect her power while they were ravaging in Salva Gildenbourne? Detect it past the bulk of Mount Thunder? And arrive so quickly? No: she did not believe it.

She no longer felt Covenant's irate, tattered summons; no longer sensed the *krill*'s shining imprecation. Grimly she focused her attention on the Staff of Law and fog.

"There!" one of the Swordmainnir barked softly.

A quick pang of alarm disturbed Linden's flames. She bit her lip, resisted her impulse to falter.

"Where?" asked the Ironhand. "My sight has lost its youth. I do not descry—"

Calm as mist, Stave said, "Chosen. Direct your strength to the mountainsides beyond the Defiles Course."

She complied at once. *Moksha*'s forces were more likely to round Mount Thunder from the north than the south.

Fresh tension spread among the Giants. Latebirth groaned. Stonemage and Grueburn cursed harshly.

"Chosen-son!" snapped Cirrus Kindwind. "Stand at my back. Move as I move. I will shield you."

To Branl, Coldspray rasped, "You must defend the Timewarden. We cannot. If the Swordmainnir do not stand together, we will soon fall."

Linden opened her eyes, but she did not need them to discern the Sandgorgons. She felt their eager ferocity in every nerve.

There were—

Oh, God!

—at least a score of them. Two score? More?

Fatal as a landslide, they sped among lingering streamers of brume, hurtled down the mountainside toward the valley.

One led the way. It had pulled some distance ahead of the others. Behind it came three, no, four more Sandgorgons. Nimble on the pads of their feet, the strange backward flex of their legs, they cascaded over the rocks. The rest of the monsters followed, a pale rush angling across Mount Thunder's contorted slopes.

For an instant, Linden froze. How many Sandgorgons had left their home across the seas? More than this? Surely not *more*?

The company could not survive so many.

Worse, Jeremiah would not be one of the victims. Lord Foul and *moksha* Raver might not be able to control the *skurj*; keep them away from the Despiser's prize. The Sandgorgons were another matter. The shreds of *samadhi* Sheol animated their minds. They would obey Lord Foul's wishes.

As if she had taken herself by the throat, Linden let out a black scream against the fog.

That was as much as she could do. She wanted to strike at the Sandgorgons before they reached the valley, do as much damage as she could from a distance. But she had already caught the reek of more gangrene.

High above the Defiles Course, a second chancre had appeared, a second suppuration. The gutrock bled vile fluids like pus.

God in Heaven! We can't—

Rime Coldspray adjusted the formation of the Swordmainnir. With Frostheart Grueburn, Latebirth, and Halewhole Bluntfist, she came to stand in front of Linden. The others positioned themselves to defend Jeremiah. He was trying to shout, but his voice broke into whimpers. Stave waited at Linden's side as if he were resting. In no apparent hurry, Branl returned along the valley bottom toward Covenant.

Ragged with strain, Covenant continued yelling at the Sarangrave.

"Linden Giantfriend." The Ironhand sounded almost nonchalant. The prospect of an impossible battle seemed to focus her combative nature. "The *skurj* we must entrust to you. If by kind fortune they approach singly, you may perhaps prevail. The Sandgorgons are mighty in all sooth, yet they wield only strength and ferocity. And we also are mighty. We are armed and armored. We will hope to stand against them. If they do not mass for a combined assault"—she shrugged to loosen her shoulders—"we will teach them to esteem us."

The pounding of Linden's pulse in her ears measured out Coldspray's words— *entrust to you.* After that, she recognized only one in three. Still she knew what was required of her.

Jeremiah had his defenders. Armed with a sword forged to fight Sandgorgons, Branl would guard Covenant. And Covenant was not helpless. If any residue of his victory over Nom lingered in the minds of the monsters, or in *samadhi*'s, they might flinch from attacking him. That left the *skurj*.

Linden believed that she could stop them—

—if they came no more than one or two at a time.

Fierce and ruddy, a maw full of fangs burst from the granite high in the cliff. With grim satisfaction, Linden saw that the monster was directly above the Defiles Course. The riverbed held much less than its former torrents; but the remaining gush was still *water*: polluted beyond estimation, yes, and stinking to the stars, but water nonetheless. Her fate was written in it.

Swinging her Staff like the handle of a flail, and hissing the Seven Words past her teeth, she sent barbed fire at the *skurj*.

The leading Sandgorgon was already nearing the valley. The others did not gain ground, but they followed swiftly.

Thinking *Melenkurion* and *minas* and *khabaal*, Linden found that the monster in the cliff had emerged near the limit of her range. She could not hit it hard enough to slay it. But she was fighting now: instinct and desperation guided her. She did not need to kill the monster directly. She could use the river. All she had to do was make the damn thing fall.

Deliberately she harried the creature. She whipped fire at its jaws, made wounds in its gullet. Then she caused one of his fangs to rupture.

Roaring in distress, the *skurj* thrashed against the rims of its egress. The stone around it cracked and crumbled.

It was not a thinking creature. It did not observe and take care: it only hunted and fed—and reacted to pain. After a moment, its own writhing broke loose a section of the cliff.

Amid shards of gutrock as loud as thunder, the monster plunged down the face of the precipice.

When the *skurj* hit the Defiles Course, steam erupted from the impact. Fouled water sprayed upward, filled the valley bottom with a rain of poison and acid. But Linden had anticipated that. As the monster fell, she raised a curtain of black flame between her companions and the river. Earthpower burned ruin out of the air. Then, as the corrosive deluge subsided, she turned her fire against the *skurj* again, burning to trap the monster in the river.

Inflicted hurts blocked the monster's escape. It shrieked like shattering as it swallowed spray and splashes, gulped down death. Then it collapsed, steaming furiously; stretched out its length in the current. A moment later, it was dead, and the Defiles Course flowed over it.

Linden wanted a shout of celebration. She looked around for it. But sudden plague-spots dotted the far side of the valley; and more appeared on the near side, within a stone's throw of the company; and the first Sandgorgon raced off the mountainside onto lower ground, charging toward Branl and Covenant.

The *gaddhi* of *Bhrathairealm* had called the Sandgorgons *more fearsome than madness or nightmare.* Baked to an albino whiteness in the Great Desert, the creatures were destruction incarnate. They could pulverize granite with the prehensile stumps of their forearms. And their heads had been formed for battering, lacking eyes or other vulnerabilities. They breathed through slits like gills protected by tough hide on the sides of their heads.

If that Sandgorgon contrived to strike Covenant, it would snap every bone in his body.

But Linden could do nothing to defend him. Half a dozen *skurj* had already thrust their heads and fangs out of the ground. More were close. Frantic and furious, she faced those threats, leaving her husband to Branl.

She had devised a new defense. Whipping flame from place to place, she concentrated Earthpower on the lambent fangs. From maw to maw, she caused eruptions like bursts of agony along the kraken jaws. Small hurts: the *skurj* were huge, and their mouths held scores of scimitar-teeth. Nevertheless their pain was acute. It enraged the monsters—but it also distracted them.

It slowed their emergence from the earth.

Gripping her glaive, the Ironhand breathed, "Well done, Linden Giantfriend. I had not considered such a ploy."

It was no more than a delay, a transient interruption. But it might create openings for the Swordmainnir.

While Linden lashed obsidian back and forth, accentuating her efforts with the Seven Words, Covenant and Branl finally turned to face the nearest Sandgorgon. As if they were sure of their strength, they strode to meet the charge. Branl held Longwrath's flamberge poised to slash. Covenant's halfhand gripped Loric's shining dagger by its wrapped hilt.

Behind them came a cluster of Feroce, perhaps ten of the naked child-forms. They held out their hands like gestures of supplication or worship. Rank green flames twisted and flared in each of their palms.

At their backs, more fog piled out of the Sarangrave, obscuring the perils of the wetland.

The Sandgorgon gathered itself, sprang over the water. For the flicker of an instant, it vanished below the rim of the riverbank. Then another leap brought it out of the Defiles Course. Silent as the fog, as the boundary between life and death, it sped toward the Unbeliever and the Humbled. Between one stride and the next, it became a juggernaut.

Covenant and Branl did not hesitate.

Instead the creature faltered. Five of its strides from its targets, it jerked to a halt. Its head turned from side to side, scanning with its arcane senses. It seemed to remember Covenant. Its blunt forearms aimed confused blows at the air.

Before the Sandgorgon could recover—before the thwarted scraps of *samadhi* Sheol's sentience regained their mastery—Branl delivered a cut that opened the monster's torso from its neck down through its chest to its opposite hip. Blood and strange guts spouted from the wound as the Sandgorgon toppled.

Branl did not pause to regard the corpse. Four more creatures were only heartbeats away. One had already leapt the river. Another was leaping.

But Covenant turned to the Feroce in spite of his peril. "That was impressive," he growled quietly. "What did you do?"

The Humbled continued his advance. His blade shed blood and strips of flesh as if its old magicks repelled the gore of the Sandgorgon.

In their one voice, moist and diffuse, the lurker's minions answered, "We have caused it to remember that it is bestial, a creature of instinct, not of intent. We have caused it to remember that you are mighty. Alas, we are merely the Feroce. We are frail, unworthy to serve our High God. We cannot impose recall upon so many, or upon such savagery."

At the last instant, Branl stepped aside from the first creature, beyond the reach of its arms—but not the length of his sword. The Sandgorgon had no defense as he slid the flamberge across its trunk below its ribs. Reflexively it clamped its forearms over the slash; but they were not enough to keep its life from spilling out.

Covenant nodded to the Feroce. "Do what you can," he said; demanded. "And tell your High God I need more than just you. I need *him*. I need him *here*. This is what alliances are for. I have to have help."

Branl spun into a horizontal cut that bit through obdurate bone, nearly severed the top half of a Sandgorgon's face and skull. But Longwrath's sword caught there, grinding between bones which could have smashed down a wall. The *Haruchai* could not wrench his blade loose quickly enough to intercept the next creature.

Wailing, the Feroce brandished their fires as the third Sandgorgon swung a crushing blow at Branl.

Even his preternatural strength was no match for the creature's. Yet he was *Haruchai*, and swift. And he had not forgotten the ease with which a Sandgorgon had killed Hergrom, crippled Ceer. He evaded the blow by diving under the creature's arm. It did not touch him.

He landed on his feet, whirled back toward the creature. But now he was too far away to protect Covenant; and he had to retrieve his sword.

At the last instant, the theurgy of the Feroce took hold. The monster slowed its rush directly in front of Covenant.

Wincing and bitter, he raised the *krill*. The eldritch blade slipped as easily as murder into the Sandgorgon's heart.

Blood sprayed from the creature's gills as it plowed into him. It was already dead. Still the impact sent him sprawling. He lost his grip on the dagger. It tumbled away across the dirt, sending dismembered flashes of argent through the new fog.

From the ground, he glared wildly at the fourth Sandgorgon as though he imagined that he could defy it with nothing more than his gaze and his anger. Spangles like glints of frenzy gathered around his wedding band; but he had fallen too heavily to wield them.

Leaping, Branl came down at that creature's back with the full force and magic of his flamberge.

The Sandgorgon staggered away in a welter of blood and bone. Its legs folded under it. It pounded its featureless face against the valley bottom while its muscles seized. Then it lay still.

More Sandgorgons were coming: too many. The first of them had reached the valley. In another moment, it would cross the Defiles Course.

Branl appeared to shrug as he reached down to clasp Covenant's hand. In one effortless motion, he snatched the Unbeliever upright. A moment later, he retrieved the *krill*, returned it to Covenant.

"Now or never," Covenant gasped at the Feroce. He could hardly breathe. Something in his chest felt broken. "You said the alliance is sealed. We need help *now*."

Together he and Branl resumed their ascent along the valley. He lurched in pain. His companion looked as deadly as Longwrath's sword.

The Feroce followed at a slight distance. Their fires flared like mewling.

Linden was not watching. She could not. While she harassed *skurj* furiously, lashing Earthpower and Law at the bright lava of their fangs, another ironwood became instant conflagration. Burning sap burst from its trunk, its boughs, even its leaves. It was close: its heat slapped at her face as an open maw appeared, rabid and ravenous. Uprooted by the monster, the tree pitched down the slope as if it had been hurled aside.

Frantic and off-balance on the cliff edge of her strength, Linden threw obsidian vehemence at the *skurj*.

Rime Coldspray stopped her. "Withhold, Giantfriend! Assail more distant threats. We will oppose those that come near!"

While Coldspray shouted, Latebirth and Bluntfist rushed toward the residue of the blazing tree.

Linden knew that the Ironhand was right. Still she lost herself in a moment of visceral terror. That monster was *close*. It could tear any Giant apart with one bite.

Jeremiah called out to her, but his voice seemed to come from the far side of the world. Roaring heat and viciousness muffled every human sound.

Yelling the Seven Words like curses, Linden flung the outrage of her heart at other *skurj*.

At least ten now howled beyond the river. Pustules in the dirt promised more. Joining the creature which Latebirth and Bluntfist faced, four had eaten their way underground to burst upward between the company and the watercourse. Linden started to hurt those four. Then she realized that they were not coming toward her. Instead they swarmed around the first monster which she had slain.

They were feeding. Eating their dead.

Just for an instant, she believed that she and the Swordmainnir had been granted a respite. But she was wrong. These monsters reproduced by devouring their dead, absorbing the energies of the fallen. Then they split. With sufficient nourishment, one became two. Two might become four—four might become eight—if one dead *skurj* supplied enough brimstone sorcery.

Horror rattled in Linden's skull. It stung her whole body as if she had been caught in a rain of pebbles. While the monsters arrived faster than she and her companions could kill them, they could not be beaten.

They were arriving much faster.

She needed wild magic; needed a dozen staffs like hers; needed help.

There was no help.

And she did not have time to drop her Staff so that she could invoke her ring. Nor did she have the *krill* or any other catalyst which might ease her access to wild magic. Nor had she learned how to summon silver havoc instantly without aid. If she could have cleared her mind, concentrated her health-sense—

She was already foundering. Any pause now might be her last mistake.

Latebirth and Halewhole Bluntfist closed on the nearest creature from opposite sides. They endured the heat only because they were Giants. Latebirth lunged a thrust straight into the monster's side. But her thrust was a feint. As the jaws of the *skurj* reached for her, she jumped back—and Bluntfist rushed in. Raging like the monster, Bluntfist swung a two-handed cut at its neck with all of her mass and her prodigious strength.

Unable to stop itself, the *skurj* fell onto a second lunge from Latebirth. Her long-sword drove between rows of tearing fangs into the back of the creature's throat; into the monster's brain. It collapsed in convulsions.

Linden and Coldspray shouted a warning simultaneously, and Frostheart Grue-burn charged; but they were too late.

Another *skurj* erupted from the ground almost directly beneath Latebirth's feet. As if it had detected her scent while it chewed through the dirt, it knew exactly where to strike. She was hauling on her sword, pulling it free, when the monster emerged. In one fluid motion, it surged upward and *bit*—

Bluntfist sprang to Latebirth's aid. Grueburn was only three strides away. As if he had forgotten that he was helpless against such foes, Stave followed Grueburn.

The monster's jaws caught Latebirth below her arms, front and back. Fangs dug into her armor.

Latebirth!

The hardened stone might have preserved her, at least for a moment; long enough for Bluntfist and Grueburn to arrive. But her cataphract was broken on one side, damaged in battle on the way to Andelain. The monster ripped through it as if it were sandstone; tore her open from chest to spine.

Oh, Latebirth—

Her killer was still swallowing blood and organs when Bluntfist and Grueburn hacked its throat to shreds. Fresh gangrene stained the earth around them.

"Ware, Swordmainnir!" the Ironhand roared at the dismay of her comrades. "The *skurj* must not feed!"

They were Giants, familiar with cruel storms and bitter fighting. They knew how to set their griefs and fears aside.

Linden did not. Sick with distress, she sent a raving blast into the first creature that snagged her attention.

It had begun a leap over the Defiles Course. Half of its length was in the air as Linden's fire poured between its jaws, ran down its gullet. With Earthpower and fury, she ignited an explosion inside the long body.

Then she had to hope that most of the monster would fall into the Defiles Course; that the river would prevent other *skurj* from feeding. She did not have time to watch. More and more of the horrific serpents had reached the near side of the valley, or had appeared there. Grueburn and Bluntfist whirled away to face another creature. Onyx Stonemage and Stormpast Galesend left their places with Jeremiah, pounded down the slope to challenge a new foe. Stave picked up Latebirth's longsword. Wielding a weapon as tall as himself lightly, as if he had trained in its use for decades, he rejoined Rime Coldspray in front of Linden.

Behind the *skurj*, a torrent of Sandgorgons raced into the valley, speeding with the single-mindedness of spears toward Covenant and Branl.

Faint amid the tumult, Jeremiah cried, "Mom, *run*! *We have to run!*"

At every moment, more *skurj* and Sandgorgons arrived, an inundating wave of monsters. Perhaps Linden would have fled—perhaps the Giants would have—if any of them had believed for an instant that they could outrun the monsters. If any of them had been willing to forsake Covenant and Branl.

From the bottom of her heart, Linden brought up a howl of flame:

"Thomas!"

He and Branl had come a third of the way up the valley. There they stopped. Apparently they had decided to stand their ground. Branl moved somewhat apart to accommodate the reach of his sword. Covenant held the *krill* ready. "Hellfire," he panted at the whimpering Feroce. "Hellfire."

Deliberately he shifted his left hand so that his ring touched Loric's gem. Then he uttered a shout of wild magic that halted the leading Sandgorgons as if he had *forbidden* them. A dozen paces away, they paused to study him.

Once long ago he had fought Nom to a standstill. He had not tried to kill the creature; but he had defeated it, forced it to submit—and to listen. He could do more. Yet his power then had not harmed Nom. It did not harm the Sandgorgons now. Their hides had some virtue against wild magic. They could withstand much of his ire.

Against so many of them, he would have to unleash far more wrath, more than he could hope to control—

He might shatter the cliff above the Defiles Course, sealing his only way into the mountain.

With argent bright in his eyes and silver burning on his scarred forehead as if his mind had become white fire, he ordered the monsters away. In Nom's name, and in his own, he commanded them to depart with their lives.

They did not acknowledge his authority. They were done with old respect and gratitude. Perhaps they now considered such emotions to be subservience. Instead they heeded *samadhi*—or *moksha* Raver speaking to them through *samadhi*'s remnants.

While more monsters sped down the valley, those watching Covenant and Branl changed their tactics. Rather than obeying their instincts, trying to batter or crush any obstacle, they showed that they could think.

First one of them crouched: then four more: then a score. One by one, they began hammering the ground with their forearms.

One was strong enough to cause vibrations that Covenant felt in spite of his numbness. Five made the earth under him shake, dislodged small stones, raised spouts from the dirt. A score—

He staggered as if he had been taken by vertigo. Flailing to stay on his feet, he had to yank his left hand away from the *krill*. For one heartbeat, two, three, Branl seemed untroubled, as immovable as the roots of a mountain. Then he was compelled to shift his feet, correcting his stance against the tremors.

As more Sandgorgons arrived, they seemed to understand what the nearer creatures were doing. Without hesitation, they grasped their advantage. Hurtling forward, they struck like albino lightning at Covenant and Branl.

Oh, they could *think*—

Yet they remained bestial. *Samadhi*'s mind was not natural to them, and it endured only in scraps of malevolence. Focusing on their foes, the Sandgorgons did not see a tentacle as thick as an ironwood unfurl itself from the Defiles Course; or they did not regard their peril.

In spite of his uncertain footing and Covenant's imbalance, Branl wrenched his companion out of the way as the tentacle swept like a scythe at the charging creatures.

The Sandgorgons were mighty. The lurker was mightier. It roared as if the tumult of fog had been given voice. With one heavy arm, Horrim Carabal blocked the charge. Swift as a spasm, the tentacle coiled around several of the monsters. Then it heaved them into the air.

Howling and savage, the lurker snatched those Sandgorgons to the river and slammed them down; held them under the fouled water.

At the same time, a second tentacle stretched upward. Guided by the invocations of the Feroce, or by its own instincts, the lurker's arm crashed like a felled tree onto the crouching Sandgorgons.

That blow scattered the monsters. It stopped the tremors.

In an instant, Branl recovered. He righted Covenant. Then he rushed into the confusion of the Sandgorgons, delivering cuts like a whirlwind of blades. Some of the creatures lost arms, or forearms. One lost a leg. Two fell dead before the others rallied against the sorcery of Lostson Longwrath's flamberge.

Covenant heard Linden's call then, but he had no chance to answer it. A screech from the lurker warned him. Turning, he saw the torn stump of the lurker's first tentacle writhe above the water, lashing the air with gore. He saw Sandgorgons spring, unharmed, out of the Defiles Course.

Ah, hell.

"*Don't stop!*" he yelled at the Feroce. "I know he's hurt! Hurt is better than *dead*!"

Summoning himself, he wrapped both hands around the *krill* once more. Then he moved toward the river. With every step, he mustered more of his power. In his grasp, the dagger seemed to grow longer, brighter, keener. The physical blade remained unchanged, but his wild magic became a longsword implied by Loric's theurgy.

He remembered the Seven Words. They were of no use to him. They bespoke Earthpower and Law. His force was of another kind altogether. He focused it with curses as familiar as leprosy.

Facing a group of Sandgorgons, with more on the way, he did not hesitate.

He had slashed one and pierced another before they appeared to realize that he had become dangerous. Suddenly chary, they retreated from the cut of wild magic.

Covenant's world contracted until it contained only Sandgorgons. Somewhere at the edges of his marred vision, innominate shapes swirled in and out of the fog; but he had no time to recognize them. Praying that they were some manifestation of the lurker's magicks—that Branl had not fallen—that Linden could contrive to preserve herself and Jeremiah and the Giants—he anchored himself on his argent blade and assailed the creatures in front of him.

His wife had cried out to him, but he had not answered. He had only one answer left: one answer—and no opportunity to try it. No way of knowing whether it would suffice.

The lurker's remaining arm pounded at the Sandgorgons again. Again. Some lurched, apparently hurt. One crumpled and did not rise again. Most withstood the blows as if they lived for such tests of their puissance.

Impassive and lethal, Branl fought on. But his foes had changed their tactics again. He could no longer spin hacking and thrusting among them. Instead they backed away, gained a little distance. Then they spread out to surround him.

And from the mountainsides still more Sandgorgons plunged downward. They seemed numberless: a horde of havoc.

Higher up in the valley, Linden flung Earthpower like screams at the *skurj*. Her Staff sent out an unremitting barrage of flame, as black as death in the Lost Deep, and as extravagant as her struggle against Roger and the *croyel* under *Melenkurion* Skyweir. Theurgy that might have carved gutrock blasted monsters on all sides. Many she hurt, delayed, enraged. Some she slew. But they were creatures of lava, spawned in magma. They could shrug aside appalling quantities of her fire. And more came: so many that her every gasp filled her lungs with brimstone and putrescence. *Moksha* Jehannum must have brought every living *skurj* here from their former prison in the far north.

Her horror was gone. She had sweated it out in heat and fury. Spots of anoxia danced across her vision like burgeoning infections. The wood of her Staff bucked and recoiled as though it might break into splinters at any moment. Her pulse had become an undifferentiated stutter in her veins, too ragged and urgent for individual beats. Even Jeremiah's sporadic shouts and warnings did not reach her. There was no room left in her for anything except Earthpower and *skurj*.

She was failing. For all her frenzy and desperation, her exertions did not suffice. The monsters far outnumbered her abilities. Even if she had been galvanized by the EarthBlood, as she had been under *Melenkurion* Skyweir, she would have been no match for the host surging against her.

Around her, her friends strove like demons against impossible odds. They fought in pairs, supporting each other: Stonemage and Galesend, Grueburn and Bluntfist. Cabledarm also had left Jeremiah. With Stave like a Giant at her side, she committed all of her strength to the fray. Exchanging feints and cuts, they wrought bloodshed among the monsters. Only Rime Coldspray stayed to ward Linden. Only maimed Cirrus Kindwind watched over Jeremiah.

In small bursts, momentary and localized, the Swordmainnir succeeded. They appeared to kill or cripple every creature they met. And Stave did as much as any titan—until an untimely snap of jaws broke his longsword. After that, he had no choice except to throw the shard of his blade down the monster's throat, and to withdraw while he searched for some other weapon. His bare flesh could not survive any contact with the monsters.

Without him, Cabledarm fought alone.

Nevertheless the companions were doomed. The *skurj* were simply too many to be overcome by frenetic Earthpower and a few Giants. And those creatures which did not attack fed. They multiplied. Much of the valley bottom had become a mad seethe of monsters as vicious as scoria, as fatal as the white core of a furnace. Many of the trees had gone up in flames, but their destruction made no difference.

Linden no longer thought. In some sense, she no longer cared. She was too far gone to count her concerns. As far as she knew, her husband and Branl were already dead. She had only moments left. Jeremiah would survive only if Lord Foul or *mok-sha* Jehannum turned the monsters aside.

Abruptly Cabledarm went down. She did not rise again. Stormpast Galesend fell with a fountain of blood where her arm had been. One of the *skurj* pounced on her before Linden could intervene.

Instantly Stave dove into the struggle, claimed Cabledarm's sword. He joined Onyx Stonemage before she was overwhelmed.

Strands of fog tumbled among the combatants, obscured details until crimson and obsidian fires burned holes in the streamers. Through the confusion, Linden saw too many Giants: half a dozen more than there should have been. Giddy with exhaustion and flame, she tried to count. Three Swordmainnir still fought. Coldspray and Kindwind made five. How could there be more?

"Welcome!" the Ironhand shouted with a tantara in her voice. "Well come in all sooth!" Then she yelled, "Assume my task, and Kindwind's, that we may give battle!"

The others—the *others*?—were not Swordmainnir. Most of them were men. They wore canvas breeches and shirts rather than armor. And they carried no swords. Two had spears. Another appeared to drive an entire spar between the jaws of a *skurj*. Linden saw a collection of billhooks with whetted edges, belaying-pins longer than one of her arms, knouts studded with sharp stones, immense cleavers.

Such weapons should have been useless here; yet they wrought confusion among the nearest monsters. Billhooks tore open the hinges of jaws, left maws unable to close. Belaying-pins smashed teeth. Knouts distracted creatures while spears stabbed. Cleavers shed blood wherever they could. In spite of their bulk, the Giants moved with the agility of sailors trained to weather hurricanes.

They were a paltry force against the onslaught of *skurj*. Still they fought as if they were singing; as if they were glad to spend their lives in a hopeless cause.

The man who had fed his spar to a monster broke free of the battle, came toward Linden and Coldspray. "Ironhand," he panted, grinning. Reflections of Earthpower and lava in his eyes resembled the exultation of hysteria or madness. "I hear and obey. Stone and Sea! We are lost."

Rime Coldspray did not pause to acknowledge him. Roaring a Giantish battle-cry, she took her stone glaive into the heart of the turmoil.

To Linden, the man remarked, "My name is unwieldy in such straits. For ease of use in peril, I am called Hurl."

She hardly heard him.

A woman with the charred remains of a knout in one hand followed Hurl; hastened past Linden. As soon as the woman neared Jeremiah, Cirrus Kindwind ran to join the Ironhand. Swinging her longsword one-handed, Kindwind dealt furious cuts at every *skurj* within reach. But she did not pursue her attack on any single creature. Her tactic was speed. Apparently her only objective was to cause pain; to weaken her foes with wounds.

Stave also relied on swiftness. Still he fought with the precision of a surgeon. He seemed inhumanly adept at slicing open the hearts of monsters. Somehow he avoided every slash of fangs, every scalding splash of blood, every brimstone touch.

It was all futile. One of the newly arrived Giants died directly below Linden. She could not save him. She had forgotten the Sandgorgons; forgotten Covenant and Branl. She had nothing left except a kind of autonomic ferocity. She had fought her way beyond the precipice of her strength and power. Now she could only flail and fall.

Yet the surprise of more Giants appeared to affect the *skurj*. It altered the focus of their rampage; or they received new commands from the evil which had replaced Kastenessen as their master. Their dim minds—or *moksha* Raver's—recognized that Linden and the Giants were trivial: puny opponents easily eaten later. A greater enemy awaited their fangs, an antagonist whose power might provide a richer feast. Wild magic might slaughter every one of the monsters; or it might exalt them, if they were able to feed on it.

In a staggered cadence, as if some *skurj* were more reluctant than others, they turned toward the lower end of the valley.

There near the Sarangrave and the Defiles Course, Covenant fought for time. He needed a respite, just a few moments for his only answer. His last gamble. He had to be able to stand back and *concentrate*— And even then, he might be too late.

But he could not take the chance while Sandgorgons forced him to struggle for every moment of life.

He saw Giants now. They seemed to come from nowhere, as if they were an incarnation of the fog. Five, no, six of them, two women, the rest men. Not Swordmainnir. They looked like sailors armed with implements from their ship. Their movements were swift and accurate, but they lacked the fluid poise of warriors.

Still they were apt foes for Sandgorgons, more agile than Covenant, twice Branl's size. One against one, their sheer muscle matched the savagery of the monsters. Their skin was not hide bred in the extremes of the Great Desert and the brutal gyre of

Sandgorgons Doom. They could not slough off crushing blows and ruinous waters. But their instincts and reflexes were not hampered by single-mindedness. They fought with intelligence as well as strength; with skills which they had earned in storms.

And they did not fight alone. The lurker's tentacle continued its battery, pounding at as many creatures as it could reach. At the same time, Branl seemed to float through the contest as if he served his blade; as if he were a weapon wielded by the eldritch flamberge. If a Giant halted a Sandgorgon with a blow or a cut, the *Haruchai* arrived bearing death.

Although the newcomers were only six, they fought like furies. Their weapons soon failed them. Knives broke on the hides of Sandgorgons. Knouts had no effect. Spears only pierced when they struck perfectly. Still the Giants were Giants, powerful of fist and arm. Few as they were, they thwarted the onrush of monsters.

Somehow the Giants and the lurker and Branl cleared a space around Covenant.

That should have been enough for him. He had been offered his chance. He only needed to gather himself.

But his damaged chest sucked air in wracked gasps; and vertigo filled his head as if he stood on an appalling height, peering down into the valley from the fatal slopes of Mount Thunder; and he had never unlearned his fear of unrestrained wild magic. He could too easily imagine shattering the high cliff above the river.

Then he was given more than a momentary reprieve. A kind of convulsion seemed to grip the Sandgorgons as if an invisible hand had taken hold of their minds. They paused; scanned the valley as if they sought more satisfying opponents. An instant later, they wheeled away.

Some of them delivered a last flurry of blows, but soon all of them were pounding back up the valley. Massed and eager, they formed a bleached river pouring irresistibly uphill. At the same time, the *skurj* began to squirm downward, horrific numbers of the serpent-monsters. As the Sandgorgons ascended, they parted only to let scores of *skurj* pass among them.

The attackers had traded targets. The Sandgorgons raced to assail Linden and Jeremiah and the surviving Swordmainnir. A tsunami of *skurj* plunged toward Covenant and Branl and their unforeseen allies.

Covenant's vision was too badly blurred: he could not tell how many Giants still stood with Linden. He recognized her only by the faltering fever of her Staff, her stained fire.

Damnation. He did not know how she would fare against the Sandgorgons. Even aided by Branl and Giants, he would not be able to withstand the onslaught of *skurj*. Even if he ripped open the mountain—

"*More!*" he cried at the Feroce. "We need *more!*"

The lurker's minions had withdrawn, flinching, toward the Flat. They may not have heard him. They or their High God may have chosen not to hear him.

Cursing himself for every lost instant, Covenant dismissed his wild magic longsword. Now or never. What good was leprosy if he could not trust its implications? If it did not enable him to bear what he required of himself?

In one quick motion, he pulled the blade of the *krill* across his left palm, drew blood sluggish with dehydration. He had no staff, no instrument of Law. Like Berek Halfhand before him, he needed blood and desperation to accomplish what even wild magic could not. Clenching his cut hand, he slapped red drops against the dagger's gem. Then he flung his gaze upward, past Linden and the onset of Sandgorgons, past the outpouring of the Defiles Course, past the towering cliff to the highest slopes of the mountain. In his mind, he shouted the Seven Words: a prayer that had no voice.

A prayer that meant, *Please.*

Almost immediately, he was answered.

Power without shape or sound exploded in him, through him, around him. A detonation both silent and invisible shocked the valley from end to end. Theurgy as old as the world seemed to ripple across the fabric of reality. It jolted the Sandgorgons in their strides; bewildered the *skurj* so badly that some of them turned on each other. Sights that should have been clear blurred and merged. The slopes on both sides of the river trembled.

After the concussion came stillness: a quiet so profound that it appeared to stop time. Existence held its breath. The Sandgorgons began strides which they did not complete. *Skurj* paused with their lurid jaws wide. Fangs or brains forgot themselves. Giants tried to flick glances at each other, or at Covenant, and found that they could not move. Only Branl—

Lowering his blade, the Humbled bowed to Covenant as if he understood. As if he approved.

A moment later, the entire sky became thunderheads, black as ur-viles, impenetrable as gutrock. The heavens poised themselves for a blast which would rattle Gravin Threndor to its roots.

As if on command, the lurker struck. From the Defiles Course, a tentacle lashed at the baffled *skurj*. It wrapped itself around one of the monsters.

Shrieking in pain, Horrim Carabal lifted the creature.

The tentacle caught fire: it burned like aged wood. Rabid flames streaked the air. The lurker's agony must have been extreme: worse than *turiya* Raver's violation; worse than self-mutilation. Yet the sovereign of the Sarangrave did not let go. Instead it flung the *skurj* eastward over the wetland.

That creature did not return.

Nor did the lurker. Its arm collapsed into the river, smothered flames in water and corruption. Sounds like the sobbing of marshes roiled through the fog. No other tentacles appeared.

Through Horrim Carabal's wailing came a deep concussion as unanswerable as a tectonic shift. Mount Thunder itself seemed to howl as gouts of sizzling rock swept downward. Storms boiled lower until they shrouded Gravin Threndor's high crown.

And from the depths of the Flat, waters rose against the current of the Defiles Course as if they had been summoned by the mountain. Dark thrashing swelled between the riverbanks.

Covenant hardly noticed the river. Dimly in the distance, he thought that he saw yellow fires break through the clouds. He thought that he saw discrete flames surge lower like the onset of an avalanche. They roared as if the very air had become conflagration.

"You are answered, ur-Lord," Branl announced distinctly. "A worthy effort in all sooth. How the forces which you have unleashed may combat *skurj*, who are themselves a form of fire, I cannot conceive. Nonetheless the summons is both valiant and unforeseen. I am proud that I am Humbled in your name."

At last, Covenant began to see the fires more clearly. They looked impossibly far away: too far away to reach the valley before the Sandgorgons and the *skurj* remembered their savagery. But now he was sure that those flames were Fire-Lions. They embodied Earthpower and Mount Thunder's enduring spirit. They could be as swift as the theurgy which had called them forth.

The Sandgorgons rallied more quickly than the *skurj*. But the monsters of the Great Desert did not resume their charge toward Linden and her few companions. Their strange senses marked the rush of a new threat. And some deep part of them—an instinct too atavistic to heed *samadhi* Sheol—responded with eagerness. They had been bred in scorching heat and flaying winds, and had been trapped for millennia within the scouring energies of Sandgorgons Doom. Their urge to prove themselves against any and every foe outweighed *samadhi*'s urgings. It outweighed self-preservation.

Together they turned away from Linden, strode deliberately down into the bottom of the valley. There they stood like a wall, awaiting the landslide fury of the Fire-Lions.

They had already demonstrated that they had no cause to fear the rising waters.

Beasts of flame became torrents on the mountainsides. They spread like wildfires toward the sheer drop above the river.

Muttering mute curses like supplications, Covenant watched the cliff and the

Sandgorgons. If *samadhi* and *moksha* did not regain control of those creatures—if the uncertainty of the *skurj* lasted just a little longer—

Behind Covenant, the Feroce gibbered for his attention. "Pure One, hear us." Their pleading was a damp clamor, scarcely audible through the tumult of Fire-Lions, the scald and crash of ancient magicks. "Our High God's flesh cannot endure the worms of fire. He must not hazard them. Yet the alliance has been sealed. Even in his anguish, our High God upholds it.

"You must seek higher ground. We have done what we have done. The Feroce can do no more."

While Covenant stared, stricken witless, Branl called, "Ur-Lord!" He sounded uncharacteristically urgent. "Heed the Feroce! The waters rise!"

"Well said, *Haruchai*," muttered a Giant as he snatched Covenant into his arms. He had a seamed face, and skin toughened by wind and sun, yet he looked as slender as a sapling, or as incomplete, like a man whose body was decades younger than his visage. Nevertheless his muscles were hawsers. "This fog masks a mounting flood. A tide gathers from the east. Even Giants cannot swim such waters."

The *skurj* turned away from the cliff, away from the Sandgorgons. Those monsters which had bitten into other *skurj*, seeking blood and sustenance, ceased their feeding. Rearing like serpents, they brandished their fangs at Covenant; at Branl and six unknown Giants.

Together the Giants scrambled out from under a breaking wave of reified lava. Covenant dangled, helpless in his rescuer's arms, trying to understand events which had become as sudden as vertigo. At the rear of the group, Branl fought alone, swinging Longwrath's flamberge in a blur of cuts. But he retreated as he slashed, moving quickly without giving the monsters his back. The thunder of the Fire-Lions sounded like ruin, the gutrock rumble of an earthquake powerful enough to tear Landsdrop apart. The tumult of water rising from the Sarangrave resembled the onrush of another tsunami.

At the full stretch of their long limbs, the Giants raced for the southern rim of the valley. A long stone's throw away, more Giants bore Linden and Jeremiah upward. Swinging a longsword, Stave accompanied them. Branl cut twice more at the nearest creatures, then turned to follow the Giants.

When the Fire-Lions met the wall of Sandgorgons, and Horrim Carabal's flood found the *skurj*, the result was cataclysm. It shook the foundations of the Lower Land for leagues in every direction. Struck by acrid eruptions of steam and fury, the thunderheads became a bludgeoning deluge that seemed to erase the valley from existence. Rain fell like the ultimate darkness.

Then the Giants raised a huzzah, ragged and grateful. The monsters were dying, all of them. Dimly Covenant realized that most of his companions had survived. He had seen Linden's fire before the end. Lord Foul would not have permitted harm to Jeremiah.

Carried by a Giant whom he had never met before, Thomas Covenant felt no relief. He had exhausted himself. Now he was too stunned to feel anything.

4.

Reluctances

 The downpour lasted until the Fire-Lions were done with the Sandgorgons; until all of the *skurj* were dead, and the lurker's flood dwindled to the east; until *samadhi* Sheol's sentience had faded entirely from existence. Then the thunderheads drifted apart as if they had forgotten their purpose. The chill of rain and darkness dismissed the fog. Glittering as if they trembled at what they beheld, stars pricked the night sky with loveliness.

Linden did not see the Fire-Lions depart. For all she knew, they, too, had perished. But she did not think so. Gravin Threndor's ancient fire and glory were inherent to the world, as natural as the Worm. She doubted that they could be unmade.

She rested under the shelter of an ironwood high up on the side of the valley, as far as possible from the craters and carnage of the battle, the plague-spots like stigmata in the ground, the clinging reek of gangrene. Leaning against the hard trunk with the Staff of Law in her lap, she waited for some semblance of strength to return.

She was too tired to be afraid. Too drained even to stay on her feet after Hurl had delivered her here. Too depleted to regard Jeremiah, or Covenant, or the Giants. Instead she floated into the lucidity of exhaustion: that numb mind-set in which unbidden thoughts followed their own logic to conclusions that might not have made sense at any other time.

In your present state, Chosen—

She was done with fighting. That much had become clear to her.

—Desecration lies ahead of you.

God, she had endured so much violence— From her struggles against Roger Covenant and the *croyel* to the horrors and killing beside the Defiles Course, she had fought and fought. With wild magic, she had shed the lives of scores or hundreds of misled Cavewights.

You have become the daughter of my heart. It was enough. She was done. Ever since Jeremiah's escape from his graves, the foundations of her life had been shifting. They needed to shift further.

She did not mean that she had given up. Carried along by the syllogisms of prostration, she arrived at convictions which did not imply surrender. She had seen her husband find his way through an appalling conundrum of *skurj* and Sandgorgons. She had seen Giants appear out of nowhere to hazard their lives; seen the lurker of the Sarangrave set aside its old malevolence and choose to endure terrible pain. Rime Coldspray and four of her Swordmainnir had given battle while three loved comrades were slain. Stave and Branl had fought as though they wielded the prowess of every living *Haruchai*. The fact that Linden and Covenant and Jeremiah were still alive meant many things. It did not entail or require surrender.

But she could not keep meeting peril with violence, striving to out-do the savagery of Lord Foul's servants and allies. She could not. She needed a different purpose, a better role in the Land's fate. She had passed through the wrath of Gallows Howe to the gibbet's deeper truths; to the vast bereavement which had inspired Garroting Deep's thirst for blood. The time had come to heed the lessons which her whole life had tried to teach her.

If she did not give up, and did not fight, what remained? She thought that she knew, although she trembled to contemplate it; or she would have trembled had she been less weary.

There is hope in contradiction.

Maybe that was true. If she did not know how to forgive herself, she could begin by offering other forms of grace to people or beings who needed it more.

The daughter of my heart? she thought. Give me a chance. Let me show you what your daughter has in mind.

She was still the Chosen. She could make decisions and go in directions which the Despiser might not expect.

After that, her helpless clarity looped back to its starting point. She was done with fighting; with violence and killing. One idea at a time, she followed the same logic to the same conclusions. Exhaustion was like that, she knew. Under the right circumstances, it shed a certain amount of light; but its own conditions prevented it from casting its illumination further.

Later Hurl came to her with a satchel of dried fruit and cured mutton. He also offered her a flask of *diamondraught* diluted with fresh water: enough of the Giantish liquor, he said, to restore her, but not so much that it would impose sleep. And when she had eaten a little and drunk more, she found that she felt strong enough to focus her eyes and look around.

The survivors were lit like reincarnations of themselves by the silver of the *krill* in Branl's grasp. Jeremiah's distress called out to her. He sat huddled against the trunk of a tree nearby, but he did not look at her—or at anything outside himself. With his arms wrapped around his knees and his face hidden against his thighs, he rocked back and forth like a child in too much pain. Stave and Cirrus Kindwind stood with him. The Giant murmured reassurances that Linden could not hear. Stave's stance suggested that he was keeping watch.

Hurl had joined most of the other newcomers a short distance away. From somewhere—presumably among the fringes of the Sarangrave—they had retrieved sacks bulging with supplies: food and more *diamondraught*; other things which they considered necessary, and which they must have carried for many leagues. As Stonemage, Grueburn, and Bluntfist gathered with them, the canvas-clad men and women handed out viands and refreshment.

The surviving Swordmainnir and several of the other Giants bore oozing scalds. Contact with the blood and entrails of the *skurj* had burned them. But they were Giants, able to endure fulminating hurts. One and all, they were grieving over their fallen comrades. Yet that hurt, also, they were able to endure, at least for a while.

Down the slope from Linden, Covenant stood with Branl, Rime Coldspray, and another Giant, an implausibly thin man who appeared to speak for the sailors. Like Stave, Branl was unscathed. The hunch of Covenant's shoulders told Linden that he had fallen hard, damaged his chest. Her nerves detected cracked ribs and some dislodged cartilage, but no broken bones. Nevertheless his manner resembled the ravaged hillsides.

"I swear to you," he was saying, "I thought it made sense. This is what happens when I convince myself I know what I'm doing. Even after Lord Foul touched Jeremiah, I thought we could sneak in here. I'm still not sure we could get in any other way. But this was a disaster.

"Hellfire, Coldspray! I just about got us all killed." To the other Giant, he added, "If you hadn't showed up—"

Or if, Linden amended on his behalf, he had not feared his own power; if he had unleashed enough wild magic to cleanse the whole valley. If he had indeed been *done with restraint*. Yet she believed that he had done well to hold back. He had little health-sense, and wild magic tended always to resist control. He might have inadvertently killed his companions.

"Enough, Timewarden," the Ironhand replied, peremptory with fatigue and loss.

"It is bootless to fault yourself for an onslaught which you could not have foreseen. Our peril here was both extreme and bitter. Yet it has not exceeded the hazards of the more direct road. And here we have found aid as unforeseen as our foes."

Linden nodded privately. Soon she would have to go to Covenant, if he did not approach her first. She needed his embrace to console her. And she wanted to explain herself as well as she could. She was done keeping secrets, especially from him.

But her son took precedence. She could only imagine what Lord Foul's visions and his own helplessness had done to him.

She allowed herself a bit more food, a few more swallows of *diamondraught*-tinged water. Then she began the immense labor of rising to her feet.

At once, Stave came to help her. His hand on her arm lifted her, steadied her. His single eye studied her as if she were no longer closed to him. In silence, he supported her toward Jeremiah.

As Linden approached, Cirrus Kindwind moved away. Clearly she needed the solace of her own people.

Every step sharpened Linden's perception of her son's despair. Her nerves assured her that his mind was still present. Although he rocked back and forth like an abused child, he had not retreated to his graves. Nevertheless he looked lost in misery.

For a moment, she paused to think. But she was too tired and sure to reconsider anything. Lowering herself down the Staff of Law, she knelt facing Jeremiah. Then she set the Staff on the soaked ground between them.

"Jeremiah, honey. Can you hear me? Are you listening?"

Hugging his face against his thighs, he rocked harder.

"Jeremiah, listen." Her voice was a sigh. "I know it's hard." How many times had Thomas said that to her? "But we're still alive." Others were not. "This isn't the end. We can finish what we started."

Muffled by his legs, Jeremiah whispered, "You can. I can't."

Linden searched herself for strength. "What do you mean?"

Slowly his head came up as if he were summoning indignation; as if her question insulted him. Memories of Sandgorgons and *skurj* capered like ghouls in his haunted gaze.

"Because I can't *do* anything, that's why." He made a visible effort to sound angry, but his voice held only anguish. "I wasn't even in danger. Foul wants me alive. But there were all those monsters, and I couldn't help you. I couldn't do anything except watch. And even when I did that, I could still see the Worm. Even when Latebirth and Galesend were dying, and it was horrible, and there was blood everywhere, and those fangs. I could still see the Worm. Every minute, it does more damage than all the *skurj* in the world, and there's nothing I can do."

As guerdon for his puerile valor—

Aching for him, Linden summoned her courage. "I know. It must have been terrible for you. That's why I want you to take my Staff."

She expected surprise, but he only looked away. "Why? It won't make any difference. I can't use it. I don't know how. It isn't mine. You'll just have to take it back. You won't have any choice."

She was tempted to reach out and shake him; but she refrained. He was too full of dismay to appreciate what she was offering him. As calmly as she could, she admitted, "We might have to take turns at first. The Giants and Thomas are hurt. They need me. But you can still get started. And I don't always have to hold it. I can use some of its power without touching it. That doesn't change anything. I still want you to have it. I want it to be yours."

"Why?" Jeremiah repeated like a groan.

"Because you need to be able to defend yourself," he needed to believe in himself, "and I don't need it anymore. I have white gold—and I can't use both. No one can. Earthpower and wild magic together are too much. So now I want to learn how to handle my ring. I want you to learn how to use the Staff."

"I can't," he said again. "I don't have any idea—"

"Jeremiah." She made his name sound like a reprimand. "We talked about this. Of course you don't know how. But you can learn. You don't even need my help. You have your health-sense and your own power. You can teach yourself.

"And if you have something else to concentrate on, you might be able to stop seeing the Worm. Earthpower and Law can do all kinds of healing. Maybe they can cure those visions. Maybe they can even keep the Despiser from taking you again."

Taking the risk, she finished, "And maybe you can find a way to make the Staff clean again. I know that I can't. That blackness is too much a part of me."

Jeremiah stared at her. The bleak torment in his gaze became a muddy roil. Its ambiguous currents twisted in unfamiliar directions, disguising their own depths. For a moment, she feared that he would pull away completely; that she had asked too much of him. That he would choose despair and dissociation.

But then he reached for her Staff.

"I'll try. I can't stand the way I am."

Blinking at an unexpected sting of tears, she said unsteadily, "Just remember what I told you. Start with your own Earthpower. Use it to touch what the Staff can do. You should be able to feel it. Then you'll be able to do more. It won't be easy at first. But you'll get better."

He ignored her now. Already distracted, he stroked the written wood, familiarizing himself with its texture, exploring its arcane script. Briefly he considered its iron heels as though they held the secrets he needed. Then he surged to his feet, holding the Staff of Law as if he wanted to swing it around his head.

Ah, God. Feeling strangely naked, bereft, like a woman who had just said farewell to her son's childhood, Linden climbed upright. She was grateful for Stave's firm grip on her arm, reliable as a corner-stone; but she had no words to offer her friend. Before she could do or say anything else, she needed to stop weeping.

"I do not scry, Chosen," the former Master remarked without any discernible emotion. "To my sight, the future holds only darkness. Yet I judge that you have acted wisely. The boy's need is great, and you have other strengths."

Fortunately Stave did not appear to expect a response. Without a sign from her, he guided her toward Covenant.

As she drew near, Covenant turned away from Rime Coldspray and the lean Giant. His gaze was feverish with pain, and the lines of his face had been cut deeper: he seemed to have aged years in the past few hours. Even without his memories of the Arch, he bore the burden of too much time. His damaged chest was the least of his hurts. At the core, he was defined by his rage for lepers; for the innocent victims of Despite. He hated the necessary fact that other people suffered so that he might oppose Lord Foul.

Wincing whenever his ribs shifted, he held out his arms to his wife.

Fearing that she had just sacrificed her son—the first step toward sacrificing herself—Linden stepped into Covenant's embrace as if she were falling.

It was a mercy that he did not speak. Words were demands. For a few moments, at least, she simply needed to be held. And no one else's arms felt like his. Even Jeremiah's hugs could not comfort her now.

But as she leaned on Covenant, she felt his injuries more keenly, his bodily hurts and his aggrieved spirit. He held himself responsible for too much. And she had done nothing to ease or heal him.

With her health-sense, she reached out for the Earthpower of the Staff. As she had done once to relieve a suffering Waynhim, she invoked healing from a distance.

At first, she focused her heart on the distress in Covenant's chest. But when she had restored the integrity of his ribs and cartilage, she turned the balm of Law on the scalds and exhaustion of the Giants.

"Thanks, love," Covenant murmured when she was done. "That helps." His arms tightened around her.

Rime Coldspray and several of the other Giants stood straighter. In spite of their sadness, they smiled.

"Thomas." Linden held Covenant closer. She wished that she could talk to him privately. The things which she had to say were difficult enough: she did not want anyone else to hear them. But she had learned to distrust that impulse. "I need to tell you something."

While I still can.

He released a pent up breath. "So tell me."

"I love you." There was no good way to say it. Words were inadequate. "I want to help you. I want you to stop Lord Foul. I want the Land to be saved, and the Earth, and the stars, and the *Elohim*," although she could not imagine how any of those deeds might be accomplished. "I want Jeremiah safe, and all of our friends, and everything that we've ever cared about.

"But I'm done fighting."

Covenant stiffened as if she had frightened him. His voice was harsh with strain as he asked, "And you think you have a choice?"

He did not let her go.

She nodded against the thin fabric of his T-shirt.

"So tell me," he repeated through his teeth.

To make room for what she had to say, she eased away until she could touch his chest. Kissing the tips of her fingers, she slipped them through the old knife cut in his shirt. "You said it yourself. We have to face the things that scare us the most. There's really no other way. Escape isn't worth what it costs.

"But the Despiser isn't what scares me the most. Even losing Jeremiah isn't. Or losing you. That might break me, but it isn't my worst fear. And the Worm—

"Thomas, I've hardly seen the Land the way it was when you fell in love with it. That first time, when we came here together, it was all the Sunbane. And since then, we've lost too much, and I've been going crazy about Jeremiah.

"Oh, Andelain has changed my life. More than once." Glimmermere and *aliantha* and percipience and the Ranyhyn had all changed her. "But I simply haven't learned how to care about this world as much as you do. The Worm isn't my worst fear."

Before he could prompt her, she said, "My worst fear is what I might become. Or what I've already become. I need to face that somehow."

"Then how—?" Covenant began. But he stopped himself. For a moment, he seemed to scramble like a man who felt the ground shifting under his feet. Then his head jerked up as if his chest had been pierced again; as if she had stabbed him. She felt the jolt of his intuitive leap. "Oh. *That* fear. Now I get it."

Linden nodded again. Trying to be clear, she said, "Days ago, you left me because you had to deal with Joan. If we live long enough, I'll have to leave you."

And her son.

Gripping her shoulders, he stared like wild magic into her face. "That's why you gave Jeremiah your Staff."

"One of the reasons," she conceded. Now that he understood, she found it comparatively easy to bear his gaze. "Earthpower and Law can't help me. I have to use my ring."

At once, he pulled her close again, hugged her as though his heart refused to go on beating without her. "Hellfire, Linden," he breathed. "That's insane. It might be exactly what we need."

She matched his embrace. "And I'm the only one who can even try. You said that, too. You have to face Lord Foul. And Jeremiah has to decide for himself. That leaves me."

"I remember," he said gruffly. "I must have been out of my mind."

Then he held her at arm's length again so that he could study the doubts and determinations following each other like ocean swells in her eyes.

"Well, why not?" he growled. "I didn't ask you and the First and Pitchwife to do my fighting for me when I decided to give up using power all those millennia ago, but you kept me alive anyway. Maybe I even expected you to do that. Why shouldn't it be your turn now? Sure, we have more enemies this time. But we also have more friends. And I think we're capable of things damn Foul has never seen before. Why shouldn't you get a chance to take your own risks?"

Linden smiled through a brief relapse of tears. "I knew that you would under-stand." Then she added, "But I haven't told Jeremiah. We aren't there yet. We might not live long enough to get there. And he has other things on his mind. I don't want to scare him until I'm sure that he needs to know."

Covenant nodded; but abruptly he was distracted. "I get it." He was no longer looking at her. "But suddenly things aren't as simple as they were a minute ago."

When she followed his gaze, her heart seemed to stop.

Holding the Staff, Jeremiah had summoned his heritage of Earthpower. Small flames spread from his hands onto the shaft. They traced the cryptic lines of the runes, blossomed briefly on the iron heels, measured the wood.

They were his—and they were stark black, as dark as ichor squeezed from the marrow of the world's bones.

"Jeremiah!" When Linden's pulse resumed its labor, it pounded in her temples, in her ears, at the base of her throat. "What are you doing?" She had asked him to change the Staff. Instead her own darkness was changing him.

He did not glance at her. "Don't bother me." His eyes echoed the hue of his flames. "I'm trying to concentrate. This is temporary. I mean, I think it's temporary. I just don't know what to do about it yet."

Scowling to himself, he muttered, "You're stronger than I thought. I can't figure out how you did it."

Linden meant to intervene. She thronged with objections, warnings, supplica-tions. But Covenant stopped her. With his hand on her cheek, he urged her to face him.

"Leave him alone for a while," he advised softly. "He wants to try. Maybe this is how he has to learn. Maybe he has to go through you to get to himself."

Covenant may have meant, Maybe he's starting to face his worst fear.

Linden wanted to believe him, but she could not. Her father had kept her locked in the attic with him while he killed himself. Her mother had begged her to end her life. Linden had given her Staff to Jeremiah of her own free will; but she did not know how to distance herself from his peril.

Yet what else could she do? She had already decided to leave him when last came to last. When there was nothing left for her except the dark.

Instead of stopping her son, she clung to her husband as if he were the only defense she had.

But slowly food, diluted *diamondraught*, and the aftereffects of Earthpower steadied Linden. By degrees, she regained a semblance of calm.

The same benefits wrought on her companions, the Giants if not the *Haruchai*, until the frenzy and desperation of battle began to fade. And as the Giants recovered, their need for tales grew.

Clearly the newcomers and the Swordmainnir were well known to each other. But much had occurred since they had parted: both groups had much to tell, and to hear. In particular, the sailors wanted to understand the confluence of events which had brought about the crisis of the Defiles Course. Because they were Giants, they knew about Covenant and Linden; but everything that pertained to Jeremiah was a mystery to them. And the Swordmainnir were eager to hear how their people had contrived to arrive when they were most needed.

When everyone had eaten, the sailors bundled up their supplies, leaving out a little food in case Linden or Covenant or Jeremiah wanted more. Then the Ironhand announced that the time had come, and her people gathered around her, aching and ready.

Linden stood among them with Covenant behind her, his arms around her. Branl joined Coldspray so that the *krill* would shed as much light as possible for the Giants. But Jeremiah seemed to have no interest in stories or woe. His immersion in his task was complete, as it always was when he worked on his constructs. His eyes watched flames while his hands made them dance and gambol on the Staff, or gave them shapes that suggested Ranyhyn, flickering portals, evanescent *Elohim*. Gradually he attuned himself. Nevertheless his every expression of magic remained as benighted as the world's doom.

Perhaps to reassure Linden, Stave positioned himself near her son; but he did nothing to distract Jeremiah.

The Ironhand began by introducing the newly arrived Giants, seven men and four women. Hurl Linden had already met. Their leader was the Anchormaster of Dire's Vessel, the Giantship which had brought the Swordmainnir and Longwrath to the Land. His name was Bluff Stoutgirth, although he was lean to the point of emaciation; and his mien hinted that he was more inclined to hilarity than to command. Here, however, his manner was grave and grieving. His sailors and Rime Coldspray's Swordmainnir had endured much together during their voyage to the Land. They felt their losses keenly.

For Linden and Covenant, and for the *Haruchai*, Bluff Stoutgirth named his comrades—Etch Furledsail, Squallish Blustergale, Keenreef, Wiver Setrock, others— but Linden doubted that she would remember them all. Still she was grateful for the knowledge that they had come from Dire's Vessel. That detail made the fact, if not the timeliness, of their arrival comprehensible.

The Anchormaster offered to tell his tale first. It was, he suspected, both shorter and kinder than that of the Swordmainnir, though perhaps no less unforeseen. With Rime Coldspray's assent, he began.

After the departure of the Ironhand's company, Dire's Vessel had remained in the anchorage of ancient *Coercri*, The Grieve of the Unhomed. For a number of days, the sailors busied themselves with the mundane tasks of repairing and maintaining their Giantship. Then they began to notice changes in the littoral's weather, disturbances in the sea. Storms lashed the coast and disappeared again without apparent cause. Downpours drenched Dire's Vessel out of clear skies. Currents ran awry, heaving the Giantship from side to side until anchors were set at every point of the compass. Still the Swordmainnir did not return. They had vanished among the uncertainties of their quest.

Five mornings ago, however, the sun astonished the crew—Stoutgirth said this with improbable good cheer—by failing to rise. Stars began to disappear from the firmament of the heavens. Mighty swells from the southeast threatened Dire's Vessel's moorings. Such occurrences augured some immense and dolorous ill, but the sailors could not interpret the signs.

Yet on the following day a new astonishment appeared. Striding forth from tales many centuries old, a man made himself manifest upon the foredeck of Dire's Vessel.

That he was a man of immense age was plain. The lines upon his visage were such that they mapped a world. Indeed, his years had been so prolonged that they appeared to erode his substance where he stood. His raiment was ancient, an unkempt robe of indeterminate hue, and his limbs wore hatchments of scars. Yet he bore himself as one who could not be bowed, and his glances had the effect of lightnings.

Unmistakably, Bluff Stoutgirth announced, the man was one of the *Haruchai*. Indeed, he was unmistakably Brinn, the companion of the ur-Lord Thomas Covenant and the Sun-Sage Linden Avery aboard Starfare's Gem: the *Haruchai* who had become the Guardian of the One Tree.

The Guardian's tidings were dire in all sooth, Stoutgirth confessed. "The Worm of the World's End is roused, seeking the ruin of all things. Therefore the One Tree withers. The life of the Earth nears its close." Yet when the Giants bewailed their lot, moaning the loss of love and wind and stone, of seas and joy and children, Brinn answered their lament.

"Yet good may come from loss as it does from gain. The decline of the One Tree has concluded my devoir. I am freed to remember the promises of an earlier age. And the Worm is not instant in its feeding. Life lingers yet in the world's heartwood. This gift is granted to me, that I may expend my waning strength in the Land's service.

"While I endure, I will guide you, for your aid will be sorely needed."

None aboard Dire's Vessel, the Anchormaster continued, could comprehend that need. Yet their hearts were lifted by the thought that they might yet be of use in the Earth's last peril. In a foreshortened Giantclave, the Master of Dire's Vessel, Vigilall Scudweather, determined that she and a half portion of the crew would remain to tend the Giantship, praying that events would allow them to serve some worthy purpose in their turn. Bluff Stoutgirth and the others prepared such supplies and weapons as they were able to carry swiftly. Then they followed the Guardian of the One Tree from The Grieve into Seareach, tending always to the southwest toward the toils of Sarangrave Flat and the renowned perils of the lurker.

For a wonder, they passed into and through the Sarangrave unthreatened. Indeed, their course was eased at every obstacle, though they had no understanding of the magicks which relieved their efforts. In another matter, however, fortune gazed less kindly upon them. The Guardian's diminishment was unremitting, and no succor of companionship or repast eased it. During the evening of the day now past, he frayed at last and faded, drifting away along the world's winds. Then the Giants feared that naught remained to thwart the Worm. Yet they persevered, for the Guardian had led them far enough to descry Mount Thunder. They knew their destination. Therefore they hastened onward, denying themselves all sorrow for Brinn *Haruchai*, until they beheld turmoil upon the mountain. And at the last, fortune smiled once more. The Giants of Dire's Vessel did not come too late.

So Bluff Stoutgirth ended his tale.

"Joy is in the ears that hear," Rime Coldspray replied formally, "not in the mouth that speaks. Upon occasion, however, both ears and mouth may know joy, for its causes are plain to all. When we foundered in strife and loss, your coming lifted our hearts. We are Giants and must grieve. Yet we are filled with gladness also. You are a brightness amid the world's dusk."

The other Swordmainnir offered their thanks and pleasure as well. But they fell silent when Covenant began to speak. Holding Linden tightly, he addressed the sailors with a familiar ache in his voice.

"Brinn talked about a service or boon. Even after he saved my life, he wasn't done. But he didn't tell me what he had in mind. Now I know. You're his last service. His boon. We weren't enough. We needed help. No matter what happens, we're going to need more."

Linden nodded. Manethrall Mahrtiir had spoken truly. *And betimes some wonder is wrought to redeem us.* The Giants of Dire's Vessel had given Covenant time to summon the Fire-Lions.

But the Swordmainnir did not linger over their gratitude. Their weariness ran deep; and there was much that Stoutgirth and his crew needed to know.

"As you have surmised," the Ironhand began, sighing, "our tale is both lengthy and unforeseen. It has cost us lives and blood and sorrow. The worth of our deeds is not ours to proclaim. Yet I will trust that worth resembles joy. It will be found in the ears that hear if the mouth that speaks cannot name it."

Then Rime Coldspray gave the Giants of Dire's Vessel her story.

At first, Linden listened uncomfortably. The Ironhand described events and purposes in more forgiving terms than Linden could have managed, especially where Linden herself was concerned. She had to stifle an impulse to add her own stringent counterpoint to the arching cadences of Coldspray's narration. But gradually the Ironhand's tone filled her thoughts, lulling her until she drifted on the currents of Coldspray's voice.

Beyond the reach of the *krill*'s gem, darkness waited as though the whole truth of the world had become night. Overhead the watching stars seemed too disconsolate to value their hard-earned reprieve. Behind the episodes of Rime Coldspray's tale, the Sarangrave's lapping waters muttered reminders of venom and putrescence. Jeremiah's study of the Staff sent small flames skirling upward, but shed no light.

Yet within the ambit of the *krill*'s argent, Bluff Stoutgirth and his comrades were transfixed. Where the Anchormaster and Hurl appeared to suppress jests at every turn of the tale, Keenreef and Squallish Blustergale looked dismayed to the heart. Etch Furledsail, Wiver Setrock, and one of the women—had Stoutgirth called her Baf Scatterwit?—stared at the Ironhand as if nothing made sense. Together Dire's Vessel's crew evinced every reaction except joy.

Nevertheless no one interrupted Rime Coldspray. Even Covenant did not, although he could no doubt have added his own interpretations. Instead he seemed distracted, as if he were thinking about something else.

Then Coldspray was done. A long silence greeted her, until Stoutgirth announced brightly, "A toothsome tale, Ironhand—a veritable feast of clear peril and ambiguous vindication, strange beings and extravagant exertions. Doubtless we will gnaw upon it, seeking its marrow, while the world endures.

"Yet you have spoken of worth. For my part, Ironhand, I do not acknowledge it." He laughed happily. "As matters stand, we resemble sailors snared in the ensorcelments of the Soulbiter. There can be no worth in the tale of those who fail and fall unwitnessed, for their doom is not redeemed by the telling of it. We must have boasting, Rime Coldspray! I will not name the deeds of this company worthy until the World's End has been forestalled. Only then may the tale be shared with those able to esteem it."

Linden frowned, thinking that the Anchormaster had insulted her friends. But the Giants heard something different in Stoutgirth's assertion; or they heard it with different ears. Several of his sailors laughed, and both Grueburn and Kindwind chuckled.

"Then," Rime Coldspray replied, bemused and rueful, "we must endeavor to win free of this Soulbiter, that we may thereafter brag of our survival."

The Anchormaster nodded. "And toward that end, Ironhand, there is a matter which you have not addressed. How do you propose to sail these fatal seas? You have overcome the unwelcome of the *Haruchai*. And your companions are figures of legend, revered among us. Your purpose must be mighty indeed, to gather such a congeries of valor and puissance.

"Ironhand, what is your intent?"

Coldspray opened her mouth to answer, then closed it. With a bow, she stepped aside, referring the question to Covenant; or perhaps to Covenant and Linden.

Covenant's arms tightened momentarily. In Linden's ear, he whispered, "This is the hard part of being a leper. I'm going to need your help."

Startled, she turned to him with questions in her eyes; but his only response was a twisted smile as he stepped away from her. The sailors and the Swordmainnir towered over him, yet he faced them as though his stature equaled theirs.

"I hope you aren't expecting me to be sure of anything. We have too many enemies, and they have too much power. And all I really know about the Worm is that we can't stop it. But I don't want to just sit on my hands waiting to die. The Despiser started all this. *Him* I think we might be able to stop. I want to put an end to his evil."

He pointed at the mouth of the Defiles Course. "I want to get into Mount

Thunder. Up into the Wightwarrens, if that's even possible. That's where Lord Foul is. I want to go find him."

Briefly his shoulders hunched as if he were strangling his fears. "But there's something else I want to do first."

While the Giants studied him, he gestured Branl to his side. Taking the *krill*, he held it up in his halfhand by its wrapped blade. Within its silver, he continued.

"The Ironhand told her story. The Swordmainnir have been through hell and blood ever since they left you. Fighting Longwrath, fighting for Longwrath, they lost Scend Wavegift. Against the *skurj*, they lost Moire Squareset. And eventually Kastenessen killed Longwrath. All of that was bad enough. But now the toll is even higher." Although Coldspray and Stoutgirth had already acknowledged their dead, Covenant insisted on the names. "Latebirth, Stormpast Galesend, and Cabledarm died for us, and Dire's Vessel lost a man I never even met. You called him Slumberhead, God knows why. He sure as hell wasn't dozing when he gave his life.

"It's too much. You're Giants, all of you. You can't ask yourselves to carry around that much grief indefinitely. You need a *caamora*. How else are you going to face what's ahead of us?"

The Ironhand glanced at her surroundings. "We have no fire," she said harshly, "if we do not sacrifice yet another tree."

All of the ironwoods set ablaze by the *skurj* had burned down to ash, or had been extinguished by rain. There was no flame in the valley apart from Jeremiah's experiments.

"And I won't ask you to do that," Covenant assured her. "I promised you a *caamora*. I intend to keep that promise.

"When I made it, I thought I could use Longwrath's body. That seemed like a kind of acknowledgment. A way to make something good out of what he went through. But the Giants we've lost here have been mangled by the *skurj*. They already look desecrated. It seems disrespectful to use them.

"So I'm going to burn myself."

To the sudden alarm of his companions, he added quickly, "I mean with wild magic. I'm going to light myself and hope that I can burn hot enough to console you.

"It's wild magic. It drains me. Hell, it even terrifies me. But it won't hurt me. The only danger is that I'll lose control. Too much might do more harm than too little."

Then he turned back to Linden. "That's why I need your help. Your health-sense. I want you to watch out for me. If I start to go too far, I want you to stop me."

Seeing the raw need in his scowl, she felt a hammer pound in her chest. How could she stop him? Oh, she believed that he would not be harmed physically. His power was *him*. But the cost to his spirit might be extreme. His reluctance was necessary to him. It counterbalanced his extravagance: it was his way of managing his fear that he might commit havoc. If he damaged his friends—if he damaged *anything*—he would not be able to forgive himself.

How could she stop him, except by possessing him?

But he did not give her a chance to protest, or to ready herself. He ignored the apprehension of the Giants, the doubts. Before they could say that they did not want him to take this risk, he touched his wedding band to Loric's cut gem.

In the space between instants, he became fire.

She could still see him. He stood incandescent in the core of a silver conflagration, a blaze like a bonfire barely contained, bound by force of will in the shape of a whirling pillar as tall as any Giant. As he burned, the *krill* fell from his fingers: he no longer needed it. Flames seemed to burst from every inch of him. They looked pure enough to render his flesh from his bones. Yet he was not consumed. Instead his magicks appeared to exalt him. With wild magic, he could have brought life and time to an end without the aid of the Worm.

Nevertheless his power was also a howl. It tormented him. It was the contradiction which lay at the center of his plight in the Land, *the one word of truth or treachery*. Without wild magic, nothing could be redeemed. With it, everything might be damned.

In spite of her dismay, Linden understood. With wild magic, destruction came easily. *That* she knew to be true. She had seen it in *caesures*; in the reaving of Cavewights. With fire, Covenant looked capable of ripping the stars out of the heavens. She did not know how to watch without weeping.

For a moment while Covenant blazed, Rime Coldspray and the other Giants hesitated. They did not know him as Linden did, but they could see how his attempt to both exert and restrain himself wracked him. At the same time, however, they recognized what he was offering. Even if they had not heard about the gift which he had once given to the Dead of The Grieve, they would have yearned to seize this opportunity.

He had chosen to risk himself. How could they refuse him?

Abruptly the Ironhand reached into the whirl of fire, caught Covenant in her huge hands, and lifted him high. There she held him while his flames attacked her flesh as if they threatened to char her bones, reaching for her heart.

Her grasp threatened his concentration; but he did not withdraw his power.

Her pain was severe, as she needed it to be. She required such anguish to cauterize her bereavements. Without the cleansing of fire, her sorrow would have become bitterness. Eventually she would have lost her ability to hear joy.

While Coldspray gripped him, Covenant fought to keep his balance between too much and not enough. But when she passed him to Frostheart Grueburn, his self-control faltered. Wild magic mounted higher.

Linden watched him with her own agony. Cries that she could not utter closed her throat. Stave had come to stand at her back. He clasped her shoulders to steady her. Jeremiah had dropped the Staff of Law. He gaped at Covenant with consternation in his silted gaze. But she was aware of nothing except silver fire and Thomas Covenant.

How much could he endure? Three Swordmainnir remained after Grueburn. Stoutgirth and his crew numbered eleven. They, too, were eager for the healing hurt of a *caamora*. How could Covenant possibly—?

How could she stop him?

Cirrus Kindwind received him from Grueburn, supported him awkwardly with her good hand and the stump of her maimed forearm. She kept him too long, and not long enough. Sensitive to his ordeal, she did not allow herself to anneal her whole lament. When she released him to Onyx Stonemage, she looked incompletely assuaged.

Linden could not stop him. She could not help him. Not without possessing him. By imposing her choices on his. By using her health-sense to enter him as she had once entered Jeremiah; as she had done to Covenant himself several times long ago.

Good cannot be accomplished—

Hoarse gasps of strain burst between his teeth as Stonemage gave him to Bluntfist.

"Mom!" Jeremiah yelled. "*Do* something!"

Near Linden's ear, Stave said sharply, "Attend, Chosen. Your ring answers."

As soon as he said the words, she felt fire spitting from her wedding band.

She, too, was a rightful white gold wielder.

—find another truth—

In the small gap of inspiration between heartbeats, she recovered her voice.

"Put him down." From her ring, she drew flames like streamers and wrapped them around her. She spoke fire. "Put him *down*!"

The Swordmainnir knew her too well. They could not resist her. Baffled and uncertain, Halewhole Bluntfist lowered Covenant to the ground.

At once, Linden rushed to him. Her arms and her love and her shining she flung around him. Then she gave herself to him—or she made him hers. With percipience, she united their powers until she found a way to balance his extremity with her physician's caution.

Together they stood in conflagration while the Giants of Dire's Vessel crowded around them. Together Covenant and Linden burned as the sailors came two at a time to grip his shoulders or hers; to be flensed by pain and find release.

A curtain of tears fell between Linden and her companions. For a moment, she was blind. She was almost deaf. But then the *caamora* was done. When she felt the last of the Giants withdraw, she relaxed her fire, taking Covenant's with her. Her ring had answered his: now his answered hers. As if they had briefly become one, they let go of wild magic until they stood, unburned and unburning, in each other's arms.

She heard the Giants singing; but they seemed impossibly far away, and she did not listen to them. Instead she heeded only the need in her husband's embrace and the relieved beat of his heart.

There is also love in the world.

5.

"No Prospect of Return"

As if the *croyel* still had the power to dredge up his buried past—or as if Lord Foul had inherited that power—Jeremiah remembered his sisters. Two of them, both barely toddling on their stick-thin legs. There was never enough to eat. Their names were—? Their names were gone. He could not imagine their faces, except as pale smudges lit by the Despiser's bonfire. They had existed in a different world, on the far side of a wall of absence. He was not sure now that they had ever meant anything to him, except as squalling mouths that needed food worse than he did. And yet he remembered that they had been his sisters.

Linden and Covenant did not know that about him. It was his last secret: he remembered his sisters.

A scornful voice told him that he should have done something to protect them.

He *should* have, even though he had gone first, he had put his right hand in the fire as soon as his mother finished screaming, and after that he was in too much pain to feel anything else. Even after he had learned how to conceal himself so that those terrible flames could not touch him again, the idea that he should have done something twisted his heart.

Why was he thinking about this now? It did not make sense. *Protect* his sisters? *How?* He was only five. His mother was always praying or crying. Just about the only thing he knew for sure was that he had to be good. He had to do what she told him. He had to obey Lord Foul's eyes in the bonfire. That was what kids did. It was how they stayed alive.

Yet they were your sisters, were they not?

I don't even remember their names.

Yet you knew their peril, did you not?

I was just a kid. I didn't know anything.

Yet you heard your mother's pain, did you not? You understood that fire burns, did you not?

I was only *five*, Jeremiah tried to protest. I had to obey.

Did you? At such a cost?

I couldn't do anything else! Everything hurt too much!

Yet they needed you, did they not? Had you refused the flames, would they not have done likewise? Are you not therefore the cause of their sufferings?

I was just a kid.

Yet you are no longer a child.

Stop.

And are you not as blameworthy now as you were then? For deeds and self-pity which imperil those whom you profess to love, are you not blameworthy still? Did you not reveal their heading and purpose by defying possession? You knew that peril also, did you not?

Stop. Yes. Stop.

How then do you now refuse blame?

Jeremiah had no answer for that voice. The sanctuary which he had designed for the *Elohim* was not an answer. It was no excuse for standing on grass as if he thought that he could outface Lord Foul. He should have protected his sisters. He could not have protected them. He should have done it anyway. He deserved to watch the Worm while Linden and Covenant failed to save the world because of him. He had told Lord Foul where they were.

So now he concentrated obsessively on the Staff of Law: as obsessively as he had worked on any construct. As soon as he recovered from the surprise of the *caamora*, the jolt of alarm, he picked up the Staff and resumed his study. Covenant was not hurt. Linden was not. Jeremiah could see that. They did not need him; and he had other things to do.

When he held the strange black wood, he felt its possibilities. In a sense, it too was a construct. It was made of parts that he could identify. The living wood. The iron heels full of old magic. The language of the runes. The blackness, Linden's blackness: the deep ebony which had taken over his own Earthpower when he had tried to change it. How those parts interacted was a mystery, but that did not trouble him. How the parts of his own constructs interacted was a mystery. He did not need to think about it. Instead he tried to understand how the parts fit together. He wanted to see the *design*.

If he could do that, he would know how to use the Staff. He would have power. He would be able to *do* things. Things that might make a difference. Things that might excuse him.

Things that might silence the scorn in his mind, block visions of the Worm. Then he would have a chance—

Linden had given him that gift. His mother: the one who loved him, not the one who had put her own hand in Lord Foul's bonfire. Studying the Staff, he believed that he would cheerfully kill anybody or anything that tried to hurt her.

But the design—the secret of Linden's gift—eluded him. No matter how hard he tried, he could not *see* it. He was beginning to sense some of the Staff's uses. A few of them might even be possible for him. And while he concentrated on those possibilities, Lord Foul's visions lost some of their harrowing vividness, their inevitability, their weight of ridicule. Still the design itself, the key that would unlock the gift, was beyond him. He could not alter the blackness of the flames.

In his heart, he was still only five.

Eventually his efforts to find his way felt less like his familiar obsession with building. They became a kind of fever, a ragged desperation that went nowhere. When Cirrus Kindwind offered him food, he ate. He accepted water. Vaguely he noticed the Swordmainnir and the sailors talking together, adding details and explanations to their stories, discussing the hazards ahead. He heard them decide to give their dead to the river, hoping that the lurker would convey the bodies to the cleaner waters of the sea. He saw Linden and Covenant wander away together—not far, but far enough so they could at least pretend that they were alone. Without thinking about it, he knew that Stave and Branl watched over the whole company. But his real attention remained fixed on the Staff.

It should have been everything he wanted. Calling upon the resources of Earthpower and Law should have been as natural as reaching out his hand.

It was not. His ability to raise and shape flames like midnight blossoms mocked him with all that it was not. His fire did not extend his percipience or ease his fatigue. It was too insubstantial for healing. It had no force. And it was always black.

The laughter in his head derided him. Involuntary glimpses of the Worm made fun of him.

Are you not therefore the cause of their sufferings? How then do you now refuse blame?

The Staff of Law required a Linden Avery—or a Thomas Covenant—and Jeremiah was just a kid.

Finally he dropped it as if he were merely worn out. With both hands, he tried to scrub the bitterness off his face. Hiding behind a scowl, he gnawed on a dry sausage for a while, drank more water. Then he looked for a patch of level ground where he could stretch out.

Almost immediately, Linden called, "Jeremiah, honey. Are you all right?"

He wanted to retort, Leave me alone! I don't need you worrying about me. But of course if he said that everybody would know how he felt.

Instead he muttered, "Just tired, Mom. I need sleep."

"Rest as much as you can." Covenant sounded distant. He was thinking about something else. Probably about Linden. "We're running out of time. I want to start before midnight."

Fine, Jeremiah thought. *You* start. I'm going to lie down until somebody takes pity on me.

But he did not mean that. He meant, I'm lost. I need help. But you can't help me. You've already done everything. The rest is up to me, and I'm not enough.

ΙΟΟ

He expected to lie awake, chewing his misery while voices laughed and the Worm ravaged. But he was more tired than he realized. He surprised himself by falling out of the world.

In dreams, he watched the stars spin. At first, they wheeled slowly, as cautious and deliberate as if they were performing an unfamiliar dance. Later they moved faster. And as they swirled, they drew closer to each other, contracting their glitter, leaving the rest of the heavens drowned in blackness, as doomed as the Lost Deep. After a while, they began to collide and join. Yet the merging of one distinct gleam with others, and then still others, did not make their shining brighter. Instead their private lives seemed to extinguish each other. Soon hundreds or thousands of them had become one, and that one was scarcely visible: a dying ember in the fathomless ruin of the night.

But at the same time, that single dulled spark became heavier. Not bigger, no. Just more massive. And it leaned down on Jeremiah, pressed its intolerable weight against his heart. He did not breathe. There was no room in his chest for air. His heart no longer beat. It could not lift blood through his veins under so much pressure. He was becoming the sky, black and blank, infinitely desolate.

He awoke with an enfilade trapped between his ribs. Memories of bullets whined past him and into him, furious as hornets. Wildly he floundered to his feet, frantic for relief.

He nearly yelped when Stave grasped his arm.

"Still your alarm, Chosen-son," said the *Haruchai*, almost whispering. "There is no imminent peril. Dreams are not omens. They bespeak only your fears." Then he added, "The Chosen slumbers yet, as do the Giants. Only the Ironhand and the Anchormaster stand watch with Branl. We do well to permit their rest."

Jeremiah resisted an impulse to cling to the former Master. There was no light: Branl must have covered the *krill*. Stave's grip felt like the only certainty in a reality which had lost its moorings. The boy half expected to see the stars continue their shrinking spiral, their fatal deflagration. But of course they remained where they were, clinging to their fate.

The air was thick with the complex reeks of the Defiles Course and Sarangrave Flat, of ironwood ash and drowned *skurj* and the charred corpses of Sandgorgons. Around Jeremiah, darkness clotted like blood. It filled every span of ground and hidden niche. When he considered the movement of time, he found that midnight was near.

As quietly as Stave, he asked, "Where's Covenant?"

The *Haruchai* pointed down the valley. "There. He communes once again with the Feroce."

Jeremiah looked toward the marshy verge of the Sarangrave. At this distance, he could not descry Covenant. There was too much sensory clutter from the restless currents and predators. The lurker still complained over its pains, whimpering wetly. But near the wetland, Jeremiah spotted glints of emerald arrayed as if they had gathered to attend a potentate. Green flames fell and rose like sighs.

Behind them, the Flat stretched eastward, growing darker with every league until its doom became the sky's.

Closer to him lay the benighted shapes of Giants. A few of them slept against the boles of ironwoods near the crest of the slope. They snored and started fretfully, troubled by their dreams. Lower down, but still above the chancres and spilth of battle, the other sailors and Swordmainnir had found patches of ground where they could feign comfort.

Overhead carrion-eaters flapped across the background of the stars. Slaps and splashes from the Flat sounded like feeding. The contorted carcasses of monsters littered the valley-floor like rubble. Bleached in the Great Desert for millennia, the dead Sandgorgons smelled only of sulfur and Fire-Lions. But the gangrene fetor of the *skurj* clung wherever their blood had been spilled. If many of them had not been sucked into the marsh when the lurker's flood receded, the stench would have been worse.

Standing with Stave in the last night of the Earth, Jeremiah pined for sunshine. He craved one more warm yellow wash of light. Trying to summon clean fire, he filled his palms with flame. But the blackness of his heritage persisted. Covered by darkness, his magicks were visible to ordinary sight only as deeper blots, stark as stigmata.

Stave still held his arm. "Chosen-son." The former Master pitched his voice for Jeremiah alone. "It may be that the task which the Chosen has offered is too extreme. She has asked of you an achievement which has surpassed her. If you will heed my counsel, therefore—"

The *Haruchai* paused, apparently awaiting a response.

"Please." Jeremiah was tempted to snort, Don't bother. You can't help me. Contemptuous laughter echoed in his ears as if it had become a part of him, a cancer too insidious and personal to be cut out. More and more, the coming end seemed like an act of kindness. But he did not sneer at Stave. Any suggestion that did not make him feel smaller— "I've already tried everything I can think of."

"It is this," Stave replied. "Set aside those tasks which daunt you. As your knowledge of the Staff grows, your strength will also. For the present, strive only to meet present needs. The lacks and requirements of this company are many. Choose among them one which lies within your compass."

"Like what?" Jeremiah asked. Stave's manner seemed to banish scorn.

"Chosen-son," Stave returned, "your senses are acute. And you will comprehend that our intended ascent into Gravin Threndor must present grave obstacles. Of these, the first is plain. The air is noisome. It discomfits us where we stand. It will become unendurable within the mountain.

"The Timewarden conceived that the Chosen would cleanse the air. However, the Staff of Law has now been entrusted to you." Stave stooped, retrieved the shaft, held it up. "Therefore the task falls to you—the task and the opportunity. An increase of strength comes from the use of strength."

As Stave spoke, bursts of surprise like little explosions ran through Jeremiah's veins. He clutched at the Staff. "The *air*," he breathed. To his nerves, the atmosphere was as distinct as Earthpower. Its insidious taints were so clear that they were almost tangible. He had wasted so much time and effort. "Why didn't I think of that?"

Stave shrugged. Finally he released Jeremiah's arm. But Jeremiah hardly noticed. His mind raced. How had he let himself believe that he had to fail? Did the *croyel* still have that much power over him? Did Lord Foul? Had he simply *assumed* that the small flames which he could raise from the Staff were trivial? Ineffective because he did not know how to make them clean? Had he *tested* them?

He had not. Instead he had let the Despiser and the Worm and even Linden's encouragement distract him. A stupid mistake, as stupid as breaking his own neck by not watching where he put his feet. And stupidity was worse than failure. It was worse than terror: it made him useless.

The purpose of life, Cirrus Kindwind had once assured him, *is to choose, and to act upon the choice.* If he could not do what Linden had asked him to do, he could do something else.

He could do *something* that had to be done.

၍

Before long, Covenant started back up the valley, trailed by a cortege of Feroce with their nauseous emerald fluttering like banners. Along the way, Branl unveiled the *krill*. At the same time, Rime Coldspray, Bluff Stoutgirth, and the Humbled made their way down from the ridge of Mount Thunder's calf. Silver spread across the sleeping Giants as the Ironhand and the Anchormaster began to rouse them.

Far back in Jeremiah's thoughts, images of the Worm squirmed. When they broke through his concentration, they stung his heart. Now he thought that he recognized the confluence of the Black River and the Mithil. If so, the Worm had crossed much of the South Plains. Furious as a perfect storm, the incarnate cataclysm flared and thundered ever closer to the hills which had once formed the boundary of Garroting Deep. And beyond the region of the lost forest stood *Melenkurion* Skyweir. The companions did not have much time left. They had probably rested too long.

But now Jeremiah could push those nightmare visions away. The fangs that were Lord Foul's eyes, and the memories of the *croyel*'s feeding, no longer consumed him. He had a job to do, a job he understood. In some ways, it resembled making one of his constructs: it involved pulling bits of good air toward him and rejecting poisons; forming a kind of breathable edifice. That may not have been how Linden cleaned the air, but he knew how to do it. The real challenge would be to *keep* doing it. It would erode constantly: he would have to rebuild it constantly. And the erosion would get worse as the company moved. Still Stave's suggestion gave him hope. Watching Covenant's approach, Jeremiah felt almost ready.

Above and around him on the slope, the Swordmainnir shrugged their shoulders into the armor, examined their weapons. Without prompting, Wiver Setrock and the woman called Keenreef portioned out another meal, although their supplies were dwindling. Other sailors complained or jested. Of no one in particular, Baf Scatterwit asked where she was. Sounding sincerely confounded, she wanted to know where Dire's Vessel and her other friends had gone. But when Stoutgirth replied with instructions rather than answers, she complied as if she had forgotten her confusion.

"She is easily bewildered," one of the men—Squallish Blustergale?—remarked casually to Jeremiah, "yet she is an adroit sailor, quick in every exigency. Aye, and doughty withal. None will outlast her on the sheets, or strive more fiercely when there is need. Also she is gentle in her bafflement. Therefore she is precious among us."

For her, Jeremiah felt a flush of sympathy. He knew too well that an absent mind fostered the illusion of safety—and that the illusion was dangerous.

Muttering to himself, he looked around for his mother.

Until Covenant had left to summon the Feroce, he and Linden had slept together on a stretch of churned earth thirty or forty paces closer to the high cliff which confronted the valley. She was awake now, brushing dirt from her clothes, combing her fingers through her hair. As she came toward Jeremiah, her right hand clung to her wedding band, turning it around and around her ring finger as if she feared that it would be taken from her.

"Jeremiah, honey," she asked when she drew near, "were you able to sleep?"

"Mom." He met her holding the Staff of Law in front of him like a promise—or a defense. "Don't worry about me. I'm making progress." He ducked his head to hide conflicting reactions: eagerness for what he might be able to accomplish; chagrin for what he could not. "I mean, sort of."

Her concern reached out to him. Argent reflections haunted her gaze like the residue of horrors. Wordless and worried, she hugged him tightly. Then she stepped back. "Remember what I told you. There's no such thing as failure. *Sort of* progress is better than nothing. Under the circumstances, it's probably impressive. We can only do what we can." The ruefulness of her smile twisted his heart. "I need to remember that myself."

Before he could think of a response, she turned to meet her husband.

Covenant came grimly up the side of the valley, walking like a man who had left behind anything that might have softened his severity, his personal commandments. The time had come to essay Mount Thunder; and Jeremiah could see that Covenant was as afraid as Linden. But for him, strangely, fear seemed to be a source of strength. In the illumination of the *krill*, his silver hair shone like wild magic, the contained conflagration of his heart.

He returned Linden's embrace briefly; linked his arm with hers as he approached the Giants. Just for a moment, he looked like he might be on the verge of frenzy or tears. Then his expression hardened. The lines on his face resembled slashes.

"I talked to the Feroce," he announced unnecessarily. "I guess that's obvious." The creatures stood a dozen steps behind him, as timorous as ever, and as compelled.

"They say they've never been inside the mountain. And they don't want to go. They call it a *Maker-place*. Lord Foul's home. It scares them.

"But the lurker didn't give them a choice. I didn't even have to argue. I only had to promise them that *that*"—he pointed down at the gullet of the Defiles Course—"isn't a Maker-place. It's like the Shattered Hills. It defends Lord Foul, but he doesn't live there. He's somewhere up in the Wightwarrens, probably in Kiril Threndor. The Feroce can help us without going that far.

"They don't know what we'll find. They aren't sure they'll do any good. But they know water—especially polluted water. They'll try to guide us. And—" Abruptly Covenant paused. For a moment, he covered his eyes as if he had been assailed by memories too painful to countenance. Then he controlled himself, shrugged stiffly. "They'll try to make the water remember where it comes from. If they can do that, it might be as good as a map."

"What does he say?" asked Baf Scatterwit. "A map? Does he speak of a chart?" She was becoming agitated.

The Anchormaster rested a lean hand on her shoulder, murmured a soft command which appeared to soothe her. She smiled at him, nodded, and did not speak again.

In a taut voice, Covenant finished, "If what the Feroce can do doesn't take us into the Wightwarrens, we'll have to find our own way."

The Ironhand nodded sternly. "Then, Timewarden, only two matters remain. You and Linden Giantfriend and the Chosen-son must eat to sustain your strength. And we must look to our survival within the mountain.

"We are Giants, lovers of stone. We do not fear to attempt the hidden passages. Also the Anchormaster and our comrades of Dire's Vessel will accompany us, for so they interpret the wishes of Brinn *Haruchai*, the last Guardian of the One Tree."

Stoutgirth grinned as if he found her assertion risible; but he did not return a jest.

"Being sailors," Coldspray continued, "they have borne with them a goodly quantity of rope. Such providence will surely serve us well."

The muscles at the corners of her jaw bunched. "Yet we must breathe. It is certain that the airs within the water's channels will be foul beyond bearing. Ere long, respiration alone will prove fatal." Her tone was exposed gutrock. "Therefore I am compelled to inquire. How can we dare Mount Thunder if we cannot breathe?"

"Maybe the Feroce—" began Covenant darkly.

Jeremiah took a step forward. "Wait." His hands itched with anticipation on the Staff. "I've been working on this." He glanced quickly at Stave. "I'm not sure, but I'm learning. Maybe I can—"

Abruptly he closed his eyes; forgot words. Now or never. His mother had trusted him with her best instrument of power. If he proved her wrong, he would have to return it. Her hopes for him—and his own—would be gone.

Just for a moment, malice pealed through the dark behind his eyelids. Prove her wrong, puppy? How can you not? You are naught but a tool, a means to an end. Your every deed serves my desires.

But Jeremiah refused to listen. The whole company was watching. And the Staff was *alive*. In small ways, it answered his Earthpower, his health-sense. He could believe that those responses would grow. And in the meantime— Right here, right now, he could feel the air, taste it; almost touch its nature. He could distinguish between health and sickness.

Deliberately he poured flames into the cups of his hands. Ignoring their taint, he wrapped them around the Staff. Then he asked the wood for more theurgy than his mere body contained. As hard as he could, he concentrated on breathing—

—on pushing away poisons and corruption—

—on rejecting putrescence and vilification—

—and on drawing the cleanliness that remained toward him.

And when he knew that he was inhaling and exhaling *life*, he extended his edifice of good air toward his companions.

See? he told the mockery inside him. I can do this. I can *do* it.

Then he opened his eyes to see the effects of his efforts.

Linden gasped as she took an unconflicted breath. "Jeremiah," she murmured. "My God—" Covenant filled his lungs and seemed to stand taller, as if the air had confirmed him. He gave Jeremiah a look like a shower of sparks from a whetstone. Rime Coldspray and Bluff Stoutgirth raised their heads, sampled the spread of vitality. Grins like promises showed their teeth. With gestures and relief, they exhorted their comrades to crowd closer.

As the whole company began to breathe more comfortably, the Ironhand announced, "This is well done, Jeremiah Chosen-son. I confess that I did not foresee it. If you are able to sustain such exertions—"

She swallowed the rest of what she might have said; the questions she might have asked.

"It'll get easier," Jeremiah muttered self-consciously. "I mean, I think it will. I'm not used to it yet. I just need practice."

Chuckling, Blustergale swung a clap at Jeremiah's back that would have felled him. But at the last instant, the Giant seemed to recall that Jeremiah was little. His hand patted Jeremiah gently and withdrew.

Stave bowed his approval. A tightening at the corner of his mouth hinted at a smile.

Behind Covenant, the Feroce squalled in soft voices, as if they feared to be overheard; but Jeremiah did not know how to interpret their cries.

✸

Now that he had begun to prove himself, he was eager to try the uncertain ascent along the watercourse. But Rime Coldspray reminded him again that he needed food—as did Covenant and Linden. Reluctantly Jeremiah let go of his magicks.

While they ate and drank, the company discussed uncertainties and perils.

This approach to Mount Thunder's heart was Covenant's idea, but he did not know whether the path of the Defiles Course within the mountain would prove passable. In the past, he had only entered the Wightwarrens from the Upper Land. Certainly the Giants were skilled climbers and delvers. The *Haruchai* were born to crags and cliffs. And they were adequately supplied for their immediate purpose—or so the Anchormaster asserted. Nevertheless they could imagine obstacles which they would not be able to surmount. Water was water, after all. Under pressure, it could find its way through constrictions which would refuse Giants or *Haruchai* or Feroce.

In addition, the Despiser clearly knew where to look for his enemies; and his servants were many. At any time, he might send Cavewights or stranger creatures to waylay the company. Long ago, horrors had formed a large portion of his forces. The companions could not assume that any stretch of their path would be uncontested.

To all of this, Jeremiah listened without paying much attention. For the moment, at least, he was content with food and the Staff of Law. Finally he knew what he had to do—and how to do it. He had already shown that he could do it. The whole company trusted their lives to him. And Stave had assured him that he would get stronger. He might even learn how to do more than improve the air.

If Lord Foul tried to take him, sixteen Giants, two *Haruchai*, and two white gold wielders might be able to protect him.

So he ate what he was given, and drank water lightly tinged with *diamondraught*, and tried to mask his impatience while he waited for Mom and Covenant to finish this last meal.

At last, the company was ready. Keenreef and several other sailors shouldered packs of supplies. All of their quirts and spears had been destroyed, but most of Stoutgirth's crew still carried weapons: billhooks, longknives, belaying-pins. The Swordmainnir had their armor and their blades. And the *Haruchai* had set aside the characteristic reluctance of their people to rely on weapons. Branl shouldered Longwrath's flamberge, while Stave bore Cabledarm's longsword.

Among such companions, Covenant and Linden looked small, vulnerable. But there was a dangerous promise in Covenant's eyes. And Linden looked withdrawn. She no longer seemed to care about details like difficult climbing and enemies. Only the way that she twisted her ring around her finger hinted that she was fretting.

Formally the Ironhand drew her stone glaive. Holding it ready, she spoke in a voice of granite.

"Here we surrender every future which we have imagined for ourselves. We have no prospect of return. Indeed, we cannot trust that we will outlive another day. Our doom is this, that we enter Mount Thunder seeking to confront the most heinous of foes—and yet the Worm hastens toward the World's End many scores of leagues distant, where no deed of ours can thwart it. Thus even the greatest triumphs within the mountain may come to naught, for no life will remain to heed the tale.

"Nonetheless I proclaim"—Coldspray swung her sword once around her head, then slapped it into its scabbard on her back—"that I am not daunted. *I am not daunted.* While hearts beat and lungs draw breath, we seek to affirm the import of our lives. The true worth of tales lies in this, that those of whom they speak do not regard how the telling of their trials will be received. When we must perish, my wish for us is that we will come to the end knowing that we have held fast to that which we deem precious."

Then her tone eased. "Doubtless this is folly. Yet when have our deeds been other-wise? Are we not Giants? And is not our folly the stone against which we have raised the sea of our laughter? What cause have we to feel dismay and hold back, when we have always known that no anchor is secure against the seas of mischance and wonder?"

Perhaps she would have continued; but the Anchormaster was already laughing. He tried to say something, but the words were lost in broad gusts of glee. For a moment, the other sailors were silent, dismayed by images of futility. But then Baf Scatterwit began to guffaw: the happy mirth of a woman who enjoyed laughing for its own sake. Her laughter broke the logjam of her comrades' fears. Carried along by her open-heartedness, the crew of Dire's Vessel roared as if they themselves were an exquisite jest.

The Swordmainnir were more restrained. They had lost too many of their com-rades. But when Rime Coldspray started to chuckle, Frostheart Grueburn followed her example, and then Cirrus Kindwind. In their subdued fashion, the Ironhand and her warriors shared the delight of the sailors.

Privately Jeremiah thought that they had all lost their minds. Nevertheless he found himself grinning. He had heard too little genuine laughter in his life; and the mirth of Giants was especially infectious. At least temporarily, it made Lord Foul's scorn and the *croyel*'s malice seem empty, like taunts from the bottom of an abandoned well.

Long ago, Saltheart Foamfollower had enabled Covenant's victory over the Despiser by laughing.

As the Giants began to subside, Covenant muttered, "Stone and Sea are deep in life." He seemed to be quoting. "Two unalterable symbols of the world." Then he lifted his head to the dark heavens, the decimated stars. From his ring, a brief flash of silver challenged the night. "I can't help it. I've always loved Giants. Any world that has *Haruchai* and Ranyhyn and Ramen and Insequent and even *Elohim* in it is precious. But there really is no substitute for Giants."

Jeremiah agreed with him.

The Ironhand answered Covenant's moment of power with a flash of her teeth. "Then, Timewarden," she said, "let us now vindicate your love."

With a sweep of her arm, she drew the Swordmainnir and Dire's Vessel's crew with her as she started down the side of the valley toward the throat of the Defiles Course.

Jeremiah followed them as if he, too, had been called. With the Staff and his own power, he drew clean air out of the ambient reeks.

After a moment, Cirrus Kindwind came to his side. Frostheart Grueburn now accompanied Linden and Stave, and the Anchormaster had claimed a place with Covenant and Branl. Escorted by Giants and *Haruchai*, Covenant, Linden, and Jeremiah picked their way between craters like maws and past rank corpses toward the cave where the Land's most ancient waters carried their burden of poisons and spilled evil into the embrace of the Sarangrave.

Apparently the Feroce had anticipated the company's movement. They already stood on the riverbank within an easy stone's throw of the cliff, a cluster of ten small creatures with emerald in their hands and naked fright in their eyes. They did not react as the first Giants approached them. Instead they stood in the stench of the Defiles Course, facing each other and quavering as if their deity had declared them expendable.

But when Covenant drew near, they turned away from their communion. Flinching, they spoke in their one voice: an eerie sound like squeezed mud, moist and attenuated.

"We are the Feroce," they said as if they were on the verge of weeping. "We are only the Feroce. At our High God's command, we attempt aid. It exceeds us. We will not suffice."

Covenant regarded them like a man who showed no mercy; but his words belied his manner. "You don't have to suffice. You just have to try. When you can't do any more, you're free to go."

"Then," replied the creatures, "we will begin. We have no wish to prolong our failure."

Together they faced the gaping mouth of the cliff. In a tight cluster, they started toward the deeper dark, a blackness that seemed to mock the *krill* and the company, the night and the forlorn stars. Although no tangible power compelled them, they moved as if they were being scourged.

Covenant watched them, but he did not follow. Instead he rasped to the Giants and the *Haruchai*, "Just remember. White gold is going to be mostly useless, at least for a while. I don't have much control. I'm more likely to cause a cave-in than accomplish anything useful. Plus I can't keep my balance worth a damn. And Linden hasn't had time to learn what she can do. We'll need all the help you can give us."

"This we have foreseen, Timewarden," the Ironhand answered calmly. "If Giants are fools, they are also rock-wise, certain of foot on any stone. With your consent, we will bear you, and also Linden Giantfriend and Jeremiah Chosen-son. In our arms, you will be warded from many perils."

Now Covenant looked back at his companions. "Linden?"

"I think it's a good idea." She made a palpable effort to sound confident; but Jeremiah heard the congested tension in her voice. "Grueburn has carried me more times than I can count. I'm not worried about her. And I don't like the way that looks." She gestured at the river mouth. "If nothing else, it's going to be slick." Her mouth twisted. "I would rather be carried. If Grueburn doesn't mind."

Grueburn's response was a snorted chortle.

Covenant nodded. "Jeremiah?"

Jeremiah felt a touch of relief. "Mom's right. I'm not as strong as I want to be. I mean with the Staff. If I don't have to do my own climbing, I can concentrate better."

For himself, Covenant did not hesitate. To Coldspray, he said brusquely, "Thanks. I should have thought of that myself."

Then he made a visible effort to relax as Bluff Stoutgirth lifted him from his feet.

In a moment, Jeremiah was sitting on Kindwind's forearm with his back against her breastplate. His lightless flames scurried up and down the length of the Staff. They were weaker than they needed to be, but they gathered enough purity to ease the company's breathing.

From her position in Grueburn's clasp, Linden glanced at Jeremiah with an expression which he could not interpret. A warning? A prayer? Was she saying goodbye?

She had found her own sense of purpose, but he had no idea what it might be.

One after another, Rime Coldspray and all of the Giants followed the receding green of the Feroce. Holding the *krill* above his head to extend its illumination, Branl walked close behind the Ironhand near Stoutgirth and Covenant. Stave took a position between Grueburn and Kindwind.

Striding as if they were about to burst into song, the Swordmainnir and the sailors left the world they knew. Beside the Defiles Course, they entered Gravin Threndor and darkness.

6.

The Aid of the Feroce

As Frostheart Grueburn carried her into the gutrock gullet of the Defiles Course, Linden lost her last glimpse of the heavens. It was cut off as if the whole of the world beyond the immediate channel, the immediate darkness, had vanished. As if the fate of every living thing, of life itself, had been reduced to this: impenetrable midnight; stone as slick as oil or black ice; Mount Thunder's imponderable tons, ominous and oppressive. As if she herself had become nothing more than a burden.

The decimation of the stars had been a constant reminder of the carnage which the Worm had already wrought. But what had been lost only made what remained more precious.

Yet she had set aside her responsibility for the world. She had chosen her task. It was necessary to her, the only choice that offered any hope of forgiveness. But it would not stop the Worm. It would not hinder Lord Foul, or save her friends, or spare her son.

At first, the watercourse became narrower, ascending in low stages like terraces or past obstructions like weirs. Beyond the Ironhand—beyond Stoutgirth, Covenant, and Branl—the Feroce clambered, elusive as eidolons, over a tumble of boulders barely wide enough to accommodate the Giants in single file. Long ages of poisons and leaking malice had pitted the stone, cut it into cruel shapes, left it brittle with corrosion. But the waters had also caked every surface with slime like scum. And wherever the tumult of the currents had left gaps, necrotic mosses clung, viscid as wax, treacherous as grease. Touching them would be like trailing fingers through pus.

While the passage narrowed, however, its ceiling stretched higher. Here the Defiles Course ran down a fissure in Mount Thunder's substance. A few arm spans up the walls, the green of the Feroce gleamed sickly on moisture and moss: the residue of the river's former flow. Above that demarcation, the *krill*'s argent faded into the dark.

The crevice was old: far older than Linden's knowledge of the Land. It had endured for eons, perhaps ever since the convulsion which had created Landsdrop. It might continue to do so. Nevertheless the gutrock overhead seemed fragile. The clutter of boulders where the Feroce led the companions demonstrated that stones did fall.

But the possibility that some tremor might release sheets of rock did not trouble her. She had more urgent concerns. More than the mountain or the darkness—more than slick surfaces and vile moss—she feared the air. It was not merely fetid and hurtful: it was thick with leached evils. Every breath brought dire scents from offal and corpses; from strange lakes of lava and ruin arising from the deep places of the Earth; from the detritus of horrid theurgies and delving. From time and rot and distillation.

And from She Who Must Not Be Named. At intervals like the tightening of a rack, Linden tasted hints of the bane's distinctive anguish, terrible and bitter. She could only bear the miasma which she drew into her lungs because Jeremiah was ameliorating it with Earthpower.

Earlier he had sweetened some of the air in the valley. He could not do as much here. The atmosphere was more concentrated. And the fact that his companions were forced to advance one at a time exacerbated his difficulties. He had to push the Staff's benefits too far. As a result, Rime Coldspray and the other Giants in the lead had begun to cough as if they were about to bring up blood. Between their stertorous gasps, Linden heard Covenant wheezing. Some of the Giants in the rear retched. The sounds of their distress rebounded from the walls; multiplied upward until they filled the crevice.

The air would continue to deteriorate as the company climbed. Leagues of unknown passages, dangerous footing, and pollution lay between the company and the more tolerable atmosphere of the Wightwarrens. And Jeremiah was already faltering.

He was not ready for this; not ready at all to have twenty-one lives depending on him for every breath.

Instinctively she yearned to reach out for the Staff's resources; to wield them herself. Jeremiah was not far behind her: only Stave followed Frostheart Grueburn ahead of Cirrus Kindwind. Linden could siphon Earthpower and Law from the wood while he held it. Her chest *hurt*. She wanted good air.

Resisting her impulse to assume the work that she had given to her son was as painful as breathing.

But she had surrendered the Staff because Jeremiah needed it more than she did. Eventually he might need it absolutely. He had to become stronger. If she took back her trust prematurely—if she made his challenge easier from the start—she would undermine his efforts to believe in himself.

Yet the company was struggling. Sweat ran from Grueburn's face, although the stone and the water were cold as a crypt. Her distress ached through her lore-hardened armor. By degrees, frantic coughing spread among the Giants. In front of Grueburn, Baf Scatterwit was taken by a spasm so fierce that she slipped. She caught herself with both hands, avoided a plunge into the river, but not before her kneecap struck rock with an audible crack. Choking on Giantish obscenities, she hauled herself upright. Then, however, she was forced to halt, hunching over to massage her knee.

From Coldspray or Covenant, ragged murmurs passed Linden's name back to her; but she did not need to hear it. She understood. Jeremiah had to do better.

"Jeremiah, honey." She was panting herself. "You're trying too hard." He did not know himself well enough yet. "It's easier than you think. It's the Staff of *Law*. It was made for this. You don't have to force it. You just have to encourage it. Guide it. Let it express how you feel."

"I can't." Jeremiah's protest was thick with dread. "That doesn't make sense."

Linden fought for patience. "Try it this way. Close your eyes. Forget where you are. Forget what's happening. Forget the Staff, if you can. Concentrate on Earthpower and air, clean air, air that keeps you alive. It's like building one of your castles. You think about what you're making. You don't think about how you make it. The Staff is just a means.

"You can do this if you trust yourself."

She could almost hear his resolve breaking. "That doesn't—" he began to insist. But then he stopped. "All right," he said like a groan. "I'll try building. That worked before. Just don't blame me if—"

He fell silent.

For a moment, the effects of his theurgy disappeared entirely. Linden drew air like shards of glass into her lungs. All of her muscles seemed to seize at once. Grueburn's gasps sounded like tearing flesh. Along the line, Giants stumbled to a halt, sank to their hands and knees. The *krill* lit them like spectres, as if they had crossed over into the realm of the Dead.

The Feroce had caused some of Sarangrave Flat's mud to remember that it was once hurtloam. Covenant had said so. Surely they could do something similar to the air? If he asked them?

Then Linden felt a stronger current of Earthpower emanate from Jeremiah and the Staff. It was tentative at first. It surged and receded. She found one healing breath, lost it again. Nevertheless her heart lifted. His access to the Staff's potential resembled the chamber hidden in her own mind, the room which could open on wild magic. Learning that the chamber existed had enabled her to locate it again. And each time, the search was more familiar. The door opened more easily. The same could be true for Jeremiah, if he refused to panic.

He was young and gifted. In some respects, his sense of himself was more flexible than hers, less conflicted by an awareness of his limitations. For a heartbeat or two, his power shrank; but it also became steadier. Then better air began to gust outward. Some of it escaped into the empty heights of the fissure. Most of it swept over the company.

Linden snatched freshness into her lungs, fought for it. It was still tainted, but it became cleaner with every breath. Groans of relief spread among the Giants as Jeremiah expanded his efforts. Grueburn seemed to bite off great chunks of air, swallow them gratefully. A fierce grin bared her teeth. Still coughing, Baf Scatterwit started to laugh. One at a time, sailors and Swordmainnir joined her.

"Well done, Chosen-son!" called the Ironhand. "Well done in all sooth! It may be that our cause is doomed. It may be that we will soon perish. Yet miracles abound, and Jeremiah Chosen-son stands high among them."

Gradually Linden's companions stood straighter. They began to move again.

The Feroce had not paused. They may not have noticed the company's difficulties. Or they may not have cared. They had their own fears. Perhaps a stone's throw ahead of the Ironhand and Covenant, the troubled green passed from sight beyond a corner. Streaks of argent lit the rubble piled along the river as if the stones had tumbled there from Gravin Threndor's dreams.

As her respiration eased, Linden thought that she heard thunder.

No, not thunder. By degrees, the sound clarified itself. It was too wet, too complex, too constant to be atmospheric. It cast spray into the ambit of the *krill*'s illumination. The company was approaching a waterfall.

Where the spray brushed her cheeks, it stung.

She could not gauge the height of the plunge by the timbre of its muffled roar; but she heard neither warnings nor chagrin from the Giants. The Ironhand did not hesitate as she bore Covenant out of sight, leaving Branl behind to light the way.

In moments, a few sailors and Onyx Stonemage scrambled to Branl's position, followed by Squallish Blustergale and more of the Anchormaster's crew. As Grue-burn neared the turn, Linden became more confident that the water did not plum-met from a great height. Still her anxiety did not relent until Grueburn carried her past the corner. Then she was able to see that the waterfall was no taller than one Giant standing on the shoulders of another.

She could not have climbed it. Perhaps Grueburn could not. But here the river's diminishment was obvious. A comparatively narrow gush of water pounded into the deep center of the channel. Beside the river on both sides, eons of a far heavier flow had left more gradual slopes. Broken rocks cloaked in mosses like shredded skin mounted upward in possible increments.

A short way up the rise, Coldspray and Covenant waited for Branl and light. Above them, the Feroce scrambled for the rim as if they were in no danger of slipping. Their emerald glow wavered and gibbered on the walls as they scuttled out of sight. Then their fires faded as if the crevice had opened to accommodate a cavern.

Linden looked back at Jeremiah. The radiance of Loric's gem revealed black ten-drils of power like vines curling away from the Staff, making the air precious. As the boy worked, however, a scowl of strain clenched his features, and the wood trembled in his grasp. He was still trying too hard.

"Are you all right, honey?" Linden asked over the shout of the water. "Do you need rest? We should be able to survive for a few minutes."

"Don't bother me." He sounded distant, wrapped in concentration. She barely heard him. "I'm fine."

"The Feroce act like they're in a hurry," Covenant offered, "but I can ask them to wait"—he glanced at the waterfall—"once we catch up with them."

When Jeremiah nodded, Rime Coldspray continued upward. Behind her, Bluff Stoutgirth gestured his crew forward. Moving as surely as the Giants, Branl passed Grueburn and Linden to rejoin the head of the line.

Accompanied by argent, the Ironhand took Covenant past the lip of the fall, out of the harsh spray. At the rim, Branl waited again. Still in single file, Giants made the ascent. Ahead of Grueburn and Linden, Scatterwit limped over the treachery of the stones. She was obviously in pain, yet she chuckled in short bursts as if her damaged kneecap amused her.

Then Grueburn crested the waterfall; and Linden stared in surprise. Ahead of her, *krill*-light played across the black surface of a lake.

It may have been vast. The height of the cavern seemed to imply that it was; and the darkness beyond the *krill*'s reach concealed the boundaries of the water. Liquid obsidian curved away to Linden's left, following the cavern wall out of sight. But ahead and to the right, the lake appeared to have no end—or her senses were con-fused by intimations of power.

It was eerily motionless, as still as stone. Water dripped from mosses high on the walls, where until recently the cavern had been filled. Thin trickles fell here and there across the emptiness, perhaps dribbling from stalactites invisible in the dark. But there were no ripples: none at all. And no sounds. Drops struck the lake and were absorbed seamlessly. Water lay flat as glass against the rocks of the verge.

The Ironhand had halted with Covenant near the curve of the lakefront. One by one, the rest of the company reached them and stopped, peering into the blind depths or the veiled distance. Branl waved Loric's dagger for a moment, watched silver sweep across the immaculate ebony. Then he stepped back.

A leaden silence ruled the cavern. From this vantage, even the waterfall appeared to make no sound. The Giants seemed unwilling or unable to speak. To Linden's eyes, the air over the lake looked as condensed and heavy as sweat.

Again her health-sense caught hints of She Who Must Not Be Named. Here they were stronger. The spilth of theurgies as old as the mountain—as old as the Land—stained the lake wherever she looked. Implied carrion-eaters tasted her skin.

Distracted by noisome things, she was slow to notice that the Feroce were gone.

Gone?

"Thomas?" The silence seemed to seal her throat. She had to swallow several times before she could say more than his name. "The Feroce? Where did they go?"

Rime Coldspray and her comrades scanned the cavern, the lake. Covenant gazed past or through Linden like a man who had lost his sight. "Into the water." His voice sounded preternaturally distinct: precise and defiant. It should have raised echoes. Instead it fell stillborn. "I don't know why. They didn't say anything."

"I am loath to believe," remarked Branl, "that they have forsaken us."

"As am I," Stave agreed. "They heed their High God."

The Ironhand coughed, cleared her throat. "Without them—"

As if she had summoned them, delicate green flames appeared on the surface near the spot where the cavern's leftward sweep interrupted Linden's view. Untroubled by the waters, the creatures arose under their fires, lifted emerald from the lake. Their passing left no mark on the water's black sheen as they climbed the rocks.

"Why do you tarry?" Their damp voice scaled into the heights. "You must hasten. There is peril, much peril. Are you deaf to majesty? Blind to wonder? You must hasten."

Tensions ran among the Giants. They prepared to move. But Rime Coldspray stood where she was. From her clasp, Covenant called to the Feroce, "What's going on? You picked a hell of a time for a swim. Did you wake something up?"

Studying the lake, Linden saw nothing, heard nothing. She felt only the noxious tickling of centipedes, tentative and eager.

"Will you not hasten?" the creatures urged. "We are merely the Feroce. There is no peril for us. Your lives are forfeit."

Covenant appeared to freeze for an instant, startled into incomprehension. Then he snapped to the Ironhand, "Go!"

At once, Coldspray surged ahead over the hazardous stones. Behind her, Giants followed as swiftly as they could. But Baf Scatterwit's cracked knee slowed her. Grueburn waved her free arm, urged Halewhole Bluntfist and the trailing sailors to pass her. Then she drew her longsword; kept pace with Scatterwit. Cirrus Kindwind did the same, bracing Jeremiah with her maimed forearm. Holding Cabledarm's longsword, Stave positioned himself between them and the water.

Linden did not glance at her son. The lake seemed to grip her. There were too many centipedes, more and more of them. Spiders. Maggots. Worms avid to feast on her sins. Only Jeremiah's tendrils of Earthpower and Law shielded her.

A bulge appeared in the water.

No, not a bulge: a *body*. A stone's throw long. A double arm span wide. Lithe as a serpent, flowing up to bend the surface and then sliding back down endlessly. As dark as the lake, but rife with strength. If it had a head or a tail, Linden did not see them. No slight ripple or splash defined the immense monster's glide.

From the rocks ahead of Covenant, the Feroce confessed abjectly, "We sought to gaze upon our High God's god. We have done so. Its thoughts are broken. They lack glory. Only ruin remains. It will slay you all."

"Hellfire," Covenant rasped. "I suppose even the lurker had to come from somewhere. If that's its mother, I've seen enough. I don't want more."

Branl stood at the waterline, poised with the *krill* and Longwrath's flamberge. Linden felt a throb of wild magic from Covenant's ring. Reflexively her wedding band answered his attempt to prepare himself. Imminent heat and argent chased away the things that scurried across her skin. The long arc of the monster's body continued to flow. If it felt the company's presence, its awareness was hidden in the depths.

Linden tried to focus her attention on her ring, seeking to support Covenant; to dismiss the bane's touch. But she was too close to the Staff. Jeremiah's power seemed to block her, or she blocked herself. Wild magic and Law conflicted.

Coldspray and then the Anchormaster rounded the curve. Dire's Vessel's crew hurried after them, crowding close to the cavern wall. Weapons ready, both Stonemage and Bluntfist had taken positions like Branl's near the water's edge, guarding the rear of the company. Scatterwit whimpered as if she feared to be left behind.

The Feroce had disappeared again. Had they gone ahead? Linden did not know. She struggled to breathe. A moment passed before she realized that the company's alarm had pierced Jeremiah's concentration. He needed help.

Here she could not call upon the Staff without touching it. The throb and itch of her ring interfered. Trepidation interfered. Leaning away from Grueburn's arms, she reached for Kindwind and Jeremiah; but she could not stretch far enough. Then Grueburn shifted closer to Kindwind, and Linden gripped the Staff by one iron heel.

She did not take it. Instead she added her will to her son's disturbed resolve, reinforced his intentions with her own.

He gave her a quick glance of thanks. Relieved, he settled back into himself. The pressure of poisons in her lungs eased. All of the Giants seemed to move more quickly. Even Scatterwit's pace improved.

"Attend!" Branl called calmly. "The water rises."

Linden twisted her head to look.

Oh, shit. Branl was right. Still motionless, still silent, the midnight lake had begun to devour its borders, fed by some source beyond her discernment. It did not lap or splash against the rocks. It simply covered them.

Led by the *Haruchai*, Grueburn, Kindwind, and Scatterwit passed the curve at the rear of the company. At once, Branl ran ahead, carrying light. Now Linden saw that the cavern narrowed in this direction. The walls leaned closer to each other until they met in a sheet of running water. At first, the sheet appeared sheer, a straight waterfall thinned by its own width. It would be impossible to climb. And there were no slopes leading up to the tunnel that opened three or four Giant-heights above the lake. The Feroce stood facing the cul-de-sac as if they had been thwarted.

But then Linden saw that the pour of water reflected argent and emerald in a cascade of spangles. Under the waterfall, the stone was broken in scores or hundreds of places, pitted and interrupted wherever erosion and toxins had found flaws.

Surely it would still be impossible to climb? The stone would be slick—

The lake rose. The added water should have drained away as fast as it came, but it did not. Somehow the lurker's mad god heaved the entire surface higher. Grueburn, Kindwind, and Scatterwit were forced to pick their way closer to the wall.

Without explanation, Stave sprinted away. Inhumanly sure-footed, he caught up with the Humbled, moved among the Giants. He handed Cabledarm's sword to the Anchormaster. Linden heard him ask for rope.

Favoring her knee, Baf Scatterwit stumbled into the edge of the lake. Her right foot went under. The impact of her weight had no effect on the water's massive lift.

Linden had no idea what would happen then. The lake's power defied her senses. But Scatterwit scrambled out again. She tried to limp faster.

Linden clung to the Staff's heel, struggled to help Jeremiah clean the air.

From a sack of supplies, a sailor produced a coil of rope as thick as Stave's arm. He looped one end twice over his shoulder, secured it by tucking it under itself. Immediately he approached the swift sheet of the cul-de-sac. As if the difficulties were trivial, he began to ascend.

Water pounded onto him. It splashed past him without affecting the eerie surface of the lake. He was drenched in ancient corrosives, distilled residues. But they did him no apparent harm. His flesh spurned the mountain's taints.

"Giantfriend," Grueburn rasped: a harsh scrape of sound. With her sword, she gestured at Scatterwit.

Linden glanced in that direction, saw Scatterwit limping more heavily than before. Far more heavily. With every step, she lurched to the right, toward the lake, as if she had lost her balance. She seemed to recover by force of will.

God—

Baf Scatterwit's right foot had been cut away, severed at the ankle. A clean slice: clean and cauterized. There was no blood. She seemed unaware that her foot was gone. She moved as if only her damaged knee pained her.

Linden started to shout a warning at the Giants; but Grueburn stopped her. Through her teeth, the Swordmain snarled, "They know." Abruptly she slapped her sword back into its scabbard. With her free hand, she supported Scatterwit so that the woman could hurry without toppling.

Panic and Grueburn's rush broke Linden's hold on the Staff. Earthpower and black flame faltered. The air dug a knife into Linden's chest. But Jeremiah tightened his grip a moment later, took up the slack. Complex stresses gleamed on his cheeks and forehead.

Between one urgent breath and the next, Linden saw Stave rise higher than Rime Coldspray's head. His fingers and toes gripped the damaged stone like claws. Another breath, and he had climbed more than halfway. Then he gained the lip of the tunnel and passed out of sight, trailing the rope behind him.

Now, Linden thought. Now he has to secure it.

There was nothing that she could do for Scatterwit.

Stave did not have time. With Grueburn's help, Scatterwit joined the other Giants. Kindwind and Jeremiah came last. Bluff Stoutgirth gave Scatterwit a look of anguish, then jerked his head away. Other sailors chewed their silence as if they sought to break their teeth. They were all ready. Covenant now clung to Coldspray's back, leaving her arms unencumbered. But the lake still rose. In a few heartbeats, no more, it would threaten the nearest feet. It would sever—

Stave's line jerked. At a word from the Anchormaster, Wiver Setrock grabbed it, tested it. Carrying more rope, Setrock swarmed upward, a sailor adept at ratlines and hawsers. Unlike Stave's, his feet slipped here and there; but those momentary skids hardly slowed him. If the corrupted water hurt him, he ignored the pain.

He reached the lip, vanished into the river's tunnel. Moments later, his line snaked down to his comrades. Then Keenreef and Hurl were climbing, each with new ropes.

The lake crept higher. The waiting Giants squeezed closer to the wall. Some of them stood in the waterfall, breathing with their mouths covered. The Feroce watched from a short distance. The water came to their ankles, then to their knees; but they did not fear it. Green and silver shone in their limpid eyes.

Linden wanted to tell Coldspray and Kindwind to go next, take Covenant and Jeremiah to safety. But when she tried to speak, her voice failed. She could not imagine how Cirrus Kindwind would bear Jeremiah upward with only one hand.

From the Ironhand's back, Covenant asked the lurker's creatures, "What about you? We need you."

"The Feroce are the Feroce," they replied as if that answer sufficed. Sinking at every step, they began to back away. As they submerged, their fires flared briefly on the water, then went out.

"Hellfire," Covenant muttered. "Bloody damnation."

To Coldspray, the Anchormaster said, "In such straits, my will commands." His tone held an unexpected edge of authority. "You and Frostheart Grueburn must ascend. Halewhole Bluntfist and Etch Furledsail will assist Cirrus Kindwind." He hesitated for an instant, then growled, "Baf Scatterwit must hold the rear."

Scatterwit responded with a laugh like the croak of a raven.

Of course, Linden thought bitterly. Scatterwit had been maimed. Therefore she was more expendable than her comrades.

Groaning to herself, Linden worked her way around Grueburn until she reached Grueburn's back. The Swordmain would need both hands—

Abruptly Jeremiah's power evaporated. "Sorry about this." Tension thrummed in his voice. "I'll get back to it."

Lifted by Kindwind, he went over her shoulder to her back. As he shifted, he braced the Staff across her breastplate so that he could hold it with his arms on either side of her neck. There he hung, hugging the sides of her chest with his legs. Then he shut his eyes; began to exert Earthpower again. Black flame twisted upward in front of Kindwind's face.

Four lines now dangled from the darkness of the tunnel. At once, the Ironhand, Onyx Stonemage, and two sailors hastened upward. As soon as they were clear, Grueburn started to ascend like a leap of fire. Through tainted torrents, Linden watched Bluntfist and Furledsail support Kindwind.

Somehow Jeremiah continued to pour out Earthpower while water hammered down on him.

The lake still rose. It was no more than an arm span away from the rest of the Giants. Only Branl stood between them and the fatal surface.

Resting his flamberge on his shoulder, the Humbled crouched at the water's edge and prodded the tip of the *krill* into a stone. There he waited, studying the lake as if he were daring it to touch High Lord Loric's blade.

A moment later, Grueburn carried Linden up into the tunnel into the deeper darkness of the river's passage. At first, she saw nothing. Granite and black water filled her senses. But then Covenant's ring began to emit a soft glow. Strain knotted his forehead, bared his teeth, as he strove to elicit wild magic without losing control. Gradually his conflicted, tenuous light revealed the surroundings.

Beyond its wide mouth above the cavern, the tunnel resembled a chute or flume angling sharply downward from somewhere far above. The diminished river filled its bottom, tumbling loudly over planes like shelves, gouged flaws, indurated obstructions. Covenant's silver bled along the splashing and spray. The Ironhand, Stave, and a few Giants had waded upward, forcing their way against the downrush to make room for their comrades.

There were no protrusions or stable boulders where Stave and the sailors could have secured their ropes. Instead Keenreef, Hurl, and two comrades anchored the lines by sitting in the river and bracing their feet in cracks and potholes. By plain strength, they supported the Giants ascending through the waterfall.

Earlier Stave must have done the same—

Grueburn and Kindwind led Bluntfist and Furledsail upward. The river fumed against their knees, boiled to carry them away. But they were Giants: they kept their feet. All of the Swordmainnir were in the tunnel. More sailors swarmed up the ropes. By Linden's count, only Scatterwit, Squallish Blustergale, and Branl remained in immediate danger.

The river here was as corrupt as it had been around the lake. It reeked of the bane's exudations.

As Grueburn joined the Ironhand, Covenant gave Linden a look like a glare of fever. By its very nature, wild magic resisted restraint. It became more dangerous with repeated use. But Linden could not help him. There was too much Earthpower in the air. The chute constricted it. Reminders of She Who Must Not Be Named assailed her. Her wedding band no longer answered his.

"It's getting harder," Jeremiah groaned. He kept his eyes squeezed shut. "The Worm—I can see *Melenkurion* Skyweir."

Grueburn and Kindwind stood in the river shoulder to shoulder. Aching to relieve

Jeremiah and Covenant—to relieve herself—Linden put her hand on the Staff again, added her determination to her son's.

"How far?" she asked him. "How far away is it?"

"I don't know." Jeremiah was near his limits. "Close enough." Then he added, "But the Worm is in a river. It isn't moving as fast."

Linden closed her eyes as well; listened to the tumid clamor of water. The Worm must have passed the boundary of the Last Hills. It was crossing the wilderland which had once been Garroting Deep. And along the way, it was appeasing its hunger by drinking from the Black River, which took its name from its burden of diluted EarthBlood.

Yet the Worm had traversed most of the Land with appalling speed. How much time remained before it forced its way into the depths of the Skyweir? A day? Less?

A moment later, Covenant's wild magic faded. When Linden opened her eyes, she saw silver streaming from the *krill* in Branl's grasp. It shone on the water frothing down the contorted length of the channel. At the same time, she heard shouts.

Hurl called, "They are safe!" And the Anchormaster crowed, "Stone and Sea! We are Giants in all sooth! And the *Haruchai* are Giants also, in their fashion. We live!"

"The lake rises still," continued Hurl. "Indeed, it swells more swiftly. Yet Scatterwit has suffered no further harm. And Blustergale has lost no more than two toes and a portion of a third. Had we been but a heartbeat sooner—"

Blustergale interrupted him, roaring in feigned indignation. "There is no pain! None, I say! Is this not an affront to fire the coldest heart? Am I not a Giant, as mortal as any, and as worthy of my hurts? Does the lurker's god think so little of me, or of Baf Scatterwit, or of all here, that it does not deign to cause *pain*?"

While Scatterwit chuckled, Bluff Stoutgirth commanded, "Enough, Blustergale. Some among us deem toes needful. Demonstrate that you are able to ascend here, and I will suffer your umbrage. Should you slip or falter, however, I will regard you justly chastened."

"The lake rises still," Hurl repeated more urgently. "Badinage and bravado will not slow it."

"Aye," the Anchormaster replied, "and aye again." He had recovered his good humor. "As you have seen fit to chide us, you will remain to mark the water's advance." Then he urged his sailors into motion.

Led by Onyx Stonemage, the others thrashed ahead.

Branl approached Coldspray, Grueburn, and Kindwind; Covenant, Linden, and Jeremiah. He held Loric's dagger so that its radiance did not shine into his eyes. Shadows obscured his mien as he announced, "The lake did not heed the *krill*."

"The Feroce were right," Covenant grumbled. "The lurker's god is crazy. That knife can cut anything." He peered into the darkness of the chute. "Now I'm worried. We don't know what's up there. We're going to need those creatures."

"They've come this far," Linden sighed. In spite of their fears— "If they don't rejoin us, it's because they can't."

"I know." Tension throbbed in Covenant's voice. His arms were getting tired. He would not be able to cling to the Ironhand's back indefinitely. But Coldspray would need her hands to help her defy the weight of the river. Grueburn and Kindwind would need their hands. "I just want to bitch for a while."

"Timewarden," Rime Coldspray replied like a reprimand, "your tales are foreshortened beyond sufferance. They are ended ere I am able to hear joy in them. And you employ words strangely. 'Bitch,' forsooth. I will deem it a courtesy if you will refrain until we are better able to heed you."

Covenant gave Linden a twisted smile, rolled his eyes. "Have it your way. I'll do my complaining when we find the damn Despiser."

"And another," sighed the Ironhand. "Is there no limit to your brevity?"

Linden wished that Covenant could laugh. She wanted to laugh herself. But she did not have it in her. The spray promised carrion. It implied horror. Even in the constriction of the flume, the sensations were oblique. Nevertheless they were getting stronger.

ɷ

Now the company did not tarry. A shout from Hurl announced that the lake was nearing the rim of the waterfall. Heaving against the pressure of the river, the Swordmainnir and the sailors fought their way upward. One of the Anchormaster's crew had tied a rope around Baf Scatterwit's waist. Giants ahead of her held the line. And Squallish Blustergale stayed with her, taking some of her weight. Together they struggled along behind their comrades.

Linden's arms ached. Cramps threatened her thighs. Nevertheless riding Grueburn's back was easier than it might have been. All of the Giants moved hunching over, ready to catch themselves if they slipped on slick rocks or secreted moss. Grueburn's posture helped Linden to hang on.

The passage should have been impossible for the *Haruchai*. Water that reached the Giants' knees struck Stave and Branl above their waists. Nevertheless the two men forged ahead as if they were incapable of faltering. The *krill* in Branl's grasp did not waver. He and Stave carried their cumbersome swords like men who had spent decades training with such weapons.

Before long, Hurl called to inform the company that the lake had reached the bottom of the chute.

Muttering elaborate Giantish curses, the Swordmainnir and the sailors continued an ascent that seemed to have no end.

Eventually, however, Rime Coldspray came to a widening. There across the centuries the river had eaten deposits of sandstone and shale out of the walls. It had dug a pit in the underlying basalt. The result was a space in which all of the Giants could gather—and a pool deep enough to swallow the *Haruchai*. Fortunately a few boulders clung to the sides. Here and there, stubborn granite ledges protruded from the walls.

Coldspray looked a question at Bluff Stoutgirth. When he nodded, she ordered a rest.

Gratefully Frostheart Grueburn sloughed Linden onto a boulder. Cirrus Kindwind put Jeremiah down beside Linden, stood straighter to ease the tension in her back. As Coldspray settled Covenant nearby, the Anchormaster arranged Stonemage, Bluntfist, and his crew, some standing to their chests in the pool, others leaning on boulders or propped against the walls. Then he asked for food and clean water.

Sailors unpacked chunks of cured beef and mutton, rinds of cheese, bread with the texture of hardpan, dried fruits, waterskins. As they did so, Linden accepted the Staff of Law from Jeremiah and assumed the whole task of purifying the air so that he could rest and eat. He had not questioned her assistance earlier: he was not loath to trust her now. Apparently he was learning to believe that she would not recant her gift.

While she had the opportunity, she extended other forms of refreshment to the Giants; eased the trembling of Covenant's muscles; nourished Jeremiah's strength. As if to himself, the boy murmured, "That's a neat trick. I want to learn it." But he did not reach for the Staff. Images of the Worm seemed to glide like ravens across the depths of his gaze.

Some of the waterskins held diluted *diamondraught*. When Linden had swallowed enough to wash the taste of pollution out of her mouth and throat, she joined the Giants eating.

She had not heard Hurl's voice for a while. Surely he was able to stay above the lake? But if the Anchormaster felt any anxiety on Hurl's behalf, he concealed it with jests.

"Thomas?" Linden asked. "What do you think? How high can that monster lift so much water?"

He opened his mouth to answer; closed it again. After a moment, he said, "By damn." Surprise and relief. With the index finger of his halfhand, he pointed down the chute.

In the distance below the pool, unsteady emerald reflected wetly on the walls.

The fires of the Feroce were still some distance away, but they were coming closer. And before long, Linden made out Hurl's bulk looming behind them. In the green glow, he looked somehow ghoulish, like an avatar of the Illearth Stone. His grin resembled the grimace of a fiend. Nevertheless he was unharmed.

The condition of the Feroce was more difficult to gauge. Linden had never been able to sense the nature of their magicks. From her perspective, they seemed smaller, weaker, as if they had been reduced by their immersion in the lake. And when they finally waded into the pool, she saw that they had indeed shrunk. Although they floated effortlessly with their arms and flames above water, they appeared to have drawn into themselves as if their encounter with their High God's god had shamed them.

"They rose with the lake," Hurl proclaimed in a tone of wonder. "I had surrendered all hope of them. Yet when the lake began to hint that it might recede, the Feroce emerged."

The creatures faced Covenant; but now they did not flinch or cower. Nor did they ask his pardon for their absence. "We are merely the Feroce," they stated. "We serve our High God. We do not question our worship. Commanded, we obey." The strangeness of their shared voice seemed to accentuate the corruption of the atmosphere, the taint of the river, the slick sheen of the walls.

"But we have beheld our High God's god. He is lessened. Perhaps he is lessened." They regarded only Covenant. Even their flames appeared to focus on him. "Perhaps the Pure One is also lessened." Their emerald shone in his eyes. It gleamed like spray on his scarred forehead. "You must hasten again. We do not question. Commanded, we obey. Yet doubt infects. It spreads. An end draws near. We fear it. It gladdens us.

"You must hasten."

"Or what?" Covenant asked carefully.

The Feroce were no longer afraid—or their fear had become a different form of apprehension. "We are naught," they answered. "Worship is all things. Or it also is naught."

"Mom?" Jeremiah breathed. "What's going on?"

Linden touched his shoulder to quiet him. She tightened her grip on the Staff.

"Then forget your High God," Covenant said almost calmly; almost mildly. "Forget our alliance. Forget that Clyme died for it, and the Worm is going to destroy every god you can imagine." He did not raise his voice, but his tone became thicker, harder. "Remember that the *jheherrin* saved the Pure One. They were weaker than you are, and maybe more scared, but they helped him anyway. Then he set them free.

"Try remembering *that*. If doubt infects, so does courage."

Linden held her breath. If the Feroce turned back now—

For a long moment, they were silent. They did not move. Their large eyes remained fixed on Covenant. Nevertheless they conveyed the impression that they were conferring with each other.

Covenant faced them steadily, waiting.

Finally they sighed like slumping mud. "We are the Feroce. We are ignorant of courage. We obey because we must."

They did not urge haste again. Instead they drifted away from Covenant, gathered in the center of the pool. There they faced each other, holding out their fires like questions for which they had no answers.

"Thomas?" Linden asked.

He frowned at her, or at his own thoughts. "I know. Not exactly reassuring." Then he grimaced. "So what else is new?"

"We should go," he told Rime Coldspray. "We're running out of time."

Yet doubt infects.

It was contagious.

Nodding, the Ironhand addressed Bluff Stoutgirth. "Anchormaster?"

"Aye." Stoutgirth grinned. To his crew, he said as if he were jesting, "Come, sluggards. Have done with feasting and sloth. While we dally, the world's doom grows fretful. Soon it may set its sails and depart unopposed."

His crew responded with snorts or groans, or with ripostes; yet they immediately began packing away their provisions. Soon they were ready.

Linden hesitated, unsure of her son. But Jeremiah asked for the Staff without prompting. "I feel better now," he assured her. "I want to practice." He faced her squarely, held her gaze. "But maybe you shouldn't help me anymore. You make it too easy. I don't have to push myself when you're doing half the work."

She winced. He was right, of course. He had to make himself stronger; had to earn his inheritance. But she already knew that she was going to abandon him again. She was even going to abandon Covenant. And when she did, she would leave without any hope that she might ever return.

Her hands shook as she passed the Staff to her son. Unclosing her fingers required an act of will.

His attention shifted at once to the wood; but she continued to gaze at him, clinging. Carefully she said, "I'm proud of you. Do you know that?"

"Sure, Mom." His tone made it clear that he was not listening.

The theurgy which he summoned from his hands and his violated heart was as black as anything that she had ever done.

೧౦౭

L ed by the Feroce, the company struggled upward. Emerald oozed like infection down the river. The light of the *krill* seemed to lurch from place to place as it struck irregular facets of stone. The channel felt interminable. Its twists and bends through Mount Thunder's gutrock blocked Linden's view ahead. She could not guess how far the company would have to climb.

Fortunately Jeremiah's use of Earthpower and Law was improving. The Giants were able to breathe more easily. And the hints of She Who Must Not Be Named which Linden had felt earlier were lessened by midnight fire in the confines of the flume.

Blustergale continued to support Scatterwit. A few of her comrades took turns holding the rope tied around her. Like them, she labored ahead, striving toward an untenable future.

So suddenly that Linden only had time to flinch and grip, Grueburn slipped: she started to plunge. But Stave stopped her by anchoring her foot. She caught herself on her hands, regained her balance. Muttering rueful apologies, she bore Linden onward.

Other Giants slipped as well. As their weariness grew, they lost their footing more often. Most of them recovered quickly, or were secured by their comrades. But one of the sailors fell hard enough to take Keenreef with him. Threshing their arms, they were swept downward. However, Wiver Setrock dropped to his knees below their rush, spread his arms, snagged his comrades before they collided with Grueburn and Kindwind. With another sailor and Onyx Stonemage at his back, Setrock helped the Giants find their feet.

Anxiety and jests echoed down the chute. Coldspray and Stoutgirth shouted unnecessary warnings. Jeremiah looked around wildly for a moment: the only sign that he had noticed what was happening. Then he returned his attention to the Staff.

Darkness. Green glaring dully. Flashes of argent. Loud water acrid with minerals and pollution. Treacherous rocks and mosses. More darkness. Covenant clung like a penitent to Coldspray's back. Jeremiah half knelt behind Kindwind, gripping the Staff across her cataphract. Linden listened to the effort of Grueburn's breathing, felt the strain in Grueburn's muscles, and could do nothing.

She had given up looking ahead when she heard the Anchormaster call, "And not before time! Doubtless all things must have an end. After such an ascent, however, I would lief have gained a less ambiguous summit."

Linden jerked up her head; saw that the fires of the Feroce no longer reflected on the walls. The *krill*'s illumination seemed to imply an open space ahead. She tried to extend her discernment upward, but she could not. Her senses were blocked by Giants and fouled water, Earthpower and exertion. Even Loric's gem had the effect of obstructing her percipience.

None of the Giants spoke as they hurried to reach a place where they might be able to rest again.

Like the Feroce, Coldspray and Stoutgirth had moved out of sight. Holding light for the sailors and the Swordmainnir, Branl stood at the edge of the channel-mouth. Now Linden was able to see that the river ran from another large cavity in the gutrock; but the scale of the space was still hidden from her.

As Grueburn labored upward, however, Linden heard more complex tones in the water's turbulence, new pitches and timbres. Another waterfall? No. The sounds lacked that deeper resonance. After a moment, she realized that she was listening to more than one torrent. From beyond the immediate rush and spray came the turmoil of other streams, two distinct sources of water, neither splashing from any considerable height.

Half a dozen sailors reached the Humbled. They passed him leftward, clambered out of sight. As Stonemage and Setrock gained the opening, they led Keenreef and more of Dire's Vessel's crew to the right. Together Grueburn and Kindwind carried Linden and Jeremiah to smooth stone at the rim of the tunnel.

Linden peered out at a large cave like a bubble in Mount Thunder's igneous substance. By the measure of the lower cavern, its dimensions were modest. She could have hit the ceiling with a rock, or skipped a pebble halfway across the dark water in front of her: a diminished lake now little more than a pond marked by rancid strands and stains higher on the walls. At the water's former height, the rocks piled around the cave's bottom would have been covered, useless to the company. At the pond's present level, she could have scrambled anywhere in the cave.

Nevertheless the air was viscid, thick with omens. The hurtful tang of She Who Must Not Be Named was stronger here. Suggestions of ire and ruin felt like insects on Linden's skin, tangible and feeding. Without Jeremiah and Earthpower, she might have whimpered aloud.

But then Grueburn carried her aside, out of the way of the Giants behind them; and Linden noticed the water's inlets.

There were indeed two, one diagonally across from her on the left, the other opposite her and somewhat to the right. The stream on the left tumbled from a fissure in the wall, a crack barely wide enough to admit a Giant. The water frothing there conveyed the impression that it cascaded from somewhere far above the cave. In the *krill*'s light, its spray shone silver.

The other stream boiled out of an opening beneath the lake's surface. Apparently it came from the base of a subtle flaw in the stone, a seam where distinct forms of rock had been reluctantly fused. Under the pressure of its own weight, water seethed into the pond.

Only the fissure on the left offered the company an egress. An ascent there would be difficult. If the crack narrowed, it might become impassable. But the water there was fresh.

God, it was *fresh*—It came from a clean spring, or from several. And the fissure was accessible. The company could reach it without enduring an immersion in the pond; without subjecting Linden to more of the bane's touch.

The Cavewights were entirely unlike the Feroce. Surely they required sources of clean water? Surely a source this abundant would lead toward the Wightwarrens?

Her heart seemed to beat in her throat as she turned toward Covenant.

Rime Coldspray had set him down on the far side of the cave's outlet. Stave and all of the Giants had now emerged from the tunnel, and Cirrus Kindwind had already lowered Jeremiah to the rocks. He leaned on the Staff, resting, but he did not relax his efforts. Stark strands of power fluttered around the company, softening the atmosphere.

He was the only one not looking at Covenant. Stave, Branl, and the Giants watched the Unbeliever, the Timewarden, waiting for him to make a decision. As if there could possibly be any doubt—

But he ignored them. Instead he faced the Feroce.

Wreathed in green, they clustered a few paces beyond him. Some of them stood with their feet in the pond, but they did not sink away. Again they appeared to commune with each other. Their fires danced like language in their hands.

Linden winced at the sight. They were definitely smaller. Shrinking. Losing faith.

Covenant's impatience showed in the clench of his shoulders, the rigidity of his back. He seemed to want some form of confirmation from the creatures, even though the company's path was obvious. After a tense pause, he demanded, "Now what? We can't just hang around here. We don't have time."

The Feroce did not look at him. Their voice quavered as if they expected to be struck down.

"You will be wroth with us. You will not heed."

"What?" Covenant's surprise echoed faintly around the walls. "I'm going to get angry because you're trying to help? Why?"

Two of the creatures pointed at the fissure. "You must not enter there. It misleads." Two others indicated the rank moil of the second inlet. "You must follow richer water." Then they crowded closer together. "Now we perish. You will not suffer us."

"Thomas!" Linden protested. She gestured urgently toward the crack. "That water is *fresh*." It did not stink of threats.

Giants nodded their assent.

"Oh, stop," Covenant growled at the Feroce. "I'm not going to do anything to you. None of us are." He squinted over his shoulder at Linden, then addressed the creatures again. "But we need an explanation. 'Richer' water? I assume you mean water with more crud in it. That doesn't make sense. Never mind that it's likely to poison us. Suppose you're right. Suppose it does run closer to the Wightwarrens. Even Giants can't swim against that kind of pressure. And we sure as hell can't hold our breath long enough to find air."

"Wait a minute," Jeremiah murmured. Ebony tendrils curled across the pond. They searched along the far wall. But he did not say more; and the alarm clamoring in Linden's ears prevented her from heeding him.

"So tell me," Covenant continued. "Why *that* water? Why is a trail we can't even follow better than one we can?"

The creatures flinched. Their fires guttered. "We are the Feroce. We obey, as we must. We cannot answer ire."

Covenant swore softly.

Quivering, the damp voice said, "We do not know your goal. We do not know the mountain. But we taste the memories mingled here. Those waters do not hold the Maker's scorn. Other powers enrich them, yes. They urge false worship, abhorrent to us, seductive." The Feroce shuddered. "Yet we are certain. Memory is certain."

"Wait a minute," Jeremiah said again.

Everyone ignored him.

"The stream of mere water. The plain path. It misleads. It does not recall light. No light has shone upon it. No sun. No flame. No magicks."

No light—?

"Stone and Sea!" rasped the Ironhand. Other Giants muttered their chagrin.

The *Haruchai* watched and listened as if they were drawing different conclusions.

"The richer waters," said the Feroce, "remember much. They recall darkness and horrible strength. Strange theurgies. Time without measure. And light. Light! In a distant age, they have known the sun. They have not forgotten.

"The memory is there."

As one, the creatures pointed at the turbulence spewing from beneath the surface of the pond.

Oh, God. Floundering, Linden thought, Light— The cascade of fresh water had never seen torches. It had never felt the ruddy glow of rocklight. Therefore its long plunge did not intersect the catacombs. Even Cavewights needed illumination.

But the other stream— Ah, hell. That impassable gush came from the Soulsease. It had once traveled the Upper Land. It had known the warmth of the sun. And far to the west, the Soulsease entered the Wightwarrens. But only a few days ago, it had lost its way through the mountain. Now it plunged toward the Lost Deep. For that reason, it was fraught with the anguish and rage of She Who Must Not Be Named.

"Thomas." Linden's voice had fallen to a whisper. She was too frightened to raise it. "I can't. There's no way—"

She could not submerge herself in water that reminded her of the bane. She would go mad.

In a taut rumble, the Anchormaster remarked, "We know little of these Feroce. We of Dire's Vessel have heard your tale, but we have not lived it. Is it conceivable that they have turned aside from our purpose? If they are no longer ruled by their monstrous deity's will, it may be they who mislead, rather than the waters."

Covenant shook his head. "I doubt it. They had a perfect chance to abandon us back at that lake, but they didn't. The lurker still wants to live. They still want to live. We're the only hope they've got."

Like him, Linden believed the Feroce. Nevertheless the company could not go where they suggested.

She should have been grateful. Instead she wanted to scream.

"I said, *wait* a minute!" Jeremiah demanded more strongly. "You aren't paying attention."

Fierce as a blow, Covenant wheeled away from the Feroce. Bracing his fists on his hips, he glared past the spread of Giants and the mouth of the downward chute. "Hellfire, Jeremiah! Paying attention to *what*?"

Jeremiah faced Linden rather than Covenant. "Look, Mom." Black fire played across the spout of fouled water, skirled up the seam of the wall. "*Look.*"

Linden stared at him, thinking, Don't push me. I can't.

But he was her son. She could not refuse him. Trembling privately at the prospect of maggots, spiders, worms, she asked Frostheart Grueburn to put her down. When she stood beside Jeremiah, close enough to borrow some of the Staff's Earthpower, she turned her senses toward the fused stone. Alarm hampered her, but she forced it aside. Unsteadily she directed her percipience into the water; into the wall.

There.

Instinctively she recoiled; closed her throat against a moan.

The rock along the seam was thin. It looked thin enough to break. And beyond it—

She bit her lip until she drew blood.

—stretched a different fissure, a wedge with its tip at the seam. It was narrow, but it widened into the distance until it passed beyond her discernment. And it was full of water.

No, she realized a heartbeat later, not full. Everywhere under Mount Thunder, the Soulsease had shrunk to a fraction of its former flow. Before that, it had been a mighty torrent. That hidden fissure had indeed been full. And the cave itself had been full as well: a fact which probably explained why the weight of water had not broken through the seam ages ago. The cave had served to equalize the pressure. But now—

Ah, now the level behind the wall had dropped. The fissure had emptied itself until the water stood, waiting to drain, little more than the height of a Giant above the pond. If the rock broke, the issuing flood would be fierce. Still the Giants might be able to withstand it. Stave and Branl might. When the river found a new level, a new equilibrium, the company might be able to ascend against it.

Writ in water. God help me.

Linden was not ready. She would never be ready.

"Linden?" Covenant called in frustration. "Jeremiah? What is it? Damn it, I can't *see.*"

In a voice so small that she hardly heard it herself, Linden answered, "That wall is thin. There's a crevice behind it. I can't tell how high the crack is, or how far it goes. But if we break the wall—"

She did not have the courage to say more.

"That's it," Jeremiah confirmed more loudly. "That's the way. We can go there."

The Swordmainnir peered across the cave in wonder. At a nod from the Anchormaster, Hurl and Wiver Setrock began to work along the wall to the right. "We are wise in the lore of stone," Stoutgirth explained unnecessarily. "We will ascertain whether our strength may suffice to open the way."

While he waited for Hurl and Setrock, he sent four of his crew leftward to refill their waterskins from the clean stream.

"The stone," intoned the Feroce, "remembers endurance. It will not surrender to fists or blades."

"That's not the problem," Covenant muttered over the clamor of waters. With Coldspray's help, he crossed the slick outlet, then scrambled toward Linden and Jeremiah. "The problem is control. Too much is easy. Just enough is hard."

Linden turned to him as if she were falling. When he reached her, she put her arms around his neck, leaned against him.

"Oh, Thomas," she whispered to him alone. "I can't do this. I can feel She Who Must Not Be Named."

"What, *here*?" he breathed. Alarm tightened his grip. "Is She close?"

Linden shook her head. "I didn't mean that. I don't know where She is. But I can feel Her power. It's leaking into the water. Just smelling it is bad enough. If I touch it—"

Horror crouched in the pit of her stomach, in all of her nerves. The bane was death to her. It hungered for her soul.

Just for a moment, Covenant held her like a man who wanted to howl. Then he mastered himself. "I understand," he said stiffly. To retrieve her from carrion, he had been forced to hold her underwater; threaten her with drowning. "I'll spare you if I can. If the Giants aren't strong enough, I'll try—"

She felt him grimace as if he had bared his teeth. "Hellfire, Linden. I might bring down the roof."

She knew what he meant. He had too little health-sense—and he feared himself too much. His passions were too extreme for restraint.

Hurl and Setrock reached the seam. While Hurl pressed an ear to the stone, listening, Setrock thumped the flaw with the heel of one palm, gently at first, then harder. Harder. Then Hurl stepped back. To the Anchormaster, he called, "Water lies beyond this stone. Linden Giantfriend and the Chosen-son gauge acutely." His voice carried like streaks of argent across the surface of the pond. "Yet the Feroce do also. The stone has suffered much across the ages—aye, and absorbed much to harden it. It will not yield to blows or iron."

Branl raised Longwrath's sword as if it were a question.

Hurl shook his head. "The theurgies of that blade are obscure. I cannot conceive that they will suffice here."

"The *krill*?" asked Branl.

The idea wrung a flinch from Linden. "No," she told Covenant. "Not the *krill*. It might cut deep enough. But whoever holds it will be too close." Tons of water and rock would crash outward— She had no choice. "I have to do it."

He pulled back his head, peered into her eyes. "Are you sure?"

She could not hold his gaze. Leaning her forehead against his chest, she sighed, "I can try. I need to start using my ring. It might even help."

When he had invoked wild magic in the lower cavern, his wedding band had summoned a response from hers: a silver throb which had muted the sensations of pincers and scurrying. Perhaps her own power would shield her from the bane's tormented, tormenting seepage.

She felt Covenant gather his resolve. Briefly he tightened his hug again. Then he wheeled away.

Shouting so that everyone would hear him, he demanded, "Listen! Linden is going to break through that wall for us, and she's going to have to do it from here." Opposite the seam. "But when she does, she'll release a hell of a lot of water. I don't want it to touch her! I don't care how you do it. *Think* of something. Just keep her out of the water!"

Jeremiah gaped at him. In surprise, the boy lost his grasp on Earthpower. The air failed in Linden's lungs. She started to gag. But then Jeremiah recovered. Renewed flames spread outward.

"Mom?" he asked anxiously. "Mom?"

Panting, she urged him, "Don't worry about me. Your job is hard enough. If I can do this, there's going to be a flood—but we'll still need air. The Giants will take care of me. I'll be fine as long as we can breathe."

The Ironhand and the Anchormaster exchanged a few quick words. Then Rime Coldspray announced, "Timewarden, it will be done. The water here is vile. It will become more so. Yet we are hardy against such affronts. With your consent, I will entrust Linden Giantfriend to Bluff Stoutgirth and those in his command. They are not hampered by armor and swords. Frostheart Grueburn will stand ready to receive the Giantfriend when our passage inward has been opened."

Covenant did not object. Linden could not.

At once, Stoutgirth called a few orders of his own. Almost immediately, everyone except Linden was in motion.

The sailors refilling the waterskins helped each other past the fissure, moving directly toward the seam. Blustergale supported Baf Scatterwit in spite of her insistence that she did not need aid. Flashing a smile of encouragement at Linden, Grueburn strode away, followed by Cirrus Kindwind carrying Jeremiah. With a boost from Stave, Covenant climbed onto the Ironhand's back. A look of nausea filled his eyes as if he had been overtaken by vertigo.

For an instant as Branl passed her, Linden considered asking him to wait with her. She could use the *krill*'s gem to trigger wild magic: she had done so once before. But the outcome then had appalled her. She remembered too well the charred remains of Cavewights, scores or hundreds of them. Her spirit still wore the stains of slaughter. She nodded to the Humbled, but did not speak.

Stave came to her side. He gave her a grave bow, regarded her with his single eye. "In such straits, Chosen," he remarked, "it may be that Giants are better able to ward you than one *Haruchai*. Nonetheless I will not be parted from you. I have accepted once an absence from your side. I will not do so again."

Of the friends who had first joined Linden after her return to the Land, Stave was the last. The Ramen were gone. Liand and Anele were dead. And in some ways, Stave had endured more than any of them. She had no words for her gratitude.

Trailing behind Stonemage, Bluntfist, and the last of the sailors, Etch Furledsail stopped with Linden and Stave. Even among Giants, she was tall: a graceful and comely woman no longer young, with grey scattered through her hair, a gleam in her eyes, and a weathered face. "It may appear to you," she offered, "that our intent for your protection entails needless hazard. I assure you that it does not. I dare not attempt true haste over the hazards of these rocks. Therefore we will bear you across the water.

"Fear nothing," she added. With a wave, she indicated Setrock and Hurl beside the seam. "Where one Giant may fail, three will succeed. And we are adept in water. Here it is noxious in all sooth." She frowned at the pond. "Still it will not harm us.

"Giantfriend, I ask only that you do not resist when the wall has been opened. To evade such torrents, we must move swiftly."

Linden said nothing. She had stopped listening. Her gaze followed her companions as they gathered on both sides of the flaw where she meant to strike, but she was not watching. Her attention had turned inward. While Furledsail's voice passed over her, she searched for the door hidden within her, the specific intersection of intention and emotion and openness, of need and willed desperation, which gave her access to wild magic.

Furledsail raised an eyebrow at Linden's silence. Stave replied with a slight shrug.

At first, Linden could not find her way. Too many things could go wrong. If she ruptured the wall, a tremendous amount of water would crash straight toward her. It would hit hard enough to make pulp of the Feroce, who still stood on the other side of the cave's outlet. Or the Giants poised beside the seam might be struck by shards, caught in the cascade, torn away. Jeremiah's concentration might falter again. Then the bane's insidious fetors might overwhelm Linden. And she could not be sure that the company would be able to force a passage along the crevice behind the wall. If that crack held more water than the cave could release—

Furledsail intended to carry her into the pond; into memories of horror and anguish—

But then Covenant called her name. Jeremiah shouted, "Mom!"

Steady as gutrock, Stave said, "You are Linden Avery the Chosen, named in honor Ringthane, Giantfriend, and Wildwielder. Much is asked of you, but much has also been given. The time for doubt has passed. Only deeds or death remain. On other occasions, you have dared Desecration. You need not fear it now."

Anchored by the voices of people who were dear to her, Linden closed her mind to the clamor of too much trepidation, too many possible disasters. She was not alone. Her husband and her son loved her. Her friends had faith in her. She could trust them.

But they could not reach into her secret places for her. That she had to do for herself. And she knew how. She had done it before. She only had to retrace her mental steps.

Following her health-sense inward, she found the intimate chamber of her power. It was masked on all sides by fears and sins, unforgiven, but it was a part of her nonetheless. She had a right to it.

Now or never. How often had she said that to herself?

When argent stark as lightning began to blaze from her ring, she did not hesitate. And she did not hold back. She was not Covenant, fraught with ungovernable potential. Causing *caesures* had required precision, supreme delicacy: attacking granite and basalt demanded only *force*.

She delivered *force* as if she had suddenly become mighty.

As the stone cracked along the seam, the whole cave seemed to shriek. Rubble and water burst from the wall like screams.

Before Linden could snatch another breath, everything became chaos.

An avalanche of water slammed into the pond, but she hardly saw it; hardly saw the Giants gripping each other so that they would not be swept away; hardly saw Jeremiah flail black fire in all directions, wild and useless. She had already been lifted into Furledsail's arms. At once certain and cautious, Furledsail moved into the pond. But she did not confront its upheaval directly. Instead she angled away to the right, past the immediate thrash and spray.

At the same instant, Hurl and Setrock dove. Hurl stretched out, long and shallow, crossing as much distance as he could. Setrock went deeper, shorter. As Furledsail sank to her waist, Hurl broke the surface beyond her.

Above the water, the lash and rebound of waves, Furledsail tossed her burden upright to Hurl.

Linden caught a frantic glimpse of Stave swimming. Then Hurl's hands caught her.

He did not hold her. Treading water, he pitched her back over his head. A blind throw—

Blind and unerring. Deftly Wiver Setrock snagged her out of the air. In the same motion, he, too, flung her behind him.

A heartbeat later, Linden lay in Grueburn's clasp at the water's edge. With wary haste, Grueburn retreated up the rocks to press her back against the wall among the other Giants. Her grin as she regarded Linden was feral with glee.

Linden's mind had gone blank. She stared up at Grueburn as if she did not recognize the Swordmain.

But somewhere deep inside her, a voice was crowing.

You did it. You *did* it.

Did you call me your *daughter*? she shouted at Lord Foul. Watch and learn, you smug bastard!

She could cheer and threaten because the Despiser was not her greatest fear. He was Covenant's problem. She had chosen a different path to the World's End.

Wild magic was a necessary step.

7.

At Last

Tumults crashed inward. They threatened to fill the cave, drown the entire company. The Feroce vanished in roaring waves. The air that came with the flood stank of minerals and trapped hate. It surpassed Jeremiah; surpassed the Staff of Law.

But the constrained volume of the river was less than it had been scant days ago, much less; and the cave's outlet swallowed the immediate brunt of the inrush. On either side, waves slammed like heavy seas against the walls, fell back onto each other. The pond became a boiling cauldron, a contained squall. Surges tore at the Giants' ankles, knees, thighs. Fluid blows hammered Stave and Branl. Yet moment by moment the flail and rebound of the waters ran down the mountain's throat.

Gradually the flood seemed to find its balance. Its force receded as the cleft drained. Turmoil slapped at the walls and the company, but did not claim them. Smaller waves sank to the level of knees and then ankles. Soon the water only splashed the feet of the Giants. Its thunderous howl faded.

At the same time, the air tumbling from the opened crevice lost some of its virulence. It had been blocked for ages or eons, and its contagions had congealed until they were thick as mire. But now it ran out like the river; and as it emptied the cleft, it drew air from some cleaner source. Gasping, Linden tasted hints of something that resembled life. When Jeremiah regained his grip on Earthpower, the whole company began to breathe more easily.

His efforts confirmed that he was unharmed.

But the Feroce were indeed gone. If they had survived the torrents, they had allowed themselves to be swept away: back to the cavern and the black lake, to the Defiles Course and the Sarangrave. Linden wanted to think that they were still alive. They had done what they could. Perhaps their High God would forgive their doubts.

A shout from the Ironhand announced that the gap into the crevice had become passable. Branl carried the *krill* closer to light the way as the Anchormaster and half a dozen of his crew dropped down into the water's former channel, then began scrambling upward. The river frothed against their legs, but they labored higher until they were out of sight.

Through the raw clamor of the current, Covenant told Branl to go ahead. With Coldspray's assent, the Humbled took Loric's dagger into the crevice. For a moment, the gem left slashes of argent on the pond's turmoil. Then the Ironhand followed, bearing Covenant with her, and her size blocked most of the light. The remaining streaks and gleams made the cave and its water look ghostly, transient, as if the whole place were dissolving; losing its place in the reality of time.

Halewhole Bluntfist went next with Setrock and Furledsail. Cirrus Kindwind carried Jeremiah after them. Then it was Frostheart Grueburn's turn. As Linden scrambled onto Grueburn's back, she saw a rope trailing from the crevice: a lifeline. Onyx Stonemage gripped the end while someone—Bluff Stoutgirth or one of his sailors—pulled it taut. Muttering her approval, Grueburn held the line to steady her as she bore Linden into the crevice with Stave behind her. Squallish Blustergale supported Scatterwit. Stonemage brought up the rear.

The lifeline was necessary. Somewhere beneath Grueburn's feet, there was stone: there had to be. But long turbulent millennia had deposited thick layers of silt as cloying as quicksand. The water pounding against Grueburn's thighs was not the greatest obstacle to her ascent. The silt was worse. She sank to her calves and higher in muck that dragged at every step. While she hauled one foot out of the mire, her weight drove the other deeper. She needed the rope.

For that reason, any Giant above her who happened to find secure footing paused to anchor the line. The result was progress in arduous surges as sailors and Swordmainnir pulled themselves or each other from one patch of solid ground to another.

How the *Haruchai* managed to ascend, Linden could not imagine. Glancing behind her, she sensed an uncharacteristic frown of vexation on Stave's visage. The strain in his muscles was as palpable as Grueburn's. At intervals, he clutched at the lifeline, obviously reluctant to require its aid.

How long could he continue? How long could the Giants? Linden had often been amazed by their endurance, but still— The crevice was too narrow for the companions to assist each other side by side, and the silt was *deep*. Each new step seemed to demand more effort than the one before.

A call from above warned the company that Stoutgirth had floundered into a pit where the mire seemed bottomless. His sailors dragged him back; but then everyone else was forced to wait while the Giants in the lead probed for a way past the pit.

Linden felt a flutter of panic. The walls seemed to be leaning in. Surely the crevice was becoming narrower? The current boiling past Grueburn's legs carried glints of She Who Must Not Be Named like flakes of shed malice: lightless, invisible, yet distinct to Linden's nerves.

If Frostheart Grueburn lost her balance— If Linden plunged into the water—

Apparently Stoutgirth's fall and rescue had released gases trapped in the pit. Heavy as fog, sulfur and putrefaction rode the stream. They burned Linden's eyes, stung her nose, bit into her chest, until the tug of running water took them away.

She could hear Covenant swearing at his helplessness. Jeremiah jerked his head from side to side, flung black fire along the river. Spray stood like sweat on his skin.

Then the Anchormaster reported success. The line began to lurch forward again.

In their turn, Kindwind and Grueburn reached the pit. Now Linden understood Stoutgirth's mistake. Her health-sense could not measure the varying depths of the silt. It was all so old, so laden with refuse and minerals, so full of the aftereffects of dire theurgies, that it refused percipience.

Helped by Bluntfist and Furledsail, Cirrus Kindwind bore Jeremiah around the rim of the pit: a narrow path. Linden shifted until she hung from Grueburn's shoulder; dangled over the pit as Grueburn forced her way around it. Stave crossed by floating on his back and pulling himself along the rope. Grueburn and Kindwind waited while Blustergale ensured Scatterwit's safety. Then Blustergale sent Scatterwit ahead. He stayed behind to assist Onyx Stonemage.

In heaves and sags, the company struggled upward. Aching for Grueburn, and for Jeremiah, Linden concentrated on clinging to Grueburn's armor—and on holding still so that she would not disturb Grueburn's balance.

Here the air was definitely better. It became cleaner, demanded less from Jeremiah, as the river dragged its atmosphere with it. Hints of the bane persisted, but they were diminished.

On into darkness, interminably. The fissure became wider. It narrowed again. At intervals, indurated juts of stone interrupted the silt. For long stretches, the muck seemed deeper. The Giants fought for breath to feed their straining muscles, their accumulating exhaustion. Their gasps filled the crevice above the rush of water. Linden could not remember when they had last rested.

Then the rope was drawn tighter. Grueburn gripped it with both hands. She began to move a bit more easily. Behind her, Scatterwit chortled, a sound as forlorn as a groan. The light of the *krill* reached farther down the cleft. It touched Kindwind's head, flared like fire in Jeremiah's hair. The wall on the left had begun to lean away from the river. The darkness overhead felt more open.

The leading Giants must have found a place where they could stand; where they could gather on firm rock and brace their feet.

"Soon, Giantfriend," Grueburn panted. "Soon."

"It better be." Jeremiah coughed the words. "I can't hold on much longer."

Linden watched the silver on the walls grow brighter as more and more of the company moved past the *krill*. In moments, she caught sight of Branl. Where he stood, the left wall appeared to fall away. But then she saw that the fissure simply became wider. Beyond a rough edge like a doorpost, that wall curved back, continuing the crevice. The river ran there, tumbling more slowly between sheer sides now farther apart. Past the turning, rough stone formed a floor like a platform above the water, vaguely level, and perhaps ten or fifteen paces across.

Bluff Stoutgirth and his immediate companions waited there, chests heaving. Coldspray had put Covenant on his feet. He stood squinting past the glare of Loric's gem, impatient for Jeremiah and Linden. With Setrock and Furledsail, Bluntfist had taken the rope. Together they hauled as if they hoped to raise their comrades from a crypt. Silt caked their legs, but they ignored that discomfort.

On the platform, some of the sailors began unpacking waterskins and bundles of food.

Eager to slip down from Grueburn's back—eager to put her arms around Covenant—Linden did not look around. Her legs stung as she dropped to the stone. Moving toward Covenant, she stumbled, had to catch herself. Then he was holding her tight. The urgency of his hug matched hers.

"Hellfire, Linden," he murmured near her ear. "I thought that was never going to end."

It was not ended now. The companions had merely found a respite.

From the downward fissure, Stonemage herded Blustergale and Scatterwit out of the river: the last of the Giants. As similar as brothers, Stave and Branl came toward Linden and Covenant.

Linden felt Jeremiah quench the power of the Staff. Instinctively she flinched. But the atmosphere here was kinder to her lungs. Although it was thick with dust and disuse, stale, acrid, the river carried most of its wastes and poisons with it. She could breathe without choking.

When she had held Covenant long enough to ease her heart, she turned to her son.

Jeremiah was sitting on the stone, hugging his knees against his chest in an effort to control the tremors in his limbs. He had dropped the Staff beside him. Dully he stared across the water, a gaze as expressionless as the far wall. Saliva collected on his drooping lower lip: a sight which Linden had not seen since he had emerged from his dissociation.

She knelt at his side, put her arm over his shoulders. "Jeremiah, honey? Are you all right? It's no wonder you're tired. You've been keeping us all alive."

His eyes did not shift. He hardly seemed to blink or swallow. His voice was a low rasp, a scraping like the sound of a creature crawling on its belly.

"It isn't fair, Mom. It's not. I'm so tired. I can't go on. I can't. But I have to have Earthpower. Without it—" Abruptly he released his legs, slapped at his face as if his weariness revolted him. "It protects me.

"You don't know what it's like. That mountain is *huge*. And the Worm is in the river. It's drinking every bit of Earthpower it can find, but it wants more. It wants it *all*."

Oh, Jeremiah—

Uselessly Linden told her son, "You'll get stronger. You're already stronger. We'll eat something, rest for a while. You'll feel better. Then we'll need you again. We'll have to go back into the river. You'll be able to protect yourself."

Leaden with depletion or despair, his head turned toward her. "What are you talking about?" He peered at her as if he were going blind. "The river? Why?" With one hand, he pointed up the wall. "That's the way. It has to be. The air's better there. You won't need me anymore."

She frowned, momentarily confused. Then she stood to look around.

Giants cast grotesque shadows, shapes that appeared to caper across the walls. Between them, however, the *krill* lit this section of the crevice clearly.

Under tremendous pressure long ago, layers of stone on this side had shifted. Diagonally beginning half a dozen paces beyond the Giants and angling erratically into the darkness overhead, ancient forces had pulled the higher reaches of the wall back from the lower. The result was a crude ledge or shelf: a natural formation that lurched upward, lying level in some places, jutting like a titan's stairs in others; obstructed here and there by piles of rubble. For short distances, it looked wide enough to accommodate horses. Other stretches were too narrow to let more than one Giant pass at a time.

It ascended beyond the *krill*'s illumination, beyond the range of Linden's senses, climbing into the secrets of the crevice. She had no way of knowing where it led. But the air drifting down was unmistakably cleaner.

Surely even stone-dwelling Cavewights required unfouled air?

In any case, the ledge went higher. It might go far enough to reach the catacombs.

"You're right," she murmured to Jeremiah. "We have to go up." Then she added quickly, "But that doesn't mean we don't need you. It just means that you can stop wearing yourself out for a while. Maybe you can learn other ways to use the Staff."

"Like what?" he asked as if she had suggested something unimaginable. He had already failed to affect the hue of the wood. He could not undo its effect on him.

Instead of giving him a direct answer, Linden said, "You're here for a reason, honey. It's no accident." For his sake, she spun a web of inferences that made her tremble. "Of course, you're here because Roger took you. He wanted a way to make me give him Thomas' ring. And Lord Foul wants revenge. He thinks that you can help him trap the Creator. He's trying to fill your head with despair so that you won't fight him.

"But it isn't that simple. Lord Foul isn't the only one who chooses who comes to the Land. He picks us because he thinks that he can manipulate us, or because he thinks that we're already his. But the Creator chooses us, too. They both picked us." Covenant had taught her this. Now she pushed it further. "The only difference is, the Creator doesn't manipulate us. He lets us make our own decisions."

Ignoring the rest of the company, Linden hurried to make her point before her courage failed.

"The Creator sees hope in you, honey. He sees things that you might choose for yourself, things that might make a difference. That's why—" Oh, God. Did she have to say this? Did she have to face it? "That's why he didn't warn me before Roger got to you. If he had given me any hint that you might be in danger, I would have stopped Roger somehow. I would have taken you away so that he couldn't find you."

She had almost done so when she had seen images of Revelstone and Mount Thunder in her living room.

"The Creator didn't warn me because he needs you."

Her claim seemed to strike a spark into the tinder of Jeremiah's aggrieved spirit. Unsteadily he stood to face her. The murk of his gaze clung to her.

"Needs me *how*? What am I supposed to do?"

For that, Linden had no answer.

"What you've always done," Covenant put in roughly. He had come to stand behind Linden. She felt the tension in his muscles, heard the clench in his voice. "Something damn Foul doesn't expect."

Jeremiah's head snapped toward Covenant. His mouth hung open.

"Maybe," Covenant went on, "you think he marked you. Maybe you think being a halfhand means he has some kind of claim on you, some kind of special power over you. But that's backward. *He* didn't cut off those two fingers. Your *mother* did. And she did it so she could save the rest of your hand. Being a halfhand doesn't make you a victim. It makes you free.

"The Despiser doesn't know you as well as he thinks he does. He can't. Filling your head with visions is just a trick to keep you off-balance. He doesn't want you to see the truth. You're only his if you choose him."

Jeremiah gaped at Covenant. Linden watched turmoil seethe like Lifeswallower's mire in her son's eyes. The whole company seemed to pause while he struggled to understand: even the river seemed to hold its breath. The *krill* cast light and shadows in all directions.

As if he were choking, Jeremiah protested, "But what I see is *real*. The Worm is *real*."

He may have meant, We're all going to die.

"Well, sure." Covenant's tone conveyed a shrug. The Despiser did not lie. "But that's not the point. The Worm isn't more real than *you* are. It's just more dramatic."

"I don't get it," Jeremiah groaned. "I can't— Lord Foul is too strong."

His confusion and need twisted Linden's heart; but Covenant did not relent. "Then let him be too strong. You don't need to beat him. Just do *something* he doesn't expect. Be yourself."

A young man with the Staff of Law and his own Earthpower: a young man with a talent for *making*. Even the Despiser in his fury and frustration could not satisfy all of his desires without the ability to create. Linden understood what Covenant was saying. She knew why Lord Foul needed her son.

But she could see as clearly as if she had entered him with her health-sense that Jeremiah did not understand. He was too young to know how much he did not know about himself. When he ducked his head to mutter as if he were ashamed, "Maybe Roger had the right idea. Maybe we should all try to become gods," she seemed to hear the *croyel* in him: the legacy of being possessed.

Yet she did not hear scorn. Bitterness, yes. Fear. Self-pity. But not contempt. He had other birthrights as well.

Surely she could try to believe that they would come to his aid when he needed them? Surely she should trust him, no matter how much his distress hurt her, or how much she feared for him? She would not be there for him when his plight came to its crisis. Trusting him now might be the last gift that she would ever be able to give him.

∞

When the companions had eaten another meal, shared their waterskins, and refreshed themselves as much as they could on the better air drifting into the crevice, they started upward. Once again, the Ironhand and the Anchormaster took the lead; but this time Covenant walked behind them with Branl and Halewhole Bluntfist. After Hurl, Keenreef, and several other sailors, Linden and Jeremiah essayed the terraced ledge accompanied by Stave, Frostheart Grueburn, and Cirrus Kindwind. Onyx Stonemage and more of Stoutgirth's crew came next. As before, Blustergale and Baf Scatterwit brought up the rear.

In places, the surface they trod resembled sheets of slate, and there the going was easy. Some of the stairs where the rock had crumbled were minor obstacles. But occasionally the sheared steps reached to Linden's waist. A few were taller than she was: they cast shadows as threatening as chasms. Like Covenant and Jeremiah, she had to be lifted to the next level.

The walls leaned toward and away from each other, tracing the variations of Mount Thunder's flaws and stubbornness. By increments, the river fell below the reach of the company's illumination. The rush of water became distant, as if it were fading out of the world; and with it the spilth or detritus of She Who Must Not Be Named also receded. In gusts and eddies, the air improved.

Like the crevice, the width of the ledge undulated. At intervals, Linden was able to walk at Jeremiah's shoulder as if she could still shield him. More often, the company was forced to go in single file. When the ledge became dangerously narrow, Cirrus Kindwind kept her hand on Jeremiah's shoulder, and Frostheart Grueburn did the same for Linden.

After some distance, Rime Coldspray and Bluff Stoutgirth came to a break in the ledge. Linden could not see how they crossed it. Giants blocked her view. Her every step was obscured by shadows. But when she and Jeremiah reached the gap, she found that the sailors had stretched a rope over it, held taut by Hurl on one end and Wiver Setrock on the other. Using the line for support, Kindwind and Grueburn helped Jeremiah and Linden to the far side.

When the last of the Giants were safe, the company continued to climb.

Linden lost her sense of duration. Nothing in the mountain's perpetual midnight marked the passage of time. Gradually the river passed out of hearing. After that, there were no sounds apart from the efforts and breathing of the companions. The *krill*'s light shifted as Branl moved, but it revealed only rock and more rock, enduring and unrelieved. Beyond it, darkness crowded thick as obsidian or basalt.

Still the river pulled air downward with it: a guttering breeze on Linden's face. For a while, she derived a sense of progress from the declining pressure of taints in her lungs. Soon, however, the changes became too subtle to be distinguished. Then weariness and strain became her only measure for the meaning of her steps.

At intervals, Jeremiah extended tentative flicks of theurgy from the Staff, but their purpose eluded Linden.

In the distance ahead, the crevice bent sharply to the left. Beyond a blind corner, another high step or shelf interrupted the ledge. This one reached the chests of the

Giants. Some of the sailors were able to gain the next level unassisted; but the Sword-mainnir were more heavily burdened, and their weariness was more profound: like their smaller companions, they needed help.

When Grueburn had lifted her past the shelf, Linden paused to scan her surroundings.

Within the ambit of the *krill*'s illumination, the ledge looked wide as a road, comparatively level. But the crevice was narrowing. After its sweep to the left, it curved gradually back to the right; and as it did so, the opposite side restricted her view ahead. Overhead the walls leaned together: she supposed that they met somewhere in the darkness, closing the fissure. Above her at the farthest extent of the light, a line across the near wall suggested the possibility of another ledge.

The far wall was pocked with holes like the mouths of tunnels, open maws where the gem's radiance did not penetrate. They looked big enough for Giants. A few were level with the company's path, but most were scattered higher around the curve.

Linden peered at those holes, frowning, until she felt Covenant's tension. It poured from him like the heat of a fever. He was glaring along the ledge ahead with his fists clenched and his shoulders tight, as if he were expecting a blow.

When she followed his gaze, she saw bones.

They littered the ledge as far as she could see: thighs and ribs, arms, hands and feet, skulls. Small heaps like crushed children. Whole skeletons piled atop each other. Femurs and ulnas randomly discarded. Smashed skulls grinning at their own ruin. Hundreds, no, thousands of them. Most of them suggested Cavewights, but some made Linden think of ur-viles—or stranger monsters.

"I don't like this," Covenant muttered. "It's probably good news. Somebody tossed them here. We must be getting close to the Wightwarrens. But hellfire! I think we're in trouble."

In the *krill*'s silver, the bones looked desiccated, bleached: they seemed to ache with age. But when Linden studied them more closely, she saw that only some of them were old. Others still wore gobbets of flesh, shrouds of blood. The breeze drifting past her held a tang of new rot—

—and another odor, one which she did not want to recognize. She remembered it too well.

The fresher piles seethed with rats. They cleaned the bones fearlessly, creatures that had never been threatened. Occasionally a dark eye glittered at Linden. Whiskers twitched. Plump bodies fought for every shred of meat.

Long ago aboard Starfare's Gem, she had seen them swarm at Covenant, possessed by a Raver and eager for his blood.

"Thomas," she whispered: a dry croak.

He reached out to her. "What is it?" When she took his hand, he gripped her hard. "Do you sense something?"

"I can—" Linden tried to say; but her throat closed. She had to force out words. "Oh, Thomas. I can smell *moksha*."

The precise evil of Ravers was imprinted on her nerves. Her memories of *turiya* were bad enough. What *moksha* had done to her was worse.

Covenant stared at her. "Damnation." Darkness and light warred in the background of his gaze. Then he wheeled away.

"Branl!" he barked. "Coldspray! We're going to be attacked!"

The Ironhand called a question; but her comrades reacted before he could answer. Bluntfist, Kindwind, and Grueburn urged Covenant, Jeremiah, and Linden farther along the ledge, closer to the wall. Between them and the plunge of the crevice, Stonemage drew her sword. Branl thrust the *krill* into Hurl's hands, flourished Longwrath's flamberge. He and Stave flanked Stonemage.

Baffled, the sailors heaved Baf Scatterwit above the edge. As she scrambled away, they stretched their arms for Squallish Blustergale.

"Are you sure?" Covenant panted to Linden.

"Of course she's sure." Jeremiah made a palpable effort to sound fierce, but his voice came out in a yelp. "We always get attacked."

"I can't see!" He shoved at Kindwind's back. "I can't do anything if I can't see."

Gripping her longsword, Cirrus Kindwind shifted to cover him more completely. Bluntfist and Grueburn readied their blades.

Herding Scatterwit and Blustergale ahead of them, Coldspray and Stoutgirth strode closer. "Setrock!" the Anchormaster commanded. "Keenreef. Furledsail. Lead us! Clear bones from our path. If we are assailed, we must have sure footing."

The three sailors surged forward. Scatterwit started after them, hopping. Two of her comrades caught her arms, dragged her aside. Blustergale and another Giant followed Setrock, Keenreef, and Furledsail to help sweep debris from the ledge.

Many of the bones crumbled when they were kicked aside. They released a fume of age.

Instinctively Linden siphoned Earthpower from the Staff, sent her health-sense farther. The holes in the far wall looked deep. They felt empty: tunnels leading nowhere. The rats had a musty fetor, the smell of carrion and ancient dust. And the Raver—

Implications of *moksha* Jehannum burned her nerves, but she could not locate their source, any source.

Hurl held the *krill* above his head to extend its light. Wiver Setrock and his companions brushed through the bones. The sailors behind them pushed more into the crevice. Rats scurried away, chittering angrily. *Moksha* remained hidden.

Abruptly Coldspray announced, "There is no gain in waiting."

"Aye," assented the Anchormaster. "If we are to be assailed, our foes must approach along our path. They cannot surprise us."

At a word from the Ironhand, Stonemage and Bluntfist started after Blustergale. With Bluff Stoutgirth, Hurl, and the rest of the sailors, Coldspray followed. Kindwind and Grueburn drew Covenant, Linden, and Jeremiah away from the wall. With Branl and Stave, they trailed behind the rest of the company.

Without a cordon of defenders around her, Linden felt exposed. The holes in the stone across from her seemed to watch like eyes, black and malicious. But Jeremiah was visibly relieved: now he could see. He loosened his arms, swung the Staff from side to side as if he were testing its reach. Determination clenched his features. And Covenant strode after Setrock, Keenreef, and Furledsail as if he feared for them more than for himself.

Branl kept pace with Covenant. Stave stayed with Linden.

Frostheart Grueburn rested a hand on Linden's shoulder, kept Linden between her and the wall. Calmly she assured Linden, "Stoutgirth Anchormaster speaks sooth. Our foes cannot surprise us here. They will seek some advantage of position or concealment."

Linden was not comforted. She could feel *moksha* Raver crouching somewhere near. Hurl's grasp on the *krill* was not as steady as Branl's. As he moved, shadows reeled across the walls, along the ledge. Threats seemed to lurk in all directions.

Urged by Coldspray, the company advanced more quickly. At the same time, Stoutgirth called to his sailors in the lead, ordered them to wait for Bluntfist and Onyx Stonemage.

Spread out along the ledge, the companions rounded the curve. Linden searched past the Giants for a glimpse ahead. Mutely she prayed for haste. The holes scattered across the far wall disturbed her. For no reason that she could name, she wanted to get out from under their black glower.

A moment later, Setrock shouted in frustration. When a gap opened between the Giants, Linden saw that the ledge ran straight for a short distance beyond the curve. Then it was blocked by a pile of large boulders. The last of the rats vanished among them.

Blustergale and his companions were still kicking away bones. Other Giants studied the boulders, testing their bulk, looking for a way past them.

As the Ironhand and the Anchormaster strode closer, Furledsail turned toward them. "The balance of this obstruction appears precarious," she reported. "We may be able to shift the stones." She hesitated, glanced at her comrades, then added, "Yet the formation is not natural. Moreover, it is recent. I deem that it was placed to thwart us."

"Oh, hell," Covenant muttered. "Hell and blood."

He sounded tense enough, anxious enough, to tear the barricade aside with wild magic. He knew what *moksha* had done to Linden.

His power might shatter the ledge.

Biting her lip, Linden pushed her senses among the boulders. She wanted to discern what lay beyond them. But before she could extend her percipience far enough, a sharp cracking sound distracted her. From high above her came a granite impact, one rock massive as a menhir colliding with another—or bouncing off the wall.

She jerked up her head. Saw nothing.

An instant later, a boulder the size of a Giant struck somewhere far overhead. It rebounded in a spray of shards. Splinters as keen as knives hissed past the ledge. The remaining mass arced away, hammered the far wall below the holes, burst into rubble. She did not hear the fragments hit water. The fissure was too deep.

Giants yelled. Linden, Jeremiah, and Covenant were shoved against the wall again. Kindwind and Grueburn crouched over them, shielded them with lore-hardened armor.

Apparently unconcerned at the edge of the drop, Stave pointed at the line or ledge a long way up the fissure. "There," he announced. "The stone fell from that height."

"Don't *stand* there!" snapped Covenant. "If it was supposed to hit us, there's going to be more!"

Stave glanced at Covenant. "Indeed, Timewarden. From this vantage, I will have forewarning. The wall provides a measure of shelter, yet it also obscures sight."

Peering upward, he said, "I discern no—" Then he spun toward the Giants near the blockade. "Beware!"

Too late, Linden felt the swift hurtle of another boulder.

This one did not strike the walls. It came straight down, hard as a meteor.

Sailors thrust Scatterwit aside as the second rock struck within a stride of where she had been. It tore off a chunk half the width of the ledge as it bounced away, squalling with debris.

More than half the width. Only an arm span remained.

Linden, Covenant, Jeremiah, and their immediate defenders would have to pass that break in order to follow their companions.

Covenant's vertigo—

"Giants!" roared the Anchormaster. "Shift the barricade! We must pass onward!"

With Keenreef and Furledsail, Setrock began straining at the pile. Others of Dire's Vessel rushed to add their strength. Hurl moved to give them more light. Scatterwit lurched after him.

One long stride took Stoutgirth past the break. Coldspray crossed behind him, then looked back to verify that the rear of the company was safe. Linden, Covenant, and Jeremiah. Branl and Stave. Kindwind and Grueburn.

A third boulder seemed to detonate against the far wall. A granite fusillade ripped across the ledge.

Blustergale went down with blood spurting from his shoulder. A shard had pierced an artery. Fragments whined off Bluntfist's armor, staggered Stonemage. A sailor whose name Linden did not recall was torn apart. For an instant, his whole body spasmed. Blood and fluids sprayed from half a dozen wounds. Trying to regain his balance, he pitched off the ledge.

A scream that she could not utter choked Linden. Heedless of the danger, Covenant ran toward the break. Jeremiah looked around wildly.

As if from nowhere, a stone spear appeared in the center of Hurl's chest. He sprawled backward, crashed against the wall. The impact knocked the *krill* from his hand. It hit the ledge, skittered away—

Shadows pounced from all directions.

Faster than Linden's fear, Branl leaped the break, dove headlong. Sliding in Blustergale's blood, he snagged the dagger at the lip of the drop.

Somehow he kept his longsword.

More spears crossed the crevice, a volley of stone shafts. Setrock and his comrades were driven back from the blockade. Now Linden saw a Cavewight standing in each of the tunnels in the opposite wall. The holes spat spears. Then those Cavewights moved aside. More creatures with spears strode into view, stepped into the force of their throws.

Rime Coldspray shouted orders louder than Bluff Stoutgirth's. At the same time, she returned over the breach to intercept Covenant. Ignoring his curses, she hauled him off his feet, swung him onto her back so that she could shield him.

Grueburn and Kindwind guarded Linden and Jeremiah with their armor. Grueburn's blade batted a spear aside. Stave knocked another out of the air.

Bluntfist sprang close to the edge, protected as many sailors as she could. Limping, Stonemage joined her. Bluntfist let one spear splinter against her cataphract while she chopped at another. Stonemage deflected two shafts. The Giants behind her dodged.

Surging upright half cloaked in blood, Branl raised the *krill*. One-handed, he swung his flamberge. A spear shattered. Pieces fell into the crevice. Bright silver spread over the ledge, along the fissure. Shadows capered, jeering.

More spears came in continuing waves.

Years among shrouds and ratlines had made the sailors agile. They twisted and ducked; shoved each other out of the way; blocked spears with belaying-pins and fists. When they could, they armed themselves with the Cavewights' weapons.

Sobbing, Scatterwit clamped her hands to Blustergale's shoulder. "Ward yourself!" he gasped. "The wound is mine. I will stanch it." But she ignored his protest.

Near Linden, Earthpower burgeoned. Abruptly Jeremiah pushed past Kindwind's protection. Yelling words which he had heard Linden use, he found an open space, aimed the Staff of Law like a lance. "*Melenkurion abatha!*" From the wood's iron-shod end, black flame blared. "*Duroc minas mill!*" Magic lashed like lightning across the fissure, scoured its way into one of the tunnels. "*Harad khabaal!*" The Cavewights there caught fire, blazed in agony.

"Take *that*, you bastards!" Like Scatterwit, he was sobbing. "I'm learning! I'll kill you all!"

To Linden, Cavewights implied Roger Covenant. She shouted Jeremiah's name, fearing an eruption of Roger's laval fury. But she hardly heard herself over the roars and efforts of the Giants, the sharp strike of spears.

As the boy readied another blast, Stave reached him. Turning his back on the Cavewights, on the spears, Stave stepped in front of Jeremiah, forced Jeremiah to look at him. Calm as a breeze amid the turmoil, the former Master said, "Wield such strength with care, Chosen-son. It is new to you. Therefore it is uncertain."

"Rockbrother!" called Frostheart Grueburn.

Stave did not glance at the Swordmain. "Also," he told Jeremiah, "the ur-Lord's maimed son may join the assault at any moment. You must prepare to oppose him."

Cursing, Grueburn left Linden, leaped to stop a spear aimed at Stave. The frantic sweep of her sword missed: she took the shaft's point on her breastplate. It glanced away, clattered on the ledge.

"Roger?" cried Jeremiah. "You want me to fight *Roger*? How am I supposed to do that?"

"With care," Stave replied evenly. "With passion, certainly, but also with care." Step by step, he urged Jeremiah back into the shelter of Cirrus Kindwind's bulk and armor.

Frantic and afraid, Linden searched the confusion with her senses; but she found no sign of Roger.

Abruptly the barrage of spears stopped. Responding to a signal that Linden did not hear or feel, all of the Cavewights withdrew from the gaping tunnels.

A moment later, the barricade beyond the company collapsed as if a keystone had been removed. Huge rocks rolled over the edge, dropped soundless into the dark. In an instant, most of the barrier was gone as though a door had been kicked open.

Along the ledge charged a throng of Cavewights, howling.

They were armed with spears and falchions, cudgels and axes. Plates of stone hanging from their shoulders served as armor. The hot red of their eyes scorned the *krill*'s wavering radiance.

Their suddenness caught the Giants off balance. A cudgel like a battering-ram struck the side of a sailor's head, knocked him into the fissure. Cries followed him down. Furledsail fell back with gore spilling from a slash below her ribs. She, too, might have gone over the edge; but Setrock sprang after her, snatched her into his arms. Her attacker Keenreef stopped with one hard punch to the center of the forehead. Then he had to wheel away from the vicious stroke of an axe.

"Withdraw!" The Anchormaster's command echoed up the wall. He sounded preternaturally unperturbed; accustomed to gales. Perhaps he was also accustomed to loss. "Withdraw, Dire's Vessel! This is work for Swordmainnir!"

But he did not retreat himself. Jerking the spear out of Hurl's chest, he advanced to meet the Cavewights. He seemed to be laughing.

Onyx Stonemage and Halewhole Bluntfist were already running to counter the charge. Rime Coldspray shouted for Branl; consigned Covenant to the Humbled. With her glaive in her fist, she raced after Stonemage and Bluntfist.

The ledge was too narrow for a massed assault. No more than four Cavewights led the attack; and even then, they hampered each other. Stonemage and Bluntfist let the remaining sailors scramble between them. Then the two Swordmainnir faced the creatures.

Coldspray stopped Stoutgirth three paces behind her comrades. She and the Anchormaster braced themselves for flung spears; prepared to cut down any Cavewight that fought past Stonemage and Bluntfist.

"*Damn* it, Branl!" Covenant demanded. "*Do* something! I can take care of myself!"

Branl studied Covenant for a moment; shrugged delicately. Then he handed Loric's dagger to the Unbeliever. Springing away over the break in the ledge, he went to join the Ironhand.

Covenant, Linden, and Jeremiah were left behind. Stave, Grueburn, and Kindwind. But soon sailors came to them dragging Blustergale, carrying Furledsail. Harried along by Setrock, Scatterwit retreated from the fray.

Linden watched Giants and Cavewights fight in darkness relieved only by the *krill* in Covenant's grasp, and by the crimson glow of eyes. At first, Bluntfist and Stonemage seemed implausibly effective. They were skilled and mighty. They had room enough between them to swing their blades. And they could afford to let creatures lunge past them: Coldspray and Stoutgirth protected their backs. Rabid thrusts and slashes were beaten aside. Bodies toppled from the ledge in welters of blood.

But the Cavewights were mighty as well, born with the strength to delve in gutrock by hand. They were nearly as tall as Giants. Their arms were longer. And they were many, more than Linden could count. Eventually their sheer numbers would over-whelm the Giants. Already Bluntfist and Stonemage were driven backward. The Ironhand and the Anchormaster were forced to retreat as well.

Branl strode between the commanders. He passed Bluntfist and Stonemage, drifted like a shadow among the Cavewights. With the rippled edges of his long-sword, he seemed to reap creatures all around him. Howls became shrieks. Bodies fell. In the press of Cavewights, his shorter stature was an advantage. Creatures fight-ing at the height of Giants could not block his flurry of cuts, his swift dance. For a moment, he stopped the advance. Linden almost believed that he would be able to turn the battle.

Still the Cavewights were too many. And they were not mindless. Quickly they adjusted their tactics. Those in the lead sprang aside, cleared a space which allowed other creatures to level their weapons and their strength at the Humbled.

Branl dodged a spear, cut off the arms of its wielder. As if in a single motion, he blocked a cudgel on one side, countered a sword on the other. He slashed at thighs, knees, ankles.

But more Cavewights came. In spite of his prowess, he was beaten backward.

Soon Covenant would have no choice. Jeremiah would have none.

At the edge of her vision, Linden thought that she saw another boulder plum-met into the depths. She saw or imagined a Cavewight sprawling through the air after it.

She shook her head to dispel the image. She could not help Branl and the strug-gling Swordmainnir. She had promised herself—

But she could meet other needs. Snatching Earthpower from the Staff, from Jere-miah, she aimed fire at Blustergale's shoulder and Furledsail's side.

She worked fiercely. She had no time for kindness. The battle was coming closer. Like an act of violence, she stopped Blustergale's bleeding, mended the bones, closed the wound; poured energy into his veins: healing as brutal as abuse. When she was sure that he would live, she treated Furledsail in the same fashion.

All of the Giants had cared for her. Some had given their lives. This was how she rewarded the living.

Then Stave called her name. She jerked up her head, flung her gaze at the fighting.

He still stood near her. Nevertheless another *Haruchai* had joined Branl. The newcomer had acquired a falchion from a fallen creature. Together he and Branl struggled to slow the Cavewights so that the Swordmainnir would not be overrun.

Another—?

Linden did not recognize him.

A heartbeat later, a second unfamiliar *Haruchai* landed lightly on the ledge. He must have been working his way down the wall. Even one of his people could not plummet onto stone with such ease from any great height.

He had the grizzled hair of a veteran: his face was a lattice of old scars. He paused to glance around at Stave and the sailors. Grueburn and Kindwind. Linden and Jeremiah. Then he stared at Covenant.

For the first time, Linden saw open astonishment on the impassive face of a *Haruchai*.

8.

Shamed Choices

Wild magic swelled in Covenant. It yearned for release. His wedding band ached on his ring finger. The ambush had already killed three of the Giants. Hurl's body lay against the wall, transformed by a stone spear into fresh feasting for rats. Two of the men from Dire's Vessel had plunged into the crevice; into the distant embrace of the Defiles Course. Still an uncountable number of Cavewights pressed forward: a storm of red eyes and ferocity squalling like ghouls. Covenant did not know how much longer the company's defenders could withstand the attack.

Stonemage and Bluntfist. Coldspray and Stoutgirth. Branl with Longwrath's flamberge. The eldritch blade's magicks were meaningless here: its edges were not. Together the Humbled and the Giants were more effective than Covenant could comprehend.

The Anchormaster's remaining sailors had armed themselves with spears. Even Blustergale and Furledsail had regained their feet after Linden's violent healing; had claimed weapons. But they could not enter the fray. The ledge was too narrow.

Covenant loathed killing, but his abhorrence for the suffering and loss of those who stood with him was greater. To save them, he would have incinerated every

Cavewight on the ledge. And he would have borne the cost; added those deaths to the stains on his soul. His ring seemed to plead for use.

Yet he suppressed its fire, swallowed his ambiguous power. He did not have enough control to strike at the Cavewights without harming the people whom he longed to save. He could not protect Linden and Jeremiah. He had never been able to spare anyone who chose to fight for the Land.

And he did not understand why the unfamiliar Master stared at him in such amazement.

Surely the *Haruchai* had come for this? Summoned by Bhapa and Pahni, they must have rushed to Mount Thunder to join the Land's last defense. Why else were they here? How else had they arrived when they were needed?

"Thomas," Linden panted. "Thomas."

Covenant barely heard her. He gripped Loric's *krill* as if he had forgotten it.

Why was this Master surprised?

Fortunately he had not come alone. Armed with a Cavewight's falchion, the other warrior now supported Branl. In perfect harmony, they appeared to flow and eddy among the creatures, delivering bloodshed and death with the grace of dancers: a cut here, a thrust there, a spinning feint, on and on, all too swift for Covenant to grasp. Maimed and dying Cavewights were flung like sleet into the fissure. And those that fought past the two Masters were met by the hard iron of the Swordmainnir, or by Stoutgirth's spear.

The strength and skill of the defenders slowed the charge. They halted it.

"Ur-Lord." Stave pitched his voice to pierce the clamor and rage, the screams of pain, the raw gasping. "Here is Canrik of the Masters. His comrade is Dast. Above us, Ulman and Ard await the outcome here." Stave's tone had a sardonic tinge, trenchant and vindicated. "They were unaware of your return to life."

Unaware—? The idea staggered Covenant. Realities shifted. The ledge tilted to one side. It began to turn. He stood on impossible stone, could not keep his balance. The crevice called his name, a chiaroscuro of alternating seductions and commands. The *krill* fell from his numb fingers.

What had Bhapa and Pahni told the Masters? Had the Cords even reached Revelstone? Had the Ardent failed in his dying gift? Then why were the Masters here?

Covenant wanted to howl silver until the ledge stopped; until everything stopped.

Through the whirl, Linden's arms found him. "Thomas!" He thought that he saw Stave holding the *krill* nearby; but he heard only his wife. "The Masters came. Stave says that two hundred of them came!" With every word, she tried to summon him back. "But they didn't know where to look for us. There are too many tunnels. They had to spread out. Four of them found a place where the Wightwarrens open on this crevice. Somewhere up there." She seemed to be pointing. "Two *hundred*, Thomas! We'll have more help as soon as the others learn where we are.

"Hang on, Thomas! You have to hang on."

Reeling, he struggled to focus on her. His hands fumbled their way to the sides of her face. He held her directly in front of him, almost nose to nose, so that she would wheel with him—or so that the truth of her would remain stationary. She was not spinning. The ledge was not. Even the world was not. It was all in his mind.

He should have been accustomed to such things. He had been dizzy often enough—

"Mom?" Jeremiah asked. He seemed to be pleading. "Are they going to save us?"

Canrik spoke. "Ur-Lord." His voice was hard. His amazement had become anger. "There are questions which must be answered." Then he seemed to relent. "They cannot be answered here.

"Giants!" he called. "Do you possess rope? We would do well to gain the ledge above. Ulman and Ard will aid us. We have no other path."

A cudgel caught the side of Stonemage's leg. She went down. Lunging, Stoutgirth spitted her assailant. Blood gushed from the Cavewight's mouth, splashed the Anchormaster's face. But Stoutgirth was not done. In spite of his leanness, he was strong enough to heave the Cavewight into the air on the end of his spear. Furiously he pitched the creature over the edge.

Stonemage's pain made Linden flinch. She pulled away from Covenant. "Help them!" she yelled at Canrik. "Stonemage can't stand!"

The Master faced her, glaring. "There is no need. The attack fails. A rout begins."

Harried by fears like furies, Covenant forced his inward whirl aside. The whole crevice continued turning, but he ignored it. Standing with his legs wide, he looked along the ledge.

Through a blur of failing sight and vertigo, he saw that Canrik was right. Only seven or eight Cavewights still fought. The other Master, Dast, pursued creatures trying to retreat. Branl spun to help Bluntfist and Coldspray with their opponents. His blade spilled entrails, flung red spray. With every slash, Coldspray drew bright gore. Bluff Stoutgirth threw his spear: a final strike that gouged chips from a plate of armor. Then he stooped to Stonemage, pulled her arm over his shoulder, hauled her upright. Together they staggered toward the rest of the company.

Blustergale did not wait for instructions. From one of the company's sacks, he produced a heavy coil of rope. Baf Scatterwit tried to take it from him: his healed shoulder was still weak. He refused her; gave the rope to Wiver Setrock. To console her, he said, "Stand ready. You will have other tasks."

She hooted a laugh. "I am ready. Am I not ready always?"

"Anchormaster!" shouted Setrock. "The Master counsels an ascent! Other Masters wait to assist us."

Manic in his mask of blood, Stoutgirth grinned, rolled his eyes. "Sluggard! Why do you delay? If we do not accept aid when it is offered, we are not merely fools. We are witless as well."

At once, Setrock moved to the rim of the ledge, peered upward. For a moment, he gauged the distance, hefted his coil of rope. Then he nodded. Crouching to gain force, he threw his coil at the ledge high above the company.

It disappeared in the darkness for a moment. Then one end of the rope came snaking down.

Covenant drew a steadier breath, watched his surroundings settle back into their necessary positions.

Stoutgirth lowered Stonemage to the ledge, settled her leaning against the wall. "Another line," he commanded Scatterwit cheerfully; too cheerfully. Anguish in his gaze belied his tone. "Rig three cradles. I will not entrust the Timewarden or Linden Giantfriend or Jeremiah Chosen-son to the strength of their arms."

He did not add that Cirrus Kindwind had only one hand, or that Blustergale and Furledsail were still recovering, or that Onyx Stonemage was hurt, or that Scatterwit herself had lost a foot.

Covenant approved. He did not believe that he would be able to hold on when fresh vertigo urged him to fall.

Questions which must be answered?

Canrik was glaring at Linden again as if she were a viper. As if he felt betrayed—

Under the force of his gaze, she seemed to shrink inside her clothes. She had endured too much distrust from the Masters; too many judgments. Her history with them hung on her shoulders like a millstone. But she did not reply to Canrik's plain ire. Instead she turned to Jeremiah. Like a woman who wished to demonstrate something, she said distinctly, "I need Earthpower, Jeremiah. For Stonemage. Do you mind?"

Apparently she wanted Canrik to understand that the Staff of Law now belonged to the boy.

Jeremiah frowned. "She's hurt." He looked baffled. "You don't have to ask. She needs you."

He seemed to mean, *I don't know how to help her.*

The idea that the Masters still saw harm in Linden made Covenant want to hit Canrik in the face. Trembling at the intensity of his own wrath, he watched her walk toward Onyx Stonemage.

The injured Swordmain sat on the far side of the place where a boulder had broken the ledge. She kept her hands clamped around her thigh to block the sensations from her knee, prevent the pain from breaking through her self-command. Linden did not try to cross the gap unaided—and did not wait for help from the Giants. Instead she halted near the breach and bowed her head, concentrating her senses on Stonemage's injured leg. As if of its own accord, fire unfurled from the Staff of Law, an ebon tracery stark in the *krill*'s shining. It spun whorls like intaglio as it reached toward Stonemage.

Beyond them, Rime Coldspray kicked a Cavewight off the ledge: apparently the last of the creatures. Breathing hard, she and Halewhole Bluntfist studied the distance for a moment, where Dast harried the remnants of the attack. Then they raised their swords to salute Branl.

He replied with a *Haruchai* bow. His expression acknowledged neither pride nor satisfaction. If he had gleaned anything from Dast's thoughts, he did not reveal it.

Briefly Covenant faced Canrik. He wanted to demand, How dare you? How *dare* you? After everything she's been through while you were sitting on your damn hands? But he restrained himself. There was too much here that he did not understand. Too much that the Master did not.

Deliberately he shifted his attention to Jeremiah. Harsh as a rasp, he asked, "Where is the Worm now?"

Like Linden, he intended a demonstration.

Jeremiah winced. He studied his hands twisting on the Staff. "It's still in the river." His voice shook with bitterness. "Still above ground. But it's getting close. I can't see *Melenkurion* Skyweir anymore. There's just a huge cliff with a crack where the river comes out."

Over his shoulder, Covenant looked at Canrik again. Did you hear that, you self-righteous bastard? You think you've got questions? You have no idea.

Everything that Linden had done for her son's sake since Covenant's return to life was justified.

Then he told Jeremiah unsteadily, "Don't worry about it." The boy was ignorant of Linden's fraught history with Canrik's people. When would she have explained it? Why would she? Galt had saved Jeremiah's life. "I know what's happening to you is cruel. I can only imagine how much it hurts. But you'll get your chance to do something about it. And the Masters will help us."

At least until their questions were answered.

As if in response, Canrik said, "The Masters have been given lies. Stave conceals his thoughts. Branl of the Humbled must reveal truth."

The openness of Branl's mind did not trouble Covenant. Of course Branl would tell the truth. He had promised to instruct his people. Covenant trusted that he would tell the whole truth.

But lies? Who had lied to the *Haruchai*? Who had taken that risk? And how had the discernment of the Masters been foiled?

Stave regarded Canrik with a flatness that seemed to imply disapproval; but he did not reproach the Master.

Around Covenant, the Giants hurried through their preparations to leave the ledge. A sailor called Spume Frothbreeze braced his feet on the wall. With a second coil of rope over his shoulder, he pulled himself upward hand over hand. Scatterwit's line had been knotted around his waist so that he could drag it behind him.

To Covenant's blurred sight, the height of the next ledge seemed unattainable. If Ard and Ulman were there, he could not distinguish them. Within moments, Frothbreeze faded into obscurity.

But the Giants did not hesitate. At once, a woman followed with the company's last rope: Far Horizoneyes. Like Frothbreeze, she climbed with the ease of long experience.

Keenreef and Setrock took the remaining supplies, hastened upward. Covenant scowled at the cradles knotted into Scatterwit's line: three of them tied in sequence so that he, Linden, and Jeremiah could sit in them and simply hold on while Giants and *Haruchai* raised them. He did not want to do this. He would lose his balance again. And all three of them would be vulnerable. If the Cavewights renewed their attack, threw more spears—

"*No.*" The Ironhand's voice snatched him out of his fretting. Although she spoke quietly, her vehemence shocked him.

Turning, he saw Bluff Stoutgirth rise to his feet with Hurl's body across his shoulders.

"No," repeated Coldspray, furious or grieving. "Anchormaster, no."

"One I lost to the *skurj*," Stoutgirth replied like a lament. "For him, I have been granted a *caamora*. But three were slain here, and two fell beyond the reach of sorrow." He bared his teeth through his veil of blood. "All were in my command, and their guerdon was death. I will not forsake Hurl to the feeding of rats."

"You *will*," countered the Ironhand. "I do not gainsay your bereavement. Nonetheless you are the Anchormaster of Dire's Vessel, and you have not been relieved of command. Storms do not abate when a Giant falls from the rigging. Nor is our peril eased by the loss of comrades precious among us.

"The world's ending will be *caamora* enough for any woe. You will not hazard your life for a corpse."

"Will I not?" Stoutgirth did not meet her gaze. "Is this your word, Rime Coldspray? Do you speak thus, you who have lost five of your Swordmainnir, and have seen the purpose of your striving across the seas fail? Ironhand, your heart is stone. Mine is water."

Coldspray clenched her fists: anger glared in her eyes. Before she could retort, however, he jerked up his head, laughed like a loon. Two strides took him to the edge of the chasm. There he crouched, braced his arms under Hurl's body, and heaved it into the depths.

Laughing or crying, he said, "Hurl I give to the river. May it bear my heart to the surcease of seas, as it does him."

His wracked mirth rose until it seemed to fill the crevice: a broken man's threnody for the world's fallen. But he did not permit his rue to hold the company back from the ropes.

ᘒᘓᘔ

When Covenant reached the higher ledge, he had to sit down. Freed from his knotted cradle, he collapsed against one wall of the crude tunnel leading away from the crevice; drew his knees to his chest and hugged them urgently; hid his face. He felt unmanned by vertigo, by impossible demands and contradictions. He had barely known Hurl. He could not even remember the names of the other slain sailors, Giants who had lost their lives without striking a blow in their own defense. And his decisions had led them to ruin. It was his responsibility to make their deaths worthwhile.

It could not be done. Nothing that he ever did would assuage Lord Foul's countless victims. Nothing would suffice to honor the valor of those who still struggled for the Earth.

Still Covenant had to try. He had to close his ears to the siren song of dizziness and futility. He had to believe—

There is no doom so black or deep that courage and clear sight may not find another truth beyond it.

He was a leper. Surely he could believe whatever he chose? As long as he was willing to pay the price?

Fortunately he was not alone. In the Land, he had seldom been alone; but this time he had been given more than companionship and aid. Linden was coming toward him. He did not need health-sense to recognize the love in her eyes, the raw concern. Jeremiah followed behind her, clutching the Staff of Law as if his sanity depended on it. Stave brought the light of Loric's *krill* into the tunnel. Branl had gone to extremes that still appalled Covenant. Two Masters—Ard and Ulman?—stood on the ledge, helping with the ropes. And there were still Giants.

God, Giants—Five of Rime Coldspray's comrades: four of the Anchormaster's sailors: all gone, as lost to the world as Lostson Longwrath. Nevertheless those who remained outnumbered the dead.

And two hundred Masters had come to the Wightwarrens. Two *hundred*—

If Covenant's ability to choose what he would and would not believe was one side of being a leper, this was the other: he did not know how to bear such abundance. He had spent decades in one world and millennia in another learning how to stand alone.

Yet he could not pretend that he was not grateful. When Linden sat down beside him and slipped her arm over his shoulders, he found that he was able to meet her gaze.

"It isn't all bad," he said roughly. "At least we're still together. Some of us made it."

He meant, I love you, Linden Avery.

Her hug seemed to say that she understood.

Blinking uselessly, he looked around. "How are we doing?" Shadows and stark silver confused the shapes gathering around him. "We can't stay here."

"We'll be ready soon," she told him. "Some of the Giants need help." Cirrus Kindwind and Onyx Stonemage. Baf Scatterwit. Squallish Blustergale. Etch Furledsail. "They're being hauled up now. That only leaves Canrik and Dast."

Of course, Covenant thought. Naturally the Masters would insist on coming last.

Two hundred of them were in the Wightwarrens somewhere. Against how many Cavewights? He had no idea. Roger had had plenty of time to summon every living creature in Mount Thunder. And *moksha* Raver remained a threat. He might still be able to command any number of Lord Foul's servants. Covenant was not sure that two hundred *Haruchai* would be enough.

And in spite of what he had said to Jeremiah, he was not confident that he could count on their help. *The Masters have been given lies.* He did not know what those lies were. Therefore he could not guess how the Masters would react to the truth.

Together, Kindwind and Stonemage were heaved onto the ledge. When the last sailors and *Haruchai* had been pulled upward, Canrik strode among the Giants toward Rime Coldspray.

"Ironhand," he said at once, "we must not tarry in this passage."

Coldspray looked down at him. "Aye. Our foes are certain of our presence. They will surely come against us. And here we cannot retreat. We will perish—we must—if we do not discover a choice of headings. Are you able to guide us?"

Canrik nodded. "Our older knowledge of the Wightwarrens is slight, but we have not forgotten our path hither. And as we rejoin with our kinsmen, our knowledge will increase.

"What do you seek? Where do you hope to discover Kastenessen"—he cast a caustic glance at Linden—"if it remains your intent to confront one deranged *Elohim* while the Land and the Earth are unmade?"

Without pausing for thought, Covenant surged to his feet. "Kastenessen?" he snapped. Lies? "Where did you get that idea? Didn't you feel it when Kevin's Dirt faded? What did you think that meant? Kastenessen gave up days ago."

Clearly the Masters knew that the Worm of the World's End had been roused—

"We are not blind, ur-Lord," retorted Canrik. "We are aware that Kevin's Dirt has ended. But we were misled, Stave does not speak to us, and Branl is"—the Master appeared to search for words—"strangely reluctant. We cannot divine your purpose."

Covenant made an effort to swallow his anger. The Masters were not his enemies. He was simply outraged that they thought ill of Linden.

"I have to get to Kiril Threndor," he rasped. "If that's not too much to ask. I want to find the Despiser. And Cavewights aren't our only problem. My son is here somewhere. He's scared enough to try anything. Plus there's *moksha* Jehannum. He's probably mad as hell.

"I don't know what's bothering you, but it's trivial. We don't have time for it."

For a moment, Canrik stood as if he had been silenced. Slowly a frown settled onto his forehead. Then he stated, "Our questions must be answered."

Without waiting for a reply, he strode down the tunnel.

Coldspray glanced sharply at Covenant; but she did not delay. Hailing her Swordmainnir, she sent Halewhole Bluntfist and Frostheart Grueburn after Canrik. Then she followed him herself, taking Cirrus Kindwind with her, Ard and Ulman; leaving Onyx Stonemage with Covenant, Linden, and Jeremiah.

A subdued Anchormaster marshaled his crew. His uninjured sailors—Wiver Setrock, Spume Frothbreeze, Keenreef, Far Horizoneyes—he sent ahead. With Scatterwit, Blustergale, Furledsail, and Dast, he trailed the rest of the company.

Instinctively Covenant took Linden's hand, rested his halfhand on Jeremiah's shoulder. Accompanied by Stave and Branl, they started along the passage.

Jeremiah did not resist, but he walked with his head down, paid no attention to where he put his feet. His hands tightened and relaxed on the Staff, urgent as heartbeats. At intervals, he jerked up his head and glared around him. But he did not speak; did not appear to notice Covenant or Linden.

Maybe Roger had the right idea. Maybe we should all try to become gods.

The notion made Covenant's stomach burn as if he had swallowed acid. He refused to believe—

Linden studied her son for a moment. Then her eyes flinched away. She looked at Covenant, pleading like a woman who had no language for her needs. Almost at once, however, she turned her attention to Stave.

In a low voice, she asked, "What's bothering the Masters? Did Pahni and Bhapa reach them?"

She might have asked, Do they think that Pahni and Bhapa lied? They can't believe that. If they do, why did they come?

"Chosen," replied Stave, "I must accord to our people the respect which I will require of them." His tone suggested that he was keeping his distance. "They will speak of their doubts and indignations when we have evaded immediate pursuit. It is their right to be who they are, and to determine what they will become.

"Yet I am free to acknowledge that the Masters have heard and questioned the Cords. True to his service, the Ardent delivered Bhapa and Pahni to the vicinity of Revelstone. Their words gave the Masters cause to come in search of you, Chosen." He gave a subtle emphasis to Linden's title. "Now the Cords accompany the Masters. If our foes and our fate permit it, you will be reunited with them.

"More than that I will not disclose."

"Damn it, Stave," Linden muttered. "That's not enough. How could they not know that Covenant is alive? Didn't Bhapa or Pahni tell them?"

How had the Cords goaded the Masters into action at last, if not by insisting that the ur-Lord needed them, the Unbeliever, the man who had twice defeated Corruption?

"We'll hear about it soon enough," Covenant put in. He did not have the heart to challenge Stave's scruples. Instead he tightened his grip on Linden's hand, trying to reassure her. "Or we'll spend what's left of our lives fighting, and we won't hear anything at all. Either way, it doesn't matter. They aren't just Masters. They're *Haruchai*. Eventually they'll help us, even if they think we did something terrible behind their backs. They have to. They're too ashamed to do anything else. They've already passed up two chances to face Lord Foul with me, not to mention once with Kevin. They don't know how to live with it."

Stave nodded like a shrug. Branl did not offer his opinion.

For a long moment, Linden studied the ungiving stone ahead of her. When she finally spoke, her voice was so soft that Covenant barely heard her.

"Don't let them get in my way. This is my last chance. We can't stop the Worm. It's my fault, but I can't do anything about it. That's why I have to—"

Abruptly she stopped.

"I know," Covenant sighed. "We're all in the same boat. The only thing that might be worse than facing our fears is not facing them."

Linden did not reply; did not lift her head. She clung to his hand as if she were drowning.

Covenant knew the feeling. He believed that she would find the courage she needed. A woman who could do what she had done would be able to do more. But he was not at all sure how he would bear losing her.

The sheer scale of his anger at the Despiser was becoming a liability. Often it had kept him going when he should have failed. But now he needed a better answer—and his anger threatened to blind him.

That was the paradox of his leprosy. In order to confront Lord Foul, he positively required numbness. He had to be untouchable: immune to every affront; impervious to the extremes of wild magic. Unaffected by the implicit betrayal of Roger's allegiance. Yet numbness might also leave him impotent. It had done so before.

When Linden left, she would take his heart with her. If he allowed fury to fill that great hole in his chest, he was sure to fail.

ᔕᘓᕉ

E ven in this unfamiliar passage, Covenant recognized the Wightwarrens. He knew them by the crudity of the Cavewights' delving—the careless walls and ragged ceiling, the irregular protrusions of stone where the creatures had neglected to finish what they started—and by the instinctive cunning with which the tunnel followed veins and lodes within the gutrock. From here, anyone who knew the catacombs well would be able to find Kiril Threndor, Heart of Thunder, where Covenant had once surrendered to the Despiser.

But he had no idea how far he still had to go. And he felt sure that the company would be attacked again before he reached his goal.

As if to prove him right, a warning shout came from the darkness ahead: the Ironhand's voice. He heard yells and effort, the clash of weapons. At once, Onyx Stonemage gestured for a halt. She went three paces farther, then stopped, waiting with her longsword in her fists.

"Mom?" Jeremiah asked uselessly. "Mom?"

"Cavewights bar the passage," Branl announced, "a small force. I surmise that they did not anticipate our ascent from the crevice. They were not prepared against us. Yet the constricted space aids them. They suffice to—"

Stave shook his head. Briefly Branl narrowed his gaze. Then the Humbled said, "They do not suffice. Four Masters assail the creatures from the rear. Openings are created for the blades of the Swordmainnir, and for Canrik and Dast. Three Cavewights have fallen. Five. Now eight." After a moment's silence, Branl stated, "The passage has been cleared."

"Is anyone hurt?" Linden asked.

Branl appeared to hesitate before saying, "Skill and armor shielded the Swordmainnir. *Haruchai* do not regard their hurts."

"In other words," she snapped, "they don't want me to insult them by offering to treat them."

Covenant ground his teeth. She was right, of course.

Stave shrugged. "There is much which the Masters do not comprehend."

"Mom," Jeremiah breathed thickly. "I smell blood."

Linden glanced past Covenant at the boy. "I know, honey. I'm sick of all this kill-ing. But we can't stop. If we don't fight, they'll kill us."

As if to herself, she muttered, "It galls the hell out of me that the Cavewights would probably be on our side if they knew how Foul is using them. They can *think*, for God's sake. They just don't think clearly enough."

And they probably love their children, Covenant added for her. They probably hate us for what we're doing. But he kept that thought to himself.

Jeremiah murmured something that Covenant did not hear. Stonemage was beck-oning them into motion.

Still holding Linden's hand, still resting his palm on Jeremiah's shoulder, Cove-nant started forward again.

Soon he, too, could smell blood: blood and more bitter fluids. In the distance ahead, the *krill*'s illumination caught glints of crimson on the floor and walls. It looked dark as ichor. The Giants and Masters leading the company had moved past the site of the fray, leaving hacked and gutted corpses behind them. Blood lay in thick pools around bodies and spilled guts. Stonemage strode through the carnage as if she could not afford to acknowledge it. Stave and Branl stepped, heedless, in swaths of red, trod with apparent unconcern over dripping corpses. But Covenant had to let go of Linden and Jeremiah so that he could pick his nauseated way among the dead.

God, it was hard not to hate the Despiser. Rage felt like the only sane response.

As the Giants bringing up the rear passed the slain Cavewights, Branl told Cove-nant, "The Swordmainnir have gained an intersection of passages. The path familiar to Canrik and his companions lies to the right, but there the air is fraught with peril. Samil, Vortin, and other Masters approach from the left. They report that their search did not tend toward Kiril Threndor. Therefore the Ironhand wishes to con-tinue ahead. She awaits only your consent, ur-Lord."

Covenant hesitated momentarily, trying to guess the consequences of every choice. Then he rasped, "Tell her to trust herself. More Masters will find us. Eventu-ally some of them will know how to reach Kiril Threndor."

Branl and Stave nodded. Branl's manner hinted at increased concentration as he conveyed Covenant's reply.

Covenant looked to Linden for her approval; but her attention was fixed on Jere-miah. The boy stood staring straight ahead as if he had gone blind. His hands shifted up and down the Staff as if he were wrestling with the Worm.

Groaning to himself, Covenant trailed after Onyx Stonemage.

When he and his companions reached the intersection, they found Frostheart Grueburn, Halewhole Bluntfist, and Dast waiting for them. Blood dripped from a cut the length of Grueburn's left forearm. A spear had gashed Bluntfist's right cheek. But their wounds seemed superficial. In the *krill*'s argent, their grins looked garish as grimaces.

They gestured Covenant and the others onward. "The Ironhand deems," Grueburn explained, "that we are no longer required in the forefront. Therefore we will ward the rear." As Grueburn added, "Though we are Giants, we counsel haste," Bluntfist chuckled. "Yon tunnel"—she indicated the one on Covenant's right—"is rife with odors. It augurs unpleasantness."

"Be careful," Covenant warned them unnecessarily. "We can't lose you."

He had to stifle an impulse to start running.

This tunnel climbed steeply; dipped down; rose again. It turned at odd angles. After a while, the clang of iron echoed after Covenant. Muffled snarls, thudding blows. Branl reported that Cavewights assailed Grueburn, Bluntfist, and Dast. But now the confines of the passage aided the Swordmainnir and the Master. They could afford to retreat as they fought, following the company. And soon they were able to beat back the creatures. The sounds of struggle faded.

Branl continued to relay information from his kinsmen. In the distance ahead, the vanguard reached a branching. Four more Masters were there. These *Haruchai* reported that they had found a cave, a space like a small cavern with a shallow basin for a floor and openings into other passages: a place where the companions could be questioned.

"I don't like it," Covenant complained to Branl. "We're running out of time." And he did not want to hear accusations from the Masters.

"In this, they speak with one voice," replied Branl. His tone concealed his personal reaction. "They require an account of our deeds and purposes."

"They will be answered," Stave returned. "Yet I also mislike the prospect of delay. We can have no effect upon the outcome of the world if we do not achieve our ends before the Worm drinks of the EarthBlood."

The Humbled shrugged. "If the Masters are denied, they may respond with denial."

"Oh, God," Linden sighed. "Just what we need."

Covenant swore to himself. Whatever else Linden had done, she had not lied to the Masters. But they might not be able to see past the fact that she had set in motion the Earth's ruin.

Aloud, he demanded, "Can't you convince them, Branl? It doesn't matter why they're here. Hellfire! It doesn't even matter if Bhapa and Pahni lied to them. We need help. Holding us back now is just surrender. We might as well kill ourselves."

The Humbled held Covenant's glare. "I cannot sway them, ur-Lord. I am not as I was. My thoughts no longer accord with theirs. They deem that they would not have acted as I have done. In their minds, they would have forestalled the Worm's awakening. This belief justifies their wrath."

Jeremiah was squirming. "That's stupid," he snorted as soon as Branl finished: scorn thick as venom. "Covenant wouldn't be here without it. And I wouldn't be *here*. I would already be helping Roger and that *croyel* become *eternal*.

"Did you tell the Masters *that*?"

"To what purpose, Chosen-son?" countered Branl. "They would reply that Corruption could not threaten creation while he was imprisoned within the Arch. And while he was imprisoned, much might have been attempted to thwart him. Only the Worm's awakening assures his triumph."

Before Covenant could think of a response that was not rage, Linden spoke. "If it's up to me," she told the Humbled, "I'll answer anything. I don't know how much time we have. I don't know if we can afford to stand around arguing. But the Masters are important. I'll do what I can."

"Chosen." Branl's visage revealed nothing. Yet when he bowed, he gave her his full respect. Then he turned away, bearing the company's only light down the tunnel.

Well, damn, Covenant thought. My wife—

Baring his teeth, he tried to grin. When that failed, he concentrated on catching up with the Humbled.

I am not as I was.

And Linden was facing the most immediate of her fears.

✢

Before long, Covenant and his immediate companions reached the place where the tunnel forked. There four Masters awaited him. He recognized Ard and Ulman. The other two were Vortin and Samil.

The *krill* lit momentary wonder in Vortin's eyes, and in Samil's, as they bowed to Covenant. It exposed their ire when they regarded Linden. But they did not linger. While Branl explained that they would help Grueburn, Bluntfist, and Dast guard the rear, the four men moved into the blackness of the passages.

Covenant heard weapons behind him again. Giantish oaths echoed like gasps along the tunnel. Bluff Stoutgirth's voice harried Scatterwit and Blustergale.

"They are swift enough," a Swordmain responded to the Anchormaster. Grueburn? Bluntfist? "Expostulation will not speed them."

Gritting his teeth, Covenant followed Stonemage with Linden, Jeremiah, and Stave. Among them, Branl strode along like a man whose uncertainties had become faith.

This passage also ascended and dipped as it wandered; but now each rise took the company higher into the mountain. Covenant had no idea where he was in relation to the ancient Heart of Thunder. His human memories of the catacombs were confused by the dangers which he and his companions had faced then. Surrounded by this darkness, this weight of stone, he could not imagine how far he still had to go.

Tired as he was, the erratic climb felt long. The vagaries of the rough corridor blocked his view in both directions: he could not see beyond the *krill*. Like the Giants ahead of him, those behind seemed insubstantial, as if they had faded from the world. Only Linden and Jeremiah were real. Branl, Stave, and Onyx Stonemage.

But then the tunnel angled downward so sharply that Covenant had to lock his knees to keep his balance. When he was free to look up again, he saw the end of the passage, an opening into a wider space. From his perspective, that space resembled a pit, black and bottomless. But the figures walking into and through it demonstrated that it was not deep.

As he followed Branl into the cave, he found his companions gathering near its center. The Ironhand and Cirrus Kindwind. Four of Stoutgirth's sailors. And Masters—

Their number confused him until he realized that more *Haruchai* had joined the company. They bowed to the Giants, gazed with closed faces at Covenant and Linden. Then they spread out around the space, leaving only scarred Canrik with Rime Coldspray.

The cave was vaguely circular, with walls that looked natural rather than hewn, and a knuckled ceiling like an array of clenched fists. The floor was a complex jumble of fallen rocks on sunken patches where the underlying granite had contracted or cooled, sending a fretwork of narrow cracks through the surface. Four more tunnels opened like throats at irregular intervals around the walls: gullets choked with darkness where the light did not penetrate. In pairs, the Masters moved to stand guard at each entrance.

"Thomas?" Linden asked softly. "Where are Pahni and Bhapa?"

"They'll come." Covenant tried to sound sure. The Wightwarrens were vast; but when the mental communion of the *Haruchai* reached enough of their people—

When or if.

She frowned. "We need them. The Masters seem to think that I can answer their questions, but I probably can't." She fell silent briefly. Then she added like a sigh, "I want to see Pahni and Bhapa again."

"Me, too," he muttered. He had already lost too many friends—and he was going to lose more. He did not know how to avoid it.

He and Linden greeted Coldspray and Kindwind, acknowledged Wiver Setrock and the other sailors. Covenant scowled at Canrik, thinking, Be careful what you say. Be very careful. But he did not warn the Master aloud. Instead he turned to watch the Anchormaster and the remaining sailors enter the cave.

Both Furledsail and Blustergale were helping Baf Scatterwit now. She had torn open the stump of her ankle trying to walk as if she had not lost her foot, and every step left smears of blood. Nevertheless she grinned hugely as she rejoined her comrades.

A few moments later, Grueburn, Bluntfist, and five Masters entered the small cavern. They arrived at a trot, but they slowed when they saw the rest of the company. Carmine streaks stained their limbs, their tunics and cataphracts; but little of the blood was theirs. They did not move like people with injuries. The two Swordmainnir approached their Ironhand. Dast, Ard, and Ulman joined the *Haruchai* keeping watch at the entrances. Vortin and Samil took places with Canrik.

Rime Coldspray's jaws worked as if she were chewing curses. "Here the Masters require answers," she grated, "though every delay serves our foes."

"We do," said Canrik, impervious to her indignation. "We comprehend exigency. Nonetheless we will await the coming of the Voice of the Masters, and of the Ramen Cords. Our thoughts have reached out to other Masters, and thence to more distant kinsmen. Handir and those with him now hasten toward us. They will stand in the presence of the ur-Lord before the end. They will demand sooth from Linden Avery, who has brought the Worm upon us, and has given rise to falsehoods."

Covenant beat his fists together, punching the hard circle of his wedding band to control his ire. Linden was right. He repeated that to himself again and again. She was right. He could do nothing against Lord Foul if the Masters refused him. Five Swordmainnir, eight Giants from Dire's Vessel, Stave, and Branl were not enough to oppose thousands of Cavewights, never mind Roger and *moksha* Jehannum and any other force that the Despiser summoned.

Distinctly Jeremiah said, "You don't know Mom." His eyes looked blank, as if he were thinking about something else. From his hands, black power ran like oil through the Staff's runes. "Why would she lie? She isn't afraid of you."

Just for an instant, Linden's features crumpled. Then she covered her face with her hands. When she lowered them again, her expression had hardened, and the gaze that she fixed on Canrik was bleak.

As if he were choking, Covenant asked the Master, "How long do you expect us to just stand here?"

Canrik regarded him gravely. "The pursuing Cavewights have been slain. No others gather within reach of our discernment. We conclude that they do not know where to seek for us. No assault is imminent." He glanced around at the Giants. "And your companions must welcome any respite."

He appeared to believe that his reply would content Covenant.

Covenant said nothing. In spite of his weak sight, he could see that the attitudes of the Masters had changed. They had recovered from their initial surprise. Now they conveyed more anger. They appeared to feel betrayed, not by Covenant himself, but by the fact of his presence. And they blamed Linden—

Days ago, they had been misled by an image of Covenant. When Roger had ridden disguised by glamour into Revelstone with Jeremiah and the *croyel*, the Masters had failed to discern the truth. They had reason for doubt.

Nevertheless Covenant wanted to yell at them. Linden had already endured too much from Handir and the other Masters. She did not deserve more.

Uncharacteristically brusque, Stoutgirth Anchormaster told his crew to distribute food and water. Before they could comply, however, more Masters began to arrive. In groups of four, they entered the cave from various passages: a score of *Haruchai*; then two score. To the Giants, they bowed impassively. To Linden and Covenant, they gave flat stares as fierce as castigations. Jeremiah they seemed to ignore. Then they spread out to form a cordon around the company; but whether they did so to defend Covenant, Linden, and Jeremiah, or to defend against them, Covenant could not tell.

Handir had once threatened to wrest Linden's implements of power from her.

I won't stand for it, Covenant told himself. I can't.

But he could not make the Masters' decisions for them. *The necessity of freedom* belonged to them, as it did to everyone else.

Still pressures rose like water within him. Soon he would have to start raging at somebody, anybody, for no better reason than because he needed an outlet.

He bit down on his tongue to stifle a shout when Handir finally strode into the cave.

The silver of Handir's hair, and the scars which seamed his visage and forearms like emblems, testified to his years and stature. He was the Voice of the Masters, accustomed to authority.

Three of his people accompanied him, but they were not alone. Among them, they escorted Manethrall Mahrtiir's Cords, Bhapa and Pahni.

At the sight, Covenant's anger fell away like a wave from a cliff. He could see that the Cords had changed. The Pahni whom he had known might have forgiven Linden for refusing to attempt Liand's resurrection. That girl might have run to hug Linden; might have shed tears of gratitude and relief. And brave, diffident Bhapa would have stood back only because he did not consider himself important enough to demand attention.

Not now. Somehow both of the Ramen had inherited Mahrtiir's spirit. Pahni swept forward like a striking raptor, and her eyes were bright with vindication, keen as whetted iron. Bhapa approached more slowly, but not because he was reluctant or daunted. Rather he walked with the firm tread of a man who had been flensed of his weaknesses.

The two of them gave the impression that they had brought the Masters from Revelstone by force of will.

Pahni offered the Ironhand a Ramen bow. The Cord's gaze flicked among the Swordmainnir, counted their losses. Then she bowed again more deeply, acknowledging their fallen. But she did not greet Covenant. Although her eyes widened when she saw the Staff in Jeremiah's hands, her attention did not linger on him.

The look that she fixed on Linden was simultaneously proud and defiant. She seemed to dare Linden to tell her that she had done wrong.

Linden started toward the girl, then stopped herself, biting her lip. Her eyes were bruises.

Bhapa's manner was more reserved. He honored Coldspray and her comrades formally. To Covenant, he bowed as well, saying only, "Timewarden." His brows lifted as he regarded Jeremiah; but he, too, did not pause for wonder. In a voice as tight as a rope, he said, "Some tidings we have received from Handir. We have been assured that Manethrall Mahrtiir has not fallen. For that we are grateful. But the tale of his transformation we must hear at another time." Then the Cord came to stand in front of Linden.

Her arms lifted to him, but he did not grant her an embrace. Instead he sank to the stone; prostrated himself before her as if she had become his suzerain, as honored as a Ranyhyn.

"Bhapa—" Linden's voice broke. "Oh, Bhapa." Tears ran down her cheeks. "What are you doing? What's happened to you?"

Severely the Cord rose to his knees. After studying her face for a moment, he stood. Dampness softened his gaze, but his manner did not relent. He spoke as if he were offering a pledge.

"Linden Avery, Ringthane and Chosen, I cry your pardon. I will account for my deeds. But I must first assure you that Cord Pahni is innocent of fault. She spoke as she did at my command. The blame of the outcome is mine and no other's."

Clarion as a whinny, Pahni announced, "He has become my Manethrall. He has honored my life with service. Where he leads, I follow gladly."

God in Heaven, Covenant thought. What have you done?

Linden bit her lip again, struggling to contain a torrent of emotions.

Just for an instant, Jeremiah looked like he wanted to put his arms around her. But he caught himself, stepped back. He had known Bhapa and Pahni only for a short time—and only through the veil of the *croyel*'s derision. He did not know how to interpret what was happening.

Frowning, Handir had contained himself while the Cords preceded him. Now he spoke.

"I am Handir," he said in an astringent tone, "by right of years and attainment the Voice of the Masters. Much lies between us. It must be answered.

"We have learned to our cost that our discernment cannot pierce the glamour of Corruption's servants. Here we behold one who appears to be the ur-Lord, yet we have seen his like before. We require some assurance that he is indeed the ur-Lord rather than a new display of glamour."

Linden flinched. Disapproval spread among the Swordmainnir. Branl allowed himself a scowl. Stave's mouth tightened.

But Covenant responded first. Handir's challenge brought back his anger in a rush.

"Oh, stop," he snarled. "Branl must have told you who I am. Are you so sick with suspicion that you can't even trust one of the Humbled? The *last* of the Humbled?

"Here, I'll show you."

Fiercely he stamped toward Jeremiah. To Jeremiah's surprise, Covenant slapped his halfhand onto the black wood, gripped it for a moment. Then he wheeled to face Handir again.

"Do you remember the test of truth? I thought you remembered everything. When Roger was pretending to be me, he didn't let Linden use the Staff. Hell, he didn't even let her touch him. Now she's my wife. My *wife*, do you understand?"

The *Haruchai* were passionate about their mates—

Through his teeth, Covenant gritted, "I don't know what's bothering you people. I don't really care. You want answers? If you keep this up, you'll all answer to *me*."

Then he stopped. Handir's evident satisfaction silenced him. Now he realized that Handir's demand had served an oblique purpose. Inadvertently Covenant had just confirmed Handir's authority; his right to judge.

It was possible that Handir had not doubted Covenant's identity—

The idea made Covenant reel. What had Bhapa and Pahni told the Masters?

With a defiance of his own, Stave said impassively, "Be at ease, Timewarden. The Masters crave stone, yet they stand upon quicksand. They are indeed misled. Uncertain of his devoir, Handir masks his deeper apprehensions."

The Voice of the Masters did not react to Stave's assertion.

"Then get to it," Covenant told Handir. "At least one of us will by God answer your questions."

Deliberately Vortin and Samil moved to stand beside their leader. They appeared to ask or expect Branl to join them; but the Humbled remained with Covenant and Linden, Jeremiah and Stave.

Sensitive to the tensions in the cave, Bluff Stoutgirth took his crew aside; out of the way. Glowering, Rime Coldspray did the same with her comrades, although the Swordmainnir plainly wanted to defend their friends. The cordon of the Masters tightened around them all. Within it, Pahni remained nearby, apparently waiting. But Bhapa stood with his back to Handir, facing Covenant and Linden. Again Covenant felt the force of the former Cord's new demeanor, his earned severity.

"Cord," Handir said harshly: a reprimand or a warning.

Bhapa ignored him.

"Ringthane and Timewarden," the older Raman began, precise as a garrote, "the wrath of the Masters is mine to endure. You had no part in their misapprehension. Their umbrage rests, not upon a falsehood, but upon a withheld truth. For this, I again cry your pardon, Ringthane. The choice was mine. Cord Pahni spoke as she did at my command."

"And would do so again," declared Pahni. "I serve my Manethrall as I do the Ranyhyn."

But Bhapa did not pause for her. "The dilemma of the Masters is this. They did not know of your return, Timewarden, because I did not permit them to know. They were informed of the rousing of the Worm. They were told of the Worm's hunger for the Blood of the Earth. But naught was said concerning your resurrection, Timewarden. Your name was not spoken. I did not concede the knowledge that you were restored to us by the selfsame deed which awakened the Worm."

In spite of their stoicism, Handir, Canrik, and the other Masters betrayed their indignation. Branl must have explained Covenant's return. Nevertheless they were unprepared for Bhapa's confession. Millennia ago, the Bloodguard had trusted the Ramen—

"Rather, Ringthane," the older Cord continued to Linden, "I encouraged them in their belief that the blame for the world's doom is yours." His tone was a stranglehold. "Speaking as I had instructed her, Pahni gave them cause to imagine that your sole purpose from first to last has been the restoration of your son, that you have given no heed to the havoc which you have unleashed. Therefore the Masters have come seeking retribution for the final crime of the Earth."

Covenant listened with his mouth open, wordless and appalled. Linden stared as if Bhapa had betrayed her: a man who had sworn himself to her. The Giants cursed softly, gripping their weapons. Only Jeremiah did not react. Apparently images of the Worm had reclaimed him.

Then Handir barked, "Enough! Am I a child, that a Raman must assume my place?"

Swift as threats, Samil and Vortin approached Bhapa. They grasped him roughly, dragged him aside.

Linden looked like she might wail. To restrain her, distract her, Covenant said reflexively, "This is my fault." Her distress was worse than his. She already blamed herself— "I should have told Bhapa and Pahni what to say. I didn't because I thought the Masters deserved a chance to make their own decisions. It never occurred to me—"

What had possessed the Cords?

Linden did not look at him. Her whole face seemed to plead with Bhapa.

Ignoring Handir's indignation, Bhapa told her, "Faithful to his word, the Ardent delivered us to the vicinity of Revelstone. There we were able to speak privately ere the Masters greeted us. The burden of my wishes I gave to Cord Pahni because her need was plain. I prayed that her passion would prevail where my own ire might undermine me."

He tried to say more; but Samil silenced him with a hand on his throat: a choke which nearly lifted him from his feet.

Without transition, Covenant's wedding band burned. Sudden fire crowded his mind, straining for release.

The threat to the Cord was too much for the Swordmainnir. In an instant, Rime Coldspray reached Samil and Bhapa, her glaive in her hands. Frostheart Grueburn followed a step behind her.

Around them, the cordon of Masters closed like a noose. Giants brandished their weapons: swords and spears. Pahni's garrote appeared in her fists.

"Handir!" Covenant snapped. "*Handir!*"

Handir's jaws bunched. He nodded once.

Samil released Bhapa. Samil and Vortin stepped back.

Covenant took a deep breath, made an effort to quench his heart's fire.

In a small voice like a cry, Linden asked, "Why, Bhapa? Why did you do that?"

Handir spoke over her. To the Ironhand, he said, "Withhold your blows. You cannot stand against us. For that reason, we will not strike. We scorn unequal combat. Samil sought only to impose silence upon the Cord."

Reluctantly Coldspray sheathed her sword. Grueburn and the other Giants lowered their weapons. As they did so, the Masters relaxed their ring around the company.

Their Voice faced Linden. "We share your query, Linden Avery. We will hear it answered. But first we must have some confirmation of what has occurred."

Before she—or Bhapa—could protest, Handir turned, not to Covenant, but to Branl.

"Are your thoughts sooth?" he demanded in the full light of High Lord Loric's *krill*. "Stave has learned concealment. Therefore he is suspect. Concealment enables falsehood. Are you now likewise capable of falsehood?

"Is *turiya* Herem truly slain? Has Linden Avery indeed restored a Forestal to the Land? Has her fated boy provided for the preservation of the *Elohim*, and for an end to Kevin's Dirt? Have you defeated Sandgorgons and *skurj*? Does the ur-Lord now seek to challenge Corruption in Kiril Threndor?"

Branl lifted an eyebrow. Then he shrugged like a man who did not deign to take offense. "I am *Haruchai*," he said. "More, I am Humbled. I do not sully my mind with lies.

"Nor," he added more sharply, "will I condone aspersion to the Ramen. As do you, Handir, Voice of the Masters, I require an account of their deeds. Yet they have been at all times steadfast and valiant companions. They have given of themselves utterly while the Masters remained effectless in Revelstone. I will endure no denunciation of them."

Handir studied Branl. He appeared to search Branl's mind.

"We are not effectless now," the older man retorted. "Two hundred Masters have entered the Wightwarrens, seeking Linden Avery and Kastenessen as we were urged. Two hundred more strive toward *Melenkurion* Skyweir, where they, too, will give of themselves utterly against the Worm, if their arrival is not belated."

At once, Pahni countered, fierce and proud, "Did the Ranyhyn consent to bear you?"

Handir glanced at her. "You know the truth of this, Cord Pahni. Do not aggravate your fault with insolence. You will be judged when you have justified your deeds."

Then he said to Covenant as much as to Branl, "Ranyhyn bore us hither. Without their aid, we could not have come so swiftly. But the Masters who ride to *Melenkurion* Skyweir do so on lesser beasts. The great horses declined to be ridden there."

The shining of Pahni's eyes resembled exultation. "Thus the Ranyhyn approve Manethrall Bhapa's purpose."

The Voice of the Masters permitted himself a vexed frown. "I do not hear you," he told the Cord. "It becomes evident, however, that I must heed the last of the Humbled. By him, as by the ur-Lord's presence, the lies of the Ramen are exposed. Now Linden Avery's query must be answered.

"Bhapa of the Ramen, it is not in the nature of your people to scheme and mislead. Why have you betrayed their legacy? Why have you concealed necessary truths?"

Covenant was holding his breath. He forced himself to let it out. The idea that two hundred Masters intended to oppose the Worm directly appalled him. He shook his head to dispel images of pointless slaughter.

Wary and unrelieved, Rime Coldspray and her Swordmainnir studied Bhapa, measuring the man in front of them against their memories of him. The Giants of Dire's Vessel did not know the Cords, but they remained poised to support the Ironhand. Only Baf Scatterwit did not seem tense. She was chuckling to herself as if everyone in the cave amused her.

Jeremiah muttered something that Covenant could not hear. The boy scowled darkly, as if he were contemplating murder. The absence in his eyes suggested that he was watching the Worm burrow into *Melenkurion* Skyweir.

Bhapa rolled his head to loosen his bruised throat. He came closer to Linden and Covenant. In the open center of the gathering, he stopped: a man who needed room for the fire of his emotions. His eyes were white flames in the surrounding gloom.

"*It was for this,*" he told Handir in a tone of throttled fury. "That you might here encounter the truth of the Ringthane, the Chosen, Linden Avery—encounter it and *know shame.*"

Then he turned his back on the clenched repudiation of the Masters.

"Ringthane"—he addressed his appeal directly to Linden—"you are dear to me. My esteem you won by your care of Sahah, who is both Pahni's cousin and half my sister. No succor known to the Ramen could have brought her back from death, yet you contrived to do so.

"My heart you won in the aftermath of First Woodhelven, when you redeemed Manethrall Mahrtiir's life—aye, and preserved also his place as my Manethrall. At that time, I could not have met the peril of these times without his guidance. Sparing him, you spared me also."

Linden listened with tears spilling from her eyes, but she made no sound.

The older Cord's voice rose as he continued. Anger grated like thunder in the background of every word.

"And since those great deeds, I have been stunned to the soul by your devotion to your son, by your valor in the greatest extremity, and by your enduring love for the Timewarden. I know nothing of *turiya* Herem, or of Forestals, or of *Elohim*. Yet I know with a certainty which surpasses utterance that the awakening of the Worm was the outcome of Fangthane's cunning, not of any desire for Desecration in you. You acted only upon your love for the Timewarden, and upon your love for your son.

"Linden Avery, Chosen, Ringthane, I am *offended to the marrow of my bones* that these sleepless ones have dared to think ill of you. They have named themselves the Masters of the Land, but they do not *serve.* True service submits itself to the cause which it serves, deeming that cause holy. This the Ramen comprehend. True service does not judge the deeds which are asked of it. It does not consent to *this* and refuse *that*, according to the dictates of its own pride. It gives of itself because the cause which it serves is worthy.

"The self-will of these Masters *offends* me. It is an offense to every good which they have sworn to preserve."

As if he were unaware of the lifting of Covenant's heart, unaware of the bright approval in the eyes of the Swordmainnir, unaware even of Linden's weeping, Bhapa said more softly, "That is my justification. I did not mislead the Masters for the Land's hurt, or for their own. I merely"—he spat the word—"*encouraged* them in their judgments and pride, praying that they would ride forth in wrath to confront Desecration. Thereby I hoped to impose upon them a confrontation with their own folly.

"If I must say more, I will add only that I did not invoke the Timewarden's name because I feared that the Masters would not heed it. When have they ever stood with him in his last need? I feared that their notions of service would compel inaction."

Then the Cord was finished. Briefly he slumped as if his passion had drained from him. But after a moment, he squared his shoulders and lifted his head, bracing himself to accept the consequences of what he had done.

Linden's only answer was to say his name like a sob as she went to him. To his look of surprise, she replied by putting her arms around him and holding him tight.

Covenant wanted to weep himself. He wanted to laugh, and to shout out his joy in the Cords, and to rail at the Masters. But he contained his turmoil, set his own emotions aside in order to concentrate on Handir.

Fates of every description stood on the lip of a precipice. One misstep now might be fatal. Covenant should have felt dizzy; but he found that his faith was equal to this moment. Bhapa had brought the Masters to a crisis of rectitude, a challenge which would search their definition of themselves to its core. And here they had the power to save or damn Covenant's intentions. Nevertheless he was content to await the outcome. He called himself the Unbeliever, but he believed in Bhapa, whose name meant "father." In Pahni, whose name was "water."

And he had always trusted the *Haruchai*.

The Voice of the Masters did not speak. His mien revealed nothing. No doubt he was engaged in a vehement discussion with his kinsmen; but they masked their thoughts.

When Linden had satisfied her gratitude, she released Bhapa. Blinking to clear her eyes, she gave him a crooked smile. Then she turned to Pahni.

Clearly she was unsure of herself with the young woman. Pahni had not spoken a word to her since Linden had refused to attempt Liand's resurrection. Instead of offering to hug the Cord, Linden asked with an ache of yearning in her voice, "My God, Pahni. How did you do it?"

How had a woman who had been little more than a girl when she found her first love in Liand discovered the strength to face down the assembled Masters in Revelstone?

In spite of her slight stature, Pahni met Linden's question with an imperious air. She looked whetted, as if she had spent days applying her heart to a grindstone. Without hesitation, she replied, "I made of my grief a form of rage. I spoke to excoriate, goading the Masters to bestir themselves. We are the life which remains. They could not stand idle while a mere Cord faulted them for permitting the world's Desecration. They had no answer for the charge which I brought against them."

They did not grieve. Therefore their bereavements ruled them.

Harsh as the call of a hawk, Pahni added, "*I* do not cry your pardon, Ringthane. I am a Cord of the Ramen. I will not regret that I have abided by the command of my Manethrall." But then her manner softened somewhat. "And I also am offended in your name. I, too, crave the shaming of the Masters."

At that, Linden covered her face with her hands.

Relieved and grateful, Covenant went to Bhapa. When the older Cord met his gaze, he said without rancor, "You took a hell of a risk. What were you going to do if it didn't work?"

Bhapa's mouth twisted. He almost smiled. With a hint of his former diffidence, he said, "Timewarden, I would have spoken of you. Your need outweighs my wrath. Had the Ringthane's name failed, yours might have prevailed—though," he admitted ruefully, "in that event the burden of shame would have become mine to bear."

Covenant nodded. Under his breath, he murmured, "You're a brave man. I'm glad you're here. But maybe you should have trusted them with the truth. This"—a twitch of his head indicated the Masters—"isn't settled."

Still Handir and his people said nothing, revealed nothing. They guarded the cave and the company, motionless as graven images while they carried on their mental debate.

Impatient for a decision, the Giants fretted among themselves. While Grueburn and Stonemage spoke in low voices to Bluff Stoutgirth's sailors, telling them more about Bhapa and Pahni, Rime Coldspray approached the Cords. She greeted them kindly in spite of her obvious exasperation, praised their courage, thanked them for their fidelity to Linden. Then, however, she reached the end of her endurance. Striding past the Ramen, she confronted Handir and Canrik, Samil and Vortin.

"Enough of this!" she called so that every Master could hear her. "While you query yourselves, our foes rally against us. Such uncertainty ill becomes you. If you will not stand with us, stand aside. We must attain Kiril Threndor."

"Must we then countenance shame?" snapped Canrik. "Is that your counsel, Giant? You who know nothing of the strictures which form and inform the *Haruchai*?"

· The Ironhand started to retort; but Handir gestured abruptly for silence. Ignoring Coldspray, he faced Covenant across the shining of the *krill*.

"Nonetheless this also is folly." He spoke with his accustomed rigidity—and yet his tone conveyed a cry of protest. "Doubtless Linden Avery has become a rightful white gold wielder. And your endeavors against Corruption have twice exceeded every expectation. Yet when the Worm feeds, wild magic cannot counter it. Only Law can withstand the Earth's destruction, but the Staff is held by a boy who has not mastered it. Why do you wish to expend our lives where no good outcome can be achieved?

"If we must be shamed, we will bear it. We are *Haruchai*. Yet it is cruel—is it not?—to insist upon our service in the name of folly. In the name of futility, ur-Lord. In the name of *waste*."

Covenant grinned at him fiercely. "You tell me. Which would you rather do? Die here fighting Cavewights? Take the chance that something good might happen? Or be swept out of existence while you stand around complaining about waste?"

The Voice of the Masters paused for only a moment. Then he said without inflection, "We will fight."

Covenant clenched his fists; stifled an impulse to punch the air. "Then get me to Kiril Threndor. Protect Linden as long as you can. Keep Jeremiah safe. And brace yourselves. We've already surprised the hell out of Lord Foul. Maybe we'll surprise you, too."

After that, he could no longer contain himself. Turning away from Handir, he shouted at the ceiling, "Did you hear that, you tormented bastard? The *Haruchai* are going to *fight*!"

The Ardent's last service had accomplished its purpose.

9.

Parting Company

Covenant wanted to talk to Linden, remind her that he loved her, do what he could to reassure her. In addition, he meant to check on Jeremiah. The boy's elsewhere gaze was changing: his whole face seemed to be changing. The silted hue of his eyes had acquired a crimson tinge, as if his irises were bleeding. And his visage looked leaner, deprived of its youthfulness by dismay and nascent horror. His hands no longer gripped the Staff tightly, no longer spilled the black flames of his transformed legacy. He may have forgotten that he held it.

As guerdon for his puerile valor—

He was losing his ability to ward himself from visions of the Worm.

Covenant wanted to say something, ask questions, understand; give comfort if he could. But he had no time. While the echoes of his defiance lingered in the cave, the cordon of Masters surged into motion.

Responding to the mental shouts of the sentries, *Haruchai* sprinted toward the chamber's openings. Around the company and the Cords, a few Masters formed a protective circle: Handir and Canrik, Samil and Vortin, Dast and Ulman. Stave held the *krill* high in one hand, hefted Cabledarm's longsword in the other. Branl readied Longwrath's flamberge.

"Cavewights," the Voice of the Masters announced, passionless as stone. "They have massed their forces. Now they advance."

Covenant spun, scanned the entrances. "Where?"

"On all sides, ur-Lord," Branl replied.

Nodding to the Anchormaster, Rime Coldspray and her comrades joined Handir's defensive formation. The sailors arranged themselves to support the Swordmainnir.

"Hellfire!" Covenant's ring itched for use. He felt an irrational desire to fling wild magic at the knuckled ceiling. "Then pick one! Which one goes toward Kiril Threndor?"

Linden's face was pallid with fright as she grasped Jeremiah's arm, prepared herself to pull him into motion.

He threw her off. "Again?" he protested petulantly. Then his voice darkened. "Of course. We're always attacked." He sounded like a different person, someone older, inured to abuse. "Somebody should tell them they're as doomed as we are."

"Jeremiah!" cried Linden softly. "Honey? What's happening to you?"

For an instant, the boy's eyes rolled back in his head. Then he bared his teeth. His gaze came into focus.

"I'm getting it, Mom." Again he sounded different, as if this time he had arisen from some other grave. "I don't care what Stave says. I'll show you."

"We do not know the way," Handir told Covenant. "None here have trod familiar passages. We must estimate our road. We are certain only that Kiril Threndor lies in that direction." He pointed above and behind Covenant. "We will endeavor to clear a path there"—he indicated the tunnel closest to Kiril Threndor's heading—"hoping to encounter other Masters. Their knowledge may extend farther."

"Sure," Jeremiah muttered. "Why not?"

Bhapa and Pahni stood with Stave beside Linden and Jeremiah. The Cords held their garrotes in their fists.

Covenant heard a noise like the sizzle of rain on hot stone: running feet. It swept closer. Before he could respond to Handir, Cavewights charged into the cave on all sides. In an instant, they filled the space with chaos and howling.

They came brandishing spears and truncheons, falchions heavy as spars, axes shaped to behead Giants. They burst into the cave from every entrance in such numbers that they could have inundated their foes, left no one standing.

But they did not come so far. Three strides into the chamber, they crashed like breakers against a seawall of Masters.

Hardly able to understand what he saw, Covenant watched the warriors meet the attack with a fanged front. At each entrance, tight wedges of three or four men bit like teeth into the brunt of the charge. Even as they fell in spurts and gushes of blood, the *Haruchai* drove confusion among the first creatures; forced them to veer away on both sides. Some of the Cavewights tripped over bodies, did not rise again. Others spilled past the formations and scattered their lives against a bulwark of Masters.

The wedges did not hold. They could not. There were too many Cavewights. But the *Haruchai* were at their most devastating when they fought singly. As their front failed, they spun among their assailants, fighting as though carnage exalted them. They leapt and ducked, avoided and struck. Punches snapped arms, broke necks. Kicks dislocated knees, smashed feet. And many of the Masters snatched up weapons. They cut like scythes through the Cavewights, reaping entrails, brains, gore.

Nevertheless the creatures were many; and they had spent millennia nurturing their hatred and savagery, their resentment of peoples who had repeatedly foiled their singular dreams. They fought with the ferocity of beasts. Slaughtered themselves, they delivered slaughter in return. Covenant watched dozens of Masters go down amid scores of Cavewights. Wherever he looked, he seemed to see *Haruchai* killing or crippling creatures—and yet at every moment the Masters were driven back. Axes took heads, ripped torsos. Spears, bludgeons, brutal swords: all wrought havoc. Even the armed warriors died, cut down from behind while they slew the foes in front of them.

Covenant could have stopped this—but only by killing everyone in the cave, rendering every living thing to ash. His thwarted heart burned, accomplishing nothing.

Still more Cavewights surged inward, striding long-legged over the mounting rubble of corpses. Their weapons flung red ruin. Step by step, the fighting closed around the company. Handir prepared his defense. The Swordmainnir waited with their blades poised.

Behind them, Linden and Jeremiah faced each other, apparently arguing. Alarm stretched her features. He gnashed his teeth as if he were biting off hunks of desperation. She may have been shouting—they both may have been shouting—but Covenant could not hear them. Howls and screams deafened him, the sickening sounds of torn flesh, the hard smack of blows, the crack of breaking bones.

As if he were answering his mother, Jeremiah raised the Staff of Law. He held it over his head like a quarterstaff, braced to hammer down fire. The look in his eyes was agony.

Abruptly Branl gripped Covenant's arm, turned him toward the tunnel where Handir had proposed to leave the cave. At the same time, the *Haruchai* between the company and that exit changed their tactics.

Imponderably graceful amid the viciousness and turmoil, those Masters drew back, leaving an open line for the Cavewights, an aisle straight toward the clenched center of the defense.

Covenant thought that he heard Linden yell, "*Now*, Jeremiah!"

Roaring triumph, the creatures rushed forward—

Now or never.

—and Jeremiah swung the Staff.

Black lightning raged from the shaft. Earthpower struck at the Cavewights, fire hot as an inferno. It set them ablaze as if their bones were kindling. Their roars became shrieks. Lit like torches, they blundered away, trying to escape.

More creatures charged. More creatures caught fire. Jeremiah screamed as if his efforts were claws tearing at his heart. His eyes wept anguish. Nevertheless he poured out power in a convulsion of killing.

For a moment—if only for a moment—he cleared a path.

"Now!" Linden cried again. "*Run!*"

This time, she was shouting at the Giants.

The company obeyed. Shielded by Masters and Swordmainnir, and then by the Giants of Dire's Vessel, Branl hauled Covenant forward. With Bhapa and Pahni, Stave herded Linden and Jeremiah. While the surviving *Haruchai* gathered to ward the rear, the Land's defenders dashed along Jeremiah's path.

A moment later, the boy's power failed. He crumpled as if his tendons had been cut. He dropped the Staff: he may have fainted. But Far Horizoneyes snatched him off the floor, cradled him without missing a step. Furledsail grabbed the Staff and kept running.

Cavewights crowded the passage ahead. They had only paused, shocked or startled by screaming. But while they were in the tunnel, their movements were constricted. With Canrik and Samil—with Vortin, Ulman, and Dast—Handir tore into the creatures, broke them like boughs in a rending wind. And those Cavewights that withstood the force of the *Haruchai* fell to the blades of the Swordmainnir.

Trampling bodies, the company gained their exit.

But now the Masters also were hampered. Their speed and agility became less effective. Dodging a spear, Ulman stepped into the stroke of a falchion. The blade opened his side, cut deep enough to reach his spine. He fell, fountaining crimson. The other warriors in the lead survived only because they were supported by the swift skill of the Swordmainnir, the lick and thrust of longswords.

The *Haruchai* holding the rear did so without the aid of battle-trained Giants. The Anchormaster and Frothbreeze gave what aid they could: still the losses among the Masters were grievous. While they struggled against swords and axes, massive clubs, they also had to contend with spears hurled over their heads to strike at Stoutgirth's crew. Leaping to intercept some of those shafts left the Masters defenseless. They were cut down or spitted.

Behind the warriors, Keenreef and Setrock swung their sacks of supplies, blocked spears with bundled waterskins and food.

As the Masters died, the Cavewights drove closer. How many *Haruchai* remained in the rear? Ten? Less?

Covenant heard Scatterwit laughing amid the clamor: a horrific sound, shrill and urgent, feverish as hysteria. It jerked him around to watch as Scatterwit thrust her way among the Masters. Stoutgirth's shout, and Blustergale's, carried after her, but she ignored them.

Lurching on the stump of her ankle, she rushed the Cavewights with her arms spread wide as if she wanted to embrace every creature within reach.

In an instant, the point of a spear jutted from her back. A truncheon crashed onto her left shoulder. An axe bit between her ribs on the right. Her laughing was cut off; but she did not falter. Four, no, five Cavewights she hugged to her chest. Using them as a shield, she drove her great strength and weight against the pursuing creatures.

For a moment, she was impossibly successful. Somehow she cleared a space between her comrades and their foes. Five paces. Seven. Ten. When the blade of an axe came down on her head, spilling brains and ruined bone, she sagged. Still her legs thrust her forward. Supporting herself on the creatures in her arms, she kept fighting.

Then she was done. Strength and life drained out of her: her legs failed: she dropped to her knees. Propped upright by corpses, she knelt there until her foes hacked her to pieces.

Screaming, the Anchormaster tried to follow her. Frothbreeze and Blustergale caught his arms, held him back.

Rage filled Covenant's throat. He could hardly breathe. "The *krill*," he gasped. "I need the *krill*!"

Scatterwit had opened a gap. If he could reach the rear before the Cavewights resumed their advance—

Stave and Branl must have understood him. Without hesitation, Stave slapped the bright *krill* into Covenant's hands. At the same time, Branl moved past Covenant. With one arm, the Humbled parted the sailors so that Covenant could pass.

While Linden cried his name, Covenant brought up a rush of wild magic.

But he did not unleash its raw force. Instead he shaped silver fire along the blade of the *krill*. As he had done against the Sandgorgons, he fashioned an argent sword fierce as the white core of a furnace.

With Branl, he went to meet the Cavewights.

Behind the two men, the rest of the company fled, following Handir's embattled cadre and the striking Swordmainnir. Supported only by the last of the rearguard, Covenant and Branl carried bloodshed among their attackers.

Covenant made no attempt to defend himself. He had no skill, and was burning too hotly to care. He left his own protection to Branl's flamberge, to the fleet prowess of the few Masters. Wielding his chosen theurgy, Covenant became incarnate killing.

With every slash and thrust, every frantic swing, he appalled himself. He had to goad himself with curses like groans in order to keep moving. Otherwise he would have plunged to his knees, crippled by abhorrence. The Cavewights were only simple in their thinking: they were not unintelligent. And they had a long history. On their own terms, they had a civilization. They had never deserved the use which Lord Foul had made of them. They did not deserve what Covenant did to them now.

He promised himself that the Despiser would pay for this; but no promise sufficed to condone such slaughter.

Branl and the Masters exacted their own toll. They were as precise as surgeons, as fluid as wind. But where they cut and blocked, punched and fended, Covenant ravaged.

The Cavewights seemed endless. Those still alive after the struggle in the cave were joined by more issuing from the other passages, entire hordes of creatures mad with blood-lust and ancient resentments. Yet even they could not withstand a blade forged of wild magic that shone like condensed stars. Nor could they match the skill of the *Haruchai*. Their screams and shrieks raced back down the tunnel, pierced the hearts of the Cavewights behind them. Their rage became fear. It became terror and panic. Fighting the press of their fellows, they tried to flee.

At first, they failed. The creatures advancing from the cave were not yet afraid. They resisted the impulse to retreat. But loud desperation filled the passage. It flooded through the Cavewights, carried away their fury. They turned to run, leaving their piled dead to guard their backs.

There Covenant flinched to a halt. His eldritch longsword frayed and faded: the *krill* dangled in his numb clasp. Hellfire, he tried to say. Hell and damnation. But he could not catch his breath. There was no air anywhere. There was only blood.

Blood and bodies, some still writhing in their last throes.

If he had been able to speak, he would have asked Branl and the Masters to forgive him. Of the *Haruchai* guarding the rear, only seven remained; and most of them bore wounds. How many of them had already given their lives? Covenant could not bear to guess.

Surely he had the right to defend himself? To fight for the people he loved, and for their world? Surely the Despiser was responsible for all of this blood?

Of course, Covenant told himself. But the fact of his antagonist's malevolence did not relieve him of culpability. He had done so much of the actual killing—

There was a price for such deeds. He intended to pay it—as soon as he could breathe again. As soon as he found his way to Kiril Threndor.

Without a word, Branl took his arm, urged him into motion. Beyond the *krill*'s reach, the rest of the company had vanished around a bend in the tunnel. But he could still hear fighting. Muffled by distance, blows and yells echoed out of the darkness. Clearly Handir's comrades and the Swordmainnir were able to beat back the Cavewights blocking their path. But the creatures had not given up. They contested every step.

They were not *Haruchai*. They had no way of knowing what Covenant had done— and could do again.

Pulled into a trot, Covenant ran after his wife and his friends, stumbling on his numb feet like a man who had never drawn a clean breath.

Past the bend, he nearly fell when the *krill*'s light revealed the body of a Swordmain among the strewn corpses of Cavewights.

Cirrus Kindwind sprawled against the wall, propped at an awkward angle by a spear driven through one eye and out of the back of her skull. Her longsword lay a few paces away, as if she had tried to throw it with her last strength. Her features had closed around the spear: they held it in place like an act of defiance.

She had been fighting in darkness. Covenant carried the only light.

Blinded by intolerable tears, he ran again, trusting Branl to guide him.

Abruptly the sounds of fighting ahead ceased.

Quiet as the dark, Branl said, "Other Masters have come to assail the Cavewights. The way has been cleared." After a moment's pause, he added, "It will not remain so."

Covenant tried to clear his vision, but he saw no sign of his companions. He found only bodies and spilled fluids rank as offal.

The tunnel turned again. It rose steeply. At the top of the incline, he had to clamber over terrible mounds of the dead. He feared to look at them; feared to see some of Handir's people, another Swordmain, the Cords. Linden or Jeremiah. His friends had been fighting an uphill battle when they were rescued.

Beyond heaps of Cavewights, he caught up with the company.

At first, he could not see past Bluff Stoutgirth and his crew. They had spread out in a wider section of the passage: their tall forms blocked his view. But then the sailors stepped aside, and the *krill*'s silver fell on other survivors.

In the vanguard, the Voice of the Masters stood with Canrik and Dast, Vortin and Samil. They had been joined by nine or ten of their kinsmen. A quick glance showed Covenant a multitude of wounds and stains. Nevertheless all of the *Haruchai* bore themselves as if their hurts were superficial; as if they had not lost scores of their people, and had never known sorrow. Closer to Covenant, still heaving to control their breathing, Frostheart Grueburn, Onyx Stonemage, and Halewhole Bluntfist waited with the Ironhand. Gore streaked their cataphracts: their longswords trembled in hands made weak by weariness. But their injuries looked shallow. Only the darkness in their eyes betrayed the loss of Kindwind.

Stoutgirth's dismay was more overt. His jaws worked as he tried to summon some sound from his throat, some shout or cry which might relieve his pain. Yet he remained mute: a man for whom all laughter had gone out of the world. At his side, Squallish Blustergale wept openly. The other sailors hung their heads in shock and fatigue.

Bhapa and Pahni stood apart from the rest of the company as if they had no place in it. They had not fought. Nor had they known any of the fallen except Cirrus Kindwind. And they were Ramen, lost without open skies to unfetter their spirits.

Among the Giants, Covenant found Linden and Jeremiah with Stave.

The boy was conscious now; on his feet. He had reclaimed the Staff of Law. Holding it upright, he scowled at his hands as they moved over the shaft, tracing the runes as if he were searching the written wood for the answers to questions which he did not know how to ask. He did not glance up when Covenant arrived. His concentration excluded everyone.

But Linden's gaze leapt at once to her husband. Her mouth shaped his name.

The sight of her made Covenant feel like weeping again. He recognized the complex consternation in her eyes: fear for her son and her friends, and more particularly for him, combined with a flagrant dread which had not yet become resolve. And something else, a kind of horror—

Until he saw her expression, he did not realize that he was drenched in blood.

He went to her at once. But he did not touch her; foul her. He did not dare. His hands made truncated gestures, then fell back to his sides. The *krill* in his grasp cast cavorting shadows that seemed to mock the faces around him.

Linden's mouth repeated his name. Thomas. And again, Thomas.

Handir moved among the Giants toward him. "Ur-Lord," said the Voice of the Masters, "we must not delay. Two paths to Kiril Threndor are now known." He must have acquired them from the minds of the newcomers. "One is the more direct. It is also the more perilous. If we must, we will attempt it. We await only your word."

Jeremiah stamped the Staff on the stone. His voice cracked. "We don't have time. Don't you understand? The whole *mountain* is coming down." He did not look up from his hands. "The Worm doesn't even feel it."

Covenant groaned. *Melenkurion* Skyweir was falling like Kevin's Watch. Hellfire—

Linden studied her son. Her face twisted. Then an obstacle within her seemed to break; or perhaps she pushed it aside. She went to Covenant, threw her arms around his neck, pressed all of herself against his soaked T-shirt and jeans as if she ached to embrace his sins, his accused soul.

"Thomas," she breathed in his ear. "Oh, Thomas."

"Ur-Lord," Handir repeated more loudly.

Covenant dropped the *krill* so that he could wrap his remaining strength around his wife. What else could he do? He had no words for his distress; no language that might soothe his clawed heart. He was going to lose her. The Worm was making his choices for him.

"Are you sure about this?" Linden asked in an aching whisper. "I mean about Kiril

Threndor?" She may have meant, About everything? "Are you sure that Lord Foul
is there?"

Are you sure that you want to face him?

"Of course he is." Covenant clung to her acceptance. "Or he will be when I get
there. Where else would he be? Sure, he wants us all dead." All except Jeremiah. The
Despiser had probably laid a *geas* on the Cavewights so that Jeremiah would be
spared. "But if that doesn't work, he wants me to find him. He wants the pleasure of
finishing me."

So softly that Covenant barely heard her, Linden murmured, "Then help me. I
can't do this."

He wanted to tell her, You can. You're the only one who can. But he did not. She
had heard his professions of faith often enough.

"Ur-Lord!" insisted Handir; but Covenant was not listening. He was already covered in blood. It was too late to count the cost. Maybe someday he would be
forgiven.

He released Linden. When she loosened her arms, he stepped away from her to
confront Jeremiah. Deliberately he placed himself in front of the boy, braced his
empty fists on his hips.

"Can you hear me?" he demanded. "I need you. You have to hear me. I need your
help."

Linden might rally if he could show her that her son was not as lost as he
looked.

Jeremiah did not glance up from the Staff. Shadows seemed to redefine his face.
In a caustic tone, as if he were speaking for the *croyel*, he snarled, "Then you might as
well give up. I can't even *see* you. I can't see anything. The Worm is under that mountain. That's all there is."

Thinking, Forgive me, Covenant barked, "*Jeremiah!* Snap out of it! You think this
is bad? It's going to get worse. Have you forgotten? Foul wants to *use* you. He's going
to do you more damage than you can imagine."

The boy flinched as if Covenant had struck him. Darkness writhed across his
visage.

"Thomas!" Linden objected.

Covenant ignored her.

"Right now, he's just softening you up. Soon he'll get serious. He'll try to tear you
apart, turn you inside out, hurt you so much you'll be *eager* to do what he wants. If
you don't help me, he wins."

Linden tried to come between Covenant and Jeremiah. Stave held her back. The
spurned *Haruchai* seemed to understand—

Jeremiah looked like he wanted to weep. In a different voice, abused and abject, he whimpered, "I can't—"

As if he had lost patience, Covenant retorted, "You *can*. You have that right. You were *born* with it. All you have to do is choose," *must* or *cannot*. He pushed his fingers through his hair, tried to harden his heart. Deliberately harsh, he rasped, "Otherwise you might as well go back into hiding. You'll be useless."

Slowly Jeremiah's silted gaze settled into focus on Covenant. He seemed to return from some other dimension of reality; some private hell. When it came, his answer was distinct.

"I don't want to go back there."

Covenant felt like cheering. Grimly he stifled the impulse. "Then trust yourself. Trust the Staff. There's a way to fight back. You just have to find it.

"And remember I need you. You might do something better than surprising the Despiser. You might surprise yourself."

"Ur-Lord," Handir demanded, peremptory as a cudgel. "Do you not hear me? Every delay is fatal. You must select a path."

Still Covenant ignored the Voice of the Masters. He had to face Linden.

She was glaring at him, furious and bitter. Her hands clenched as if she wanted to hit him. He had hurt her son.

Before she could speak, he said harshly, "Maybe I'm wrong." With the fingers of his halfhand, he massaged the scar on his forehead. "Maybe I'm not. Look at him. What do you see?"

For a moment longer, her indignation raked Covenant; but she could not refuse him.

When she focused her senses on Jeremiah, her eyes went wide. Realizations scudded across the background of her gaze. In a startled tone, she breathed, "You brought him back."

Covenant nodded. He felt suddenly drained, weak in every limb, as if he had passed a test which might have broken him.

To Handir, he said in a wan voice, "The direct road. Jeremiah is right. We don't have time for anything else."

He knew what *direct* meant. It would require more killing.

Rime Coldspray stood over the old *Haruchai*. "If the path is perilous," she asked, "what form do its hazards take?"

Handir frowned up at her. "For a portion of its length, Ironhand, we will be exposed to assault on all sides."

She snarled a curse. Then she gave Covenant a look full of reflected argent. "Aye, Timewarden. If we must kill and die, then let us do so swiftly and be done."

At once, she turned to the sailors. Sure of herself now, she told them to help the Masters guard the rear of the company.

Branl had retrieved the *krill*. As he restored it to Covenant, he said, "Be wary, ur-Lord. Your son has not yet opposed us. *Moksha* Raver remains. And we do not doubt that Corruption has other servants."

With a mental command, Handir sent the newly arrived Masters to support the sailors. Joined by Canrik and Dast, Samil and Vortin, he started along the passage. The Swordmainnir followed at his back. Gesturing for the Cords, Covenant accompanied Branl. Stave urged Linden and Jeremiah forward.

Through the thick midnight of the Wightwarrens, Covenant bore the only light. He tried to hold it steady, but his arm wavered like his thoughts. Be wary. Roger and Cavewights and *moksha* Jehannum. Cirrus Kindwind. Baf Scatterwit. Scores of slain *Haruchai*. And for what? Not for him. Not even for Linden. Lord Foul was not afraid of them. He believed that he had already triumphed. Nothing that they did could stop the Worm.

No, it was all for Jeremiah: all the threats and bloodshed, all the striving and woe. So that the Despiser would be able to take him.

Covenant could only pray that Jeremiah would eventually find a way to resist.

§

Before long, the company's progress became a running battle, frantic and almost continuous. The tunnel branched more frequently, intersected other passages; and at almost every junction, massed Cavewights waited, or small bands of Masters, or both.

With their acquired weapons—heavy falchions, spears nearly as tall as Giants, axes that Covenant could not have lifted—Handir, Canrik, and their comrades led the way. Deceptively swift, they slipped among their foes, slashing or stabbing at exposed limbs, throats, groins. Together they disrupted one attack after another.

And behind them came the Swordmainnir. Rime Coldspray and her women fought in a kind of fury, pitiless and brutal. Their blades flung blood. Crimson stained the air, streaked the walls, glazed the floor. They wore it as if it nauseated them, but they did not falter.

Cavewights went down, screaming or already dead. *Haruchai* fell as well. New warriors joined the company. Together they hastened from one struggle to the next.

For the time being, at least, Lord Foul's forces did not attack from the rear. Masters reported that Cavewights crowded the tunnel behind them; but the creatures appeared content to follow at a distance. They feared Covenant's wild blade—or they desired a surer chance to strike.

Guiding by newly acquired memories, the Voice of the Masters turned left at one branching, passed straight through two intersections, angled sharply to the right at a third. The passage lurched upward in stages like terraces. The cries of the dying trailed like spectres behind the company.

Thirty or more *Haruchai* had now joined the company. The losses of the Cavewights were far greater. But there were thousands of Cavewights. Tens of thousands. At present, the tunnels themselves were the company's best defense. Covenant and his companions survived primarily because Handir's route avoided another open killing field like the cave.

At Covenant's side, Linden hurried as if she were hunkering down inside herself, trying to make herself too small for her fears to find her. Nevertheless she remained Linden Avery. With Jeremiah's consent, she borrowed Earthpower from the Staff at intervals and spread it among the Giants, fed vitality to Covenant's dwindling reserves. To Bhapa and Pahni, she offered the same gift; but they declined it. They were Ramen. They could have run through these passages indefinitely, fleet as horses in spite of their loathing for enclosed spaces.

To the Masters, she gave nothing. She knew better.

Along the way, Jeremiah made his own use of Staff-fire. Instead of extending flames outward, however, he appeared to draw them into himself. They ran up his arms as if he intended to broil his own skin, excoriate himself. Then they faded into his chest. And as he absorbed the Staff's magicks, his eyes darkened until they seemed to refuse light. They glittered at Covenant's silver like chunks of obsidian.

Covenant had no idea what the boy was trying to accomplish, but he did not question it. He had provoked this reaction. Now he had to trust it.

The gem's shining restricted his view ahead, but he thought that he saw—

Abruptly he lowered the dagger, shaded it with his free hand. "Branl?" He was breathing too hard to articulate a question. "Branl?"

"Indeed, ur-Lord," the Humbled replied as though he understood.

There: in the distance above Covenant, beyond the dark shapes of the Swordmainnir hastening upward temporarily unopposed: a faint glow. Reddish, but not crimson; warmer and more yellow than the laval eyes of the Cavewights. It seemed to flicker as Giants interrupted it, but Covenant could guess what it was.

Then Linden grabbed his arm, breathed his name; and he was sure.

Rocklight. The company was approaching one of the lit regions of the Wightwarrens.

The glow grew stronger. Summoned by Handir, Masters from the rear ran past

Covenant and Linden, Jeremiah and the Cords. Fresh rage and iron rang along the passage. Hard impacts. A rabid stutter of screams, howls, frenzy.

"We will ward you," Stave said suddenly, "but you must also defend yourselves. A multitude awaits us." He touched Jeremiah's shoulder. "Do you hear, Chosen-son? You must turn your thoughts to our peril. It may be that our lives will require your aid."

"What do you want from me?" Jeremiah panted. "More killing? That's not what Law is for. I can't forget the Worm. I'm not strong enough."

Linden regarded him with desperation in her eyes.

"Then don't worry about it," said Covenant between sickened breaths. "You're getting ready for a different kind of fight." As was Linden. "Leave this one to the rest of us."

To Giants and *Haruchai*. And to Covenant himself, who had already shed enough blood to drown him.

He gave himself no other choice. In a former life, he had turned his back on power. Now he demanded it of himself.

Rocklight washed over him. Rime Coldspray and her comrades passed an opening, spread out to both sides. Blows and shouts pounded down the tunnel, but the sounds were strangely muffled. A gulf seemed to swallow their force.

Straining for air, Covenant went a step or two ahead of Linden and Jeremiah; ahead of Stave. The *krill* he held at his side so that it would not blind him. With Branl, Bhapa, and Pahni, he drove his weakness out of the tunnel onto a ledge as wide as an avenue.

There he found himself facing a rocklit chasm.

It was not a fault or flaw in the gutrock, although it resembled a crevice: long and high, but not wide, little more than a stone's throw from wall to wall. Rather it had been fashioned, dug out over centuries or millennia. The ruddy light everywhere testified to the effort and theurgy which had formed the space. Overhead, and to left and right, it stretched beyond the reach of Covenant's dimmed sight. But when he moved closer to the rim of the ledge, he could see the bottom of the excavation: a crude trough crowded with debris, as full of refuse as a midden.

In spite of Stave's warning, he stopped and stared, momentarily unable to do anything except look. For a few heartbeats, he forgot fighting; forgot his peril entirely. He needed time to comprehend what he saw.

A ledge opposite him resembled the one where he stood. It was the lowest of five, six, no seven levels like communal passages, each carved into the wall two or three Giant-heights above the next. And at the back of each horizontal cut, each shaped road, were openings like doorways. They measured out the chasm in both directions at intervals of perhaps twenty paces. Stone doors closed some of them. Others stood open, revealing lit chambers.

Habitations. Covenant could hardly think. He struggled for air as if he were inhaling dismay. Dwellings. Homes.

Homes implied families. Families implied children.

There were hundreds of doorways near enough for his failing vision; and the chasm was long. If the wall where the company had emerged mirrored the one across from it, the space held thousands.

Thousands of homes. The Cavewightish version of a city.

Ah, hell. Covenant had brought bloodshed to a place where the creatures were vulnerable, where their mates and children could be killed. A place which they would defend for reasons better than obedience to the Despiser.

Everywhere he looked, he saw Cavewights mustering. On every level, armed bands gathered and ran, converging—

Any uncontrolled wild magic here would incinerate children.

—on bridges that spanned the chasm.

Hellfire! There were dozens of the damn things, wrought granite roads as wide as the ledges. A few stretched straight across, level to level; but most of them arced, connecting the walls at differing heights. On Covenant's left, the nearest bridge reached to the third level opposite it: another farther away on his right extended to the fourth. An elaborate and apparently random network of spans crisscrossed the space, giving every ledge access—direct or indirect—to every other.

And on every bridge, Cavewights raced across the air, rushing to give battle.

—*exposed to assault on all sides.* Bloody damnation!

Covenant wheeled on Branl. "We have to get out of here! These are their homes! We can't start killing their *children*!"

The Humbled shrugged. "We do what we must. Foes now throng the passage at our backs. We have sacrificed the choice of retreat.

"Our path lies there." He pointed to the nearest bridge. "From the third level opposite, we must cross to the fifth above us. At that height, a passage leads toward Kiril Threndor. Its constriction will defend us once again."

"Then *run*!" Covenant yelled. "Before they can stop us!"

He could not unleash wild magic here. Even to save the Earth, he could not.

"Thomas!" Linden clutched his arm, tugged at him. "Look!"

For an instant, his mind reeled. Then he dragged his attention away from possibilities which horrified him.

On both sides, his companions were already fighting.

To the left, the Ironhand and Frostheart Grueburn slashed like furies through the press of Cavewights. Among them, Handir and half a dozen Masters dodged and struck. Onyx Stonemage and Halewhole Bluntfist had gone to the right. With more *Haruchai*, they held their ground against three times as many creatures. The cacophony of battle was terrible. It seemed more terrible because it dissipated in the high chasm as if it were meaningless.

The Giants of Dire's Vessel had arrived behind Covenant. The last six or seven Masters prepared to block the tunnel, protect the rear of the company.

Now Covenant spotted more Masters on the levels above him: groups of four widely scattered. They were too few to save his companions; too far away.

"*Coldspray!*" he cried as if he were falling.

The Ironhand and Handir exchanged shouts. Coldspray bellowed commands at Bluff Stoutgirth. The Anchormaster answered with curses. His glare held madness.

Clutching their unfamiliar weapons, the sailors charged to the right. With strength and mass, if not with skill, they rushed to support Stonemage and Bluntfist.

Bhapa and Pahni hesitated for a moment, spoke to each other. Then they followed the Anchormaster.

Together *Haruchai*, Giants, and Ramen began to force the Cavewights backward.

At the same time, Coldspray and Grueburn appeared to redouble their efforts. They chopped down creatures, tore through flesh and bone, flung bodies off the ledge. Handir and Canrik fought as one, striking high and low simultaneously. Samil and Dast knocked Cavewights off their feet. Vortin and his comrades broke necks, cracked skulls, disabled limbs.

For a moment, Covenant did not understand. The Ironhand had divided the company. Surely she had made it weaker? But then he realized that she had also divided the Cavewights. They were fighting for their homes now, not for Lord Foul. They rushed to oppose two threats instead of one.

Near Covenant, Coldspray's tactics seemed to accomplish nothing. Only savage fighting pushed the creatures back.

Nevertheless fewer foes gathered on the bridges which the company had to cross.

Coldspray and Grueburn gained the foot of the nearest span, the shallow arc to the third level. Handir and his warriors fought to secure the Ironhand's position.

Cavewights tried to burst from the tunnel at Covenant's back. Masters repulsed them.

Branl hauled Covenant after Coldspray. Covenant caught Linden's hand, pulled her with him. Stave brought Jeremiah.

"Mom!" Covenant could barely hear the boy. "What do you want me to do?"

"Stay with Stave!" she called back. "He'll tell you!"

Coldspray and Grueburn started onto the bridge. Ahead of them, a fresh onslaught of Cavewights came howling down the span. Branl and Stave followed the two Swordmainnir with Covenant, Linden, and Jeremiah. Somehow Handir and his comrades finished their immediate foes.

Swift as swords, Handir and Canrik ran to join the Ironhand. Dast and Samil. Vortin and a few *Haruchai* guarded the rear.

At the mouth of the tunnel, Masters died one by one. Numberless Cavewights gained the ledge. Some sped after the group escorting Covenant. Others pursued the sailors.

With Bhapa and Pahni, warriors reached the crossing to the fourth level. Stoutgirth and his crew fought as if they were caught in a hurricane. Stumbling on a slashed leg, Far Horizoneyes fell from the ledge. Blustergale scattered creatures with every swipe of his spear. Stoutgirth's shouts sounded like hysteria as he herded his crew onto the bridge.

Coldspray and Grueburn surged upward. Confusion spun through Covenant, lethal as vertigo, fatal as blades. The chasm gaped below him. It breathed his name. If Branl and Linden had not held him—

Dizzy and wandering, he followed the Swordmainnir.

They were still a dozen strides away from a collision with charging Cavewights when other creatures began to fling spears from the upper levels.

Partially protected by their cataphracts, the Ironhand and Frostheart Grueburn did not pause. Cursing fiercely, Coldspray hastened to meet her foes. Grueburn slapped shafts aside with her longsword or her open hand.

Handir and his warriors formed a shield around Covenant, Linden, and Jeremiah. The *Haruchai* countered a barrage of throws. Handir caught one spear, blocked another. A third pierced his chest, cast him silent as a stone into the chasm.

Snagging shafts from the air, Canrik and the other Masters advanced as though their leader's death changed nothing. When one of Vortin's comrades mistimed a catch and was gutted, none of the warriors flinched.

Covenant felt the shock as Rime Coldspray crashed against the torrent of Cavewights. She should have fallen: the impact would have split a slab of marble. Yet she stood. At her back, Grueburn braced her with one hand—and Canrik, Dast, and Samil attacked as if they were born to the use of weapons—

—and the enfilade of spears stopped. The creatures thronging along both walls could not throw now without hitting their own kind.

Cavewights plunged like detritus from the bridge as Coldspray and Grueburn powered ahead.

Out of the heights, a boulder struck the span where the sailors and the Cords raced upward. Bouncing away, the stone took two Masters with it.

After that, Covenant lost sight of Stoutgirth and the others. He hardly knew where he was. His boots skidded in blood: he could not imagine how Branl and Linden kept him on his feet. His mind was whirling madness. He seemed to rise borne on a gyre of carnage.

Then he was gasping on the flat shelf of the third level, and Linden was shouting his name, urgent as fever, and the bridge back across the gulf to the fifth level was only a dozen paces away. Cavewights came from both directions, but he had no time for them. He caught his balance on the sight of the span he had just crossed. Up the curve slick with slaughter, more Cavewights rose like executioners; like deserved death. They poured from the passage where the company had entered this habitation, gushed upward in a flood released by the dying of Masters.

They were too many. That was all: they were just too many. The Swordmainnir and the *Haruchai* were already fighting desperately, drenched in blood. Trusting Covenant, Linden, and Jeremiah to Stave, Branl sprinted to support his kinsmen. Jeremiah trembled on the verge of panic, ready to hurl black devastation in all directions. Linden stood with him, but she looked lost, unable to help him: appalled or paralyzed. A deranged part of Covenant wanted to demolish the whole place, children and families and everything living. He and his companions could not survive *more* Cavewights.

Suddenly calm, almost at peace with his dizziness, he went to face the creatures rising in rage up the bridge. Once again, he shaped wild magic along the blade of the *krill*, formed a longsword of fierce argent. With it, he began hacking great hunks of granite out of the span.

When the Cavewights there saw what he was doing, they froze.

Three blows cut halfway through the indurated substance of the bridge. The fourth sent shivers down its length. The stone screamed at its own weight.

Shrieking, the creatures turned to flee. Most of them reached the lower ledge before the bridge fell in thunder. The rest plummeted.

Still swinging, Covenant nearly followed the wreckage into the depths. Stave dragged him back.

Covenant did not pause. Every thought was gone from his head: every notion or awareness except a compulsory desire to get his people out of here. He would never rid himself of the taste of blood. Brandishing slaughter, he ran to help his companions reach the next bridge.

✵

H e and those with him were only able to gain the fifth level because new groups of Masters entering the habitation converged where they were needed. Fresh and unbloodied, they threw their lives into the mass of Cavewights.

They were *Haruchai*. In a distant region of the Land, two hundred of them rode to oppose the Worm of the World's End with their bare hands. Fighting and dying like men who had never known fear and did not count the cost, they helped Rime Coldspray and Frostheart Grueburn clear the top of the span.

Of the Masters ascending with the Swordmainnir, only Canrik and Samil remained. Branl alone guarded the rear, contesting every step with Longwrath's flamberge. Somehow Stave kept spears away from Covenant, Linden, and Jeremiah.

Fortunately the tunnel toward Kiril Threndor was near. And the Cavewights blocking the way had been scattered by unexpected Masters. From the opposite wall, more creatures came, loud as thunder, vehement as lightning; but most of them were not close enough to strike.

Still they were too many, as they had been from the first. They would follow the company into the passage ahead. Eventually they would kill everyone.

At Canrik's urging, Coldspray and Grueburn led their companions into the blind dark of the tunnel. He and Samil joined Branl and Stave guarding the rear. The surviving Masters arrayed themselves at the opening, braced to die so that the Cavewights could not pursue.

"No," Covenant panted at them. "Come with us."

He had seen too many *Haruchai* killed.

Branl silenced him. "Will you seal the passage, ur-Lord?"

Covenant struggled to breathe. "Yes."

He could not have done so in the earlier tunnels. The company might have needed to retreat. Now he had gained a path to the Despiser. There was no going back.

"Then," said Branl flatly, "these Masters will aid the other Giants and the Cords."

Covenant tried to move; tried to lift the *krill*. Are you serious? You want me to leave them out there? His arms refused to obey him until the warriors outside the tunnel met his frantic gaze and nodded their approval.

Even here, they made their own choices. He could not gainsay them.

Groaning curses, he forged fire along the blade of Loric's dagger for the last time. Unsteady as a man who had forgotten the use of his limbs, he slashed silver at the walls and then the ceiling. With wild magic, he cut down great chunks of stone until the passage was sealed.

After that, he collapsed inwardly. He could still walk, still go where he was guided; but he could not think or speak. Images of slaughter filled his head. Wounds gaped at him like the grins of ghouls. The tumult of falling stone volleyed against the boundaries of his mind. So much killing. So many dead. And he had lost the sailors. He had lost everyone with them.

He had brought carnage into the dwelling-place of the Cavewights: just one more item on the long list of his crimes.

What was it all for? Covenant knew his own reasons, but Lord Foul's daunted him. The Worm could not be stopped. At last, the Despiser could be sure of his long-sought freedom. Then why had he been so profligate with the lives of his servants? Did he simply *enjoy* sacrificing them? Or did he secretly fear that Covenant might yet find a way to thwart him?

No. The Despiser knew Covenant too well.

But Lord Foul did not know Linden and Jeremiah: not with the same intimacy. The fane which had preserved the *Elohim* and delayed the Worm demonstrated that he had underestimated Covenant's wife and her adopted son. Without their efforts, their opposition, he might already have escaped the Arch of Time.

Maybe that explained the brutality of his defenses.

The tunnel rose. Dragging the weight of his sins behind him, Covenant trudged upward.

At his side, Linden stared ahead, wide-eyed as a woman who saw a holocaust waiting for her. Jeremiah wrung the Staff as though he wanted to twist it apart. His every step was a flinch. Leading their few companions, Coldspray and Grueburn slumped like derelicts. Only Stave and Branl, Canrik and Samil paced the ascent like men who could not be appalled by any sacrifice.

A rift cut across the tunnel. It split the floor as though it had been made by an axe sharp enough to wound mountains. It yawned at Covenant, too black to be relieved by the *krill*'s shining. But it was thin: a fracture no wider than his thigh. Pretending to ignore it, he stepped across.

More fissures appeared. They were little more than cracks, yet they served to remind him of the times when violence had torn through Kiril Threndor, Heart of Thunder.

He was getting close—

When the Giants halted, he nearly walked into them. Blinking and stupefied, he looked around.

They had entered a chamber like an exaggerated vesicle, a natural formation left behind by some accident of volcanism. The passage continued, but Coldspray and Grueburn stood wavering as if they had come to the end of themselves: they looked like they wanted to lie down. The cavity was more than large enough to accommodate them prone. It could have held a dozen sleeping Giants.

To one side rested a pair of large boulders. They seemed strangely out of place. Covenant could not imagine how they had come to be here. But plenty of room remained, and the floor was approximately level. When he found himself swaying on his feet, he realized that he was tired enough to stretch out and rest in spite of the Earth's peril.

And yet his weariness was a drop in the ocean of Coldspray's and Grueburn's exhaustion. Even the *Haruchai* were probably worn down, although they concealed it.

Grueburn's longsword dangled from her fingers. "Is it conceivable," she asked, plaintive as the cry of a distant tern, "that we are done with combat? I cannot raise my arms."

"'The mightiest of the Swordmainnir,'" muttered Coldspray dully. "So I have vaunted myself, and so I am. Behold." She lifted her glaive. "My hand is firm." It shook like a dying leaf. "My eye is keen." Fatigue glazed her gaze. "Beyond question, I am—" Abruptly she dropped her sword. Her shoulders slumped. "Stone and Sea! I am undone by woe and killing. I cannot spit out the taste of blood. It will fill my mouth to the end of my days."

Sighing, Covenant roused himself enough to respond, "Join the club."

Jeremiah said nothing. He appeared to have lost interest in everything except his ambiguous struggle with the Staff of Law. Folding his legs, he settled himself against one wall, sat cross-legged with the black wood resting across his thighs. His head he kept bowed as if he did not want anyone to see the darkness deepening in his eyes.

Linden studied him for a moment, then turned away. She had spent too long clenched inside herself; too long crowded with needs and fears which she had not allowed herself to express. She was a rightful white gold wielder: for hours now, she could have struck her own blows. Yet she had contained herself, passive as dust amid the winds of battle. Somehow she had withheld—

But I'm done fighting.

In spite of endless provocations, she had kept faith with her decision. The cost of so much restraint must have been severe. Now she seemed ready to explode.

Nevertheless her voice stayed clenched as she asked the Ironhand, "What about the others? We left them to die."

Her bitterness resembled the edges of Longwrath's sword.

Coldspray shook her head. "They will not perish while they are able to fight and flee." She spoke as if she sought to reassure herself. "Having lost us, they will retreat for their lives. My commands were plain. And Halewhole Bluntfist and Onyx Stonemage are Swordmainnir. They comprehend that they must not sacrifice the Anchormaster's crew and the Masters of the Land—and assuredly not the Ramen Cords—to no purpose. Rather they will seek an egress from the habitation."

Then her tone frayed. It seemed to tear. "Now we have played our part. Ask no more of us. We can go no farther."

Once before, Covenant had seen despair in the eyes of a Giant, when Saltheart Foamfollower had tasted the ecstasy of killing Cavewights—and had found that he wanted to kill more. That despair had kept Foamfollower alive when all of his people were murdered. Coldspray's surrender, and Grueburn's, made Covenant want to weep.

He drew a shuddering breath. Well, then, he told himself. This is as good a place as any.

Hell and blood.

To the Ironhand, he said, "Don't worry about it. You've brought us far enough. Nobody could have done more."

Then, wincing inwardly, he told Linden, "If you're going to do it, now's the time. You won't get another chance."

On the walls, silver made dark streaks like the ichor of mountains.

Alarm flared across her face as she turned to him; but she did not protest. Instead she tightened her grip on herself, increased the pressure until it threatened to break her. "Already?" she asked without hope or humor. "Are you sure? I still want to live."

Her gaze said, I still want to live with you.

"Kiril Threndor isn't far." Covenant choked for a moment. He had to swallow a rush of grief. "You can't go there with me. Neither can Jeremiah. This is it."

As if he were asking for forgiveness, he added, "I'll take Branl. Jeremiah will have Stave and Canrik and Samil."

She looked away. Her eyes avoided Coldspray and Grueburn as if she felt shamed by the prices which they had paid for her. Instead she regarded her son again.

To no one in particular, she said, "All right. I chose this. Some of those poor Masters might still be alive if I had made a different choice." She seemed to choke momentarily. "Or Baf Scatterwit. Cirrus Kindwind. God, I loved her—

"Losing them will be wasted if I change my mind now."

Covenant's vision blurred. He squeezed his eyes shut to clear them. Taunting her, Lord Foul had called Linden his *daughter*. He was wrong.

From the floor, Jeremiah asked suddenly, "What're you talking about?"

Linden did not let herself look away. "Jeremiah, honey—" Her voice was breaking. "I have to go."

In one motion, Jeremiah surged to his feet, lifted his gaze into the light of the *krill*. His eyes were as black as the Staff. Even the whites had become midnight.

"Go where?"

"I can't put it off any longer." She sounded tight enough to snap. "I need to face the only thing that scares me worse than losing you. You and Thomas."

His face twisted. Protests clawed at his features. "But you'll come back," he said as if that were not a question. "That's what you do. You come back."

She flinched—but she did not falter. "I don't think so, honey. Not this time."

Jeremiah stared horror at her. "You're going to leave me? You're going to let Lord Foul have me?"

"No, Jeremiah." Her tone sharpened. "I'm not going to *let* him anything. But I can't fight him for you. Even if I took back the Staff and stood right in front of you, I couldn't help you." More gently, she said, "I wish that I could spare you, but I can't. If you don't want him to take you, you have to stop him yourself.

"I know it's hard—"

Her son cut her off. Vicious as a denunciation, he sneered, "'I know it's hard.' You keep saying that. You don't know anything. I've already tried to fight. I'm not strong enough. The *croyel* thought I was easy. How am I supposed to stop the Despiser?"

Linden shook her head. Her distress made Covenant ache. "I don't know. But I believe in you. You can do it."

"I *can't!*" His shout was like the tearing of flesh, full of pain and awash with blood. "I'll have to watch the Worm destroy *everything!*"

Covenant's balance shifted. Only grief kept him from dropping to his knees. Only a whetted empathy kept him from raging at Jeremiah. But grief and empathy were enough. He braced himself on them when everything else spun away.

"You can always decide to give up," he said as if he were steady and sure; as if he had strength to spare. "You have that right. If it's what you really want." Or the boy could join Lord Foul. "But I need you. I'm going to need you absolutely. And Linden can't help me. Nobody else can. There's only you.

"But first we have to let Linden go."

Jeremiah flung a look black enough to kill at Covenant.

A heartbeat later, the boy turned his back on his mother.

"Then go." He sounded as lightless and fatal as the path toward Kiril Threndor. "You never loved me anyway. I was just an excuse. You don't want to have to blame yourself for letting me put my hand in that bonfire."

"Jeremiah—" Linden was weeping now. "Honey—"

Ah, hell, Covenant thought. Visions of the Worm had raised all of Jeremiah's demons. He had spent days suppressing them. They ruled him now. Deliberately he sat down again, put his back to his mother; to Covenant and their companions. His hands wrestled ebon flames along the wood of the Staff as if he wanted to rewrite Caerroil Wildwood's runes.

Maybe we should all try to become gods.

The Giants watched blank-eyed, caked in drying blood, mute as cenotaphs. Branl studied Jeremiah with a speculative frown, as if he were considering where to cut the boy.

Covenant gave the *krill* to Stave. Then he took Linden's arm and pulled her away. While she stifled sobs against his chest, he held her tight.

With as much tenderness as he could manage, he promised quietly, "I'll talk to him, love. He doesn't know it yet, but he's just proving your point. You can't do his fighting for him. No matter what happens to him, he's the only one who can do anything about it."

"Oh, Thomas." Distress shuddered through her, harsh as spasms. "I'm so scared. What if he gets it wrong?"

For a moment, she could not go on. She slumped against Covenant as if she had lost the will to stand on her own.

He hugged her in silence. He had no words—

But gradually she responded to his embrace; drew a steadier breath. Freeing one arm, she wiped her face, smeared tears and blood across her cheeks. "And I swore that I would love you as long as you never let me go. Now I'm the one who's leaving. I have to let both of you go."

Covenant held her as hard as he could. "I understand. You can't get rid of me this easy." Then he said more seriously, "In any case, I'm like you. I believe in Jeremiah. He has to feel this way. If he doesn't, he won't ever get past it."

At one time, Covenant himself had embraced despair—

"Also," Stave put in like a man who had been biding his time and was done with patience, "you will not depart alone." The *krill* shone full on his face; on the scar of his lost eye. "Linden Avery, I have said that I will not be parted from you again. The Chosen-son I entrust to Canrik and Samil, and to the Swordmainnir. You I will accompany."

Surprise seemed to loosen some of Linden's tension: surprise or relief. She ignored the former Master long enough to kiss Covenant quickly, wipe her face again. Then she turned to Stave.

"Do you know where I'm going?"

"Mayhap." Stave may have smiled. "Or mayhap I am mistaken. I care naught. At one time, I declared that Desecration lies ahead of you. Now I am persuaded that there is no Desecration in you. I will not stand at your side to ward against you. I will do so because I have not learned humility, though you have endeavored to teach me. I crave further instruction."

His assertion sounded like an example of *Haruchai* humor.

Linden tried to say his name. Apparently she could not. Instead she went to him, put her arms around his neck.

Past her hair, Stave met Covenant's gaze. "You have wed well, Timewarden," he said as if his characteristic stoicism had become a form of jesting. "I will strive to ensure her return."

Covenant nodded. What could he have said? There were no words in all the world for his gratitude.

When Linden released the former Master, he returned Loric's dagger to the Unbeliever.

Covenant took it; gripped it. His throat was as tight as his grasp on the *krill*. He had to force himself to ask Linden, "Are you ready?"

The corner of her mouth twisted: a failed smile that nearly broke his heart. "I'm never ready. I've given up waiting for it."

He rubbed his scar roughly, tried to compose himself. "Then remember I love you. I *love* you.

"And don't worry about Jeremiah. You did your part. I refuse to believe anything you did for him is wasted. The rest is up to us."

Her mouth said, "I'll try." Her eyes said, Thomas of my heart.

The Giants offered her no farewell. Frostheart Grueburn set her teeth on her lower lip: a woman stifling protests. Tears streamed openly down her cheeks. Rime Coldspray hung her head as if she could not bear her weariness—or her dismay.

Jeremiah did not look at any of them.

Together Linden and Stave moved to a clear space a few steps from the walls and the Swordmainnir. There they waited like contradictions or counterweights. His poised relaxation balanced her trembling tension. After a moment's consideration, he tossed Cabledarm's sword to Canrik. No weapon would serve him now.

Grim as a deliverer of damnation, Covenant stood beyond Linden's reach. He could not afford to hesitate now. He had no time; and his resolve might fail at any delay. He knew where she was going. He was more afraid for her than he was for himself.

As if he had begun preparing for this days ago, he gave fresh wild magic to the dagger's gem and thrust the blade into the stone between his boots. When the hard surface caught silver, he dragged the *krill* to the side, cutting granite like damp clay. Step by step, he sliced a circle around Linden and Stave.

Along the line of his cut, his power shone as if rock were the fuel for which it yearned.

He did not need a large circle to enclose his wife and the former Master. In spite of his awkwardness and grieving, he returned to his starting point quickly. Then he forced himself upright. Wild magic reached for the ceiling. Through its brightness, he met Linden's gaze.

For his sake, she kissed a promise onto her wedding band, held it up with her hand clenched.

Weeping like Grueburn, Covenant slapped his ring against the *krill*'s gem.

The world will not see her like again.

Care for her, beloved, so that in the end she may heal us all.

Too late, Jeremiah cried out, "Mom!" Linden and Stave were gone.

Covenant turned away as if he were falling.

Elena, he thought obliquely, I'm so sorry. I'm doing what I can. Somebody else has to care for you.

ᔧᐤᒃ

S till he had no time. He could not afford his own weakness, or the wailing of his wrenched heart. He had to keep moving. He would find some form of peace soon enough.

Ah, God.

Jeremiah was standing now, showing Covenant a face fretted with ruin. "I keep doing that," he said in such misery that Covenant wanted to turn away. "It's like I don't even remember her until it's too late." His head hung as if he were talking to the floor. "By the time I understand what she's doing, she's already gone. I don't even say goodbye."

I'm never ready.

Covenant knew the feeling.

He allowed himself to postpone speaking to Linden's son for a moment. While he tried to gather up the shreds of his courage, he asked Branl, "How much farther?"

The Humbled glanced at the tunnel ahead. "Kiril Threndor is near, ur-Lord." Then he frowned. Tension in the lines of his face betrayed anxieties which his tone concealed. "Yet my heart misgives me. I cannot credit that Corruption has no other defenses close about him." Briefly he appeared to consult with Samil and Canrik. "Also, ur-Lord, I do not discern Corruption's presence. His malice is particular. It cannot be mistaken. That some great evil awaits us is plain. Yet it is not Corruption. He is absent"—Branl cocked an eyebrow at a sudden thought—"or veiled by glamour."

Covenant swore privately, but he could not pretend that he was surprised. Lord Foul knew that he was coming—and the Despiser was cunning.

Rubbing numbly at the scar on his forehead—the mark of his sins—Covenant turned to Jeremiah.

"It's probably a good thing you can see the Worm." He did not try to be gentle. "You'll know when it's time."

Jeremiah jerked up his head. "Stop that." His doom was stark in his eyes. Tattered and soiled, stained with old blood, his thin pajamas made him look as unloved as an empty house. "Stop saying things you know I can't understand. You keep saying you need me, but you won't tell me how or why. You act like you think I'm important, but I don't know what you're talking about.

"Why can't I come with you?"

Covenant grinned without humor or kindness. "It's fun, isn't it. You're like all the rest of us. Nobody ever hands you an answer. The only thing you can do is guess. Then you have to take your chances."

At once, however, he reached out, wrapped the fingers of his halfhand around the Staff of Law. Another test of truth: he wanted the boy to believe him.

To his touch, the wood felt dead; almost brittle. Ripe for consummation.

Startled, Jeremiah quenched his flames. But he did not look away. His gaze clung to Covenant's. For a moment, his eyes resembled the Harrow's, deep as voids, hungry for some life that was not his own. But slowly they became harder, flatter: the black of obsidian and anger.

Distinctly Covenant said, "You can't come with me because I don't want you that close to Lord Foul until I can distract him. But I do want you to come. I think you'll know when. You'll be able to sense it." He glanced at the Masters. "Or Canrik and Samil will. Or watching the Worm will tell you."

Jeremiah stared.

Holding the Staff and the *krill* so hard that his forearms ached, Covenant tried to explain.

"I need you because I don't think I can beat Lord Foul by myself. You aren't strong enough? Neither am I. He's too much a part of me.

"When the Worm drinks the EarthBlood, the Arch of Time will start to crumble. That's when Foul can escape. More than anything else, he wants *freedom*. If he has to, he'll even give up trying to trap the Creator. Being stuck here—" Covenant let go of the Staff. He shoved his fingers into his hair and pulled, trying to drag his thoughts into language. "There's no word big enough for that kind of despair."

If Jeremiah understood nothing else, he would understand *that*.

Again Covenant found himself swaying, unsure of his balance. His intentions became impossible as soon as he articulated them. He wanted to fall down; just hit the floor and lie there while he could still choose the moment of his last collapse.

But he had made promises to Linden. Hell, he had made promises to practically everybody, one way or another. And he could not turn his back on Jeremiah's distress.

"I need your help to keep him busy. If we can, I want to make him miss his chance. As long as he's stuck here with us, he'll be vulnerable. Then I might be able to find an answer of my own."

Is that plain enough for you? Hellfire, Jeremiah! It's all I've got.

The boy glared blackness. His breath came in ragged chunks, as if the labor of his heart did not leave room for his lungs. He swallowed as if his mouth and throat were full of blood.

"I *can't*. Don't you understand? He's the *Despiser*. He can take me whenever he wants. I won't able to do *anything*."

"Oh, stop," Covenant snapped. He might have yelled, We're out of time! "There's always something you can do. You have talents. You have the Staff. And you know what *possession* is like." *He broke me. I hate being used.* "If nothing else, you can just hide. You can hide as long as you want."

Jeremiah had freed himself from years of dissociation. Maybe he would be able to find his way out of Lord Foul's grip.

The boy bared his teeth as if he wanted to take a bite out of Covenant; but Covenant was done with him. Intuitively, if not with any of his truncated senses, he felt the end of Time approaching. He had to go.

"Help me," he finished. "Don't help me. It's up to you. I'm out of time."

Like a man who had recovered his balance, he turned his back on Jeremiah's stained struggle; on the lost boy's naked need. At one time, Covenant had risked the Land's ruin for the sake of a snake-bitten child. More than once, he had approved when Linden had made similar choices. This was different. No matter what Jeremiah believed about himself, he was not helpless. He was *not*.

And Lord Foul did not understand him. After all of this time, the Despiser still had no real idea what he was up against.

As Covenant left Linden's son, Rime Coldspray spoke. In the *krill*'s light, she looked like a closed door. Her voice was rusted iron, a blade gnawed by neglect. Yet her gaze was sure in its mask of blood.

"Do not fear, Timewarden. While we live, we will stand with the Chosen-son. If we cannot guide him, mayhap Canrik and Samil will do so. They have shown their worth. They will not fail in Stave's stead, or in Branl's."

Mute as an unmarked grave, Frostheart Grueburn nodded her assent.

With that hope, Covenant followed Branl out of the chamber.

ॐ

T he Humbled held Longwrath's flamberge ready. He walked lightly, silent as a breeze. *That some great evil awaits us is plain.* Behind him, Covenant stepped over cracks in the wracked stone, carrying the illumination of Loric's courage and lore into darkness. The tunnel twisted from side to side as if it were writhing.

I cannot credit that Corruption has no other defenses close about him. Here and there, flecks of mica or quartz in the walls caught silver and glittered like eyes.

More fractures flawed the gutrock. The forces unleashed here must have been appalling: High Lord Prothall's struggle with Drool Rockworm for the old Staff of Law; Lord Foul's fierce and increasingly frantic efforts to destroy Covenant's spirit. Clutching the *krill*, Covenant rushed past thin splits that called out to him, urging vertigo and surrender. He had surrendered once. Not again. Not now. Linden had gone to meet her worst fear. He intended to do the same.

Then argent caught the edges of an opening ahead. Covenant smelled sulfur, the dire reek of brimstone. He felt distant heat like the withering touch of Hotash Slay long ago. And attar.

"Ur-Lord," Branl said sharply. "Be warned. There is might and evil. Though I cannot name their source, they vow death."

Attar, Covenant thought. The sweet sick stink of funerals; of preserved corpses. Lord Foul.

The *Haruchai* as a people did not know that smell. They had never confronted the Despiser.

Hardly aware that he was struggling for breath—that sweat ran like tears down the galls of his visage—that his hands shook as if he had fallen into fever and delirium—Thomas Covenant accompanied the last of the Humbled into Kiril Threndor.

He knew this place. He would have recognized it in any nightmare. Here he had been killed with his own power, his own ring. Here he had ascended in agony to participate in the Arch of Time, to defend with his soul the most necessary of the Laws which made life possible.

The space was a chamber like an abscess in the deep chest of Mount Thunder, Gravin Threndor: round and high, large enough to hold scores of Cavewights worshipping, and acute with patches of rocklight like plague-spots. Random illumination oozed like pain from the walls. The walls themselves looked like they had been shaped by a brutal blade, cut angrily into facets that cast radiance in all directions. From the ceiling, the light was thrown back like a spray of shattered glass by stalactites that resembled burnished metal: reflections so bright and broken that they seemed to swirl on the verge of madness. Some of the stalactites, too, had shattered, leaving gaps like gouges overhead, scattering their debris across the floor. Around the cave's borders, tunnels opened like unuttered screams. Among them were scattered a few boulders that resembled the stones where Covenant had left Jeremiah, displaced by violence or theurgy from where they belonged.

Here was the source of the gutrock's fracturing, here in Kiril Threndor. Those cracks were memories of terrible battles, recollections expressed in the language of wounds. Within the chamber, more splits spread insanity across the floor. From their depths, darkness swirled into the air. In places, the surface had buckled, tilting slabs at tormented angles.

But the fissures did not touch the time-worn dais in the center of the chamber. Flaws avoided that stone as if they had been denied; as if no form of harm could alter the fundamental substance and meaning of the low platform.

Two steps into Kiril Threndor, Covenant halted. He no longer noticed the stench of attar. He did not regard the allure of cracks in the floor, or the entrances from which Cavewights might pour forth at any moment. He was transfixed where he stood by the figure on the dais.

The sight was as *wrong* as a knife to the heart; as hurtful as the piercing which had twice ended his life, once in the woods behind Haven Farm, once here at the Despiser's hands.

Roger Covenant.

Obviously waiting, Roger faced his father. A grin like a rictus stretched his fleshy cheeks. The slouch of his shoulders and the heaviness of his torso betrayed his disregard for his mortal flesh; his disdain. On his shirt and pants, he bore the scorch-marks of his battles with Linden. The puckered skin of healed burns showed through holes and tears in the fabric. For his deeds, he had paid a price in pain—

His hands were empty of weapons, of any instruments of power. But his right was Kastenessen's, hot and ruddy as lava, flagrant with power. It blazed like the jaws of the *skurj*. It, too, must have cost him excruciation.

He gnashed his teeth at Covenant. "Well, hi, Dad." His mouth sneered; but his voice was a tortured thing, twisted on a rack of unappeasable desires until its joints opened and its sinews tore. "You took your own sweet time getting here."

His eyes were Lord Foul's, carious as rotting fangs.

10.

All Lost Women

Linden had chosen this. It was not a reaction to the Despiser's manipulations: it was her own doing. She had stepped off the path of his desires. If she served him now, she could not pretend that she had been misled or tricked.

Her choice. Her doing, for good or ill.

And she had promised herself that she would remember; that she would allow no effect of shame or pain, horror or failure, to confuse the fact that she had acted of her own free will. She would not blame Lord Foul, or fault Thomas for failing to spare her, or think less of Jeremiah because he had been weak.

She had made that promise to herself. Nevertheless she forgot it in the first instant of translation. She forgot who she was, and why she was here, and what she had intended to do. Such things were washed out of her by a scend of enchantment. Her world had become magic and majesty, and nothing was required of her except wonder. Something more than translation had occurred. She had entered a realm of transubstantiation where delight was the only possible response. Here she found contentment in awe and tranquility, the ineffable mansuetude of the redeemed.

The rich rug luxurious under her feet was distilled solace. It overlapped others as hieratic as arrases depicting scenes of worship, humility, sanctification: tableaux in which the devout ached with joy. She could have gleaned comfort endlessly from each of them; but her eyes and her heart were enticed by rapture on all sides. Somehow the richness of the rugs was both complete and transparent, solid and evanescent. They lay on a lucent floor pristine as aspiration, enduring as marble. Enhanced by the intervening substance of the rugs, the stone seemed polished to the point of incandescence. She was only able to bear its marmoreal radiance because she had been exalted to the tone and timbre of her surroundings.

Gazing around her, rapt and delirant, she saw a space like the ballroom of a grandiloquent palace; saw beauties in such profusion that she could not hope to appreciate them all. Loveliness effloresced in every direction. Near the walls, braziers of burnished gold offered flames redolent with incense and purity. Among the rugs, delicate filigree shafts like spun glass clean as crystal stretched upward to form arms that supported chandeliers as bright as the splendor of worlds. Beyond them, wide staircases graceful as wings swept toward higher levels and finer glories. Yet their treads and their immaculate banisters did not call her to rise and explore. She was satisfied where she stood, more than satisfied; already so dazzled and enraptured that any ascension—any movement—would diminish her perfect peace.

High above her, mosaics sang like choirs: a reverent hymnody audible only as praise. They displayed constellations and firmaments like burgeoning creations, like galaxies and stars and worlds always new.

Yet more delicious to her senses than any other munificence was the fountain. A geyser in the center of the floor, it reached high, flawless and faceted as a single diamond, until it spread its arching waters wide: a feathered spray of droplets as precise as wrought gems. There no small jewel fell. Each clinquant bead hung in abeyance, suspended, motionless. Static and lovely as ice, the fountain displayed its own splendor: an icon of transcended time, sealed against change as though its perfection had been made eternal—and eternally numinous.

Bespelled, she gazed about her like a figure in a dream, forgetting life and love and peril for the sake of an ecstasy that surpassed comprehension.

But Stave stood in front of her. She did not know him; or she did not see him; or he had no significance capable of distracting her from wonder. The scar of his lost eye dragged a frown across his visage. His hands gripped her shoulders and conveyed nothing.

"Chosen," he said as if he spoke from the far side of the world. "Linden Avery. Will you not hear me?"

She gazed past him or through him as though he were only a figment, too tenuous to require notice. He may have been no more than a blur in her vision. Soon her sight would clear, and he would be gone.

"This place is known to me." Every word vanished as soon as he uttered it, absorbed by astonishment. "I have learned to set aside its power." For no apparent reason, he studied her closely. "It is known to you as well, Linden. We stand where we have stood before, among the mazements of the Lost Deep. Then, however, Earthpower and the Staff of Law enabled you to turn aside from enchantment. Now you must reclaim yourself by other means."

In a small voice, Linden asked, "Why am I here?" But she was not talking to Stave. She simply did not understand how she had come to be blessed by so much beauty.

His frown deepened. "A query with many replies, Linden. One is that I have guided you hither, knowing no better place for your purpose." He hesitated; gave a slight *Haruchai* shrug. "I have no apt language for such matters. It is my belief that translations by wild magic are directed by clarity of intent. Heretofore our courses and destinations were determined by the Ranyhyn. Matters obscure to us were plain to them. Now we have found our way unaided."

His hands tightened on her shoulders. "Here, however, you did not choose our course. The burden of clarity was mine. As I once conveyed you to Revelstone without your consent, so also I have brought you to the Lost Deep. If I have erred, the fault is mine."

He was fading. Linden could hardly see him. By slow increments, an exquisite pleasure erased him from her sight. Soon her eyes would be clear, as untrammeled as the palace, and as precious. She wanted nothing in life except to see and hear and touch and smell—

"Why have we come?" he continued as if he did not know that he was almost undone. "Another reply is that the bane rises. Though the distance is great, Her emanations are distinct. Seeking your son, Linden, we roused She Who Must Not Be Named. Thereafter it was conceivable that She would relapse to somnolence. She had been deprived of her prey by the Timewarden. Doubtless Her wrath was great. Yet She had also fed upon the soul of High Lord Elena. At another time, She might have resumed Her ancient sleep.

"Yet now I perceive that She could not. The flood which was released against the *skurj* has filled the abyss of Her slumber. Indeed, those waters are withheld from the Lost Deep only by the lingering theurgies of the Viles. Such an inundation cannot harm a being such as She Who Must Not Be Named. Nonetheless it vexes Her. Therefore She rises."

The man's tone became more urgent, although he existed only as vagueness. "She *rises*, Linden. And I fear—" His fading hands shook her. "Linden, hear me. I am *Haruchai*. I fear nothing, yet I tremble. I fear that the bane will ascend to Kiril Threndor. I fear that She will discern the scent of Corruption and the puissance of the Timewarden. I fear that She will fall upon them in fury and lay the Timewarden waste.

"For that reason I have guided you here. It is my hope that you will call out to Her with wild magic. It is my prayer, Linden, that you will draw Her to us before She nears Kiril Threndor."

He must have wanted something from her. Why else did he mar the palace with his voice, his hands, his insistence? But each word evaporated as soon as his mouth shaped it. He might as well have made no sound. He persisted in her sight as nothing more than a dwindling imperfection among the meretricious entrancements of the ballroom.

"Linden." Although he sounded as calm as snow-clad peaks in clear sunshine, he conveyed a subtle desperation. "You must hear me. All of life tilts on the edge of a blade, and I am afraid. My hand remains able to strike you, and to strike again, until I am heeded. Alas, my heart will not suffer it. You must hear me."

She did not. She had forgotten him. She had almost forgotten that language had meaning. His words slipped past her. Then they were gone. Only ensorcelments remained.

But Stave was not alone. At his back, an array of creatures crouched in the act of rising to their hind legs. Black things, no more than a dozen. And grey ones, smaller, half that number. Above the cruel slits of their mouths, they had no eyes. Wet nostrils dominated their faces. Pointed ears twitched on their skulls. Their heads and bodies were hairless.

Stave turned and bowed to them as if they had earned homage.

They made chittering sounds like his, language without meaning. One of them taller than the others held a jerrid of black iron, a scepter like a short javelin. A fuming liquid as dire as poison dripped from the iron. The tall creature snuffled at Linden, then turned away. With low growls and snarls, it used the point of its jerrid to sketch incomprehensible symbols in the air. Acid drops scattered here and there; but they evaporated before they touched the floor.

For a moment without measure or duration, nothing changed. Linden remembered nothing. Only the ballroom endured. Like Stave, the creatures faded, the black ones and the grey. Like him, they were almost gone.

Then a subtle tremor ran through the fountain, a vibration so brief and untenable that it defied sight. She could not believe that she had seen it. She hardly recognized her own fright.

Slow and horrid as a plunge from a nightmare precipice, a single jewel of water high in the fountain began to fall.

Light shone all around the small bead. It looked like an epiphany; like the essence of the Earth's gems; like the last gleam of the ravaged heavens. It fell and fell forever, infinite and fatal; and while Linden watched it, her heart did not beat, her lungs did not draw breath. When at last it reached the floor, the largesse of the rugs, it made a tiny splash: the first faint quiver of a world about to shatter.

Somewhere in the distance, hundreds of leagues away, the Worm—

Linden blinked. A small frown knotted her forehead. Her heart offered up a weak beat.

The creatures continued their guttural invocation—and another bead of water began its interminable demise—and Stave stood in front of her again, clutching her shoulders.

When he repeated her name, she wanted to weep.

A second little splash. A few ripples. In rugs? In marble?

A third rare jewel of water, and a fourth, dropping from perfection into time and ruin. When they struck, they made a pattering sound, delicate and awful.

Oh, God, she thought. Stave. The Worm. The bane.

Ur-viles and Waynhim. Once again, they had come to her rescue when she did not know how to save herself.

In this place, rescue was an atrocity. It destroyed a supernal achievement, the triumph of lore which had preserved the palace through the ages. And the effect on Linden was no less cruel. Raindrops brought back memories like devastations. Thoughts were carnage and cataclysm.

Jeremiah. Thomas!

Somehow she reached out to the *Haruchai*. Her voice was softer than the accumulating drip of the fountain. Her eyes should have been full of tears.

"What did you say? About the bane?"

His back straightened. His chin rose proudly. His eye shone.

"She rises, Linden. If you do not call out to Her, She will assail the Timewarden. She will consume your son."

Damn it! Linden wished that Stave had hit her. She wanted to pummel herself. She had chosen to face her worst fears. Then she had forgotten all about them. And while she had lost herself among marvels, the Earth's peril had increased beyond bearing.

She Who Must Not Be Named might take Thomas and Jeremiah.

In a different life, a bullet had struck Linden. A scar over her heart matched the perfect circle in her shirt. There was no going back. Choices made could not be recanted.

Thomas had unforeseeable strengths. He might survive. But mere Law and Earthpower would not suffice to ward Jeremiah.

For Linden's sake, or for the Earth's, the ur-viles and Waynhim had disrupted the prolonged theurgies of the Viles; sacrificed their own heritage of splendor. Around the ballroom, a light drizzle fell. The fountain cast a fine mist that gathered into droplets. Drips leaked from the music of the ceiling. Ripples ran down the stairways. Gradually the chandeliers released their lights. Spots of water stippled the woven rugs, the immemorial floor.

No going back. Now or never.

God help me.

Linden delayed only long enough to say to the ur-viles and Waynhim, to the eyeless features of the loremaster, "You keep helping me, no matter how much it costs, and I still don't know how to repay you." Then she wheeled away.

Clenching her fists, she raised her face to the leagues of blind stone above the Lost Deep. Rain spattered her cheeks and forehead. Its sheer age stung her eyes. In her mouth, the drops tasted like dust.

As if she had always known what she could do, she invoked her wedding band. She had no more use for despair and recrimination; inadequacy. Only power would serve. Like a woman screaming, she flung a roar of wild magic into Mount Thunder's gutrock.

"*I'm here!* You lost me once! Come get me now!"

Her theurgy could have torn vast stone to powder; could have brought the weight of the mountain crashing into the caverns of the Lost Deep. But her health-sense was precise. She did not hurl silver against the rock: she tuned it to pass through Mount Thunder's substance, sharpened it to a pitch that only the bane would be able to hear.

"Come and *get* me! I can save you!"

Melenkurion Skyweir was already falling. She felt its massive collapse like atmospheric pressure on her skin, heard it like the grumble of impossible thunder. At any moment, the Worm would begin to drink EarthBlood from the world's heart.

Slowly the drizzle became rain. Details among the mosaics blurred and ran as their melodies dwindled to liquid. The staircases slumped, shrugging thin streams from their sides. The shafts of the chandeliers bowed as if they had lost faith in themselves. Rills curled around Linden's boots, flowing nowhere. Argent made raindrops as bright as exploding stars.

"I can tell you how to save yourself!"

She felt Stave's hand on her shoulder. His touch seemed almost diffident as he asked for her attention. But she did not acknowledge him until her power and her shouting failed; until she could no longer sustain her summons.

Silver stains danced like little suns across her vision as she turned back to her friend.

Through a veil of rainfall, Stave told her, "It is enough. If your call is not heard, no other will suffice."

The ur-viles and Waynhim barked to each other like dogs, excited or fearful. The loremaster gestured resignation or encouragement with its jerrid. Water glistened on the skin of the creatures as if the fluid were dying, giving up its last magic.

"Therefore I must speak," continued the former Master. "I will not be vouchsafed another occasion to do so."

Linden glared and squinted, trying to clear the spots from her eyes. Wet hair straggled across her cheeks.

"I must state plainly, Linden, that you have become wondrous in my sight. Here my life is forfeit. It may be that the bane will heed you. Me She will not suffer. In Her sight, all men are betrayers. I will be devoured."

Water streamed on Linden's face, scattered from the lines of her jaw. Drops snapped against her skin. Here my life is forfeit. How had she failed to consider this? For hours, she had imagined her intentions as though they threatened only her. But of course Stave was right. He could not withstand the bane. She Who Must Not Be Named would not tolerate him.

"As farewell," her final companion told her, "I must say aloud that I regret nothing. My fears are gone. You risk much, as you have ever done. Whatever now ensues, know that I am made proud by my place at your side."

She Who Must Not Be Named only slew men; only killed and ate them. She had no other use for them. Women She consumed in an entirely different fashion. She craved the torment of their living spirits when their bodies were destroyed. Her hunger was for the anguish of their souls, undying and endlessly tormented. It resembled or confirmed or justified Her own agony.

In some sense, literally or metaphorically, the bane was here because Lord Foul had betrayed Her; seduced and ruined Her with lies; gaoled Her within Time. Now She could only suffer—and feed on the sufferings of any woman who came within Her grasp. *Diassomer with fear and dread*— Unforgiven Elena, Covenant's daughter by rape. Emereau Vrai, Kastenessen's mortal lover. An Insequent whom the Ardent had called the Auriference. Hundreds or thousands of women across the ages of the Earth. As far as She was concerned, all women and every love had been betrayed.

If She had not forgotten Her true name—Her real scope and power—She would have brought everything to an end long ago.

Linden peered through splashes and rivulets at Stave. The rain was becoming torrential as millennia of lore failed, unloosed by these few ur-viles and Waynhim according to the arcane dictates of their Weird. Lashing drops and spray fraught with residues stung like acid. She tried to find her voice; swallowed bitterness so that she might shout refusals at her friend. If he would not ask the Demondim-spawn for protection, she meant to plead on his behalf.

But she did not. She was already overwhelmed.

I am made proud by my place at your side.

In the small space between instants, the rainwater running over her body became vermin. It became centipedes as long as her hand, feasting maggots, spiders with hundreds of pincers, lice that scuttled and squirmed, worms burrowing. Noisome things crawled and clawed and pecked everywhere, intimate as lovers, avid as eaters of death. Desperate to quash the feeding, she thrashed like a madwoman, hit herself frantically, dug at her scalp until she drew blood.

Stave may have shouted her name. If he did, the rain slapped his voice from the air.

Cascades filled her mouth with biting insects. They laid their eggs in her eyes, breeding. When she tried to breathe, she gasped abhorrence into her lungs and retched. Beetles and centipedes scuttled down her throat.

—written in water. The Despiser had named her fate. Water was horror. It was eager excruciation. It transformed her to carrion and shrieking.

Now Lord Foul laughed at her from an insurmountable distance. *You have become the daughter of my heart.* Laughed as he must have laughed at She Who Must Not Be Named. Soon Time would begin to crumble, and he would be free. Linden had brought this on herself. She had given it to the world as if it were the sum and consummation of her life. It would never stop. Across every inch of her flesh, it drove her mad. She could not bear it. If she had been given a knife, she would not have hesitated to flay the skin from her bones.

Such desecration should have finished her. But it was endless. It could always get worse.

And while Linden flailed in torrents, the bane shouldered Her way into the cavern.

Her power was immense. No doubt She could have shaped Herself to slip through the passages of the Lost Deep. Yet She did not. Damage suited Her: She liked wreckage in Her wake. As She entered, the rolling bulk of Her fury made a ruin of the stone. With every shrug, Her advance flung rubble at the walls. Her many faces were etched in fire. Mute screams stretched their mouths. Torment gouged their eyes.

Without knowing what she did, Linden stopped thrashing. The scale of the bane's extremity and rage demanded her absolute attention. Suddenly worms and maggots were no longer sensations. They became insights.

When She Who Must Not Be Named spoke, the impact of Her voice seemed to stop Linden's heart. The ferocity of the sound changed the rain to steam and scalding.

"Do you speak to me?" The roar crushed Linden's hearing. "Do you speak to me of *save? Do you dare?* My pain cannot be redeemed. It can only feed and *grow*.

"You are mine. I will relish you. I require only a moment to chew the marrow from the bones of the man who has betrayed you to me. Endure your suffering. It will be brief. Then I will consume you, and you will know the ecstasy of eternal woe and regret"—She gathered Herself to cry like a beast—"*and agony!*"

Linden could not protest. The bane's intent was just. Linden deserved centipedes and spiders. Horror was her true heritage: the legacy of her pitiful, self-pitying parents. By audacity and blind carelessness and insufficiency, she had awakened both the Worm of the World's End and her own worst nightmares. She had brought this doom upon herself.

Nevertheless it was intolerable. The bane would kill *Stave*, her friend when she had no other. The knowledge that he was about to die for her sins was more than she could bear.

Days ago, the foundations of her life had begun to shift. Now they settled into new alignments. Like a woman rising from her own grave, she changed. In a rush, her whole reality was transformed. Faster than the febrile stutter of her heart, maggots and squirming and misery became a wail of wild magic.

She had no power to equal the bane's. She Who Must Not Be Named transcended everything mortal. Nevertheless Linden was Thomas Covenant's wife. He had wed her in love and joy. In passion and courage, he had made of her a rightful white gold wielder. She was not helpless.

Swift as her pulse in her veins, she spun silver puissance around her treasured friend, caught him in a fist of bright flame: a fist or a circle. She had no *krill* to enable a translation, but she had other resources. She had the unthinking reflexes which had allowed her to step outside the sequences of time during the collapse of Kevin's Watch. She had the whetted senses with which she had created *caesures* without stumbling into Joan's madness. And she was not hampered by her husband's necessary reluctance.

While the bane surged forward, Linden grasped Stave and *threw* him. Away from this moment. Away from this place, this stone, this fate. Trusting his instincts—his *clarity of intent*—to choose his destination, she spared him the cost of her choices.

Perhaps he would forgive her.

When he was gone, she wrapped herself in wild argent a heartbeat before the bane pounced on her, shrieking.

The ur-viles and Waynhim did not try to help her now. Shrouded in rain, they stood apart like witnesses: creatures condemned to watch the extinction of their obscure hopes.

The bane's rage took Linden, snatched her into incandescence and infernal torment. But the bane did not *have* her. Vermin and pestilence did not have her. She was cloaked in her own fire, cocooned heart and soul. Within the bane's appalling body, she was not devoured. Instead she left the sensations of horror and eaten death behind as if they had become irrelevant.

According to Kasreyn of the Gyre, white gold was an imperfect tool able to fashion perfection in a flawed world. But she did not seek perfection. She wanted only to preserve herself until she could at least try to keep her promise.

She thought of herself as an embolism, a tiny clot or bubble in the flagrant bloodstream of She Who Must Not Be Named. Untouched because she was trivial. Wild magic warded her against time, against mortality. She controlled nothing. She could not harm the bane. But she could remain herself. She could think and strive. The vast being roared in frustration and bafflement, thwarted hunger; but Linden ignored Her.

Linden Avery had chosen this fate. She knew why she had done so. She knew that she was lost. She would die as soon as her resolve and her fire failed. Nevertheless she did not falter. While she could, she pursued salvation.

Through the tremendous roil of wracked souls, the seething turmoil of the bane's victims, Linden searched for Elena.

Elena Lena-daughter, child of rape, prey of Despite. Seeking to oppose Lord Foul, she had broken the Law of Death to raise Kevin Landwaster's spectre—and by that crime, she had become the Despiser's servant. When Linden had seen her among the Dead in Andelain, Elena had still borne the galls and wounds of her self-Desecration. Yet Linden had given her no pity, no kindness. Of Elena's later sacrifice to the bane, Linden knew only what she had been told. But she remembered too well what she herself had done to the first Law-Breaker. Now she considered it the least forgivable of her sins.

As if she had the right to judge—*she*, who had set the world's last crisis in motion—she had denied to Elena the understanding and consolation which Berek and Damelon and Loric had given Kevin. Instead of mercy, she had offered Elena only demands: the selfish expostulations of her own guilt.

Stop feeling sorry for yourself. It doesn't accomplish anything.

That memory still made Linden cringe. It had brought her here. Because of it—and because the implications of carrion required this—she had forsaken her husband and her son and the imminent destruction of the Earth.

Throughout the bane's clamoring chaos, she drifted, searching for Covenant's daughter.

Scores of faces wailed in front of her and fled. Hundreds. Thousands. She believed that she knew how to save them all. Or perhaps she only hoped. But she had to start with Elena, who had been four times betrayed: by the circumstances of her birth, by her own actions in the cave of the EarthBlood, by Linden, and by being cast into the inferno of the bane's mad agony.

Elena was here. Finding her was only a matter of time—and Linden was immune to time while her strength lasted.

When the aghast ravage of Elena's face appeared, Linden clutched it with silver before the spectre could be swept away.

Elena did not struggle, yet Linden could barely hold her. The bane's wrath lashed the eidolon in every direction. She Who Must Not Be Named pressed down on Linden's shield with all of Her accumulated mass: the weight of ages. Only Linden's cocoon preserved her. Only wild magic kept Elena with her, face to face.

"Oh, Elena." She spoke in flames. She had no other voice for her remorse and shame. Her words were the lament of her wedding band: the grief of an absolute promise broken absolutely. "I'm so sorry. You didn't deserve what I did to you. You and Caer-Caveral brought Thomas to me. I should have been grateful. But I couldn't think about anything except how much I hurt. I treated you like it was your fault. I wanted you to be stronger than I was. I wanted you to forgive me, but I couldn't say that. I can't forgive myself.

"I'm like Kevin. I chose my own Desecration. You just made a mistake. You don't deserve—"

Elena's cries made no sound that Linden could hear. Nevertheless the High Lord's protests silenced Linden. They appeared like avatars in her mind; like reifications of every injury which had ever flensed Elena's heart.

Why have you come? My suffering is enough. I do not desire the sufferings of others. I did not call you to this doom.

Terrible pressures distorted Elena's features: stretched them until they tore; compressed them into granite knots. Her eyes were wounds.

Do you conceive that I was compelled to eternal horror? The Dead are not so cruel. I acceded to the pleas of Sunder and Hollian out of love for my father, and because you are his beloved, and because you must be preserved.

Linden Avery, you multiply my torment. You have damned yourself. I must go mad, as She is mad. Why have you come?

At an unconceivable distance, the thunder of *Melenkurion* Skyweir's destruction boomed. Surely the Worm had begun its feeding at the wellspring of the Earth's Blood? Surely the world's remaining life could be measured in heartbeats?

Linden did not care. She had been trained as a physician, a surgeon, a healer. She knew in her bones that her first and only responsibility was to find an answer for the need in front of her.

"To free you," she answered in conflagration. "I'll free as many of you as I can. I'll tell the bane how to free Herself. But I have to start with you. You're the one I hurt."

Thomas Covenant's daughter, as precious as her own son.

Elena's wailing was inaudible. Still Linden heard her. Her voice seemed to burst from her eyes, from the veins throbbing in her temples.

You cannot. Do you hear? You cannot. We are souls. Her anguish binds us. As we are, we cannot be divided from Her. We must live again to be free of Her. We must have flesh. We must be truly separate, spirit from spirit, thought from thought. Pain from pain. To release us, you must unmake our deaths.

We cannot be freed!

That cry rent Linden's heart. It nearly snapped her resolve. For a moment, she could only gape at Elena. *Unmake* your death? *How?* Elena was not Thomas: she was not imprinted on Linden's nerves, Linden's needs, Linden's love. Her body was gone beyond comprehension. And Linden did not have either the *krill* or the Staff. She had only her ring.

Don't tell me that I have to leave you like this!

But then her preconceptions shifted. She had spent her life making promises that she did not know how to keep. She had never sufficed to keep them. And yet she had accomplished more than she could have imagined. But not because *she* was more—or not only because she was more. No, she had been able to do so much because she was not alone. From Liand and Anele and Stave to the Ranyhyn and the Swordmainnir and Thomas himself, she had been aided in every deed. She had been given gifts—

They had taught her truths which should have been obvious, but which had nonetheless eluded her. Berek Halfhand had seen Gallows Howe in her, a mound of ruin made barren by bitterness and slaughter. In Garroting Deep, however, she had discovered a deeper truth beneath the drenched dirt.

More than bloodshed and revenge, the olden forest had yearned for restitution. The trees would have turned their backs on killing entirely if they could have recovered their ravaged expanse and majesty.

She understood that now. She recognized, if the bane did not, that healing was both more arduous and more worthy than retribution. And sometimes healing required measures as extreme as the patient's plight. Surgeons amputated or extirpated. They performed sacrifices. They transplanted. They did not judge the cost. They only did what they could.

And even here, in the Lost Deep at the onset of the World's End, Linden was not alone.

In a blaze of wild magic, she reeled against the current of the bane's savagery, dragging Elena with her.

The bane's resistance was brutal and blind, undirected. She Who Must Not Be Named could shatter entire landscapes, but She did not know how to fight within Herself. She had never needed to do so before. Linden seemed to struggle endlessly— and to find what she sought in an instant.

Through the flame and hunger and abhorrence of the bane's boundaries, she saw the Demondim-spawn.

Under a deluge of collapsing theurgies, the ur-viles and the Waynhim stood together as if they had finally become kin, united by a common interpretation of their Weird. As one, they studied the bane with senses other than sight; or they studied Linden.

Time and again, they had helped her when she had not known that she needed their gifts. Like Thomas. Like the Land itself.

Peering at the creatures, she understood at last that they had not unbound the ancient magicks of the Viles merely so that she would be able to remember and act. They had cast down their purest heritage for reasons greater than her needs and desires. Their Weird demanded more. They had undone the wonders of the Lost

Deep for the same reason that they had aided her and the Land repeatedly: so that they would be vulnerable now. So that they would be accessible—

If you can ever figure out a way to let me know what you need or want from me—

What had the ur-viles and the Waynhim ever wanted, except to escape their loathing for their own forms?

Linden waited until the loremaster met her gaze; until the tall creature nodded its assent. Then she did what she could for Elena.

Risking the shroud of wild magic which protected her, Linden flung Elena out of the bane; tossed her like a wisp of hope or a kept promise into the waiting embrace of the loremaster.

The creature appeared to swallow. The spectre of Elena seemed to vanish. Linden could not be sure. She Who Must Not Be Named was roaring: a howl that stunned Linden's chest, rattled her mind in its chamber of bone, stopped her ears and eyes and mouth and lungs. She hardly knew who or what she was.

Time was fraying at the edges around her, starting to unravel. Soon its deterioration would unweave the world. Reality would lose its shape. Existence would cease.

Still wild magic shielded her. Her own needs shielded her; her own loves. She was not done.

She grasped the first spectre shrieking past her: a woman who could have been anyone, Diassomer Mininderain, Sara Clint, Joan herself, anyone at all. As she had with Elena, she gave the savaged soul to the loremaster, or to all of the Demondim-spawn. Then she reached for another victim.

Before Linden could do more, the bane found a defense. Her ferocity seemed to have no beginning and no end as She began to compress Herself, condensing Her might and bulk around Linden, making Herself more solid. Linden no longer drifted on currents of fire and fury. Pressures great enough to rive mountains clamped down on her. Forces which dwarfed her threatened to rupture her eardrums, burst vessels in her lungs, squeeze blood from her eyes. Lost women were held motionless in their unutterable screams.

But Linden did not need ears or eyes or air to hear She Who Must Not Be Named.

"You diminish me! You dare to diminish me! You will not! You speak of save, but your purpose is *betrayal*. I will not permit you!"

Linden had no voice. It had been crushed out of her. She could speak only with wild magic: the blazing paradox, *save or damn*, which formed the keystone of life.

"This isn't betrayal. It's kindness. I can save all of these poor women. I can tell you how to save yourself."

"*How?*" The bane's roar was a sneer, contemptuous as vitriol. "You are nothing! What do you offer that I have not attempted endlessly?"

Linden could not move. She was effectively dead. The bane's power was too much for her. Nevertheless she answered.

"The Arch of Time is breaking. If you don't believe me, look for yourself. You can see it. The Worm of the World's End is drinking the EarthBlood. Everything is going to be destroyed. Your prison is starting to fall apart.

"While it falls, you can slip out. You'll be free. But you have to go now. Otherwise I don't know what might happen. You belong to eternity. If you don't leave—if you stay inside Time—you might be extinguished along with everything else."

Perhaps She Who Must Not Be Named craved extinction, an eternal end to Her suffering. If so, Linden had failed. But at least her own anguish would end as well.

"All I want," she insisted in fire, "is to release your women. You don't need them anymore. Not now. They're part of this world." They were dross, imperfections. "If you take them with you, they'll only hinder you. They may even prevent you. You won't be truly free."

The bane contracted around her. Terrible strength made pulp of her flesh and organs, her bones, her mind. Nothing existed for her except the raw rage of She Who Must Not Be Named.

"Fool! Madwoman! Treacher! Do you conceive that I desire *freedom*? You do not know me. Freedom is *agony*. It is *abhorrence*. It is not *redemption*. I am anguish because I have forgotten who I am.

"The destruction of this world is nothing to me. I cannot die. *I must have my true name!*"

Convulsions shook Mount Thunder to its roots. Shocks distorted the definitions of existence. Slabs fell from the ceiling and were pulverized. Granite sifted like ash onto the heads and shoulders of the ur-viles and Waynhim. Stone lurched under their feet. Yet they stood as if they were rooted by pride: legs straight, backs regal, arms open to welcome released souls. The loremaster's eerie visage shone with an inward exaltation.

Linden felt ripples like imminent *caesures* trembling toward her, confusing the structure of instants. There were no risks left except this one.

"Then give me Emereau Vrai." Kastenessen's lover: the only woman who had ever been loved by an *Elohim*. He had given her some of his magicks. How else had she been able to create the *merewives*? Perhaps he had also revealed secrets which no one mortal—which none of the bane's other victims—could have known. Why else had his people considered his crime so heinous that he deserved his Durance? Linden had heard long ago that he had been punished for harming an ordinary woman with his love; but she did not trust that explanation. When had the *Elohim* ever been so protective of individual lives? Emereau Vrai might know—And if she did, the

Demondim-spawn might be lorewise enough to understand her. "Let me show you that I'm telling the truth."

I'm a woman, damn it! I don't want to seduce you.

The bane contracted in fury. Her vehemence increased. It was unbearable, unanswerable. Though Linden clung to wild magic—to her wedding band—to the promise of Thomas Covenant—she was little more than a spark, a fading ember within the virulence of She Who Must Not Be Named. Hundreds or thousands of women shrieked their pain and despair, but they made no sound.

Then the pressure eased. Yowling to Herself, the bane receded slightly. Linden remembered to breathe. She blinked at the blood in her eyes.

An excoriated face appeared in front of her. A voice that registered only in Linden's mind said, I am Emereau Vrai. Does Kastenessen love me still? I am betrayed to this doom, but not by him. It was his kindred who made of me a plaything for damnation. All that I have done, I did because he was taken from me.

You have spoken my name. Know that I forgive nothing. Alone among this host, I approve my fate. She Who Must Not Be Named is my god. My anguish is worship.

Linden might have said, Of course he still loves you. In his heart, he never let you go. He made himself insane for you. But she did not have the strength. Her life and her will were almost gone. She needed the last of herself to clasp Emereau Vrai and send Kastenessen's lover into the arms of the Demondim-spawn.

They accepted her gladly, barking their homage amid the devastation of the Lost Deep.

Then Linden was done. Wild magic drained out of her, and she was swept unshielded into the excoriation of the bane. As far as she knew, she only remained alive because she had slipped into a fracture between instants. When the currents of the bane's fury carried her back into the sequences of time, she would die.

Yet that fracture—or some other pause—held her. She did not die, or move, or think. Entire realms of pain slid past her as if she had become untouchable.

As if she had finally become worthy of her husband.

With senses other than vision or hearing or touch, she recognized the Demondim-spawn. They stood like kings in the wreckage of their eldritch legacy. Every visage among them now shone like the loremaster's. The proportions of their bodies were changing, as if they were becoming human; sharing the loremaster's transfigured spirit. They seemed taller.

In unison, they chanted at the bane: a paean or invocation as alien as their guttural speech, and as incomprehensible. With every rise and fall, every beat, their hymn appeared to accrue peril, as if they were hazarding more than their own destruction; as if the accumulation of their words threatened the pediments of reality. And yet their eagerness was plain on their eyeless faces. Somehow they had arrived at a crisis of extermination or apotheosis toward which they had striven for millennia.

They may have been extolling the bane—or forbidding Her.

Her response was a cry that sent spasms through the gutrock for leagues in all directions:

"I AM MYSELF!"

When Linden's heart beat again, she was no longer inside the bane. Instead she had the sensation that she was being carried; cradled with the tenderness of a lover. Powers that surpassed understanding protected her from the ruination of the Lost Deep.

She was given a moment to watch the bane release souls into the waiting arms and mouths and bodies of the ur-viles and the Waynhim: a torrent of long anguish so suddenly relieved that she could not name what became of it. Then the bane began to rise like music, intangible as mist, and potent as divinity, through Mount Thunder's stubborn foundations; and Linden was lifted with Her, passing among the mountain's complex rocks and cavities as if she were as transient as a wraith.

11.

Of My Deeper Purpose

For a moment that felt like a protracted sob, Jeremiah watched Covenant and Branl recede along the passage toward Kiril Threndor; watched the silver of the *krill* fade like the last light in the world. Then he folded back down to the floor. Sitting with the Staff of Law gripped across his thighs and images of the Worm chewing at the edges of his mind, he stared into absolute blackness and tried to believe that he was not out of time. That the subtle trembling of the stone did not announce the collapse of the Arch. That Covenant would come back to him, since Linden had said that she would not. That he would be spared.

His mother had not even bothered to explain where she was going; or why.

He was angry; too angry to speak or grieve. Linden and Covenant had left him with an impossible burden, as if he were somehow responsible for saving the Earth. As if he were not still the same boy who had been too small to rescue his sisters from Lord Foul's bonfire.

On some level, he knew that he was also angry at himself. Angry because he hated his own childishness. Because he felt useless and stupid. Because he had not tried to get an explanation from Linden, or to change her mind, or to say goodbye. Angry because Covenant expected too much from him. But that anger belonged to some other Jeremiah—to a piece of who he had become when Kastenessen had broken him—not to the boy who had been left by his mother and his first friend.

Sure, he understood Covenant's reasons for walking away. *I don't want you that close to Lord Foul until I can distract him.* The words sounded like they made sense. *But I do want you to come. I need your help to keep him busy.* That was simple enough.

But it was not simple at all. Covenant had also said, *You aren't strong enough? Neither am I.*

And *Then let him be too strong. You don't need to beat him.* And *Just do something he doesn't expect.*

So what was *that* supposed to mean?

And what would it accomplish? Nothing that Jeremiah or Linden or Covenant himself ever did would stop the Worm. It was already drinking EarthBlood: Jeremiah could feel or see or hear it. The whole world did not contain enough power to prevent its own death.

What good would it do to make Lord Foul *miss his chance?*

As guerdon for his puerile valor—

Jeremiah was angry, all right. Of course he was angry.

In some ways, sitting there in Mount Thunder's stark midnight hurt more than being possessed by the *croyel.* That bitter creature had made him truly helpless, as unable as a corpse to affect how he was used or what he became. But he was not helpless *now*: not literally. He had the Staff of Law and his own Earthpower. He could kill Cavewights. Eventually he could maybe teach himself how to help Coldspray and Grueburn recover. If nothing else, he should have been able to fill this cave with light and warmth. But the Staff's possibilities only taunted him. They emphasized all of the things that he could not do.

Covenant and Linden might as well have asked Jeremiah to remake the world.

Gnawing his futility, he ignored the exhausted rasp of the Giants' breathing, the useless stoicism of the *Haruchai*, the slow drip of blood from too many wounds. He had nothing to say to his companions. They could not help him.

Maybe Roger had the right idea. Maybe we should all try to become gods.

The idea was a cruel joke.

He should never have listened to Linden. He should never have accepted her Staff. He should have stayed in his graves, hidden. He would have been better off. Nobody would have expected him to produce miracles.

"Chosen-son?" asked Rime Coldspray: an abraded whisper. "Jeremiah? Do you hear me?"

He wanted to snarl at her. The floor trembled under him. A fever gripped Mount Thunder's gutrock. In the distance, the implied roar and clatter as *Melenkurion* Skyweir collapsed shook the world. He could feel it. Towering plumes of dust and ruin cast a pall across the Land's last dusk. He could see it.

Covenant was wasting his time. Linden had thrown her life away.

But naturally the Ironhand and Grueburn did not hear what Jeremiah heard. He was alone.

"I'm busy," he muttered. "What do you want?"

"Chosen-son." Rime Coldspray made a palpable effort to speak clearly. "I am loath to burden you further. We are not altogether sightless in such dark. And I do not doubt that the vision of the *Haruchai* exceeds ours. Nonetheless some small flame would comfort our spirits.

"I do not ask a *caamora*," she added as if she feared that he would misunderstand. "I am undone by weariness, and have no heart for lamentation. Yet fire and light would be a kindness." She sighed. "Mayhap they would enable me to remain upright until we are summoned by the Timewarden's need."

"Aye," breathed Grueburn. She sounded too weak to say more.

"Then you should sit down." Jeremiah remembered seeing a couple of large boulders against the walls. They were invisible now, blank to his health-sense, indistinguishable from the surrounding stone; but the Giants could rest on them. "Don't you feel it? The floor is starting to shake. The Worm is sending out ripples. The more it drinks, the bigger they'll get. Soon you won't be able to stand. You'll last longer if you don't try."

"Stone and Sea!" the Ironhand panted. "Does the world end? Does time remain for the Timewarden to accomplish his purpose? Have we come so far at such cost, and arrived too late?"

"How should I know?" countered Jeremiah sourly. "I've never watched a world die before." Then he rasped, "Of course we're too late. That's what all those Cavewights were for. Lord Foul sent them to slow us down."

We were doomed, he added to himself, as soon as Mom and Covenant started thinking I could hold up my end.

But Canrik said like a reprimand, "He is the ur-Lord, the Unbeliever. Twice he has wrested life from the clutch of Corruption, for the Land if not for himself. We are

Masters and have doubted much. Now we are done with uncertainty. While Branl remains able to speak to us, we will fear nothing."

Jeremiah grimaced. "Fine. You do that. Fear nothing as long as you want. Just don't say I didn't warn you when this place starts to shake so hard you fall down."

The darkness of the cave and the darkness inside him mirrored each other. He could not distinguish between them.

"Ah, Chosen-son." Coldspray's voice seemed to scrape the floor. It sounded as unsteady as the stone. "Your straits are indeed bitter. I know not how you may be consoled.

"Yet surely you also would find comfort in light."

"Don't you think I'm trying?" Jeremiah retorted, caustic as lye. "I've been trying ever since Mom"—he raised the Staff, slammed it back onto his thighs—"gave me this thing. But I can't change what I am. It's all just black."

The Staff had turned against him soon after he had begun trying to use its stained resources. Before that, his power had been the warm yellow of sunshine. He could have provided at least a taste of kindness for Coldspray and Grueburn. But his efforts with the wood had not changed it. Instead it had stripped away his denials, his defenses.

It had exposed the truth—

The Ironhand sighed again. "Ah, then." She may have shrugged. "Lacking other illumination, I will emulate the certainty of the *Haruchai*. I will trust that Linden Giantfriend and Covenant Timewarden will exceed every expectation, as they have done from the first. And also—" She groaned softly. "Also I will heed your counsel, Chosen-son. Until we are summoned to Kiril Threndor, I will rest."

Jeremiah heard the creak of her joints as she forced herself to move. He felt the mute crying of her muscles, the catch and strain of her respiration, the lurch of her pulse. With Grueburn, she went to the wall opposite him. The weight of their armor and swords seemed to make their shoulders moan as they lowered themselves to lean or sit, apparently on the boulders.

"The ur-Lord has begun," Canrik announced. "He confronts two great evils. Branl now discerns that Corruption has taken possession of the ur-Lord's son. They stand as one." A moment later, he added, "In such a conflict, Branl is of little use." His tone had a grim tinge. "His flesh cannot withstand the fire and fury of the *skurj*. Therefore he cannot ward the ur-Lord."

Taken possession, Jeremiah thought. Oh, joy. In spite of his own despair, he felt a reflexive pang for Covenant's son. When Roger lost his partnership with the *croyel*, he must have decided that Lord Foul was his only path to godhood; his only way to survive the shattering of the Arch. But he should never have trusted the Despiser. He must have been so desperate—

Then Jeremiah forgot about Roger. The ur-Lord has begun. Time was running out—and Jeremiah was still as helpless as a kid.

More than anything else at that moment, he wished that he had refused the Staff of Law. How could he have believed that *he* would be able to make a difference?

The Worm appeared to drink slowly: it looked ecstatic. Nevertheless shockwaves multiplied among the Land's bones, ran through the gaps between instants. Far to the southwest, time was beginning to twist and flow. Mountains which had once leaned against *Melenkurion* Skyweir slumped as if they were melting. Confusion distorted the foothills. Trees which had died thousands of years ago in Garroting Deep flashed into existence and blurred away.

Melenkurion. The Seven Words. Abruptly Jeremiah decided to try them. He could not imagine what they might do, but he had to try *some*thing. Anything would be better than simply waiting to die.

Melenkurion abatha. Duroc—

He blinked; scowled into the darkness. There was light in the cave. How had he not noticed it before? It was faint, yes. But still—

It had to be new. It must have appeared while he was distracted by the Worm.

Faint but distinct: a disturbing actinic blue, eerie as necromancy. Except where it was blocked by the Giants, it limned the boulders as if they had begun to bleed magic. And yet it conveyed nothing to Jeremiah's nerves. His health-sense insisted that the light did not exist.

In the strange glow, he saw the *Haruchai*. Vague as ghosts or will-o'-the-wisps, they faced Kiril Threndor with their backs to him and the Giants and the stones. He could feel their tension, their desire to aid Covenant.

He blinked again and again. What was causing that acrid blue? And why was it only visible to ordinary sight?

He tried to say Coldspray's name, or Grueburn's. He struggled to speak the Seven Words aloud. But his mouth and throat were suddenly too dry.

He and his companions were not alone in the cave.

With a ponderous ease that made him flinch, the boulders began to expand.

They unfolded like crouching behemoths: monsters of living rock that had concealed themselves by curling down until they resembled balls. Now they stood, pitching the Swordmainnir headlong. Jeremiah saw lumpen heads without necks, actinic eyes, massive arms and legs outlined like sketches in phosphorescent blue.

Soundless as figments, voiceless as hallucinations, the creatures moved.

Coldspray and Grueburn crashed to the floor. At the sound, Canrik and Samil wheeled. As if they did not need time to gauge their peril, they sprang at the monsters.

Burning eyes flared. Jeremiah watched in horror as one of the creatures moved to meet the Masters. A swinging arm hit Samil like a bludgeon, threw him against the wall. Jeremiah heard the horrid smack of smashed bone when Samil's skull split. The *Haruchai* collapsed in a mess of blood and brains, sprawled lifeless as a doll.

Canrik evaded a killing blow. He delivered a kick to the monster's shin, a strike that nearly broke his leg. Then he was swatted away like a clod of dirt. Only a frantic twist in the air kept him alive when he collided with the wall.

At the same time, the other stone-thing approached the Giants. Lifting one heavy foot, the creature stamped at Coldspray's back, tried to crush her spine.

She struggled to roll aside; failed. But her armor protected her. The stomp drove the air from her lungs. Her backplate cracked from neck to waist. Nevertheless she was not broken.

Then Frostheart Grueburn heaved herself to her knees, swung her longsword in a wild cut at the monster. The iron bounced away, ringing like a shattered bell: it almost tore itself from her grasp. The stone-thing appeared unharmed. But her blow forced it to step back while it recovered its balance.

Panting curses, the Ironhand wrenched herself upright, gripping her lore-hardened glaive in both fists.

Canrik came to attack again. He moved as quickly as he could; but even his great strength could not mask his limping, or his unsteadiness.

"No!" Coldspray gasped. "Await an opening! We must combine our efforts!"

He staggered to a halt.

At once, she raised her blade as if she meant to chop at the monster's head. Then she surged forward, committed all of her bulk to a straight kick at the creature's chest.

Jeremiah thought that he heard the thews of her knee tear, but she did not cry out. The stone-thing was driven two steps backward, three—

—and Canrik leapt onto the creature's back, clamped his hands over its eyes—

—and Grueburn rushed the other monster. Discarding her longsword, she tackled the creature, wrapped her arms around it, forced it away from Jeremiah. By plain force and desperation, she strove to pitch it into a fall—

—and *moksha* Jehannum slipped into Jeremiah as easily as an indrawn breath.

After that, Jeremiah only knew what was happening to his companions because the Raver cast glances outward. Everything that he might have chosen for himself was taken away.

∞

T he first jolt of possession was cruel as the heat of a wildfire. It burned through Jeremiah leaving nothing but ash. Yet the scalding emotional violation passed in an instant. It was gone before he could even try to scream.

In its wake, it left an utter and unutterable peace.

The tranquility of complete helplessness dismissed his fears, his bitterness, his frantic floundering. Sudden as a crisis of the heart, every responsibility and desire and need was lifted from him. Nothing more could be asked of him—he could ask nothing more of himself—because there were no choices left. He was free at last of anything that resembled humanity.

Oh, he was conscious of *moksha* Jehannum's presence and power, aware in every nerve and fiber. He knew that he had been claimed. He felt the Raver's vast glee, a sensation of triumph like ecstasy or delirium. He recognized the Raver's insatiable hunger for havoc. He knew that he had finally become *moksha*'s tool, and Lord Foul's: a thing that only lived to serve the Despiser.

Yet the effect was not hurtful. It was pure relief, a soothing that mimicked bliss. This act of possession was a gift, a benison, a benediction. It eased him like an act of grace. He had finally become the boy he was meant to be; the boy he should have been ever since he had thrust his hand into Lord Foul's bonfire ten years ago. He had come home to himself.

Do you now discern truth? asked the Raver kindly, eagerly. Long have you striven to evade our intent, long and at great cost. Long have you concealed yourself from suffering, though your wounds festered with every avoided day. Do you now grasp that there can be no surcease or anodyne for an implement, except in its condign use? Do you comprehend that there is both freedom and exaltation in the acceptance of service?

This all true believers know. They submit every desire and gift to the will of beings greater than themselves, and by their surrender they gain redemption. Self-will accrues only fear. It achieves only pain. The highest glory is reached solely by the abdication of self.

Do you understand? Do you acknowledge at last that you are the Despiser's beloved son, in whom he is well pleased?

There the Raver paused. He appeared to be waiting for a response from Jeremiah; a sign of acquiescence. But Jeremiah did not reply. He had forgotten himself and did not remember what was at stake. He was simply at peace. The only part of him that seemed to have an independent existence was the part that regarded the Worm. Yet that sight conveyed neither dread nor anticipation. It had no personal implications. It merely *was*: a fact as real as possession, and as inevitable.

Moksha did not prod him. Patient as the ages, the last of Lord Foul's Ravers waited as if together he and Jeremiah could take all the time in the world. When moments or hours or years had passed, and still Jeremiah had not stirred from his relief, *moksha* Jehannum looked away as if he were mildly interested in the fate of Coldspray and Grueburn and Canrik.

In spite of their exhaustion, Jeremiah's companions fought. With a shout that seemed to rend her heart, Frostheart Grueburn succeeded at toppling her foe. But the stone-thing twisted as it fell, pulled her beneath it. When it landed on her, the impact broke her cataphract as if it were dried clay, tenuous and brittle. Air burst from her lungs.

Nevertheless she rolled away as the monster shifted to strike her. Its blow shook the floor; or the Worm's feeding did. A fretwork of cracks marred the rough surface. Gasping frantically, and shedding shards of armor, she regained her feet.

The other creature flailed blindly, trying to fling Canrik from its back. But its arms could not reach him. Somehow he kept his hands over its eyes. It could not see Coldspray. Through *moksha*, Jeremiah heard or felt the wail of pain from Coldspray's damaged knee. Still she was the Ironhand. She did not relent. She kicked the stone-thing in the chest again; growled through clenched teeth; kicked again. At the same time, Canrik exerted all of his strength to drag the creature's head back. Off balance, the creature stumbled toward the wall.

When it hit, Canrik would be crushed.

They were Jeremiah's friends. Even Canrik—

Samil was already dead.

A vague unease drifted through the boy's tranquility. He felt himself or the Raver frowning.

To *moksha*, Jeremiah admitted, I don't know how.

How? asked the Raver. He sounded bright as new coinage: shining gold stamped with Lord Foul's feral eyes.

I don't know how to be a tool. He hardly heard himself. I don't know enough. I'm like a knife that's too dull. I haven't been sharpened. I'm not ready.

Well said. *Moksha* Jehannum's approval had a salacious tinge; a hint of slaver. All implements must be refined to their purpose. The Despiser's intent is glorious beyond utterance. No mortal born is apt to his hand. You must become greater than the greatest of your former aspirations. You must transcend every demand placed upon you by those lesser beings who sought the profit of your gifts, misnaming their desires love. By submission, you will attain the stature of eternity and awe. The Raver chuckled: a sound like the jaws of a trap closing. As will I in the perfection of my service. Then his attention became more acute. For that reason, I am within you.

Cruel blue silhouetted the fighting beyond Jeremiah. The monster with Canrik on its back appeared to recognize its opportunity. It heaved its granite mass at the wall. But at the last instant, Canrik sprang away. He uncovered the creature's eyes just in time to let the stone-thing see Rime Coldspray thrust her glaive at its throat.

Blue glared like delight. Her blade's point splintered: her sword skidded aside.

Fragments as keen as poniards scattered to the floor. Weakness and her own force dropped Coldspray to her knees. Despair gripped her features like nausea.

Frostheart Grueburn did not hazard another clinch with her foe. Evading heavy blows, she retreated, circled. As soon as she could, she dove to retrieve her longsword, rolled back to her feet. An instant of consternation twisted her mien when she saw the notch that her first blow had left in the iron. But she had no other weapon. Parrying frantically while the metal shivered and shrilled, she retreated again.

Reason? asked Jeremiah.

Indeed, the Raver answered. Take no offense when I observe that you are sadly ignorant. There is no fault in you. The *croyel* was sent to teach rather than to torment you. Alas, it was a petty being, seduced by its own desires. It did not prepare you. Therefore I have intervened.

My task is to whet the dull blade. Yet you are not mere iron. Neither force nor fire will refine you. You require knowledge.

That knowledge I will grant. Behold!

Moksha Jehannum gestured in Jeremiah's mind, and the Staff of Law appeared there as though it had been translated out of his clasp. His hands still held it: his fingers curled like claws on the black wood; like an atavistic denial. Nonetheless he saw its image, precise and tangible, with the vision of thought.

This instrument, said *moksha*, I will not touch. It is loathly and vile, fashioned to thwart me. In your grasp, however, it is mighty, capable of wonders. When it is made to serve your gifts—and when those gifts in turn serve the Despiser—it is potent to affect eternity, shaping order out of shapelessness.

I will guide you to the lore of its proper wielding.

Oh, Jeremiah breathed. Order out of shapelessness. The idea pleased him. Constructs. Building. His one joy. To his granted peace was added an unforeseen happiness, a sense of possibilities.

We do what we must so that we may find worth in ourselves.

He was beginning to understand that there was more than one path to godhood.

Beyond the Staff in his mind, the Staff in his hands, the Giants and Canrik still struggled. Though their strength was waning—though every step and effort drained the life from their muscles—they circled and evaded, apparently trying to maneuver the monsters away from Jeremiah. But the stone-things were no threat to him. They protected him. They had been sent to keep his companions away from the Staff of Law.

Yes, Jeremiah said. Yes.

Moksha's approval seemed to make reality bend and ripple. His voice seemed to be the Worm's.

Then observe closely. That noisome wight, the hated Forestal of abhorred Garroting Deep, has written his will and power upon your instrument. He is among the most despised of our foes, yet even he must serve our lord and master. Such is the Despiser's majesty and cunning. Harken well while I read the runes.

Their import will distress you. This saddens me. The Raver did not sound saddened. I desire only your exaltation. Alas, all knowledge is hurtful. Yet it is also needful. And your discomfort will be brief. You will swiftly return to joy.

Jeremiah nodded his consent. Masked within himself, within the private quietude of graves, he began to ask questions which the Raver did not hear. His time as the *croyel*'s host and victim had taught him that possession was torture. He had only been able to endure it because he had no choice. Why, then, had *moksha* entered him bearing only relief and ease? Why did the Raver trouble to lull him with peace or pleasure?

He suspected that he knew the answer. He had heard too many people talk about *the necessity of freedom*.

And Kastenessen had broken him; but that violation had not destroyed him. Now he realized that the experience had taught him something useful. He knew how to be more than one Jeremiah at a time, each distinct from the others. He could think his own thoughts as well as the Raver's.

What Lord Foul wanted from him, he told himself secretly, was not something that could be compelled. Like wild magic, his talent could not be coerced beyond the small uses which the *croyel* had made of it. No matter how much he was whetted, he would not be able to exceed anything unless he agreed to it. At some point, the Despiser would need Jeremiah to serve him by choice. To submit. The tranquility which *moksha* gave or imposed was a lure.

The idea did not disturb Jeremiah. The Raver's mastery did not allow resistance, or the emotions of resistance. It banished distress. Nevertheless there was more than one Jeremiah—and some of them could be concealed or dissociated in ways which did not attract *moksha* Jehannum's attention.

Bubbling with glee, *moksha* read the Staff. His magicks lit the abstruse symbols, not with fire or shining, but with a deeper black that scorned human notions of darkness. His disembodied finger traced the script as he interpreted it. Yet he did not explain it in words. Instead he gave Jeremiah images.

While the runes came to life, Jeremiah found himself standing on the ruined dirt of Gallows Howe surrounded by the ire of trees.

His presence there was only a vision. He had not passed through time to an age when Caerroil Wildwood's outrage ruled Garroting Deep. His body still sat on the floor of a cave in Mount Thunder, holding the Staff of Law across his thighs, feeling tremors rise through the gutrock; apparently watching his companions fight with their last strength. But his mind—

His mind had followed the Forestal's symbols into the recesses of *moksha* Jehannum's memories.

Everything that Jeremiah beheld, *moksha* viewed with hate, with savagery and revulsion. The dirt under his feet had drunk the deaths of Ravers. Their assumed bodies had dangled from the gibbet of the Howe while their spirits had shrieked in agony. Anywhere else in the Land, anywhere at all, *moksha* or *samadhi* or *turiya* could have simply slipped away when their flesh was taken, sparing themselves the horror of being slain. But in Caerroil Wildwood's demesne, they had been denied that luxury. The Forestal had *forbidden* them. They could not escape.

The recollection made *moksha* Jehannum froth with fury and frustration. Nonetheless what the Raver sought was here, in the innate lore of forbidding; in Caerroil Wildwood's ability to draw power or sentience or resolve or rage from every leaf and branch, every twig and trunk and root, throughout his loathed realm—and then to express that force in ways which *moksha* and his brothers could not withstand.

For the Raver, Gallows Howe summed up everything that he abhorred about forests. But his hatred was more than that. It was wide as well as deep. It included every tree of every variety everywhere: young and old, graceful and gnarled, upright and outstretched. Alone they were each as vulnerable as kindling. Together they were as mighty as mountains. Therefore *moksha* hated them with a vehemence that trembled in every particle of his being. They were everything that he was not: stately, grand, generous, welcoming, austere, fecund. Their existence justified every stretch of ground where they flourished—and the Raver hungered for their extinction.

Jeremiah saw all of this as *moksha* Jehannum saw it. He felt the Raver's fulminating outrage so keenly that he appeared to share it. And he knew that *moksha* wished him to share it. But he also saw the Howe and the Deep with his hidden eyes. He knew the wrath and grief of the innumerable trees. He understood how those passions formed the essence of the Forestal's power. More, he recognized that the forest's vast appetite for bloodshed was not inherent. It was a response to a terrible crime.

The force which lay behind it was not rage, but rather a bereft adoration for the green and living world in all of its fragile guises. The substance and sorrow of everything that Caerroil Wildwood had been and done was his love.

And Garroting Deep was an emblem of the Land. *Moksha*'s hatred of trees was only one manifestation of a more encompassing evil: the fury and despair that despised or feared every aspect of the Land's rich beauty.

This, too, did not trouble Jeremiah. He felt no indignation, no desire to protest.

Instead he considered it among his private selves. He resisted nothing, and so nothing was taken from him. Passive as a victim, he kept his thoughts to himself, as he had done for most of his life.

Frostheart Grueburn still circled on unsteady legs, flailing with her blunted longsword. Rime Coldspray hacked and hacked at her foe until her glaive was shattered to the hilt. Canrik twisted between the stone-thing's legs, trying to trip or topple the monster. But that tactic failed him. The creature was too strong, too heavy.

Still the *Haruchai* struggled. And he had resources of stamina which exceeded even the Swordmainnir: he could still think. When he realized that he was too weak to bring down the monster, he slipped away. Snatching up a long sliver of the Ironhand's sword, he sprang again onto the creature's back. His ragged dirk he pounded into one of its eyes.

The force of his blow sliced open his hand. Blood spurted between his fingers. But the sliver penetrated. Actinic blue blazed for an instant. Then the eye went dark.

The stone-thing had no voice. It could not scream. Nevertheless the reflexive slap of its hands at its face was as wounded as a shriek. One hand swept the shard from its eye. The other caught Canrik's wrist. A fierce swing flung him away.

Entirely by chance, the monster threw him into the tunnel toward Kiril Threndor. He vanished from the cave.

Jeremiah did not see what became of him. He did not know how the Giants stayed on their feet. Yet this sight also did not distress him. He watched his friends impassively, as if he had already succumbed.

He understood forbidding now: the how of it, the why, the necessary power. He had absorbed it without the hindrances of language because *moksha* and the Despiser needed him to understand it. It was essential to Lord Foul's deeper purpose. But Jeremiah's epiphanies went further. On Gallows Howe, with Garroting Deep unfurled like a banner around him, he realized that forbidding was essential to other purposes as well, to desires which were not the Despiser's.

Forbidding was Earthpower, of course; but it was Earthpower transformed by trees and their Forestal into an entirely different form of magic.

To *moksha*, Jeremiah said, I need more.

If forbidding alone had been enough, the Forestals could have defeated Lord Foul themselves.

Indeed. *Moksha* Jehannum's approval was incandescent. Abhorrence is but one refinement. Other whetstones are needed to perfect the blade.

While Jeremiah watched, helpless and unmoved, the Raver took him on a coruscating plunge through other memories, other expressions of recalled lore.

His passage was a whirlwind, a giddy chiaroscuro, a torrent of glimpses and insights. He did not try to grasp them: he hardly looked at them. Instead he simply accepted them; allowed them to be imprinted on his nerves, written into his brain. Some were millennia old: a jeweled casket sunk deep into the mire of the Great Swamp, a tapestry sealed in a cavern lost among the snows of the Northron Climbs, a periapt as crowded with knowledge as a tome. Others were immeasurably ancient: the creation of Forestals from the substance of an *Elohim*, the complex theurgies which had fashioned the Colossus of the Fall, the invocation of Fire-Lions. He did not need to make sense of them because they were already his, ready for his submission and use.

But among the swift confusion of those recollections, Jeremiah found one memory that filled *moksha* Jehannum with a particular delight. It was the Raver's recall of that horrific, wonderful moment when *moksha* had taken possession of Linden.

Perhaps her straits should have appalled Jeremiah; yet they did not. He was intimately familiar with the excruciation which the Raver had inflicted on her, the relish for her torment. He had survived such things himself. And he knew that she had somehow expelled *moksha* Jehannum for Covenant's sake, or for the Land's. She was Linden Avery. *Moksha*'s cruelty could not define her.

However, some of her own memories lived among the Raver's; and *those* wrung Jeremiah's heart. They erased his calmness, dismissed his given relief as if it were nothing more than a mirage. For the first time, he learned what his mother had suffered when she, too, had been just a kid.

Remembered by *moksha*, Jeremiah stood in the attic with her, watching her father bleed out of his cut wrists, and helpless to force the blood back into his veins. Already gashed and dying, that aggrieved man had locked her in with him so that she would not be able to go for help. In effect, he had compelled her to witness his surrender to self-pity: her father.

She had been only eight.

Mom. Jeremiah wanted to wail. *Mom*. But the Raver was not done.

Crowing, *moksha* remembered Linden's mother. At about Jeremiah's present age, she had been at her mother's bedside while her mother had prayed for death. According to *moksha*, the woman's illness may not have been terminal. But Linden had heeded her mother's pleading. Her mother had blamed her, Linden, for causing her husband's death; for making her life unsupportable. And Linden had been left alone to provide care. Wipe away sweat. Mop up dribbling mucus. Tend bedpans. So when Linden had exhausted her own misery, she had—

Jeremiah did not know how to bear it.

—taken wads of tissues and forced them down her mother's throat; forced more and more of them down until her mother would never blame anyone else again.

The Raver reveled in those events. *Moksha* wanted Jeremiah to understand that his mother had always been a victim and a killer. The woman who had claimed to love him was as pitiful and weak as his natural mother. Linden's parents had made her who she was. She would never be anything more. Because of her—*moksha* Jehannum insisted on this as if the truth were beyond question—Jeremiah had always belonged to Lord Foul. From the first, he had been raised to serve Despite by women who had earned their own victimization.

The gift that Lord Foul offered now was more than mere peace, more than simple relief: it was transcendence. Jeremiah's submission would be rewarded with a place in eternity, a form of godhood in which his wounds and struggles would have no meaning. He would be free at last of his inherited unworth.

Moksha urged this vision of Jeremiah's future as if it were perfected delight. And Jeremiah heard the Raver. He recognized what the Raver wanted from him. But he was no longer listening. Within his secret silence, he cried out for the woman who had chosen to be his mother when no power in life could have required her to claim him.

Yes, he told Lord Foul's servant. Yes.

Entirely dissociated from his real circumstances—entirely concealed from his possessor—he meant, Watch your back, you piece of shit. I'm coming for you.

Just do something *he doesn't expect.*

Spasms shook the cave. Forerunners of temporal rupture broke chunks of rock from the ceiling, scattered debris across the floor. Grueburn staggered from side to side gasping for breath, barely able to stand. Canrik lurched back into the cave. He kept his fist clenched to stanch the bleeding of his hand. Desperation twisted his features as he searched for a way to aid the Giants.

Ineffective as a cripple, Coldspray stood directly in front of Jeremiah. The one-eyed monster advanced on her, ready to strike. She waited for it as if she had come to the end of herself and could no longer raise her arms.

But when it reached out to wrap her in a crushing embrace, she lifted the remains of her glaive and hammered the pommel into the creature's good eye.

As the light of that eye died, the blinded stone-thing lashed out. In mute pain, it tossed the Ironhand aside as if she had become trivial.

Now, however, the monster could not see. Confused by its hurts, it seemed unable to locate Coldspray. Instead of pursuing her, it continued its advance. Swinging its massive arms, it came toward Jeremiah.

One inadvertent impact would be enough. He would not survive even a glancing blow. Lord Foul's plans for him—

Inside Jeremiah, *moksha* Jehannum snarled an obscenity. Distracted, he snatched Jeremiah's halfhand off the Staff of Law, drew a swift symbol in the air.

The creature began another step. Halfway through the motion, it suddenly collapsed into dust: a pile of remains stirred only by the tremors rising through the floor.

During that brief instant, Jeremiah took his chance.

He had absorbed astonishing kinds and quantities of lore from the Raver, more knowledge than he could have named. Forbidding was a part of it. An expression of Earthpower called a Word of Warning was a part. The wood-magicks of the *lillianrill* were a part, as were the elaborate healings which the Lords had once wrought in Trothgard, and the music with which Caerwood ur-Mahrtiir had invoked a bower among the wastes of the Lower Land. He knew how the great tree-city of Revelwood in the Valley of Two Rivers had been fashioned.

But that was not all: he had learned more. If he had been released, he could have devised a prison which would have snared *moksha* Jehannum until Time was extinguished. Given a few uninterrupted days, he could have repaired the damage that ancient violence had done to Mount Thunder's heart. With a few years and a Forestal's aid, he could have made a garden of the Lower Land.

But the Raver had not released him, and he had only an instant. When his opportunity came, he did not hesitate.

One small sip of Earthpower from the Staff restored his inherited theurgy. Then he rose up from helplessness to trade places with his possessor.

In the space of a single heartbeat, he trapped *moksha* Jehannum inside himself.

The Raver struggled, screaming. Of course he struggled. He knew everything that Jeremiah did. He had long ages of experience to guide him. He had frenzy and ripe terror. And Jeremiah was only mortal. He lacked the intransigent metal of a *Haruchai*. He did not have the great spirit of a Giant. He had no inborn capacity to defy possession.

But he had resources which Lord Foul's servant could not match. Linden had blessed him with long years of care and tenderness. Anele had given him power. He had learned how to walk away from the helplessness with which he had protected himself. And he was not afraid to grasp the Staff of Law.

Moksha howled horror at the ceiling. He thrashed and writhed, raked frantic claws across the barriers which Jeremiah raised against him, sank sharp teeth into the flesh of Jeremiah's resolve. Wild and despairing, the Raver fought.

Yet Jeremiah refused the fight. He did not need to measure his strength against his foe. Instead he relied on knowledge which *moksha* did not share. Retracing his own past, he *dissociated* the Raver; committed Lord Foul's servant to the graveyard where he himself had once lain, hidden and lost. Almost effortlessly, he dropped the Raver into the waiting earth.

With Earthpower and newly acquired lore, he clamped down on *moksha* Jehannum until he could no longer hear the Raver's screams. He piled dirt over the malign spirit, stamped the grave flat. Then he turned away.

At one side of the cave, Rime Coldspray tried to regain her feet, but she could not. Trying to evade the second monster, Frostheart Grueburn had crumpled to her knees. Canrik had found another splinter of Coldspray's glaive. Now he looked for an opening, a chance to sacrifice his other hand.

Gritting his teeth, Jeremiah rose up in power. A detonation like a thunderclap from one heel of the Staff tore the stone-thing apart. Rendered to powder, it fell.

The floor heaved. The ceiling shed more rocks. Cracks yawned open, grated shut. Here and there, wounds split the walls. Patches of gutrock oozed and ran as if their essences were being squeezed out of them.

"I'm sorry," Jeremiah panted: a faint echo of his friends' gasping. "I mean, I'm sorry that took so long. First I didn't know how to do it. Then I had to wait for a chance."

A chance which the Swordmainnir and Canrik had given him.

"Do not heed us," the Ironhand managed to say between broken breaths. "The Timewarden— The Worm—"

Jeremiah did not have time to think. Covenant needed him. Canrik was already waiting for him at the tunnel toward Kiril Threndor.

He took the time. "You're joking." His tone hinted at *moksha*'s glee. He had enjoyed immuring the Raver. "I can't leave you like this. You don't look strong enough to stand.

"This is Mom's Staff. It doesn't really belong to me. But I know how to use it now."

Then he released a second blast of Earthpower.

This detonation was as fierce as the force which had destroyed the stone-thing; but it was an entirely different kind of theurgy, a more natural magic. It hurt Coldspray and Grueburn, but it did not damage them. Instead it delivered violent healing, a ferocity of repair. He had learned too much too quickly: he was not capable of gentleness. And the Worm was feeding. Concussions spread through the substance of the world. Disruptions of Time mounted toward the last crisis of the Earth. He had to reach Kiril Threndor and Covenant.

In a moment, he was done. He stamped the Staff on the floor once because he had no words for what he felt. Then he gathered himself to follow Canrik.

Until he saw Rime Coldspray climb to her feet and test her limbs, trembling as if she were feverish—until he felt Frostheart Grueburn standing near him, and Canrik watching with open surprise—Jeremiah did not notice that the cave was full of warm light. He had taken it for granted—

The Staff felt like recognition in his hands. It sent out broad swaths of flame as kindly and soothing as sunshine. Its shaft shone with the cleanliness of healthy heartwood. Along its surface, Caerroil Wildwood's runes remained, distinct as promises, but their meaning was no longer obscure. They were an offering and an appeal: they enabled and prayed.

To Jeremiah Chosen-son, the descendant of Sunder and Hollian in spirit if not in body, the Forestal's script pleaded for restoration.

12.

You Are Mine

 At the edge of Kiril Threndor's high chamber, Thomas Covenant stood motionless, held by shock and fury while he scrambled to absorb what he saw.

Anger was not what he needed here: he knew that. If he had failed to see the truth for himself, he could have heeded High Lord Berek among the Dead. *He may be freed only by one who is compelled by rage*— Ire would mislead him when he absolutely had to be the master of himself.

But he could not control what he felt.

Well, hi, Dad. That was his son. His *son*, wracked like a plague victim by power and malice. *You took your own sweet time getting here.* His son with Lord Foul's putrescent eyes.

The Despiser had claimed Covenant's lost boy at last. Lord Foul had taken possession—

The sight set a spark to the driest tinder in Covenant's soul. Between one breath and the next, he became conflagration; incandescent wrath. Wild fire flushed across his skin in waves like the urgent knot and release of his heart. Flames spat from his eyes, lashed out from his arms and chest. His vehemence cast argent through the diseased chiaroscuro of rocklight. Bright killing gathered like a blade in the scar on his forehead.

Berek had warned Linden. He had warned Covenant. But he had said nothing about the means by which Lord Foul might gain freedom.

"What's the matter, Dad?" Roger glared as though his whole being had been consumed by scorn; as though he had been torn apart and put back together wrong. Denied anguish contorted his visage. At every moment, he looked more like a maimed thing, twisted beyond recognition. His right hand was sick lava, fuming and rotten. "Aren't you glad to see me?"

His plight demanded pity. For Covenant, pity was rage.

A step ahead of Covenant, Branl regarded the figure on the dais. He held Longwrath's flamberge negligently, as if he had no further use for it. "Ur-Lord," he remarked as though he had been studying a particularly uninteresting icon, "I now comprehend why I was unable to discern the presence of Corruption. His aura was both blurred by Kastenessen's *skurj*-born theurgy and disguised by his human vassal. Here his evil is plain. Corruption has taken your son, or your son has given himself. We must oppose both or neither. We cannot harm the spirit while the flesh shields it."

Hell and blood. Covenant had no answer for the Humbled. He had none for Roger. Wreathed in flame, he tightened his grip on the *krill* and started forward. Fissures marred the floor in front of him like the outcome of his anger; but he ignored them. Dizzying reflections and stalactites and tortured slabs of granite meant nothing to him. With every stride, he raised Loric's dagger higher. The radiance of its gem filled his voice.

"Let him go," he snarled at the Despiser. "This is between you and me. *Leave him out of it.*"

"Dad!" Roger feigned surprise. He feigned dismay. "You still don't get it." He lifted his inhuman hand to match the *krill*. A brimstone stench covered the reek of attar. The redder heat of magma daunted the rocklight. "None of this would have happened if you and that damn woman hadn't interfered. All I wanted was the *croyel*— the *croyel* and Jeremiah—but you wouldn't let me have them. If you had stayed out of my way, I wouldn't be here.

"This is *your* doing, Dad. It's the only choice I had left."

"I don't care," Covenant retorted. "You did this to yourself. Nobody forced you. All you had to do was take pity on your mother," on poor, deranged Joan, who had no defense, "and none of this would have happened."

"Really?" drawled Roger. His grimace mimicked a sneer. "You actually think that? You should care. I'll tell you why. Since you seem oblivious to what's been going on, I'll explain it.

"My *mother*"—he spat the word—"was useless. She couldn't help me. She was just a distraction to keep you away from me. The *croyel* and Jeremiah were my way out. While I had them, I didn't have to *serve* anybody. *I* didn't have to care. But you took that away, you and that damn woman. You slammed the door on me, *Dad*. This is what I have left.

"I'm not going to die no matter what you do, and do you know why?" Pressures within Roger clawed terrible shapes across his face. Lurid fires filled his eyes. Threats dunted from his halfhand. "Lord Foul is going to take me with him. That's the deal. I gave myself to him, and he's going to give me eternity. We're just waiting until the Arch crumbles enough to let us out. Then we'll be gone. It'll be like you and this whole disgusting place never existed.

"I'm letting him do what he wants because *he's going to save me!*"

Halfway to the flawless dais, Covenant halted; froze on the verge of howling his fury. The pain in Roger's voice stopped him. He could almost hear the hollowness of his son's soul.

Branl was right. Of course he was. Covenant could not strike at Lord Foul without hitting Roger first. He would have to kill his son in order to hurt the Despiser—and he had already killed his son's mother.

He needed a better answer. Somehow he had to set anger aside, swallow horror. Roger's sarcasm and arrogance masked the truth. The young man was appalled by what he had done to himself.

"No," Covenant snapped, wrestling for composure. "He won't take you with him. Whatever he offered you won't be what you think it is." He had cloaked himself in fire and outrage as if they were a shield, but he could shrug them off his shoulders if he dared. If he could find the courage. "You're scared, Roger. You're too scared to think. You aren't using your brain.

"You're physical. Don't you understand that? You're mortal. Time is all you've got. It's the only thing that makes life possible. Without it, you're nothing. You're just—"

The floor heaved, shaken by Roger's impatience or the Worm's feeding. Cracks groaned in the walls. The stalactites scattered rocklight and silver in pieces sharp as shards. Covenant lost his balance, staggered until Branl caught him.

"Well, duh," Roger snorted. "Of course I'm physical. That's why he needs me. That's why I can trust him. He needs me to get rid of you.

"I'll give you this, Dad. Lord Foul is afraid of you. You've surprised him too often when he thought he had you beat. But that won't happen this time. That's what *I'm* for. That's why he made a deal with me. I'm going to make sure you don't surprise him again."

Resisting a rush of frenzy, Covenant shouted, "No! He's just *using* you. He doesn't *need* you. He can be as physical as he wants whenever he wants." Covenant had not forgotten the tangible impact of the Despiser's contempt when Covenant had faced the Illearth Stone in Foul's Creche. "But you can't be as eternal as you want. You're *dross* to him. You're more than a hindrance, you're a prison. He can't escape the collapse of Time while he's inside you. If he tries that, he'll die when you do. He won't get out unless he leaves you behind.

"And when he does, you won't be able to follow him, and you sure as hell won't be able to accompany him, because you're just *you*. You aren't made for eternity. You're just a frightened man who can't stand being afraid. Giving yourself to Foul isn't hope, it's *panic*."

Roger was roaring like his hand, poised to strike; but Covenant did not pause. "You're going to die like the rest of us," he insisted. "No deal can save you. Foul can't make you a god. He knows that as well as I do. If you can convince yourself otherwise, you've been serving him longer than you think."

"*No*, Dad." Tremors like hysteria shook Roger's voice. Pain wrenched at the corners of his mouth. "You've got it all wrong. Lord Foul doesn't lie. He promised I would stop being afraid. He promised what's happening now is temporary. He promised I would never be in pain again."

Sure, Covenant wanted to reply. It's all true. You *won't* be afraid. You'll be dead.

But a sudden surge of power from the dais closed his throat. Abruptly Roger's voice changed. "*Enough.*" It became the sound of crushed boulders, falling mountains. It had the depth and resonance of a tectonic upheaval. "That promise I will honor. I will put an end to your fawning. Now you will be silent. I will speak to this doomed wight who deems himself my foe."

Involuntarily Roger bit down on his tongue. Blood leaked from his mouth. His eyes bled venom.

At the same time, behind or within or through Roger, Covenant saw another figure, a towering shape taller than Giants, mightier than the spectres of High Lords. Authority and rocklight limned the form; but within its outlines was nothing but absence, an emptiness like the chasm of the Lost Deep. The figure's sole feature was its fanged eyes. They resembled Roger's, yellow and bitter. But the ferocity in them, or the despair, was fiercer than Roger's denied terror.

"Ur-Lord," Branl warned unnecessarily. "Corruption manifests. Yet he also retains possession of your son."

"Oh, good," Covenant snarled at the Despiser. "I'm glad. Now I can talk to you directly.

"You really ought to be ashamed of yourself. You don't need surrogates. You should have the decency to let Roger go. Or if you can't manage decency, you should at least have the dignity. Using him just makes you look craven."

Lord Foul expanded. He made himself too big to be confined by Kiril Threndor. Yet his lambent silhouette remained visible, as if he had superimposed himself on the rock.

"We are well met, Timewarden." He did not shout, yet every word was a blast of ruin. "In times past, I have named you groveler, anile and foolish, but I now perceive that you have become worthy of me. Your death has been made certain. No exertion is required of me to assure it. Nevertheless I acknowledge that at last you merit extinction at my hand."

"Sure." Covenant readied the *krill*. As much as he could, he ignored Lord Foul's fierce shape, concentrated on Roger. "Try it. I'm not going to surrender again. And I am done with restraint."

The Despiser laughed like grinding stones. "Yet you have not forgotten folly. That pleases me." His eyes and Roger's bit at the air. "I find delight in your misbelief that you are potent to oppose me.

"Have you forgotten, Timewarden? Does mortal recall fail within you even now? I have assured you that you are mine. You have been my servant always, though you have twice refused submission. Each and all of your efforts to thwart me have conduced to my present triumph. Because you have dared to oppose me, I will be made free."

Covenant shook his head. "Maybe *you're* the one who's forgotten. We've talked about this before. It goes both ways. If I'm yours, you're also mine. Maybe I've always been yours, but I made you mine when I let you kill me.

"And apparently you've forgotten Linden. You tried to tell her the same thing. According to you, everything she does guarantees your escape. But she's still here. She's still doing things you didn't expect and couldn't imagine. She may even find a way to keep you here when reality falls apart."

The Despiser swelled. He appeared to gather vehemence. But Covenant did not flinch.

"And haven't you forgotten Jeremiah? Don't you need him? Isn't he essential to your *deeper purpose*? How can you even hope to use him when he has the Staff of Law?"

Lord Foul's laughter was savage. It felt unanswerable.

"Indeed, the boy holds the Staff of Law. But my servant *moksha* has taken possession of him. Even now, he awaits my will. Through him, Law itself promotes my intent."

Oh, hell! In spite of his fire, Covenant faltered. *Moksha* had Jeremiah? The walls of the chamber seemed to contract around him. Futures for which he had prayed faded like hallucinations. He had gambled on the boy: gambled and lost.

How would Linden bear it when she learned that her son served the Despiser?

At that moment, Roger struck. His halfhand hurled a bolt of incineration at his father.

Reflexively Covenant caught the blast with Loric's *krill*; blocked it with the gem's radiance and an outpouring of wild magic. Argent against laval crimson, flame against the savagery of molten stone, he fought to save himself.

But he hardly knew what he was doing. He lost track of Branl. The dagger bucked in his grasp: Roger's force tried to tear it from his numb fingers. The coruscation of powers blinded him. Briefly Kiril Threndor inverted itself. He depended from the floor, felt himself falling toward the ceiling. Then the whole chamber reeled, giddy as vertigo.

He clung to the *krill* instinctively, sent his heart's need like lightning through the blade's cut jewel; floundered to survive.

His son's might appalled him. Roger was stronger now. The severing of his human hand from Kastenessen had not weakened him. Nor had Kastenessen's passing into the fane of the *Elohim*. Roger's given fist retained the ravaging force of the *skurj*. And Lord Foul stood behind him or within him, supporting him.

Soon the *krill* would start to melt. It had to. Nothing mortal-made could endure Roger's virulence, or Covenant's wild response.

Upright beyond the ceiling and the stalactites, the breaking gutrock, Lord Foul watched. His eyes gnashed approval.

Blasts like magma knocked Covenant's weapon from side to side. Feral heat chewed into his hands, gnawed at his arms. And his dead nerves betrayed him. They spared him from the worst of the pain, but they also weakened his grip. The hilt twisted. The skin of his fingers seemed slick as spilth. He could not hold.

He had to hold. The moment of his last crisis was upon him. Catastrophes burned in the bones of his forehead. Everything that he required of himself while life remained in his body depended on his ability to grip and hold.

Somehow he withstood Roger's assault. He had more than the *krill*: he had wild magic. In some sense, he *was* white gold. The power possible for him was limited only by his humanity, his flesh and sinew and passion. Loric's dagger was not melting. Even Covenant's hands were not. They were preserved by the theurgies that saved and damned; by the contradiction of renewal and ruin that formed the keystone of the Arch of Time. As long as he did not let go—

But he could not do more; could not advance to threaten Roger or the Despiser. Together they were too strong. Roger's savagery demanded his utmost, and his utmost was not enough.

And while he fought to withstand lava and malice, he gave no heed when the boulders against the walls opened themselves and became monsters.

Two of them. Three.

Apparently the Despiser was not satisfied. He desired Covenant's death too much to let Roger fail.

The stone-things were vacancies. Despite their actinic auras, they were only visible to ordinary sight. Branl did not sense them. His attention was fixed on Covenant's struggle. One step at a time, he circled obliquely closer to the dais. But he was looking for an opening, a chance to attack while Covenant distracted Roger. He was not watching for other threats.

As massive as monoliths, and as silent, two of the creatures lumbered toward the Humbled from opposite sides. The third advanced on Covenant.

Covenant saw nothing except white fire and ruddy brimstone; felt nothing except the tearing heat of Roger's theurgy. Roger had called him *oblivious*. He was oblivious now. There was no room in his heart or his mind for anything beyond the extremity of his need to hold on.

But Branl was *Haruchai*. He may have been as transfixed as Covenant; may have felt as desperate. Nevertheless he was a warrior to the bone, defined by combat. A heartbeat before the nearer stone-thing drew close enough to hit him, he saw it.

Whatever he thought or felt at that moment, he did not hesitate. Spinning away from the dais, he swung a two-handed cut at the side of the creature's neck.

The clang of iron shivered among the stalactites. The flamberge bounced back, singing with stress.

The monster lurched to a halt. A third of its throat had been sliced open.

Branl needed an instant to regain control of his blade. Then he swung again.

This time, the creature folded to its knees. Slow as a sigh, it collapsed on its face and became dust.

Febrile with pain and hate, Roger fed the mounting holocaust. Through the glare, Covenant descried Roger's features. Their agonized contortion seemed to cry out, wailing of needs and fears that surpassed sound, exceeded the firestorm of powers. Roger's mouth shaped words which Covenant could not hear.

Dad, Covenant's son seemed to be saying, help me.

Abruptly his own dread and hurt fell away. The burning of his hands lapsed into numbness. His grip steadied the *krill* against Roger's onslaught. Wild magic rose to a pitch too acute for perception. *Moksha* Jehannum had taken Jeremiah. Covenant did not know what had become of Linden, but he knew that She Who Must Not Be Named was too strong to be defeated. And the Worm of the World's End was feeding. Forces mightier than Covenant's struggle shook Mount Thunder to its roots. He was losing everything that he had ever striven to preserve. Nevertheless he was not daunted. He still had something to fight for.

His son was possessed. Roger bore the immedicable wound of Kastenessen's hand. He had been a fool—a fool and a coward—but that changed nothing. He had not chosen his parents; had not caused his mother's weakness or his father's absence. Now the extravagance of his distress made Covenant's voluntary hurts seem trivial.

A different kind of anger dismissed Covenant's pain; his earlier wrath. This new ire resembled his old, familiar rage for lepers. It was a passion colder, calmer, and more complete than his desire to hurt the Despiser: a sympathy so furious that it felt like exultation.

Clenching Loric's dagger, he concentrated his outpouring of fire through the gem. Then he began to force his way toward the dais. One step at a time, he advanced against torrential magma and malevolence.

"No!" the Despiser shouted. "I will not permit it!"

While Branl stood over the fallen stone-thing, the second creature came at his back. One sweep of its granite arm smashed his shoulder, flung him at the wall. Noiseless amid the cacophony of magicks, the flamberge clattered to the floor. He struggled to rise, but his legs failed him.

In that instant, Stave appeared in Kiril Threndor as though he had dropped from the ceiling. Somehow Linden had translated him here. He would not have left her side willingly.

Nonetheless he was *Haruchai*: he did not need time to gauge what was happening around him. As his feet touched the floor, he dove for Branl's longsword. A roll brought him upright with the flamberge in his fists. His momentum carried him into a straight lunge at the creature which had struck the Humbled.

In spite of its antiquity, the blade retained some vestige of Kasreyn's lore. It drove deep into the monster's chest. When Stave wrenched out the longsword, the stone-thing toppled to one side. Dying, it turned to powder and drifted away.

Reflections of brimstone and wild magic flashed in Stave's eye as he hastened to stand between Covenant and the third monster. His mien was a taut mask of outrage and grief.

Linden, Covenant thought. Oh, God. What have you done?

But he did not stop fighting.

"No!" Lord Foul roared again. "I will not *permit* it!"

Scourged by his possessor, Roger shifted his aim. Fierce as a scream, he turned his power away from Covenant.

A mistake—In the space between instants, Covenant thought that the Despiser had misjudged his foes—or had simply been overcome by his own fury. The *Haruchai* could not oppose him. Covenant was the real danger.

Then, however, Covenant saw the frenzy in Roger's eyes—saw the Despiser's bitterness dulled by a more human anguish—saw Roger hurl coerced scoria, not at Stave, who shielded Covenant, but at Branl, who could not.

The Humbled lay gasping against the wall. One shoulder had been shattered. Other bones were broken. His legs refused to hold him. Still he managed to wrench himself aside.

Roger's blast did not destroy him. Instead it made a smoking ruin of his wrecked arm, stripped the flesh from his ribs. Even that lesser damage might have killed him;

but Roger's attack cauterized as it burned. Branl was stricken unconscious: he did not bleed. His chest still heaved for air.

Roger had done that: *Roger*. It was as close to an act of mercy as he could manage. In spite of Lord Foul's mastery, Roger had left Stave alive to protect Covenant.

And Covenant—

Covenant recognized his chance.

In a stumbling rush, he ran at Roger, gained the dais. Faster than he could think, he slashed with the *krill*.

One swift stroke severed Kastenessen's hand.

The hand exploded; or Lord Foul's presence in Roger did. The concussion tossed Covenant away. He hit hard enough to crack his skull. A whirlwind of little suns wheeled across his mind. He lost the dagger somewhere. Blood started from his eyes. It ran from his ears. He could not feel his arms, his legs. A gyre of disconnected instants sucked at the verges of reality.

"*You*," raged the Despiser, "will not *prevail*!"

A clutch of theurgy yanked Covenant from the stone, threw him farther. He skidded like scattered bones over slabs and fissures.

He had no strength, no weapon. He might as well have had no limbs. Another throw would finish him.

Sightless and desperate, he answered with wild magic. His mind became white fire. Violent flames poured from every part of him that still had living nerves and could feel pain.

"You bastard." Roger seemed to be shrieking at Lord Foul, but Covenant heard only whispers. "You lied to me."

"And do you now take offense, little man?" snorted the Despiser. "I do not regard your umbrage. I do not speak lies. If you heard falsehood, it was of your own making. Now you will suffer the outcome of your folly. Take comfort in the knowledge that your abjection will be brief."

Radiating fire like waves of fever, Covenant tried to blink the blood out of his eyes; struggled to see.

He lay on a canted sheet of basalt. Vaguely past its rim, he glimpsed the unharmed dais, the broken clutter of stalactites. The furious shape of Lord Foul still dominated the chamber, too immense to be opposed or endured.

Branl lay where he had been struck. Stave had vanished or fallen. Had he confronted another monster? Covenant had no idea how many stone-things still moved in Kiril Threndor.

But over there, to the left of the dais, stood Roger, unpossessed and human. Fountains of blood had streaked his clothes, stained his face. Facing the Despiser, he huddled over his pain with his gushing wrist clamped under his arm to slow the bleeding. He glanced at Covenant; at Covenant's undifferentiated, useless flail of power. Then he turned back to Lord Foul.

Tremors ran through the floor. They staggered Roger, rocked Covenant mercilessly. The Despiser and the dais they did not affect.

Lord Foul's biting eyes loomed over Covenant. "As for you," he sneered, "beaten Unbeliever, impotent Timewarden, I have reconsidered your doom. Though I hunger for your death, I also crave your despair. Therefore I have asked of myself which end will wound your spirit more grievously, a death in agony at my hands, or an occasion to witness the final devastation of all that you hold dear. Remain as you are, and you may observe my return to majesty. Continue to oppose me, and I will snuff your frail life as you would a lantern."

Squinting, Covenant located the *krill*. It was too far away.

Grip and hold.

Try it, he panted, although he could not speak. See what happens. He could hardly move. You haven't won yet.

Nevertheless his shining faltered. He let his power fall away.

Then he found himself rising to his feet. Stave lifted him from behind, supported him when he could not stand alone.

The last of Lord Foul's stone defenders was gone.

The chamber juddered as if it had been struck by the leading edge of a tsunami. Covenant's guts and chest knotted, threatening to retch blood. But Stave's arms sustained him.

Softly Stave breathed, "*Moksha* Jehannum has taken the Chosen-son." He had dropped the flamberge. He had no more use for it. "Canrik cannot succor him. The Ironhand and Frostheart Grueburn cannot. Samil has been slain."

"Linden?" Covenant coughed: an effort that seemed to grind the broken ends of ribs against each other.

"I know not." Stave did not disguise his bitterness. "She cast me from her ere she was claimed by the bane. I desire to hope that she lives, yet I cannot."

A moment later, the former Master whispered, "I do not comprehend, Timewarden. Time comes unbound. Soon it will unravel entirely. Why does Corruption remain?"

Through a mouthful of blood, Covenant panted, "He's enjoying himself too much." After uncounted millennia of imprisonment— "He knows he's already won. He's just waiting for Jeremiah."

And while Lord Foul waited—

Covenant wanted to strike. He ached for the strength to stop the Despiser. But he was too weak. Too badly hurt. Sick with grief for Linden and Jeremiah. He had nothing left except waiting.

Roger deserved a better father.

Roger was crying. He may have wanted words, but he could only manage sobs. A young man who had dreamed of eternity—

"Timewarden," Stave demanded, uncharacteristically urgent, "some deed we must attempt. We cannot condone this doom."

I know, Covenant thought dimly. I just need a chance to breathe.

He needed something to believe in. Something to hope for.

What kind of idiot thinks he can save the world by himself?

He had forgotten how seductive despair could be.

"Hear me, Timewarden," ordered Stave. "I will endeavor to retrieve the *krill*. Should I succeed, you must wield it. You must—"

Covenant gripped Stave's arm weakly; tried to restrain the *Haruchai*, although of course he could not. Spitting blood, he croaked, "Wait. He wants Jeremiah. We still have time."

Too much wild magic would only hasten the fall of the Arch. It would ease the Despiser's departure.

Stave did not move. He may have trusted Covenant. He may have simply hesitated.

Lord Foul's gaze had turned away. He appeared to peer through rock toward the cave where Covenant had left Jeremiah. His eyes dripped eagerness. He was as vulnerable as he would ever be.

We still have time.

Covenant had abandoned Linden's son to *moksha* Raver.

Suddenly the Despiser's eyes flared. They blazed like torches. His outrage stunned Covenant's ears. Kiril Threndor lurched in the mountain's chest as though Mount Thunder had suffered a fatal crisis.

Stave said something. He may have been shouting, but Covenant could not hear him.

Roger was moving.

Broken as a derelict, as the wreckage of his dreams, Roger stumbled toward the dais. He crouched. When he rose again, he clutched High Lord Loric's dagger.

As he raised his arm, fresh blood pumped from his severed stump. Red splashed across the stone like an accusation.

His screaming seemed soundless as he hammered the blade into Lord Foul's impalpable shape.

A puny attack, too low and frail to accomplish anything. And the Despiser was mighty: he was scarcely physical. Nevertheless wild magic coruscated in the dagger's gem. Loric had forged his blade to mediate between irreconcilable possibilities. It was the highest achievement of his vast lore. Somehow it *hurt*—

In spite of Lord Foul's vast power, the *krill* appeared to nail him where he stood; fix him in one place. He gathered his fury into a fist. With a single punch, he crushed Roger to wet pulp. But he did not leave the dais. Did not slip past the restrictions of time.

Roger—

Now Covenant heard Stave yelling, "The Chosen-son has freed himself!"

At last. Now or never.

Covenant was battered and deadened, too weak to support his own weight, broken in ways which he was too fraught to name. But he was still a white gold wielder, a by God *rightful* white gold wielder. And he had made promises. *I am done with restraint*. He hit Lord Foul with fire as fierce as a bayamo.

The Despiser thrashed, howling. As if the effort were insignificant, he expelled the *krill*. Then he turned on Covenant. Enraged and savage, he countered with so much force that Covenant's bones should have been pulverized.

Stones heaved. Igneous slabs were tossed like dried leaves. Repercussions ripped down the remaining stalactites, filled the air with whirling debris.

But Covenant withstood the blast. Wild magic withstood it. He had surrendered once. Never again.

Jeremiah had found a way to defeat *moksha* Jehannum. Help was coming. All Covenant had to do was survive. And keep hurting Lord Foul. Prevent his escape. The Despiser must have believed that he would still be able to claim Jeremiah before Time collapsed in on itself. Covenant had no intention of letting that happen.

Powers mounted in Kiril Threndor. Incinerating silver and Lord Foul's sledgehammer blows staggered the chamber. Covenant only knew that Stave still lived because he, Covenant, had not fallen to his knees. He no longer saw anything, heard anything. Yet he *felt* everything as if his nerves were white gold, as if his senses were wild magic. He recognized every concatenation of Lord Foul's malevolence. He could have named each of his own responses.

His millennia within the Arch of Time had not been wasted on him. His heart and his mind and even his leper's body understood wild magic. He was half translated out of reality himself, refined by fire and determination until he hardly needed his own physical existence.

He could not keep the Despiser here: he knew that. Instants were fraying. Moments bled into each other. Causes and sequences were becoming confused. Lord Foul might outlive such uncertainties: Covenant could not. He fought only to distract his foe, to engage the Despiser's endless hatred. To make the Despiser *miss his chance*.

Then the chance came, Lord Foul's or Covenant's.

With flame and effort rather than sight, Covenant saw Jeremiah enter the chamber; saw Jeremiah running wreathed in Earthpower as clean and necessary as sunlight. The heartwood Staff in his hands blazed with a purity that pierced rocklight and argent, defied Lord Foul's savagery.

Behind him came Coldspray, Grueburn, and Canrik, but this contest was not for them. Like Stave and Branl, they had done more than Covenant could have asked or imagined. Their part in the Land's fate was finished. Only Jeremiah had the power to alter the terms of Covenant's struggle.

And Jeremiah knew what was needed. While Covenant fought to block Lord Foul, preclude Jeremiah's possession, Jeremiah fashioned his magicks—

The Despiser's instant reaction was glee, triumph, exultation. He reached for Jeremiah as if he were pouncing. But wild magic tore through the hands of Lord Foul's power, shredded his grasp. Covenant ripped apart the Despiser's clutch while Jeremiah wrought Earthpower.

In the guts of Mount Thunder, the consequences of the Worm's feeding expanded. Shock after shock, they mounted toward their final outcome. Waves ran up and down the walls as if the rock had become water. Granite pain dripped from facets of rocklight. Unnatural heat and cold gusted at Covenant's face like gasping, like strained exhalations of time.

In a moment or an hour—in no time at all—Lord Foul appeared to realize what was happening. He appeared to recognize that he had to flee. If he wanted freedom, he had to abandon his *deeper purpose* against the Creator. He would be trapped otherwise. He would cease to exist.

Shrieking like the deaths of stars, he turned away.

But he was already too late. Because Jeremiah—

Oh, God, Jeremiah!

—had learned how to *forbid*.

With Earthpower and extravagance—the whetted extremity of a boy who had been hurt too much and was finally done with helplessness—Jeremiah forbade Lord Foul's escape.

In horror, the Despiser wheeled to face his foes again.

Covenant he ignored. Wild magic ripped through his fleshless form, sent fiery harm careering everywhere along his disembodied nerves; but he was not dissuaded. He knew pain too well: he had spent eons wrapped in his own agony. Damage and diminishment could be repaired. His chance for freedom would never come again.

Every force at his command, Lord Foul focused on Jeremiah. But now he did not strive to take possession. Instead he sought to destroy.

He knew more about forbidding than Jeremiah did. He was stronger than the boy would ever be. When Covenant wounded him, he could call on long ages of despair to secure his concentration.

At first, Jeremiah wielded the Staff with an exalted certainty. He had freed himself from *moksha* Raver: he had earned his power. And he had spent too much of his life immured in dissociation. His need to repudiate Despite defined him. Nevertheless he was only himself; only human. Lord Foul was the Despiser, eternal and insatiable. Although Covenant fought as hard as he could, flailed desperately and did ferocious damage, Jeremiah began to falter.

The Staff trembled in his grasp. His arms shook. His eyes were cries of dismay. He gave his utmost—and it was not enough. Bit by bit, his forbidding began to crumble.

"*Jeremiah!*" Covenant yelled: a shout of conflagration. "Hold on! *I'm coming!*"

With Stave's help, he floundered toward the dais, flaying his foe as he approached. But he already knew that he would fail. He could have torn open Mount Thunder's entire torso—he felt destructiveness on that scale within him—but he could not block Lord Foul's flight. Wild magic was the wrong kind of power. Like the Despiser, white gold aspired to freedom; and any forbidding required the structures and commandments of Law.

Jeremiah dropped to one knee. Blood burst from his mouth. Earthpower pouring from the Staff began to gutter. In another moment—

Jeremiah! Oh, God!

Without warning, an overwhelming thunder swept through Kiril Threndor. It staggered the whole mountain. For an instant, Covenant thought that the Worm had drunk its fill; that the World's End had come. Then he saw more clearly.

A hand like the fist of a god struck down the Despiser. Strength that threatened to crack Covenant's mind left Lord Foul crumpled on the dais, almost corporeal, almost whimpering. A transcendent touch secured Jeremiah's forbidding. As if as an after-thought, something supernal deposited Linden at Jeremiah's side.

A heartbeat later, the thunder passed on, leaving the Earth to its own ruin. In the power's absence, the rising convulsions of the Worm's feeding felt like a reprieve.

Linden clasped Jeremiah, helped him stand again. Her return renewed his resolve, his strength. Fresh Earthpower crowded the chamber. Refusals tightened around the Despiser.

Covenant believed that he was deaf as well as blind. Wild magic was all that kept him alive. Nonetheless he heard Linden say, "She Who Must Not Be Named is gone. I gave Her what She needed. This must be what She calls gratitude.

"I love you, Thomas."

It's enough, Covenant thought. Thank you. It's enough.

But he could not afford to pause. Reality was coming undone around him, and he had not confronted his worst fears.

He could do that now. Linden had come. She was whole and here. The emblem and summation of all betrayed women had given Covenant that gift.

Mustering his own gratitude, he urged Stave to support him until he gained the dais.

The Despiser was smaller now, beaten down or reduced by the bane's retribution. He was almost Covenant's size. He hunched into himself as though he sought to hide. As though he wanted to be smaller still.

With wild magic and leprosy, Covenant reached out to him. With pity and terror, Covenant lifted Lord Foul upright.

This was his last crisis. There could be no more.

"Do you understand?" he asked like a man bidding farewell. "If I'm yours, you're mine. We're part of each other. We're too much alike. We want each other dead. But you're finished. You can't escape now. And I'm too weak to save myself. If we want to live, we have to do it together."

The Despiser met Covenant's gaze. "You will not." The voice of the world's iniquity sounded hollow as a forsaken tomb. His eyes were not fangs. They were wounds, gnashed and raw. "You fear me. You will not suffer me to live."

"Yes," Covenant answered, "I will."

He was blinded now, not by fires and fury, but by tears as he closed his arms around his foe. Opening his heart, he accepted Lord Foul the Despiser into himself.

∞

When it was done, Thomas Covenant turned to the people who had redeemed him. If he could have looked at himself, he would have seen the scar on his forehead gleaming.

"Thomas," Linden breathed. Earthpower and argent shone like wonder in her gaze. "Oh, Thomas. I don't understand. I don't know what it means. I'm just glad that I got to see it."

Stave nodded his acknowledgment. His assent.

Canrik's face was hidden. Squatting beside Branl, he did what he could for the Humbled. Rime Coldspray and Frostheart Grueburn simply stared, too exhausted to recognize their relief.

Kiril Threndor stumbled as if Mount Thunder itself had flinched. Chunks of the ceiling broke loose. Fissures clenched the walls, unclenched. In the distance, the mountain's shoulders shrugged avalanches. Covenant felt the Earth's foundations failing. But Jeremiah's forbidding protected everyone in the chamber. He hardly seemed to notice his own prowess.

"So am I," the boy admitted. More sourly, he said, "Too bad we won't get to enjoy it."

Covenant tried to smile. "What are you talking about?" He spoke to Jeremiah, but he poured out his heart to Linden. "This is our chance. We can't stop what's happening, but that doesn't mean we can't try to save the Earth. I know that sounds impossible, but maybe it isn't. We don't have to create an entire reality from scratch. We just have to put the pieces of this one back together.

"If we follow the Worm—and if we pick up the pieces fast enough—and if we know where they belong—"

Perhaps the Arch and the world could be rebuilt from the fragments of their destruction.

"We have everything we need," he assured Jeremiah. "Two white gold wielders. The Staff of Law. Linden's health-sense. Your talent. Hell, we still have the *krill*. And I think—" His face twisted with pain and chagrin and hope. "I'm not sure, but I think I know everything Lord Foul knows."

The Despiser had striven for eons to escape his prison. His knowledge of the created world was both vast and intricate.

Jeremiah stood straighter. His hands tightened eagerly on the Staff. "I've learned a few things myself."

"And I've seen She Who Must Not Be Named without all of that agony and bitterness," offered Linden. "I know what She means."

In spite of its galls and strain, hers was the most beautiful face that Covenant had ever seen.

"We can do this," he said as if he were sure. "We can do it together."

There is no doom so black or deep—

Linden looked at Jeremiah. "Then you had better get rid of that Raver. He's holding you back."

Moksha had probably exacerbated Jeremiah's faltering earlier.

Jeremiah nodded. He closed his eyes. For a moment, he grimaced. He may have feared losing what he had gained from the Raver; feared losing a part of himself. But then he became a brief flare of Earthpower and forbidding.

Darkness billowed out of him. *Moksha* writhed uselessly, seeking a body that could sustain him. But the Giants were too weary to be used, Branl was too severely injured, and Stave and Canrik were too obdurate. Howling, the Raver fled.

Braced on Stave's shoulder, Covenant left the dais. When he had reclaimed Loric's dagger, he stabbed it into the stone where Lord Foul had stood. It had held the

Despiser there briefly. Perhaps it would do something similar for Mount Thunder's heart.

In the light of the gem, Covenant went to stand with Linden and Jeremiah.

Their faces were starting to blur. Bits of them seemed to fade in and out of solidity. The ichor of the mountain streamed from the walls, spattered from the ceiling. The dust of pulverized gutrock rose like spume from the cracking floor. For an instant, Branl appeared to be whole again. For another, he resembled a desiccated corpse. Canrik's wounds and those of the Swordmainnir wavered between past and future.

"If it will be done," Stave said, or had said, or would say, "it must be done now. Do not fear for us. We are at peace. Our deeds here would content the heart of any *Haruchai.*"

"And of any Giant," Rime Coldspray managed faintly.

Covenant took the time to embrace Linden; to give her the best kiss that he had in him. He delayed long enough to ruffle Jeremiah's hair. Then he said simply, "Now."

With his halfhand, he clasped Linden's left. Sharing his burdens, he raised both arms, held high his bright wedding band and hers. After an instant's hesitation, Linden reached out to grip the cleansed Staff between Jeremiah's hands, trusting the influence of the *krill*, or the accelerating collapse of Law and Time, or her own rightful use of wild magic to protect her from incompatible theurgies. She smiled at her son. He was concentrating too hard to smile back.

A final convulsion tore through Kiril Threndor. Wracked beyond endurance, the whole chamber became rubble.

Lifted by fire, Covenant, Linden, and Jeremiah stepped into the wake of the World's End and rose like glory.

Epilogue

"The soul in which the flower grows"

Together in deep night, Thomas Covenant, Linden Avery, and Jeremiah walked west from the slopes of Gravin Threndor through the enduring woodland of Andelain.

At first, they could hear the distant turmoil of the Soulsease as it rushed between the walls of Treacher's Gorge: a plaint like a lament, compelled and swift. But gradually the sound faded among the rich hush of the trees. Stately Gilden and high oaks comforted the heavens. Broad-boughed sycamores and gnarled cottonwoods spread their limbs in welcome. Occasional rills chuckled through the dark, and lush greenswards cushioned walking. Amused breezes wafted their small jests here and there, caressing the Andelainian largesse with tranquility as pellucid as Glimmermere. Along the hillsides, *aliantha* and flowering forsythia gathered like guides or guardians, confirming a path through the night.

The three carried no light, although Covenant and Linden could have etched the trees with argent, and Jeremiah bore the restored Staff of Law as well as his legacy of Earthpower. They preferred to make their way among the monarchs and nobles of the Hills without other illumination because they themselves had become light. The three of them glowed gentle silver as though they lived half in the realm of the Dead; as though they were in transition, passing into or leaving a dimension of refined spirit. And the scar on Covenant's forehead held a more concentrated lucence both oneiric and definitive. He wore it like an implied coronet, the crown of all that he had loved and done.

The ambiguous auguries of their marred clothes were gone. Instead of ruined red flannel or a cut T-shirt or blood-soaked pajamas, instead of jeans and boots, they were clad in robes of fine sendaline supple as woven ghost-silk, soothing to their hard-used skin, and their feet were bare. In their passage beyond Kiril Threndor, they had been made clean.

Lifted by the verdant luxury of the grass, they walked easily, and the crisp air was an elixir in their lungs. On some other night, an atmosphere which had not known the sun's touch for days might have left them shivering. On this night, the chill was refreshment, balm: an anodyne for iniquity and travail.

The three figures luminous as spectres did not feel distance. They did not notice time. They had done what they could to answer their own questions, and were free of impatience. Certainly Covenant and Linden could have walked for hours in silence, content with Andelain, and with the communion of their clasped hands. But Jeremiah was young. He spoke first.

"We did it."

Linden smiled at him. "We did."

After a while, Jeremiah asked, "Did we do it right?"

"I think so," Covenant said. Old and present pains complicated his tone. He did not share himself with his essential enemy without cost. "It's hard to be sure." Too much had been lost.

Then he gestured ahead. There a glade bedecked with wildflowers opened among the trees. "But we did that part right."

Past the boughs, the reaching twigs, the abundance of leaves, a vast multitude of stars emblazoned the heavens, distinct and glittering and inspired, complete in their loveliness. Their myriads made magnificence of the sky's black void.

The three stopped in the heart of the glade. For a time, they simply gazed upward, rapt and reveling.

"Of course," Covenant added, "we had help."

From an innominate distance, Infelice came to stand with them. Sumptuous in her gems and beauty, the suzerain of the *Elohim* was herself an incarnation of stars. "Indeed, Timewarden," she said like the chiming of faraway bells. "We who were preserved from the Worm have given our aid, though our diminishment has been grievous. Chiefly we have concerned ourselves with guiding the Worm's return to its proper slumber. Doing so, we have assisted in the restoration of the One Tree to its full leaf and bloom. Yet these were lesser tasks gladly undertaken. The greatest deeds were yours, Timewarden, and yours, Wildwielder, and also yours, Chosen-son. Your achievements transcend us.

"You have made the world new."

Jeremiah nodded, grinning.

"But all those people," Linden said sadly. "Millions of them. Tens of millions. All that devastation. I did that. I have to live with so much death—" She did not continue.

Covenant tightened his grip on her hand.

Infelice shook her head. "Yet had you not roused the Worm," she replied, "he whom you name the Despiser would have wrought graver harm by some other means. Damning the Earth, you enabled its redemption. Therefore do not fault yourself, Wildwielder. Though it shames me to confess it, your folly has surpassed the wisdom of the *Elohim*. We erred in our opposition, erred cruelly. Now we accept the outcome without regret."

" 'Beings from beyond Time,' " murmured Linden.

"Indeed," the *Elohim* said again. "For that reason, if for no other, there can be no fault in you. You were chosen for your task. You did not seek it out. Nevertheless you have found it within yourself to prevail."

Then she faced Covenant. "For your sake, Timewarden, I am grieved. You have elected to bear the lasting burden of this restoration. You have given the living Earth a gift which exacts anguish. The Despiser is not defeated. He strives within you. While you live, he must be defeated continuously. I have come to proffer my obeisant gratitude—and also to inquire how you contrive to endure your triumph. Your willingness defies my comprehension. I could more readily grasp the surrender of your spirit to the Arch of Time. Your acceptance now surpasses me."

Covenant grimaced. He almost smiled. "It's easier than it looks. Or it's harder. Or maybe it's just worth the effort." He ran his halfhand through his hair. "I don't know how else to explain it. Lord Foul makes us strong."

"Strong?" Jeremiah objected. "The Despiser? He would have slaughtered the whole world and laughed about it."

"Well, sure." Covenant shrugged. "But ask yourself why he's like that. Berek said it. 'Only the great of heart may despair greatly.' All that malice and contempt is just love and hope and eagerness gone rancid. He's the Creator's curdled shadow. He—" He grimaced again. "I'm not saying this right."

"He gives us the chance to do better."

Jeremiah and Infelice studied him, frowning.

"In any case," Covenant added, "taking a stand against him is what makes us who we are." He looked more sharply at the *Elohim*. "When we don't, we aren't anything. We're just empty."

Uncharacteristically gracious, Infelice bowed. "A just charge, Timewarden. I perceive now that it is condign. I am content to acknowledge it.

"Contemplating the paradox of your folly and wisdom, I bid you joy."

Riding a delicate loft of bells, she took herself away.

Linden watched her husband's face and smiled like a new day.

As if he were answering her, Covenant said, "I can feel my fingers. They seem to have nerves again, what's left of them. And the soles of my feet—They used to be numb. Now I know I'm standing on grass. I can almost feel individual blades.

"I've always thought you were beautiful, but I had no idea you're *so* beautiful."

She kissed him for a time while Jeremiah rolled his eyes. Then the companions walked again.

The Hills displayed themselves like treasures. Leagues may have passed, unmeasured by Andelain's kind ease. In the east, Mount Thunder's dark bulk showed against the paling sky. Intimations of morning lifted birds into the air. Chirps and twitters began like introits, the preliminaries of worship. Every in-drawn breath was a sacrament. Every exhalation released care.

And from out of the fading night came Wraiths to do homage.

Fleet as candle-flames, and glad as an aubade, throngs of living fires danced among the trees, two or three at first, then scores, then innumerable hundreds. Sharing warmth and brightness like wealth, they gathered in the air. Harmoniously they measured the sequences of a stately gavotte around Covenant, Linden, and Jeremiah. One at a time, they wafted closer to kiss blessings onto Linden's forehead, and onto Jeremiah's. But in front of Covenant they appeared to falter as though they were abashed or frightened, dismayed by awe. Eschewing his forehead, they touched lightly on his wedding ring, then scampered away, relieved and eager, piquant as trills.

When the Wraiths had bestowed their approval and were done, the companions resumed their effortless travel.

Later, on a rise crowned with larch and plane, they heard a snatch of song. There they paused to listen.

Swelling around them, melodies arched and ached among the boughs. A counterpoint as deep as roots joined the music, and leaves offered a fluttering descant: the strophes of an ode to spring and fertile burgeoning, to anticipations of ripe summer. Soon the whole woodland seemed on the verge of full-throated song. But then the chorus shrank or condensed until it became Caerwood ur-Mahrtiir striding upward with the earned remains of his staff cradled in one arm.

Calling his name, Linden started toward her dear friend. After a few steps, however, she halted at the sight of the crowd ascending behind the former Manethrall.

Tall figures followed the Forestal, creatures sculpted and kingly in their perfection. A few were grey, the rest as black as the departing night. Like Caerwood ur-Mahrtiir, they were eyeless. But he had lost his orbs in battle: they had been fashioned without the need for ordinary sight. Where gaping nostrils had once dominated their faces, they now had more human noses which they appeared to bear proudly; and their mouths could smile. The straight strength of their limbs matched the symmetry of their forms and the sovereignty of their carriage.

The tallest of the creatures accompanied the Forestal a step behind his right shoulder: the loremaster. The rest of the transformed ur-viles and Waynhim stopped a few strides away. The loremaster carried its fearsome iron jerrid in one fist, but the other creatures had exchanged their eldritch knives for wands like twigs with which they appeared to shape the verdant music.

"Mahrtiir?" Linden began. "Caerwood ur-Mahrtiir? You have no idea— Are these—?" Unable to complete a question, she said through her tears, "I am so glad to see you!"

"We are well met," mused the Forestal, "well met in all sooth, Ringthane, Linden Avery, friend. And well met also, Covenant Timewarden and young Jeremiah. Among unforeseen wonders, you are a particular delight. Though I sang against the Worm with every aspect of my given strength, I did not prevent the world's death. Nor could I evade it. Yet I am here. Indeed, all who clung to life at the moment of the Earth's extinction live still. While the restored Arch endures, you will be remembered and honored among all of the wide world's forests."

"But how did you get here?" asked Linden. "We left you— I don't even know how far we've come."

"Andelain is here," answered the ur-Mahrtiir. "Salva Gildenbourne is nigh. When the Worm had turned aside from my service to the fane, I wished to meet my passing among the trees and richness and innocence which I love. Therefore I sang to these woodlands, and was conveyed hither."

At once, he continued, "I will not linger. The sight of you suffices for me, Linden Ringthane. A task immense and needful awaits, and I am avid to begin while my powers freshen within me. Much of lands and peoples, of wood and mountains, has been laid waste, much that cannot be restored. Yet much remains. And there can be no true healing that does not commence with trees.

"I am become the Earth's Forestal."

"Alone?" Linden inquired like a plea. "Alone, Mahrtiir?"

Caerwood ur-Mahrtiir sang mirth. "Assuredly not, Linden Avery, friend. With me are these ur-viles and Waynhim, the last of their kind. Aye, they are Demondim-spawn, given life by lore rather than by natural birth. But they are also High Lord Elena redeemed from torment. They are the Auriference and Emereau Vrai and Diassomer Mininderain and many other women. They are the dark yearning of *merewives* and the sunlit absorption of *Elohim*. And now they are also Forestals.

"Encountering each other here, and filled with wonder that we had been spared, we spoke at length, these regal creatures and I. I proposed to them a new interpretation of their Weird, one suited to their perfected forms and exalted spirits—and they adjudged the meter and harmony and timbre of my music worthy. I will not labor for the Earth's renewal alone.

"In sooth," the ur-Mahrtiir admitted, "our task is too great for us. But we are not daunted. We will grow, Linden Avery." His singing rose until it shivered every leaf, flourished along every bough; and every creature sang with him. "We will *grow.*"

"Guardians," Linden murmured as the Forestals carried their melodies through the Hills toward other, more distant forests. "In the Creator's stead." *How may life endure in the Land, if the Forestals fail and perish, as they must, and naught remains to ward its most vulnerable treasures?* "I would never have guessed that Demondim-spawn were the answer to Caerroil Wildwood's question."

"They weren't," said Covenant. "You were. You and Mahrtiir. You kept that promise, just like you kept your promise to the ur-viles and Waynhim."

"And you saved my daughter. Here I was, planning to punish myself eternally for what happened to her, and you—"

Jeremiah scowled, feigning disgust. "*Please* don't start kissing again. It's gross."

Linden laughed until her son laughed with her. Then the three of them resumed their walk into the west.

Behind them, Gravin Threndor—mighty and long misused—grew distinct as the sun ascended from its imposed ensepulture. Across the heavens, the stars appeared to withdraw, making way for daylight. The greying sky became pearlescent with promise. Winged flights graceful as birdsong articulated the air and the treetops like runes in motion, a script constantly modulating toward new interpretations. Implied flames touched the tips of the highest sequoias.

"Amazing," Linden breathed. "Something as simple as sunrise. I didn't think that I would ever see it again."

Covenant grinned. "You call that amazing? *I* didn't think I would ever see well enough to know the difference."

"I can't wait," Jeremiah said. But whether he felt impatient for the sun, or for some other wonder, he did not explain.

Gradually light came to the heights of Andelain. Bright day spread down branches and boles as though Mount Thunder had granted it passage. The mountain wrapped its cloak of shadow closer about itself. Sunshine enlivened the leaves with memories of music.

And in a wide hollow defined by stands of mimosa, by wide-spread jacaranda and flowering rhododendron, with a giddy brook running past an abundance of *aliantha*, Covenant, Linden, and Jeremiah found the friends and companions with whom they had shared so much weariness and strife.

Rime Coldspray and Frostheart Grueburn were there, Onyx Stonemage and Hale-whole Bluntfist. The Giants of Dire's Vessel, those who had survived their many battles: Bluff Stoutgirth, Squallish Blustergale, and their few comrades. Canrik and perhaps two score other Masters, all that remained of two hundred. Manethrall

Bhapa. Cord Pahni. Branl, the last of the Humbled, who had killed Clyme and sacrificed an arm and become certain. And Stave, the former Master.

They had been healed and refreshed, all of them, and their raiment restored by the re-creation of the Earth. They lacked only the silver glow and sendaline of *beings from beyond Time*. They had come together in the hollow to feast on treasure-berries, drink pristine water, and share their astonishment.

They must have been conveyed here while the fraying strands of Time were rewoven.

They did not immediately notice Covenant, Linden, and Jeremiah. But then the three were announced. Among the trees at the edge of the hollow, Ranyhyn whinnied a proud welcome: Hyn and Hynyn, Rallyn and Khelen, Rohnhyn and Naharahn. And as their call carried over the Hills, full sunlight struck the horses, burning away the last vestiges of dusk from their glossy coats. Among them, the Ardent's mount cropped grass as though it had no use for mere relief and wonder.

But the star-browed Ranyhyn did not remain to receive greetings or gratitude from Linden and Jeremiah, as they must already have done from Stave and Branl, Bhapa and Pahni. They were eager to rejoin their herds and their Ramen. They galloped away, taking Mishio Massima with them, and trumpeting praise to the new day.

Giants and *Haruchai* lifted their heads. Bhapa and Pahni looked around.

A moment later, jubilation and awe filled the air. Linden wept for gladness, and Jeremiah wavered between shouts and tears. Covenant spread his arms like a man who yearned to embrace everyone simultaneously, and his scarred forehead shone like incarnated starlight.

Then there were shouts and much laughter among the Giants, hugs and clasps and affectionate congratulations. As one, Stave, Branl, and the Masters did more than bow: they sank to one knee and lowered their heads in homage. Unable to contain himself, Manethrall Bhapa put his hands on Linden's waist and lifted her high until she begged him to put her down. With more restraint and sadness, Pahni offered her hopes for Linden's happiness, and for Covenant's.

Jeremiah joined the mirth and effusion of the Giants. Linden took the Ramen away from the others to make her peace with Pahni's bereavement, to speak of Caerwood ur-Mahrtiir, and to share her heart with friends who had been as faithful as Liand. For his part, Covenant spoke first with the Ironhand and Stoutgirth Anchormaster, while Stave, Branl, and Canrik attended him.

His efforts to find words for his gratitude, the Giants brushed aside. "The thanks are ours to give," Rime Coldspray proclaimed. "We are wont to avow that joy is in the ears that hear. Upon such occasions, however, it is also in the mouth that speaks. Though our hearts are galled by loss, they also overflow with gladness. Wherever

Giants remain in the Earth, the names of Covenant Timewarden and Linden Giant-friend and Jeremiah Chosen-son will be uttered in celebration and reverence."

Bluff Stoutgirth nodded his approval. But he smiled with difficulty, and his need for a *caamora* was plain. He was a sailor, not a warrior: his losses bore a different emotional weight than Coldspray's. Nevertheless he accepted them with a spirit slowly lifting.

Covenant had only one question for them: what now?

The Anchormaster answered without hesitation. "With the Giants at my command, I will return to Dire's Vessel. It is my hope that we will sail at once for our homeland. I pine for the harborage of Home. I ache to learn the fate of our kindred. And I yearn for new ears to soften my sorrow with their joy."

Covenant understood. He had his own sorrows to assuage. "And you?" he asked of Coldspray.

Before she could reply, Stave spoke.

"With the Ironhand's consent, we will welcome her and her Swordmainnir to Revelstone. We have much for which we wish to atone. First among our faults, doubtless, is the ignorance which we have inflicted upon the folk of the Land. Yet more immediate to us here is the manner in which we have rebuffed the friendship and valor of the Giants. We hunger to make amends."

Covenant cocked an eyebrow at the outcast Master's use of *we*. But he did not interrupt.

"Also," Stave went on, "I would seek a boon of the Ironhand, and perhaps of her comrades also, a boon which pertains to Revelstone, and which Revelstone may sway her to grant."

Now both Coldspray and Stoutgirth stared at him, as surprised as Covenant.

Stave faced them with a smile: another surprise. "You crave explanations." Amusement sparkled in his eye. "Know, then, that I am Stave, by right of years and attainment the Voice of the Masters. I speak for these *Haruchai* assembled here, and also for those who have retained the benison of their lives elsewhere."

More gravely, he said, "Your example, Covenant Timewarden, and also that of Linden Avery the Chosen, and indeed of Jeremiah Chosen-son, have turned our thoughts to new paths. We have concluded that the Land has no need of Masters. Rather it will be better served by Lords. Therefore we wish to claim a different purpose. If you do not gainsay us, ur-Lord, we will form a new Council, emulating with our best strength the service begun by Berek Lord-Fatherer.

"And the boon which we will ask of the Ironhand is this, that she and her Swordmainnir join with us in that Council. By their kindness and merriment, we hope"—he smiled again—"to avoid the snares of our long past and severe judgments until the time when the folk of the Land discover a desire to stand among us."

Jeremiah had wandered closer while Stave spoke. Now the boy said, "I can tell you where to find Kevin's Wards."

"And we will welcome that knowledge, Chosen-son, when our need for it is ripe."

Covenant shook his head, but not in disapproval. "I don't know what to say. It sounds practically ideal. But you'll have to give up your rejection of Earthpower. Or lore. You'll have to start from scratch."

"As we should, ur-Lord," Stave replied. "The Earth has been vouchsafed a new beginning. The *Haruchai* also must begin anew."

After a moment's thought, Covenant observed, "You'll need a High Lord. You, Stave?"

"I?" Stave countered. He seemed to hear a jest in Covenant's question. "No. I do not stand so high in my own estimation. And I do not doubt that the day will come when the Voice of the Masters must speak for the *Haruchai* rather than for the Land. The Council of Lords and the High Lord must regard wider concerns.

"I have named Canrik to lead the first Council. He is newly acquainted with uncertainty, and will gain much from an immersion in the necessary doubts of the Lords."

Canrik nodded, expressionless as any Master or Bloodguard.

"But Branl—?" Covenant asked. "Surely he's earned it?"

"I will not shoulder that burden," the *Haruchai* halfhand stated flatly. "Clyme's death mars my heart. I desire a different atonement. I will return to Gravin Threndor, seeking High Lord Loric's *krill*."

He held up his remaining hand to forestall objections. "Certainly the Cavewights will greet me with enmity. However, Corruption no longer goads them to madness. And they, too, must feel awe at their continuation in life. It is my hope, therefore, that soft words and a refusal to do harm will dissuade them from bloodshed. They are not mindless, ur-Lord. And I am not helpless in my own defense, though I will cause no more hurt. Mayhap I will elude death until they perceive that we are no longer foes.

"Should I succeed, I will bear the *krill* to Revelstone. And should I fail—" Branl shrugged delicately. "I will die content in myself. I will not perish grieving."

Covenant thought of Cail, who had been rejected by his people, and had gone to find his fate alone. Branl was rejected only by himself. Still he would have to find peace on his own terms.

Finally Rime Coldspray said to Stave, "The boon you seek is too great to be granted readily, Rockbrother. My comrades and I must speak of it at length. Indeed, many Giantclaves await us, and we will spend whole seasons in delight and sorrow and hope. But first we will gladly accompany you to Revelstone. How can we refuse? We are Giants."

Together, Stave, Canrik, and Branl bowed their thanks.

After a while, Linden came to join Covenant and Jeremiah. Resting one hand on her son's shoulder, she pointed into the west. "Who do you suppose that is?"

Looking there, Covenant saw a lone figure standing in sunlight at the rim of the hollow. A woman, he thought, although he could not be sure. The figure's head was wrapped in cerements like the Theomach's. Ribbands as garish as the Ardent's ornamented the figure's upper body, while from its waist hung a motley skirt as haphazard and arcane as the Mahdoubt's.

To Covenant's gaze, and Linden's, and Jeremiah's, the figure replied with a beckoning gesture.

At first, Covenant smiled. "It looks to me," he said wryly, "like the Insequent are finally giving credence of the idea of acolytes." He almost chuckled. "In fact, if I had to guess, I might say that's *the* Acolyte."

But then his eyes darkened, and for a moment he resembled a man who had never recovered from his oldest wounds.

"It's time. We have to go."

As he spoke, the figure drifted out of sight.

"Go?" Jeremiah protested at once. "Why? We just got here."

Linden studied her husband quizzically, but she did not contradict him.

"The Chosen-son speaks for me as well," began Rime Coldspray.

"And for me," put in Bluff Stoutgirth.

"We have sung no songs to honor you," Coldspray added. "We have not truly begun to voice our wonder and gratitude, our esteem deep as seas. We have not told you of our love. And we have heard neither Linden Giantfriend's tale nor Jeremiah Chosen-son's. In sooth, we are scarcely able to estimate your own.

"What compulsion requires you to depart, Timewarden?"

Covenant rubbed his glowing scar to disguise a clench of woe and regret. "Unearned knowledge," he answered brusquely. "Right now, we're too dangerous. Jeremiah and me. Maybe even Linden. Jeremiah needs time to figure out what he's going to do with everything he got from *moksha*. He has to learn what it all means and decide how he wants to use it. Linden freed She Who Must Not Be Named. She freed Elena"—his voice caught for a moment—"and who knows how many other lost souls. That must have been shattering. She hasn't had a chance to recover. And I'm carrying the Despiser around inside me. What he knows isn't a problem for me. I used to be part of the Arch of Time. But he's *Lord Foul*. If I let him, he might spit in your faces. Or he might find a way to use my ring. I hope I can persuade him to relax. Maybe I can even convince him to think of me as something more or better or at least kinder than his worst enemy.

"We all need time."

And possibly a teacher, he mused ruefully. If so, one of the Insequent might serve. The Theomach had certainly guided Berek Halfhand well enough.

Softly Rime Coldspray said, "Though you conceal it, your hurt is evident, Covenant Timewarden. None here would choose to deny you. Do not take it amiss when I confess that your departure will sadden us."

With an effort, Covenant set aside his aching. He reached out for Linden's hand, smiled at Jeremiah. "It isn't permanent," he said more cheerfully. "It can't be. Our old lives are finished." By degrees, his distress receded. "There's no going back. You can't get rid of us this easy."

Then a new mood came over him, one that he had not felt for a very long time; and he found himself laughing as if he were a man for whom laughter came naturally.

Take *that*, he told his inner Despiser. And all this time, you thought I hated you.

When he subsided, he said to his friends, "I can't tell you how good it feels to know we can see you again whenever we want." Still chuckling, he added, "But we won't until we're ready."

Linden gave him a smile that sang in his heart; and Jeremiah nodded awkwardly, discomfited by recognitions for which he had not prepared himself. Together they walked away in the direction taken by the Insequent: the Unbeliever and his new wife and his obliquely adopted son.

And as they walked, spring rainclouds gathered to the southwest. In the distance, sudden showers streaked the air, falling like chrism to the reborn ground. Struck by sunlight, the showers returned a rainbow to the heavens: one bright instance of the world's inherent splendor.

When it faded, Covenant, Linden, and Jeremiah appeared to fade with it. But their silver lingered for a time, until the day moved on.

Here ends

The Last Dark

and

"The Last Chronicles of Thomas Covenant"

Combined Glossary for The Chronicles of Thomas Covenant

Abatha: one of the Seven Words

Acence: a Stonedownor, sister of Atiaran

Ahamkara: Hoerkin, "the Door"

Ahanna: painter, daughter of Hanna

Ahnryn: a Ranyhyn; mount of Tull

Aimil: daughter of Anest, wife of Sunder

Aisle of Approach: passage to Earthrootstair under *Melenkurion* Skyweir

a-Jeroth of the Seven Hells: Lord of wickedness; Clave-name for Lord Foul the Despiser

ak-Haru: a supreme *Haruchai* honorific; paragon and measure of all *Haruchai* virtues

Akkasri: a member of the Clave; one of the na-Mhoram-cro

aliantha: treasure-berries

Alif, the Lady: a woman Favored by the *gaddhi*

amanibhavam: horse-healing grass, dangerous to humans

Amatin: a Lord, daughter of Matin

Amith: a woman of Crystal Stonedown

Amok: mysterious guide to ancient Lore

Amorine: First Haft, later Hiltmark

Anchormaster: second-in-command aboard a Giantship

Andelain, the Hills of Andelain, the Andelainian Hills: a region of the Land which embodies health and beauty

Andelainscion: a region in the Center Plains

Anele: deranged old man; son of Sunder and Hollian

Anest: a woman of Mithil Stonedown, sister of Kalina

Annoy: a Courser

anundivian yajña: lost Ramen craft of bone-sculpting

Appointed, the: an *Elohim* chosen to bear a particular burden; Findail

Arch of Time, the: symbol of the existence and structure of time; conditions which make the existence of time possible

Ard: a *Haruchai*; a Master of the Land

Ardent, the: one of the Insequent

arghule/arghuleh: ferocious ice-beasts

Asuraka: Staff-Elder of the Loresraat

Atiaran: a Stonedownor, daughter of Tiaran, wife of Trell, mother of Lena

Audience Hall of Earthroot: maze under *Melenkurion* Skyweir to conceal and protect the Blood of the Earth

Aumbrie of the Clave, the: storeroom for former Lore

Auriference, the: one of the Insequent, long dead

Auspice, the: throne of the *gaddhi*

aussat Befylam: child-form of the *jheherrin*

Baf Scatterwit: a Giant (woman); crew aboard Dire's Vessel

Bahgoon the Unbearable: character in a Giantish tale

Banas Nimoram: the Celebration of Spring

Bandsoil Bounds: region north of Soulsease River

Banefire, the: fire by which the Clave affects the Sunbane

Bann: a Bloodguard, assigned to Lord Trevor

Bannor: a Bloodguard, assigned to Thomas Covenant

Baradakas: a Hirebrand of Soaring Woodhelven

Bargas Slit: a gap through the Last Hills from the Center Plains to Garroting Deep

Bareisle: an island off the coast of *Elemesnedene*

Basila: a scout in Berek Halfhand's army

Benj, the Lady: a woman Favored by the *gaddhi*

Berek Halfhand: Heartthew, Lord-Fatherer; first of the Old Lords

Bern: *Haruchai* slain by the Clave

Bhanoryl: a Ranyhyn; mount of Galt

Bhapa: a Cord of the Ramen, Sahah's half-brother; companion of Linden Avery

Bhrathair: a people met by the wandering Giants, residents of *Bhrathairealm* on the verge of the Great Desert

Bhrathairain: the city of the *Bhrathair*

Bhrathairain **Harbor:** the port of the *Bhrathair*

Bhrathairealm: the land of the *Bhrathair*

Birinair: a Hirebrand, Hearthrall of Lord's Keep

Bloodguard, the: *Haruchai*, a people living in the Westron Mountains; the defenders of the Lords

Bluff Stoutgirth: a Giant; Anchormaster of Dire's Vessel

bone-sculpting: ancient Ramen craft, marrowmeld

Borillar: a Hirebrand and Hearthrall of Lord's Keep

Bornin: a *Haruchai*; a Master of the Land

Brabha: a Ranyhyn; mount of Korik

Branl: a *Haruchai*; a Master of the Land; one of the Humbled

Brannil: man of Stonemight Woodhelven

Brinn: a leader of the *Haruchai*; protector of Thomas Covenant; later Guardian of the One Tree

Brow Gnarlfist: a Giant, father of the First of the Search

caamora: Giantish ordeal of grief by fire

Cable Seadreamer: a Giant, brother of Honninscrave; member of the Search; possessed of the Earth-Sight

Cabledarm: a Giant; one of the Swordmainnir

Caer-Caveral: Forestal of Andelain; formerly Hile Troy

Caerroil Wildwood: Forestal of Garroting Deep

Caerwood ur-Mahrtiir: a Forestal; formerly Manethrall Mahrtiir

caesure: a rent in the fabric of time; a Fall

Cail: a *Haruchai*; protector of Linden Avery

Caitiffin: a captain of the armed forces of *Bhrathairealm*

Callindrill: a Lord, husband of Faer

Callowwail, the River: stream arising from *Elemesnedene*

Canrik: a *Haruchai*; a Master of the Land

Cavewights: evil creatures existing under Mount Thunder

Cav-Morin Fernhold: former Forestal of Morinmoss

Ceer: one of the *Haruchai*

Celebration of Spring, the: the Dance of the Wraiths of Andelain on the dark of the moon in the middle of spring

Center Plains, the: a region of the Land

Centerpith Barrens: a region in the Center Plains

Cerrin: a Bloodguard, assigned to Lord Shetra

Chant: one of the *Elohim*

Char: a Cord of the Ramen, Sahah's brother

Chatelaine, the: courtiers of the *gaddhi*

Chosen, the: title given to Linden Avery

Chosen-son: Giantish name for Jeremiah

Circle of Elders: Stonedown leaders

Cirrus Kindwind: a Giant; one of the Swordmainnir

***clachan*, the:** demesne of the *Elohim*

Clang: a Courser

Clangor: a Courser

Clash: a Courser

Clave, the: group which wields the Sunbane and rules the Land

***clingor*:** adhesive leather

Close, the: the Council-chamber of Lord's Keep

Clyme: a *Haruchai*; a Master of the Land; one of the Humbled

***Coercri*:** The Grieve; former home of the Giants in Seareach

Colossus of the Fall, the: ancient stone figure guarding the Upper Land

Consecear Redoin: a region north of the Soulsease River

Cord: Ramen second rank

Cording: Ramen ceremony of becoming a Cord

Corimini: Eldest of the Loresraat

Corrupt, the: *jheherrin* name for themselves; also the soft ones

Corruption: Bloodguard/*Haruchai* name for Lord Foul

Council of Lords, the: protectors of the Land

Courser: a beast made by the Clave using the Sunbane

Cravenhaw: a region between Garroting Deep and the Southron Waste

Creator, the: maker of the Earth

Croft: Graveler of Crystal Stonedown

Crowl: a Bloodguard

***croyel*, the:** mysterious creatures which grant power through bargains, living off their hosts

Crystal Stonedown: home of Hollian

Currier: a Ramen rank

Damelon Giantfriend: son of Berek Halfhand, second High Lord of the Old Lords

Damelon's Door: door of lore which when opened permits passage through the Audience Hall of Earthroot under *Melenkurion* Skyweir

Dance of the Wraiths, the: the Celebration of Spring

Dancers of the Sea, the: *merewives*; suspected to be the offspring of the *Elohim* Kastenessen and his mortal lover

Daphin: one of the *Elohim*

Dast: a *Haruchai*; a Master of the Land

Dawngreeter: highest sail on the foremast of a Giantship

Dead, the: spectres of those who have died

Deaththane: title given to High Lord Elena by the Ramen

Defiles Course, the: river in the Lower Land

Demimage: a sorcerer of Vidik Amar

Demondim, the: creatures created by Viles; creators of ur-viles and Waynhim

Demondim-spawn: another name for ur-viles and Waynhim; also another name for Vain

Desolation, the: era of ruin in the Land after the Ritual of Desecration

Despiser, the: Lord Foul

Despite: evil; name given to the Despiser's nature and effects

dharmakshetra: "to brave the enemy," a Waynhim

Dhorehold of the Dark: Forestal of Grimmerdhore

dhraga: a Waynhim

dhubha: a Waynhim

dhurng: a Waynhim

diamondraught: Giantish liquor

Diassomer Mininderain: in myth, a woman betrayed by Lord Foul and imprisoned in the Earth as punishment

Din: a Courser

Dire's Vessel: Giantship used by the Swordmainnir to convey Longwrath

Doar: a Bloodguard

Dohn: a Manethrall of the Ramen

Dolewind, the: wind blowing to the Soulbiter

Doom's Retreat: a gap in the Southron Range between the South Plains and Doriendor Corishev

Doriendor Corishev: an ancient city; seat of the King against whom Berek Halfhand rebelled

drhami: a Waynhim

Drinishok: Sword-Elder of the Loresraat

Drinny: a Ranyhyn, foal of Hynaril; mount of Lord Mhoram

dromond: a Giantship

Drool Rockworm: a Cavewight, leader of the Cavewights; finder of the Illearth Stone

dukkha: "victim," Waynhim name

Dura Fairflank: a mustang, Thomas Covenant's mount

Durance, the: a barrier Appointed by the *Elohim*; a prison for both Kastenessen and the *skurj*

durhisitar: a Waynhim

During Stonedown: village destroyed by the *Grim*; home of Hamako

Duroc: one of the Seven Words

Durris: a *Haruchai*

EarthBlood: concentrated fluid Earthpower, only known to exist under *Melenku-rion* Skyweir; source of the Power of Command

Earthfriend: title first given to Berek Halfhand

Earthpower: natural power of all life; the source of all organic power in the Land

Earthroot: lake under *Melenkurion* Skyweir

Earthrootstair: stairway down to the lake of Earthroot under *Melenkurion* Skyweir

Earth-Sight: Giantish power to perceive distant dangers and needs

eftmound: gathering place for the *Elohim*

eh-Brand: one who can use wood to read the Sunbane

Elemesnedene: home of the *Elohim*

Elena: daughter of Lena and Thomas Covenant; later High Lord

Elohim, the: a mystic people encountered by the wandering Giants

Elohimfest: a gathering of the *Elohim*

Emacrimma's Maw: a region in the Center Plains

Emereau Vrai: Kastenessen's mortal lover, now victim to She Who Must Not Be Named

Enemy: Lord Foul's term of reference for the Creator

Eoman: a unit of the Warward of Lord's Keep, twenty warriors and a Warhaft

Eoward: twenty Eoman plus a Haft

Epemin: a soldier in Berek Halfhand's army, tenth Eoman, second Eoward

Esmer: tormented son of Cail and the Dancers of the Sea

Etch Furledsail: a Giant (woman); crew aboard Dire's Vessel

Exalt Widenedworld: a Giant; youngest son of Soar Gladbirth and Sablehair Foam-heart; later called Lostson and Longwrath

fael Befylam: serpent-form of the *jheherrin*

Faer: wife of Lord Callindrill

Fall: *Haruchai* name for a *caesure*

Fangs: the Teeth of the Render; Ramen name for the Demondim

Fangthane the Render: Ramen name for Lord Foul

Far Horizoneyes: a Giant (woman); crew aboard Dire's Vessel

Far Woodhelven: a village of the Land

Father of Horses, the: *Kelenbhrabanal*, legendary sire of the Ranyhyn

Favored, the: courtesans of the *gaddhi*

Feroce, the: denizens of Sarangrave Flat, worshippers of the lurker, descended from the *jheherrin*

Filigree: a Giant; another name for Sablehair Foamheart

Findail: one of the *Elohim*; the Appointed

Fields of Richloam: a region in the Center Plains

Fire-Lions: living fire-flow of Mount Thunder

fire-stones: graveling

First Betrayer: Clave-name for Berek Halfhand

First Circinate: first level of the Sandhold

First Haft: third-in-command of the Warward

First Mark: Bloodguard commander

First of the Search, the: leader of the Giants who follow the Earth-Sight; Gossamer Glowlimn

First Ward of Kevin's Lore: primary cache of knowledge left by High Lord Kevin

First Woodhelven: banyan tree village between Revelstone and Andelain; first Woodhelven created by Sunder and Hollian

Fleshharrower: a Giant-Raver, Jehannum, *moksha*

Foamkite: *tyrscull* belonging to Honninscrave and Seadreamer

Fole: a *Haruchai*

Foodfendhall: eating-hall and galley aboard a Giantship

Forbidding: a wall of power

Forestal: a protector of the remnants of the One Forest

Fostil: a man of Mithil Stonedown; father of Liand

Foul's Creche: the Despiser's home; Ridjeck Thome

Frostheart Grueburn: a Giant; one of the Swordmainnir

Furl Falls: waterfall at Revelstone

Furl's Fire: warning fire at Revelstone

gaddhi, **the:** sovereign of *Bhrathairealm*

Gallows Howe: a place of execution in Garroting Deep

Galt: a *Haruchai*; a Master of the Land; one of the Humbled

Garroting Deep: a forest of the Land

Garth: Warmark of the Warward of Lord's Keep

Gay: a Winhome of the Ramen

ghohritsar: a Waynhim

ghramin: a Waynhim

Giantclave: Giantish conference

Giantfriend: title given first to Damelon, later to Thomas Covenant and then Linden Avery

Giants: the Unhomed, ancient friends of the Lords; a seafaring people of the Earth

Giantship: a stone sailing vessel made by Giants; *dromond*

Giantway: path made by Giants

Giant Woods: a forest of the Land

Gibbon: the na-Mhoram; leader of the Clave

Gilden: a maple-like tree with golden leaves

Gildenlode: a power-wood formed from the Gilden trees

Gleam Stonedown: a village decimated by *kresh*

Glimmermere: a lake on the plateau above Revelstone

Gorak Krembal: Hotash Slay, a defense around Foul's Creche

Gossamer Glowlimn: a Giant; the First of the Search

Grace: a Cord of the Ramen

Graveler: one who uses stone to wield the Sunbane

graveling: fire-stones, made to glow and emit heat by stone-lore

Gravelingas: a master of *rhadhamaerl* stone-lore

Gravin Threndor: Mount Thunder

Great Desert, the: a region of the Earth; home of the *Bhrathair* and the Sand-gorgons

Great One: title given to Caerroil Wildwood by the Mahdoubt

Great Swamp, the: Lifeswallower; a region of the Land

Grey Desert, the: a region south of the Land

Grey River, the: a river of the Land

Grey Slayer: plains name for Lord Foul

Greywightswath: a region north of the Soulsease River

Greshas Slant: a region in the Center Plains

griffin: lion-like beast with wings

Grim, **the:** (also the na-Mhoram's *Grim*) a destructive storm sent by the Clave

Grimmand Honninscrave: a Giant; Master of Starfare's Gem; brother of Seadreamer

Grimmerdhore: a forest of the Land

Guard, the: *hustin*; soldiers serving the *gaddhi*

Guardian of the One Tree, the: mystic figure warding the approach to the One Tree; formerly *ak-Haru Kenaustin Ardenol*; now Brinn of the *Haruchai*

Haft: commander of an Eoward

Halewhole Bluntfist: a Giant; one of the Swordmainnir

Halfhand: title given to Thomas Covenant and to Berek

Hall of Gifts, the: large chamber in Revelstone devoted to the artworks of the Land

Hamako: sole survivor of the destruction of During Stonedown

Hami: a Manethrall of the Ramen

Hand: a rank in Berek Halfhand's army; aide to Berek

Handir: a *Haruchai* leader; the Voice of the Masters

Harad: one of the Seven Words

Harbor Captain: chief official of the port of *Bhrathairealm*

Harn: one of the *Haruchai*; protector of Hollian

Harrow, the: one of the Insequent

Haruchai: a warrior people from the Westron Mountains

Healer: a physician

Heart of Thunder: Kiril Threndor, a cave of power in Mount Thunder

Hearthcoal: a Giant; cook of Starfare's Gem; wife of Seasauce

Hearthrall of Lord's Keep: a steward responsible for light, warmth, and hospitality

Heartthew: a title given to Berek Halfhand

heartwood chamber: meeting-place of a Woodhelven, within a tree

Heer: leader of a Woodhelven

Heft Galewrath: a Giant; Storesmaster of Starfare's Gem

Herem: a Raver, Kinslaughterer, *turiya*

Hergrom: one of the *Haruchai*

High God: title given to the lurker of the Sarangrave by the Feroce

High Lord: leader of the Council of Lords

High Lord's Furl: banner of the High Lord

High Wood: *lomillialor*; offspring of the One Tree

Hile Troy: a man formerly from Covenant's world; Warmark of High Lord Elena's Warward

Hiltmark: second-in-command of the Warward

Hirebrand: a master of *lillianrill* wood-lore

Hoerkin: a Warhaft

Hollian: daughter of Amith; eh-Brand of Crystal Stonedown; companion of Thomas Covenant and Linden Avery

Home: original homeland of the Giants

Hooryl: a Ranyhyn; Clyme's later mount

Horizonscan: lookout atop the midmast of a Giantship

Horrim Carabal: name given to the lurker of the Sarangrave

Horse, the: human soldiery of the *gaddhi*

horserite: a gathering of Ranyhyn in which they drink mind-blending waters in order to share visions, prophecies, and purpose

Hotash Slay: Gorak Krembal, a flow of lava protecting Foul's Creche

Hower: a Bloodguard, assigned to Lord Loerya

Hrama: a Ranyhyn stallion; mount of Anele

Humbled, the: three *Haruchai* maimed to resemble Thomas Covenant in order to remind the Masters of their limitations

Hurl: a Giant (man); crew aboard Dire's Vessel

Hurn: a Cord of the Ramen

hurtloam: a healing mud

Huryn: a Ranyhyn; mount of Terrel

husta/hustin: partly human soldiers bred by Kasreyn to be the *gaddhi*'s Guard

Hyn: a Ranyhyn mare; mount of Linden Avery

Hynaril: a Ranyhyn; mount of Tamarantha and then Mhoram

Hynyn: a Ranyhyn stallion; mount of Stave

Hyrim: a Lord, son of Hoole

Illearth Stone, the: powerful bane long buried under Mount Thunder

Illender: title given to Thomas Covenant

Imoiran Tomal-mate: a Stonedownor

Inbull: a Warhaft in Berek Halfhand's army; commander of the tenth Eoman, second Eoward

Infelice: reigning leader of the *Elohim*

Insequent, the: a mysterious people living far to the west of the Land

Interdict, the: reference to the power of the Colossus of the Fall to prevent Ravers from entering the Upper Land

Irin: a warrior of the Third Eoman of the Warward

Ironhand, the: title given to the leader of the Swordmainnir

Isle of the One Tree, the: location of the One Tree

Jain: a Manethrall of the Ramen

Jass: a *Haruchai*; a Master of the Land

Jehannum: a Raver, Fleshharrower, *moksha*

Jerrick: a Demimage of Vidik Amar, in part responsible for the creation of *quellvisks*

Jevin: a healer in Berek Halfhand's army

jheherrin: soft ones, misshapen by-products of Lord Foul's making

Jous: a man of Mithil Stonedown, son of Prassan, father of Nassic; inheritor of an Unfettered One's mission to remember the Halfhand

Kalina: a woman of Mithil Stonedown; wife of Nassic, mother of Sunder

Kam: a Manethrall of the Ramen

Karnis: a Heer of First Woodhelven

Kasreyn of the Gyre: a thaumaturge; the *gaddhi*'s Kemper (advisor) in *Bhrathairealm*

Kastenessen: one of the *Elohim*; former Appointed

Keenreef: a Giant (woman); crew aboard Dire's Vessel

Keep of the na-Mhoram, the: Revelstone

Keeper: a Ramen rank, one of those unsuited to the rigors of being a Cord or a Manethrall

Kelenbhrabanal: Father of Horses in Ranyhyn legends

Kemper, the: chief advisor of the *gaddhi*; Kasreyn

Kemper's Pitch: highest level of the Sandhold

Kenaustin Ardenol: a figure of *Haruchai* legend; former Guardian of the One Tree; true name of the Theomach

Kevin Landwaster: son of Loric Vilesilencer; last High Lord of the Old Lords

Kevin's Dirt: smog-like pall covering the Upper Land; it blocks health-sense, making itself invisible from below

Kevin's Lore: knowledge of power left hidden by Kevin in the Seven Wards

Kevin's Watch: mountain lookout near Mithil Stonedown

Khabaal: one of the Seven Words

Khelen: a Ranyhyn stallion; mount of Jeremiah

Kinslaughterer: a Giant-Raver, Herem, *turiya*

Kiril Threndor: chamber of power deep under Mount Thunder; Heart of Thunder

Koral: a Bloodguard, assigned to Lord Amatin

Korik: a Bloodguard

Krenwill: a scout in Berek Halfhand's army

kresh: savage giant yellow wolves

krill, **the:** knife of power forged by High Lord Loric; awakened to power by Thomas Covenant

Kurash Plenethor: region of the Land formally named Stricken Stone, now called Trothgard

Kurash Qwellinir: the Shattered Hills, region of the Lower Land protecting Foul's Creche

Lake Pelluce: a lake in Andelainscion

Lal: a Cord of the Ramen

Landsdrop: great cliff separating the Upper and Lower Lands

Land, the: generally, area found on the map; a focal region of the Earth where Earth-power is uniquely accessible

Landsverge Stonedown: a village of the Land

Landwaster: title given to High Lord Kevin

Latebirth: a Giant; one of the Swordmainnir

Law, the: the natural order

Law of Death, the: the natural order which separates the living from the dead

Law of Life, the: the natural order which separates the dead from the living

Law-Breaker: title given to both High Lord Elena and Caer-Caveral

Lax Blunderfoot: a name chosen by Latebirth in self-castigation

Lena: a Stonedownor, daughter of Atiaran, mother of Elena

lianar: wood of power used by an eh-Brand

Liand: a man of Mithil Stonedown, son of Fostil; companion of Linden Avery

Lifeswallower: the Great Swamp

lillianrill: wood-lore; masters of wood-lore

Lithe: a Manethrall of the Ramen

Llaura: a Heer of Soaring Woodhelven

Loerya: a Lord, wife of Trevor

lomillialor: High Wood; a wood of power

Longwrath: a Giant; Swordmainnir name for Exalt Widenedworld

Lord: one who has mastered both the Sword and the Staff aspects of Kevin's Lore

Lord-Fatherer: title given to Berek Halfhand

Lord Foul: the enemy of the Land; the Despiser

"Lord Mhoram's Victory": a painting by Ahanna

Lord of Wickedness: a-Jeroth

Lord's-fire: staff-fire used by the Lords

Lord's Keep: Revelstone

Lords, the: the primary protectors of the Land

loremaster: a leader of ur-viles

Loresraat: Trothgard school at Revelwood where Kevin's Lore is studied

Lorewarden: a teacher in the Loresraat

loreworks: Demondim power-laboratory

Loric Vilesilencer: a High Lord; son of Damelon Giantfriend

lor-liarill: Gildenlode

Lost, the: Giantish name for the Unhomed

Lost Deep, the: a loreworks; breeding pit/laboratory under Mount Thunder where Demondim, Waynhim, and ur-viles were created

Lostson: a Giant; later name for Exalt Widenedworld

Lower Land, the: region of the Land east of Landsdrop

lucubrium: laboratory of a thaumaturge

lurker of the Sarangrave, the: monster inhabiting the Great Swamp

Magister, the: former Forestal of Andelain

Mahdoubt, the: a servant of Revelstone; one of the Insequent

Mahrtiir: a Manethrall of the Ramen; companion of Linden Avery

maidan: open land around *Elemesnedene*

Maker, the: *jheherrin* name for Lord Foul

Maker-place: *jheherrin* name for Foul's Creche

Malliner: Woodhelvennin Heer, son of Veinnin

Mane: Ramen reference to a Ranyhyn

Maneing: Ramen ceremony of becoming a Manethrall

Manethrall: highest Ramen rank

Manhome: main dwelling place of the Ramen in the Plains of Ra

Marid: a man of Mithil Stonedown; Sunbane victim

Marny: a Ranyhyn; mount of Tuvor

marrowmeld: bone-sculpting; *anundivian yajña*

Master: commander of a Giantship

Master, the: Clave-name for Lord Foul

master-rukh, the: iron triangle at Revelstone which feeds and reads other *rukhs*

Masters of the Land, the: *Haruchai* who have claimed responsibility for protecting the Land from Corruption

Mehryl: a Ranyhyn; mount of Hile Troy

Melenkurion: one of the Seven Words

Melenkurion **Skyweir:** a cleft peak in the Westron Mountains

Memla: a Rider of the Clave; one of the na-Mhoram-in

mere-**son:** name or title given to Esmer

merewives: the Dancers of the Sea

metheglin: a beverage; mead

Mhoram: a Lord, later high Lord; son of Variol

Mhornym: a Ranyhyn stallion; mount of Clyme

Mill: one of the Seven Words

Minas: one of the Seven Words

mirkfruit: papaya-like fruit with narcoleptic pulp

Mishio Massima: the Ardent's mount

Mistweave: a Giant

Mithil River: a river of the Land

Mithil Stonedown: a village in the South Plains

Mithil's Plunge, the: waterfall at the head of the Mithil valley

Moire Squareset: a Giant; one of the Swordmainnir; killed in battle by the *skurj*

moksha: a Raver, Jehannum, Fleshharrower

Morin: First Mark of the Bloodguard; commander in original *Haruchai* army

Morinmoss: a forest of the Land

Morninglight: one of the *Elohim*

Morril: a Bloodguard, assigned to Lord Callindrill

Mount Thunder: a peak at the center of Landsdrop

Muirwin Delenoth: resting place of abhorrence; graveyard of *quellvisks*

Murrin: a Stonedownor, mate of Odona

Myrha: a Ranyhyn; mount of High Lord Elena

na-Mhoram, the: leader of the Clave

na-Mhoram-cro: lowest rank of the Clave

na-Mhoram-in: highest rank of the Clave below the na-Mhoram

na-Mhoram-wist: middle rank of the Clave

Naharahn: a Ranyhyn mare; mount of Pahni

Narunal: a Ranyhyn stallion; mount of Mahrtiir

Nassic: father of Sunder, son of Jous; inheritor of an Unfettered One's mission to remember the Halfhand

Naybahn: a Ranyhyn; mount of Branl

Nelbrin: son of Sunder, "heart's child"

Nicor, **the:** great sea-monster; said to be offspring of the Worm of the World's End

Nom: a Sandgorgon

North Plains, the: a region of the Land

Northron Climbs, the: a region of the Land

Oath of Peace, the: oath by the people of the Land against needless violence

Odona: a Stonedownor, mate of Murrin

Offin: a former na-Mhoram

Old Lords, the: Lords prior to the Ritual of Desecration

Omournil: Woodhelvennin Heer, daughter of Mournil

One Forest, the: ancient forest covering most of the Land

One Tree, the: mystic tree from which the Staff of Law was made

Onyx Stonemage: a Giant; one of the Swordmainnir

orcrest: a stone of power; Sunstone

Osondrea: a Lord, daughter of Sondrea; later high Lord

Padrias: Woodhelvennin Heer, son of Mill

Pahni: a Cord of the Ramen, cousin of Sahah; companion of Linden Avery

Palla: a healer in Berek Halfhand's army

Peak of the Fire-Lions, the: Mount Thunder, Gravin Threndor

Pietten: Woodhelvennin child damaged by Lord Foul's minions, son of Soranal

pitchbrew: a beverage combining *diamondraught* and *vitrim*, conceived by Pitchwife

Pitchwife: a Giant; member of the Search; husband of the First of the Search

Plains of Ra, the: a region of the Land

Porib: a Bloodguard

Power of Command, the: Seventh Ward of Kevin's Lore

Pren: a Bloodguard

Prothall: High Lord, son of Dwillian

Prover of Life: title given to Thomas Covenant

Puhl: a Cord of the Ramen

Pure One, the: redemptive figure of *jheherrin* legend

Quaan: Warhaft of the Third Eoman of the Warward; later Hiltmark, then Warmark

quellvisk: a kind of monster, now apparently extinct

Quern Ehstrel: true name of the Mahdoubt

Quest for the Staff of Law, the: quest to recover the Staff of Law from Drool Rockworm

Questsimoon, **the:** the Roveheartswind; a steady, favorable wind, perhaps seasonal

Quilla: a Heer of First Woodhelven

Quirrel: a Stonedownor, companion of Triock

Rallyn: a Ranyhyn; Branl's later mount

Ramen: a people who serve the Ranyhyn

Rant Absolain: the *gaddhi*

Ranyhyn: the great horses of the Plains of Ra

Ravers: Lord Foul's three ancient servants

Raw, **the:** fjord into the demesne of the *Elohim*

Rawedge Rim, the: mountains around *Elemesnedene*

Reader: a member of the Clave who tends and uses the *master-rukh*

Rede, the: knowledge of history and survival promulgated by the Clave

Revelstone: Lord's Keep; mountain city formed by Giants

Revelwood: seat of the Loresraat; tree city grown by Lords

rhee: a Ramen food, a thick mush

rhadhamaerl: stone-lore; masters of stone-lore

Rhohm: a Ranyhyn stallion; mount of Liand

rhysh: a community of Waynhim; "stead"

rhyshyshim: a gathering of *rhysh*; a place in which such gathering occurs

Riddenstretch: a region north of the Soulsease River

Rider: a member of the Clave

Ridjeck Thome: Foul's Creche, the Despiser's home

rillinlure: healing wood dust

Rime Coldspray: a Giant; the Ironhand of the Swordmainnir

Ringthane: Ramen name for Thomas Covenant, then Linden Avery

ring-wielder: *Elohim* term of reference for Thomas Covenant

Rire Grist: a Caitiffin of the *gaddhi*'s Horse

Rites of Unfettering: the ceremony of becoming Unfettered

Ritual of Desecration, the: act of despair by which High Lord Kevin destroyed the Old Lords and ruined most of the Land

Rivenrock: deep cleft splitting *Melenkurion* Skyweir and its plateau; there the Black River enters Garroting Deep

River Landrider, the: a river of the Land, partial border of the Plains of Ra

Riversward: a region north of the Soulsease River

Rockbrother: Swordmainnir name for Stave

Rockbrother, Rocksister: terms of affection between humans and Giants

rocklight: light emitted by glowing stone

roge Befylam: Cavewight-form of the *jheherrin*

Rohnhyn: a Ranyhyn; mount of Bhapa after Whrany's death

Roveheartswind, the: the *Questsimoon*

Rue: a Manethrall of the Ramen, formerly named Gay

Ruel: a Bloodguard, assigned to Hile Troy

Ruinwash, the: name of the River Landrider on the Lower Land

rukh: iron talisman by which a Rider wields the power of the Sunbane

Runnik: a Bloodguard

Rustah: a Cord of the Ramen

Sablehair Foamheart: a Giant, also called Filigree; mate of Soar Gladbirth; mother of Exalt Widenedworld

sacred enclosure: Vespers-hall at Revelstone; later the site of the Banefire

Sahah: a Cord of the Ramen

Saltheart Foamfollower: a Giant, friend of Thomas Covenant

Saltroamrest: bunk hold for the crew in a Giantship

Salttooth: jutting rock in the harbor of the Giants' Home

Salva Gildenbourne: forest surrounding the Hills of Andelain; begun by Sunder and Hollian

samadhi: a Raver, Sheol, Satansfist

Samil: a *Haruchai*; a Master of the Land

Sandgorgons: monsters of the Great Desert of *Bhrathairealm*

Sandgorgons Doom: imprisoning storm created by Kasreyn to trap the Sandgorgons

Sandhold, the: the *gaddhi's* castle in *Bhrathairealm*

Sandwall, the: the great wall defending *Bhrathairain*

Santonin: a Rider of the Clave, one of the na-Mhoram-in

Sarangrave Flat: a region of the Lower Land encompassing the Great Swamp

Satansfist: a Giant-Raver, Sheol, *samadhi*

Satansheart: Giantish name for Lord Foul

Scend Wavegift: a Giant; one of the Swordmainnir; killed by Longwrath

Search, the: quest of the Giants for the wound in the Earth; later the quest for the Isle of the One Tree

Seareach: region of the Land occupied by the Unhomed

Seasauce: a Giant; husband of Hearthcoal; cook of Starfare's Gem

Seatheme: dead wife of Sevinhand

Second Circinate: second level of the Sandhold

Second Ward: second unit of Kevin's hidden knowledge

setrock: a type of stone used with pitch to repair stone

Seven Hells, the: a-Jeroth's demesne: desert, rain, pestilence, fertility, war, savagery, and darkness

Seven Wards, the: collection of knowledge hidden by High Lord Kevin

Seven Words, the: words of power from Kevin's Lore

Sevinhand: a Giant, Anchormaster of Starfare's Gem

Shattered Hills, the: a region of the Land near Foul's Creche

She Who Must Not Be Named: an ancient bane slumbering under Mount Thunder, now composed of many lost women

Sheol: a Raver, Satansfist, *samadhi*

Shetra: a Lord, wife of Verement

Shipsheartthew: the wheel of a Giantship

shola: a small wooded glen where a stream runs between unwooded hills

Shull: a Bloodguard

Sill: a Bloodguard, assigned to Lord Hyrim

Sivit: a Rider of the Clave, one of the na-Mhoram-wist

skest: acid-creatures descended from the *jheherrin*

skurj: laval monsters that devour earth and vegetation; long ago, the *Elohim* Kastenessen was Appointed (the Durance) to prevent them from wreaking terrible havoc

Slen: a Stonedownor, mate of Terass

Slumberhead: a Giant (man); crew aboard Dire's Vessel

Snared One, the: ur-vile name for Lord Foul the Despiser

Soar Gladbirth: a Giant; youngest son of Pitchwife and Gossamer Glowlimn

Soaring Woodhelven: a tree-village

soft ones, the: the *jheherrin*

Somo: pinto taken by Liand from Mithil Stonedown

soothreader: a seer

soothtell: ritual of revelation practiced by the Clave

Soranal: a Woodhelvennin Heer, son of Thiller

Soulbiter, the: a dangerous ocean of Giantish legend

Soulbiter's Teeth: reefs in the Soulbiter

Soulcrusher: Giantish name for Lord Foul

South Plains, the: a region of the Land

Sparlimb Keelsetter: a Giant, father of triplets

Spikes, the: guard-towers at the mouth of *Bhrathairain* Harbor

Spoiled Plains, the: a region of the Lower Land

Spume Frothbreeze: a Giant (man); crew aboard Dire's Vessel

Spray Frothsurge: a Giant; mother of the First of the Search

springwine: a mild, refreshing liquor

Squallish Blustergale: a Giant (man); crew aboard Dire's Vessel

Staff, the: a branch of the study of Kevin's Lore

Staff of Law, the: a tool of Earthpower; the first Staff was formed by Berek from the One Tree and later destroyed by Thomas Covenant; the second was formed by Linden Avery by using wild magic to merge Vain and Findail

Stallion of the First Herd, the: *Kelenbhrabanal*

Starfare's Gem: Giantship used by the Search

Starkin: one of the *Elohim*

Stave: a *Haruchai*; a Master of the Land; companion of Linden Avery

Stell: one of the *Haruchai*, protector of Sunder

Stonedown: a stone-village

Stonedownor: one who lives in a stone-village

Stonemight, the: a fragment of the Illearth Stone

Stonemight Woodhelven: a village in the South Plains

Storesmaster: third-in-command aboard a Giantship

Stormpast Galesend: a Giant; one of the Swordmainnir

Stricken Stone: region of the Land, later called Trothgard

Sunbane, the: a power arising from the corruption of nature by Lord Foul

Sunbirth Sea, the: ocean east of the Land

Sunder: son of Nassic; Graveler of Mithil Stonedown; companion of Thomas Covenant and Linden Avery

Sun-Sage: one who can affect the Sunbane

Sunstone: *orcrest*

sur-jheherrin: descendants of the *jheherrin*; inhabitants of Sarangrave Flat

suru-pa-maerl: an art using stone

Swarte: a Rider of the Clave

Swordmain/Swordmainnir: Giant(s) trained as warrior(s)

Sword, the: a branch of the study of Kevin's Lore

Sword-Elder: chief Lorewarden of the Sword at the Loresraat

Syr Embattled: former Forestal of Giant Woods

Tamarantha: a Lord, daughter of Enesta, wife of Variol

Teeth of the Render, the: Ramen name for the Demondim; Fangs

Terass: a Stonedownor, daughter of Annoria, wife of Slen

Terrel: a Bloodguard, assigned to Lord Mhoram; a commander of the original *Haruchai* army

test of silence, the: test of integrity used by the people of the Land

test of truth, the: test of veracity by *lomillialor* or *orcrest*

The Grieve: *Coercri*; home of the lost Giants in Seareach

Thelma Twofist: character in a Giantish tale

The Majesty: throne room of the *gaddhi*; fourth level of the Sandhold

Theomach, the: one of the Insequent

Thew: a Cord of the Ramen

Third Ward: third unit of Kevin's hidden knowledge

Thomin: a Bloodguard, assigned to Lord Verement

Three Corners of Truth, the: basic formulation of beliefs taught and enforced by the Clave

thronehall, the: the Despiser's seat in Foul's Creche

Tier of Riches, the: showroom of the *gaddhi*'s wealth; third level of the Sandhold

Timewarden: *Elohim* title for Thomas Covenant after his death

Tohrm: a Gravelingas; Hearthrall of Lord's Keep

Tomal: a Stonedownor craftmaster

Toril: *Haruchai* slain by the Clave

Treacher's Gorge: ravine opening into Mount Thunder

treasure-berries: *aliantha*, nourishing fruit found throughout the Land in all seasons

Trell: Gravelingas of Mithil Stonedown; husband of Atiaran, father of Lena

Trevor: a Lord, husband of Loerya

Triock: a Stonedownor, son of Thuler; loved Lena

Trothgard: a region of the Land, formerly Stricken Stone

Tull: a Bloodguard

turiya: a Raver, Herem, Kinslaughterer

Tuvor: First Mark of the Bloodguard; a commander of the original *Haruchai* army

tyrscull: a Giantish training vessel for apprentice sailors

Ulman: a *Haruchai*; a Master of the Land

Unbeliever, the: title claimed by Thomas Covenant

Unfettered, the: lore-students freed from conventional responsibilities to seek individual knowledge and service

Unfettered One, the: founder of a line of men waiting to greet Thomas Covenant's return to the Land

Unhomed, the: the lost Giants living in Seareach

un-Maker-made, the: in *jheherrin* legend, living beings not created by the Maker

upland: plateau above Revelstone

Upper Land, the: region of the Land west of Landsdrop

ur-Lord: title given to Thomas Covenant

ur-viles: Demondim-spawn, evil creatures

ussusimiel: nourishing melon grown by the people of the Land

Vailant: former High Lord before Prothall

Vain: Demondim-spawn; bred by ur-viles for a secret purpose

Vale: a Bloodguard

Valley of Two Rivers, the: site of Revelwood in Trothgard

Variol Tamarantha-mate: a Lord, later High Lord; son of Pentil, father of Mhoram

Verement: a Lord, husband of Shetra

Verge of Wandering, the: valley in the Southron Range southeast of Mithil Stonedown; gathering place of the nomadic Ramen

Vernigil: a *Haruchai*; a Master of the Land guarding First Woodhelven

Vertorn: a healer in Berek Halfhand's army

Vespers: self-consecration rituals of the Lords

Vettalor: Warmark of the army opposing Berek Halfhand

viancome: meeting place at Revelwood

Victuallin Tayne: a region in the Center Plains

Vidik Amar: a region of the Earth

Vigilall Scudweather: a Giant (woman); Master of Dire's Vessel

Viles: monstrous beings which created the Demondim

vitrim: nourishing fluid created by the Waynhim

Vizard, the: one of the Insequent

Voice of the Masters, the: a *Haruchai* leader; spokesman for the Masters as a group

Vortin: a *Haruchai*; a Master of the Land

voure: a plant-sap which wards off insects

Vow, the: *Haruchai* oath of service which formed the Bloodguard

vraith: a Waynhim

Ward: a unit of Kevin's lore

Warhaft: commander of an Eoman

Warlore: Sword knowledge in Kevin's Lore

Warmark: commander of the Warward

Warrenbridge: entrance to the catacombs under Mount Thunder

Warward, the: army of Lord's Keep

Wavedancer: Giantship commanded by Brow Gnarlfist

Wavenhair Haleall: a Giant, wife of Sparlimb Keelsetter, mother of triplets

Waymeet: resting place for travelers maintained by Waynhim

Waynhim: tenders of the Waymeets; rejected Demondim-spawn, opponents and relatives of ur-viles

Weird of the Waynhim, the: Waynhim concept of doom, destiny, or duty

were-menhir(s): Giantish name for the *skurj*

Whane: a Cord of the Ramen

white gold: a metal of power not found in the Land

white gold wielder: title given to Thomas Covenant

White River, the: a river of the land

Whrany: a Ranyhyn stallion; mount of Bhapa

Wightburrow, the: cairn under which Drool Rockworm is buried

Wightwarrens: home of the Cavewights under Mount Thunder; catacombs

wild magic: the power of white gold; considered the keystone of the Arch of Time

Wildwielder: white gold wielder; title given to Linden Avery by Esmer and the *Elohim*

Windscour: region in the Center Plains

Windshorn Stonedown: a village in the South Plains

Winhome: Ramen lowest rank

Wiver Setrock: a Giant (man); crew aboard Dire's Vessel

Woodenwold: region of trees surrounding the *maidan* of *Elemesnedene*

Woodhelven: wood-village

Woodhelvennin: inhabitants of wood-village

Word of Warning: a powerful, destructive forbidding

Worm of the World's End, the: creature believed by the *Elohim* to have formed the foundation of the Earth

Wraiths of Andelain, the: creatures of living light that perform the Dance at the Celebration of Spring

Würd of the Earth, the: term used by the *Elohim* to describe their own nature, destiny, or purpose; could be read as Word, Worm, or Weird

Yellinin: a soldier in Berek Halfhand's army; third-in-command of the tenth Eoman, second Eoward

Yeurquin: a Stonedownor, companion of Triock

Yolenid: daughter of Loerya

Zaynor: a *Haruchai* from a time long before the *Haruchai* first came to the Land